I0818271

The Collected Stories of Carol Emshwiller

vol. 2

Introduction by Barry N. Malzberg

nonstop press • new york

THE COLLECTED STORIES OF CAROL EMSHWILLER
Vol. 2

Carol Emshwiller

First Edition:
2016

Book designed and edited by Luis Ortiz
Production by Nonstop Ink
Cover art by Ed Emshwiller

Hardcover ISBN: 978-1-933065-34-2
Trade Paper ISBN: 978-1-933065-38-0

PRINTED IN THE UNITED STATES OF AMERICA

www.nonstoppress.com
PO Box 580444, Flushing, NY, 11358

Contents

INTRODUCTION

Carol Emshwiller: The Hunting Machine

Four or five years ago I petitioned the President of the Science Fiction Writers of America to give Carol Emshwiller the Grand Master Award. "There is no writer who has had a more significant effect upon the field of science fiction in the last twenty years than this writer" I wrote. "She has quietly changed everything, both focused and unfocused the category, made it synchronously more of what it is, more of what it isn't. Quietly she has been doing this for fifty years. Unquietly her achievement should be recognized."

To which modest petition I received in response what my older daughter — happily escaped from retail now but a veteran of twenty years in that abbatoir — describes as "Nut Letter /37", the letter you send to the customer who did not like the salesperson's hairdo or the smell surrounding the perfume counter. "Dear Barry/Thank you very much for your suggestion/We shall certainly give this serious consideration." So much for "serious consideration". Maybe the old banking dictum is correct: "You can get more with a kind word and a gun than you can from a kind word alone."

Others have in the years following been named in her place and I do not disparage any of these worthies, none of them are undeserving but Carol Emshwiller should have been noted before them just as on the inception of the Grand Master Award in 1975 Robert A. Heinlein was the first, the obvious, the irreplaceable choice. What Carol Emshwiller has been quietly conducting for this half century has been a literary revolution which has dragged the often uncapitulating various categories of fiction into a new amalgam, a new set of protocols and a forced sinister revelation: so-called "literary" fiction, science fiction, fantasy, feminism, horror, entropy have been set up like prize bears in a carnival gallery and almost carelessly Carol Emshwiller has knocked them off the shelves, sent them to a jumble on the floor and then has casually reassembled them in ways which had previously seen impossible. Her female narrators (almost all of her stories are in a first person as deadpan casual as Holden Caulfield or Bridget Jones) are intensely human and with equal intensity trans-human; in their odd and pointillist perception, in their cool dislocation they are examples of what Alice Sheldon (aka James Tiptree, Jr.) wrote me in 1974 (arguing that there should be more stories by women in *Final Stage,* an anthology of "ultimate science fiction" stories I was editing with Edward L. Ferman) are women as culture's truest aliens, voyagers from a planet other than our own with the same name, custodians of a circumstance we cannot measure. Most of her stories are *assembled*, are aggregate rather than plotted, that pointillist accumulation of odd and deadly detail, filtered through sensibilities superficially tilted but in fact unfiltered, perceiving social structure and myth as arbitrary contrived deceit. Like Shirley Jackson and for some of the same reason (a woman totally immersed within and utterly unaccepting of the "conventional reality) she provides that odd and terrible disjointedness, that dislocation which as in "The Lottery" can utterly overwhelm.

Carol Emshwiller, wife of the artist Ed Emshwiller and co-host or guest of hundreds of the science fiction community parties of the 50's and 60's began as the relatively incognito, very pretty wife of an artist central to that community, elected relatively incognito to try writing herself, published a remarkable first story "The Hunting Machine" with editor Robert Lowndes in the late 50's (incognito in this case being served by a conventionally extrapolative, brilliantly paced traditional story) and then, cautiously but with carefully managed prolificity became quietly prolific, showed the Damon Knight editing *Orbit* a way he had never suspected science fiction could go and along with the tide of science fiction were the expressionless, carefully deadly literary stories which appeared in the quarterlies. There was a collection for Harper & Row in the 70's, *Joy In Our Cause* most of whose contents were not science fiction but which was published by the science fiction editor Victoria Schochet, predictably it caused little stir. But Carol Emshwiller was never interested in causing a stir. She had more important game in the rangefinder of her hunting machine.

If the late Grace Paley, I came to note somewhat unpleasantly decades later, had had real talent and production she might have made half of Carol Emshwiller. (No one of course had asked me.) Paley certainly had the observation and the anger in full measure, Carol Emshwiller did not have the Paley connections but then again these stories were not written by someone who was at all interested in connections.

Well, one could carry the case down the road but Carol Emshwiller is her own case on her own road. A few years ago she managed something which is I believe never to be repeated: on an April Friday she was announced as the winner of the Phil Dick Award for best sf or fantasy paperback original and on Saturday she won the Nebula. Even Michael Chabon couldn't do that. (He won the Nebula for best novel on Saturday but the Policeman's Union had to settle for runner-up for the MWA Best Novel Edgar.)

A splendid writer, one of our very best: irreplaceable. In occasional meetings we got along splendid and I wish there had been far more than "occasional". Her work has lasted six decades. That's the beginning.

Barry N. Malzberg

Adapted

Did you see my signal in the window, my cornstalks? I wrapped the bottoms of them in brown paper because I don't have the right sort of vase anymore. All mine are too blue or too green or white.

You know, once I wanted to put the whole back yard into corn and I said I would bring the stalks in to put in the vases, for why in the world, I said then, are cornstalks less beautiful than flowers? They are green thick and a big bunch of them in the house would have a wildish look of abundance and when they dried and turn tan they would be like sand, like some of the desert brought inside. Who made all these silly rules about beauty I said once

But I was too busy that year to dig up the backyard grass, except for a little patch like most everyone had, for lettuce and tomatoes. You were that summer and I was chasing after you. You were always bringing the inside out and the outside in and, even if I felt you were right to do so, I swept out the sand every night and brought the toys inside again. Sometimes I found my spoons in the sand pile and now and then something from my underwear drawer. Once I found a vase from the top shelf over the refrigerator. There was nothing that was out of your reach. You climbed like a monkey though you could hardly walk.

I think not planted that corn was a big mistake, then, when we had out first house. I should have done it, time or no time. I should have done it, time or no time. I should have no swept out sand a few nights and dug up that tough grass instead, because the real reason I didn't do it wasn't because of the time at all, but because I thought it would look peculiar to have the whole back yard in corn. I thought the neighbors might not like it. I thought they might think I was strange.

Well, I *was* strange then, but strangeness is not so easy to keep. I shut my eyes and opened my hands as wide as I could and, though it seemed to cling, little by little, year by year, it fell away.

There was a time, when I was your age, when I liked being different. I used to like to look into a mirror and I even did not mind my long, thin nose and sharp chin. I would wonder about myself, staring into my own eyes, and every time I did it I would feel a kind of excitement. I could see how different I was, and I could see a look about me (it seemed to come more and more as I grew older) of something going to happen. I didn't know at all what it could be but sometimes I would think if it as flying. I could fly if I wanted to, I'd think, only what I meant was ,,, well, not fling at all but something I could do that had to do with this floating feeling inside me. I knew of children who had jumped from trees thinking that they could fly, but I never tried that. Though I would say to myself, and be sure of it, I can fly, that was not what I meant.

I was rather proud of my looks then, though I wouldn't stand up straight and look at people. "The spittin image of your father," my mother used to ay, always with a kind of fear in her voice and a kind of anger. My father had not been seen or heard from since two months after she met him. "Two months and eleven days of bliss," she would say fiercely and that was all she ever did say about him.

I think I first learned from her to hunch my shoulders and hang my head, though that got worse later. Mother was more embarrassed by my height and my nose than she was of my slumping, so she never told me to stand up straight.

And then, when I was nineteen, your father came, blond and perfect and brown that summer, the crisp, yellow hairs on his chest and down his legs, making him a man edged in gold, in the sun on the beach. I couldn't believe he'd look at me at all, though big eyes were in fashion then. I slumped, I wilted, and I hung my head. "You have the most perfect eyes I've ever seen," he'd say, but I got so I hated to look at myself in the mirror. I always wore low heels then, for even though your father was tall, I was taller. And the day before he asked me to marry him I dyed my hair so it was jet black and not a kind of grayish half-black. I always felt it helped and I've kept it this way ever since. You've never seen me with my real hair color. It's like yours.

So we got married and you came along and your father was not like *my* father, he stuck to me and to his job managing the little grocery store, and soon we got that fires house, and that was my chance, really, to be myself for the first time. I was free of my mother and free, by then, from your father in a certain, different way. I could have planted the backyard all in corn. I don't think your father would have cared so much, but I planted tomatoes and lettuce and then rose bushes and zinnias. In the windows I hung green curtains with white and pink pattern. I remember just once I said that I rather felt like having a bright red ceiling. "At least in one room," I said. And our father said, "And why not paint the floor black and paste silver stars on it,"and he laughed, so I did the ceiling cream downstairs and the light green upstairs. It almost seemed I purposely did them the colors I disliked the most. But after a while I didn't mind them and the ache I had to have just one read ceiling went away.

Things went along as in any family then, and you grew bigger and went to school and didn't take so much time and I decided to take things up like the other young mothers did and a strange thing happened.

I had decided to try some art and I enrolled in a beginning class in an adult education art course. After the class had gotten into it a bit, the teacher would take us outside in fair weather to do landscapes.

One time we were sitting on a small hill doing a group of young, rather uninteresting willow trees along a new artificial pool. It was hot and there were quite a few ants about, crawling over out legs and getting in the watercolor boxes. The others were restless, talking and getting up to shake off an ant or two and after a while most of them walked across the park to a little drug store to get ice tea.

They asked me to go with them, but I was already started on my picture and I said , no, rather rudely. I think, though I usually take great pains to be sweet to people. You know how I am. I think ever since I realized I was different I've tried hard to be sweet to others. Well, this time I know I was rude, but this time I didn't care. I had begun to like the stiff, new-looking scene. I had begun to see it in a different way. It was as if it were all moved much closer and I was looking at tiny details and this was an open spot in a forest instead of an open spot in a suburban housing development. I felt thick trees all about in the place of the low, long stores of the corner shopping-center and the split-lever houses behind them. This was an oasis of sunlight in a jungle instead of an oasis of shade and I began to paint it like that, not thinking what colors were right or that the detailed lines I made with my blue-inked ball point pen of the veins in the leaves and the texture of the back and the bugs could only be made up because I certainly couldn't see them. I felt as if I could.

The others came back, but I had set up my things to the side and no one came to see what I had done. I didn't wake up to it myself until I had finished. I knew it was finished without even taking a last, long look and I turned to wash my brushed and shut up my box. I was thinking of getting an iced tea for myself before we left though I didn't care for iced tea and I really wasn't feeling so very hot. Heat has never bothered me, you know, but of course you do know, for it has never bothered you either.

And then I turned to get my purse and I caught sight of the painting out of the corner of my eye and I looked at it straight on then, really looked, for the first time, and I felt a jolt as if everything inside me had suddenly stood up while I was still sitting there. I've only felt that way one other time in my life and that was yesterday.

The picture was tangle of blue pen lines and then browns and reds and dots of yellow. It was still a picture of those five young willow and the stiff lawn sloping to the pool, but one sensed the dark jungle close around it. It seemed a scene of mathematical orderliness and lemon-cool sunlight in the midst of hot chaos. In the corner of the foreground there was the branch of a pinish tree. The only part of the picture that was green, almost black. It was done in great details, even the shapes of the needles drawn with those spider-webbing blue lines, but I had never seen a tree of needles quite like that ever before.

I quickly hid the painting under some sheets of fresh paper and when the teacher asked to see it, I said I hadn't been able to do anything that day because it was too hot and because if the ants. When I got home I tore up the painting and put it in the garbage and I didn't take any more art classes. I even didn't take music, though that was what I would have liked to try next.

I tried some history course at the college then, and later Psychology, but after that art class it seemed I couldn't get interested. I wasn't learning anything that I really cared about at all, and I kept having the feeling that everything I was learning and memorizing so carefully was only partly true. Then I decided to go on a reading program. I joined two book clubs and I read all the bestsellers, but there wasn't a single book that I could day I enjoyed except one silly little book, not very well written, about a girl named Sarania who thought she could fly, but in the end she found she couldn't at all.

And then, but I'm sure you remember, I decided to go for swimming lessons. How I loved that. I got caught up in it without even thinking and I'd come home late and we'd have spam or a can of hash for supper. I hardly noticed what I was doing. There was that feeling in me again of something going to happen. I felt like a caterpillar would feel if he could think about butterflies.

It was when the pool was cold that I loved it best. I would imagine I was diving into a deep, black, mountain lake and I would swim and swim while the others would shiver. "How can you do that?" they'd say, and "It's always the thin ones that are tough."

I took you sometimes on Saturdays. You were ten then. I guess those were the last times we felt close to each other. You learned so fast everyone was amazed. You were like a little seal with just your nose out of water and your black eyes bright and your long, dusty-colored hair dark with water and plastered close to your head. We would swim together to the bottom of the deepest end and blow bubbles at each other and then come up and laugh. You, with your sharp little nose and long, thin hands and feet, you were beautiful to me then. And, because I looked like you, I almost thought I was beautiful too.

But after a while your father complained about the meals and the dust about the house. "Now and then I wouldn't mind." He said, "but it's been everyday for over a month." And I began to think again and I began to have the same feeling I had when I painted that strange picture and I realized my feelings about swimming were the same but had come on me slowly so that I hadn't noticed them.

I stopped swimming then and I wouldn't let you go either. You never would look at me after that, straight into my eyes like we used to when out heads would pop up out of the water and we'd take a big breath and laugh. You've always held your eyes away since then, and you took on my slouching walk, my hanging head, and I, I never told you to stand up straight.

It was after the swimming I began to do nothing. "I guess I'm just a housewife," I'd tell my friends and laugh and I did try to keep a nice house. I always have, tried, but it was even harder to do the housework when I had no classes to think about, even ones I didn't particularly like, and not much to do with you. About all I did for you in those days was to chauffeur you to your piano lessons and back. How you hated the piano, as much as or more than I did when I was your age. Remember how you begged to play the oboe at school? And your father said, "Why not, even if it is peculiar for a girl. After all, someone in the band has to play it." But I said no, and your father was used to me then and didn't bother to ask why. He knew I wouldn't be able to give a good reason but would only get upset and talk nonsense.

You didn't know, but every morning, first thing in those days, I'd take three aspirin. That was before Dr. Wilton got me the tranquilizers. Somehow I would get through each day, portion it out in cigarettes and coffee and aspirin.

Then I got what I felt was a wonderful idea. I would have my face changed. That, I thought, would put and end to my strange thoughts of being different, those crazy night-time ideas that I could fly or do something equivalent to that. If my face was like other peoples', then, I felt, I would have a new beginning and really *be* like other people instead of pretending. I could relax then and just be my new self

So then I got that job in the department store because I couldn't ask your father for all that money. I was quite happy — not with the job, but just sure that I was going in the right direction and that things would soon be better.

I worked almost that whole year and then (you were thirteen and it was spring) I went to New York for three weeks and had my nose changed and a little taken off my chin. I had them widen my nostrils so no one could say they were either wide or thin and some taken off the end of my nose so that no one could say it was either long or short.

When I came back, it was the first of May, you gave no sign that I was changed. You never spoke of it and you never looked at me.

But our father loved my new nose. He said it was the most perfect nose he'd ever seen. He said it matched my eyes now and that he couldn't stop looking at me with my perfect nose and prefect eyes. And I could see that, for he was always looking and pulling me to him. "It's like having a new wife," he said, "A brand new, beautiful wife."

It was like the honeymoon again for a few weeks, but I remember that first night after I came home I got out of bed alone around midnight and went to look at the moon and there was a dog barking in the park and our young fruit trees, just in blossom looked frail and silly to me because I was thinking of the forest, and I forgot, looking out at the night like that, that I was only tall like my father now. I forgot I no longer had his face and I felt again that peculiar thing about me. I could fly if I wanted to. I thought. I could fly. Yet I didn't really want to, and never *had* wanted to except sometimes at night like this. And just as I was thinking *it*, then, I remembered my new nose and chin and I stopped looking out to the window and curled up on the floor and cried for a long time. I've never cried again, not even yesterday.

It was soon after that Dr. Wilton got me tranquilizers. I had quit my job. I did not enjoy it for its own sake and extra money meant nothing to me, so, about three weeks after I had my face changed, I went to se Dr. Wilton and he said I was fine and got me the tranquilizers.

And then I sort of discovered nuts. Of course I'd had nuts before, and always liked them, but now they became my passion like candy is to some people or alcohol to others. I could not be without a box of mixed nuts near me and I ate as I worked and I grew into the thing I am, this giant, tall and fat, my perfect nose looking small and my carefully carved chin hardly there at all. And my real self, tall and very thin and long nosed and with mud-grey hair, my real self seemed like a dead twin sister. One who had some great talent that was never realized. I took a tranquilizer every morning and every afternoon and I laughed over bridge with neighbors and I said, "I guess I'm just the house wife type," but I don't think I will ever say that anymore.

You see, yesterday I saw a man and seeing him was like everything sitting up inside me just like that time when I painted that picture. It was like love, too, love at first sight, only it wasn't exactly love.

He was very, very tall, and thin as you are, he had a long nose and sharp chin, and his hair was the color of soft, dry dirt ... like yours.

I held the grocery bundle and leaned back against the car. All the years seemed to fall away and I was back before I met your father, and wonderful things were going to happen, things I could see when I looked in the mirror, and this was it. This was the time.

He was standing on our walk and he seemed to be looking about the house for some sign, looking at each window as if to find a room inside with a bright red ceiling, or cornstalks in brown pots showing at the windows, or perhaps a yellow pane of glass in one. And he looked at the lawn as if searching for the little round suns of dandelions, but I had pulled them all out. He looked up and down the street then, as if for some other house that might have some sign, and he took a paper out of his pocket and looked from it back to our house, and then he turned to go.

I took a grip on my grocery bag and started towards him, my legs like willow branches, and I walked right to him looking into his eyes. I asked with my eyes, I begged, but I could not bring myself to speak. I kept thinking, in a minute he'll know me, in one moment more. *We*, I thought. I can say *We*. I'm his kind. But I walked up to him and past him and he didn't recognize me. Dressed in my fat and my dyed hair and my new face I passed him. He looked right at me, my whole *surface*, and didn't recognize me at all.

Going up the steps I saw him walking away, on down the street, watching house. "Father," whispered, though he was younger that I (more your age) and seemed also husband, brother, son. I went into the house and sat a long time in the hall and I could not cry. Then your father came in, and you later, and I made supper and we ate and afterwards you studied and practiced the piano and your father read and we heard the news on the radio and we went to bed and then got up again in the morning and ate breakfast as we have done and done and done. But I did get cornstalks and put them I the window. I don't know anymore if it's the right sort of sign. I have tried to thin I other ways so long that my mind no longer flies away of itself.

But it's for you, and you'll know what to do. I knew better at your age than ever again. And he, or someone like him (our kind), will come back, sometime for sure. And when he comes, or someone like him, I want you to go with him and I'll stay. I'll stay with your father and be what I've made myself into. But you, Darling, sit up. Don't slump so any more.

***The Magazine Fantasy and Science Fiction,* May 1961**

Glory, Glory

I was walking down the Bogashtha Stah with my husband when suddenly a well-dressed old man (in our kind of suit and tie) bowed down to me and touched his forehead to my left shoe. "Oh my God, my living God," he said in quite good English. "You are my one and only." My husband started laughing even before I'd realized what had happened.

"Ooo, ooo," my husband said, "I married a goddess and didn't even know it."

Then a young girl came running out of a corner flower shop-flower hovel is more like what it was-with a bouquet that she laid at my feet, and she also bowed down. She even kissed my shoe, and this is not a very good city for kissing shoes in. "No, no," I said, trying to lift each of the people at the same time. "No need for that." What I said, I don't know why, sent my husband into another fit of laughing.

"Need!" he said, "need!"

The old man had quite a hard time getting back up even though squatting down is a common position in this culture, and even with me and the girl helping. My husband was, all this time, leaning against the wall (one of their ancient walls of huge stones which everybody wonders how they brought here and from where) still laughing. "I'd help," he said, "but I can't right now. Hoo, ooo, there must be something about you I haven't noticed. Let me take a good look," which he didn't do. He just kept laughing and pounding the wall with his fist, though not so hard as to hurt himself

We hadn't been in this country more than half a day and we were suffering from the altitude and were exhausted though we'd had a little nap. Nothing in the guide book had said anything about something like this. And I'm not an imposing person. At barely five feet, how imposing can you be? Though here the people are generally as short as or shorter than me. My husband, on the other hand, is quite tall even in our own land and, of course, towers over everyone here. I was wondering why they hadn't picked him to bow down to. He seemed a much more logical choice and he is an important man.

I tried to give the bouquet back to the girl but she wouldn't let me. (She spoke no English.) "Take it," the old man said. "It's of no use to her now that it is given in your name."

What name? I wondered, for they couldn't possibly know my name, but I took it. My husband still leaned against the wall weak from laughing.

"And why not?" I said. "What's so funny?"

I knew I should be laughing at myself, too. Not take myself so seriously, and I wouldn't have if my husband hadn't kept on and on and not even looked at me to see if there really was anything special about me, though I knew there wasn't. As we continued, only (as we'd said to each other before), "only a little bit lost" — for behind us, on that same Bogashtha Stah, was our hotel — as we kept walking other passersby didn't even look at me. Perhaps I had my face buried in the bouquet. I did keep sniffing it. It wasn't as if I was used to getting flowers anymore. It had been a long time since I'd had some. I kept saying how nice they were, partly just for spite, and they really were nice. The flowers here are spectacular and strange... sexy flowers with long, fuzzy stigmas, branched stamens, pendulous styles. I'd never seen the like before.

But then it did happen again. This time a boy — a ragged little thing sitting on the curb-looked at me and his face lit up with such delight that I was delighted myself, especially to see such a look on the face of this forlorn little creature, and then he, also, fell to his knees, forehead on sidewalk. Then a young couple just behind him did the same and then a woman my own age, rather plump, as I am, though she was very short and, of course, brown-skinned and had those lovely almond eyes. She bowed down as the others did and then raised herself to kiss my dress. And then the people brought more flowers, four, five bouquets, big ones, and spread them out in front of me as though I was to walk on them, and more people came. They smiled and I smiled back, rather tentatively because I didn't have any idea what was going on. But suddenly I felt my arm grabbed from behind just above my elbow and in a grip that hurt. For a moment I panicked and tried to twist away, but I couldn't, and then I saw it was my husband. He hurried me through the crowd at a trot, scattering the flowers, trampling them, bumping into people and making me do it, too. When we got to the corner he jumped on an already moving bus and pulled me up with him.

"That was a dangerous thing to do," I said when I had caught my breath. "I'm too old for that." Really, I was put out at having been pulled away from those flowers and smiling faces, and so roughly that my arm still hurt. Also he had laughed at me for something I thought rather nice.

"Too old for *this,*" he said, *"this!"* And then he turned his back on me and when there was a vacant seat he took it for himself, though that's not his usual way. He has always kept a certain decorum in our relationship even when we're alone. It helps make things go smoothly between us, and I appreciate that.

We rode without speaking for what must have been a half an hour. I knew he needed to cool off so I kept silent. The bus was now circling a slum. I was worried, but I thought all we'd have to do to get back would be to cross the street and take the same numbered bus back, though there wasn't a number on it, but a symbol. I looked it up in my phrase and symbol book. It meant big tree and big, big tree. The bus crossed a long rather rickety bridge and my husband began to look a bit worried, too. He stood up and, at the other side of the river, we got off, crossed the street and waited for a bus going back. This was the edge of the city. Huts were all along the banks of the river , but behind them were fields of what looked to me like red amaranth though I wasn't sure. Several dirt roads converged at the bridge. One road was so small, little more than ruts, it looked as though it hardly mattered at all.

We'd both cooled down by then and we were both worried, which brought us closer to each other. I felt like reaching out and holding hands, but I didn't, especially since I knew the whole thing was my fault. When things happen like that on the street, I should do as I've been taught all my life, look straight ahead, pay no attention, above all no eye contact, and keep walking. I know that. "I'm sorry," I said. "I shouldn't have let it happen. I should have known better. I *do* know better."

He grunted that he'd heard. It wasn't much of an answer, but I felt better for having apologized anyway, and that's the important thing, or so they say.

We waited. A few buses came but so full of people and goats and turkeys that we hesitated to get on, though my husband went to the doorway of each and asked "Bogashtha?" but the drivers all said, no, or what we took as no, so we waited and waited, sitting on a marker stone. Finally my husband said, "Next bus that comes we take, no matter what."

By now the sun was as though sitting in a notch between two of the mountains, and about to go down. As soon as it did, the wind began to blow and it got colder. Many people began to cross the bridges on foot now, most carrying big, raggedy bundles. They all seemed tired and hardly noticed us at first, but then it happened again. Two women saw me and there was that same look of joy as before. I felt my own spirits lift as theirs did. Other people looked at me then, too, and they stopped being tired and bowed down, some, again, putting their foreheads on the ground. I said, as I'd said before, "Please. No need for that."

This time my husband was too tired to laugh, but gave a disgusted "Humph." And then they began to lay things at my feet ... odd things that they happened to have with them, a star fruit, a cashew fruit, a purple melon, a little bag of strange, round seeds

"We can't eat any of this," my husband said, but I was so hungry I thought I would in spite of the dangers we'd been warned about and I nibbled a star fruit without even trying to wipe it off, which probably wouldn't have done much good against all the things they'd told us we might catch.

Then some of the women saw that I was shivering and gave me their shawls, old and ragged shawls, but they had that special beauty that these people weave into everything they wear, those reds and pinks and honey yellows. I suppose the shawls looked funny over my packable nylon print dress and with my pearls, but I felt better as soon as I wrapped them about me. The people laughed and nodded when I did it, but I hated, anyway, to take anything of theirs. They had so little, but it did seem as if it was a pleasure for them to give things to me. My husband said the shawls probably had fleas on them, but by then I cared less about fleas than I did about keeping warm. After all, I only had on my light dress while he had his suit jacket.

I had very little money with me as I always depended on my husband for that, but I decided to hand it all out to them — they hadn't asked me for any, but I wanted to. My husband said it was like overtipping and would ruin their whole economy... make them discontented, but I did it anyway. After all, I didn't have that much.

"You're enjoying yourself, aren't you?" my husband said. "You love all this attention." I realized he was right. I *was* enjoying myself. Nothing at all like this had ever happened to me and I liked it.

Then a man came up to us who spoke some English and asked me to say' a few words to the people. "Please, Mrs.," he said, "speak of this unexpected meeting. Just a few words," and he said he would translate.

"Good Lord!" my husband said. Of course he knew I'd never spoken in public in my life and he was right to worry that I'd make a fool of myself, but I did want to thank the people. I felt so much warmer wrapped up in their shawls and I was happy with the reds and oranges and the soft wool of them. Softer than most. Odd, here they were with almost nothing of material wealth and yet their clothes were the softest and warmest I'd ever felt.

I thought, then, how hardly any of them could speak English anyway, so I did speak. "All these nice things," I said. "You are so kind." I was trying to speak clearly and simply so if they knew any English at all they could understand. "We were cold and hungry, but now we'll be fine because of you. Thank you. Thank you."

Then the translator began to talk and he went on and on, his voice rising and falling with emotion. It wasn't possible that he was translating what I'd said unless he was repeating it ten or twelve times with different words and inflexions. It's the usual thing, I thought. Nobody ever pays any attention. I've often said I might as well be talking to the wall.

My husband tried several times to interrupt and even became quite harsh with him, but the man wouldn't stop. Then my husband tried to pull me away as he had before, but the translator grabbed my other arm so that I was jostled back and forth between them even as the translator talked. They were both strong men, though the translator was small, and, though my husband gave several hard jerks, the translator managed to keep hold of me. My shoulder hasn't been the same since and I had bruises — five little black and blue spots for each of their fingers — on each of my arms.

When the translator finally stopped talking, the people cheered and surged toward us. There must have been a hundred or more by now and, though they were all smiling, it was frightening. Then two small but stolid men lifted me to their shoulders before I or my husband knew what they were doing and began to trot down the road with me — down that tiny road that led away from the bridge and toward the mountains, and all the people followed and began to sing.

The translator trotted by my side and said their song was about how, "Mountains will rise yet higher." I wanted to ask him what that meant, but I wasn't sure I could trust him to give any right answers anyway. "A known song," he said, "a very, very, very known song. 'Uphold us with your own right hand.' You," he said, pointing at me. "Birds will be fed. As a child, birds."

I could see my husband also in the crowd, towering over all the others, but he was having a hard time staying near me. The translator had been having a hard time, too, but now he was holding on to my ankle so as not to be swept away from me. I wondered that my husband hadn't thought to do it, but perhaps he hadn't had the chance. I could see he was struggling, though, and I felt warmed that he would work so hard for my sake. The translator saw me looking back and said not to worry, that he would take care of me, which did not reassure me.

We went on and on, the ground rising sharply now that we had passed the fields so that I worried about those who carried me — these small men hardly as tall as I, and I'm not thin ... not at all thin. I wondered how they had the strength. I saw my husband far behind now, looking red and out of breath even though he had no one to carry, though of course there was the unaccustomed altitude.

Then the road became a mere trail. Hardly room for one person.

I was carried sideways and the crowd thinned out to a long, long line. I was frightened when I looked at the steep drop to the right of us, but the men were like mountain goats.

Whenever the trail allowed it, the translator held on to my foot and talked to me. "For you," he said. "This is all for you and in your name." I asked him what name, but he would only answer, "Yours, Mrs."

It was almost dark when we rounded a curve and before us was a hanging valley, steep, but not too steep to stop there for the night. Fires were already being started, but everyone came and called out to me. "They're asking you to speak," the translator said. "Open your arms. Point out the moon and its star."

"You'll just tell them anything you please. Why should I speak at all?"

He squeezed my foot until it hurt. "You must. It doesn't matter what you say. These are your lucky days. The moon shines in your eyes and in your white hair. Moon is the name of the mole on your chin. You have a star on your cheek."

Yes, I do have a star — one of those blood vessel bunches. I forget what you call them. I was going to have it fixed. I didn't think it would ever be important.

Then here was my husband, climbing up toward us. I thought maybe he'd given up. He could have turned around and walked the easy way, down and over the bridge and gotten help in town. That probably would have been the logical thing to do, but here he was, for once not logical, pale and panting, and I felt that warmth for him again. Perhaps this would be a whole new beginning for us. He might rescue me, though it was hard to tell if I needed rescuing or not and, actually, I wasn't sure I wanted to be rescued even if I needed to be. At least not yet. Things were happening. I'd always wanted things to happen and nothing much ever had. For a long time I'd been feeling that I was trying to play the part of myself as though I were a character in a drama that wasn't even about me.

"Speak," the translator said. "They won't put you down until you do." I saw that that was true, and that, for their sakes, I should speak and so I did. I said how the thing on my chin was a mole and the thing on my cheek was just a bunch of blood vessels that I'd forgotten the word for, and that I was an ordinary person. Then the translator spoke. He was too tired to go on very long this time, but I was sure what he said had nothing to do with what I'd said. Once the people even cheered.

Then they put me down on a pile of blankets that had been prepared for me. My husband came up and collapsed beside me. Women brought us soup, just one bowl for us to share. (I tried, surreptitiously, to give the most to him while I could see that he tried, surreptitiously, to give the most to me.) My husband said that the translator had told him not to worry, that help would be on its way soon, that he, the translator, would see to it, and my husband had given him a hundred-dollar bill. I thought about what he'd said about their economy and how I'd hardly given out ten dollars worth of coins, but I didn't mention it. Perhaps it was different giving it all to one person. We were too tired to talk much. Again I said I was sorry and curled up close to him. I felt guilty that I'd somehow gotten us out here cold and dirty and in even more altitude than before, wrapped up in ragged blankets that smelled of hay.

In the morning we both felt better. How could we not? Wisps of clouds hung over each mountain top and mist streamed up our hanging valley from below. I hadn't seen anything so mysterious in a long time, if ever. I felt like a child, everything new and so much yet to know and see. Women came then and gave me a big skirt so I could urinate in privacy under it as they do, and we all went off-all us women, to the far side of the valley... they, laughing and talking. Then I had the idea that I would bow down to them as they had done to me, so I did that, and it made everybody happy. They taught me the words for sun, sky, mountain, cloud ... I'm pretty good with languages and I'd already picked up other words. I was trying hard because of not trusting the translator. I knew their words for secret or sacred and non-secret or non-sacred. The translator's accent was so bad I couldn't be sure which was which.

"Women," the women said, laughing, "women, yes, yes," and I knew what they were saying, both their words and what they meant by it. "Men," they said, and pointed with their thumbs to the opposite side of the valley, turning toward it but covering their eyes at the same time. I also covered my eyes and laughed.

Then we women and the men came back together in the center of the valley and everybody had a bowl of grains of some sort. The translator sat beside me as we ate. "That is not the language of the city," he told me. "That is only ordinary mountain language. It is not worth learning. I can speak all the languages," he said, "from the lowest, which they speak here, to the highest, as the proof is this English I am speaking."

I was disliking the translator more and more. I couldn't stand him near me. I preferred the women even if I didn't understand them. "Go away," I said, which was quite unlike me. I even told him he was spoiling my breakfast, but then I realized how irritated I was sounding and tried to soften it. "You've been a great help," I said, "but I really would rather try to manage as best I can by myself"

"Mrs., I am still helping," he said. "Believe me, this language is no good." Then the two little men lifted me again and this time my husband grabbed my leg and held on. "Speak," the translator said.

I didn't hesitate. I knew what to say. First I gave their greeting words — the ones I'd heard so often that morning. They were delighted. Then I pointed with my thumb — not like hitchhiking, but straight out as I'd seen them do — pointing at the translator. "No," I said and waved him away. (I knew about the dangers of wrong gestures. I'd seen programs about that on TV, but I took the chance anyway.) Then I closed my mouth and covered it with *my* left hand, still pointing at the translator and would not speak until the women pushed him away. "You'll be sorry," he said. "Without my help, it is forever." After that I said all my new words with my arms raised and out. I said, sky, and sun, and mist. Then I said that word that meant either secret or sacred, and I pointed to myself and said, non-secret, or non-sacred, and they laughed again. I nodded and smiled back at them and everyone thought it was all very funny and so did I. Then we were on our way, again at a trot — my husband beside me this time — up, up, and over the mountain pass, and rounding down, and the view was like nothing I'd ever even imagined I would be privileged to see. Beyond and beyond, always more mountains, and far below another hanging valley, sister to the one we'd camped in the night before except for huge old trees scattered about it, and houses there, and things that glittered and lots of red, and you could hear a sound as of several piccolos a little out of tune. Faint. You could almost think it was the ringing in your ears.

The translator hovered, always a few yards behind us, and my husband, still holding my ankle, kept saying, "I don't know how we're going to get out of this mess without that man." I didn't answer. Besides, all I really cared about right then was how beautiful everything was.

Then we rounded a switchback and met five women coming up from below shaking wind-chime kind of things and playing little tin flutes that looked to be from the five-and-ten. When they got to me they kissed my hands and feet and they all said, "Thank you," in English but only one could really speak it, though not very well. "It's you," she kept saying. "It's really you."

"Who?" I said. "Tell me who?"

"Mountains will rise yet higher," she said. "Birds will be fed. As a child, birds."

The five women played us down the mountain and soon we were at the entrance proper to the valley where carved wooden gates crossed the walkway from the rising cliff on one side to the drop-off on the other.

"If we go through these gates," my husband said, "we'll be prisoners. I'm going to give that translator another hundred dollars." At that moment I didn't care. Besides, feeling like a prisoner was nothing new to me. My husband must have seen something of this on my face. "If I were you," he said, "I'd not make that translator angry. He's the only one who can help us. I know he's utterly without conscience but he's sensible."

"Sensible," I said, and I was wondering of what use hundred dollar bills were way out here.

"You've let this go to your head. You're thinking very well of yourself, that's easy to see, but you know you never even finished college." He was always reminding me of this, but this time in particular it didn't seem right, neither college nor hundred-dollar bills.

We went through the gates and entered the valley. Blue jays were everywhere and so tame that they sat on people's heads. And then those old, old, old trees ... Ribbons and mirrors hung about them and beyond was the village, low, long, red houses, some quite large.

They brought me to what seemed the very oldest tree of all, and sat me down facing it. The woman who could speak a little English said, "We want your forehead on the ground in front of her." So I did that, as they had done for me. I liked doing it,. smelling the earth, touching it with my forehead. I even rested my cheek on a circle of lichen on a nearby stone. It was certainly a tree worthy of worship: rather short, but the widest I'd ever seen, and one whole side of it was dead. Still, here in front, one part struggle on, alive.

Then they tried to get my husband to do the same but he wouldn't. I told him I thought it might be best to do it, "under the circumstances," I said, "and it's nice to do — you'd be surprised." But he said he wouldn't bow down to any tree no matter what the circumstances. He was looking quite unlike my husband by now (and I suppose I was looking even less like myself than he looked like himself, for I had that big striped skirt on and several shawls). He was dirty and his suit was wrinkled and had sweat marks on the back and under the arms. He no longer had his tie. His left breast pocket looked funny now with its three little pens.

They all lined up and began a ceremony, singing and dancing, patting trees as if they were friends. Even the children came and danced with them. Some so small they must have only just learned to walk. I went to the old, old tree and put my arms around the part that was still alive and kissed it. I did it without thinking. I had the idea that, if I ever did get back home, what a nice thought it would be to know that my kiss was thousands of miles away and maybe three miles high. They noticed, of course, though they said nothing, but I didn't care who saw, I just wanted my kiss there: Hello and/or Good-bye. Whichever.

Then a bundle was brought out by the woman who could speak a little English. "A little bird," she said. "A flying snake," and she unwrapped it so I could see.

It lay so still at first I thought it was the statue of a child, painted utterly lifelike, brown with shiny black Chinese hair, and with those almond Indian eyes. He was naked and on his head was a crown of brilliant jay feathers. But then he blinked and made a soft sound. "He is in your name," the woman said, and, "He is secret and sacred." (She used both words in English.)

"My God!" That was my husband who had come up beside me. "My God, now what!" And then the child smiled and reached out to me and I to him, but the woman held him back. "No," she said, "you serve him in other ways. May you live long enough so that many small things should not suffer."

They brought me a bouquet of poison oak mixed with prickly teasels. They brought me buffalo burrs and Spanish dagger fronds. They brought me bitter fruit. I took everything. I didn't mind.

"You will enter a cave. There will be a long, steep tunnel. At the end of it you will be born into the place where a priest will already be dancing death. There will be many other things never seen in the light of day, but there will be women on each side of you and women front and back. Every new moon you will be asked if you accept what it is you must do. You will say yes though there will be times you'll want to say no. But most of the time you will live as we do and be looked up to, as we are all looked up to here. If you don't agree to this, you are free to go now, but it must be now."

It's odd that just when the woman said we were free to go and go now, my husband suddenly got very angry. He lashed out, punching men and even women, and yelling, saying everybody was insane. It took the small men several minutes to throw him down and tie his arms behind his back. They were brutal, but they had to be. He was like a crazy person though he was calling everybody else crazy. (Of course it wasn't the first time he'd called *me* crazy.)

Even when he was somewhat calmer, he still shouted out. He said I wasn't capable of answering for myself because I was as far from reality as they were. I'd even, all on my own, kissed a tree. I was escaping from the truth. He said my answer was no, and that I didn't have the sense to say it. He shouted no, then. "No, no, and no!" All this didn't make me angry anymore. I knew I had to decide, calmly, for myself.

"Reality" and "escaping." Those were the words that stuck with me. I have never thought my life to be particularly real, and it occurred to me that I didn't relish it much either, and I liked this whole adventure, including, or especially, the hardships. I do know pain and hardship aren't reality any more than joy is,but this place had both, and I'd not had either one. And it was full of beauty, and rituals, and the great, old trees, and mist, and earthquakes, and laughter. And I was to have a part to play. I'd never had a real part in anything before. I said yes.

"Crazy," my husband said, still panting from the exertion in this altitude. "You've no concept. No concept at all." I said I knew I had no concept, but that I was willing to accept whatever this would turn out to be.

"You'll regret it."

"I'm sure there'll be times I will," I said, "but my life is already full of regrets."

So then a group left to take my husband back. There were just six of them including my husband and the translator. "We come back and get the Mrs.," the translator kept saying. "The police will come if you pay for it, Mr." But I'd never let anyone take me from my new real life.

***The Start of the End of It All and Other Stories*,** 1990

A Is For Abel, B Is For Bird

I sing-song out, "Abel, Abel, under the table." That's where he is, all hunched up in a little ball, scared of me, I hope, except he looks calm. "Abel isn't able. Abel isn't able —to do anything. He can hum, though. I heard you. You can't pretend you didn't."

That boy's been treated too kind. Maybe he'll talk pretty soon just so he can tell on me. But probably nobody would listen, especially not his mother. Maybe not much use in talking around here. Maybe that's how it all began.

They say he never did talk. Not ever. With his big brother it's different. He talked just like anybody else and then his daddy died and all of a sudden he didn't anymore. So far, that is. With his big brother it makes some sense, but Abel is nine years younger and never did know his father. He's just copycatting. But a child needs talk around, good or bad, it doesn't matter which. At least *I* expect to do a lot of it.

They live far out. I had to hitch a ride with somebody going that way, but they wouldn't take me on in so I had to walk from their front pasture. The ditches were overflowing and the pasture was too wet. Odd for the desert, but I'd heard about too much water coming down from the mountains this year because of too much snow up there. I thought I'd have to walk through mud, but the road was pretty clear. I could see the house and barns not so far off. You couldn't miss them with those Lombardy poplars around. I didn't have a lot to carry, but my books are heavy. I had to stop and rest a couple of times. The road is a desert sort of road, perfectly straight and no trees, so I kept hoping somebody would look out the window and see me and come and help me. Of Course now that I've been here a day or so, I know better. I'm surprised the mother got out of bed to greet me at all. (Abel must have been hiding. I didn't meet him till supper. Stuck out here all by himself — I mean with just these three people, he can't have known many strangers.) The mom was all mussed up from having just got out of bed. She looked embarrassed. She said she didn't realize I was coming today, but now that I know her a little bit, I know she always forgets what day it is.

She had stains all down the front of her dress.

Those two brothers look alike except the big one is dark and Abel is a red head. Well, a pink head like their mom, except she's getting gray. (Just try to get her to say something. She will if she has to but she doesn't have to very often.) They thought school would make the big one talk, but they say he ran out the back door every time they put him in the front until they gave up. That's why they got me for Abel. They didn't even try school.

The ranch belongs to the big one even though he's only seventeen. I'm only two years older than he is. If I hadn't already said, I could pretend I was the same age as him.

I do like the big one. I like that he's quiet. And there's things I like about this place, too, though it's all tumble down. You can see how nice it could be with just a little help. I thought to get a can of paint myself or find nails and a hammer. They wouldn't notice if something got fixed anyway. The big sister and brother only do what's necessary for the stock, and the mom does even less than necessary. She does the house stuff. The chickens don't die and the Jersey gets milked.

(I thought that grown up sister was a man when I first came. She seems a lot more like a man than the big brother. I'll bet she doesn't even own a dress. Her clothes are all loose so she looks thick. She stamps around in men's boots. I heard her swearing. Her mother doesn't care. She gave me her room. I don't know where she sleeps now. I wouldn't be surprised if she wasn't sleeping out in the cow barn.)

They couldn't always have been this way — everything gone to pieces. They have a closed up parlor I sneaked into. There's a fancy organ in there. Mice ran out of it when I went into the room. I could see where they'd used the felt to make themselves a nest. Everything is nice in that room. The sofa has gold-colored upholstery. There's a lamp with beaded red fringe. You can tell they never use it. There's sandy dust all over. I'm going to clean it up and teach in there. I need a place where things aren't falling apart. I won't ask permission, I'll just do it and see what happens. I haven't had a whole lot of elegance in my life. *So far,* that is.

Of course if you want to look out at something nice, there's always those snow-capped mountains. Some people might think I'm a little bit crazy because I talk to mountains when I'm off by myself. I started when I was about three years old. I always did it after I got whipped. I never talk to the highest, just the second or third highest. When I was little I thought the highest wouldn't bother listening to a little girl with little-girl problems. I still do it that way. I wonder if I could get Abel to talk to a mountain? I wonder if there's one he likes better than all the others?

Talk or no, I'm supposed to stuff some learning down him. They said to get to know each other first, but what's to know about somebody who never says a word? He can nod and he can hum. That's what's to know. I told him, "I ask a question, and I don't get some kind of head shake, then one pinch to the funny bone." That hurts and doesn't show. I demonstrated. That's how he ended up under the table.

I tell Abel I never knew my father either. I say, "That doesn't make me special. I was whipped regular as clock-work. Catch me not talking and they'd have put a stop to that soon enough. And I say: If you can hum, you can talk, and I say, if you think you've got everything just the way you want it here, well, not anymore you don't.

And then I go right down under the table myself and pull him out and give him another pinch to the elbow, but this time I have a good grip on him. He doesn't make a sound but I can tell I hurt him, but he doesn't look scared and I want him scared. I tell him I'm an old witch. I say I'm a hundred years old. I say, "Look at me. You can see the witch color in my eyes." I hold my face real close to his and, he looks and then shuts his eyes after. (My eyes are just like anybody else's but he'll think they're not. You tell a little kid things like that and they just about always believe, and, even if they don't exactly believe, they half believe.)

I say, "You watch out when it gets to be the full moon."

So then I tie an old lead rope around his ankle and tie him to the organ and we get to work. "Pay attention to the old witch," I say. I keep my hand near his elbow. He knows why. At first I thought maybe he was stupid as well as mute and that nobody in the family would admit it, but he understands fast enough.

A is for apple, juicy and red.

B is for bird, so sweet to be heard... I change them.

A is for Abel who's ugly as sin.

B is for bee all ready to sting.

C is for crybaby, D is for dumb, E is for empty, F is for false, G is for *Gotcha!*

And I grab him. I'm the only one that laughs.

"Now draw me these letters. Or else you know what."

He does, and nicely, too. That's what I call one time learning, or maybe two time. A couple of pinches is all it takes. Most people don't know about those nerves. I guess I really *am* like a witch. But if anybody has witching eyes, it's Abel. His eyes are sort of the same color as his hair except darker, kind of orangy. I got a good look at them when I made him look at mine.

Next morning the big sister and brother go off to wherever it is they go out — for maybe two days (the sister says she can't say for sure how many) to bring the cows down from the mountains. She says sometimes the cows get where you wouldn't believe. After they leave, the mom cleans up the kitchen and then goes back to bed, which is her usual way. We'll have the whole place to ourselves, me and Abel. Except I can't find him. We have our biscuits with bacon grease and then he's gone. I search all over all kinds of cubby holes. Abel is small for his age (if they've got his age right) he'll fit into all sorts of little places. At least I get to know this place better. It really is a run down mess.

Well, I should have been looking up. I should have been thinking monkey. He makes me think of a monkey anyway. Little monkey face and those sad eyes. Orangutan kind of hair color. Those eyes of his are going to be a lot sadder after I get my hands on him. Maybe he thinks I'm scared to get up on the roof. I don't know how he did it, but I'm going to use the ladder. At least it's not the barn roof. That's three times as high. So we chase each other across the ridge and I win, except I tear my skirt. Abel probably tore his pants, but they already have so many tears you can't tell.

No one has ever told that child not to do *anything*. He's climbed everything he wanted to since — well probably *before* he could walk. I don't know how he survived to get to be nine.

This time I tie Abel to me and we go off for a long walk — out where nobody can see or hear us. We sit under a willow beside the stream. There used to be a dam here, but it's been broken through and never repaired. You can see where there was a nice pond. I sing the alphabet song three times. Then I tell Abel to move his lips along with mine so I can see, and that I don't have to hear anything. He does. Obedient little fellow. You'd think he'd refuse. What could I do if he did except the same old pinching?

I won't beat on him. I don't *ever* do *that* kind of thing. Anyway, I know my pinches hurt just as much. I know because how I learned about them was that they did it to me. But I didn't learn how right away. I had to practice. Even on myself. When I got good at it I got to be a scary person. I always denied it when the other kids tattled on me. Lots of times a teacher looked at somebody's wrist or elbow and said, No harm done that she could see. Teachers liked me because I worked so hard. I always got good grades. I always won the prizes. The teachers never believed anything anybody said against me. They thought the other children were jealous. They gave me good recommendations and then, of course, my grades and prizes proved it. I don't have a bad temper. I don't need one. Things usually work out my way. I'm always very calm. That scares people, too, which stands me in good stead.

It's good the brother and sister are gone because both at noon dinner and also at supper, I tie Abel to his chair and the mom doesn't even notice. She's a terrible cook. Dinner is left-over bacon (left over from when?) and left-over biscuits. Abel takes it like it's always this way. He hums as he eats and kicks the table leg. It's annoying but the mom doesn't say not to. I'll put a stop to that later. (He does this because the big brother isn't here. When he is, Abel eats sitting on his lap. I should put a stop to that, too. You can see why Abel wants to be just like him.)

That night we have beef stew. I think the big sister must have made that. At least the mom found the energy to warm it up. Or maybe it sat at the back of the stove all this time. We'll probably have it tomorrow and the next day, too.

There's a lot of it.

That night I tie Abel to the bed, but, of course, he unties himself. He's gone *before* breakfast this time. I look all around again, up and down tops of roofs and way out, but I don't find him. (I do find some old dried up paint -which I throw out -and some hammers and nails.) Abel comes in on his own for noon dinner. I guess he got hungry without his breakfast — those biscuits and bacon grease.

I grab him and pinch him real good. Wrist, too. I know I hurt him but what I see in his eyes isn't fear — unfortunately. There's something calm there. Sort of as if, if he could or would talk, he'd say, "Oh." Just, "Oh," like, "So this is how it is."

I say, "Don't you want to learn anything? You want to be stupid all your life like you are right now? I'll bet your dead daddy wouldn't like that." He looks away, like he's thinking about it.

"Your dead dad would wallop you good if he knew all what you do."

But Abel shakes his head, no. Slowly, several times. I can almost hear him say his daddy wouldn't.

"Yes he would. You never knew him. What do you know."

But he shakes his head again. "Your mom doesn't count. She's too tired to whup you otherwise she'd have done it a long time ago." He keeps on shaking his head.

"Be that as it may," I say, "now you've gone and done it. I'm going to pull out all my witching. I'm making this big magic circle. You go outside it, you'll die in excruciating agony. So: the front fence, the rear pasture, the near ditch at the end of the vegetable garden. That leaves you more room than you need."

Then I pretend to cast a spell. I talk all sorts of nonsense. I make up a fancy sign that I scratch in some of the fence posts and on the ditch gates. Then I make a couple of tiny branding irons out of fence wire, and I make a little fire and when the brands are red-hot I brand Abel D for dumb (I guess he'll learn the letter D fast enough) and then an arrow. I put these where they don't show and where they'll hurt the most, or, anyway, the second most hurtful spot: under his arm. "That arrow always points to me, even if it has to turn around to do it," I say. "Watch it good and you'll see." On myself — on the back of my hand right where he, and everybody, can see it, I burn another arrow. I tell him when he stops being dumb I'll change his D to a secret lucky sign. But I tell him I don't expect he'll ever get that far along. I tell him the arrow means I'll always be able to catch him, so I don't have to bother tying him up anymore.

So after we finish with all this I decide I'll not go on with the alphabet right now. I have a big animal book with hand colored pictures and animal information. I sit Abel down next to me and read to him out of it, and pretty soon he's really listening. Tigers and elephants and ostriches, and, by the way he looks and listens, I don't think he's ever heard of any of them, even elephants. I think: now I've got you, but I give him a couple of pinches to show him that just because he's behaving himself doesn't mean I'll stop doing it.

They have quite a few books here, but all from a long time ago. (The home medical advisor says things you wouldn't believe. And half the book, maybe more, is taken up with sick horses and hoof problems.) That book and the government bulletins on farming might make Abel pay attention, too, so I read to him about poison weeds that kill horses or make cows have two-headed calves. There's even a picture. I tell him he could read all this himself if he learned how. "Starting with the alphabet," I say. Just as I figured, we have that same stew again for supper.

In spite of all that pretend witching, the next morning Abel is gone again, and I find him outside my magic circle. Not only that, I find a funny little squiggly sign right under all my witch signs. I should have made a bigger brand on him that would have hurt more, like four arrows in all four directions, or five. Maybe witches have five directions. Or most likely seven.

He isn't hard to find this time. You can practically see him from the house even though he's far off. I just went to say hello to the mountains as I like to do first thing, and I see him out past the horse field. At first I think he's a vulture. He's higher up in a tree than I could ever go up in the tiny branches at the top. When I get out there, I sit down under the tree to think what to do next. I tell him his hands will get stiff as a corpse and he'll come down in a big crash and break his neck and never walk again let alone climb anything. "You'd better come down now while your hands still work."

He's swaying back and forth like there's a hurricane up there. He's doing that on purpose. I'll be blamed if anything happens and it looks as if something will. That child is fearless. "You can't scare me," I say, "I'll just witch you down." Not that I've had much luck with witching so far.

So I pretend to weave another spell. He's just looking down at me with that, "Oh," kind of look, so I get louder and I start dancing around. I keep saying, "Sink Down," and "Low" and "Descent," between all the gobblede-gook. I say, "Gravity … gravity will get you," though I'm pretty sure Abel hasn't ever heard of that and won't until I tell him about it.

But all of a sudden Abel starts to make a terrible racket, shrieking and howling and his voice is like none I've ever heard. It wobbles and wavers and goes on and off by itself. It's scary. I suppose I should be happy to know he can make any sort of sound at all. If anybody is a witch it has to be Abel. But then he stops the racket and lets go of those little top-of-the-tree branches and comes crashing … or starts to … but then he grabs again and stops himself. It's like magic. (He's so light and little. I wonder if the others have noticed how thin he is?) He squats there on a bigger branch like a bird ready to take off.

I say again, "You can't fly, you know," but I say it because he looks so much as if he can. "I won't ever, ever pinch you anymore." But why should he believe anything I say? "I don't want you to hurt yourself. I like you. You're the nicest person I ever did teach." It's true, too, he is, though maybe it's just that he keeps quiet. "I know you wonder why I've been hurting you. I just did that to make you talk." Of course I didn't. I did that to everybody I ever taught and practically everybody I got next to. I'm thinking how I hardly ever tell the truth. "It's *true,*" I say. "Look. This proves it."

There's a nest of beavertail cactuses a ways from the tree. I go over and put both my arms right in the middle of them. I don't feel the pain. But then I realize that if I try to catch him in case he falls, my arms will prick him as if he fell right in the cactuses. Still, I might save him. "I promise I'll never hurt you again," I say, "cross my heart." Except what will I do to make him learn — or do *anything? I* know he hates me. I wanted him to.

"You're not dumb. I'm sorry I said that and I'm sorry about the D I put on you. I'll change it."

But he's going to jump. I don't know how I know. His face is as impassive as it always is. He hasn't moved. He still squats on his branch, balanced, not even hanging on to anything. Then he spreads his arms like wings and drops straight down — into mine — my prickly ones. Safe. "See," I say, "I knew you couldn't fly."

He looks up at me with his witchy eyes — again as if to say, "Oh, so this is how it is." And then I start to cry which I never do, and my prickles start to hurt, and he looks as if his prickles, that he got from my arms, hurt, too, but he doesn't cry.

Well, their mom finally bestirs herself enough to help us get the prickers out, except there's no way we can get them all. She puts a poultice on the rest, made out of Jimson weed and turpentine and lard and tobacco and goodness knows what all else. She gives us hot wine and puts us to bed. She doesn't ask how it happened. She really seems to care about Abel. I thought she didn't. And she treats me kindly. Everybody here is kind. That is, when they remember you exist. They don't even remember Abel.

The big sister and brother come home pretty soon. Abel is asleep from the wine and I'm kind of groggy. The big sister asks how it happened, but I pretend to be too groggy to talk about it. As I lie there, still half drunk, I think how I like that Abel is, as they say, a clean slate, and that nobody but me will tell him anything — gravity and elephants — the whole world, mine to give. And then I get a real good idea of what to do with him. There's this little bitty circus that comes around to all the little towns. It's only one ring, but how many rings can you watch at the same time? We could go. They have plenty of money, they just don't use it for anything but cows.

I tell the big sister how much Abel likes my animal book. I say Abel should go to some other places and that, as soon as our prickles are better, I can find out about where the circus is. I say we should stay away maybe a week and let Abel get a good look at the world.

The big sister likes this idea a lot. She must trust me. But the mom objects. I hadn't thought she would. Maybe she saw more of the things I did than I realized. And she does kind of cling to Abel. I didn't see that at first. It Isn't noticeable until you get to know her some, but the big sister convinces her. She says, "Talk or no, it'll be good for Abel to leave the ranch." (First chance I get I'll burn a smear over those brands I put on him. I'll leave mine, though. I like it.) When we're out there by ourselves, I'll work on Abel really hard. He won't get away with anything, like I won't let him hum while we're eating. And he won't get away from me. I'll bring along the lead rope.

I might get him a harmonica. I'm surprised nobody thought of that before, the way he hums all the time. Except they don't think of anything. That child doesn't own one single thing. Well, there's his pumpkin patch that he waters pail by pail, dipper by dipper, and he has a couple of railroad spikes. The railroad goes right through here. They stop the train and pick you up in the middle of nowhere, if you let them know ahead. That's how we'll go after we get well enough and after I find out where that circus is.

The mother brings out some old clothes from when the big brother was Abel's size. I guess without this trip nobody would have thought to get them out until Abel couldn't get his backside into his pants, which is just about right now. The so-called "new" clothes are pretty worn out, too, except for a nice mannish jacket they must have used for dress-up only. The minute Abel sees it, he lights up all over. The big sister says it's just to be for good but Abel wants to put it on right away and she lets him. Like I said, he's treated much too kind. Why should he talk when he gets what he wants anyway, with just a gesture?

"Don't you dare climb anything with that on." I whisper it in his ear when I help him into it.

So Abel goes off just walking around as if to show the jacket off to the pigs and chickens and meadowlarks. The jacket's a lot too big. He doesn't know how funny he looks in it. The mother watches him walk away. She's frowning at him. I never know what her expressions mean (though mostly she doesn't have any expression at all, which is just like Abel). But then she gives me money to have Abel's picture taken and she says she'll give him some money and I should let him spend it on anything he wants, even if it's silly. Well, am I supposed to be the teacher or not? I don't say that though.

I have a hard time keeping Abel from bringing his railroad spikes along to town. I keep taking them out of his box and he keeps putting them back in until finally I tie up his box with plenty of knots and put it in my room. He's the one who has to carry it, and I don't want a worn out boy on my hands, though I don't think it would be so easy to wear out Abel.

It's at the circus that I lose him. I just turn around and he's not there. I didn't have him tied to me. Who would need to be tied up at the circus? is what I thought. He was stuffed with red candy and red pop — red was the only kind of anything he wanted. At the hotel he even finished off his beets. First thing, he bought himself a man's tie, but neither of us knows how to tie it properly. Abel looked like he was going to cry when I couldn't do it. That's the first I saw him at all even close to tears. He didn't even cry when I branded him. I pinched him good and that sobered him up. Maybe that's what decided him to run away again. He shouldn't be hard to find though. I could tell the police — if it comes to that: funny colored hair; too-big jacket that he won't take off no matter how hot it gets; flopped over, sideways tie that he won't take off either. But I'm not going to tell anybody quite yet. I'll try to find him myself.

I think of all the things he liked best: fire eater, tallest man in the world. (The fat woman scared him. He shut his eyes. He shut his eyes for the two-headed calf, too. I couldn't make him look, even with a pinch. Those things don't bother me. I can stand anything that's real and the truth.) He liked the snake charmer. *There's* something that wasn't true. I could see right away that snake wasn't even poisonous. I told Abel but he didn't seem to care. "S is for sssssnake," I said, "and S looks like a snake, too." I wrote that down for him, S and SNAKE. "Pay attention. This whole thing isn't just for fun, you know. I don't care anything about fun."

I wondered if he'd gone back to the hotel? He liked looking out the window, down where people passed by all the time.

So after checking the side shows I start back to the hotel and I find Abel first thing, sooner than I thought, at the edge of the field where the circus is. He's getting pestered by a bunch of boys. He must hardly know what another boy his age is like. They keep pushing him and every time they do he falls over backwards with that, "Oh," look of his and then he gets up and gets pushed over again. You'd think he'd learn not to get up.

I give my special yell. It's a really crazy yell. It's saved me lots of times. I suppose the circus people wonder what sort of animal is out here. Those boys run off right away and then I hear this funny voice saying, "Whiskey, whiskey." It's a crow. That's what Abel bought with the rest of his money; that, and two more bottles of red pop (I checked his pockets, there's only four pennies left). What will his mom think? It's not my fault, it's hers for letting him buy anything he wanted. Should I try to sell it back? Or get rid of it some way? Abel can't tell on me at least. I can do anything I want to, as when have I ever not?

It's a scraggly looking bird. I don't know why he would want it — except it's as run-down as everything on the ranch but the horses and the cows.

"Abel, this crow won't talk for you. It has no sense except its normal crow sense — though maybe not even that, being cooped up like it is. I'll bet it only has five or six words at the most. Of course that's a lot more than you have. Your dead daddy wouldn't like this at all. He wants you to do the talking. He'd whup you good if he saw you with this dumb bird.

The crow says, "Hello, hello, boy. Whiskey, whiskey." It hops and flutters in a lopsided way because of its clipped wing. "Tommy wants whiskey. Good boy."

"And this crow can't fly any more than you can. Are you aware of that?"

What will they think if, "Tommy wants whiskey," are Abel's first words? Or maybe only words ever? But maybe I can use this crow some way. Talk to a mountain? Talk to a crow?

We walk down a ways and find a bench. We sit and Abel drinks his cherry pop and I drink his strawberry pop. He doesn't seem to mind.

"They won't let you take this crow into the hotel, and, anyway, it probably has lice and God knows what else." The crow has already shat all over the top of the bench.

"Look at that," I say. "You want that all over your bed? But maybe if you talk to it — maybe then, I'll find a way to get it up to our room secretly." (Just try to keep something yelling, "Whiskey, whiskey, whiskey," secret.) "I'll do the best I can. Give it a name and call it that out loud just once and I'll write it down for you." So I write ABEL and put it on him and MARY CATHERINE and put it on myself. It's not the first time I've done that for him. Abel takes the ABEL and puts it on the crow's perch.

"You mean you're naming the crow Abel?" And he nods yes. "You can't do that. We'll get you all mixed up."

That's the first I've seen him laugh. I didn't think he could. Or would ever want to, especially not in front of me.

"All right then, Abel Tiny and Abel Teeny Weeny. So if you want me to go to all the trouble and risk-of-my-neck trying to get Abel Teeny Weeny into the hotel room with us, you have to say something. I don't care what. Say, Oh, or, Boo, or, elephant, for heaven's sake."

He shakes his head, no.

"Well say, no, then. Just no. That's a good handy word. You can get pretty far with just that."

But it isn't as if I don't know he won't. It's not going to happen out of the blue like that. If I'm going to win every battle, I'd better make sure every battle is one I can win.

"All right, we'll write things instead. We'll work till supper time and then we'll have a picnic here on the bench so we won't have to worry about getting the crow into the hotel — hum if you like — and I won't have to be embarrassed about your head on the table and all that humming. And then we'll go to the evening circus. You can stay up as long as you like. Nobody has ever told that child to go to bed anyway, but I think it's a good idea for me to treat him as if he'd been brought up like any other boy. Give him some idea of the way normal people are.

(At the hotel Abel and I are in the same room. They put in a folding army cot for Abel but I think he would just as happily sleep on the floor. And he hasn't got one tiny bit of modesty. He's like a wild animal. Traipses around naked as though it was the most natural thing. Nobody has thought to teach him the rudiments of anything at all. I tell him we don't do that. That he should keep his pants on except when with men and boys. "Women don't like to see that," I say. Actually I kind of like him jumping around naked, but I'm supposed to be the teacher. And I want to shock him. People learn faster if you shock them and the learning sticks better. Learning has to hurt some. That's my theory.)

I make Abel write elephant and snake and crow and horse twenty times each. All by himself he draws the crow and writes ABEL underneath it. Then we go back to the circus, crow and all. The crow came with a black cover so we cover him up. I hook the lead rope to Abel's belt under his jacket and tie him to this scarf kind of thing I wear around my waist. People will notice anyway. Abel is such a noticeable boy. He looks like a clown himself. His hair color doesn't even look real and, no matter how much you plaster his hair down, two minutes later it sticks straight up. (One of these days I'm going to cut most of it off.) So we'll get noticed anyway, and, after getting a good look at Abel, people are sure to see the lead rope.

But I must have tied a bad knot, and then I was watching the acrobats, which are my favorites, and after them the clown acrobats come which are just as good, and maybe are the same people, and suddenly there's Abel. Above them, up by the top of the tent, hanging on to some sort of tent rope. He's got the crow on it's perch in one hand. The lead rope is dangling out from under his jacket like a long, white tail. How did he climb up there with only one hand?

At the same time I see him, everybody else does. They think he's part of the clown act. They laugh and clap. Now he's up there with no hands at all, just his legs wrapped around the rope, and everybody claps all the more. He's untying the crow. There's two clown acrobats going up after him.

He lets the crow go. For a minute it looks as if even the crow thinks — or hopes — it can fly, clipped wings or not. It flaps like crazy, but it drops, as I knew it would — flaps just enough to break its fall some and ends up in the sawdust, hopping and flopping.

I feel my heart beating so hard I think I might die. I want to yell out for Abel to climb down and that he should use both hands, for heaven's sake, but everybody's making too much noise. (I hope he doesn't have any secret railroad spikes hidden in his pockets.) I see the clowns are talking to him and I see Abel nodding yes and no. Now the first clown is almost up to him and grabs the dangling lead rope. As if it was planned, Abel lets go right then. There he dangles, his belt up under his arms. I hope it holds. The crowd loves it. It's the funniest act of any. I laugh, too, but mostly because Abel is safe — so far. I laugh and laugh, but I feel all wobbly. Lots of people are standing up, but I don't think I can. And then things quiet down a bit and I hear, clear as day … I hear Abel say, "Caw." And then again, and lots of times. At least it's not whiskey. People laugh like anything.

Another clown down on the ground has picked up the crow and is cawing out to Abel, and they have this crow conversation while they're bringing Abel down, and then all three clowns are in it. Then he's down again, they take him in back behind the bleachers.

So I go back behind the bleachers, too. My legs are like … I hardly know what. And the first thing Abel sees me back there, he says "Caw," right at me He's got this look in his eyes as if: You wanted a word? So you got one.

The clown is still cawing out at Abel and Abel is cawing back. You can see he loves doing it. His voice sounds funny. As if he really doesn't know how to use it. Kind of an animal voice. More like a real crow than it ought to be. It worries me about whether he can manage other words, though. Caw doesn't take a lot of moving your mouth around. I wonder if he could say any other word, especially if it wasn't an, ah, word?

"Are you his mother?"

"Certainly not." (How could anybody think that?)

I can feel myself blushing. I hate when I do that. I don't even know why I'm doing it. Why would I blush in front of three ridiculous clowns With false noses? Of course they're acrobats. And they are the same ones that did the show just before, because one slips off his clown suit and under it there's the skin-tight acrobat suit. When he does that, I blush again just when I thought it was over. And I step on Abel's dangling lead rope and almost pull him down and trip myself up, too. I'm wishing I'd never heard of him and that tumble-down ranch and I'm ashamed of the lead rope. "He keeps climbing things," I say, and they say they noticed that. And then they say, "This is our crow, you know. Somebody stole it."

"He didn't do that. He used up all his money on it. Somebody else must have stolen it and sold it to him." (They probably don't believe me.) "But he'll give it back anyway."

Abel looks like he really will cry. He tries to hold it in, but this time he can't. Tears and he's actually making a sound —a little animal sound. One of the clowns takes out a bandana —three times as big as usual — and wipes them up, but they keep on coming.

"This is a special crow:' one of the clowns says. "He has a little cap and jacket. His tongue's been clipped so he can talk. He can turn summersaults."

So the long and the short of it is, I get rid of the crow which I never wanted to be bothered with anyway. I grab the lead rope and we sneak out the back way. I make Abel take off his jacket and tie so nobody will recognize us, but they probably will anyway.

"If you cared so much about that crow, why did you let it go free, anyway?" But he just goes on making that little sound. Makes me think of a kitten.

"Well, now you've gone and done it. You're never going to go see a circus again as long as you live and that's that." (At least it's a sound. I figure any sound at all is good practice for him.) "And caw is not a good word. Find a better one or we're going home on the next train."

But all this cawing. We can't go home with that. What if they say, "Pass the stew," and Abel says, "Caw?" What if they pick us up at the train tracks and they ask us, did we have a good time? and Abel says, "Caw?" I have to stop him, and we have to stay here until I do.

There's still plenty of light since it's hardly eight o'clock, so I get a good hold on Abel's lead rope and start us up along the creek that runs through town. I'm thinking to go a long ways up to be out of ear shot just in case Abel makes a lot of noise. He's still making that little mewling sound every time he takes a breath. He's just pretending to cry. I know all about nine year olds. I tell him, "Life is full of disappointments and you have to get used to it and the sooner the better. You disappoint me all the time. Here you have a real man's tie and a real man's jacket, not to mention getting to go to the circus. What more do you want? What do you think life is all about anyway? And me? What do you think my life is like, having to watch out for you all the time?"

Of course he just keeps making that sound.

We keep on climbing... up through the aspen and willows that line the creek.

And I start thinking about how Abel doesn't have any sort of animal of his own and that he needs one. There are plenty out there at the ranch but I don't think any of them are Abel's. (A pumpkin patch just isn't the same.) Seems as if nobody even thought to get him a horse and let him go out and help push cows. They forget how old he is like they forget everything else about him.

"You're not nine years old. You're a little dwarf and you don't even know it yourself. You're small so they think you must still be a child. On the other hand, if you really *are* a child, you can't be nine. More like seven."

Abel doesn't pay me any attention that I can tell. He's up ahead as far as the lead rope allows. If I pulled on it I could pull him down real easy.

"You ought to have a horse you know. I don't know why you don't except they forgot to give you one. And you could get your own crow. Climb up and get yourself a chick and train it from the start. You could climb up no matter how high it was."

That makes him look back at me for a second, but I can't tell what he's thinking. I do pull on the rope just to see what will happen and no great harm done but a little dirt on his so-called "new" pants.

I'm thinking when we're well out of ear shot I'll give him what-for so he'll never dare say caw again as long as he lives, but as we walk, I begin to realize that the more I hurt him, the more he'll get even with me. He always finds a way. He'll say caw exactly the time it'll be the worst for me, so I decide we'll just go up here for a walk and I'll be nice to him. Except I *have* been nice. Just about as nice as anybody could be. Has anybody else bothered to take him to the circus?

I pull on the rope again and I sit us down right then and there. (If I'm not going to give him what-for, we don't need to be far off.) I say, does he realize not one single person but me has bothered doing anything for him at all? "And am I to blame that they took back your crow? If you hadn't gone off climbing where you weren't supposed to, you'd have it still, so that's your own fault. That should teach you something, though I don't suppose it will. What have you learned through all this? Anything at all?"

I pinch him good even though I've decided not to anymore. Well, this will be the last time.

"Caw," I say. "Hear what that's like? Caw, caw, caw, and caw. What if that was all *I* would say?"

He's looking that look — that: Oh, so-this-is-the-way-it-is look. His witchy eyes right into mine.

"Caw," I say. It comes out all by itself. "You're driving me caw."

Why does he just sit and stare like that? I want to say, let me go, because all of a sudden it doesn't seem as if he's tied to me, but that I'm tied to him.

I get up and start back down. I'm in front this time. I don't want to see those orangy eyes of his. I limp. I flutter. I make sure not to try to say anything for fear it will be caw.

Crank, No. 8, 1998

Josephine

Top of list ... always at the top of list, rain or shine, day or night: Find Josephine. Nothing can be done until she's back here at the Old Folks Home where she belongs. Talent night she's our main attraction. We couldn't do much without her. She wobbles on her slack wire but she hasn't fallen yet. The ceiling is so high she can do the slack wire act in there in the living room though she has to watch out for the chandelier. She's not much higher than four or five feet up. When she sings she tinkles out the music on a toy xylophone. Once she brought her wind chimes down to the living room, put them in front of a fan and sang to that.

We pretend not to see how wobbly she is. Everybody else is worse. She's the only one with the courage to dance and sing no matter what. Or maybe it's not courage, just innocence.

Because of Josephine we often have townspeople visiting our performances. We don't know if they come to admire her or to laugh ... at her and at us.

I'm the MC, stage manager, entertainment committee. I'm less important than those who perform. I suppose I do have some poise, though I've been told I rock from foot to foot. Why would the Administrator pick a man like me for finding Josephine? Why pick somebody who has a limp?

No, I *am* the perfect person to send off to find her. Somebody she can have a good laugh at. She'll trip me and I'll be looking up from the sidewalk, right into her greenish tan eyes. There she'll be, found at last, but she'll run off somewhere else before I can get up and hobble after her.

We live in a grand, though ancient mansion. It was the summer house of millionaires. They donated it to the town for us old people. The living room and dining room are often closed off—too hard to heat.

The breakfast room is the room everyone loves best and spends the most time in. It has windows on three sides with window seats under them. Five tables—enough for all of us. But I'm hardly ever in this room except to eat, nor is Josephine. Too many card games and too much Bingo.

Josephine seldom comes out of her room except to eat and on show-and-tell night. (That's the only time we open the living room and let the heat come up.) Or she comes out to run away. She's *always* lost. If not right now then she would be in another minute.

I wish I wouldn't have to be the one to find her. For the sake of the doing of a good deed, I do it.

She often says, "If not for *you* finding me, I'd not bother getting lost in the first place." I know that's true. When I find her (or should I say, when she lets herself be found) there's such a look of ... well, it's complicated, disdain, but if that were all I wouldn't do it. There's relief, too. You'd think I'd find finding her worth it for that look, and I might if it wasn't for my arthritis. I've been using a cane lately. (Josephine gets lost in any kind of weather. Thank God tonight it's clear.)

You'd think by now the people in the neighborhood would bring her back when she strays, but they don't. They're afraid of her. Her hair is wild, the look in her eyes is wild and she makes nasty comments on their noses. She doesn't dress like anybody else. So many scarves you can't tell if she has a dress on under them or not. That must unnerve them. And the dress, which is under them, is more like a scarf than a dress. Everything she wears is like that, and it's always pinkish or pumpkin colored or baby blue. She always wears big dangly glittery earrings.

I step out on the porch. I admire the night for a few minutes as I always do. I hobble down the front steps. Our mansion has a few acres around it and trees so you can think yourself in the country, but no sooner out the gate and you're in town.

Sometimes I think Josephine is hiding just around the corner, watching me try to find her right from the start. Probably wondering which direction I'll look in first. Loving how my shirt tail's out, my belt unbuckled still. (I came straight from my bed.) Loving, especially, my big sigh.

I smooth at my mustache. I had no time to wax it and it's getting in my mouth. I can feel it's as draggled as the rest of me.

First I check the bushes on each side of the stairs to see if she's crouching there. She can hold as still as a frightened fawn.

I always bow when I find her. I do that because noblesse oblige. I wear my old boater just so I can take it off to Josephine. If ever she can be found smiling (that little I've-got-you-now smile) it's because of me.

I limp off, one helpless person in search of another equally inept.

Poor Josephine, here she is, in town somewhere, but I know yearning to be in a forest instead. She often says so.

Once a young person came knocking on our door asking for Great Aunt Josephine. (Just like Josephine, her eyebrows were so much the same color as her freckles they might as well not have been there.) Our Administrator lied. He said, nobody here by that name. She said she had papers. But he said the papers must be wrong and he could prove it with other papers. I suspect the Administrator is in love with Josephine.

The others here call the Administrator fuddy-duddy and fussbudget behind his back, but they don't expect that sort of talk from me. I call him Administrator. (I'm sure they call *me* fuddy-duddy and worse behind *my* back.)

Left, right or straight ahead? It hardly matters. Sometimes she leaves me a sign, a little piece of unraveling rosy fabric from one of her scarves or a plastic flower stolen from the dining room tables, but no sign here now that I can see. I go out the gate, cross the street and down the hill. For no reason. I wish I could see more stars, but then I grew up in town. This is what I'm used to.

I whistle so Josephine can keep track of me.

I think I love her … or I must. At least in some way, else why do this practically every day? Every night? And with only a modicum of complaining? (And that, only to myself.) I think she cares for me, too. She's used to me, at least, and wants to torment me. That could be love.

Since I can first remember anything at all I've been in love. As if love came with consciousness itself. I fall in love all the time—always unrequited. I know there's something wrong with me, and I know that it shows, though I've no idea how people can see it as quickly as they seem to. But lots of people are prissy fuddy-duddies and manage to marry even so, while I've hardly even had friends. But I've stuck to my principles. I've been courageous in the face of misadventures. Even catastrophes. People can count on me. Josephine must have seen that in me from the start.

I suspect the Administrator knows only too well that I'm not the sort of man women fall in love with. I'm the safe one to send after her. Nothing will happen between Josephine and me. She practically told me as much herself. She said I was too polite. "Picky, picky, picky," she's said and more than once. I must admit I stick to my dignity as best I can.

As usual I'm not watching where I'm going. I'm looking up, wishing I could see more stars but of course there's too many street lights. I've so seldom been in a place where you can really see them. Here in town they seem unimportant. Even the moon, were it up, would seem unimportant. That's what I'm thinking when down I go.

At first it doesn't hurt, but then I try to get up.

"Josephine. I've hurt myself." I whisper it. How could Josephine help anybody?

I try again to get up. I *will* get up.

I can't. I have my belt. (I'm shocked to find it still unbuckled and my shirt tail still out. I try to be, if not elegant ... who can be elegant with no money and with the bathroom down the hall and no lock on the door? People see you in all sorts of *déshabille*. Even so, I always try to be well groomed. But I must be more addled than I thought.) I try coiling my belt about my leg. It's not going to help. I look around for my cane. I wonder if I should use it as a cane or a splint. I take my shirt off, twist it and use it to tie my leg up tight.

I was cold to start with but now I'm colder. The way I'm shaking, I may be in shock. I lie back. I tell myself, have a bit of a rest. Maybe the pain will lesson in a few minutes.

No way to keep any dignity now. Josephine will come to laugh. I am prissy and a fuddy-duddy, but I'm not a coward. I follow wherever Josephine leads. Once into the river. I had found her but she slipped out of my grip as we crossed the bridge and jumped in. I jumped in too. She knew I would. She can't swim even the little bit that I can. We were swept downstream half a mile before I managed to get us out. I had my arms around her. Even as I was busy trying to keep our heads above water, I thought: I have my arms around Josephine!

Neither of us told anybody though I suspect the Administrator had to be aware that we came back soaking wet. We left smudges all across the hall and up the back stairs. Did Josephine care that I spent my middle of the night cleaning up the worst of it as best I could? Of course she didn't, she thinks I'm much too neat and prim about unimportant things like a little bit of water—except there was also mud.

I see her. I *think* I see her. She's above me, poised on a tree branch as though about to do her slack wire act. It's shadowy up there, the light from the street light doesn't reach. But perhaps it's just a plastic bag. Josephine, what with all those scarves, has that same flimsy, maybe-there, maybe-not-there look all the time.

I wait, shaking. Wondering, still, whether it's better to use my cane as splint or cane. I try again to get up. I can't. I shout at myself, *"Do it!"* I push myself up on one knee. *"Doooo it!"* But I can't.

Then I hear Josephine whisper, "Don't do it," right in my ear, her hand on my shoulder exactly as lightly as you'd think her touch would be. She has her malicious grin but she's already found a splint. A discarded slat of some sort. She takes off some of her scarves. She puts one around me. It must be silk. (Of course silk, Josephine would never have anything but silk.) I feel how warming it is right away. Her hands are warm, too. And she has the touch—the healing touch. She takes my shirt and belt from around my leg and binds it to the slat with scarves. Then she puts her arms around me and warms me with her own body. She says, "I love you," but then she adds, "Loyal sycophant."

Every time I find her she calls me that, or "Flunky." Sometimes, *"My* good man," emphasis on the *my*. She always smiles that mocking smile and says, (and what a ridiculous thing to say) "I'll make you a blueberry pie, I'll cook up a half a dozen escargots, *my* good man." They'd never let her anywhere near a stove or any kind of fire. It's another kind of torment just as saying, "I love you," is to torment me, too. Even her arms around me is meant to add to my misery.

My boater (ridiculous to wear such a hat in the middle of the night) is lying beside me, more out of shape than usual. It already was a little the worse for wear. (You can't get hats like this anymore, except maybe at a costume store. And I haven't any money anyway.) Had I found her as I usually do, I'd have bowed and removed it and held it over my heart and Josephine would have smiled her little I'll-get-you-yet smile. I guess she has me where she wants me now.

We rest a bit and I am warmed and feel less pain. She strokes my forehead. She even smoothes my mustache away from my mouth. Here's her, Now-I've-got-you-smile, only now it's: Now-I've-*really* -got-you and she has a sly look of making plans. I suppose I'll have to do whatever she decides. But then I always do.

She helps me up. My leg, bound to the slat in silk, is as stiff as a cast. But I'll have to use my bad leg now. "I can't go far."

"It's not far."

Not far? What in the world could be, not far? Especially to somebody with two bad legs.

There's a muddy rivulet flowing across the sidewalk near us. Josephine says, "This little trickle is the fountain of youth."

I can't help but laugh out loud. There's a faucet dripping somewhere. Maybe some lawn sprinkler has dribbled all the way down here where there aren't any lawns.

"You're thirsty," she says. "Drink. Lean and drink."

I am thirsty, but I won't drink this.

"All right then, if you won't be young and gay again, let's go."

She has put my boater back on my head for me. At a rakish angle of course. That's to tease me, too. Here I am shirtless, though wrapped in her scarf. Did she bother to help me back into my shirt? She lets it lie there. I don't have that many shirts. She must know that. Back at our mansion there's not much we can hide from each other. I've turned the collar, but this side is now as worn out as the other.

She helps me. Here she is, hardly coming up to my shoulder and yet strong enough to really support me. Of course she's strong, how can you be a dancer and slack wire walker, tree climber without being strong. I've noticed before how muscled her legs are.

This is exactly what she's always wanted, I can see it in her eyes. Her mouth twitches. She can't hide her smile though she's trying.

We walk over my shirt and go. I'd much rather stay here and wait for help. I'd like to be carted off to the hospital. That would be a nice change. I'd be able to eat by myself. I'd be all cleaned up. Josephine could come visit. She wouldn't. She would. She'd like to see me in bed with maybe my leg in traction.

I haven't paid attention to where we've been going. I've been too concentrated on how to keep going than to notice where. Here we are in some alley I've not seen before.

I'd like at least to wait until the pain subsides, but Josephine pulls me. "Come on, my own, you can rest in a minute."

I go where she wants me to as I've always done, but I'm feeling dizzy and nauseous. I know what that means, I'm going to faint if I don't sit down, and right away.

Next thing I know my own groaning wakes me. I stop as soon as I realize it's me making that racket. I'm crumpled up in the back seat of a roadster. Top down. I may be thin but even so I can't imagine how Josephine got me there. Here she is driving down the road, no lights. She's driving by the street lights. I wonder how long I've been out of it. My leg is propped on the door. My boater is on the floor. I'm covered with a dusty, moth-eaten army blanket.

The car seems as old as Josephine. Has she stolen it? If she has, why didn't she steal one that has working headlights?

I fade off and when I come to I'm groaning again. It's because the road is suddenly bumpy. We've gone beyond the streetlights. Josephine drives slowly, by the stars.

The road is little more than two ruts now, and soon the trees above us close off the stars. And Josephine is driving by instinct. Or perhaps the ruts force the car in the right direction.

This must be her forest. The one she's wished to be in all this time. But why didn't she come here long ago, by herself? Or did she need a sycophant? A watcher? As if her whole life means nothing without me to observe it?

We go on and on. I'm gasping at every bump and there's nothing but bumps. It's like being on a small boat in choppy seas. I'm actually feeling seasick.

Dawn is coming. I can see Josephine's windblown mop of hair in silhouette against the grayness. I see the glint of her dangly earrings.

I call out, "I'm going to be sick."

She stops the car and helps me lean over the side. She holds my forehead. She calls me, "My dear," but I'm too miserable to think anything about it.

As to my dignity, that she teases me about every day, there's none left. My vomit and my sweat are all over me.

"We're already there," she says. "We're home."

Home!

But we bounce on, and dawn keeps coming. Things are turning pink. We round a corner into a clearing, and there's a sudden breeze. We stop near a lake full of whitecaps—pink whitecaps. When Josephine stops the car I can hear the lapping. On one side of us there's a clapboard cottage in need of paint and on the other a tumbledown shed. Ahead of us a rickety dock slanting at a crazy angle.

I'm so sick and exhausted I don't want to move. I pull back when Josephine tries to help me out. She gives up and goes inside, screen door slamming (at first I think we're being shot at) and comes out in a few minutes (another rifle shot) with hot tea. It tastes odd, dusty and stale, but it helps right away. Powerful stuff. No doubt some Josephine-type secret herbs in it.

Now she helps me in. The shutters are closed so it's dim inside. Moth eaten deer head on the wall, a half a dozen fishing rods crosswise on its antlers. Its eyes glitter with what little light there is.

Josephine plops me down on an overstuffed chair. Dust flies up and I sneeze. She props my bad leg on a foot stool. Then she goes into another room and comes back with a white shirt. Seems brand-new. But then she sees how filthy I am, sidewalk dirt and vomit, tea stains.... She brings a basin of warm water and towels and soap. Cleans up my top half.

She says, "No wonder...."

First I think, no wonder what? But then I know: I'm much too thin and my chest much too concave so of course no wonder. No wonder I'm nothing but a toady.

"I'm going to leave you here alone and go get groceries."

"Get me crutches."

I can see she won't. Why should she, now that she finally has me completely in her power?

"Please."

She looks away. At least she won't lie. There's always that about her. I appreciate it.

"I'll get night crawlers. If you want to fish right now, dig one up. You can drop a line at the end of the dock."

What a silly thing to say. Well, maybe not if she wants to tease me with suggesting things I can't possibly do.

"Watch out for snapping turtles."

Indeed.

She's off (she reaches to pat the neck of the deer head on her way out, then comes back and kisses him on the lips. Sawdust trickles out.) Here I am, sunk (too deep) in the chair. But clean—top half anyway—and with a new shirt.

I pull myself up, sneeze again from the dust, and prop myself on the arm of the chair. Using my arms and my one good/bad leg I support myself over to a harder chair. The deer's eyes follow me like those in front-staring portraits always do. There's disapproval in its look.

If I tip this hard chair from one side to the other, I can make progress. Without Josephine's herbs I'd not be able to manage it without pain. It takes a long time. When I get to the closest window and open shutters, here's Josephine driving up. I notice now the roadster used to be red.

I watch her bring in packages. She seems much more efficient than she normally is. Likely her confused look, and wandering away all the time was one more game.

I wonder where she's been because the first thing she does is hang wind chimes in the doorway. It sets to tinkling right away. Can't she do without that sound for half a minute—even here with ripplings and rustlings?

She doesn't pay attention to me but busies herself in the kitchen. There's not exactly running water but there's a pump next to the sink and every time Josephine needs water I hear it creak-creaking. It sounds as if it's in more pain than I am. Josephine sings and hums. I've never heard her sound so happy. She brings me broth—store-bought broth, the kind we always have at the Home.

"There's real broth simmering on the stove," she says, "but it'll take a while."

She plops herself down in that overstuffed chair and puts her feet on the footstool she'd pushed over for me. She gives a big sigh just like the one I always sighed before I started off looking for her. Before I realize it (probably before she realizes it) she's asleep. She does look exhausted. After all she drove all night but I wish I'd stayed in the chair myself.

There's a screened-in porch. I wobble my chair out there and find a love seat just right for lying with my leg up on the arm. I fall asleep almost as fast as Josephine did. I dream a sick dream of being, not only a toady but a toad in fact, and of herbs that keep me helpless. In the dream I try to wrestle myself out of my own torpor. I fight to wake up and find myself fighting with the wicker back of the love seat and then I'm on the floor fighting the floor and then Josephine is beside me and I'm fighting her.

She slaps me, hard, on each cheek. It feels good because it wakes me out of my bad dream. How did she know to do that? Could she ever have been a nurse?

She sits on the floor beside me and pulls me across her lap, calls me, my dear, again.

I lie in her arms, poplars rustling, waves rustling.... There's a bird chirping right outside. I hear it all as if clearer than I've ever heard anything. I feel Josephine has me just where she wants me but I'm where I want to be, too.

After a while she puts a cushion under my head, goes and gets me more of that same dusty tea. She helps me back to the soft chair with the footstool and brings me broth that was on the stove all this time. In these few hours it has turned into real homemade broth with cloudy ribbons in it and little flecks of something or other. I've no idea what.

There's one other room, a little bedroom with a sagging iron bed. The white paint from the iron is chipping and lies all over the bed and floor. Josephine brushes it off and puts me to bed there. It has a lumpy, sagging mattress but I fall asleep instantly. I feel drugged, but I'm glad I am.

In the morning I wake to thumping and bumping and then something falling part way down stairs. Turns out there's an attic and there was an old desk chair on castors up there. She's carried it down the steep stairway, castors dropping off and down first. I don't think I could have done that even without a broken leg. She rolls it next to the bed, helps me on it and pushes me out to the kitchen.

She has opened all the shutters. With the morning sun pouring in you can see the dust rising. You can even see our footprints across the floor. But Josephine doesn't clean up, instead (and it actually comes true, just as she said) she bakes me a pie. Not blueberry but mulberry. She's already been out picking things. For supper we have fiddle heads cooked in butter and fried puff ball steaks.

I eat, dressed in another clean white shirt. It smells of having been hung on the line in the sun.

In the evening she rolls me out on the rickety dock away from under the trees so we can see the stars. My God, stars so dazzling and dizzying.... It looks as if any minute you'll fall right off the earth into them. She knows them all: Cassiopeia's chair, Betelgeuse, Aldeberon, the teapot, the swan....

Next morning she pushes me out on the porch so I can watch her as she rows herself out in the old flat bottom boat and fishes. She catches a sunfish and a pike.

That evening we sit on the porch and listen to the birds settling down for the night. We watch the sun setting over the lake. First comes the wishing star and then more. Here on the porch, complete stillness, but all sorts of rackets going on outside, rustlings and tweetings, peepers peeping, bullfrogs karumphing.

Days pass like this. Soon I'm well enough to take little walks.

She hasn't been teasing me lately. Or, rather, her teasing is more playful. Even her warnings make me laugh. ("Watch out for the bears." "Watch out for rattle snakes." "Watch out for roots that trip." "Watch out for ground hornets nests." "Watch out, watch out, watch out.") Then she'll put my dilapidated boater on my head, always at a rakish angle. "And don't step on any wild strawberries." I'm beginning to love a life like this. I'd like to learn to drop a worm into the water. How hard could that be? I'd like to pick gooseberries. First though,

I'll dust this place. Josephine isn't going to do it. She doesn't seem to notice. I'm the one sneezing all the time.

I notice she has her parasol here, just in case of a slack wire. It suddenly appeared, crosswise on the antlers along with the fishing poles. It reminds me how much I miss Josephine's act. It's nice seeing birds perching on her head and feral cats coming when she calls but not as nice as that balancing act of hers.

We have our rituals: Our cleaning of the lamp chimneys, our lamp lighting, our last cup of tea before bed, Josephine patting the neck of the deer head and giving it a goodnight kiss, sawdust dripping out every time.

My leg is better when the Administrator finds us. I'm able to hobble with my cane almost as well as usual. I've cleaned up. I've fished and picked berries. I've chopped wood and gathered kindling. We've been out with a flashlight and caught frogs for frogs legs.

By now we're so used to our wind and water sounds, our wind chimes, our screeching pump, that we hear him right away and from a long ways off. We look at each other over our lunch of crawdads and miner's lettuce. There's a sudden panic. We see it in each other's eyes. We're like children, caught in an act of mischief. Of course at first we don't know it's the Administrator. What we know is, this can't be good. Then, through the trees, we see the big black car the Administrator always drives.

I say, "Where?"

She says, "Follow me."

But I change my mind. I say, "No, we're grown ups."

I've taken my usual role. Exactly what Josephine doesn't like about me the most.

"*You* may be," she says and is gone.

He comes alone. Black suit, striped tie and all—even way out here in the woods. He has a pistol in his belt. I can't imagine why, what with two (probably more addled than we think we are) old people.

I step out to meet him. *Bang!* goes the screen door. (I'm usually good at remembering to be careful.) I hold out my hand but he ignores it. "Well, well," he says. "Well, well, well." He looks all around: our shed, our paint peeling cottage, our rickety dock. He can't stop saying, "Well."

Then we hear singing—raspy, wobbly, old lady singing. We look up and there's Josephine. Talk about not being a grown up! She's dancing ... I can't believe it, first across the cottage roof, holding her pink parasol for balance. Then ... I can't believe it even more. My God, she's stepping out on the wire where electricity used to come into the house back when it was paid for. She's in no hurry. She turns, scarves twisting, goes back and forth, gives a little jump. We're mesmerized—as we always are when she does her act. After a minute or two of this, she goes off along the wire, and when a good tree comes along with nice straight branches, she hops out on those and then over to another tree and another. A scarf floats down. We lose sight of her after that.

If he takes me away, what will happen to Josephine? She won't stay here without me. She'll come back to the Home of her own accord. Is that what he's counting on?

I surmise … many surmises I had not surmised before. I couldn't stand the Home if Josephine wasn't there. She and I … once I really think about it, we both love being outside day or night in any weather. I didn't realize it but I loved chasing after her. It was our excuse for a little bit of freedom and adventure. I loved the responsibility and Josephine loved the misbehavior.

The Administrator looks at me in such rage! As if it's all my fault, *all* of it.

He shouts warnings and her name. And, "You'd better this or that, or else this that and the other." And then he shoots in the air.

I say, "You can't scare her. She doesn't scare," so he turns and points the pistol at me.

"Maybe I can scare *you.*"

"Maybe."

He shoots in the air again. "Take me to her."

"No."

I couldn't anyway. God knows what hiding places Josephine has out there in her woods and I don't know a single one. He makes a barking sound then turns and shoots out our front window. I hear something fall inside. From the sound of it, bull's eye! The deer head has gone down. I can't say I'm sorry. That deer head never did approve of me. He puts the pistol down at his feet. I think to grab it. I could run … hobble.… Perhaps I can run faster than I think. Throw the pistol in the lake. But as usual I deliberate too long. He takes handcuffs out of his pocket, puts one cuff on my wrist and looks around for someplace good and solid to handcuff me to. There's no place. Finally he handcuffs me to the pipe that takes the water from the well in to the kitchen pump.

"At least *you're* not going anywhere."

He reloads and off he goes, following the wires, but first he shoots one more shot—at our jay. Misses. (That jay perched on Josephine's head almost every time we left the cottage.) I fear for her, but I fear for him, too. I try to squeeze out of the cuff until my wrist is raw. I move the cuff up and down the pipe. And then, thump, here is Josephine, right beside me, dropped from the roof. She gives me such a smile!

As if she'd heard the shots and thought to find me lying dead and yet here I am alive. "Thank, thank, God, God, God, God!" she says. She throws her arms around me and kisses me hard right on the lips. This time there's no irony in it.

She didn't have to come back. She could have stayed lost in the woods. I'll bet she has dozens of hiding places. I wouldn't be surprised if she didn't nest in the trees as chimpanzees do. I wouldn't be surprised if she didn't eat all sorts of leaves. We've already dined on nettles.

She gets a wrench from the kitchen and twists at the joint where the pipe enters the cottage. It's so rusty it won't move, but it does break and she slides the cuff off the end and I'm free. She says, "Nobody knows he's here." There's that sly look again. "Are you sure?" "Why else would he come alone? And with a pistol? He wants me. You he'll kill and throw in the lake." Just what I was thinking to do with him. "He used to come to me at night until I started running away."

I'm shocked. Except.... Well, *maybe,* but it could be as ridiculous as that filthy fountain of youth. "This is the perfect place for him. He'll tie me to the bed and come here every weekend. Feed me nothing but oatmeal. I know him."

Oatmeal—that part I know is true. It's our usual breakfast at the Home. "I couldn't tell about it back there. Everybody thought I was too addled. They'd never believe me." That's true, too. Even I don't know what to believe. We hear shots close by. And then a squawk. Might be one of our ravens that we've been putting food out for. (I know it's only a raven, but it makes me angry. I may not be able to be as impartial as I wish to be.) Another shot, then lots of squawks. They're defending their own. I've a good mind to head off in that direction and help them.

Josephine must see it on my face. She says, "Go." I go. Weaponless except for my cane. Off into the woods with no sense of direction except raven calls. Like it or not I will be ... I *am* her hero.

I tramp on May apples and wild strawberry plants, mushrooms (toadstools I suppose), pass by a puff ball and think, must remember where it is. The ravens stop. I stop. I listen. Without the ravens I have no direction to go in.

Yet I go on, more slowly now, listening between each step. I come upon a hut of leaves and branches, floor covered with a bed of ferns.

But why isn't anything making any noise? Why not even the ravens? There's just a stirring of leaves and the easy going lapping of waves somewhere over on my left.

Then I hear him crashing towards me. I hunker down and wait and wonder what to do with no weapon except a cane. I think maybe crook it round his neck or trip him.... I think how he's a much bigger man than I am. Younger, too.

Instead of him I see a doe leap past. I hear a shot from right behind her. I'm thinking this is not a doe. Her mate was mounted on the wall and now lies on the floor. That deer head has looked at me with such suspicion all this time. I don't know where these thoughts come from. I know that can't be true. But then I see the glint of gold. Is the doe really wearing a long dangly earring or is it a trick of sun rays coming through the leaves in little spots of light? Did she wink? Or, rather, blink at me as she dashed by?

After the doe, here he comes. I no longer wonder if I should do this or that. I grab his leg as he goes by. I make him miss his second shot. How dare he! How dare, and even if the doe isn't Josephine? How dare? And in our forest! I'm on top of him, fearless. There's one more shot. First I'm thinking: Missed me! Then I'm thinking: He did it to himself.

It seems to me Josephine somehow choreographed the whole thing on purpose. Sent me off, then risked her life for … I don't know what. Me I suppose.

By the time I find my way back to the cottage it's dark, but, as I enter the clearing, it's a dazzling, shiny dark with Josephine … my God! above me, on the telephone wires again dancing to a background of the constellations, skirt and scarves billowing out, parasol.… Quite extraordinary. And dancing better than I ever saw her dance. It would have been a joy to everybody back at the Home. Alas that only I am here to see it.

"My love." I finally dare to say it. "My only, ever and always love."

She hears. She says, "I am your heart's desire."

Is that yet another joke or irony? But of course it's simply real and true. I answer, "Indeed." Indeed.

Sci Fiction, May, 2002

Overlooking

If you want to hug a tree, here's the perfect place for it. They all belong to us, and we wouldn't bother, but we don't mind if *you* do it. There's no better ones than these to hug, stunted, weathered, half-dead. They're more used to hardships than any of us, so, good to hug them.

We're crepuscular. And grayish, which makes us hard to see. We're wide awake when you're tired.

You bring dogs to sniff us out, but we outwit them. If caught, which is rare, we lie about ourselves. We pretend we're *you*.

When it's cool we wear squirrel hats and jackets. From a distance, you think we're those wild furry people you keep talking about, but those wild people are of another sort entirely. But if you think we're them, all the better.

In certain spots, way up here, there are more of us than of you. You come in small groups or alone. It's *us* you're looking for. Sightings? If we want you to have them, then you'll have them.

But we watch *you*—follow you, here and there; set up blinds you think are piles of brush. We use your own field glasses. (You often lose them. When we come out to clean up after you, there they are. Sometimes cameras, too. We don't use those. How would we get film developed way out here? Though sometimes we play a joke on you and take pictures of each other and then leave the camera back where one of your kind will find it, develop it, and wonder: Who are these odd people making funny faces?) We giggle when we see you, crunch-crunching around, your big feet on dry leaves or slipping on wet moss.

We giggle when you think you've caught a glimpse of us. *That's* not us.

Lately the woods are full of you—*and* tin cans *and* plastic water bottles, sunglasses.... There's hardly a place to sit alone and contemplate anymore. And God forbid (your God) that we should stand, anymore, at the top of anything, silhouetted against the sky!

Don't think we don't have weapons. Silent ones, unlike yours. You don't know you're hit till you're hit, and you never know which direction it came from. Crossbows with darts. So silent, we can shoot and miss more times than several, and *you* don't know you're being shot at until you're shot.

As to *your* weapons, we make sure our babies' first words are, "*Don't shoot.*"

I'm the mother. I don't mean really. I mean I'm the oldest and wisest. I lead my group around at an arthritic limp and everybody calls me Maaaah. I haven't had any other name since… I can't remember when. If I approve of something, then that's what happens.

When one of us gets hurt, it's me they call. They know, by now, that I know about all there is to know around here.

In order to avoid *you*, we have nothing to do with the highest and therefore most popular mountains. What difference does it make, high or a little bit less high?

But we've captured one of you.

I was sitting here reading from your manuals about us. Most of the books insist we *do* exist. A few say maybe. Some say we don't. There are many of you who swear you've seen us and have pictures to prove it. They're lying and the pictures are fakes. Others write about how those people are crazy. We're like flying saucers, maybe *yes,* maybe *no*. Except it's not exactly us they write about. It's those others who live farther back. It's said those others are so cold they sleep with rattlesnakes to keep them warm. We don't believe that, any more than we believe *we* don't exist.

You say we're seven feet tall and fuzzy. *That's* not us.

So I was sitting here in my favorite shady spot reading when they brought one of *you* in. An old man almost as old as my own old man got to be. I wondered why they'd bring a grown man up home this time of year. Our women are running around as if it was mating time. All because of this poor old man. It's the gang caught him. They'll do anything just to be different or to shake their elders up.

I like the old man's looks. Grey-haired like us and nice and bony. Younger men are too baby-faced for my taste. I never liked that look even when I had a baby face myself. Such faces are all right for the young, but softness of that sort is scary in a man when one must trust one's life to him. Mostly it's our men who keep *you* from us. They will sacrifice themselves if need be.

You can see on his face that this man can't figure out if we're us or his kind. I suppose we look odd. (*You* never look odd to us. We've seen you much too often.)

This man has the usual paraphernalia: Camera, backpack, field glasses, big notebook full of notes and maps. In his backpack, food, including three little easy-open cans of apricots. I sample one right away. Since I'm the maaaah, I have the right.

I ask the gang, "Why have you brought this one up here among us? If you don't know that's got to be the end of him, you should go down with the fathers and stay there."

"He knew."

"He didn't, but now he does."

"He did, too."

"There's nothing to know."

But then I see he's hurt. His arm hangs in an odd way, and he's holding on to it.

"We didn't do that. He had that already."

I don't trust these young ones. They're at a bad age. Well, but they usually tell the truth.

"Bring him here and hold him down."

(Up this close those young ones smell bad. It's a sign of maturing.)

I put my foot in the man's armpit, grab his wrist, and pull and twist and pop his shoulder back in place. I bandage him so it won't move.

If he didn't look good to me, I wouldn't have.... Well, yes, good-looking, or not I would have. Would I do less for a wounded turkey vulture than for this man? I nursed a vulture all spring. Everybody knows that.

I give this man broth. I don't tell him what's in it. We know *you* better than you know us. Best he not know. To him it'll taste as buttery as snails.

"I'm Maaaah," I say.

Right after, when he says his name, I don't listen. Why know a thing like that when... well....

I've been inside your cabins lots of times—even when you were there. Sometimes, as I walked right past you, I could hardly keep from laughing out loud at how you didn't even know I was in your shadows. I made myself peanut butter sandwiches. I drank your milk. There was one particular cabin—large for a summer house. It was all woody inside. Smelled of cedar and pine. Big wood pile outside.... (You never miss what wood we take.) Usually your cabins have chandeliers made from wagon wheels and horse shoes, but here there was a cut-glass chandelier, small though; in the cabinet, tea cups with gold on them; on the table, silver candlestick holders. I really did want one of those. Each held three candles and had silver leaves all up and down it. I went up to our home and thought about it for a couple of days, and then I came back down and took one. After all, there were four. After all, I'm the maaaah.

I could have made this man soup from *your* supplies, because once your campers get started, you don't realize how heavy your packs are and how tired you'll be, and how you'll lose your appetite because of altitude. You hide things along the trail that you think to pick up on the way home. We watch from our watching spots, thinking: Ha, ha, you'll search and search and wonder how you could have forgotten so soon, and only a couple of days later. You even wrote where you hid it in your little book on flowers or the little one on birds or the little book where you write about this trip you're taking right now, and you still can't find that food.

(Why do you leave your food so as to cut down on the weight and not your books? More often we find glasses and cameras than we find those little nature books or your notebooks.)

By now this man will be wondering, where are those furry ones? You're *always* getting us mixed up with them.

I say, "I can take you where you want to go."

But he has to rest up a bit first, so I can still sit here in my shade listening to the ravens. It's the stone that doesn't roll—that sits as I do—that gathers moss. That accounts for my greenish tinge.

I say, "You can catch a glimpse of them."

Now look at this. Already he's clumping around, snooping, peering but seeing nothing, standing right on our vegetables. Of course our gardens don't look like gardens to *you*, they just look like the normal forest floor. (Our walls look like just more greenery or random piles of sticks. You walk right through them. This man already has done it several times.)

But our rattlesnake is waiting there, in the garden.

I should have listened when that man said his name. I hadn't thought there'd be any need to call him.

I say, "I'll go with you and lead the way."

(I'll go with him even though the gang thinks he's theirs.)

This year those young ones won't wear hats. Even in the rain. (They chew your used-up gum. Smoke your cigarette butts. They want to try everything.)

I do love that gang. I love the overgrown, the clumsy and wild and insecure and smelly. Or, on the other hand, I love the stunted, the dry, the half-dead. This old man has eyes as gray as shadowy water.

What attracted me right away were his stringy muscles, the hair on his arm, that wispy mustache, mostly white. What attracted me was how he laughed when he tried on our hats.

There has to be a reason why he came. What if he's tired of being one of *you* all the time and would rather be *us*?

Helicopters come, flying low. They keep searching back and forth. They're noisy. Even the noisy gang doesn't like it. Even this man doesn't like it. If he wanted to, he could show himself and get himself rescued. I couldn't stop him.

The gang goes out and cavorts around in plain sight. We're as pale as the slate-like fragments of limestone we sit on. We wear cobwebs. They make us wispy and dim. We can disappear right before your eyes.

Since the man isn't showing himself, he might as well look out over those fuzzy others in their habitat. "

In situ," I say. "Just look over, don't go down. You have to promise not to."

I give him a lesson for the journey as I've already done, and many times, to the gang. "Some mosses you can eat, and some pine needles. You can eat the roots of Solomon seal if you don't mind a little—quite a bit, that is, of grit. You can eat ants. You can roll in dust as a sun screen or plaster on mud."

He's taking more notes. (I *do* love the way all of you cling to your notes and your bird books.)

When I was young I once showed myself right in the middle of the trail. I just stood there, all greenish and gray. It was to one of you about my own age, climbing up, geologist's hammer hanging on his belt. I liked his looks though I couldn't see much under his hat. Well, I liked his *legs*, strong and brown and covered with curly golden hairs.

I stood in a spot where the sun streamed—one of those shiny golden streaks—down—just on me. I wanted to be his vision of a forest nymph of some sort, and that he'd never forget me, but he looked at me, staring so, that I got scared and skipped away, not as gracefully as I'd hoped. It turns out I'm the one has the memory forever. That man might have been this man right here.

There was an episode in a cabin, I the succubus. It was dark but not completely. There was a moon—gibbous, of course. I'm not sure who the man was, but it might have been this one. (I caught a glimpse of legs with curly hair.) I was no more than a shadow in a shadow, but I was hoping there was a glistening around my edges.

At first he didn't want to, but I don't think he was frightened. He resisted. Just in case, I had feathers in my hairdo and a bag of wild strawberries. I whispered things. I sucked.

Then after twisting about a bit, one position and another, I lay under, as a succubus should.

Once he got started, I lost count of how many times. After all, he was a mountain climber and in perfect shape as all those who come here usually are. I felt he loved me. Too bad I hadn't seen his face, neither then nor on the trail in the shadow of his hat.

Misty or Dandy, I forget which, could be his own son.

We begin the journey to the looking-over site.

I flit and flutter, slither and slide. My old man used to say I was like a hummingbird or a butterfly. I wonder if this old man can see that? We always think of you as not noticing much.

He takes my picture.

He says, "I've always believed in you creatures. When I looked out the windows of my cabin, I saw shapes dancing. I locked my doors, even so I saw, in the corners, shadows that seemed on top of shadows. Now and then I missed a package of frozen green beans." (Maybe *I* took those beans.)

Flit and flutter, skip and slide and so forth.... I wanted to be "Shrouded in mystery" as you always say we are, but I was thinking too much about how I looked flitting. I'm the one who stumbles. I had not thought such a thing would ever happen. *You're* usually the ones who fall. I scrape myself, top to bottom. I hurt my good leg. I tear my grays.

That man picks me up. His arm, my leg.... We'll have to help each other. At least it's *my* forest.

So, and with many hardships along the way, including the aforementioned, having climbed up and over from one valley to the next, having slept in a hollow with leaves over us, having chewed on wintergreen, having eaten whole meals of nothing but chanterelles, we arrive at the looking-over point.

I dress him in a stick hat and a few vines. He'll look like that candelabra of mine (or perhaps it's his), leaves all up and down him. He gets his camera ready and we enter the blind. I push a peep hole for him, and one for myself, and we look down on the fuzzy ones' habitat.

Cottages of stone and wood, gardens with little flags to label the vegetables, bird baths, goldfish ponds, here and there a ceramic rabbit. There's an iron deer.

I say, "There's a deer," and, "Here they are, the furry ones. Don't they look nice, all glittery in their golden coats?"

Except they're not there. He'll think I made this all up.

I say, "Their little ones are *so* cute."

He's got his field glasses out now. He says, "Where? Where?"

"You can't see it from here, but their eyes are green."

Why am I saying all this, *I'm* the romantic notion. *I'm* the hope. *I'm* the story. He's been writing me down every day. We're the wish-you-existed-after-all people.

I think he's going to go on down even though he promised not to. I don't think I'm strong enough to keep him from it.

I say, "We're as important to the forest as these fuzzy ones. If we weren't here, some other creature would have to take our place. Put that in your notebook."

But he's going on down.

Of course the gang has followed us. There's not a place they don't roam (or anybody they don't follow), outskirts of towns, back yards, mountain tops.... Those young ones not only won't wear hats, this year they expose their navels. They cut cute little three-inch holes in their shirts. Where did that idea come from? As if it has to come from anywhere. Those young ones think all sorts of things. But it could be worse.

We try to keep them out of danger, but they don't listen. I used to be that way myself. They're at an age when they're easily mortified, just as I used to be, and they never apologize.

However, it's when your little kids get lost in the woods that our young ones show their best side. First they take them by the hand and lead them to a place full of flowers. Then they feed them berries. After that they take them to where *you* can find them, and they sit with them until you do. Or, if you don't come, they bring them home to us.

He says, "Well, where are they?"

I say, "But it's *you*: The mysterious ones and don't even realize it. Perhaps it's even *you*, the ones important to the trees. You hug them and kiss them. You sit in the tops to protect them. Sit sometimes for *months*. What could be more like us than what *you* do?"

But he's crawled out of the blind. He's standing up in plain sight, field glasses at his eyes, camera dangling.

"Why don't you sit and contemplate for a few minutes. Give them time to manifest themselves. There's one now. Over to the right, halfway behind the rose bush." (There isn't.)

I could have sneaked away and gone down there myself in one of our fur suits, but I forgot to bring one.

I have my crossbow and a dozen darts. I told him the dangers are few, but one never knows. I said, "No harm in being ready."

We always aim for the lower leg. Then, there they are at last, the fuzzies! A dozen. Of course it's our young ones. I can practically see who's which by the way they cavort. Dandy, the thinnest and oldest, doing his usual leaps over hedges. They're doing everything right, climbing fruit trees, digging in the marigolds. . . .

Except it's too late already. My finger's on the release. There'll be just a little swishing sound. I let go right where I aimed, into the big muscle of the lower leg. Those darts are small and sharp. At first he doesn't know what's happened, and then he's on the ground. Not so much because of pain. *Yet*. But because his leg gave way. He thinks it collapsed by itself.

It's too bad, but I don't think he even had a chance to take one single picture of the furry ones. (Nobody would have believed the pictures anyway.)

Does he realize I'm the one who shot him?

I throw the bow into the brush. Best to pretend I don't know he's shot.

There's no blood. There never is.

He's examining his calf. He's going to pull the dart out.

"Don't do that! . . . till I get my bandages ready."

He won't be able to go much of anywhere, especially not in a hurry.

Those young ones finally realize what's happened. They come up to us, still wearing their fur suits. Dandy is the first to get up here. He's more or less the leader. I suppose exposed belly buttons was his idea.

Oh, for heaven's sake, they've even done that to their fur suits—cut little holes. They love to take chances.

I say, "He got shot."

"We didn't do that." They all say it, practically in unison.

"Well. . . . I suppose not."

It's *so* easy to put the blame on them. They expect it, too. All I have to do is keep my mouth shut.

"Make one of those little stick stools. Four of you to carry him and two can help me. Then, when we get to the edge, you know what to do."

And they do it. Showing their navels and all. And with clicks and clucks and lots of giggling. They don't even realize, but when have young ones ever?

There's this longing in you. *All* of you. Even if you were sure we didn't exist, you'd still hope. We intend to live so as to fulfill *your* dreams and expectations—be of some worth to those of *your* ilk. Who would there be to sneak and follow? Come upon you suddenly? Who would live at the corners of your lives? Who would there be to be *us* if not us?

You stop and listen. *All* of you do. Every snap and rustle has a meaning. You look. You turn around fast to see what's behind you.

You want to believe in us and we... *I*, especially, want to be believed in. It's always been my main goal.

That man went over with his field glasses and camera and notes and birding book and tree book, even one left-over can of apricots.

I wish I knew which cabin used to be his.

I wish I knew his name. I should have listened when he said it.

I wanted to keep him, but of course that was never possible.

Well, at least we didn't break any of our own rules. At least I don't have to know what happened. I mean, not *exactly*.

The Green Man: Tales from the Mythic Forest, 2002

The Prince Of Mules

What do you know from the top of a hill but the lay of the land? I can see two little towns, one on each side, and—closer—a ranch. I see cow hides all along the fences. I see skulls over the gates. I know rattlesnake skins are there, too, and maybe a skunk pelt, but I can't tell from here. There's hardly any green except in thin lines coming down from the mountains and a couple of irrigated pastures.

And there's the irrigation ditch digger, Blackthorn. Today he's working just below my hill. I know it's him. Who else would be out in a ditch, his clothes so black and floppy, letting himself get too hot in the middle of the day?

He has an ugly, brutal face. I don't think he's brutal but lots of people do. They distrust him because his eyebrows are too black and bushy and one eye is always off in the wrong direction. People think that eye is looking at something they can't see—something they're missing out on that might be important. Or beautiful.

They say he looks like a scarecrow but what he looks like is the crow. Eye, one of them, the blackish blue of crow's eyes. Nose...not hooked like an eagle's, but reaching straight out. That nose says: Go somewhere. Get away. Do something else.

I see his lips moving (of course not from up here, but when I pass by down there now and then). He's always talking to his mule. I've heard tell you can talk softly to a horse but, when it comes to a mule, all you need to do is little more than mouth the words.

But it isn't as if I'm not a crow kind of person myself. And people don't like the looks of me either.

My house is off alone, half way up the hill, boulders all over my, so called, yard. Sage. Rabbit brush. (And rabbits.) A skunk lives under the shed but we get along...so far. Same goes for the rattlesnake. So far. I probably get taken for a witch, what with a snake and a skunk for familiars. If I really was one, I'd witch away my knee pains, and I'd witch myself some money. And I'd witch myself some company. (I've lived with nothing sweeter than the rattlesnake's grin. I take as friend whatever looks at me at all.)

Blackthorn and I, we should get to know each other. Would he come up here for iced tea? Or lemonade? I don't have any beer. Come to think of it, I don't have any lemons either.

"Hello down there. Halloooo."

Can he hear me from here? I wonder if he can see me waving?

"Hallooo. Mister Blackthorn."

He sees me. He shades his eyes and looks but doesn't wave.

He lives even farther up than I do. His hut is so much the color of everything else, you can hardly see it until you're practically in the doorway. I climbed up there once when he was out in the fields. I looked in the one and only window but it was so dim and dusty I couldn't see much. There was a white washbasin with pitcher in it—both chipped. There were socks on the floor. There actually was a book—on the floor beside the socks—one of those old-fashioned, leather bound books with gold lettering. I couldn't read the title. I was surprised and pleased to see he actually had a real book.

But the shed for the mule, now—that was spic and span. Smelled sweet of straw and hay and mule. Smelled so good I took a chance and lay down there for a while.

I call again. "Hallooooo."

Again he looks up but, just as he did before, he goes right back to digging. He's got to be tired and thirsty. Suppose I hold up a big glass of iced tea? Suppose I had a pail of water for the mule?

I go in, change my blouse to a cream colored one (mule nose color actually) with lace around the neck, and come back out with a pitcher and a pail. I hold them over my head.

"Halloooow!"

Finally!

When the time comes to say my name, what would be unusual and romantic and make him remember it? And me?

So he and his mule come all the way up here, two switch backs and then a long sideways.

He lets the mule drink first. (Of course!) He calls her sweetheart. How he does sweet talk that mule! "Come sweetheart. Come, Penny, drink." (When has anybody ever called me sweetheart? I think and think, but I'm thinking never.)

He says she came with the name Bad Penny, but he calls her Pennyroyal.

It looks like that's all he's going to say. Sometimes people who don't talk much like to have other people chatter away so they don't have to think about talking, they don't even have to listen; and yet others like silence around them to match their own.

"Do these ditches need you? Every single day like this?"

"Without me and Penny everything would be as dry as it is right here." His good eye takes it all in: me, my tin pitcher, my boulders.... The other eye is off at its own secret spot. I can tell he's never noticed me before, even after all those times I was walking back and forth in front of his ditch whenever he was working near my hill.

"Did you ever think of going someplace else?"

"I've been elsewhere."

He drinks my whole pitcher-full right out of the pitcher and without stopping. I should have had as much for him as for the mule.

I like his eyebrows. I even like his eye that roves off seeing...God knows what visions.

By now I can tell what my name should be. I say, "I'm Molly," so as to be more mule. Though, on second thought, perhaps I should have said Jenny so I could be Jenny to his Jack. I wonder if his first name is Jack.

How keep him here a little while longer? "Could you open this jar?" (He could.) "Could you move this heavy box for me?" (Of course.) "And I can't reach this shelf."

He does all the things and with an old crow's grace. An old crow's flashing eye.

I feel so good I want to say, Sweetheart, to something myself, except Penny's the one getting all the caresses. Does she need so many when there's others (not so far away) who haven't had any? As to looks, she's nothing special, just the general mule color, dark with a cream colored nose, but she's sleek and shiny, which is more than I can say about him. Or myself.

Perhaps, in that wandering eye, Penny is a beautiful woman as pale all over as the star on her forehead, her hair the same black/brown of the turkey vulture feathers he has in his hat.

What is he seeing with that off kilter eye? Suppose he looked at me through that? What would I turn into? But perhaps, for starters, I need to become more mulish. Mules always know what they want to do and when. They're never wishy-washy. They know what's best for everybody. I suppose he depends on her for his own safety. I'm afraid I don't have that knack.

My ravens quack, quack, quack around us. Something else is going, "Tweet, tweet, churrrrr. Tweet, tweet, churrrrr." He lifts his head and listens—points his going somewhere nose and listens like a poet. Who'd have thought?

"Could I have a ditch? One connected to the arroyo just in case there's ever a little bit of water in it?" (There hasn't been any water in it since I came here.) "It wouldn't have to be long or deep. I'll pay."

I seem to have decided (without deciding) on too much talking though I'm not yet committed to it completely. I keep silent as I hand him more tea. I think of all the things I'm not saying, as: Take me to your shack, old crow man. Or take me even farther up, to the mountain lion's den. I saw a place up there where the grass was matted in a cozy circle. I saw the scat.

What I do say is: "When I die I had always wanted to come back—if there's going to be any coming back to it—as a raven. I had wanted to be smart and cocky, but now that I see Penny, I think, perhaps, mule is better."

What I don't say is, who ever caresses a raven?

What I do say is: "I have stones as if instead of trees. All my shade is from boulders. I'm surprised anything grows here at all but some things find a way. They get a toe hold. Like I do."

I don't say: My stones are warm and motherly after a day in the sun and I lean against their big round bellies every evening. They're warm well into the night.

He has looked at me again. One of his fleeting glances that slip sideways and down before you know you've been looked at.

What I do say is, "I thought I heard a stream or maybe it's leaves blowing. I heard another, tweet, tweet, churr from some other place entirely. And it's cool somewhere not far from here." I spread my arms, the better to feel the breeze. "Admit it. There's another world somewhere, all shiny and sweet smelling. Not a bit like here."

He spreads his arms, too, but to show my hill and my view. "Why do you want to see more than this right here, the gray fox colors of the underbrush, and, not far, the fox herself and her kits."

Spoken like a poet. And what more do I want than the warm bellies of the granite? And there is a tree, one, and more up where he is.

But I think there is a world of the other eye, and in it he would be the wiry black prince of mules. And he would have shaved in that world. His hat would smooth itself out and clean itself up and the turkey vulture feathers would become the feathers of a hawk. No, eagle.

I say, "I saw sparkles. Diamond shapes, all different colors and all in a row. I heard swishing sounds as if a stream or of poplar leaves in the wind. I heard wind chimes. I felt how cool. I shivered. Look how I shiver. I saw.... I thought I saw Penny. She was wearing a nightgown sort of thing. Even now your other eye is glistening. I see tears on that cheek."

I step forward to wipe the tear but he jerks back.

"My other eye sees nothing."

"And does the nothing have a light blue cast?"

"There's no other place than here."

"I don't believe it."

"Believe what you will. People always do, and they like the odd and scandalous and fantastic better than the real."

"What about Pennyroyal?"

"She is as you see."

But I know better.

Except now he's on his way down—already on his way, back to his ditch.

"It's too hot!" I'm screeching it. Then I screech again. "Dangerous to work in such heat!" (What kind of bird is that, that screeches so? None I ever knew.) "A man of your age...." Screech, screech.

He's going. He's down. And he didn't say if he'd dig me a ditch or not.

But I know happiness is possible because I don't want a lot of it. How sweet it would be to sleep in the hay with Penny. That's not much to ask.

Like his nose says, I'll go forward, do something, go elsewhere. I will know what I want. I will become more mule.

I go back in and pack up my nightgown and a snack. (The nightgown might be important.) I sit on one of my rocks and wait until I see Blackthorn and Penny leave the ditch. (She doesn't even have a lead rope. She follows him home on her own. I would, too. I will.)

I wait until it's almost dark and then I take my bundle and climb up into the piñons. There's a light in his shack but dim. No doubt an oil lamp or candles. I peek in. Blackthorn is at the little table, leaning over it, side view. (I do like that going-someplace look of his nose.)

With that lamplight I can see more than I could before. Things are nicer than I thought, though I see sandy dust all over everything. (I could clean that up in no time.) There's a patchwork quilt on the cot, secret Star pattern. There's a humpbacked trunk. Hard to put anything down on top of that but there's not only a couple of dirty shirts lying across it, but a tin cup balanced at the top of the curve. I hope it's empty. The washbowl and pitcher look even more chipped and cracked in this light, and dirty socks are on the floor again—or still. Maybe a couple more pairs. They need darning. I'll do that.

Then I notice I'm on the side of his rambling eye and it's rambling right over to the window—to me. I don't know what he sees, but there's no reaction. It's as if that eye is blind, but maybe it's that he's seeing wonderful things and wouldn't be paying attention to me anyway.

And now he has that poet's look of listening. Have I made a noise?

The odd eye is still right on me. It glistens in the lamp light. His good eye was crow-blue-black. This one is light blue.

I think of clouds tinged pink, rainbows of course… balconies, gazebos, long white gauzy gowns that blow in the wind, raven hair…"tresses," as they say, also blowing. And Blackthorn…. In the world of that blue eye, he would wear clothes that fit him better, though they'd still be black. Penny would have a long courtly nose (as she already has) and her tresses would make her face look all the more narrow, but what makes somebody beautiful? Not their nose. Not perfect teeth. Not big caramel colored eyes. (She does have that.)

"Harriet?" Now it's his good eye which is turned towards me. "Harriet?"

How did he know my real name? Another sure sign of…well, several things. If he knows my name then for sure there is another world out there somewhere.

I hear wind. Branches squeak as they brush against the roof of the shack. I feel the evening breeze. Or is that in that other place?

He says, "Enter."

Enter what? Does he mean into that other land? And how? Since I don't know how to go there, for now, and though I'm right by the door, I just step through the little window. It's small and high, but I step through just as though it was easy—except I fall when I land on the other side. I'm down by his knees. I dare to touch his ankle. He's not wearing any shoes or socks so I touch bare skin. I look up into his eyes...eye, that is. You have to pick which one you want to look into.

"Please get up."

But his ankle is warm and damp. I haven't touched skin to skin with anybody for longer than I can remember. I lay my cheek across his instep. It smells of ditch.

"Please get up."

I kiss his foot.

But I'm way, way, way.... I'm way....

...on a hill holding the ankle of (of course!) a black stallion. (Who would be holding the ankle of a gelding!) There's moonlight. There's a breeze. Blue-black clouds scoot across the sky. It's a witch kind of land. Scary. I knew it would be. I knew all this.

The stallion paws with the hoof I'm not holding, impatient. I know he means, "For Heaven's sake get up! I asked you to before."

I do. I should at least be wearing something flowing so I'd match the setting. (I knew I'd need my nightgown, but where is it now?) But I'm dressed as I was, lacy mule-nose-colored shirt and loose old lady jeans. For sure, here, I'm no younger than I was in the other place. I could feel that in my knees as I got up.

He shakes his head, hard, up and down, mane flying, impatient still. (In this world it's the good eye, the black one, that seems odd.) He walks away, looking back at me. I follow. The grass here is soft against my legs just as I knew it would be, not like my grass, all scratchy and in clumps. Not far away I hear water running. It sounds like a small stream, nothing of the flash flood about it. He, the stallion, comes to a rock and stops beside it as though I should use it as a mounting block.

I wonder if, in this world, I might know how to ride. Maybe know how to stay on even if bareback with nothing to hang on to but the mane. And how do you steer?

I mount. Now I'm glad I'm not wearing something flowing. Except, without a skirt and scarves, there'll be nothing to blow out behind us as we gallop. Only his mane and tail, not my hair. It's much too short. And would gray hair count anyway?

He starts away at an easy trot—but I've already fallen off the other side. We go back to the mounting stone. This time I get a better grip on the mane. I hadn't thought his back would be so slippery and bounce so.

There will be a castle. Or perhaps a smaller cozy summer castle (I'd like that) where they (we) pretend to be ordinary people. Pennyroyal, the princess all in white. Her beauty is in the look in her eye. (Everybody says so.) And in the tilt of her head. There is no kinder princess. (Everybody says so.) She does nothing but smile. But her voice is a little like mine was when I screeched. (Now I know that sound I made, birds don't do that, it's mule.) She smiles. At me. She calls me, Sweetheart. (Everybody calls me, Sweetheart!)

I curtsey. Sort of a curtsy. It isn't until I try it that I realize I don't know how. Where do the arms go? How low is low enough?

I'm thinking Penny is his little sister so I could be his wife. That is, if he ever can, in this world, not be a stallion. Perhaps all it takes is my kiss, (like with frogs) but on his lips, not just his ankle where I kissed him before. Was it that kiss that started all this? That turned him into a horse in the first place?

When I leaned my cheek against his foot back in his cabin, I'd thought how nice it would be if I could clean up the shack, scrub and dust, do the dirty socks and shirts, darn, wash the dishes. Pull down hay for Penny. Sleep in the sweet smelling shed. Be his little helping elf. Or anything he wants me to be. I even thought: When can I start?

But here, I've already started—shoveling out the stables. "Sweetheart, could you kindly go...." And I was even stroked a bit before I go there.

Here...even here...what they need is a scullery maid. I'm to sleep in the stables. It's not at all the same as it would have been if I'd been set to clean Penny's stall and sleep with her and clean his shack up, up there under the piñons.

How to get out of it? The stallion must know. If I could get him to take the bit, I'd bloody up his mouth if I had to, to make him go back to that hill where the entrance to all this might be. Maybe might be.

Or if I could wake up and it would all have been a dream (it looks like a dream and feels like a dream) and I would be there my cheek still on his foot. If that happened, I'd not kiss, as I did, I'd bite.

Or if I could go into his stall and bite his foot now and be instantly transported back to his shack. (I do creep in to try that and he heehaws as if he was a mule.)

Or what if I could put out his eye? But which one! That's important. If the wrong one, then I might be here forever.

And all this after I gave him water from my tank. It isn't as if water grows on trees around here—back there I mean.

If I ever do get back, I'll have to end up hugging the warm rock bellies like I used to. I'll have to make do with whatever slithers by. But I don't care anymore. I'll wave at crow or snake or sweet gray fox....

Those townspeople were right. Jack Blackthorn! I should have known all this (as they did) from his name and his off-kilter eye and from those bushy eyebrows.

Leviathan 3, 2002

Water Master

If the Water Master says, yes, then your apple trees will grow. If he says, yes, you'll take a bath, have a drink, and you might even have a little patch of grass.

He checks the irrigation ditches and gates all day long. Leans over to pinch the sand between his fingers. Never looks up to see the birds or the mountains. Never notices the sky except as it's reflected in his water. He has to watch for secret ditches or for open gates that are supposed to be closed.

When I say, Hello, and he answers the same, he doesn't look up. I don't know what color his eyes are. Blue, I would imagine. I would hope. He always wears a wide brimmed black hat pulled down low. I don't know what his face looks like except that it's lean and lined. I don't suppose he cares who I am. Besides, I only grow prickly pears, squaw tea, tepary beans, and mesquite pods. I don't need the Water Master's water. At least not much of it.

Water is what's on his mind and rightly so. I can understand that. Nothing is better, how it bubbles up and sparkles, silvery in the sun, frothing, foaming as it rushes, roaring down from way up there to here. How it leaps so high over rocks. How it trembles in backwater pools. How it tastes. Cool.... Cold.... How dangerous it can be.

Those who steal water are the worst, therefore the Water Master wears a bullet proof book of "The Hundred Best Loved Poems" over his heart (given to him by the town. We need to keep him healthy) and pistols at his sides. Shoot first, think afterwards, that's what a Water Master does. *Has* to do. Those who open gates in the middle of the night after the Water Master has closed them ... those people are in trouble even if they think they're doing all right so far.

He lives way up by his dam, in a big house or so they say. All the things to build it but the stones came up on mules. Furnishings, too: Bathtubs, beds, mirrors so large you wouldn't think they could get around the switchbacks. I've heard tell there's an orchard and grapes and artichokes and rose bushes. There's plenty of water up there, that's where it comes from.

Even so, I'm sorry for him, looking at the ground all day long, seeing not much more than lizards. Lizards down here that is, goodness knows what crawls around up there. It's a hard, long climb to where he lives but he goes up and down almost every day, checking our raging river as he goes.

His name is Amos Acularious, but nobody calls him anything but Water Master. I think his grandparents and parents were shepherds. I wonder how one gets from shepherd to Water Master? It doesn't seem right. They say it's the river, chooses its own master. I don't believe it. And even if true, why would it choose a shepherd?

Even though all those Acularius's were nothing but shepherds, and even though Amos Acularius is so thin there's nothing much to him, and even though he wears a fringed jacket which makes him look even thinner, every girl would like to marry the Water Master and live in that big house. They've heard how shiny the floors are, how the roof gleams with copper, how water runs, icy cold, from half the faucets and even, though hard to believe, hot from the other half.

I, on the other hand, have long since decided never to marry. In fact that's been my policy from the start. It was because of diapers. (I changed my first diaper at the age of seven.) Because of dishes, too. (As the oldest child in my family, I had plenty of both those.) Besides, by now I'm too old for marriage, anyway. Except so is Amos Acularius.

There hasn't been much snow on the mountains this year. They say our Lake of the Mountain is low. Many of the ditch gates are shut in order for the lake to fill. Even so it isn't filling. Onions and rutabagas and apple trees are dying. Perhaps my tepary beans will save us all.

Nobody is supposed to go up there. That was decided a long time ago when the first Water Master was appointed. (I say appointed, but everybody else says chosen by the river.) That's his private place where he can work water wonders in seclusion. Bring a wife up and live his own life. Have his little Water Master children. Little skinny mountain goat kind of children, I suppose, brought up on the cliffs.

But something is wrong. Nobody has seen Amos Acularius for several days. They've formed a group to go up. A sort of posse. They're angry. They think maybe it's a lie that the lake is low. Maybe there's plenty of water but Amos Acularius has been persuaded to let our water fall over to the other side of the mountain into some neighboring town or other we don't know anything about. There's talk of bringing up a bomb.

Even if he is skinny and ugly (though I've hardly seen more of his face than his unshaven bony jaw with deep lines at the sides) I wouldn't want him hurt. I'm going up by myself. Secretly. And before that posse goes. They're still getting themselves together. Arguing. Even though they're angry, nobody wants to go up this time of year. It's not only harvest time, but this is the season for mountain storms. I wonder if any of them will actually get around to going up? But I'm going. I'll hide and watch what happens. I'll be there before any of them even starts. All I need is lunch and a sweater. It's a perfect day for a climb.

As I go I keep looking back to see if anybody has started up behind me yet. Nobody has. I like looking back at our little town, nestled in close along the river bank, even though that river is dangerous. Folks have drowned. Folks have been swept away—God knows where. I won't be able to see it much longer. A fog is rolling in—up here, of course not down there. It's all blue sky down there. I've seen these clouds before, hanging around the mountains. Pretty soon the tops will be hidden from everybody down there and I'm about to be swallowed up in it. I won't get lost. It's easy to see when I'm on the path, and all along I've been listening to our waterfall. I could follow by the noise alone.

When I'm most of the way up (I *hope* most of the way, I've climbed for three hours) the fog begins to seem a little wispier, I see … I *think* I see Amos A. in the smoky distance.

I feel my heart lurch—in fact my whole body lurches, just from thinking it *might* be him.

I follow, well behind. Luckily the fog is still fairly thick. I climb right on through it, up and out the other side. Suddenly the air is clear and the sky—such a dark blue. Below me, everything is all fogged in. I can't see our town at all.

I look ahead. I'm at the edge of a lake. I gasp. I can't help it. This is it, *the* lake. *Our* lake. Here's where everything comes from. Without this lake and the torrent rushing from its dam, there'd be no town. There'd be no us. Here it is, all shiny in the sun. Little lapping waves. And here the dam itself. The dam of life, the water roaring out.

I fall on my knees (I don't mean to do it, but I do) I fall and look and keep looking, and keep thinking: This is it. *It!* It's *it!*

The lake is nestled in a bowl. A golden bowl because, on each side, aspen are in their most golden phase. I'm not exactly on the shore. I'm up above the dam. The lake is longer than I had imagined, I can't see where it ends, in the distance there's a row of snowy mountains.

I finally come to myself and look away. Now where is that big house? All I see is a hut partly built into the granite. Even my own little place is bigger than this.

And where's that orchard and all those roses? Nothing here but stunted lupine and pennyroyal. (I don't see the pennyroyal, but I can smell it.)

I knew it, I knew it. There has always seemed to me to be something wrong with Amos Acularius being our Water Master. He doesn't look right. He looks more like a half starving, beaten down servant than lord of the water. Here he is living like a sheep herder. At the mercy of his dam and his lake and his torrent.

And here comes the Water Master, himself, come to lift me to my feet. I see up under his hat for the first time—those blue, blue, *blue* eyes. I knew they'd be like that. I get all shaky again. I feel a rush of heat. It's the eyes—that must be the reason he's Water Master.

And the scars. He has scars all over him, face, hands and all. Perhaps that's why he always keeps his head down and his hat pulled low and always wears long sleeves down there in town. Scars and blue eyes. He's wearing a torn T-shirt and I can count all his bones.

I'm so trembly I can't get up even with him pulling at me. His hands are rough and callused, but his voice is clear as water. "Come. Come, get up." If we were any closer to the dam and he, not leaning so close to me, I'd not hear him at all.

I can guess the reason for the scars and scrapes. I'll bet he went down in his raging torrent. That's what the scars look like anyway. He couldn't have come down from here, right under the dam. Nobody could live in this torrent. It must have been farther down, much nearer the town.

(If he came part way down in his raging river, he'd have ended up by my house. You'd think he'd have come to me for help. Did he walk away after? Right past me? I wish I'd known to look out the window. I could have been harvesting my tepary beans and he could have walked by me all bloody and bruised, head ducked down as usual—though probably hatless for once in his life.)

When I can't get up, he says, "It's always that way when you first see it." But that's not the reason (anymore) that I can't get up. It's that I'm looking straight up into eyes that exactly match the sky behind him. His face is a combination starving shepherd and yet Water Master, too. He needs a shave, and his cheeks are deeply lined, his eyes have crow's feet at the sides, but his nose is a Water Master kind of nose, sharp, regal, and with a bump in the middle. Clearly he's as old as I am. We're weathered about the same.

He never came for one of us girls. He must have known how we all wanted to come up here but he never came for any of us. When I was younger (and he was younger, too,) even I had wishes. I didn't admit it to myself. I always said the opposite.

Perhaps he went down the other side and took a wife from somewhere over there. But if this hut's his only home, all the girls would have been unhappy. And what's up here to be friends with except jays and marmots. I couldn't live here. I wouldn't, even if he asks me to.

I do manage to get up though my knees are wobbly. I have to hang on to him. What a bundle of strings his arms are. The sound of the water roars all around us, more so as we get nearer the dam. I can't even think with that going on. I'm beginning to believe everything they say about the river. It can overpower anything, even your thoughts.

He leads me (his hand holds my upper arm in an iron grip) towards his hovel.

Inside it's dark and damp. Smells damp, too. Not like any of our places down there in the desert. We smell of sand and sage.

It was so shiny outside, sun on the water, little silvery waves ... I can't see a thing in here. Now where is that wife of his, come over from the other side? I want to see if she's as ugly as he is, though I couldn't see her if she was right in front of me. But pretty soon I *can* see. Nobody's here. I feel another sort of lurch.

Surely there's no wife—or if there is, she's a messy one. But there's all different kinds of messes. This one is odd. It's mud. All over the floor (actually, after a few minutes I can see that that mud *is* the floor). There's muddy clothes lumped under his little table, muddy boots by the door—two pairs, equally muddy. How could any wife live with this mud floor and all these muddy clothes?

I can think better in here with the door shut against the sound of the torrent.

"Sit down," he says. "I'll get tea. Are you all right? You were red, but now you're so pale."

I *thought* I was blushing but I hoped he hadn't noticed.

It's cool in here. I hug myself, not for warmth, but to hold myself together. My legs feel as if they'll give out any minute. I sit. The chair wobbles. Either the floor is uneven or I'm sinking in. I start to lean back, but the chair has lost its back. I stop myself just in time. I lean forward instead and put my head on my hands to try to hide how nervous I am. Even his scars make me nervous. Even his ugliness. If I had a hat like his I'd pull it low right now to hide how I feel.

Even here, in the dim light of a dirty window, his eyes look like two little bits of sky left over from out in the sun. All the bluer with his skin so brown around them.

He goes to a hook behind the door and gets a cleanish shirt that he puts on over his torn T-shirt. A yellow slicker with hood is hanging there along with his pistols on a cartridge belt.

He looks shy and pleased as he hands me the tea. (You'd not think such a weathered man nor a man his age would be shy anymore, but I suppose he's not used to people.) The cup is … hard to believe here with all this mud, but the cup is fine china, translucent and gold rimmed. Just the sort of cup all of us thought would be up here in the big fancy house.

He does look as if he has a secret. A happy secret. There's an odd smile twitching at the corners of his mouth. As if there *is* a fancy house somewhere up here, complete with orchard and mirrors, and I just haven't been able to find it. It's not just his look, but his elegance. Mud along the bottoms of his pants but he sits, and on the edge of his table, as if in some fancy living room and holds his cup (tea for goodness sake! Who would be drinking tea up here?) holds his cup as if it was the finest china. Mine is, but his is coarse stoneware, thick and chipped.

Down there we always say nobody ever hears him laugh or even sees him smile, but right now he's smiling a little V shaped grin and looks as if he really means it. Why has he kept this smile of his secret all this time?

I should warn him a posse is coming up, and people are angry. But I don't want to spoil his smile. I don't want to say how angry people are. Instead I say, "I suppose there's nothing you can do." Of course he stops grinning, anyway. I might as well tell him. It isn't fair not to. "They're angry. A posse's coming up. I think they have a bomb. I came to warn you."

Of course I didn't. I just wanted to see what would happen up here when they came, and to see for myself if all the water was going down the other side.

"Nobody has seen you for a week, and the water is less and less."

"What is there to do? Did you see how low the lake is?"

He grabs his fringy jacket and tells me to put on my sweater. "I have a look-out spot up on that ridge."

He doesn't take his pistols. Should I remind him?

"Is your poetry book with the metal cover in the pocket over your heart? It should be."

"What poetry book? I haven't time for poetry. Except maybe to look out at it everyday. There's a lot to do even when the gates are shut. Now that the water is low, I've been clearing out the dam."

Is nothing they told us down there true, neither poetry book nor big house? Not even one single thing? It seems that what we believed was true isn't and what we believed isn't might well be.

We go out into the shine and sparkle of the lake and the gold of the aspen. Everything numinous. He's right about looking out at poetry, though I'd call it … I don't know, looking at religion maybe. I almost drop to my knees again, though why should a good view be any more religious than a bad one?

(I wonder what it would be like to live here and see this every day? Maybe it's worth the mud.)

We have to cross the dam first. There's just a narrow walkway with a railing only on the side where the water comes down. You wouldn't last long if you went over the dam here, even with the water this low. There's a lot of spray, too. I'm shaky and I grip the railing so hard I can hardly make myself let go when I take another step. Amos A. strides along as if it was a perfectly ordinary path and doesn't look back until he's on the other side and here I am, only half way. It's not even that long a dam. All the water is funneled through this narrow gap. It's hardly as far as our little bridge in town, but here the water leaps towards me as though to pull me down into it. Globs fly up as though it had hands.

He smiles. (I never would have thought, all these years, that he'd smile a smile so like a child.) He comes back for me. Holds my hand the last few steps.

At the far end we start up the cliff above the lake. I watch him ahead of me. Nobody should wear such tight pants when their legs are as skinny as his are.

It's *much* steeper than the climb I climbed to get up here. I'm breathless, not only from that, but from Amos Acularius right here in front of me. He's a nimble man. He'd be at the top by now if not for me and he's not even breathing hard. He reaches back now and then to help me. When he does, I look up under his hat again. Even if I had something to say, his eyes wash the words right out of me. All I want to say is, "Your eyes are blue."

We follow where a little foot wide waterfall used to be but now it's dry. He points at it with his thumb and says, "I can't help this."

At the top we turn around and there's the whole lake below us. The view is even more spectacular than when I first came upon it. Mainly because we can see more snow capped mountains in the distance. The white sets off the gold. There's still fog lower down where the trail from town comes up. It feels as if we're on an island in the sky, and there's no outside world at all. I wish it were true.

Here at the lookout point, there's a gnarled limber pine. Reminds me of him. We sit under it. He's not even out of breath.

Sit and look. Except I'm more conscious of his knobby knees and his muddy worn out pants right next to me than I am of the view. I wonder how long this silence should go on. I wonder if I should say something but I can't think what.

Sit and look. Then he says, "They always blame the Water Master."

They. That's us—us townspeople. Probably even me though I never needed much water. Is that why he's hardly ever looked at us or talked to us? He knows already how we blame everything on him. Especially anything bad. Maybe he knew that one of these days we'd hate him.

"Just because I control the dam, they think I can control the clouds."

I want to answer that *I* don't think that, and maybe I don't now, but I did. Even though I didn't think about it, I blamed him—even before there was anything to blame him for.

We sit quietly again. There are so many things I want to ask, as: Did you notice how I didn't need your water? Did you notice how I didn't need a ditch? And: What about all those scars? But what I *really* want to ask is if he's married, so instead I say, "Where are the children? Are they safe?"

"What children?"

Well, that's a relief. Though he could still have a wife somewhere. Maybe she didn't want to bring children into such a muddy world, and where they might fall into the raging river just as her husband had. Or did she jump in and he jumped in to rescue her but couldn't save her?

"Is your wife going to be safe?"

"There's no wife."

But of course not. Who would marry such a countrified, sheep-herder kind of man who lives in a shack with a mud floor and has stunted lupine for flowers.

"Do you actually live in that little hut?"

"Where else?"

"Isn't this a bad place to bring up children? I mean in case you have some sometime. Your wife would go crazy what with the mud and the danger and nobody to talk to—though of course there's you." "Then I guess it's a good thing I have no wife."

And a good thing his hat is low again (though at a rakish angle this time). Then here comes the posse, out from the fog—well, one of them, anyway, carrying a rifle and with pistols at his sides. Goodness knows what's in his backpack.

"This has happened before," Amos Acularius says. "They'd prefer finding you dead—guarding your dam to the death." He looks over at me. Smiles. I'm all right this time because I'm looking at his lips. I'm already thinking (I can't help it) how I'm too old to have any little Water Master babies that would have eyes like that or V shaped smiles. Then I'm thinking: Will he mind ... about not having any children? And then I'm thinking: *I'd* mind.

He says, "I would." He's talking about dying for his dam though it takes me a minute to realize it. "I don't want you to." I'm blushing again. He actually puts his sweaty bony arm across my shoulders. I suppose it's a kindness for the blushing.

Thank goodness we mostly keep looking down at the dam. "I may have to," he says. "It depends." We watch the man go into the hut. When he comes out, he has the pistols from the back of the door. He holds them by their cartridge belt and looks all around as if to hand them to the Water Master—as if he doesn't want to shoot an unarmed man. Why is the Water Master up here at his look-out spot and without his pistols? You can't guard a dam from here. Though so far there's only one man to guard it from. Except does he have a bomb?

We wait. No more men come up out of the fog. They must be far behind or maybe this man is the only one. I wonder why they've sent him up here all by himself? I know that man. I recognize him by his hat—brown leather and with a shorter brim than most. I'm not surprised they'd pick him to come up first. He's always the angriest about everything. I don't think I've ever seen him not. The look in his eyes is what I used to think was in the Water Master's, and that that was why the Water Master wouldn't look at anybody. Now I think the Water Master didn't look at people because he thought he was ugly (which is true) and because of all those scars.

The man puts down the pistols and unhooks his rifle. Then he takes off his back pack, rummages inside it and pulls out a package. He walks a little ways along the dam and sits on the edge with his legs hanging over (just seeing him do that scares me) and eats his lunch.

Amos A. and I look at each other. He's so close this time and his sweaty arm still across my shoulders.... I look away fast. We're still in the shadow of the tree though the shadow has moved.

Amos Acularious takes his arm away and moves closer to the edge of the bluff we climbed. Out from under the shadow of the tree he'll be visible from the dam, though I don't suppose the man will think to look up here.

I study Amos A's back. How he has such a longish neck. There's something delicate about him, (translucent like his tea cup) though I've felt his strength as he helped me climb.

The man has finished his lunch and is taking longish, tied together, red things out of his pack.

Amos Acularius says, "You sit tight."

Before I can think to answer—to shout, *Don't!* he's sliding down the slope in front of us as if it was a long, long child's slide.

It took us twenty minutes to climb up here, but he's at the bottom in less than half a minute. I can't see him because he's made a land slide. And he makes a racket—a swooshing, gravelly sound, and a great cloud of dust.

I'm scared to jump off the edge and slide, but I'm not going to sit up here all by myself waiting and watching—maybe watching bad things happening to Amos Acularius. Rocks are still coming down behind him. I jump, anyway, shut my eyes and jump, into his landslide and make my own. I'm all the way down before I have time to think about it.

It keeps on trickling down after our plunge. I can't see a thing. Then I finally make out Amos A. at the edge of his dam, a grayish figure, his black clothes covered with dust.

I see the man look across at Amos. Amos A's arms are out at each side. The fringe hanging down all along them makes him look, not only like a Water Master but master of all the gray granite. He's so dusty he's like a part of the cliff we slid down.

The man stands still as though startled and maybe frightened—surely impressed. Amos Acularius even impresses me and I can only see his back. Except he always has impressed me, even when he toured his gates down there in town.

But maybe his arms are out like that for a different reason. I move up next to him. He's shouting. Maybe he's swearing. Even this close, I can't hear because of the rushing water. Except he doesn't look angry. Maybe it's a prayer—for or to the rushing, roaring torrents. Could that be? Could he be talking to the water?

The man comes to himself after a minute and he starts shouting, too. *He* looks like he's swearing though of course we can't hear. Knowing him, he probably is. Then the man sets his dynamite, carefully, in the middle of the dam. Lights the fuse. Amos Acularius does *nothing!* Keeps talking to himself. Just stands there and lets them be set and lit.

I want to shout: You can't depend on prayer or spells with dynamite. I pull on his fringe. "Amos!" (I dare to call him Amos.) "Do something! Hurry!" But it's as if I'm nothing but a fly—hardly even a bother.

The man moves off the dam as we move on to it. Amos A. grabs my hand and trots me across. He'd go faster if he wasn't pulling me. He's still mouthing things, but I can't hear. I'm too scared about the dynamite to be scared of the water rushing down so near, and with hardly any railing. We cross right by where the fuse is fizzing and Amos doesn't try to stop it. I keep yelling, Amos, Amos, as if he could hear me. I try to hold him back but he pulls me on. I try to pull away so I can put it out myself, but he won't let go.

At the other side, he throws me, face down, and himself on top of me, his arms wrapped around my head, not his own. I've always done the protecting (all those brothers and sisters). I've never, in my whole life, been protected by anybody—not that I remember, though I suppose as a baby I must have been.

I feel his body all along my back—all along where I've just been scraped and bruised, but I like the feel of him, even though I hurt. I hope we never have to get up.

The dynamite goes off but with the sound of the water I can hardly hear it. Mostly I feel the shaking of the ground.

Stones clatter down around us and on top of us, though hardly any on me because Amos is protecting me.

We lie, until it stops. It feels like a long time, but I know it can't be. Then we look up, over and down at what used to be the dam. It sounds out even louder than before and the sound is different. Angrier—though it always sounded angry.

"Well, they've got water down there now. Will in a minute anyway." Amos Acularius, still on top of me, speaks right into my ear or I'd never have heard him. How can he say that so slowly and calmly after what just happened? "For a while, more than they bargained for. Are you all right?"

"But you? You must be bruised all over your back."

He helps me up.

I think he's saying he's all right but I can only guess since he's not that close anymore.

The man is staring at the Water Master. You can see the rage on his face. He's yelling, and for sure it's cursing though we can't hear. He pulls one of the pistols from its holster, cocks it, aims it right at us. Shoots one shot. We hear it ping as it ricochets against the rocks.

Amos Acularius walks right straight to him. Grabs him, gun and all. They tussle. Amos is clearly stronger. It only takes a minute before Amos turns him around and bends his arm up behind him and walks him towards the river bank. The bank is in a different place now. Already the lake is even lower and yet the torrent below, where the dam used to be is much higher and much more vicious. I've never seen anything like the way the water rushes down now.

Amos walks him to the new edge and throws him off. I see a brown hat fly away and I catch a glimpse of feet in boots. Then, in less than half a minute, the man is long gone.

Amos Acularius stands on the broken edge watching the water rush down. I come up beside him. He leans close, his hand on my shoulder. Is he going to kiss me? I'm not sure if I should pull back or lean forward, but he just wants to speak into my ear so I'll hear above the sound of the water. I feel his breath on my cheek.

"He won't die," he says. Shouts.

"How can he not?"

"The river won't let him. The river will save him. Throw him from pool to pool and never pound him into the rocks. He'll end up looking like me that's all."

He takes his hand from my shoulder. He walks up to the weapons, picks up the rifle and throws it in the river, then throws the man's and his own pistols in, too. He takes off his fringy jacket and throws it in.

"This goes with the job," he says. It belongs to the river. He takes my arm and leads me, just as he did before, into his shack and shuts the door against the roar of water. "I'm free," he says, and begins packing up his things, bunching them in to a muddy duffel, clean and dirty lumped in together.

I plunk myself on the wobbly chair. I look down at the rips and scrapes all over my pants.

"This happens after every major drought. There's a new Water Master every time. Takes about twenty … thirty years. He'll be it now. That's how you get to be Water Master. I'm free." Then he notices I have my arms around myself again and I'm shaking more than when he first handed me tea. That seems like a long time ago. He stops packing and gets me tea again. Sits beside me on his table as he did before. "I don't mind being Water Master, though you can never really master water (you think you can, but you can't) but I don't care that much for the townspeople. They hate you for spoiling their town—like it's being spoiled right now, as we sit here. They'll hate him. They never learn it's not his fault, wasn't mine either. I'm glad to be rid of them."

He reaches as if to touch my shoulder, but doesn't quite. As if he wants to caress but doesn't dare. "But I'm glad you came."

"I know that man. He's cruel. He doesn't care about anybody." "He'll be different once he knows water. Once the water knows him. Water changes you. And living here alone will change him. Seeing gold, like it is now, and the silver lake. That'll change him, too."

"But you never looked up. I was sorry for you, never looking up."

"I did. I looked out at it every morning and every night. And down there in the village, I looked. I saw you." He takes the empty cup and saucer and wraps his clothes around them. "It's my grandmother's cup. The only thing she had of any value." Then he unwraps it and hands it to me again. "Would you like to have it?"

"Where are you going?" "Some place where they never heard of a Water Master nor ever needed one. Where there's no hanging mountain lakes and no dams. Will you come? I noticed you before—how you never needed water."

He's looking straight at me again. Maybe his eyes can hypnotize and I've been hypnotized all this time. But I like it. "Grandma's tea cup. It's yours if you want it." I don't expect he'll ever be able to say, I love you. I'm not going to wait around for that. I hand it back so he can wrap it up again. "I'll come."

Sci Fiction, February, 2002

The Paganini Of Jacob's Gully

Used to be, I was the Paganini of Laggish. If my brother and I didn't play (he on the parlor bagpipes), there was no party. I played the Devil's instrument and so fast that, like Paganini, I was thought to be in league with Him. The faster I played, the more they said I'd sold my soul, or worse. Who could play this fast and frenzied but the Devil or one of his demons?

How did it come to be that the Devil always plays the violin? Dexterity, I suppose, but I can also play so sweet and slow I make you cry. That's like an angel.

My brother said my life was in danger. He said I should escape. He told me not to play this fast anymore, ever, no matter where I ended up. I changed my name from Hamish to James and ran away from Scotland to America.

Not just America, but to the opposite edge of it, westward, riding my donkey, cross-of-Jesus on her back, my fiddle wrapped tight against rain and dust. I'll die if anything happens to it and that's not just a figure of speech. I want it in my coffin with me. I want my arms around it. I've managed to keep it glued and in more or less decent shape through all kinds of weather. I've managed to keep the bow strung with horsehair I yank out of tails myself.

I learned to play when I broke my back. I wasn't supposed to move. My brother, William, traded a calf for a violin. I lay flat as I was supposed to and looked at it—thought about it. My brother got me a little book on how to play it, but no bow. He thought I wouldn't be ready for that for a while. When I was well enough to sit up, I plucked it like a guitar. I plucked so much I got calluses on the tips of my fingers, so I was ready when William got me the bow. Then he got our dance caller to gave me a lesson or two. I took the fiddle with me up on the moors when I was out watching the sheep. Our dog would howl along with my playing.

Sometimes I'd play so bright and wonderful I'd lift myself right into the air.

I seemed to reel and jig and twirl as I played, but I could never do that when I wasn't playing. My back didn't grow properly after the accident. For a long time I didn't know that I was any different from everyone else. I was crooked but I was loved. I didn't think my crookedness mattered until I went off to school for a couple of years. I was in pain, too, but I thought that was the way it was. I thought everybody was in pain.

I played away their laughing at me. I played away their insults and scorn. Later, after I'd left school for the moors and all day at the fiddle, I got my schoolmates' niggardly admiration. Maybe more their jealousy.

For a while it got so they couldn't have a dance without me and my brother. My magic was my violin. Out here it's the coyotes sing back to me.

The accident.... I remember just before, but not after. I was nine. I was skinny and small for my age, but lots of times I'd led that same bull out to pasture. Usually there weren't any cows in the field on the way. This time the bull pushed down the barbed wire fence as if it was nothing and headed for those cows. He had a ring in his nose, so you'd think he'd behave even for me. I hung on. I scraped over the downed barbed wire and over stones until the bull turned back towards me. I remember his face close to my face, all bloody from his nose ring. I remember his luminous brown eye, his yellow ear tag. I remember being tossed.

I was never going to be like my brother, though that's what I always wanted. One leg is shorter than the other. One shoulder higher. I ended up as if made to curl around a violin. Or perhaps I twisted that way from cuddling it under my chin all day long as I grew.

Out here I don't do as my brother said to. He told me never to play this fast again, but I'm true to my skill. True, you could say, to my long, fast fingers. I can't help myself.

It pains me to walk, but I have my jenny. (I named her Maggie for William's girl.) I can ride if I need to, though mostly I walk beside her. She has enough to carry.

I've found other players to play with now and then. We set them stomping.

I'm often flirted with. That's not unusual here in America. Flirt with the Devil. Tempt fate. Some women like to do that. Stroke his long fingers. Bless his hands. (Bless the Devil's hands, for heaven's sake!) They never flirted with me back in Scotland. They were afraid of me, but they didn't torment and tease me.

I don't want those easy girls. I used to think, even with my shape, somebody might come to really like me, but now, at my age, I don't think so anymore. I haven't thought about my birthdays since I left Scotland. I lost track of time and I lost track of my age. I must be close to forty by now.

But being crooked isn't all there is to it. I'm not exactly the handsomest there is. My looks go with being the Devil, shiny, droopy black hair, face too long, shaggy eyebrows, and the worst, nose like a vulture.... And it doesn't help that I've not lost my Scottish burr.

"Plays like the Devil and even looks like him." I've overheard that said. And, "Look at the nose on him."

Sometimes somebody else will say, "But he has a nice smile."

I keep smiling.

I can make the violin cry like a baby. I can make it laugh. Make it baa and meow. People think there's somebody in there. Even after I let them look through the *f* holes, they still think so. They think I've imprisoned all sorts of creatures.

(Off and on I have a mustache, but I never would dare have a goatee.)

I spend a lot of time playing in bars along with the piano player (in towns that are little more than one bar and one piano), accepting free drinks and then pouring them into the spittoon or whatever is handy. (I don't want to get drunk with *them,* or *anybody,* for that matter.)

I play at dances, too. Those are mostly outdoors. Just like back in the old country, people come from miles around. Back there they walked, here they ride. There's always a couple of men around who play some instrument or other. Mostly mandolin and fife and banjo. The banjo player's as fast and furious as I am, but nobody takes him as the Devil. The Devil doesn't play the banjo.

This time I was playing at Wilkerson's bar, just me and the piano player. Wilkerson's is little more than a roadside corner where four ranches come together. I'd been flirted with unmercifully. I never dare ignore those women. That would be insulting. If they make too overt a request, I always say, "Another time," or, "Next time." This time one of the women leans over me where I sit, her big breasts right under my nose. I think any minute they'll flop out. She kisses my hand and talks about my magic fingers and then she puts my hand right inside her dress. (Didn't have to go very far to be on her breast.) I pull away and look to see if anybody noticed. They have. They laugh and yell, "Go for it, busker."

But some must have been jealous. (Envious of the twisted?) After, when I was all set to leave, thank God my violin is packed up and strapped on the jenny, I come back in to fill my canteens. I should have used the pump down the street. At least I escaped with my fiddle in one piece.

And my hands are all right. I never hit out to defend myself. I have to save them. That's another reason to be a mild man that smiles all the time. Sometimes I do feel like hitting somebody, even with my fiddle, but I have to control myself. *Have* to. It would be as if using your best friend as a weapon.

I manage to pull myself up on Maggie. She's got everything I own on her back, including the violin. I hate to add to her load, but I have to get out of here faster than I can limp now. She knows what's going on, otherwise she'd balk at a load like this. She'd be mulish.

I head along the creek first. I need to heal myself until I can play again. I can't judge distances or time right now. I half pass out. Finally I let myself fall off. I hope she keeps quiet in the morning. Nothing like a good morning hee-haw to wake a whole town. I don't even know how far we've gone or where we are except we kept to the stream.

For once I don't sleep wrapped around my fiddle as I usually do. For once Maggie has to spend the night all packed up. I don't even loosen her cinch.

And for once she doesn't sing out at dawn. She's smart. She knows she shouldn't. Instead of her hee-haw it's her lips nibbling on my cheek that wakes me. As if to see how I am. As if to wonder why we're not up and away by now.

I manage to pull off her pack and rub her down. Then I check my bruises, though what's the difference, one pain more or less? My right eye is swollen shut. I soak it with icy stream water. I lie on the bank as I do it and work on a new piece. First I call it, "Go to the Devil." Then I call it, "Here Comes the Devil." I work on it all day, but I work as I worked when I broke my back, lying flat and thinking about it. It's a habit of mind. Used to be I mostly looked at my ceiling— bottom of the thatch it was back then—now I look at the sky through cottonwood branches.

Maggie grazes nearby. She scares coyotes and wolves away. She'd warn me of strangers of any sort. She's fearless. She'd face a mountain lion. I never beat her even when she balks. I know there's always a good reason. Her balking has saved me lots of times. And, unlike horses, she has sense enough to save herself.

I don't feel any better as the day goes on, but that's to be expected, and I'll probably be worse tomorrow. I should move farther away while I still can. I pack up and head off. I have to find a place to hide as I heal. I walk this time. Maggie has had enough troubles. I don't ever need a lead rope. She follows by herself.

I pass through another town. Three lads follow and throw stones at me. I don't pay them any mind. Reminds me of back in school. One woman tells them to stay away from the tramp. Another walks with me for a minute and tries to talk to me, but I don't want her sympathy, especially not now when I'm hobbling along even worse than I usually do.

And I'm ashamed of my bruises, though I had nothing to do with them. I save my hands to such an extent that I let my face take the blows instead.

A few blocks farther down I sit on the edge of the watering trough and wait while Maggie drinks.

Here comes that same woman. I wish she'd go away. I'm not only all beat up, but my clothes are torn. I look even more like a tramp than usual. I had thought to repair them later, when I find myself a safe place to rest up.

"I heard about what happened up at Wilkerson's," she says. "I'm sorry."

Wants to be in league with the Devil, does she? And nice-looking, too.

"I'm a little bit sorry myself."

Her eyes are gray-green-tan.

"Come by my place. I have a steak I could put on your eye. After, you could eat it."

I get up and check Maggie's load just to get away from the woman. I think of my new piece: Here Comes the Devil.

"I live on the far side of town. You'll go right by my place anyway."

I don't want her walking beside me, slowing her pace to my hobble. She doesn't look to be the kind of woman to saunter. I say just plain, No! and start hobbling along to show her how slow I am. She keeps beside me while I keep to the far side of Maggie. Can't she see who I am? Or is my face so swollen and purple I no longer look like the Devil?

At least I'm still heading away from Wilkerson's. She must chafe at having to walk at my speed. I think she'd normally be striding. She keeps glancing over at me and my jenny. I wish she wouldn't. Her hair, black as mine, is pulled back tight, but it's wispy and fine and won't stay in its knot. It gives her a nice tousled look.

Tempting fate, is she? Like those other women always do? "You might get in trouble for helping me."

"But I have herbs that heal."

I've been walking faster than is comfortable. At least the way is flat until we come to her house. There's a little group of houses up hill from a creek. Hers is the first, thank goodness.

I thought to walk right on by, but I'm so tired and discouraged. Partly because I was trying to hurry for her sake and trying walk straighter for my own pride. I stop, but I won't go in. I haven't set foot in a home for a long time. I let her sit me out in a canvas lawn chair under her grape arbor.

She sits on the edge of another near by.

"How could they do that… to somebody who…."

She can't say it so I say it for her. "To a cripple like me."

That makes her blush. I think how back home we'd call her bonnie.

"I've never heard you play, but I've heard about it. Everybody has."

"I can't right now."

"Would you stay and rest until you can?"

"I don't know how long that'll take."

If I wanted to, I could make her cry in half a minute. There's one tune always does it.

She takes the packs off Maggie before I can stop her. She brings me tea and bread, puts her steak on my eye.

I've been too much in bars. I distrust women. I find them as garish in actions as in dress, though she's not. Yet I distrust her.

Perhaps there's something in the tea or I'm more tired than I think. Or perhaps it's the relief… being looked after for a change. Let her and my Maggie be in charge of things. I lean back in the lawn chair and fall asleep before I have the chance to think not to.

I don't wake up till twilight. It's Maggie wakes me again. She must wonder what we're doing here. The sun is behind the mountains. I stroke her velvety nose and rub her poll. We watch it get darker. I'm too comfortable, and every time I move, I hurt. We won't go far tonight. Maybe down by the arroyo we walked past on the way here. Camp behind some of those boulders.

The wind picks up. The woman comes out with a hurricane lamp. "I let you sleep but you must be getting cold now. It's way after supper time."

"I'll leave as soon as I get packed up."

"No!" (A worried, too-loud no.) "I meant for you to come in and eat here. You can stay the night. I have room."

I try to get up, but I'm so stiff and sore I can't. I lie back again and pretend I changed my mind.

"Come in and have some supper?"

"I'll just spend the night right here if you'll let me. I'll be fine."

But she sees what's wrong, grabs me by my elbows, and I hers, and we pull. But these canvas folding chairs are so unstable. It collapses. We fall, she on top of me. I like that she starts to laugh. I laugh, too, but then she's upset that she might have hurt me. So many "I'm sorrys" in a row.... And she blushes.

"Don't worry, I don't hurt any more than usual."

She's a tough, muscled woman. I could feel that, and you can see it in her hands.

Then, she pulling and I pushing, we finally get me up. She leads me inside, her arm around me. I'm so stiff I'd never have made it without her help and without trying to seem to her at least a partly whole man. I'd not even have tried if not for her being there. I'd have stayed on the ground.

The room is small and smells of stew. It's dim with the dusty glow from the lamps in their sconces. Another lamp is on the table, a soup tureen beside it. There's bread and cheese.

She sits me at the table. I'd rather lie down and forget about eating.

She sits near me. She says, "I'm Vera." Then, "I like your accent."

At least there's one thing about me to like. *If* true.

I don't know why, but I tell her my name is Hamish, not James. I guess I feel too at home, and I like that she likes my brogue.

As she serves me, she says, "I have oats for your donkey."

"Don't. Maggie mustn't have oats. Give her a carrot or an apple if you like, but she'll do fine on bitter brush."

She tries to get me to sleep on her cot in her bedroom while she sleeps on the couch. I refuse, but, again, I sleep well, as though I've been waiting all this time just for a chance to lie down on a too-short couch with a hump in the middle. The ground would have been more comfortable.

Seven miles down river along the valley, there's a town called Jacob's Gully. They actually have a church, and they have a little opera house. Holds a couple of hundred people. She says Caruso sang there, and Madam Schuman-Hank, Galli-Curci. She wants me to play in that opera house. She says she can arrange it. She knows they want me.

I say yes, if I can ever play again.

She takes my hands, shuts her eyes, and holds them as though meditating over them or saying a prayer. She says, "Are they all right? I have a heating cream you can put on them that draws out pain." She turns them over. Looks as if she'd like to kiss them. I don't like it when those other women do that, but she's not like them. Then, like everybody else, she says, "What long fingers!" My hands are the only things about my looks I'm proud of.

She says she'll see to it I make some real money. She sets a date and marks it on her calendar. "Will you remember?"

She's right about me forgetting. She makes me a little calendar of the next few months. "Will you be all right by then?"

"I hope so."

She wants me to stay and recover here with her. She says she'll make a better bed for me than this couch.

I don't want to. I don't like people looking at me limping, hunching over even when I'm in good health. I leave that afternoon. I can't keep her from giving me salves and tonics, then corn-bread and bacon.

"Come here first," she says. "We can go down to Jacob's Gully together."

I say I will.

But before I can make that date, it happens again. I get beat up in the bar in Paradise Gap. There are lots of places called Paradise around here. The snow-topped mountains make it all so beautiful. This Paradise is on the edge of a gorge, alongside a river, and with lots of big cottonwoods. This time my violin is ruined.

I was starting to play… not the famous Devil's Trill, but *my* Devil's Trill. Just as hard to play as that one. Maybe harder. Tables seem to jiggle. Glasses rattle. Dust rises. It's the preacher himself says it. "No normal person can play like this." (What's a preacher doing in the bar anyway? Stirring up trouble, seems like.) This time somebody grabs my violin and splits it over his knee. Usually I just let myself get beaten, but now I fight. I don't care how ruined the fiddle is, I want it back. I break a couple of fingers, but on my right hand, so that's not so bad. Besides, I don't have a violin anymore anyway.

Finally somebody says, "Let him go." Somebody helps me up and hands me what's left of my fiddle. Somebody puts my hat on my head. I can walk.

I head away from everything and everybody, straight up into the mountains. Into the snow. When it comes to walking, I'm not in as bad shape as before, but my violin is hardly a violin anymore. I'll not make that date in Jacob's Gully.

I collapse when I reach the beginning of the evergreens. I lie there hugging the pieces of my fiddle. Every now and then I chew on jerky. (I don't know what Maggie chews on, but she's sister to the wild ass. She'll get along.) When my jerky's gone, I'll have to get up and do something. Or perhaps I won't.

I try to forget about that opera house and Vera, but I keep looking at the calendar she made me. I mark off the days, and when the day comes, I think of her wondering where I am. But perhaps she heard about me just as she did last time I got beat up at Wilkerson's.

Perhaps she heard they'd ruined my violin. I hope she didn't spend a long time waiting.

There's an interval called "Diabolus in Musica." The tritone. Hardest to sing of all. Banned by the Greeks and then later by the Church. Called the most corrupt interval in music. Feels like in no key whatsoever. I hum it to myself. It *is* hard. Doing it makes me feel sicker and more dispirited than I already am.

Used to be… everything is used to be… I could make trees rustle, creeks sparkle, birds twitter. I could play hail storms. I could play thunder.

Finally I get up. I go to a town I've never been to. They know me anyway, everybody does. Being the way I am, I could never hide. Big nose, limp, leaning-over kind of man…. Even if I grew a bushy beard it wouldn't help.

I camp out under the cottonwoods just outside of town, far enough away so Maggie's greeting the dawn won't bother anybody. I'll have water from an irrigation ditch nearby. There's a mama duck living on its banks. She walks across the road every morning with six babies following her, heading for the river. And back again every evening. People let me alone. I know I'm not helping my reputation by playing hermit.

I set my fingers and tape them up tight. I hobble into town to look for the right aged wood. I shape a new neck and attach it to the old scroll. I glue everything back together. I hobble out, even farther from town, to try it. I hardly dare. If worse comes to worst, I could go back to herding sheep, though around here the job seems only for Basques. I could become an ordinary beggar instead of a busker. Switch to a jaw harp. Play the spoons.

I haven't played in so long my fingers have soft tips for the first time since I broke my back, and they've lost some strength. I thought I got the neck the same length, but I'm playing out of tune. Practice will fix that—and everything else. The sound has changed some but it's still pretty good. I'll get used to it as I've had to get used to my whole life.

I get a dance job. I don't know how they find me but word does get around. That means real pay. I circle the day on the calendar Vera made for me. I'm to join my busking buddies at Paradise Gap for a dance. There'll be four of us: Concertina, mandolin, and another fiddler. I always turn out to be the leader with any group I play in. I don't push myself forward but they always automatically defer to me.

(Those country fiddlers hold the violin to their chest, support it with their hand, and never go beyond first position, but they're clever with their tunings. I hold my fiddle with my chin, and I couldn't play at all if I changed the tuning.)

Do the townspeople understand that I'll be one of those players? I don't know how they dare ask me back, though it was just three or four drunken bums beat me up, not the whole town.

I come into Paradise Gap with my cross-of-Jesus wild ass as if into

Jerusalem.

But *she* comes. I'll not play as I thought to.

She strides up to me the afternoon before the dance—strides, like I knew she would, and wanted to, back when she had to shuffle along with me.

"Hamish," she says. "I heard. Are you all right?"

I think again how much I like hair pulled back like that and how I like even better that it won't stay in its knot. As before, she's not wearing a bonnet, and she's, as they say, brown as a berry.

"I hope you didn't wait for me."

She strokes Maggie and Maggie nuzzles her.

"Last I saw you, you were all black and blue."

"I couldn't get word to you about the concert. I was...." What should I say, that I was lying on my back in the snowy woods looking at the sky? "I was... away."

I change my plan. I have to. First I'll play so as to make her cry, and then, when they want a rest from dancing, I'll show off. I could even break all my strings but one as Paganini did, and show what I can do. I'll play the Devil's Trill.

I've made loose women fall in love with me through fast fingers alone. At least they seemed to for the moment. A moment is better than never.

This is a dance out under the stars. It's not at all like it is in a bar. It takes place right in the middle of the village—actually right in the middle of the main road. The moon is out. Hurricane lamps line the dance area, but you hardly need them though they do give a happy glow to everything. There's maybe sixty, eighty people, all in a good mood. Babies are lined up along one shadowed wall with mothers taking turns looking after them. The small fry dance, too. Everybody dances, reels, jigs, polkas, square dances.... I and the other fiddler take turns calling: "Picken' up the Pawpaws," and "Pass around the jug...." All these women and children present makes the whole tone different. There's hardly even any swearing.

As the evening goes on, couples move back to spoon in the shadows. I wonder how I could have thought to do as I'd planned. Even if Vera hadn't been here, I'd not have done it. Losing my violin for a month must have driven me crazy.

Vera dances. Here I am, making the music that pushes her into other men's arms, though she does look at me and smile when she passes near our little stage.

As I planned, at the first break I play the Devil's Trill. I get cheers and yells, catcalls, too, but happy ones. Then I limp off to rest with the others. I wipe the sweat off my face and the violin, especially the fingerboard. She comes. I'm embarrassed by the sweat marks under my arms and all down my shirt front.

She brings me a mug of cider, moves a chair so as to sit beside me (I couldn't have moved it for her), lingers her touch on my arm. I can see how she feels in her eyes—in all of her. She's shining all over. This is the first time somebody I want to love me has loved me. (If this has anything to do with love at all.)

Later, as the night goes on, we play mostly waltzes, and later still, when everybody's getting tired, us included, love songs. The spooners get spoonier than ever, some hardly bothering to go back into the shadows. The music makes them fall in love even if they aren't. Married couples fall in love all over again. Everybody yearns for love—any kind of love.

Usually I don't think about wanting to dance, but as I play I yearn to have somebody in my arms. I yearn to be listening to myself instead of playing.

I had thought to walk... hobble down to Vera's house with her afterwards. I feel sick with yearning. I know she'd ask me to stay the night, but I can't breathe, I'm trembling, my knees wobble, and I can ill-afford to have anything more wrong with my legs. I pack up and then I go as if to the outhouse, but I hide across the street in the shadows of the alley by the general store. I watch her from there: How she asks after me, how she looks around until almost everyone's gone, how she gives up. But to be limping down to her house after all those love songs, and with the full moon.... I can't do it.

The dance had lasted most of the night so it isn't until dawn that I finally leave town. I know of a hidden camping spot, sheltered in an arroyo. There are a few trees, so there's shade. Though I've played the whole night through, I can't sleep. I spend the day playing. I play to the sagebrush. I play to the rocks. I play to a family of foxes (a mother and three kits), I play to a jackrabbit. I let the wind carry, first my love songs and then my reels and jigs, out across the desert. At twilight the coyotes answer. I play until I can't think or feel anything anymore. I pack up my fiddle and sleep with my arms around it.

When I wake it's still dark or dark again. I might have slept the clock around, though I'm not sure. I make a fire of tough, dead sagebrush and make myself coffee in my frying pan—my one and only pan. I have no food but I'm not hungry. All I want is to run away and forget my whole life. I was seducing her, that was the whole purpose. I sighed, I yearned, I made love... all with my music, and she believed me. I should leave so she can forget me. Or I should have gone with her so she'd again see me shuffling. I could sit in her soft chair and then not be able to get out of it. She could ask me to reach into a high shelf. Though I'm skewed, I'm taller than she is, but I'd not be able to do it even so. She'd soon enough learn I couldn't help her down from a horse, or up into a carriage, carry her loads for her. My looks would be the least of her worries.

I'll cross the pass to the other side of the mountains. It'll be cold up there. Cold always makes my back worse. My shuffling will be slower than ever, but I'll cross to San Francisco.

But first I'll go back to Paradise Gap bar where they broke my fiddle. I'll fit myself to the Devil's reputation. I'll flirt with those women. I'll let them put my hands anywhere they want. I'll make those drunken bums even angrier than they were before. Then I'll play... corruption, debauchery, discordance, chaos. She'll hear about it and know what I am.

I do exactly as I planned. I play fever. I play madness. I start with the banned interval. Tritone over and over, higher and higher. Then I start to play my "Here Comes the Devil" piece, but I don't finish it. Before I can, I drive them crazy, and myself, too.

I forget everything just as I forgot my accident when I was nine. All I remember of that is I was flying through the air. That's what happens now. Last thing I remember, I rose above them all, I flew... flew and fell.

As a child I had seemed to dance as I played, though I couldn't dance. Sometimes I had seemed to fly. I flew now, as in a dream. I looked down on them: Sweat flying, music flying, fingers.... I was hail and hurricane, dust devil, lightning....

Until I was tossed exactly as by that bull. I fell... from higher... *had* to be higher than the ceiling, because there was time. As I fell, slowly, as from a great distance and with plenty of time to think, I thought, there... ! Look, Vera, see what I am!

They say everybody in the bar either passed out, as I did, or beat each other up and ended in the infirmary with me. I spent the night there and didn't know it till they told me later. They rescued my violin, and in one piece. They rescued Maggie.

Vera came for me as soon as she heard. Turns out everybody wanted to take care of me. The doctor thought I'd do well here with her.

I vaguely remember the ride down in the back of an empty hay wagon. I remember the sky with little white clouds moving by above me. I remember it was bumpy and pained me.

I wake up, first back on that hunched-in-the-middle couch, and then Vera tells them to carry me into her cot where I'll be more comfortable.

I'm feverish. I dream frightening, grotesque visions. Someone places cool cloths on my forehead. Sometimes I feel someone stroking my face. My mother had died even before I broke my back, but I thought myself with her. She was the only one ever did that.

The stroking stops when I come out of my fever and start to get better. I wonder if I dreamed it.

People begin to visit. All sorts of people. Some I remember from the dance. Musicians I've played with come. People bring fresh-baked bread, cake, tomatoes from their gardens, apricots. There's hardly a day people don't come by. Sometimes they don't want to disturb me, they just bring the things, and leave right away. They set up another date for me to play a concert at Jacob's Gully.

One day Vera moves a more stable chair for me out under the arbor. She's on a folding one. The grapes are ripe. We're eating some. Somebody has just left me a fresh-caught trout.

She says, "You always look surprised when they bring you things."

"I am."

"They care about you. They even like that you played Paradise Gap bar right out of business."

"And what if I never played again?"

"You've been too much in bars."

"*Look* at me."

"*I am!*"

"Can't you see? Back in Scotland they took me as the Devil himself. For God's sake I even had to escape."

"That's not what they think here, and *don't shout!*"

Suddenly she's close to crying. "It's only a few drunken bums that beat you up and they'd be fighting with anybody. Last weekend they tipped over the piano at Wilkerson's. They threw the piano player in the river."

She kneels by my chair, hugs my knees, and puts her head in my lap. I lean away and spread my arms to each side. I don't know what to do. I don't dare touch her. Then I lean forward and move my hands closer. I dare to *almost* touch her.

But she's crying. I touch. I put one arm across her shoulders, cup her head in both my hands. I kiss her flyaway hair. I hold her tight. Tighter. Then I lift her face and kiss her forehead, kiss the tears from her cheeks, from her chin.... I say, "Everything's all right now."

Report to the Men's Club and Other Stories, 2002

Desert Child

An unbeliever once wrote: God is alive and well and living in the desert. She wrote, "Surely if he's anywhere at all. . . ."

—SUSAN COULSON

You can smell him, strong and bitter. He pricks and bites. There's either too much of everything or not enough. When water, too much water, when dry, too dry. Too cold at night, too hot in the daytime. The ground shakes. All summer long, smoke from distant fires. You hear him in the buzz of bugs, the rattle of rattlesnakes.

There's no wind now, but there has been—winds that pick up sand and swirl it into devils.

Whatever God—He, She, or It (laughing, ah *ha*! ah *ha*!)... whatever's out there—brings, it's never reasonable. As though there could ever be reasons for any of this.

You'd think we wouldn't live here. You'd think we'd let the ragged, mangy, fearsome creature slither back, fill our huts with sand, return our little oasis to the desert that It owns and won't let go.

There's this man... whatever desert thing that's out there left him to make do with what there was to make do with. Stretched him to nothing but string and bone. Dried him, scarred him, gave him a limp, took away his voice so there's nothing left but a whisper. His gray handlebar mustache is the only flourishing thing about him.

I don't think he's as old as he looks. I'm trying to build him up with oatmeal and goat cheese. That's all I have to build somebody up with.

I can count on him for help, though, even if I don't ask, and I don't. He sees a thing needs doing and does it. After, I sometimes see him lean back and stretch as if his back was sore.

We don't even know what his name really is. They call this place Archer's Corner, but there's no corner and he's not Archer, though he was here by himself before we came. First I met him, he said, "Everybody calls me Red." And I said, "They should have changed that to Gray a long time ago." At the time I thought he might have smiled, but maybe he just squinted. Now that I know him better, I know he doesn't see well.

Though he was here before we came, he always acts as if it's he who doesn't belong. I suppose he has squatter's rights. Nobody's tried to kick him out so far.

There's something about him that draws me. Not grace, but it's as if there's a special grace of the graceless.

It's not quite so desert-like here. We have our creek, coming down icy cold. We have willows along its edges. There's a wild blackberry patch. We only have to go down the path a little way for water. The creek was inclined to swish your pail away if you weren't careful, but Red (Gray) made a dam of stones and pulled over a log to still the stream in one place so the children could get water by themselves. He walked along the river a while ago and brought back two pails, mismatched socks, diapers, all hooked on branches way downstream.

He does all the work the other men either won't do or don't have time for. He put up the swing and the teeter-totter for the children. There's only five children here, and one's just a baby, but he thought it was worthwhile anyway.

It's because of him, I can sit down for a minute. The wood gathered, my goats safely in and milked, the water's brought for the men to wash up, the soup's at the back of the stove in the mess hall, there's bacon and corn bread. Red chopped the firewood and brought the water up. For now I have a minute to sit and darn a sock and think about the child.

No-see-ums, sand mites, crows, the magpie, and now this girl. They say a magpie is a bad omen. I don't see why. I always feel good when I see one, though I always salute, as they say to do, to ward off bad luck. I don't believe in bad omens, but I salute anyway.

I live apart from the others (by choice) in a hut under a cottonwood, past the cook house, and the little cold cave where we keep the goats' milk and cheese, but not far from the playground.

Our village isn't much. Nine huts, some little more than tents or half-tents, some little more than doghouses for men. We'd call our village Dog Town if there wasn't already a gold mine by that name, for the same reason. The huts are set out helter-skelter, paths between, leading to the mess hall and beyond, to the river.

No huts are far from the river except mine and Red's. Horses and carts are kept farther downstream. My goats are near me. I want to be able to hear them in case of trouble. That's another reason I live away from the others. They don't want to be near my goats. The goat pen is coyote-proof. Even mountain-lion-proof. Red built it for me.

The men are here for the tungsten. There are only a few women and children, come to be with their men and help out. I've no people of my own here. I was hired to help with the cooking and the laundry.

Last night I heard the squeak, squeak of the swing and looked out the window and there was that girl.

Who ever heard of a child alone out here in our playground swinging in the moonlight? Though I expect she goes into the goat pen to be safe, maybe cuddles up with the kids to keep warm. There's no place for her to have come from. We're a long ways from anywhere. It's as if she dropped from the sky.

She must live off the smell of sage. How else could she stay alive, scrabbling about from rabbit brush to black brush? Perhaps she milks our nannies in the middle of the night.

The children saw her first several days ago, but they never said a word till Jenny told me. They knew their mothers wouldn't want her around, considering they're always talking about another mouth to feed (that's what they say about Red all the time, and he eats like a bird). They saw her in the playground swinging just as I did. She runs every time they get near, but she came out once to Jenny. Wouldn't you know… to somebody three years old. I suppose she thought Jenny couldn't tell about it, but she could and just as clear as could be. Jenny said she was dirty and that she had funny eyes and that she'd been whipped. "Worse than any of us," she said, eyes wide with the wonder of it.

"How do you know?"

"I saw the marks."

I'm the one looks after all the orphaned and wounded creatures (including poor old Red). The mothers are right, we don't want another mouth to feed, but a child is a child, and right and wrong is right and wrong.

I went out when the moon was high and put a piece of corn-bread on the teeter-totter, then came back and sat in the shadow on my stoop and watched. I had a lariat looped and ready to go. Who I caught (in a manner of speaking) was old Red/Gray. I told him what I was doing and how, so far, she hadn't shown herself, though the moon was about to go down. I told him what Jenny had said.

He sat beside me and rolled himself a cigarette. It was the closest he'd gotten to me (or anybody) in all this time. Any other man would have taken the lariat from me and said he could do it better.

With the moon still up and the old man's company, I felt as happy as I have in a long time. We didn't say a word, just looked at how everything was silvery, and listened to the creek—sounding silvery.

Finally he said, "When we get her, what will we do with her?"

I liked how he said we. "What do you think we ought to do?"

"It might be harder than you think. I'll bet she won't be anything like these children here. Jenny's right, she's been treated bad."

I had a funny feeling he was talking about himself more than about this girl. "*You!*" I said, but I stopped myself from the rest of it, though I got chills up and down my spine from thinking of it. I changed my "*You!*" (which I'd shouted out louder than I meant to) to "*You'll* help."

He looked at me as if he suspected what I was really going to say.

I said, "If I could just coax her to come to me." (I was thinking, if I can coax her, maybe I can coax him, old Gray/Red, to come out of himself a little.) "If I could just convince her we don't whip children. Anyway, *I* don't."

He looked at me. Thought. Said, "She won't come."

"How do you know?" But I knew how he knows or thinks he knows.

"You'll have to tame her first."

All the time I was thinking: Well, just how tame are you, old man?

I wish I could think of things to talk about that would make him tell me about himself, but I don't ever hardly even dare say thank you for all the things he does for me.

We sat a while longer. Coyotes howled, and I started to worry about the girl. I got up, thinking to go take a look in the goat pen to see if she was safe.

"Don't," Red said.

So I didn't. Then I said, "It's time we gave up for tonight."

"Leave the corn-bread."

"Goodness knows what'll eat it."

We don't have that much cornmeal. You can't grow it here because some critter always gets the ears before we do. Red fenced a tiny garden for me—fenced it a foot deep under the ground and across the top, too, because of the gophers. We got some squash and green beans, but you can't grow corn that way.

There are a couple of men here I stay away from. Most of the men are more bluster than bite, but there are two.... They shot my tame raven. (That raven could even say a few words: "Land's sake," and, "Oh p'shaw." Things I say to myself when I'm alone. It could bark like a dog. I'd named him Jack.) I saw one of them shoot it while the other stood by. I thought to run out and stop him, but I didn't dare. They already call me old witch and old crow. I was glad Red was off someplace that day. He'd have tried to stop them and got himself hurt.

Anyway, two nights later, somebody shoots the girl. I don't know who did it, but I suppose one of those two. I heard the bangs as if right in my ear. Two. Whoever did it must have been standing by my window. I heard the crunch-crunch of somebody running off right after. If I talk about it, next thing they'll be shooting me. They'll say they thought it was a coyote. A coyote on the swing? They wouldn't say fox. Everybody knows how much I like foxes. Or maybe they would say fox just to torment me.

I run out. Red is there already. There she is, not dead though.

She's not a cute child. Stringy. Starving. And I've never seen anybody this dirty. She's wearing a sort of sack and nothing else. Scratchy. Not burlap but might as well be. There's something odd with her eyes. The iris is striped both black and green, and there's a membrane at the corner that isn't supposed to be there. As if she were a lizard. Tied around her neck with a blue cord there's... a thing. I have no idea what it is. Smooth, gray—looks to be basalt with green streaks of copper across it. You can find rocks like that around here, but this one is polished and shaped and contains a square chunk of magnetite.

She's conscious but she doesn't make a sound. Like any wounded wild thing I'm afraid she'll bite. Red is, too. We both keep back. She looks to be shot in the side. One bullet must have missed. At least they didn't use the old buffalo rifle. Looks to be a .22. Thank goodness.

Then she reaches up to me and I know she won't bite. Besides, the way she reaches, bite or not, I don't care anymore. She says, "Ah. Bah." I take it as "Ma."

I reach for her. But it's Red gathers her up first, gentle as could be, and puts her in my arms after I stand up. I take her to my cabin and put her on my table, my pillow under her head. Red boils water and sharpens a kitchen knife. While I'm waiting for him to be ready, I cut the sack she wears off with my sewing scissors. I cut away a lot of her matted hair, too. There's just not going to be the combing of any of it.

We try to give her wine to knock her out some, but she won't take it. Locks her mouth and turns her head away. Red says to leave her be, so we have to get the bullet out while she's wide awake. She doesn't make a sound. In fact, she has no expression all through it, neither when refusing the wine nor when Red is cutting into her. I wish she'd yell. I wouldn't feel quite so bad if she'd make a noise.

Getting the bullet out, Red knows what he's doing. I'm not surprised. It's as if I always knew he could do most anything.

Poor old man. Afterwards he looks older than ever, exhausted and in some sort of pain of his own. I try to get him to drink some of the wine before going off to his tent. "Elderberry," I say. "I made it myself." But he won't.

We wrap her in the quilt and put her on my cot. After he leaves, I lie on the floor (my clothes on), but I can't sleep. I'm cold. The girl has my quilt wrapped around her.

Later I hear her crying. She does it so quietly, at first I don't know what's making that breathy, panting sound. I think: It's about time she let herself feel something. I want to touch her, but I know better than to show I heard.

At first she's in no shape to be out and about. I don't think people know we have her… except maybe the one who shot her. Or they don't care. And nobody cares much what I do as long as I keep doing my jobs, and nobody cares what Red does at all. He stays with her when I'm out busy with what I was hired for. He tells her stories. One evening I came back and sit on the stoop listening—that whispery voice of his that doesn't sound out. I can't hear much, but just the raspy, breathy sound is soothing. I hate to go in, because I'll have to make supper for the girl first thing and she won't eat it anyway. She's starved for sure, but she won't eat just anything. She sniffs, thinks, then decides. As if she's not used to our food. I try to tempt her with special things, but her taste seems hit-or-miss. I just can't tell what she'll hate next. When I finally do go in, Red has already made stew. I should have known. She's picked out all the carrots, laid them carefully on the quilt, but ate the rest.

"Well, I can tell you're not a rabbit."

She hides her head under my quilt and says her usual, "Bah. Ah."

So far that's all she's ever said. I don't think that "Bah" is "Mah." I'm beginning to wonder if she can talk at all. I think there's something wrong with her tongue. I try to look in her mouth, but she scratches me. I don't have to look all the way in. I can see her tongue when she says "Bah." It seems too short. And I think she never saw a teapot or a fork. She turns things over and wonders about them. I don't think she ever saw an oil lamp or matches.

As soon as she's able to be up and around a bit, and we leave her alone now and then, she steals. Hides things in packrat places. Knives, scissors, food (even carrots), summer hats, winter hats, sweaters, canteens she fills with water or goats' milk (the milk sours quickly). She doesn't eat the food she hides. She wraps it carefully, as though she thinks to keep it. I have to smell it out when it gets rotten. (Mice are coming in more than ever.) There's a purpose in all this. She's getting ready to take off. Though I can't imagine how she could carry all this or where she'd go.

I give her things, but it doesn't help. I give her my warmest wool socks. First thing I know they've disappeared.

So far I've managed to avoid calling her anything. Odd, because I always name my wounded or orphaned creatures, my crows, my baby skunk.... (Red says it's a wonder I haven't nursed a wounded mouse.) They all had names. I think it's that I'm a little afraid of her. What does she want with knives and scissors? Then I come home one evening and hear Red calling her Sage. "Better than Snake Weed," I say, though I'm thinking she might be more like snake weed.

I've already put the rest of the sharp things up where I don't think she can reach, but I know she could get anywhere she wants. She's a lot smaller than I am, but she's a lot more spry.

Then there's the lamps. I keep them in the wall sconces all the time. I hide the oil and the matches up in the eaves with the knives, but if I can get up there, she could get up better. I think the matches are going, one by one.

By now everybody knows she's here with me. They're calling her the witch's child. They call her that because I'm their witch. Any woman of a certain age and even moderately ugly, one that likes to live away from others, gets to be a witch. Once everybody got sick and they blamed it on me though I got just as sick as any of them. And they're suspicious of anybody that takes in wounded wild things as I do. Of course having a raven made me all the more a witch. It's as if instead of a black cat.

Sage has mostly been quiet all this time. I always did like quiet people—like Red—but I'm thinking I should talk to Sage or she'll never speak. Maybe she could at least understand a few more words than my, "Oh p'shaw!" I start naming things. "This here's a cup. This here's a lamp. This, a blouse. This, a sweater. Feel how this is wool. And this, cotton. This here we're doing is washing our hands."

She likes my blue blouse with the lacy collar best. (On her, it's a dress.) She looks frightened whenever I take it to wash it. She actually sits under the line waiting for it to dry. Then puts it on still damp.

Now that she's been cleaned up and hair cut.... It's too short, but she doesn't look bad even so. Her nose is small and pointy, her hair is white-blond. My blue blouse suits her better than it does me. She looks not at all like a witch's child, much more fairy—more fey, though they don't stop calling her that. Knowing them, I know they never will. (I'm the one with witch-colored hair, straight, black, streaked with gray.) Her eyes make her look so odd. Even I wonder, now and then, if she really *is* a witch's child.

But then she starts being the witch's child in truth. She starts to steal knives from everybody, not just me. When the children try to get near her, she claws them. Of course she clawed me earlier on when I tried to look in her mouth. I should have cut her nails a long time ago. They look extraordinarily strong. I wonder if I could have.

Then.... It's a soft, cool, moonlit evening—everybody outside to be in it. Lopsided gibbous moon. Shadows long. The shadow of the teeter-totter and the swing looking out of shape. Catty-cornered. Everything catty-cornered.

We've heard mountain lions screeching and caterwauling, sometimes right here in our little village. This is worse. I have no idea what it is or where it comes from. I think of all sorts of animals, wounded, dying, or, more like it, furious, frenzied. It seems to come from everywhere. It's like a screech owl and banshee and pack of fighting cats all at once. The whole camp stands still. All you can do is drop what you're holding and cover your ears.

Then it stops and I see her—my blue blouse—up at the top of one of the cottonwoods by the creek.

Men gather under the tree. Practically right away two of them start chopping it down, one on each side. They make the cuts, one above the other. The tree will fall exactly were they want it to.

There are several men leaning on their rifles. How can grown men, some with children of their own, even think to shoot a child? Of course they don't think she really is one. And, well, she's been making a lot of trouble.

The tree falls—exactly where they wanted it to, slanting along the river. All sorts of smaller trees come down with it. I can't believe she's not hurt. But then I see my blue blouse off towards another, smaller, tree. They shoot. At first I think at her, and I run forward to protect her, but then I see the dust fly up on the ground around her. They keep shooting. It's just for fun. As if there hasn't been any shooting fun for a long time.

I yell, "Wait! She'll come to me." I don't know why I say that. She never has before. She's never done one single thing I said, even when I knew she understood.

Then—lucky or unlucky, I don't know which—the magpie flies out, straight up from where the tree went down. Flies off with a squawk. Everybody steps back. They all salute. They look at me as if it's my bird—the witching bird, worse than my raven—but they let me through.

I scramble over the brush towards my blue blouse. The brush grabs at me. I'll be nothing but scratches. My clothes catch on the branches, but I pull away and rip them.

I don't know how much language she's picked up. Probably more than she lets on, but I don't say much more than, "Sage," and, "Come," and, "Everything's all right," which it isn't. I say them like I talk to all my creatures. It's the tone of voice that counts.

No doubt she'd be able to get away from me if she wanted to. No doubt she knows they'd shoot her—yet again. I'll not be surprised if they shoot me. Though how are they going to run their mess hall, get all their laundry done, without me? One man has brought out a whip. I'm not sure whether that's for me or Sage.

Where is Red? My poor old man? I hope he stays hidden. He'll get himself in trouble if he tries to protect me.

I reach out to her and she to me. I grab her wrist, my hand circling around it all the way. How thin she still is.

It takes a while for us to get out from under all the branches and twigs. Both of us get more scratches and our clothes more torn than ever. Nobody moves or says a word. They just wait. A boy throws a stone. She deserves it, the way she's been treating the children. One of the men gives him a slap. There's just that one stone. It doesn't start anything. Everybody just stands and waits.

Finally we get away from all those branches. Now I'm really scared, but they move away as if they're afraid of us. I move carefully and hang on tight to Sage. I start back to my hut, but before we get there, I hear the whip. At first I just hear the crack of it, and then it lands on us. We run. Right on past my shack. We feel the whip once more before we head straight out into the desert.

This is all done in silence. Then I hear one loud "Good riddance." Meant for both of us, I'm sure. They'll have a hard time without me, but I'm sure they think it's worth it to be rid of the girl. Then they shoot a dozen times. I look back. It's not at us. It's in the air. Just for fun again.

By now it's dark, but there's that gibbous moon. At first we go as fast as we can. We stumble and fall, but hurry on. Then I turn towards the stream. I don't want to get lost, and we'll need water. She outruns me. Out scrabbles me. Part of the time she's on all fours. Hands and feet, not knees. It's a better way in the almost-dark. Pretty soon I have to slow down.

Sage is far ahead already, but I have to stop and rest. I think, Well, there she goes. That's the last of her. I sit on a downed willow. Nothing but desert on each side of the creek. There's no place to go except along its banks. It's still warm now, but it'll be cold soon. I wonder how long we'll last. If *I'll* last? Sage has done it before. *She'll* last.

I don't wish she'd never come. Any more than I wish my wounded raven had never come, though he was a lot of extra work, too. And he did peck me, especially at the beginning. That was just in order to find out what I was made of. Could be Sage acts as she does for the same reason. Wondering what I'm made of, same as I wonder about her.

Coyotes yip. Not far off. The breeze is picking up. Are my goats locked in? What with all these goings-on, I suppose the people forgot them. Or they remembered, and there'll be goat stew by tomorrow, poor things. When they were babies I brought them in to my hut when it was cold. We were friends. I'll miss them. But "Good riddance" cuts both ways. I haven't been happy here. Red is the only person I really like. (Not counting the children, that is.) I hope he'll be all right without me. I wonder where he was through all this. I wonder where he is. Witch! I wish I really was one.

Then I hear crunch, crunch, crunching. Uneven. Somebody with a limp. Somebody breathing hard. I don't wait to make sure. "Red?"

Of course Red. And with bundles and a full backpack. No wonder he's breathing hard. He collapses in front of me but only for a minute, then starts to unpack some of the things, sweaters, blankets, clothes, salve for scratches and whip wounds. Matches. Fishing line. I couldn't have conjured up more good things if I'd been a witch in truth.

He lights a small fire. "They may see it. For sure they'll smell it, but they won't bother with us anymore." He begins to lay out milk and cheese when… of course, though this time no crunch, crunches… here is Sage, come silently, from the other direction. Hunkering down like an animal as if to tell us, Don't hurt me, I'll not do any harm. She's never liked being hugged before, but this time she lets us. We both hug her at the same time. I get the feeling that Red's hugging me and wouldn't dare do it any other way. I'm hugging him, too, and I wouldn't dare do it any way but this.

Then we both work to soothe her scratches. Then Red puts salve on my scratches and whip marks. (Am I to be thought a witch because I have a cream that takes the pain away? I suppose so. I was the one kept the yeast for the bread alive. That's suspect, too.) My blue blouse is a rag, but Red has thought to bring another, and another for me. Two sweaters, a blue one for Sage.

We change clothes and wrap ourselves in blankets. Sage cuddles up with me. Red, discreetly, behind us. I have a funny feeling, sleeping next to a thing that can make that noise, but I guess I don't have to be afraid of mountain lions. She could out-yowl any of them. The wind picks up. The fire goes out. Rather than get up and feed it logs, I move back against Red. He turns and puts his arm around us. It feels perfectly natural.

At dawn we pack up and move—upstream, towards the mountains. Red insists on carrying most of the bundles. I hate to see him limping along, leaning over. I think I'm in better shape than he is. I insist on carrying one blanket and some of the food or I just won't move. I make Sage help with a small bundle of food and the smallest canteen. (Empty now. We'll need to fill them later, when the creek will be deep in a canyon and we can't climb down to it.) She doesn't object.

As we go higher, she gets more and more nervous. Or maybe excited. Even with the extra weight of the bundle, she gives a little jump every now and then, but I don't think it's out of happiness. She's starting to pant. Pretty soon she's the one leading. We don't mind until she tries to turn us away from the stream, off into the desert. I'm guessing it's a hundred in the shade. Maybe more. We try to ask her why, but she can't tell us. She says her usual "Bah" and "Ah." She points… not as we do with a finger, but with her fist. She punches out towards the left. When we go on upstream, she doesn't follow.

Red says, "Let's let her show us what she needs to."

I had hoped to get higher and cooler. We'll miss the shade. We didn't bring hats. Even Red didn't think to bring any. We can't go out there without them. Before we leave the brush and trees, we make some hats… or, rather, hattish things out of branches with leaves. We fill the canteens.

As we head out—into what looks like emptiness, but isn't— lizards scurry, a rattlesnake warns from a few yards away, but Sage hardly bothers to step aside. I wonder if she knows what it is. Stink bugs raise their hind ends to stink us, a horned toad lumbers away, lucky not to get stepped on, a road runner runs off....

By afternoon we're all worn out. Even Sage doesn't jump anymore. Mostly it's the heat that tires us so. I take the small canteen from her. We've drunk quite a bit from all of them. I'm getting worried we may run out before we can get back to the creek. Of course we could hike back by moonlight, when it's cooler. Cold, actually. We'll have the opposite problem.

But then I hear buzzing. At first I think it's the desert. It does seem a desert sound. I notice it stays with us, and then I see it comes from that stone around Sage's neck. Red and I give each other a look. Sage walks faster, but poor Red.... I take the big canteen from his shoulder. He lets me, though he insists on keeping most of the bundles.

We come to a place where rocks have been as if tossed from above. There are more and more as we walk on. And then we come to the edge of a crater, and in it a huge, twisted, shattered thing. Big as a house and kind of like one. *Two* houses. *Three!* One side all black and the other all white. I never saw anything like it. Red and I just stand there while Sage squats down beside us and hugs herself—as if she were cold.

They lived for a while. Four of them. They had barrels of things to drink, but some were broken. At any rate, they're all empty now. They're chubby, soft, with big stomachs and thin legs. I wonder if they'd have been able to climb out of the crater if they tried. They sat in the shade of the wreckage on hammock-like things of wire and cloth, their empty barrels beside them. They moved as the sun turned. You can see the back-and-forth marks in the sand. When the sun rose to noon and no shade at all, they wore bits of metal and cloth for hats. If they're anything like us, they wouldn't last long without their drinks.

What would you do if you wanted to save your child? Or what if she was the only one left who wasn't hurt? And you knew you couldn't last in this awesome and awful place. How far to water? How far to help? You'd send the only able-bodied one out, or maybe out to save herself if she could.

But, no. As Red and I walk in among the creatures, we see an entirely different story. Sage, the little slave, sent to do the hardest, most dangerous work of going for help. The others, too high-class to do it. "We'll just rest here in the shade until you bring back food and water." How could they know how long it would take? The scratches on Sage's back that looked like beatings *were* from beatings.

But then why did she come back here? Eagerly. *Maybe* eagerly. At least agitated. It's that stone she wears. Maybe she couldn't help but come. When we got close enough it started to call her.

Red and I walk in among them while Sage hunkers down hugging herself again, turned away from the wreck, shivering even in this heat but expressionless as usual.

None seem wounded. They're fine. They wear silky things, and they all wear blue—the exact blue of my blouse—while she came to us dressed in that brown, scratchy bag. One by one, Red checks them. All are dead. He also checks the mouth of one of them. "Their tongues are like ours," he says.

We put our arms around each other. I rest my head on his shoulder, and he rests his head on top of my head. We stand this way for a few minutes. Then he says, "We'll hide out for a while. Up along the stream in the mountains."

"She can't talk… ever. Did they do that to her?"

"I suppose."

"I'll teach her to read and write."

"And when she gets to be some civilized… it's the wild things will civilize her… then we'll go to town. The big town…."

"… and get her another blue silk blouse."

"Maybe two. And some for you."

Then Red goes to Sage. She flinches when she sees the knife, as though of course something bad will happen to her, but she'll bear it anyway, whatever it is. He cuts the stone off. It's not easy. It buzzes more than ever for a moment, then stops when the cord is cut through. He throws it high and away—way over the top of the crater. A real baseball kind of pitch. He holds his shoulder afterwards. He shouldn't have done that.

It's coming on twilight. Cooling down. Our water's almost gone. We need to get back to the river before morning or we'll be in trouble. We put on sweaters, take a last drink—partly to lighten our loads—and climb the bank.

For once the desert takes us in as if we belong to it, everything luminous, numinous…. Radiant. Stars…. Turning, turning. The Big Dipper swinging round the Little Dipper. North over our right shoulders. Shooting stars as if for luck.

Report to the Men's Club and Other Stories, 2002

Report To The Men's Club

"There was nothing else for me to do, provided always that freedom was not to be my choice."

—FRANZ KAFKA

Respected members of the Men's Club, you have conferred upon me the highest honor that you are capable of conferring, though it is certainly not, in your eyes, your highest honor. It is, in fact, something that you yourselves take for granted, even though I am sure you are always, on some deep level, aware of the magnificence of it, so that you walk with a surer step, see with clearer eyes, and always have a little half-smile hovering about your lips. Needless to say, it's something that I never hoped to achieve... could not possibly have hoped for, and, therefore, could not have striven for directly even though, on the other hand, I can say that some part of me has been striving for it all my life, from the very moment I began to understand which of us were the girls and which were the boys.

Yours is a unique group. In any other similar organization, I might not be fully accepted as one of you (though it's true, often those like me have been accepted at an entirely different level as lesser members of some such group), but here in this group, after the reception you have been kind enough to give to me as well as to my researches, I am sure that I am, at long last, to be numbered as one of you.

It was not after the formal initiation, where you allowed me to partake in the solemn ceremony—very moving, I may add, and of great beauty—of the drinking from the golden cup, the wearing of the crimson hood, the slow marching to that unique beat that is yours alone... it was not after that that I felt most particularly one of you, but it was in your allowing me to take part in the informal initiation. I mean no disrespect by this comment, but it should not be hard for you to see that that particular ceremony should be the most meaningful to me.

And I realize, gentlemen, how hard it must have been for you to go through with that ceremony and to paint the blue stripe just there. How you must have yearned to avert your eyes, turn away, in fact, from the whole business. You must have felt, deep inside, that you had made a terrible mistake, but you went on with it. You persevered. And I, I would have lain as still as possible in order to help you, but I knew that it was customary to fight, and so I fought with all the strength I had, and I'm proud to say that I, and you, too, were as covered with blue after my fight as you were from the fight of the man the week before. By now the blue has worn off, but not the memory of it, nor my gratitude for those hilarious moments of brotherhood.

We are the sons of hunters, not of lovers. (I trust that now I may use the word "we" and include myself with all of you.) If all the lovers of the world were laid end to end, they would not be able to make one tiny dent in some great concept of the universe, and so we are not lovers. We put aside the body and pay little attention to its messy functions. Particularly messy, I must admit it, Gentlemen, particularly messy are the functions of the body of a woman. Birth itself a messy business and more than most men can stomach. (I speak from experience.) We are best left out of it altogether. And I, in spite of having once been enmeshed in such things, am, by your ceremonies, by your blue paint, if only figuratively speaking, now am cleansed.

All my life I have been a student of mankind. *Man*kind. I have watched men. I learned their ways, the thoughtful stroking of the chin, the walk with elbows out, the long, wide stride. I repeated what I saw. I sat with legs apart, and, if not an "I can lick you" look in my eyes (for, after all, I couldn't), then certainly my gaze was level, never coquettish or cute. In fact, "cute" was what I never was, I'm proud to say. I made sure of that from before the age of three. I refused, above all else, to be cute even if I was forced to chop off my own hair to accomplish it. Mother was frantic. She wanted bows in my hair. (I can honestly say that I have never worn a bow for longer than a few seconds.)

Mother was not a woman to be reckoned with, but rather to be swept aside as one hurried towards the important things in life. A sad fact, but a true one. I saw this as a small girl when we went to the beach. Mother sat under a big umbrella with the baby while Father, along with all the other fathers and older children, frolicked in the water. "In the swim," as it were. I ranked myself, then and there, among the fathers and vowed that when I grew up I would never sit on the bank with a baby (though I must confess that I have done it, and more than once).

I have been thought to be amenable to training by many of the men I have encountered, not to mention my father, to whom I will be forever grateful for giving me a name (Leslie) that could be of either sex. (Lucky for me I had no brother, though too bad for Father.) It was from him that I learned never to be without a graphing calculator in my back pocket (though it was hard to have a back pocket most of the time). Perhaps my father saw something in me from the start— something of the enigma I wanted to be. I was frantic to be noticed by him and put on the most outlandish performances, sometimes climbing trees and screaming from the topmost branches (though I was terrified of heights) in hopes of attracting his attention.

But men are, as you know, Gentlemen, preoccupied with more important things than one small girl could ever hope to be, even one at the top of a tree. I did attract his attention, though not in ways I hoped. Often it was simply in the matter of climbing down. Mother could not help me in that regard (another sign of her inferiority).

Father always said a girl should know how to give one swift punch to the Adam's apple or one swift kick to the you-know-where. I practiced these. Perhaps I sensed, even then, what the future held.

Of course there soon came the problem of having breasts. What were these things doing on, of all bodies, *my* body? I had thought that, simply by the strength of will, I could at the very least stay neutral—not take sides so completely in this matter. So then I thought, at least I'll not be a woman like any others. I'll keep the faith with men. See their side of every question. And I'm happy to say I've done so to this day.

Also I'm happy to say that my mind is uncluttered by the imagination, that I stick to the facts, have not veered off into emotionalities. (Even when I had children of my own, I made a point of avoiding any talk of them in favor of more important subjects.) And I often make snap judgments worthy, if I may say so myself, of a military man.

But do not think I have lived without ecstasy. Though it is exactly that ecstasy—that falling gently into the damp, erotic, messy needs of the body—that misled me for a while. I became confused. My sources of pleasure were, after all, the very same as my sources of disdain and shame. I suffered in my ecstasy. I suffered, hardly knowing that I did, and yet, looking back on it, I know I did. I had come down from my trees, my rooftops, my high dives... down from all my dreams. In short, Gentlemen, I fell in love with one of you. Every day I asked him how he was coming along in the world I had left behind, and he answered me cheerfully enough for a while, but he soon grew tired of my endless probing, though even after he no longer answered me except in grunts and clearings of the throat, my goal still was: How improve the quality of life for the opposite sex. For myself, I hoped only to *inspire* excellence in him and in my children. I did not hope to find any excellence in myself.

Only a lunatic, you will be saying to yourselves, would have put up with this for a minute. I can only agree with you, but that's where ecstasy can lead those of my sex.

But you are wondering, when was it that I began my preparations for being one of you in earnest? When I was not quite in my fourteenth year, I began a series of tests. Even I could not guess the meaning of them: Ice-cold showers, hands held over candles, a knife wound in my cheek, and so forth. I bear the scars to this day, as you can see. (As to the life I subsequently led masquerading as a boy, strange to say, I have few scars—though, since the initiation of last week, I've used a cane and have this sling.)

Was I self-destructive? Obviously I was, no matter that I would protest it and no matter how many reasons for it may have been in the forefront of my mind at the time. Or, and more important, was I mainly yearning for my freedom? Ah, there, gentlemen, well you might have thought so, but that would have been your biggest mistake, for freedom has never been my wish. I can assure you of that. I wanted to take my place among the powerful. Note that I don't say I wanted power. I simply wanted to be numbered among those that make the history and the money. I wanted to be among the people that the word "mankind" refers to.

But I soon saw that I might well destroy myself altogether if I continued to show myself no mercy. There was nothing for it but to attempt a daring escape across rooftops, fording streams, and off into the bogs of the arboretum....

As can well be imagined, guards to keep me prisoner in my life, as it should be lived, were everywhere, for it was in everyone's best interests that I stay. Children were on the stairs (their skates, their jump ropes to trip me, hoses in the garden, rakes left, tines up), Grandmother in the kitchen, Mother in the backyard, Father, though he had seemed to be in sympathy with my earlier efforts to better myself, was now aligned with all the others and stationed himself at the front door. (By then, my husband was long gone.) At night, too, someone was always awake and watching, if not a child with the pretext of a bad dream, then a grownup with insomnia. But I managed to bide my time until my oldest son was just my size, and, dressed in his clothes, my hair cut short, I walked past all my jailers quite easily one beautiful spring afternoon.

I brought nothing from that place except that one suit of clothes. After all, I had not earned a penny for all the work I did each day. I felt that nothing there really belonged to me, not even the apple that I put in my pocket. I left with all my longings newly kindled, but even then I could not put a name to what I wanted. It is you, Gentlemen, who have made it all come true at last—that for which I longed most.

What, after all is said and done, distinguishes us... us men from the women. What but the fact that we are *not* enmeshed in the body and that we do *not* fluctuate at the mercy of our glands—that the moon does *not* affect us. Isn't it, then, by all these *nots,* as well as by all our male values and virtues, that we are set apart from simply "being"? It is, in fact, exactly these questions, as you all well know, that I have made the essence of my investigations, and which I have recorded in what you have, most kindly, called: "Extraordinary detail," and that I have published under the title *Man*... simply *Man,* for that one word is enough—has always been enough. You have found this work worthy of some small notice, and for this I thank you.

But I have spoken too long already, and so, since I have presented my most important points, I'll not bore you with any more of my personal history: How I joined, for a time, a gang of runaway boys; nor will I mention the kindly intellectual who found me half-starved in the gutter and who took me in and brought me up as his own son. (I had, by then, reached a fairly early menopause, possibly due to my hardships, so more children were, happily, out of the question.) Without the help of this man, I would certainly not be here among you. I wish to give a special thanks to him.

So, as I step—or, rather, hobble; I've still not quite recovered from that wondrous initiation—down from this podium, I'll not be stepping down at all, but up. One giant step up into *Man*kind. Too bad Father isn't here to see me now, though Mother would probably say (not even knowing she was quoting Kafka) that it was hardly worth the trouble.

Report to the Men's Club and Other Stories, 2002

Nose

Being nowhere but here and nobody but me. Nothing to do but play solitaire or sit and watch the snow. And it isn't even a real snowstorm, just little worthless flakes, melting as they hit the ground. Might as well be rain. Feet will get wet. I'll stay here and look out the window. Other people will go out in it and raise their faces to the wind. I'll be nice and dry.

But that's what I thought two minutes ago. I grab my raincoat and my floppy yellow hat. I'm out in it and I don't even know why. Why would anyone? Especially me? I hate wet feet. Why go? And isn't beauty where you find it? Even in the rust in my bathroom? In the food spots on my blouse? In the cracks of the ceiling?

Even so, I'm out of here. If only to some park bench. I could sit and pet wet stray dogs.

It's because of my nose. I stay in because of it. I go out because of it. My whole life is because of it. It's not only large, but it has a big bump in the middle. I'd be happily married if not for that. I'd have children. They'd find me beautiful just because I was their mother. Of course, my face is too long and narrow anyway. If there was a witch's part to be played I'd be chosen first, but I haven't even been chosen for that. I haven't been chosen for anything. And my hair's not witch's black. Dishwater blonde, they used to call that, though now it's streaked with gray.

(Even in my baby pictures I have almost that length of nose and that bump. Who ever heard of a baby with a big, bumpy nose?)

So here I am, running. There's the need to escape once and for all. Of course I'm not so stupid… not quite *that* stupid… to think I can escape myself. *Or* my nose. Even now, as I trot away from every¬thing I ever knew or thought about or wanted or didn't want, I know I'm still peering out from behind my nose.

But it's now or never. Everything is *always* now or never. I just didn't realize it until I suddenly saw those cracks in my ceiling and I thought: Fix it. Do it now or it will never be done. And I knew I wouldn't get around to it. I knew it would be never.

Running still and I'm not tired. That's because I've been on my Stairmaster, sometimes all afternoon. (What else is there to do?) I may have been preparing for this moment all this time and didn't realize it.

Hop and skip over broken sidewalk and chewing gum. Flap out into traffic. And survive it. Jump again. I don't heed nor need the WALK/DON'T WALK signs. I think of mother. There wasn't much more to her than warnings. I don't not do anything she said not to, or do anything she said to. And look, not dead anyway. Still hopping and skipping, happy to have survived the street and my nose and everything else... up to right now.

Away we go, nose and I. But I'm stopped by smells. I've been too much inside. I forgot all about bus exhaust. I smell everything. I smell sour old age and babies. Laundry, clean and dirty. Soap: Eucalyptus, bergamot.... I'm back and forth from delighted to repelled so fast I can't keep track. For now I'll just stay repelled. No, better to stay delighted.

I've not seen a nose like mine in a long time And not because I wasn't looking. I looked at everybody until I finally gave up, though I didn't really give up, I just didn't look quite so hard.

One doesn't see noses like this anymore, just as one doesn't see crooked teeth. Perhaps I should have had my nose fixed a long time ago, but I grew up in the Sixties, when things were supposed to be natural. Besides, I didn't have the money.

I saw the look in people's eyes: Why didn't she ever have it fixed? Now, if they look at me at all, I see them thinking: She's so old, fixed or not, it won't do much for her.

The nose.... (Note I don't say *my* nose. Sometimes it hardly seems anything so looming could be mine.) The nose never pointed in the right direction to find another like me, though, more likely, it *did* find those people, but all the others had had their noses fixed, so I never knew they had been like me. I suppose their mothers saw to it before it ruined their lives—made them shy or sly or outcasts like I am.

What is the meaning of love, or, if not love, what is the meaning of hate? Why do people wonder always about love (which eludes them) and never wonder about hate, which doesn't? They know hate more intimately than they ever know love.

But more important (to me), what is the meaning of noses? Or a nose? And what do we know of the face hiding behind it? Peeking out—frightened? A face by now a little the worse for wear, though full of yearning still?

It's as if I've been transported to a city where everybody's nose is perfect. *And* teeth *and* jaw line. Foreheads high and smooth. Everybody wrinkle-free.

They've been scraped and sanded and lifted. Where are the *people*? Are these really them?

And then there's my teeth! I never thought that much about my teeth because my nose so overshadowed them. Who would be bothered looking beyond the nose to the teeth? Not even me.

But now I'm thinking of every part of myself. Even my stomach. Even my breasts. Especially my breasts, because I'm running and they're flopping about. I've been dashing about like a crazy person, and come so far so fast I don't know where I am, but here's a park and benches. I sit down to catch my breath.

And here is somebody, all in black, raincoat and umbrella, sitting down beside me. A big fat hulking man, hunched as if ashamed of his size. I can't see much of him, except it's easy to see he has a perfect, slightly upturned nose. He's hunkering down, not to fit under his umbrella, but to try and fit his nose.

What has the world in store for someone trying to hide behind this kind of nose? Looking out as if from behind a very small bush or a large flower.

(Coffee is being ground somewhere. Bread baking. There's the general smell of wet.) I look out at him athwart my nose bump. (It cuts my vision into two parts as though I were prey instead of predator, but I feel predator compared to him.)

Something about his hunkering makes me bold. Back in the days when one was stuck with the nose one was born with, there were kings and queens—*emperors*, even—with noses like mine, long and pendulous, though maybe not with *quite* such a big a bump in the middle.

And look, here we are already out of the snowy rain into a coffee-smelling coffee shop. And I'm glad for having been bold. Florian.

Being called Florie or most likely Flowery must have been almost as bad as having the wrong nose. His is fixed, though that was a big mistake. You can tell he was meant to have a big one. Everything about him goes with big. His mother had it changed when he was too little to object and before she realized what his face would be like. He'd object now, and maybe she would, too. It took away his power. Now he prowls around as if he's looking for it. How to add to his face? He holds his lower jaw pushed forward. (His teeth are large and perfect and very white. They look fixed, too.)

Under these circumstances, how could we have found each other? But it was inevitable. I'm the one who has his nose. I see it in his eyes—how he looks at me, so yearning, his long, long (and long-lost) nose in mine. I have enough for both of us. All he sees of me is that. It's love at first sight.

I keep my eyes lowered. I don't want my love for him and his nose—the one he used to have—to show quite so soon, though he must guess it.

He hovers over me. Leans delighted. He's big enough to hover even sitting down. His strong, fat, hairy hands.... I keep my eyes on them.

He says, "Smell that coffee."

(I smell mostly you.) He smells good, too, of wet raincoat, of umbrella.... And I smell croissant, strawberries, the plastic rose in the center of the table, the plastic table cloth. And through it all, the damp… the sweet, sweet, damp smell of male in general.

I know, with his little ordinary nose, he can't smell much of this, nor of me as a woman.

"Florian," I say, just to say his name. It's almost as if I've named him myself, exactly my favorite name though I didn't know it was until now. Why didn't I run away a long time ago? But would someone by the name of Florian have come along back then?

We sit by the window. It's the best seat in the place. The storm is getting more so. Now it's not just little damp flakes, but big lumpy ones. It's like a scrim, and the city's getting beautiful behind it. I'm thinking: Of course, everything is matching my happiness.

I'm at a loss for words—at a loss for feelings, actually. I'm empty of all need. Not even any hopes. What's to hope? This is all I've ever wanted. From now on, in my whole life, I'll not forget the smell of jasmine tea and wet wool.

I say, "When? I mean your nose, and who did it?"

"My mother. I was twelve. Then I was thin and willowy around a nose that was as if for another person."

I'd have found him a long time ago, if not for her. As it was, he had to find me. Had to search by sight alone. Couldn't sniff me out with what he has left of his nose.

Nosing things out, sorting smells.… It's not as easy as you'd think. I can smell accidents about to happen. Does he expect me to keep him safe? A big, fat man like he is… (his hands are twice as big as mine and look so strong) and little me, looking out for him, not letting anything bad happen? I'll do it.

I used to have lots of good reasons to live alone, but now I can't think of a single one.

I say, "Yes." It pops out by itself.

He says, "I know."

So it's settled just like that.

The nose knows how to get from here to there, so I'll be the one to lead us where we have to go.

I say, "Follow me."

He says, "Lead on."

And the nose does know. We're at the river. We sit under a bridge. We put our arms around each other. Why wait? It's what we've always wanted.

Kiss? It's not as easy as I thought. Noses in the way. His not so much, but mine especially. At first we can't figure out how to do it. You'd think we'd know by now, but neither of us does. We almost give up. We do.

Should I kiss his cheeks? I'll bet his are soft as pillows. I put my hand to my own to see how mine will feel to him. Bony, that's for sure. Long. Too much chin.

But then we try lips again. And, necks cricking sideways more than is comfortable, we manage.

There's no turning back now, so we don't. We go ahead, risking. That's all right. It's what I knew I'd have to do in order to succeed in finding whatever I would find, though I didn't know it would be Florian. What I know now! I'll never be the same again. I've found who I am, here behind my nose. And who Florian is behind his. If you can call that being behind anything.

His big, flat face.... Without his real nose, it looks babyish, while I look like a vulture. I suppose that's what he likes in me.

Off we go again. (Ours will be the love story of the century, even though the century has only just begun.)

Off we go, skip and splash, raise our noses. Or I do. I smell the weather changing for the better. I smell blue sky. I smell need. I smell—it's all over both of us—sex.

Do you know they chopped the noses off ancient statues and ground them up just as they did penises, to use as aphrodisiacs? And do you know? The ground-up noses worked just as well.

Report to the Men's Club and Other Stories, 2002

It Comes From Deep Inside

I saw a painting and fell in love with it. I don't know why. It wasn't that well done, and it was clear the artist didn't know anything about art. I know art. I've been through art school, I've had aesthetics, I paint, but I didn't care if this painting was well done or not, I loved it at first sight. I fell in love with the artist, too, though I'd never met him. I figured he was gentle and noble in a simple way, just like his painting. The name in the lower right-hand corner, in rounded, careful... actually childish writing, was Sam Gray. One would wish a more colorful name for an artist. Gray! How could that be? Well, all the more like the painting with its billowing yet innocent gray clouds.

The painting was of a storm over the mountains. The clouds took up three quarters of it. At the bottom, as though insignificant, were the mountains, all in a row. Also at the bottom there was a small, square, red thing that I finally figured out was a cabin.

Right away I recognized Basin Mountain off to the side, so I had an idea where that cabin was and where Sam Gray might be. The painting cost a hundred dollars. I couldn't afford it. I knew the artist was inept and untrained—had no eye whatsoever, but I bought it anyway. As I gave the money to the lady in the little art gallery, I asked questions. She said lots of art came down from that place, paintings of gnarled trees, meadows of wild flowers, tumble-down shacks, gray granite cliffs with a dun mule or two in the foreground, or gray granite cliffs with lupine and fireweed.

It's from the painting that I discovered the art colony. Their secret place is deep in a canyon—a high canyon, up in the mountains. I came in on them from the only way there is to come. (They could close off this one trail and keep their art unadulterated by outside influences forever if they wanted to. I suppose not very much that's postmodern will find its way up there.)

I packed up and started out for Basin Mountain. I dressed the part, not for climbing, but for art. My running shoes are white, purple, and green. (I always wear an orange blouse in case of getting lost, and with long sleeves in case of bugs.) I wore slinky green pants even though they were wrong for hiking, but artists always wear the wrong things on purpose. I looked like an artist without even trying. Or, rather, only trying a little bit. But you have to dress the part, else how would anybody know you were one?

I had bug spray and sun goo. I had breakfast bars. I had apples. I had a big floppy hat.

I wonder about the man called Gray—if he might be dressed all in gray as an arty trick, sort of like how city artists wear black. But considering the innocence of the painting, I doubt it. If he's all in gray, it's more likely to have been what he happened to have handy on this particular day. That is, assuming I find him on this particular day.

I follow the creek that rushes down their canyon. I'm pleased with how the trail winds round and round. It was shady from the start. I'm pleased with the trees. No vehicles of any sort could ever come up here. I was pleased with that, too.

As I climb I practice art talk, such as: "It's a distillation of the vitality of my inner experience. It contextualizes my life." But maybe it shouldn't be all about me, but about the spirit in the world right now. I'll use the word *zeitgeist*. Maybe *gestalt*.

(I may try a little high-class French when I come upon them. I'll say, "*Vous voilà enfin.*" Or should I say: *Tu?* Especially if the first person I meet is Sam Gray?)

Suddenly I'm stopped. Both sides of the trail fall away and I'll have to cross a dangerous unstable ridge of talus. Isn't it just like artists to make you cross a place like this to get to them. Here, in life as in art, the danger of slipping—of crashing down into the chasm of nonentity.... (I do know reminders of death are always a good thing in art.) I can't decide whether to cross the dangerous ridge or sit down and do a dangerous drawing instead.

(I wonder how they bring their art across this to the shop in the valley. Mules would do, I suppose.)

I tell myself to take the most difficult way in art as in life. I sit down to draw. All the better if I can come across Sam Gray with a drawing under my arm. I'll try to make it simple and naïve, but splashy. When I meet him, I'll hold the drawing so he can't help but see it.

I make several so as to have choices. I keep drawing, on and on, until it's too late to try to cross the ridge tonight. I move back and set up my tarp, eat a couple of breakfast bars. I try to write a poem describing exactly what I see, as my poet friend said to do, but talus and scree are not conducive to poetry. Even the snowy peaks, and more snowy peaks behind them.... I mean how many snowy peaks can you describe at one sitting? I let my poem blow away. I think to drop my drawings, too, but I need something to show Sam Gray. I decide a not-so-good-drawing is better than nothing. Besides, how would he know the difference, being such a bad artist himself?

I look at my drawings to pick one. Not necessarily the best. They are full of happy accidents, such as ground-in dirt and blood from my scratched elbow.

I can't sleep on these rocks. (I didn't bring my pad because I thought I'd be there by now.) Also, I start to worry about the end of art as we know it. In art as in life, you can go too far. Perhaps art has gone too far already.

In the morning I wake to a gorgeous sunrise. I try to describe it but you have to be fast. I write quickly: Purple to orange to yellow to pink, funny lenticular clouds.... I'm so busy writing it down I don't have a chance to see it at all.

But now there's the narrow ridge to cross; or should I not, so as to live to paint another day?

I sit and worry for a while. I think, you can get too old for art. They say you can't, but you can. It's because you've already done everything—gone through the bad language and the language play and then the odd punctuation; done the sex part (dildoes and menstrual and such). Pretty soon you find yourself using the same old tricks you always used. You can get too wise, too. And then you get dizzy as you age. You'll hardly make it to your easel. So dizzy you'd never be able to cross a ridge like this. I'd better cross it now, while I'm still in pretty good shape. I'll go fast and I won't look down.

After the scary ridge, it's all easy. The trail widens to where artists could walk hand in hand, which makes me think all the more of Sam Gray.

As I go I keep looking around. I think to find him sitting on some outcropping, painting. I think I see red and orange and black paint on the stones, but that turns out to be the usual lichen.

Pretty soon I see their houses... bungalows, that is, each one is entirely different from the other. And there's that red shack at the far end. The only person I see is a boy with thick glasses and a sharp-nosed, intellectual look. He's painting. He has green and yellow paint on his jeans. Of course. Children do art all the time. Try to stop them. I'm shocked. I didn't know there'd be children.

"Are you all artists here?"

"Yeah."

I can hardly breathe with the wonder of it. I've always wanted to belong to an art colony.

"*Sam* Gray," I say. "Is he handsome?"

"I don't know. I don't think so."

Of course he doesn't know. To a child, only the very young are beautiful. To a child, everybody grown up is old.

"Where is everybody?"

"They've gone up by the glacier to paint ice. I didn't want to. I wanted to paint our house instead. See, I already did."

And there it is, a big, bad, muddy painting. But the boy is only nine.

But art should speak to the common man, and young and old alike. I guess it does—in the long, long, long run, that is. I mean nobody anymore thinks

Beethoven is just the cackling of hens and the braying of donkeys, as they used to say. However, if I paint with dung, I won't tell anybody. If I paint the virgin, I won't say who it is. If I mix urine with my paint as a protest against how we live now, all slicked up and shiny, I won't say. It'll be my secret protest.

I head off towards that funny little red cabin.

"Nobody's home."

"All the better then."

I look in the windows. It's just jammed with art in there, on the walls and on the floor—my favorite kind of mess. There's even art in the kitchen. And hardly any dishes. As far as I can tell from here, all the art not very good.

I'll die if I can't be part of the colony, with or without Sam Gray. Every single friend I'd have here would be an artist of some sort. There'd be nothing but art talk all day long. People will be eccentric of course. I'll be eccentric, too. I wish my drawing was splashier some way. If I knew how to make it that way, I'd have done it in the first place, though how splashy can talus ever be? Of course there is that little smear of blood on it.

Here they come now. You can tell they're all artists even from this far away. They have flowers in their buttonholes. Some have earrings in the wrong places or safety pins for earrings. They're hopping about and patting each other on the shoulder or (actually!) their rumps. (Trust artists to be doing things like that.) They wear all kinds of shiny things, and big hats just like mine, and some shirts… well, you'd think it was Hawaii, only the designs are all squarish or diamonds or like streaks of lightning. One wears a cape that billows out behind him. Some of the women toe out. They seem to be walking around in a sort of third position.

I'll be kind, even to those who paint better than I do, just as one always is kind to those who paint less well.

There's a piñon right next to the red hut. I hide behind it and look them over. There are lots of women—some a little horsy. Their boobs bounce when they walk (of course no bras)—but several men, too. I see one I hope is Sam. He has a nice straight nose, lined face, and bushy eyebrows, but he isn't dressed like an artist at all, more like a gas station attendant with an olive drab jump suit. He actually has his name embroidered on his pocket. Jasper. Maybe he's the handyman.

Every art colony needs one. Even so, I like his looks.

There's another man who looks pretty good, too. And much more artistic. This one looks French. Except Gray isn't a French name. Perhaps it used to be Gris. His mustache is ridiculous. Did he form it like Hitler's in order to shock? It does. That's one kind of art.

I wonder what it feels like to be able to shape something on your face like that—to form it to some sort of arty addition you might want on your upper lip. Hide defects, accentuate good points. No wonder women are always putting on make-up. They might not if they had something to shape on their faces.

There's another man, but he's too chubby. You get that way from sitting around writing poetry and reading too much. He's wearing red plaid pants.

None of these men stops at the hut.

The handyman hangs back to pick up waste paper. I come out of my hiding place and catch up to him. He's startled to see me. He stares and looks shocked.

"Where in heaven's name did you come from? We're the only ones supposed to be here."

We? I wonder if he considers himself one of them even though he's only a handyman. He's not Sam Gray, unless he's wearing somebody else's jump suit, though of all the men I've seen so far, he's the one I had hoped was. I ask anyway.

"Shhhh."

He takes off his hat and wipes his sweaty forehead on his sleeve. His forehead is pure white, innocent and young, while his lower face is tan and old. I want to tell him to put his hat back on or his forehead will get to be as weathered as the rest of him.

The inside of his hat is full of little slips of paper on which I can read a word here and there. I see, MAJESTIC, IMPOSING, MAGNIFICENT, STATELY, NOBLE, ELEGANT.... All sorts of poetic words. At first I think he's not a handyman after all, but then I wonder if these bits of paper are discarded words from the poems of the others, and he's been picking up after everybody else, and he's carried the rejected words home in his hat so as not to pollute the region with too much grandeur. With so many artists around, it probably wouldn't take long for this place to get to be a rubbish heap of discarded elegances and ornamentations.

He says, "Leave as soon as you can."

"I would die for art," I say. "I would even die for not-very-good art."

As if inadvertently, I let my drawing of the talus fall out of my pack and unroll. I see now it's as boring as I feared it was. Why did I make it so symmetrical? I tell him, "That's my blood, there in the corner."

I thought my little scratchy lines would make it more interesting. I gave it black shadows. None of that helped. It's still just as boring as talus is in real life. You'd think I'd sketched a pile of helter-skelter shoe boxes.

I say, "Talus is dangerous."

All this talk doesn't make my drawing any better.

"I'm an artist just as you all are. Doesn't that count?"

He's already taken a good look at me but he takes another. He stares at my drawing, too. He has black, beady eyes. I don't know whether to think of them as sexy or scary.

"Art," I say, "comes from the heart," and, "It comes from the fires deep inside. I feel it here." I squeeze my left breast with both hands.

I can see he's interested.

I think up titles not-very-good artists might like. I say, "I'll paint pictures called THE GOLDEN CHIMES OF SUMMER or RAINBOW OVER IMPETUOUS RIVER. I'll cling to my mood swings. To my melancholy, if necessary." (Would a good title make my talus drawing more interesting?) "I call this one TALUS THREATENING THE PATHWAY OF LIFE."

One look at my drawing and they think I'm perfect for this place. Turns out I get to have a funny little bungalow. So far I haven't made it my own in any artistic way. I don't know whether to spend my time on it or on my art. I know some artists get side-tracked into making their living space their art and never have any time for anything else. Or they work on their very selves. I wear things only artists would wear, but I don't spend a lot of time on it. I let my hair fly around. I flow, waft, whistle things like Beethoven's Ninth.

Even so, I didn't get off to a very good start—unless crying is arty. Maybe it is. Artists are supposed to be super-sensitive, so I guess it's not so bad that I cried all day my first day here (or, rather, tried not to cry and *mostly* succeeded) because Sam Gray had painted my favorite painting and yet here he was, nothing but a little man half my size and as gray as his name—eyes, hair (what there is left of it). Clothes. They looked as if they'd been washed, colors with whites, until everything got dulled down to one dirty color. He squinted and blinked. His eyes teared all the time. He thinks he'll go blind pretty soon, so he's painting more of his bad paintings as fast as he can. He has no time for anybody. I like all his paintings more than I would admit to anybody. I don't even like to admit it to myself.

Sam's is the smallest hut of any, yet has the most art. The others I'd call bungalows, his I call a hut. He's the most dedicated of all of them. The day I came he was painting away at wild roses in front of a dead juniper. He's too old to climb around with the others looking for good subjects. (I'll bet he couldn't cross the ridge if his life depended on it.) He doesn't take the time to think if he should paint this or that, he just paints it.

After meeting him I had tears rolling down my cheeks all day, so I got lots of sympathy. The fat man brought me a bouquet of dried grasses. One of the horsy women brought me cookies in the shape of... well, either leaves or vaginas. Another brought me a Frisbee in the shape of a winged phallus. It flew as well as any Frisbee I ever had.

There's Leonora, America, Nicco, Montgomery, Heather, Melody, Harmony.... There's actually a Minerva (one of the horsy ones). Their names are so arty I wonder if they chose them themselves. (Too bad I already told them my name is Mary Anne.) I wonder if Sam Gray is really Sam Gray. Could be he wanted to be different from the others, simpler maybe, like his paintings, and changed his name from something fancier.

The handyman seems to be head of the whole thing. Now how did it happen that a handyman got to be so important? Even so, he's the one I wish would notice me. I look as sad as I can when I'm near him. Maybe I'll leave some words around for him to clean up. Love words, or sex words, better yet commitment words.... Though when have artists committed to anything but their art? Ardor, passion, that's what artists have, and they go wherever that leads. Except I like Sam Gray's painting for the opposite reasons, so tender, simple, innocent, and so committed.

Since we're all second best here and some of us are even third best, you'd wonder why we bother with art at all. It's the art of it, is why. It's the tripping little steps and the scarves. It's the hand with the thumb always towards the two middle fingers, first finger and little finger out. It's pointed toes. It's the sky (turquoise, pink, salmon, mauve), splashed down in big, watery brush strokes on expensive paper.

They tell me they've.... I should say "*we've,*" now that I'm part of it. We've been warned that we're not the sort of artists wanted in the world, and that there's much too much art anyway. (We know that.) We've heard that the better artists of the world would like to destroy this place and all of us in it—finish off the not-so-good art in one attack. They may even now be amassing in the valley.

We know their coming and destroying us would be a good thing. We agree with them—art shouldn't be allowed. It should be done secretly in attics. Nobody should ever get paid doing art. It's a privilege. You should be arrested if they catch you at it.

On the other hand, it could be said it's an offense to *not* do art. Like not looking up when a flock of geese honks by. Like not dancing when the beat is lively.

So even though there's much too much art in the world, how can we not keep doing it anyway?

Rejected by Sam—though no more rejected than he rejects everybody—I think to return across that dangerous ridge. I wonder if I still have the guts. Maybe I could cause a landslide that would make the ridge even more dangerous than it already is so that the better artists couldn't get at us. It wouldn't take much. If I could find even a little bomb of some sort around here, I could do it. I could be the one to save us all.

If they do have a little bomb, I wonder where they keep it?

They're going to have an art dance for the Fourth of July. We're supposed to come in costume. I can't imagine what the costumes will be like. How could they find stranger get-ups than they already wear every day?

Since the dance is in the afternoon, this will be a good time for me to leave with my bomb. Though artists understand when you want to be alone.

Sam won't be going of course. He'll be painting as usual. He says his eyes are worse than ever and he doesn't have much more time.

The handyman will be going. Surely he's the one has our bomb, if anybody does. Artists don't have things like that. So now I've two reasons to woo him, and since one has to do with the good of the whole colony and isn't just about me, I suddenly have the courage to do it.

First I ask him right out, "How do you defend yourself here, just in case?"

"In case of what?"

"Attack by...." I'm about to say, "the first-rate artists," but that seems rude. I wonder what to call them. But then I think, if Minerva can have flying phalluses as her art, why can't I have a bomb?

"How do you make a bomb? It's for art."

He doesn't look a bit suspicious.

"Will you help me? Or do you have one handy? You know, in case of attack."

Jasper is coming dressed as he always is—in his gas station jump suit. I ask him: How come he's the only one doesn't want to look like an artist? I say, "Since when do you have to be an artist to try to look as if you are? I mean, just one little thing would do it, like one earring or longer hair. It doesn't take much."

He says, "I don't dress any other way than this."

I don't wonder about it. I've known lots of men like that. My father wore the same shiny-seated navy blue suits as long as I knew him. He must have had three or four. Maybe more, how could you tell? I knew a man who wore a baseball jacket zipped up to his neck no matter what the weather. I've known men who never took their cowboy hats off.

"But about bombs?" I say. "I'm coming dressed as a bomb. One that's already exploded. I need to know things."

He says, "There's grenades and sticks of dynamite. You know what they look like."

Turns out it's true, he does have things: "Just in case." And he shows me.

And he shows me more than that. And more.

He's a hairy man. All over. Not what you'd think artists would be like, so I'm all the more sure he's not one.

His hut is different from the others, too. It's as simple as his jump suits. There are several more suits, all just alike. I know because he doesn't have a closet. He keeps the clean ones hanging on the back of his bedroom door. (He shut the door to keep his cat out so we wouldn't be disturbed.) (Trust him to have a clean animal.)

If he does art, or has any, it's not in here. Neither is the bomb. He brings it out from a back room. A grenade.

"I'd like two."

He actually lets me have them. Maybe because it'll be the Fourth of July.

But this is after.

He makes love as if he were the way I thought Sam Gray would be, before, when I fell in love with his painting. What I fell in love with was how Jasper is, though I thought he wasn't. Jasper is the kind of man that comes down hard on his heels and glares around, side to side. You'd think waste paper was the main enemy, *and* anybody who didn't put it in a trash basket, so I was a little worried. But he's not like that at all. From the first touch, middle finger across my upper lip and then across my lower, then along my chin, my collar bone.... After that I knew how it would be.

Everybody is getting ready for the party, except Sam is, yet again, painting his little red hut. It's almost like a signature, the way it appears even when you know it wasn't there in real life. Sometimes it's hardly more than a red speck. But this time the hut is in the foreground, large and much too red.

Who ever heard of the big red side of a hut, not even a window in it (he's painting the back), being mostly the whole painting? Just a little tan and green around it and a little blue along the top, almost as if a frame. It'll look even funnier when it does have a frame. Even my pile of helter-skelter shoebox-sized talus is more interesting. But as usual, I can see that I'm going to like it. Maybe most of all. Maybe I should wait until it's done before I go.

I sit behind him as he paints and watch his bald spot. Usually he complains when people watch him paint, but this time he doesn't. It's as if he wants me there, and even that he guesses where I'm going. Or maybe (more likely) it's that I'm the most inept, most recently arrived, and least important person here, and he thinks he can push me around. Besides, he knows how I like his paintings.

"My paintings are piling up." He doesn't even look back at me as he's speaking. "I need for them to be taken to town. I *need* them to be sold."

I can't imagine what he needs money for. We don't use money here. Besides, artists don't care about money. I think somebody gave a lot of grants for this place. Maybe the government. What does the government know about art! Or maybe some of these people were on the grant committee, people sympathetic to any kind of art at all, and the artists used the grants to set this place up.

"Why sold? You can't need money."

"No, no, I care nothing for money."

I can hear I've insulted him.

"Nor fame either. Not for myself, at any rate. What I need is for my paintings to be out in the world. I need for them to be studied. For their own sakes. They should be deconstructed." (I can't believe it, he knows about semiotics. You'd not think so from the look of his art. Of course, *I* know all this stuff, and it doesn't make *my* art any good.) "Get them the notice they deserve."

He has ten or so packed up on a little two-wheeled cart all ready to go.

"If I can have the one you're working on now, I'll take them."

He doesn't even say thank you. He knew I'd do it. It's as if he knows I was in love with him before I met him. Of course, I'm not anymore.

"Don't let them stay all rolled up. It's not good for them."

I could say I'll take them and then let them go up with me and my bombs as part of an art-bomb happening. "Performance art," they call that. Sometimes "destruction art," like when Nam June Paik broke violins. And then there were all those pianos getting chopped up. Those were supposed to be the death of music. This will be the death of art. Maybe the death of me, too. The paintings will be going up with me, which will make it all the more meaningful.

The day of the party I take all morning to make my exploded bomb costume. Then I put it on, on top of my backpack with the bombs in it, and I go to check up on the party. Just as I figured, everybody seems dressed pretty much as usual, though a little bit more so. Portia has come as a big vagina (or a cookie). Minerva is a winged phallus. One comes as a big turd. I can't see who that is under all that goo. That French-ish man comes as Hitler (he looks a lot like him anyway, but now he wears the uniform) in order to shock everybody even more than turds and vaginas.

The party's only just started and Jasper is already cleaning up out from under people. His usual way. You can't put down a half-finished drink before it's cleaned up right out from under your nose. There's a lot of homemade beer made out of all sorts of things: Elderberry beer, gooseberry beer.... All of them the best I ever tasted.

Everybody likes my costume. I'm wearing a lot of pieces of things plastered all over me and hanging down. Some are stuck on with wires Jasper gave me so chunks seem to be flying off. It's easy to hide my backpack under all this junk, but it's not very comfortable. I'm thinking maybe I should forget the whole thing and just sit here and drink beer. But then I think how it's for the good of all these second-best artists—that they should be safe to brew their beer and have their parties and paint and dance.

I want to say goodbye to Jasper some way, but I don't want him to know I'm going. He's so busy cleaning up I have to grab him to stop him for a minute. "Jasper! Relax and have fun. Drink some beer. Dance."

If he does, I won't go. I'll take off my backpack and dance with him. I'll get drunk and not worry about saving everybody.

But he doesn't.

My bombs weigh quite a bit, and everything else does, too, and the costume is getting in the way. I can't move my arms very much. Pieces of my costume that are on wires hook against the trees and bushes when the trail goes through woodsy places. I pull and sometimes push the cart with Sam Gray's paintings. It hooks on rocks. I'm getting blisters.

Even so, I try to stay aware as I go, because they say the present moment is the only one that counts, and these might be my last, so I'm aware of my costume rubbing against my knees, and my backpack pulling on my shoulders, there's my blisters. I'm sorry that these have to be part of my last awarenesses.

I'll get recognition of a sort. Maybe not for art, though why not? For sure it'll be a happening: Big blast, broken talus flying up. I hope I get to see it—start to finish, not just the start.

Should I cross first and then set off the bombs, or should I set them off on this side and not cross?

I hope I don't inadvertently make it easier to cross.

I hike up and down and up again. The trail gets harder. Coming here it was more down than up—*after* I crossed the ridge, that is. I stop to rest and think. This is right where the trail broadens out so artists can hold hands. I sit on one of the stones on the side and prop the cart against a bigger one or it'll take off back down the trail by itself. I throw away some of my costume that sticks out, though from now on the trail is above the tree line.

I think how, if I blow myself up, then right now I should be doing something I enjoy this last hour of my life. Of course the last few moments before the bomb gets to me will be spectacular. At least I'll enjoy that.

For sure it'll be exciting, and for sure more exciting than anything I could paint. Or even anything Sam Gray would. The only trouble is, nobody will see it but me. Sort of like that tree that's always falling in the forest and nobody there to hear it. It's the same problem. Will it be art if I'm the only one around?

Here goes anyway. For the sake of the gesture. For the sake of the shock. For politics and art and for the good of everybody down there and especially for Jasper.

I cross to the far side (with the paintings) and, one after the other, I pull the pins and throw. I always said I'd die for art if need be and now I'm going to.

Well, maybe not.

I'm dizzy and I have a lot of dust and grit in my mouth. My face must be all scratched up. It probably looks like my hands. I'll bet I look not only like an exploded bomb, but, definitely, as if I've been in an explosion. I feel like it, too—kind of wobbly. If I'd planned it for weeks I'd never have come up with a work of art this good.

Also the paintings are not as badly off as you'd think. I unroll a couple and take a look. They're shredded around the edges; dirt has gotten in. Actually, they're better than they were. Performance art paintings. I'll bet they're worth more than ever as destruction art where the art is only partly destroyed. As if the artist couldn't quite decide if he wanted to destroy art or not. As if Nam June Paik had only broken a little piece off a violin. It's a whole new movement. The half-destruction of art. This is a big contemporary thing. My not dying, and only getting dizzy and bloody, is part of the same movement. I hope it's more than *épatéing les bourgeois.*

I don't look back to see if I made the ridge easier to cross or harder. I head down towards town. I'm weak and dizzy, but I can manage, down to where those first-rate artists are massing. I can join them now because this costume and all this added dust and scratches and blood makes me a really good work of art. I'm probably more outrageous than any of them. It was hard getting to this point. Nobody ever said art was easy, but I didn't expect it to be quite this hard. I didn't expect to have to leave my lover... my maybe lover, and my bungalow, and to have to almost die. I should have known, though. That's the way art is. That's what has to happen for an artist to get to be good.

They've called my work, and all our work up there: "Socially irrelevant in a time of crisis." They won't ever say that again about mine.

Too bad the people down in town and those back at the colony have missed the best part. Actually, I did, too. The explosion itself is wiped right out of my head. I don't remember a thing about it. I feel half-dead; though, on the other hand, I feel more alive than usual, too. Really good art always does that.

Report to the Men's Club and Other Stories, 2002

Prejudice And Pride

All those old-fashioned ways of holding back on sex until you can't stand it that the lovers are still apart. Why don't they call out to each other instead of waiting till the door shuts between them? Why don't they turn around at the last minute and do what they ache to do? Why keep holding back, as though for the reader, that the reader should read on and on. faster and faster, skipping pages on the next part where the lovers (yet again!) do not say that they love each other? And he. Fitzwilliam, having glimpsed her ankle … or not even that, focused, rather, on her long, pale fingers as she plays, and of course rather well, the piano-forte. Her fingers make him think of her body, though he can hardly dare to let himself do so. He can think of other women's bodies, but not hers. The thought of hers is too much for him to bear.

And she … reads his eyes, though she hardly dares to look straight into them. His gaze turns her stomach as though upside-down every time she almost looks at his face. Of course she doesn't think about his body. But. Yes, she does, though doesn't let herself know she's doing it. And she sees more than she admits to herself, her eyes lowered, looking just there. But after all, she is a country girl. She can't be ignorant. They have horses. (Seeing them, with their sex down, almost to their hocks sometimes, used to frighten her when she was a child.)

Then their is that left ankle he has glimpsed, and the other also. When they finally do marry, he will fondle her pale, narrow feet. When they finally do marry, it is assured that he will get an erection at the proper times, for even the lightest, slightest brushing of his hand over her (as yet covered) — and almost as though by mistake, though they both will know that's not so — breast will be enough.

Afterwards, at breakfast, they will stare into each other's eyes, she, by then, daring to look at him.

They are rich, and the servants will bring a breakfast of the rich: Eggs, sprats, ham, tea with cream, a sweet yellowish bread with raisins.... But they will hardly eat any of it. Instead he will kiss all ten of her fingertips, and then back again, all ten, in the other direction. Then each knuckle. (He will have said that her fingertips touched to his lips are all he needs of nourishment.) When he kisses, and for several seconds (how warm his lips are), the palm of her hand, she will feel it up and down her spine.

This will all have taken place in the garden on a spring morning, they having been married in the spring.

Of course at first they don't like each other. Except there is always this electricity that passes between them. Thank goodness he keeps getting invited to places where she is visiting, and vice versa, he, so proud and mysterious, with mysterious, dark, Roman good looks, but with the bright, light eyes or the Picts. When her uncle accuses him or being too proud, her aunt says. "There is something a little stately in him, to be sure, but it is confined to his air and is not unbecoming."

He has secret sorrows: The almost-rape or his little sister and recent deaths in the family. Of course these make him all the more appealing.

Her name is Elizabeth, though it might just as likely be Margaret, Charlotte, Eleanor, or Constance.

He said of her, "She is one of the handsomest women of my acquaintance," but this was much later. At first he had said she was "tolerable," but not handsome enough to tempt *him*.

I once saw a roebuck stalking a doe. He was about the size of a Great Dane and had a full set of antlers. The doc was grazing as though unmindful of him, but he wasn't interested in food. He never, for a second, took his eyes off her. Such was his concentration that we tourists were as though invisible to him. He moved stiffly, step, then freeze; step, freeze.... This was in a virgin forest, streaks of sunlight slanting down —on them and on us. At first we had thought he was the statue of a deer, How else be so stiff and still? But he had taken a step — half-step, really, and then become like a statue again, hoof raised. His concentration on her more sexual than any act of actual sex could ever be.

This is how Fitzwilliam looks al Elizabeth, and she feels her heart tip Over. His gaze, like the roebuck's, steel wires between herself and him. Though his eyes are pale ... blue-tan, still they pull .... No, simply hold in place. The roebuck was nor trembling, but he was *almost* trembling. Fitzwilliam also does not tremble.

When they finally do go to bed (trembling), Fitzwilliam (how could it be otherwise?) comes too soon, hardly having penetrated her. They will *not* mention it. (He had only touched her breast a little bit, and it was covered up still, this time by her nightgown, but that touch was enough — or, rather, too much for him to contain himself.) But a little later he will try again, and this time all will be right — her first bumpy ride of sex, and painful, too. The sheets will be as though a chicken had been killed there. Or was it only in southern countries that that was done? At any rate, there will have been no need for a chicken. ("Oh, Elizabeth, Elizabeth, have I caused you pain? You whom, of all people in the whole of the wide world, I would want least of all to hurt?") (One would expect that they went to Bath or Brighton on their honeymoon.) They will probably not be able to make love again for a few days until she is somewhat healed, so it's good that.,two nights later, when he actually fondle her *bare* breasts, he, again, comes immediately.

It is to be hoped she does not die in childbirth.

Sometimes I think I would like to have lived back in those times, but had I done so, I would probably have been the scullery maid. I would probably be called (curdy) Hill or Rodgers or Morgan. Not have a name anything like my own foreign-sounding name — neither my foreign-sounding maiden name nor this one.

And you, Old Man. you'd probably have been the man's man. But no, you haven't the manners nor the mood for that. You'd have been the swearing, sweating coachman. And did you ever look at me like that roebuck we saw last summer looked at his doe? Perhaps you did, and perhaps it is my own damn fault that that look, if it ever was, is no longer there.

Report to the Men's Club and Other Stories, 2002

After All

It's one of those days, rainy and dull, when you remember all the times you said or did the wrong thing, or somebody else said the wrong thing to you, or insulted you, or you insulted them, or they forgot you altogether, or you forgot them when you should have remembered. One of those days when everything you say is misunderstood. Everything you pick up you drop. You knock things over. You slip and fall. And your nose is running, your throat is sore. And it's your birthday. You're a whole 'nother year older. At your age, one more year makes a big difference.

At least I'm alone. No need to bother anyone else with myself, and my temper, my moods, my dithering and doubts, my yackety-yacking when others want to keep quiet. And my voice is too loud. I laugh when nothing's funny.

Having had a night of nightmares about what might have happened if this or if that bad thing had come about. (Good no one's here, because I would be telling them the whole dream detail by detail.) Stop me if I go nattering on. I talk and talk even when I mean to keep quiet. Especially when I mean to be quiet.

There ought to be something else to talk about that wouldn't be my long, long dream or the weather, where the sunshine, gruesome and garish, causes spots before my eyes. It's time to go somewhere. Anyplace else is better than here. It will be a makeshift journey. No purpose except to get away. I didn't pack. I didn't plan. I won't bring a map. I can't depend on strangers because of my beady eyes. I have a mean smile.

You see, this evening I was sitting in the window of my cottage looking out at my piece of desert with squawking quail in it. (Tobacco! Tobacco!) I was thinking to write a story about somebody who needs to change (the best sort of character to write about), and all of a sudden I knew it was me who had to change. Always had been, and I didn't realize it until that very minute. So I have to be the one to go on a journey, either of discovery or in order to avoid myself.

I won't pack a lunch. I won't bring a bottle of water. I know I don't look my best but I don't even want to. My hair.... I don't want to think about it.

If you crawl out the hole in the back fence, right away you're on the road to town. "A pointless coming and going," they'll say, and I'll say, "That's exactly what I'm after." I've lived all this time a different kind of pointless coming and going: Concerts and plays and then reading all the books one should read—that everybody else was reading, so how could you not read them? But this will be a different kind of pointless. I don't care what they think.

They!

Why can't they just take me for granted like most children do? Being chased by your own children. How could that happen? Being followed and watched.

I suppose to catch me out, non *compos mentis. Mentos*? If that's what it's called. *Mentis sanos*? If I can remember the words for it, how can it be true? Except I don't remember.

They'll see me if I leave in the daytime.

It's one of those nights with a fingernail moon. It's one of those nights with a cold wind. Who'd expect Grandma to be out in this weather and at this hour? Who'd expect Grandma to be walking down the road to town, leaning against the wind. (It's been a long time since I was allowed to drive.)

That's my son behind the arborvitae. My middle daughter by the carport. (Carport without a car.) I see her shadow. My oldest? I don't know where she is.

"Mama, you're not as young as you think you are." (I *am*. I *am*. Exactly as young as I think I am. I'm maybe even a little more so.)

I'll be set upon by this and that. Snarling dogs let free to roam at night. Maybe there's other snarling people like myself out here. Hard rain or hail. Smells that sting the nose. Sky, a preposterous overdose of stars. If I fall asleep behind a creosote bush, what will come get me?

I suppose I ought to trust in some sort of god or other. There's one under every bush. At least I hope so. Feats of faith. I can do that.

Here I am, gone. Forever. So far, forever. I regret my books. The children will keep all the wrong ones. The good ones will get thrown in the garbage. My best scarf—they'll think it's just any old scarf. They don't know I got it from my own grandma. I told them, but they forget.

What I've done for them! It was endless! Of course that was a long time ago.

But after that, what I've done for my art! If that is art. I don't know what to call it. I could call it leisure time. My hard-working leisure time. Most of it spent looking out the window.

But art is... was my life. I mean looking out the window so as to think about it was.

I always had plenty of ideas. I didn't exactly have them. They grew—little by little, a half an idea at a time. First, part of a phrase and then a person to go with it. After a person, then a little corner of a place for the person to be in.

Can I make it through town before morning? It's six miles to the other end of it. If I do, I might be able to get my usual nap. I could rest in the ditch by the side of the road.

I've disguised myself. Big floppy hat, sand-colored bathrobe.... (I forgot not to wear my slippers.) I had a hard time deciding how I could be unobtrusive and yet not be like myself, because I've always tried to look unobtrusive. There's those earth colors which I always wear anyway.

I already stay in the corners and the shadows. I already never look people in the eye. I already hunch over. Now I'm shuffling because my slippers keep falling off.

I hear footsteps. When I stop to listen, they stop, too. I knew one of them would follow. I wonder which it is? You can't get rid of your children.

"I'm laughing at you... whoever you are. Ha, ha, ha. Hear that?"

Well, I can't keep stopping and listening and laughing all the time. I'd never get anywhere. I have to keep going if I want to get somewhere or other in time for anything at all. It's bad enough when your slippers won't stay on.

If I had a diary, I'd write: Next Day, or, Day Two. (I'd have to write the days that way because I don't know the date, I hardly even know if spring or summer, but that's not a sign of non compose... whatever... because I never did pay attention to things like that.)

I'd write: Had a nice nap by the side of the road, and that I don't know if long or short, but a nice one. (With my sand-colored bathrobe I'll bet I looked like a pinkish/tan rock.) I'd write how I must begin working on myself. They say writing things down is a good way to begin, so I'll do that. Or will when I get the diary.

If I'd brought money I could have bought one in town. Except I went through town at about dawn and the stores were closed. (If I'd brought a watch I'd know when.)

Whoever is following me has not made themselves known except in rustlings and snappings and scuffling sounds. I have to admit I'm a little bit scared.

Living in a clearing in a forest might be nice. A mountain pass would be nice, too. I'd like a view. A view can make you happy. And with a view you'd be able to see who's creeping up on you.

I've decided. I turn, sharp left, leave the road, and start straight up. It's hard going in these slippers but I have a purpose. I'm taking charge of my own life. I know exactly what I'm doing, and when, and how much and why, and the time, which is right now.

It's a cute... you could call it a cute pass, up there where I'm heading. The cliff walls on each side hug a marshy spot. There's an overhang to sleep under. Old icy snow to chew on. Though it's high, it's sheltered enough for there to be fairly large trees. The ground glitters all over as if with tiny chunks of gold. (If it was gold, it would be gone.) There's things to eat. I'll nibble lambs quarters and purslane. Do they grow up there? I'm probably thinking of the olden days back East. Anyway, there's wild rose hips, so small I wonder that I've ever bothered eating them but I always do.

Even from here, well below that pass, you can see fairly far. I study the landscape. The orange lichen that dots the boulders looks like something left in the refrigerator too long. The sky looks as if it's got the measles.

I see movement on the hillside below me. For sure there's something down there. I catch glimpses from the corner of my eye.

It's inevitable, your children will track you down. There they are. I didn't actually see them, but something is out there, I'm sure of it, creeping up on me. What do they want? What do they have in store for me? *If* they can catch me. Of course it is my birthday—or was, a couple of days ago. Perhaps they want to have a surprise party. Perhaps their arms are full of presents, paper hats, tape recorders for the music for dancing.... What if they're bringing champagne? What a lot to carry! No wonder they haven't been able to catch me.

If they bring me sweets, they'll have forgotten I can't eat chocolate. If blouses, they'll be too big. (A mother is supposed to be bigger than the children, but they forget I'm the smallest now.) If paper hats, I suppose I'll have to put one on. If horns, I suppose I'll have to blow one.

Maybe, if I can get far enough ahead, they'll give up. I try to hurry but it's getting steeper. At least, if they're carrying all those things, they're having a hard time, too. The champagne will be the heaviest. I suppose they'll have those plastic champagne glasses you have to put together, and I suppose they think that'll be a good job for Grandma. I won't do it. They can't make me.

If I *did* have a diary, and if I did write anything in it, it would be misunderstood anyway, just like everything I say is, so the first thing I'd write (page one, January first) should be: *That isn't what I mean at all.*

But I'd rather write about how my feet hurt and how it looks like rain.

Once I get up there, I may have to stay forever. I might not be able to climb down. A long time ago when I was still spry, I came up to that very spot to die, but I didn't die after all. I waited and waited but nothing happened except I had my usual dizzy spell. I had to climb back down, though I had to wait until the spell passed. Good I hadn't told anybody.

This time I haven't thought (even at my age!) about what would be the best way to die. I know I should, but, after I didn't die back then at the top of my favorite pass, thinking about it began to seem a waste of valuable time. I was contemplating art. That seemed the important thing to do.

But, from now on, what to hope for out of life (and art)? Or is it the art part that's done with? I'm still full of longing... so much longing... for.... I don't know what, but I'm breathless with it.

I lie down with a rock for a pillow. I rest a long time. When I wake up, I think: Day two or day three or day four? Even if I had a diary I'd be all mixed up already.

But now I'm thinking perhaps my own attic is the best place to disappear into. I could go down to the kitchen any time I wanted. I could get clean underwear. They say, "East or West, home is best."

I start back. It'll be easier going down because I won't keep stepping out of my slippers all the time.

Something streaks by. Lights up the whole sky. Dizzying, dazzling even in the daytime. (Talk about spots in front of your eyes!) Well now, *there's* something beautiful. One nice thing is happening on my birthday. (If it still is my birthday.)

The ground shakes. Boulders come bounding down—whole sides of mountains....

Who would have thought it, the end of the world as if just for me. Right on time, too, before my slippers give out entirely. We're all going together, the whole world and me. Isn't that nice! Best of all, I'm in at the end. I won't have to miss all the funny things that might have happened later had the world lasted beyond me. So, not such a bad birthday after all.

Report to the Men's Club and Other Stories, 2002

The Doctor

He dates his third wife often but she'll not come back to live with him. Even before it got this bad she said he'd have to clean this place out first. Have to get new couches not so clawed and peed-on. Use a lot of spray for the smell. But there's no way to clean it up now without burning it down.

She left him five years ago. She had good reasons, lots more than just this mess. One was, he was a partying person and she wasn't. (Of course if she came back now there couldn't be any parties anyway, at least not for a long while of cleaning up.) And of course you never can know people's reasons for leaving—nor for coming back.

The doctor has a rugged sexy good looks. He's still attractive even though in his seventies and even though he broke his back which left him with a crunched down look. He used to be six feet three but now he's only six feet. As a young man he had dislocated or broken his fingers so often they look terrible now, crooked and with swollen joints. One wonders how he can be a surgeon, thread his needles, and tie the fancy little knots anymore.

The house is a huge Victorian with a front stairway and a back stairway, five bedrooms not counting the maid's room, two upstairs bathrooms and one downstairs (only one toilet still works, but the doctor is alone, he doesn't need more than one). The front parlor is all bay windows and the back parlor is all wood paneling.

There's empty fields behind the house and little patches of forest on each side. Sometimes deer come in to the doctor's back yard.

The third wife said if he'd clean the place up even a little bit she'd think about coming back, but he's like those old men who've never thrown away a Life Magazine or a piece of string. With him it's mostly medical journals. He's not thrown one away since he's been in medical school, nor any books either. Lots of other junk around, too, parts of old motors, rusty tools.... Two dead cars are in the garage. He has to park his diesel sedan in the driveway.

When the doctor and his third wife bought this house, the wife kept things more or less cleaned up. If she was still with him things wouldn't have gotten quite so out of hand. She never did like having all this stuff, but it was in some control and mostly out of sight. Actually the house was full of junk from the moment they moved in.

The doctor loves a big house like this. When his wife was still with him they could invite guests to stay over. He likes to play the *pater familias*. Of course he can't do that anymore. Now he does it in a smaller way. Whenever he goes to a party he always brings big chunks of cheeses and special black bread. Sometimes a ham. Sometimes a five pound bag of pistachios. Always more food than anybody can use in a week.

His dog died shortly after his wife left him. He buried it in the back yard. That dog.... Twelve years before he had taken home a sick mangy puppy, slept with it on his chest and got mange himself. It was a type of mange that human beings are not supposed to get. The puppy grew up to be the dog that died.

But on the other hand, the doctor taught heart surgery by having the students operate on dogs.

The house badly needs painting, but the doctor doesn't notice. If he did, and though it's a huge job, he'd probably plan to paint it himself. He'd buy the paint and keep it in the garage or the basement and now and then think about doing it.

The cats started more recently when the doctor discovered a family of feral cats in his garage and began feeding them. One was pregnant. It was getting colder so the doctor made a little cat door into his basement. It gave them the run of the house.

He's not sure how many cats are in there now. And he thinks he saw a possum.

The cats are mostly tabbies, some gingers, a calico or two.... Only one is white. That's his favorite. White cats always have a hard time hunting. They're so easily seen. And she's smaller. She's the underdog cat. He has always loved underdogs best. Besides, she's so luminous. She seems to glow in the dark. He named her Nimbus. He wonders about her fur. He looked at it under the microscope to see if he could see what caused the sheen. Too bad he doesn't have a normal white cat to compare it with, but wild white cats don't last long. He wonders how this one survived to grow up.

They're all still pretty wild. They won't let him pick them up. So far only two sit on his lap. They're nocturnal and the doctor's not home in the daytime to keep them awake. There's a lot of action through the night. They've staked out their territory and defend it with caterwauling. The doctor has learned to sleep through it.

He leaves paper grocery bags on the floors all around the house because the cats like to go into them. Also cardboard boxes here and there.

Even though he can't pick any of them up, if he sits quietly (and he makes a point of sitting quietly) one might jump into his lap.

He doesn't go on vacation anymore because he can't leave the animals. He doesn't attend medical conferences. Even going away for a weekend might be dangerous for them. Nobody could ever be persuaded to come in here to feed them. He wonders what they would do if something happened to him.

The minute he comes in, he says, "Hello" to all the cats in the kitchen. (Some of them are good at meowing back to him.) He comes in the back door, the front door is never used and wasn't even when his wife was here. There's a nice little porch out front but it's never been used either.

The doctor brings in forsythia and pussy willows to force into bloom. On hands and knees he puts in tulip bulbs, thinking all the time that, instead, (if, that is, he had actually noticed the need for paint and bought it) he should be painting the house or at least starting to. He has no illusions about what a big job it is and how long it'll take but he thinks himself capable of anything regardless of his age.

The doctor brings in a large cocoon. It was hanging on a limb right over where he parks his car. He's surprised he didn't notice it before since that's exactly the kind of thing he always notices. He brings in the whole branch and mails it on the wall over the breakfast nook. High enough so the cats can't get to it.

What is born in the warmth of the kitchen is a moth of unusual beauty. The doctor can't bring himself to put it in alcohol, pin it and put it up on his wall along with the others in his collection even though it's the largest and most beautiful of any of them.

The moth won't survive these cats. He takes it upstairs and puts it in the master bedroom where there's a big bay window. (He doesn't sleep there anymore.) He shoos out the cats and shuts the door. Of course it won't last long. It doesn't have a mouth. It's purely a sex creature, alive, not to eat, but to copulate.

Fairy dust covers his hands.

The third wife never comes around to the house. It pains her to look at it. He won't let anybody in anyway. They always meet someplace else—at a nice restaurant or at a movie. Last date they had, the third wife thought the doctor looked a little odd, kind of fuzzy...greenish, mossy.... And he smells odd. Not so much the damp man-smell of sweat, though that, too, but musky and marshy—a smell of growing things. It's sexy but it worries her.

The house itself is sending out waves of pheromones that bring yet more creatures to the little cat door into the basement. Nobody can guess what's in there now.

Finally the smells bring the third wife.

It's so dim in there and there's this odd strong smell. She's not sure if a good smell or bad one. At first it makes her choke. She goes back out but then she sees eyes...two huge scary black eyes peering out at her from an upper window. What might be up there looking out with such big eyes? Maybe the smell is the smell of death. (Unlike the doctor, the third wife doesn't know what death smells like.)

The third wife puts her hand over her nose and mouth and goes back into the kitchen, moving slowly. It's hot outside, but not bad in the house. It's three stories high, and it's shaded by big trees, and the doctor has pulled all the shades to keep it cool.

At first she sees shiny eyes all around her and there's scuffling noises. She steps around boxes and stacks of magazines. She steps a paper bags. Something yowls and tears out of it in a fury.

Then she sees Nimbus on a high kitchen shelf. The doctor has already told the third wife about her—how he looked at her fur under the microscope—how it had a glassy quality.

The third wife is wearing white. She's almost as luminous as Nimbus. One wonders how long she can be in here and keep her skirt and blouse clean.

She calls out, Are you there? It's me. It's me. Calls out, Honey? Dear?

One wonders who, or how many, out of all these creatures, might answer.

Does she dare go on, farther in? Is the doctor even home? But what about those strange big eyes in the upstairs window? The Doctor might be up there helpless, at the mercy of.... Or sick...maybe sick from his own house-smells.

She heads up the narrow back stairs that go straight from the kitchen. She wonders: Is he still sleeping where he used to sleep? There are two big bedrooms, a big bed in each. He might be in either. Though what if those rooms have gotten filled up with junk? He might have had to move to a smaller one.

Then she thinks maybe she should have called the hospital first, to see if he was there. You never know when he might be operating. He's called out at all hours. (She always thought it odd that he never seemed to mind. She remembers one Christmas dinner, all the family there, the turkey just brought out....) But she's come too far now, she might as well take a look.

The upstairs hallway is narrow and dark by the back stairs but broadens out for the fancier bedrooms. It's daytime, but it's awfully dim back in the narrow part of the hall. Cats have followed her. The white cat, in its catty way, circling her feet, first one side and then the other. She has to be careful not to step on her.

At the far end, where the hall broadens out, there's a window with a dirty lace curtain. The window sends out dusty beams of light. The third wife can see...or she thinks she sees, tiny creatures in the dust, flying in the light. But how would you know the difference, dust or bugs?

But where *is* the doctor? She calls, "Honey? Are you there?"

She'll go on. She has to see if the doctor is all right.

The white cat still circles her legs, purring now.

"Honey?"

She was right about the first big bedroom. Nobody could sleep in there. There isn't room. The shades are drawn against the heat and the third wife sees the gleam of a few sets of eyes. She backs out and shuts the door.

It's from the window of the second big room that she had seen the huge eyes staring at her while she was still outside. She doesn't want to look in there, she's scared to, but it might be important.

As she opens the door, something flutters out from behind the curtain. That's what the eyes were. Big wings with huge eyes on them. And it seem as if it's looking at her but of course that can't be. Those eyes are phony—meant only to scare, but they work, She can't help but step back and huddle into herself.

The big, big-eyed moth follows her out of the room and back down the hall, always just a few yards behind. It seems to be growing. The third wife wonders if that's really happening or if she's just scared. And she wonders if it's true about moths not having mouths. Maybe *some* do.

She finally gets to the little maid's room. As she opens the door somebody says, "Come in. I've been waiting for you. Waiting and waiting." The voice is deep, resonant. Growly. Is it really her husband's? Perhaps he's sick. He sounds sick. But it's a voice full of love. The third wife wonders how she ever could have brought herself to leave him.

The white cat goes in first. She lights the room with her glow. But the third wife's white blouse glows, too. The moth comes in last. The third wife thinks it's grown to the size of a blanket.

There's something long, lumpy, and greenish lying on the maid's little bed.

The wife lies down beside...it...him...whatever it is that's so warm and soft...that smells both very good and very bad. Lies down and sinks in. First she thinks, I'm sorry I came and right after that, I'm glad I came.

She says it, "I'm glad I came," and, "I'm glad you're all right."

The thing beside her growls. She always thought he was sort of like a bear.

The neighbors across the street don't call the fire engines. They don't mind such a ramshackle eyesore burning down—good riddance, though too bad about the oak paneling and the oak staircase. And there are too many cats. Besides, they know the doctor is almost always at the hospital so there's nobody there to be rescued. They had been glad the deer preferred the doctor's yard to their own—glad possums and raccoons stayed over there. Even the crows like the doctor's land best.

Up from the flames comes a big black cloud and out from it, sparkling ashes rain down.

Everybody in the little town nearby wakes up and looks out the window. They think somebody has set off firecrackers. They haven't seen such a good show in a long time.

Polyphony, 2002

Boys

We need a new batch of boys. Boys are so foolhardy, impetuous, reckless, rash. They'll lead the way into smoke and fire and battle. I've seen one of my own sons, aged twelve, standing at the top of the cliff shouting, daring the enemy. You'll never win a medal for being too reasonable.

We steal boys from anywhere. We don't care if they come from our side or theirs. They'll forget soon enough, which side they used to be on, if they ever knew. After all, what does a seven year old know? Tell them this flag of ours is the best and most beautiful, and that we're the best and smartest, and they believe it. They like uniforms. They like fancy hats with feathers. They like to get medals. They like flags and drums and war cries.

Their first big test is getting to their beds. You have to climb straight up to the barracks. At the top you have to cross a hanging bridge. They've heard rumors about it. They know they'll have to go home to mother if they don't do it. They all do it.

You should see the look on their faces when we steal them. It's what they've always wanted. They've seen our fires along the hills. They've seen us marching back and forth across our flat places. When the wind is right, they've heard the horns that signal our getting up and going to bed and they've gotten up and gone to bed with our sounds or those of our enemies across the valley.

In the beginning they're a little bit homesick (you can hear them smothering their crying the first few nights) but most have anticipated their capture and look forward to it. They love to belong to us instead of to the mothers.

If we'd let them go home they'd strut about in their uniforms and the stripes of their rank. I know because I remember when I first had my uniform. I was wishing my mother and my big sister could see me. When I was taken, I fought, but just to show my courage. I was happy to be stolen—happy to belong, at long last, to the men.

Once a year in summer we go down to the mothers and copulate in order to make more warriors. We can't ever be completely sure which of the boys is ours and we always say that's a good thing, for then they're all ours and we care about them equally, as we should. We're not supposed to have family groups. It gets in the way of combat. But every now and then, it's clear who the father is. I know two of my sons. I'm sure they know that I, the colonel, am their father. I think that's why they try so hard. I know them as mine because I'm a small, ugly man. I know many must wonder how someone like me got to be a colonel.

(We not only steal boys from either side but we copulate with either side. When I go down to the villages, I always look for Una.)

"TO DIE FOR YOUR TRIBE IS TO LIVE FOREVER." That's written over our headquarters entrance. Under it, NEVER FORGET. We know we mustn't forget but we suspect maybe we have. Some of us feel that the real reasons for the battles have been lost. No doubt but that there's hate, so we and they commit more atrocities in the name of the old ones, but how it all began is lost to us.

We've not only forgotten the reasons for the conflict, but we've also forgotten our own mothers. Inside our barracks, the walls are covered with mother jokes and mother pictures. Mother bodies are soft and tempting. "Pillows," we call them. "Nipples" and "pillows." And we insult each other by calling ourselves the same.

The valley floor is full of women's villages. One every fifteen miles or so. On each side are mountains. The enemy's, at the far side, are call The Purples. Our mountains are called The Snows. The weather is worse in our mountains than in theirs. We're proud of that. We sometimes call ourselves The Hailstones or The Lightenings. We think the hailstones harden us up. The enemy doesn't have as many caves over on their side. We always tell the boys they were lucky to be stolen by us and not those others.

When I was first taken, our mothers came up to the caves to get us back. That often happens. Some had weapons. Laughable weapons. My own mother was there, in the front of course. She probably organized the whole thing, her face, red and twisted with resolve. She came straight at me. I was afraid of her. We boys fled to the back of the barracks and our squad leader stood in front of us. Other men covered the doorway. It didn't take long for the mothers to retreat. None were hurt. We try never to do them any harm. We need them for the next crop of boys.

Several days later my mother came again by herself—sneaked up by moonlight. Found me by the light of the night lamp. She leaned over my sleeping mat and breathed on my face. At first I didn't know who it was. Then I felt breasts against my chest and I saw the glint of a hummingbird pin I recognized. She kissed me. I was petrified. (Had I been a little older I'd have known how to choke and kick to the throat. I might have killed her before I realized it was my mother.) What if she took me from my squad? Took away my uniform? (By then I had a red and blue jacket with gold buttons. I had already learned to shoot. Something I'd always wanted to do. I was the first of my group to get a sharpshooters medal. They said I was a natural. I was trying hard to make up for my small size.)

The night my mother came she lifted me in her arms. There, against her breasts, I thought of all the pillow jokes. I yelled. My comrades, though no older than I and only a little larger, came to my aid. They picked up whatever weapon was handy, mostly their boots. (Thank goodness we had not received our daggers yet.) My mother wouldn't hit out at the boys. She let them batter at her. I wanted her to hit back, to run, to save herself. After she finally did run, I found I had bitten my lower lip. In times of stress I'm inclined to do that. I have to watch out. When you're a colonel, it's embarrassing to be found with blood on your chin.

So now, off to steal boys. We're a troop of older boys and younger men. The oldest maybe twenty-two, half my age. I think of them all as boys, though I would never call them boys to their faces. I'm in charge. My son, Hob, he's seventeen now, is with us.

But we no sooner creep down to the valley than we see things have changed since last year. The mothers have put up a wall. They've built themselves a fort.

I immediately change our plans. I decide this will be copulation day, not boys day. Good military strategy: Always be ready for a quick change of plan.

The minute I think this, I think Una. This is her town. My men look happy, too. This is not only easier, but lots more fun than herding a new crop of boys.

Last time I came down at copulation time I found her—or she found me, she usually does. She's a little old for copulation day, but I didn't want anybody but her. After copulation, I did things for her, repaired a roof leak, fixed a broken table leg.... Then I took her over again, though it wasn't needed, and caused my squad to have to wait for me. Got me a lot of lewd remarks, but I felt extraordinarily happy anyway.

Sometimes on boys night I wonder, what if I stole Una along with boys? What if I dressed her as a boy and brought her to some secret hiding place on our side of the mountain? There are lots of unused caves. Once our armies occupied them all, but that was long ago. Both us and our enemies seem to be dwindling. Every year there are fewer and fewer suitable boys.

Una always seems glad to see me even though I'm ugly and small. (My size is a disadvantage for a soldier, though less so now that I have rank, but the ugliness...that's how I can tell which are my sons...small, ugly boys, both of them. Too bad for them. But I've managed well even so, all the way up to colonel.)

Una was my first. I was her first, too. I felt sorry for her, having to have me for her beginning to be a woman. We were little more than children. We hardly knew what we were doing or how to do it. Afterwards she cried. I felt like crying myself but I had learned not to. Not just learned it with the squad, but I had learned it even before they took me from my mother. I wanted to be taken. I roamed far out into the scrub, waiting for them to come and get me.

The pain in my hip started when I was one of those boys. It wasn't from a wound in a skirmish with the enemy, but from a fight among ourselves. Our leaders were happy when we fought each other. We'd have gotten soft and lazy if we didn't. I keep my mouth shut about my injury. I kept my mouth shut even when I got it. I thought if they knew I could be so easily hurt they'd send me back. Later, I thought if they knew about it, I might not be allowed to come on our raids. Later still I thought I might not be able to be a colonel. I don't let myself limp though sometimes that makes me more breathless than I should be. So far it doesn't seem as if anybody's noticed.

We regroup. I say, "Fellow nipples and fellow pillows. . . ." Everybody laughs. "When have they ever stopped men? Look how womanish the walls are. They'll crumble as we climb." I scrape at a part with the tip of my cane. (As a colonel, I'm allowed to have a cane if I wish instead of a swagger stick.)

We're not sure if the women want to stop copulation day or boy gathering day. We hope it's the latter.

Boost up the smallest boy with a rope on hooks. The rest of us follow.

I used to be that smallest boy. I always went first and highest. Times like this I was glad for my size. I got medals for that. I don't wear any of them. I like playing at being one of the boys. Being small and being a colonel is a good example for some. If they knew about my bum leg I'd be an even better example of how far you can get with disabilities.

We scale the walls and drop into the edges of a vegetable garden. We walk carefully around tomatoes and strawberry plants, squash and beans. After that, raspberry bushes tear at our pants and untie our high tops as we go by. There's a row of barbed wire just beyond the raspberries. Easy to push down.

I feel sad that the women want to keep us out so badly. I wonder, does Una want me not to come? Except they know we're as determined as mothers. At least I am when it comes to Una.

Una has always been nice to me. I often wonder why she likes me. I can understand somebody liking me now that I'm a colonel with silver on my epaulets, and a silver handled cane, but she liked me when I was nothing but a runty boy. She's small, too. I always think Una and I fit together except for one thing, she's beautiful.

We swarm in, turn, each to our favorite place, the younger ones to what's left over, usually other young ones. But then here we are, swarming back again, into their central square, the place with the well, and stone benches, and their one and only tree. Around the tree are the graves of babies. The benches are the mourning benches. We sit on them or on the ground. There's nobody here, not a single woman nor girl nor baby.

Then there's the sound of shooting. We move from the central square—we can't see anything from there. We hide behind the houses at the edges of the gardens. Our enemy stands along the top of the wall. We're ambushed. We flop down. We have no rifles with us and only two pistols, mine and my lieutenant's. This wasn't supposed to be a skirmish. We have our daggers, of course.

Those along the wall don't seem to be very good shots. I raised my pistol. I'm thinking to show them what a good shot really is. But my lieutenant yells, "Stop! Don't shoot. It's mothers!"

Women all along the wall! And with guns. Hiding under wall-colored shields. Whoever heard of such a thing.

They shoot, but a lot are missing, I think on purpose. After all, we may be the enemy, but we're the fathers of many of their girls and many of them. I wonder which one is Una.

The women are angrier than we thought. Perhaps they're tired of losing their boys to us and to the other side. I wouldn't put it past them not to be on any side whatsoever.

Our boys begin to yell their war cry but in a half hearted way. But then... one shot...a real shot this time. Good shot, too. One wonders how a woman could have done it. One wonders if it was a man who taught her. The boys are stunned. To think that one of their mothers or one of their sisters would shoot to kill. This is real. We hadn't thought they'd harm us any more than we ever really harm them.

It was my lieutenant they killed. One bloodless shot to the head. For that boy's sake I'm glad at least no pain. He was wearing his ceremonial hat. I wasn't wearing mine. I never liked that fancy heavy hat. I suppose they really wanted to kill me, but had to take second best since they couldn't tell which one I was. Una would know which one was me.

The boys scatter—back to the center square with its mourning tree. The women can't see them back there. I stay to check on the dead lieutenant and to get his dagger and pistol. Then I limp back to where the boys are waiting for me to tell them what to do. Limp. I relax into it. I don't care who sees. I haven't exactly given up, though perhaps I have when it comes to my future. I'll most likely be demoted. To be captured by women.... All twenty of us. If I can't get out of this in an efficient and capable way, there goes my career.

I hope they have the sense to come rescue us with a large group. They'll have to make a serious effort. I hope they no longer fight and at the same time try to save the women for future use.

But then we hear shooting again and we look out from behind the huts near the wall and see the women have turned their guns outwards. At first we think it's us, come to rescue us, but it's not. That's not our battle cry, not our drum beats.... We can't see from behind the walls so some of us go up on the roofs. There's no danger, all the rifles are facing outwards, but our boys would have braved the roof without a word, as they always do.

It's not our red and blue banners. It's their ugly green and white. It's the enemy come to take advantage of our capture. We wish the women would get out of the way and let us go so we could fight for ourselves. Those women are breaking every rule of battle. They're lying flat along their wall. Nobody can get a fair shot at them.

It goes on and on. We get tired of watching and retreat to the square. We reconnoiter food from the kitchens. We eat better than we usually do. The food is so good we wish the women would let up a bit so we can enjoy it without that racket. Where did they get all these weapons? They must have found our ammunition caves and those of our enemy, too.

The women do a pretty good job. By nightfall our enemy has fled back into their mountains and the women are still on top of their wall. It looks as if they're going to spend the night up there. It's a wide wall. Not as badly built as I told the boys it was.

We find beds for ourselves, all of them better than our usual sleeping pads. I go to Una's hut and lie where I had hoped to have a copulation.

Cats prowl and yowl. All sorts of things live with the women. Goats wander the streets and come in any house they want to. All the animals expect food everywhere. Like the women, our boys are soft hearted. They feed every creature that comes by. I don't let on that I do too.

This whole thing makes me sad. Worried. If I could just have Una in my arms, I might be able to sleep. I have a day dream of her creeping in to me in the middle of the night. I wouldn't even care if we had a copulation or not.

In the morning boys climb to the roofs again to see what's up. They describe women lying under shields all along the walls and they can see some of the enemy lying dead away from the walls. I need to climb up and see for myself. Besides it's good for the boys to see me taking the same chances they do.

I send the boys off and I take their place. I look down on the women along the wall. I see several rifles pointed at me. I stand like a hero. I dare them to shoot. I take all the time I want. I see wall sections less crowded with women. I take out my notebook (no leader is ever without one) and draw a diagram. I take my time until I have the whole wall mapped out.

I could take out my pistol and threaten them. I could shoot one but it wouldn't be very manly to take advantage of my high point. Were they men I'd do it. But then they do the unmanly thing. They shoot me. My leg. My good leg. I go down, flat on the roof. At first I feel nothing but the shock…as if I'd been hit with a hammer. All I know is I can't stand up. Then I see blood.

Though they're on the wall, they're lower. They can't see me as long as I keep down. I crawl to the edge where boys help me. They carry me back to Una's bed. I feel I'm about to pass out or throw up and I become aware that I've soiled myself. I don't want the boys to see. I've always been a source of strength and inspiration in spite of or because of my size.

One of those boys is Hob, come to help me, my arm across his shoulders. I lean in pain but keep my groans to myself.

"Sir? Colonel?"

"I'm fine. Will be. Go."

I wish I could ask him if he really is my son. They say sometimes the women know and tell the boys.

"Don't you want us to...."

"No. Go. Now. And shut the door."

They leave just in time. I throw up over the side of the bed. I lie back—Una's pillow all sweated up not to mention what I've done to her quilt.

Una can make potions for pain. I wish I knew which, of the herbs hanging from her ceiling, might help me. But I'd not be able to reach them anyway.

I lie, half conscious, for I don't know how long. Every time I sit up to examine my leg, I feel nausea again and have to lie back. I wonder if I'll ever be able to lead a charge or a raid for boys or a copulation day. And I always thought, when I became a general (and lately I felt sure I'd be one) maybe I'd find out what we're fighting for—beyond, that is, the usual rhetoric we use to make ourselves feel superior. Now I suppose I'll never know the real reasons.

The boys knock. I rouse myself and say, "Come." Try, that is. At first my voice won't sound out at all and then it sounds more like a groan than a word. The boys tell me the women have called down from the wall. They want to send in a spokesman. The boys want to let him in and then hold him hostage so that we'll all be let out safely.

I tell them the women will probably send in a woman.

That bothers the boys. They must have had torture or killing in mind but now they look worried.

"Tell them yes," I say.

It must smell terrible in here. I even smell terrible to myself, and it's uncomfortable sitting in my own mess. I prop myself up as best I can. I hope I can keep to my senses. I hope I don't throw up in the middle of it. I put my dagger, unsheathed, under the pillow.

At first I think the boys were right, it's a man, of course a man. Where would they have found him, and is he from our side or theirs? That's important. I can't tell by the colors. He's all in tan and gray. He's not wearing any stripes at all so I can't tell his rank. He stands, at ease. More than at ease, utterly relaxed, and in front of a colonel.

But then...I can't believe it, it's Una. I should have known. Dressed as a man down to the boots. I have such a sense of relief and after that joy. Everything will be all right now.

I tell the boys to get out and shut the door.

I reach for her, but the look on her face stops me.

"You shot me in the leg on purpose, didn't you! My good leg!"

"I meant to shoot the bad one."

She opens all the windows, and the door again, too, and shoos the boys away.

"Let me see."

She's gentle. As I knew she'd be.

"I'll get the bullet out, but first I'll clean you up." She hands me leaves to chew for pain.

As she leans, so close above me, her hair falls out of her cap and brushes my face, gets in my mouth as it does when we have copulation day. I reach to touch her breast but she pushes me away.

I should kill her for the glory of it...the leader of the women. I'd not be thought a failure then. I'd be made a general in no time.

But, as she pulls away the soiled quilts, she finds my dagger first thing. She puts it in the drawer with her kitchen knives.

I think again how...(and we all know, only too well) how love is a dangerous thing and can spoil the best of plans. Even as I think it, I want to spoil the very plans I think of. I mean if she's the leader then I could deal with her right now, as she leans over me—even without my dagger. They may be good shots, but can they wrestle a man? Even a wounded one?

"I chose you because I thought, of all of them, you might listen."

"You know I won't ever be let come down to copulation day again."

"Don't go back then. Stay here and copulate."

"I have often thought to bring you up to the mountain dressed as a man. I have a place all picked out."

"Stay here. Let *everybody* stay here and be as women."

I can't answer such a thing. I can't even think about it.

"But what else do you know except how to be a colonel?"

She washes me, changes the bed, and throws the bed clothes and my clothes out the door. Then she gets the bullet out. I'm half out of my head from the leaves she had me chew so the pain is dulled. She bandages me, covers me with a clean blanket, puts her lips against my cheek for a moment.

Then stands up, legs apart. She looks like one of our boys getting ready to prove himself. "We'll not stand for this anymore," she says. "It has to end and we'll end it, if not one way, then another."

"But this is how it's always been."

"You could be our spokesman."

How can she even suggest such a thing. "Pillows," I say. "Spokesman for the nipples."

Goodness knows what the mothers are capable of. They never stick to any rules.

"If the answer is no, we'll not have anymore boy babies. You can come down and copulate all you want but there'll be no boys. We'll kill them."

"You wouldn't. You couldn't. Not you, Una."

"Have you noticed how there are fewer and fewer boys? Many have already done it."

But I'm in too much pain and dizzy from the leaves she gave me, to think clearly. She sees that. She sits beside me, takes my hand. "Just rest," she says. How can I rest with such ideas in my head? "But the rules."

"Hush. Women don't care about rules. You know that."

"Come back with me." I pull her down against me. This time she lets me. How good it feels to have us chest to chest, my arms around her. "I have a secret place. It's not a hard climb to get there."

She pulls back. "Colonel, sir!"

"Please don't call me that."

Then I say...what we're not allowed to say or even think. It's a mother/child thing, not to be said between a man and a woman. I say, "I love you."

She leans back and looks at me. Then wipes at my chin. "Try not to bite your lip like that."

"It doesn't matter anymore."

"It does to me."

"I liked.... I like...." I already used the other word, why not yet again. "I love copulation day only when with you."

I wonder if she feels the same about me. I wish I dared ask her. I wonder if my son.... Is Hob hers and mine together? I've always hoped he was. She's made no gesture towards him. She hasn't even looked at him any more than any other boy. This would have been his first copulation day had the women not built their wall.

"Rest," she says. "We'll discuss later."

"Is it just us? Or are you saying the same thing to the enemy? They could win the war like that. It would be your fault."

"Stop thinking."

"What if no more boys on either side, ever?"

"What if?"

She gives me more of those leaves to chew. They're bitter. I was in too much pain to notice that the first time. I feel even sleepier right away.

I dream I'm the last of all the boys. Ever. I have to get somewhere in a hurry, but there's a wall so high I'll never get over it. Beside, my legs are not there at all. I'm nothing but a torso. Women watch me. Women, off across the valley floor as far as I can see and none will help. There's nothing to do but lie there and give the war cry.

I wake shouting and with Una holding me down. Hob is there, helping her. Other boys are in the doorway looking worried.

I've thrown the blanket and the pillow to the floor and now I seem to be trying to throw myself out of bed. Una has a long scratch across her cheek. I must have done that.

"Sorry. Sorry."

I'm still as if in a dream. I pull Una down against me. Hold her hard and then I reach out for Hob, too. My poor ugly boy. I ask the unaskable. "Tell me, is Hob mine and yours together?"

Hob looks shocked that I would ask such a thing, as well he should. Una pulls away and gets up. She answers as if she was one of the boys. "Colonel, sir, how can you, of all people, ask a thing like that." Then she throws my own words back at me. "This is how it's always been."

"Sorry. Sorry."

"Oh, for Heaven's sake stop being so *sorry*!"

She shoos the boys from the doorway but she lets Hob stay. Together they rearrange the bed. Together she and Hob make broth for me and food for themselves. Hob seems at home here. It's true, I'm sure. This is our son.

But I suppose all this yearning, all this wondering, is due to the leaves Una had me chew. It's not the real me. I'll not pay any attention to myself.

But there's something else. I didn't get a good look at my leg yet, but it feels like a serious wound. If I can't climb up to our stronghold, I'll not ever be able to go home. I shouldn't, even so, and though my career is in a shambles...I shouldn't let myself be lured into staying here as a copulator for the rest of my life. I can't think of anything more dishonorable. I should send Hob back to the citadel to report on what's happened and to get help. If he was found trying to escape, would Una let the women kill him?

I try to get Hob alone so I can whisper his orders to him. Only when Una goes out to the privy do I get the chance. "Get back to the citadel. Cross the wall tonight. There's no moon." I show him my map and where I think there are fewer women. I want to tell him to take care, but we don't ever say such things.

In the morning I tell Una to tell my leaders to come in to me. I'm in pain, in a sweat, my beard is itchy. I ask Una to clean me up. She treats me as a mother would. Back when my mother did it, I pulled away. I wouldn't let her get close to me. I especially wouldn't let her hug or kiss me. I wanted to be a soldier. I wanted nothing to do with mother things.

All the boys are looking scruffy. We take pride in our cleanliness, in shaving everyday, in our brush cuts, and our enemy is as spic and span as we are. I hope they don't launch an offensive today and see us so untidy.

I'm glad to see Hob isn't with them.

I find it hard to rouse myself to my usual humor. I say, "Pillows, nipples," but I'm too uncomfortable to play at being one of the boys.

I'd prefer to recuperate some, but the boys are restless already. I can't be thinking of myself. We'll storm the wall. I show them the map. I point out the less guarded spots. I grab Una. Both her wrists. "Men, we'll need a battering ram."

Wood isn't easy to get out here on the valley floor. This is a desert except along the streams, but every village has one tree in the center square that they've nurtured along. As here, baby's graves are always around it. In other villages, most are cottonwood, but this one is oak. It's so old I wouldn't be surprised if it hadn't been here since before the village. I think the village was built up around it later.

"Chop the tree. Ram the wall." I tell them. "Go back to the citadel. Don't wait around for me. Tell the generals never to come here again, neither for boys nor for copulation. Tell them I'm of no use to us anymore."

The women won't be able to shoot at the boys chopping it down. It's hidden from all parts of the wall.

When they hear the chopping, the women begin to ululate. Our boys stop chopping, but only for a moment. I hear them begin again with even more vigor.

Here beside me Una ululates, too. She struggles against me but I hang on.

"How could you? That's the tree of dead boys."

I let go.

"All the babies buried there are boys. Some are yours."

I can't let this new knowledge color my thinking. I have to think of the safety of my boys. "Let us go, then."

"Tell them to stop."

"Would you let us go for the sake of a tree?"

"We would."

I give the order.

The women move away from a whole section of the wall, they even provide their ladders. I tell the boys to go. There's no way they could carry me back and no way I could ever climb to the citadel again.

No sooner are the boys gone, even to the last tootle of the fifes, the last triumphant drum beat.... (We always march home as though victorious whether victorious or not.) Hearing them go, I can't help but groan, though not from pain this time) No sooner have the mothers come down from the wall, but that I hear, ululating again. Una stamps in to me.

"What now?"

"It's Hob. Your enemy.... *Your* enemy has dropped him off at the edge of your foothills."

I can see it on her face.

"He's dead."

"Of course he's dead. You are all as good as dead."

She blames me for Hob. "I blame myself."

"I hate you. I hate you all."

I don't believe we'll be seeing many boys anymore. I would warn us if I was able, I would be the spokesman, though I don't suppose I'll ever have the chance.

"What will the women do with me?"

"You were always kind. I'll not be any less to you."

What am I good for? What use am I but to stay here as the father of females? All those small, ugly, black haired girls.... I suppose all of them biting their lower lips until they bleed.

Sci Fiction, January, 2003

Coo People

We've lived hidden in your cities for longer than we can remember. Top floors, mostly. Word of mouth...*our* word of mouth, tells us we've been here since your cities began. How we've managed it is, we pretend we're you, dress like you, wear your kinds of hair-dos, when your eye glasses have little wings at the sides, ours do, too. We walk around looking at things that you'd look at, otherwise we'd be staring at your ceilings all the time. We thumb through your *Playboy* and *Cosmopolitan* whether we like them or not, we get the *TV Guide* and watch what you watch so we can talk about it with you, we jump and yell as much as you do at your baseball games, we read your best sellers, look at your art shows. It's all pretend. We've forgotten our own kind of art. We don't even dare think about it. We may have lost our art forever though it's better than yours. Or so we always tell each other. We used to have our own language, too. We say it was so full of asides and embellishments that it was of a beauty inconceivable to anyone but us.

Even your doctors can't tell we're us. Of course they wouldn't suspect anyway since they don't know we exist.

If you knew about us, we don't know what you'd do. You've never liked the different. Especially you don't like those people who are fairly close to exactly what you are yourselves. So—dull and drab...invisible is what we aspire to. How else live among you and get along as well as we do?

We only trust each other. We only dare tell each other about ourselves when we're old enough to handle the information. That's about ten years old. To us, all the wonderful things about ourselves are more interesting than sex. Unimportant, some would say, but wonderful anyway. "Dear child, you're entirely different from everybody else except us and you were born to dance."

Most of the time we know who we are. There's our springy walk, our singsong voices, our screechy laugh. And we're double jointed. If you can't bend your thumb down to touch your forearm, you're not one of us. (Even if you *can* do it, you may not be one of us, anyway.) And, though just a teeny tiny bit, we can fly. I shouldn't call it flying. It's more like lift. We can lift a little bit and if frightened or exhilarated we can, *maybe*, make it over a car—a small one. There's not much need for such a talent. It's hardly worth having. And when your life depends on never being noticed, it's a big bother because when we get excited, sometimes we have to hold each other down. And *always* we have to hold down our babies. Until they get their balance that is. By the time they can sit up, they can usually keep themselves down except when they're too happy. We sew little weights into their clothing. Otherwise you'd know that we were us. We take the weights out when the child has more control, though with some children....

We came to the cities in the first place—or so we always tell each other... (Oral history is all we have. It's too dangerous to write things down)...came because we wanted your city advantages: opera and ballet. *Especially* ballet. That little bit of lift makes us good dancers, though we have to make sure not to overdo it.

I'm just in the corps de ballet. It's never good for us to be soloists.

Nijinsky was one of us. He went mad because of having to keep himself secret without any time off. He should have had a vacation from dancing now and then, before it was too late, and gone back to one of our secret retreats to rest up from always being surrounded by *you* people. We need to go away every once in a while or we'll go crazy just as Nijinsky did.

I can't think what use that little bit of lift could be except as a help in ballet. (Though it's also good for magicians lifting beautiful women with no visible means of support. In our case there actually is no means of support.) As far as I know, it's just a bother trying to hide it and trying not to do it when we're excited and happy. It's always safer for us to be sad.

But now I go coo, coo, cooing as if a mourning dove. I try to stop, because who else but one of us would do such a thing? But I'm too happy. If I didn't coo I'd lift by mistake. I sing, coo, as if a song of spring even though we've already had the first snow. You don't look as crazy if you coo in springtime. I hope people do think I'm crazy so as not to think I might be one of us, and then go on to realize that we exist.

(I think we coo because our mouths like the shape of it.)

But oh, coooo, I've met a man. Unfortunately he's one of you. He doesn't look like us. He's dark and broad and muscled. I can't imagine him having any lift at all.

He has a broken nose. I like it. He also has a bald head with a fringe of black hair around the edges. I like that, too.

First thing this man said to me was, "I know who *you* are."

I got scared. I thought he meant he knew about *us*, but he just meant he knew my name. I don't know how. Perhaps he's been to the ballet, though he doesn't seem the type.

We talked for a minute. He just moved in to my building. He lives on the first floor. We couldn't stand living that far down. I felt so good that he'd stopped to talk to me, I heard very little of what he said. I just looked into those glittery black eyes. I wish I'd listened. I wonder what it was he was telling me.

I know a few things about him from listening to people in the lobby. He's a fireman, so he does all sorts of things it would be better for *us* to be doing considering they often involve heights, but we're not strong enough for that. We have a lot of endurance, but we're willowy. They say he loves the risks but we can't take any in case we reveal ourselves. They don't think he rescues because he cares about people, he just wants to take another risk. He likes storms and fires and earthquakes—all sorts of catastrophes. And he rescues even when he's on vacation. He just can't stop. It's his passion.

We must, as is easy to see, only mate with our own kind, otherwise we might lose our double joints and our only talent. Whatever children *this* man might have would be the opposite of us: Wild and free and into everything and much too big.

I've tried not to fall in love with your kind, and, up until a few days ago, it was easy not to, even though there are many men among you that could be said to be my type; but I never cared anything about them.

Right after I first met him, I saw him at our apartment roof party. He didn't dance, but he was swaying a little bit. You'd not think a man of his nature would sway. We looked at each other. He might have winked. (He doesn't seem the type to wink either.) Perhaps he was looking at somebody behind me. I looked to see who was there, but even though she was beautiful, I'm not sure which of us he was looking at. I'm not so bad looking myself—if you like your blond hair lank.

I sneaked up behind him and eavesdropped. I heard him tell yet another beautiful girl that he was going off to the mountains, to Manchester Peak to join their search and rescue team for a vacation. I'll go to that mountain, too. I'm going to see if he'll rescue me. Of course he might be out rescuing somebody else at the time I'm in trouble, but I'll take that chance.

He doesn't like the city. I suppose he stays because of all the fires and rescues, though of course there's plenty of rescuing to be done in the mountains. Maybe he doesn't like rescuing out there because those mountain accidents are so often from carelessness or stupidity. (Exactly what I'm going to be: stupid.)

So I'm off to climb Manchester Peak where that man is vacationing. I mean I'll *start* to. I hope I don't have to go too far. I hope a snow storm comes. I'll listen to the weather report and if it says not to go I'll go.

Since it's Fall, it's a risky stupid season for going as high as I plan to go, but it has to be a real rescue. He'd know if it was phony. Up in that altitude I suppose I'll be able to lift all the more. Or will it be the opposite because the air is thinner?

I hope I don't inadvertently skim over snow drifts to make things easy for myself when I sink in up to my crotch. I hope I remember (even when I get tired) to at least have my toes dragging in the snow so I look right in case somebody sees.

I have to get the paraphernalia for it. Carabiners, ropes, pitons, ax, and such. A lot to carry but I have to look as if I'm making a serious (if stupid) try. (I doubt if I can lift with all this stuff, but I can drop a lot of those things along the way so as to leave a good trail.)

Of course I might get rescued by some entirely different person. Most likely some old hermit who lives in the mountains all year long in a smelly hovel and never says a word to anybody. There are still a few of those around.

I wonder if it would be a good thing to sprain my ankle? And when would be the best time for it, early on or farther up? (We never sprain our ankles. Our lifting is a reflex. Hard not to do it when we're about to fall down. I wouldn't know how, but I suppose I could figure out some way—slip my foot between two rocks and then.... I don't even want to think about it.)

So here I am exactly where I want to be, out in the middle of nowhere cooing in a whisper, one coo to each breath, and looking up at the snowy tops of things: snowy trees, snowy mountains.... We like white best of all. It's so airy. Of course we like blue, too. It's so sky.

I begin dropping things right away, carabiners first. After those the pitons. (I hope the snow doesn't cover everything up.) Then I let go the ax. I may be sorry but, if I drop such an important thing, that's a sure sign I'm in trouble. Leaving that takes as much courage as spraining my ankle would, but I laugh out loud anyway because of where I am and what's (maybe) going to happen.

It isn't until I'm stuck, having slipped... *let* myself slip (*we* don't slip) onto an icy ledge and can't go up or down, *nor* sideways (exactly what I wanted to have happen) that I think: What if he watches me even right this very minute to see, now that I'm in real trouble, what I'm going to do next? I can't wait to see what I'll do next myself. Actually I don't do anything. I wait.

But.... Oh for Heaven's sake! Here's one of those wizened old, hermit kind of men I was thinking about before. He's above me, leaning towards me with an unraveling old rope, unraveling black knit cap, unraveling black sweater, whiskey voice, that hardly sounds out. I can't hear him. I have to guess what he's saying. It's most likely, "Grab the rope."

I almost tell him to go away. I'll not let anyone come between me and what's supposed to happen. But I think twice and I do grab the rope. At least I won't have to test how I lift in this altitude. I won't have to find out whether, if I jump off a cliff this high, I'll be able to land softly.

At the top I reach and grab his hands—or rather his unraveling mittens. I stare at him. He's a willowy man. I'm wondering if he's one of us. I'm wondering if he's wondering if I'm one of us, too.

I see he has my carabiners hanging all over him, and, at his belt, clipped on by one of my carabiners, he's got my brand new ax.

The mind's eye sees more clearly than the eye. The mind's eye ought to trust itself. Understanding comes later—*usually* does, and always in the middle of the night.

And it *is* the middle of the night, though so far I've not understood anything. I'm bedded down in an alcove, covered with half a dozen old army blankets, listening to the old man snore. This is probably where he sleeps but he's on the floor across the room by the dry sink.

He only has this one room and it's full of art—if you can call this art. I don't know what art is any more than I know who I and we are, but the room is full of complicated things with curlicues and convolutions, twists and whorls. You can hardly tell where one begins and another ends. Or maybe they are all just one sculpture. There's hardly room to walk around. It's not like your art at all. It's stormy looking and lumpy.... There's a hint of wings. (Hermes was one of us, wings on his feet where they ought to be.)

The old man told me this is how he spends the time when it storms. I asked him, but how did he happen to be out so as to rescue me?

"I fear my dog has met with coyotes and either been killed by them or run off with them. Most likely killed. I was looking for him."

He has a funny accent. I can't place it. He actually rolls his r's and he asked me if I'd "et." You don't suppose.... Could it be that that's from speaking our old lost language?

I wish I knew more about what our art used to be like. Who would dare carve things like this but way out in the woods? (Hack out is a better way to say it.) There's nothing shocking to it as to sex, but it looks shocking anyway. Maybe there is sexuality to it and I just don't know enough to see it. Or maybe it's the power of it that shocks me. Or maybe just that so it's different.

Nothing is worse than different. We're all taught that first thing. All of you are also taught that, too. And nothing is more the same than ballet. Full of rules of how it used to be done so we can do it exactly that way now. Even our bows are choreographed according to how they used to do it. It's said, "Good ballet is never blunted by verisimilitude." There's no verisimilitude to blunt this man's art either.

But I don't want to think about it. I turn away and try to sleep though all these sculptured things looming over me are scary.

And I *do* have a midnight revelation. I wake up suddenly when I finally realize that that fireman probably isn't in search of me at all, but of *us*! All of us, maybe including this old man? Maybe he's been sent out by the government? I can't let him hear this old man's accent. I can't let him see this...art.

Even so, perhaps when he winked, it really *was* for me.

In the morning I look out the door first thing—at the sun and the shiny snow and see somebody wearing camouflage. A broad man, looking at the shack through field glasses.

I start to coo again. I can't help it. The old man gives me a look I can't read. Well, we hardly ever talk about being us unless we're at one of our retreats and even then we don't talk much about it. We just give each other raised eyebrows and such. I stop my cooing right away and switch to an entrechat starting from fifth position. I *have* to do something. If he's us he'll know I'm us, too, and if he's not us, he'll think I'm crazy.

Then I see the dog, limping up to that camouflaged man. You can't fool a dog no matter how much you look like a tree in fall foliage. Besides, it's a little late for all this brown and yellow. The dog has a bloody stump where his tail used to be. No doubt coyotes, like the old man said. The bald man squats down and pets him, examines his wound. Now *isn't* that a nice thing for a big bald man with a broken nose to do!

He sees me, there by the door. He pulls off his hat by one of its earmuffs, letting the sun shine out on his bald head which makes him even more lovable. So not only dark and dangerous, but more polite than need be under the circumstances. He could have just waved.

I don't want him meeting this old man and seeing his odd art, but here he comes, crunch, crunching across the snow. I give another coo. The old man humphs a humph as if: I knew she was us, or, on the other hand: I knew she was crazy.

(Come on in. Rescue me. Take me back with you. I'll keep my voice on an even keel. I'll not sing-song. I'll not smile too much. I'll never coo in public. I'll pull my long limp hair back tight and weave it into a bun so it doesn't fly around by itself. I'll not screech when I laugh.)

"Coo.... I mean come. Come on in."

"You shouldn't be up here. There's another storm on the way. There isn't much time."

I do love how his voice rattles out from someplace way down deep in his chest.

I lift. I actually lift out of pure joy. I stoop to greet the dog at the same time as I lift in order to hide it. It must have looked kind of funny, down and up at the same time.

That bald man has to lean over to get through the door, and there's hardly room inside for somebody as big as he is. Even so he wanders back and forth, peering at the "art" close up, touching things. The old man stays in a corner and mutters to himself. He had just asked me if I wanted breakfast but now it's clear he's not going serve either of us anything.

After looking around the bald man takes out his first aid kit and treats the dog's wounds.

After that, the man and I start back down, first through trees, but then the mountain opens out to wide views, all sky with nothing in the way of it. We like the "big sky." Hard to explain but I like this man for exactly the same reason.

I want the storm to catch us. I want us holed up behind a rock or under a tree so he'll get to know me. I lag behind and he keeps saying, "For Christ's sake hurry up. Look at the clouds rolling in." To slow us down even more, I turn and look and right behind me there's two perfect stones next to each other, and just room enough for a foot between them. I do it. I step in and twist.

It hurts more than I expected. I did a good job of it, my pants are ripped and my boot is all scratched up, but then I get to have his big warm hands all over my leg and foot. He has everything he needs in his first aid kit. He tapes up my ankle in a sort of figure eight, and as stiff as a cast so it hardly hurts at all. (Luckily we never get the misshapen feet all ballet dancers have.) After that I get to have his big warm arms around me as he carries me to a better place than on this slippery snowy slope.

That's what he *says* he's doing, but he's got ideas, too, just as much as I have. We don't make it off the slope. As he carries me, he slips. On purpose. I *think* on purpose. We slide down a long snowy bank and would have gone over the edge of the cliff if I hadn't stopped us with a hard lift. He's so heavy. I don't know how I had the strength for it, but here we are, stopped right at the edge.

He says, "You're one of those others."

"What others?"

"Don't try to fool me."

So he does know. I say, "I saved you," to distract him.

He twists my arm, but not too hard. Just a little warning. He could have broken it with no trouble at all. For sure he likes me.

We ought to move back. I'm too used up to lift again for a while and we might go all the way over and *then* what? I try to squinch myself back, but he holds me. I love his hug, but I'm scared.

"I'm scared."

"Tell me who you and that old man are and what you're up to way out here in the middle of no where? What's he making? What's all that stuff?"

Nobody ever tells me anything. They never did. From an early age...as soon as they told me I wasn't them but us, I wanted to understand us and (especially) me. Nobody would answer anything I asked.

Maybe those things all over the place in there aren't art after all.

"I don't know who we are. They told me we were us, but they never said what being us was. They've kept us secret even from ourselves. All I know is there's this one thing—this lift. And besides, I can't do it again until I rest up. We have to move back."

Finally he lets us. It's so steep and slippery I have to crawl. He does too. He pulls me along. At the top we crawl sideways to get over on safer ground, completely away from the slope. I have the thought to push him over the cliff. That's what I should do, knowing that he knows, but I don't do it.

Safe...a little bit safer, we catch our breath and I get to have his arms around me again. I'm glad I didn't push him over.

We're both shaky. We hug and tremble. With me the trembling isn't from having just escaped and having just used up all my lift, it's that my face is pushed (I pushed it there on purpose) right into his thick neck. His neck comes straight down from his jaw to beyond his collarbone. He looks like the kind of man who'd say, "Try to choke me," or, "Hit me in the stomach." He'd say, "I'll bet you a hundred dollars you can't hurt me." *I'd* bet him a hundred dollars he's said both those more than once.

There's a sudden darkening as if already dusk. There's wind and snow. Just like that, the storm starts. He carries me yet farther back, and pulls me under a tree whose branches come to the ground on all sides. We sit, hugging. I'm still breathing into his neck. He's as shaky as I am. Now why would a man who loves storms and all sorts of dangerous things be trembling so?

Now his hand is on my breast. He's taken off his cloves and reached inside my parka. His hands are large and shapely. I noticed that before. I've always liked good hands. And now those very hands are all over me.

"Actually you're not so different from everybody else."

I'm worried because our breasts are smaller. I say, "But I am different." I'm thinking mostly of my breasts.

"I don't care."

Maybe breasts don't matter that much. Maybe he really doesn't care.

Green pine boughs surround us and beyond them snow comes down. A real white out. The whole world has turned my favorite color. We're cozy in here under the branches. His knees are threaded in with mine. Our feet, in our big boots, are clumped up together. I take off my gloves and put my hand on the sweaty back of his neck, under his scarf. He's damp…radiating….

We kiss. How warm his lips are even now in this snow storm. How soft… soft generous lips. (I noticed them before, too.) You wouldn't think they'd be so soft with such a hard muscled man.

He needs a shave, but I don't mind getting scratched up. And I only have a few twinges from my ankle.

"Coo," I say, a long low, "Coooooooo."

The storm is making a racket, branches scratch against each other, the wind whistles, but I couldn't be warmer. I couldn't be more enfolded, engulfed, enclosed…. While I coo and squeak, he grunts and growls and bellows.

Now how did this happen?

We sleep. His fuzzy chest is still bare and my ear is still right on top of his heartbeat. It sounds out louder than the wind whistling around us.

At first he's nicely relaxed, but pretty soon he snores and snorts and jerks. The storm does the opposite, it quiets and soon a full moon shines out. It's even fairly bright in here under our branches. I can even see how long his eyelashes are. I noticed them before. I noticed everything before.

I should be thinking about how to get rid of somebody who knows for sure about us, but how can you do that to a person when you've heard his heart beating under your ear all night long?

We can't marry one of you. That's unthinkable though I've thought of nothing else. There have been times when I pretended I'm one of you—what I've wished for since I met this man. When I thought of being you, I flitted down the sidewalk, skipping myself over chewing gum and spit in a way that could only be us. But we're a dying breed. If we don't take care we might be gone altogether.

Those who aren't careful (those who risk, loving the wrong person) meet with an accident. I mean from our own kind. There's one of us in charge of that. We don't know who. Maybe it's the old man who rescued me. But out here I suppose I'm the one in charge. I should get rid of this man before that old man comes along and kills us both. Or one of us, depending on whether he's us or you.

We wake at first light. We lie in each other's arms, listening to snow melting sounds. That is, I do, but he's been thinking. "What about…." he says, and grunts. I'm hoping he's going to say, What about the two of us? but he says, "What about all that…stuff? I could tell the pieces will fit together into something huge. Could be a weapon or a whole bunch of them."

"It's art."

(Isn't it? Does it really fit together into one big dangerous thing? And even if it does, why isn't that art? Art is more important than some device or other for the end of your kind…or my kind.)

"It's *art*!"

But he's not convinced.

"If you care for me at all, you'll take my word for it. It's art."

"It's not even beautiful."

"Nowadays nobody is so…." (I almost say, unsophisticated, but I stop myself in time. He already feels unartistic compared to me.) "Nowadays nobody thinks art has to be beautiful. It's to make us think. Besides, beauty is learned."

"Maybe."

But I want to make him feel good.

"Rescuing is more important than any art could be though art takes just as much courage."

"I'd like to see what those things look like put together."

"Even if it all fits together why can't it still be art?"

I *want* it to be art. Your kind or our kind, I don't care which. We need more art and fewer weapons. Though, on the other hand, maybe we have too much art. It's hard to keep track of. Hard to sort through. I'd prefer less. But I would never say that in front of him.

He kisses me. A long wet kiss. For no reason at all.

I say, "Marry me."

He looks at me—those glittery black eyes—just looks. He could at least have said, Maybe.

We come out from under our tree into a world of shine…white, with blue sky above. I'm *so* happy. (Except that he didn't say, Maybe.)

The man looks all around and then looks all around again with his field glasses. He drops on one knee, ducks partly behind our tree, hands the field glasses to me and points. There, behind us, is the old man. He's sitting on a boulder, looking all around with *his* field glasses. He has a rifle across his knees. And here comes his dog, right to us. Wagging what's left of his bandaged tail.

If only I had a clue…one little real clue as to which this old man is, us or you, and whether all that stuff is art or a weapon. If I should yell to that old man, Don't shoot. I'm on your side, I want to know which side that would be.

My man (I'm thinking, my man, though I'm not sure if he is or isn't) says, "Stay here," but I'm not going to.

He starts up the slope, walking boldly in spite of the rifle across the old man's knees. My man is fearless. I knew that before.

I scramble along behind him, lifting a little so as to save my sprained ankle.

The old man, looking right at us, yells, "Stop or I'll shoot." I don't know if he means he'll shoot me, clumping along behind, or my man. Neither of us stop.

My man doesn't have any weapons. He just has his first aid kit and ropes and things for rescuing people. He wouldn't care if you were us or you people or a skunk or a mountain lion, he'd rescue you anyway.

"Grab him," the old man yells. "Push him. Let him fall over the cliff before he destroys my work."

Now I know which he is.

No I don't, I just know which of us he wants to get rid of and why.

I yell out, too. "He rescues people! That's all he does. He'll rescue you if you need rescuing."

"Not me. Never one like me."

"He has no weapons."

The cold or snow or something (maybe it's the bowl shape of the mountain side) gives our words an odd hollow sharpness—an extra clarity. Words as if in silhouette. Even my big man's gravely voice sounds out with purity.

I see my man's breath as he shouts up the slope. "Don't shoot. We'll talk."

"Push him. He wants to destroy my work."

He's right to worry. You always... *always* do that: throw art off cliffs, roll it into the sea, burn it, knock it to pieces, chop it up, smash it.... You people cut off marble penises and grind them up for aphrodisiacs. You people threw the Mayan statues down their long stairways. You scraped off the faces of kings you didn't like. You burned codexes. Makes me think it must be art for sure if somebody wants to destroy it.

Though on the other hand you people invented all these arts in the first place. We didn't even invent ballet.

By lifting harder, I'm now up beside my man. He's still clumping through the snow, but if he could stride, that's what he'd be doing.

The man shoots, but my man doesn't go down. Just keeps slogging along. I'm the one yelling, "Don't shoot," and everything else I can think to yell. "Stop. Please. Don't."

The old man stands up and starts down towards my man. My man walks up to him and then right on past, not paying him any attention. I think to attack the old man myself but I don't want to leave my man. I get between the old man and my man. The old man points the gun at me but doesn't shoot, just follows. So here we go, all of us and the dog, back to the shack. And there, just inside the door, my man squats down and takes off his gloves and takes out... is that his little camp stove? And then I see he's set the place on fire. But he's a fireman!

I say, "This is burning books. Isn't this like burning books?"

"It isn't art!"

He steps away and pulls me with him, to a safe distance. We watch. The old man, too. Everything goes up, poof, like an old Christmas tree. There's no way to stop it. My man sure knows how to set a good fire.

But *now*...just like that, my man flops down and I see blood. It's dripping... more than just dripping, out his sleeves. It's all over his hands. The dog licks at them.

I lean over him. I can't believe it. I lean close. I don't see that mist of breath. I don't feel it on my cheek. My big rescuing man is dead. How can this be? And his very last words were, "It isn't art."

I hear my "Nooooo!" echoing all over this snowy bowl. I turn. I don't know how I find the strength but I grab that that wiry old man, and push and push and drag—him and his rifle—all the way down the slope and over the cliff. He yells the whole way, but I couldn't tell you what or even in what language. I can't hear or understand anything. I don't care which he is, us or them.

After, I sit with my feet hanging over the edge. Sit and sit and sit, not thinking. Pretty soon I go back to sit by my man. I guess I can say he's mine now. He can't say he isn't. By now the fire has burned itself out some and the sun has gone behind the mountain. I guess I sat there, on the edge of everything, longer than I thought. I'll have to spend the night here just sitting, but it's what I want to do.

I push the dog away. I take off my glove and hold my man's cold, bare hand. How could such a warm furnace? How could?

At first I just sit and don't think at all and then I do, and hope. If what I hope is true, it's already too late to keep our purity untainted by you people. But I don't know what to think anymore. I've been *so* careful. I've even danced cautiously, all the time thinking: Stay down. I'm tired of it.

I'll leave the ballet. Take the tailless dog and leave. I'll join the circus. It's good for us to be in the circus, we're so much safer there. If we lift by mistake, everybody thinks it's some trick or other. I'll hang on by my teeth and get raised to the top of the tent. All of us can do that, no trouble at all. Tightrope walker might be nice. I could have a pink parasol.

Except, if I'm pregnant. It'll be hard when I have to lift for two.

I can't be sure for a while yet, but I want a little black haired boy with big feet and hands and long eyelashes. I don't care whether he can lift or not. When he climbs a tree and falls, he'll come straight down like everybody else does.

It never would have worked. I don't think he liked art much, anyway.

"Form follows function? Beauty? Truth?" Those are old notions. Besides, *we've* never lived with much truth. We can't. We don't even try. But there's all kinds of reasons for art.

His very last words were, "It isn't art." He never said, I love you. He never even said, Maybe. I wonder what he meant by not saying, Maybe?

Polyphony #2, May 2003

Repository

Lots of reasons to be glad and stay that way. Food now. Things to do. A place to sleep. A path. A place at the top of a hill to sit and look.

This is after.

Something has happened, but we don't remember what. Should we try to find out or leave well enough alone? This may be the enemy's hilltop we sit on admiring the enemy's view. Or perhaps this hilltop used to be ours. Who is the enemy? And more important who are we? Willing captives, that's for sure. Willing slaves with nothing much to do.

Many of us have wounds more or less healed. I myself have scars and something wrong with my leg. It's not so easy for me to climb to the view we love.

My only memory from before is a feeling of letting go. I remember thinking: I'm dying, but that's all right. I remember thinking of things I'd left undone but I didn't care. I thought, even right at the time: I never knew dying would be like this—serene, not sad, as if it didn't matter.

I wonder that I remember some things so clearly while others seem gone or just beyond my reach no matter how hard I try to bring them back?

Waking up here, at first I thought it was where dead warriors go for their reward, but why would we come here with our limps, our lost eyes, lost arms and legs, our burns? There's not a man among us who isn't wounded in some way. Perhaps, instead, it's a rehabilitation center. Except nobody is being rehabilitated.

Could we find a better way to live than this even if we had planned it ourselves? Nature all around us, soft things to wear, heat at night, pools here and there, sun shades, an arbor?

Some of us are making the barracks more homey—putting up partitions as if this is what life will be from now on. As if this is our future so enjoy it. But can one be joyful without a past? Or can one live with nothing of any importance to prepare for?

I seem to be the only one wondering who we are and why we're here and should we stay without objecting? Nobody else does. This is their heaven. Now and then there's even things to shoot at. That makes them happy though they only have slingshots they make themselves. They shoot lizards (try to), beetles, butterflies. They aim at humming birds. They shoot each other...shoulder and buttocks. I hope nobody gets an eye put out.

Most of us here are younger than I am. I think I might have done things like that myself at one time. If I did, it no longer interests me.

Having reached this stage (all of us grown up) we must have been looked after until we reached it. Somebody must have told us not to run holding knives, not to talk with our mouths full, not to take more than our share, not to climb too high in whatever tree there might be, and so forth. We can add and subtract. We can spell. And somebody must have said, "We don't eat that," "We don't do that," "We don't say that word," else why would I feel guilty every time I say those words myself and notice when the others say them? And somebody must have taught me the names of these flowers, lupine, larkspur, paintbrush, aster, wild iris...and to love them. Or does one love these as naturally as one loves the stars?

Into our space comes someone worse off than any of us. A bloody body—alive but barely, flopped here, on the edge of our garden.

Till now nothing new has happened since we came, but we don't know how long we've been here. By the time we started marking off days we'd already been here quite some time.

The others want to throw it out...burn it...get rid of it.... They distrust it even though it's too badly hurt to be a threat. What if it's the enemy? "Look," we're saying, "Its not wearing yellow and its head isn't shaved."

Everybody wants to drop it off The Edge. We don't know who we are but at least we know we're not our enemies.

I tell the others I'll take it into my cubby and take care of it. Even if it is the enemy I may learn something. They can have it back later.

I carry It to my cubby. I let It have the cot while I sleep on the floor. I seem to know how to care for It, as if I'd once worked at caring for people. I'm wondering what I used to be. The others defer to me in many ways. I try to remember what I used to know.

Some of our skills come back. Or, rather, appear. Some wish there were musical instruments so we could check ourselves out on them. Some play on sticks or rub stones together. Someone made a box sort of thing and beats on that. Some with better legs than mine jump around to the tapping of the others.

When they do this they watch me to see if I'm watching. They like it when I smile. They need my nod. They won't have it much longer. It told me things. I keep what It says secret. There's no need for all of us to feel this yearning.

It sings me songs I already know but had forgotten. It says we used to have names and that we let our hair and beards grow.

It said, Go up, but It lost toes to frostbite. I had to cut them off myself.

It said there were doctors. It thinks I must be one.

I asked It to come with me. "Lead the way," I said. "I'll carry you."

"I'd not make it."

"We'll kill you. We don't like the different. We take you as a spy. We'd have thrown you over The Edge by now if I didn't guard you."

"I've been in pain a long time."

"Dead, I'll let the rest of us have you. We'll throw you over."

It said it wouldn't mind.

It tells me we once had wives. It says It had one of its own. It tells me we all had mothers. They were the ones who taught us those first things about not running with knives, and to keep ourselves and out language clean.

I have thought to go in search of mine, but how long do mothers last? And how old am I? I study my face in one of the ponds. I see gray at my temples.

Or should I go in search of my wife? Or a wife?

First It seems to rally. I think It will live. And then It doesn't. It sighs and then It moans. It breathes as if climbing our hill. Now and then It says, Maaaaa. That's It's last word.

I let us have It. We throw It over The Edge.

They keep busy fixing up their cubbies.... They're building another arbor. Lumber appears. Every now and then new shoes and hats appear.

They took down the hummingbird's nest. It had two eggs in it. It was made of cottonwood cotton and spider web strands. They tore it apart to make sure that was all it was made of, and that was all.

They netted the goldfish. They dared each other to swallow them and they did swallow them. They dared each other to swallow spring peepers and they swallowed those, too. It has escalated to beetles and stink bugs. Spiders.

This is definitely the place where old warriors go. As long as there's something to shoot at, things to dare, it's our heaven. And as long as there's something to make beer out of...or they'll ferment bread. I don't think I can say that I haven't done many of these things myself. I remember odd horrible tastes. When I drink their beer I remember being drunk before.

I'm ready. I have Its bloody coat. I have Its bloody mittens. I have a staff. It said I'd need one. I make a shirt into a backpack. I fill it with rations and tie it on. I tape up my bad knee.

We will try to stop me. If I really am a doctor we will need for me to stay. I wonder if we will follow me and try to bring me back. I'll leave in the middle of the night. We always sleep like soldiers after a long march.

Thank goodness all we have are slingshots, but a few of us have rediscovered the twirling kind. We can do damage. But we won't be expecting anything out of the ordinary. We'll not wake up to catch me leaving.

It's always foggy around the hills at our back. It said to walk through with a scarf around my mouth. It said it would be three hundred steps before I'd leave the fog behind. "Keep going up.

"After the fog, trees will begin. There'll be cliffs. Keep on. For the first night and first day and next night, don't stop. Then hide yourself under rocks and rest. After that, go on at night. Hide in the daytime. At the top of the third ridge you'll come to a path. Follow it to the left. There's a cottage. A woman lives there. Her name is Lark. Mine is Ray. Tell her about me."

I wish I could remember my name so I could tell her who I am.

I sneak away and hobble up through fog. As I enter it a horn goes off and keeps on sounding. Loud. It had not told me about this so I wonder about all the rest It said. I hear things scuffling near me. Every now and then I hear something roar. Once I think I see a shapeless shape rear up, darker against the fog. I see the gleam of teeth. I think, This must be what happened to It before it was thrown down to us. I keep on but I wonder if perhaps It wanted me to be found out, captured, and end up as It did, first torn and bloody and then thrown over The Edge. I seemed to be important to us so this may be a way of getting rid of me.

When I come out from the fog, the horn stops. And it's dawn. When I look back to our Heaven, all I see is cloud, but way beyond it there are rows of white topped peaks. You can't see The Edge at all. Ahead of me are closer hills that I must climb. My bad knee has started to give way at every third or fourth step but I don't fall.

I remember trees like these. Pine cones. I remember squawking jays. I remember long, coach whip snakes that climbed the trees. As I remember that, the thought of a garden comes to me. There's a back door and I'm sitting on the steps and there's the snake, and then, out of nowhere, I know my name.

I yearn to sit and watch dawn rising behind me over our fog, but I do as It said. I don't stop. I eat as I climb. With my bad knee, I know if I stopped I'd have to warm the stiffness up all over again.

When I finally reach the ridge with the path along the top I'm so tired I can't remember if I'm supposed to turn right or left. I can't remember how many days or nights I've hobbled. I drop where I am, in plain sight. My yellow suit and It's bloody jacket must be brilliant against the snow even though I brushed them with dirt the first morning.

Later I half wake and crawl to a more sheltered spot. When I wake indeed, I've forgotten my name again. I should have written it...scratched it on bark or a pebble. If it comes to me again, I will.

I'm to turn left. Now that I'm more rested, I do remember.

I'm really limping now—shuffling. It never told me how far it was to Lark's cottage. It talked of walking nights but it didn't say how many. It didn't tell me if it was taking my limp into consideration. It said, "Keep to the ridge, but when the path dips down, stay on the path."

I wait a bit to see if it's dawn or dusk. When I see it's dusk I start out.

My leg is worse than it ever was since I first came to the Repository. I don't know how much farther I can go. Thank goodness for my staff. If I stop and rest too long, my food will run out. Should I keep on going even if I can only crawl? At least there's moonlight.

Later…I've no idea how much later, I give up. My food is gone and has been for some time. In the beginning, I strode off thinking I was strong in spite of my limp. Perhaps I'm older than I thought. Or our life is too soft and easy back in that Heaven.

I think to flop myself down but I'm not paying attention anymore. As I give up, I fall off the ridge. I slide on my back along a steep slope, gravel coming down with me. How could It have thought I'd be able to keep my footing in the moonlight of only half a moon?

Part way down I slow. I try to stop myself but then I see a light. I deliberately let myself slide farther. If I couldn't slide I'd not make it. Then I'm down and landed in a creek. At least the cold jars me so I rouse enough to pull myself out of it. I find I'm in the middle of a road. Small. Dusty. Just one lane. I lie there. The light is not far, maybe a hundred yards, but I can't make it. I can't make any distance at all. I curl up, cold and wet. I don't dare call out. Besides, who would hear me with the sound of the creek? I sleep or pass out.

In the morning they come. Several men in granite colored suits on their way to someplace else. Two carry me back to the cottage where the light was the night before. They plop me in a chair in front of a desk. I fall out of it but they prop me up again. Someone says, "Welcome to headquarters company."

A woman.

I remember women. This one is thin, but those are breasts. I remember breasts, large and small. I remember other things, things that make my penis twitch. She has tan hair cut short but I remember long hair, too, long enough so it got in my face…in my mouth. My name is on the tip of my tongue.

"Welcome, welcome. You've come from Ray."

"Ray is dead."

"News of Colonel Ray will be sent from command center to command center."

"You are Lark?" With a name like that I hadn't thought she'd be so thin and wrinkled and weathered. All this time, without realizing it till now, I'd kept her in mind as young with brown wavy hair, a wide countrified face, and serious brown eyes. I thought she lived alone. I thought she was the one who would rescue me.

"We've been waiting for you. Ray volunteered to bring one back if he could find one, or die in the attempt."

I occurs to me suddenly that, for all our friendliness, our whispering midnight talks, our songs, I never knew which side Ray was on—whether he was one of ours or one of theirs.

"Sorry, I can't introduce myself. My name is on the tip of my tongue. I dreamt that I remembered it but when I woke it was gone again."

"What comes back might be the name of your best friend or even your worst enemy. If you need a name I'll give you one later, for now you're doctor number 12. Go wash yourself, and eat and rest. This boy will help you."

She rings and here's a boy. He can't be more than ten or twelve. He's dressed in a granite colored suit as the men were. He leads me through a wide door and into the mountain. The house is just the front for a complex of caves.

First I ask him his name, but he says names don't matter. He says they call him by his age. "Ten and a half," he says.

If I knew my age I could have a name, too. Forty-three? Forty-four? I look that old. I tell him to call me Forty-four. He ducks his head, but I see his secret smile.

Then I ask him who we're fighting and why?

He says, "It's us against them. That's how it always is."

"But who?"

"We call them Jack Asses. Mostly just Asses. Sometimes Mud Rats. Sometimes Ploops. They're stupid."

I'm wondering if they really are. I'm wondering if I used to be a Ploop, but I'm too tired to think about it or even care right now. And I'm too tired to eat or wash. I drink some milk and fall into a bunk still dressed as I am, still muddy. I don't even have the energy to pull off my wet boots though I know I should.

Later, cleaned up and rested and dressed in one of those granite colored suits, the boy takes me back to Lark. I ask her the same questions I asked the boy. She answers as though she doesn't know either though she pretends she does. I don't think she cares. She says it's no longer a problem of the right side or the wrong side. It's gone beyond that. Now it's a matter of kill or be killed. Loot or be looted. Conquer or be conquered. There's nothing else to do.

Lark recruits. Lark plans. Lark has the maps and charts. She has a radio but she mustn't use it. She says, "We're sending you in. You know mountains, you know cold, you know snowshoes, you know weapons, and you know your craft. You will stay just behind the lines and tend the wounded."

"If I help I want to know what I'm dying for."

"You will serve," she says.

I tell her I will not.

Next I know I'm walking down that dirt road with others, all of us dressed as chunks of granite, some darker granite and some lighter. Ten-and-a-half is with me, helping to carry the medical supplies.

Perhaps she's right, nothing to do but be on the side you're on at any given time.

Besides, it's a job I like. It's worthwhile whichever side this is. The men look up to me. I'm older. When I tell them, "You'll be all right," they believe me and die encouraged—looking forward to home. These men are younger than those back with me in the Heaven. I'm wondering, will they go there if wounded? Their memories half gone? Knowing only that they belong together? That, at least they are not their own enemies—though was even that true?

We always cared so much about being us and not them but I am no longer us, though I must once have thought I was.

Lately, I have, on occasion dreamt my name is Wesley. I remember…I seem to remember being called Wes. I wish I had more time to stop and think about it but there's hardly time even to eat and we sleep only a few hours whenever there's a moment's respite. Poor Ten and a Half. But he works with a will. Sometimes he falls asleep on his feet—just drops where he is. I carry him to the nearest cot though lately there haven't been any extra cots. Lately I've put him in my own bed. I don't have much use for it.

There's one other doctor here and two male nurses. Our tents are set up between two rocky outcroppings so we're sheltered from the worst.

Yesterday a man came in wounded in the leg by mistake by his buddy. I hear they're daring each other into no man's land to taunt the enemy. Today I nurse a man who'd been burned by his friends in what was supposed to be a joke, but they misjudged the power of the charge.

I have to leave him and the other wounded. The battle escalates. I move forward to be with us even though us may not have much to do with me.

I tell Ten-and-a-Half to stay behind and help out here, but when I look back I see he follows. In a way I'm glad. I need him, but I worry. He's a good boy and deserves to have a little more of his life. Or one day he should be sent to medical school. He'll make a good and caring doctor. I must remember to speak to Lark about it.

I limp, I've lost a hand, an eye, but lots of reasons to be glad. Things to do. Food. A path. A pond. A hill to climb.

This is after.

Something has happened.

I remember thinking: I'm dying, but that's all right. Something important has been left unsaid, but I didn't care. I was thinking, even right at the time: I never knew dying would be so serene.

Waking up here, at first I thought it was where dead warriors go for their reward but why would we come with all our mutilations? Perhaps it's a rehabilitation center.

There's a badly burned blind boy in the cubby next to mine. He and I wonder together how old he is. I make him a cane. I paint it white.

The Magazine of Fantasy & Science Fiction, July 2003

The General

One of the enemy has escaped into the mountains. An important general. He knows our language, he knows our ways, but we don't know his nor where his men are, nor even if there are any of his men left at all. We were holding him in our maximum security facilities and we had thought to torture him until he told us what he knew of his own army. We had called in others to torture him because we don't believe in torture, but he escaped before they arrived.

There's a large reward for his capture. For a sum like this, even his own men would turn him in. He can't count on anybody. There's no way that he can survive very long anyway. It's too cold and everybody is on our side around here. Most likely they'll fight among themselves over the reward. There'll be a few more of us dead.

We had dressed him in orange. He'll have to steal some clothes. We hope he won't kill any of us to get them. He must be very stupid to try to escape in a place like this and at this season. The weather can only get worse. But perhaps death is better than our (deliberately) rat infested, latrineless cells. He has been trained by us in our own schools to laugh at death. Most likely his body is already out there somewhere. We've sent local children to search the rocks and bushes. They know the area better even than our experts. We'll give them pennies and salt for any clues they pick up. We warned them if they find him and he's not dead, they should run, as he is extremely dangerous and has probably obtained or made a weapon.

I'm on a trail now. At first I just headed out, not following any road or path, but there's no way to cross these mountain passes and not be on one. Every now and then there's a hut. This time of year they're all empty. I don't dare spend the night in any. I stole clothes from one, long underwear, and a worn out sheepskin jacket. I found a knit cap. They shaved my head so I needed a good hat. Everything I took was worn out and smelled bad, but I wear them anyway. I stole food and a blanket. I was wearing leg irons. At the hut I found tools to break them off. I'll be able to go a little faster now. I stole a sickle but dropped it later. I don't want to be tempted to lash out at anyone, especially not with a sickle.

I sleep several yards from the trail in any handy sheltered spot. Or if there are scattered boulders I cover myself with the blanket and lie along them as if I were just another stone. I haven't met a single person up here, but I don't dare relax.

I sleep the sleep of exhaustion. I'll think to myself: This is a good spot, and that's all I know until I wake up.

I'm aware that I'm walking through great beauty but if I sit down to appreciate it for a minute I fall asleep. Sometimes the moon has risen and I lie back and think to look at the sky and take some time to realize I'm in a wondrous place and this is a luminous moment, but no sooner do I have that thought than I'm asleep.

Notices have been put up on every corner:

> WANTED REWARD. Wild and dangerous man. Medium height, shaved head, dark eyes. He'd as soon kill you as look at you. By now he may have weapons. If you harbor him or give him food, you'll be considered as guilty as he is. There's a micro chip imbedded in his shoulder where he can neither see it or reach it. Anyone who has removed it will be considered as traitorous as he is. The sentence for helping him is death.

The irony is, we brought him up ourselves in our own military schools. We thought contact with us would civilize him, but he's no more civilized than he was at the age of nine when we took him in. At that time he said he'd kill us all and, in spite of all these years in our care, that's what he still wants to do.

We thought he would soon see that life with us was preferable to the primitive ways of his own people. We had thought he would realize our superiority. Anybody with any sense, we thought, even a child with any sense at all, could see we had the science, the money, the schools, the work force, the wealth.... And we were ready to share our wealth with him. He was, after all, at the top of his graduating class. The top! We were surprised that a savage child had beaten out our own. We took it as a sign we could mold the wild ones to our civilized ways if we caught them in time. We were glad to have him on our side. Until he defected, we suspected nothing.

I wake with a child looking down on me—so bundled up I wonder how she can move at all. A dirty child but I'm dirtier. At first I think a boy, but then I think, girl. I see her skirt and coarse hand-knit wooly petticoat hanging below it. I'm not a good judge of the ages of children, but I'd guess about nine or ten years old. Beside her there's a bundle of sticks she's been gathering.

I distrust everybody. I wake up in a rage as usual, ready to strike out. I think, here's one of them, but then she smiles and I smile back.

I can't help groaning as I try to sit up. I'm always so stiff, waking after a day of climbing. (When I was younger I never had this problem. I suppose it'll only get worse.) I ask her, "What are you doing way up here this time of year?" and she asks, "What are you?"

Her name is Loo. I tell her I'm Sang. Not too much of a lie, especially if you take it to mean blood and pronounce it "sans," and now I am sans everything. (For a long time I was called rubbish.)

It's been three days and we still haven't captured him, therefore sweeping changes from the top on down. Higher ups have been brought in. Those in charge are no longer in charge. How can one half-starved man, possibly wearing orange, and with a micro chip have escaped us all? We have the know-how and the where-with-all.

Loo won't go home without more sticks. I help her. She's all smiles when she sees how much I get. I shoulder a dead log, too. I think to chop it up when we get... wherever. First we climb on the main trail and then turn off on a smaller path, so small you have to know it's there to follow it.

We come to a hut of stone and weathered wood. It looks like part of the mountain. It's a hut as if out of a painting of a troll's house in a book of fairytales. The roof slopes almost to the ground. I remember fairytales from before I was taken, otherwise I'd not know about them.

Loo's grandma greets us at the door. I look past her and see it's like a troll's hut inside, too. Heavy handmade furniture, a worn down board floor, a squat black stove a squat black kettle steaming....

Loo and her grandma must have gotten marooned up here some way. I don't ask how. The grandma has a hard time walking from the stove to the doorway. Perhaps she could no longer climb down. Yet to leave her here alone with just a child for help.... I don't see how they get by. They don't look in good shape.

I don't go in. I stand in the doorway. I say, "I am your enemy. I'm a fugitive. You risk your life if you take me in. I have a chip imbedded in my shoulder. I tell the grandma about the reward though I don't say how much. I hardly dare. It's a sum hard to resist. It would make anyone rich for life.

For answer the old women motions me in, motions me to sit down, motions me to take off my jacket and mittens, and then hands me a cup of strong strange tea. It tastes of pine needles. They have two rooms. Two nanny goats stay in with them.

I say, "You don't realize."

The grandma says, "I realize." Her voice is a breathy growl.

She shows me men's clothes hanging behind the door, but she won't talk about them. In fact she'll hardly talk at all. Just gives me stew full of tiny bones. Then she gets out a paring knife and motions me to lean over the table. I do. It'll give her a chance to cut my throat if she feels like it.

(I had covered my shoulder first thing with pieces of foil from the dump on the outskirts of town so they couldn't home-in on me.)

Afterwards she makes me a different sort of tea for the pain. The way I'm slurping down every odd tasting thing she hands me, she could poison me in a minute, and I'll bet she has whatever it takes to do it.

She wraps the chip back in my foil and puts it by the door. She says, "Take this out on the trail tomorrow. Throw it over the cliff."

They make me a bed under the table I just bled on. I think to thank them but, warm and full of hot food, I fall asleep before I can get the words out.

We've sent out six units. We've commandeered the first huts along several trails as base camps. One unit has discovered a place where someone spent the night. No one is on the mountain at this time of year so who but the general could have slept there? We moved all our units to this one mountain trail.

An early snow falls all night and is still going on in the morning. I go out in it. I'll not do as the grandma said. I'll get rid of that chip at the top of one of the peaks. I'll unwrap it so as to give them a false clue. Useless and foolish, I know, but I want to do it anyway. Perhaps if it's so hard to get to they'll not bother. They'll think I'm already dead up there and let me be. They'll say it's just like me to die at the top of something. I wish I'd saved my orange suit to use as a flag.

I say I may not be back tonight, but I'll be back soon. I'm thinking it'll take all day to climb a mountain even if I'm more than half way up right here.

The grandma bundles me in handknit scarves. She winds them around me under my stolen jacket. I don't know if I can climb in all this. She wants to give me dried acorn cakes but I don't let her. I don't believe they have much food anymore than they have much firewood. Soon as I get back I'll chop up more.

The grandma lends me her staffs. She uses two. I'll need two also. "Bring them back," she says.

We've found the chip, brown from his blood. One unit climbed to the top of the mountain thinking what the General can do, they can do. Thinking he would be there laughing down at them. Or dead, but with a smile at having forced them to climb there. He was no doubt laughing, but he wasn't there. One member of the unit fell on the rocks near the top and broke his ankle. One got altitude sickness. They have been flown out. We appointed new squad leaders.

There's fish. I caught some myself on the way up when the trail dipped down beside a creek. I ate them raw. Now I catch more on the way back to the cabin.

When I get there, Loo says she saw a group of men in white suits filing up the trail. They're two day's climb away. Loo takes me yet farther up into a cave, well off the path. Rattlesnakes sleep there. If I make a fire they'll wake up.

There's already a bed of old rotten hay. Loo gives me a bundle of food. She insists. I say I'll eat rattlesnake. She says, "Yes, but this, too." Then she chops off the heads of several big ones to take back to the grandma. They're so cold they don't come to. "In the morning I'll bring some back fried," she says. She leaves me the ax and goes.

There's a little sort of porch in front of the cave. I watch her till she's out of sight, lumpy little figure, accepting everything that comes along—though what else can children ever do?

I sit down on a rock and look out at the mountains—for once without falling asleep. A long time ago these peaks used to be the border—a no man's land several miles long between my country and theirs. But no need for any borders now. It's all theirs. The beauty is still as it was and will be no matter who owns it. Does it matter? Grandma and Loo? Why do I even wonder what side they're on?

The search parties below have already camped for the night. I see their smoke.

I start to chant to myself as I did when I was a child locked in solitary. I rock back and forth. I remember the cell, too small for a man, but big enough for me. I remember my classmates called me "Rubbish" all the time and I called myself that to myself. If I slipped I'd look at my feet and call them Rubbish. If I dropped something I'd call my hands Rubbish. Rubbish, I said about myself.

My parents were murdered before my eyes and I, taken to an enemy school to be educated as one of them. I didn't even know their language. Even when I began to understand, I refused to speak it. I didn't know their food. I finally got hungry enough to eat it. I profited by that education. I got to know them as I used to know my own. Better in fact. I almost forgot my own language. I almost forgot our ways. I was told my people were a lower order of civilization, but I couldn't see much difference.

In the beginning of military school I ran away a lot. Escaping wasn't hard, it was not being found afterwards that I never managed. The enemy was everywhere. After four or five times it seemed useless. The punishment was solitary confinement. (They don't believe in hitting children. Besides, we were not to be marked in any way.) I burned my uniform three times, but there were plenty more. After a while I obeyed. It seemed a waste to go to all that trouble of running away for nothing.

I tested myself every chance I got. Heat, cold, fire, hunger, thirst.... On our matches, I stood out in storms and let icy rain trickle down the back of my neck while the others took shelter in a shed. I wondered how high a ledge I could jump from. (I found out by breaking my ankle.) I tested myself in the cold until I almost lost my toes. After that I realized I might go too far, cripple myself and defeat my own purposes.

Being in solitary...that was a test, too, and I passed it to my own satisfaction.

How I managed was through chants and songs. I chanted myself up into the trees I used to climb. I chanted to make myself into a cat. I practiced stalking the mice in my cell. When I finally caught one I made it into a pet. First I named it Sang, and then I named it Sans.

I never cried. Crying was a waste of valuable energy that I needed to fulfill my promises. My father would have told me that.

But then I realized there was a better way than all this escaping. (My father would have said that, too.) I did as I was told. I spoke their language when called upon, I excelled at everything, and became, at the age of twenty-eight, their youngest general ever. Years later, I fled and became one or ours.

They trapped us in our caves. Killed us except for me. I was saved for worse things than mere death.

We had learned to laugh at death. (They taught us that.) Death holds no terror, but we didn't learn to laugh at the torture of our loved ones, therefore I have no loved ones, neither wife nor children. After they killed my parents, my aunts, and my grandmother, I made sure there was nobody else, ever, to take from me.

In those early days I fell in love so often I thought to change my plans and be their general after all, I would marry and live on the hills above the towns, but I stayed true to the vows I made when I was nine.

At our graduation from military school, a eulogy full of kindness and humor so that we not only laughed at death, but laughed along with the dead. Their dead were to be my dead, and yet I thought only of my own. Even though I could hardly remember them alive, I thought only of their deaths.

It was hard keeping to my resolutions when I got to know the enemy. I began to care for them—those who treated me well, though many didn't, but I had knelt by my parents, covered with their blood, and swore...not to any God, but to myself—to the man I would become. I said, "You! You, as a man. You will remember this right here and now. No other thing will ever be as clear as this." And that has turned out to be true. I've remembered nothing more clearly than the blood, and the gurgling and coughing and the jerking back and forth of dying.

I ran, and thought to hide in a closet full of my father's uniforms as if they might save me, but they guessed where I was. I bit them, so then they put me in a dusty bag that smelled bad. I remember the taste of their sweaty, salty wrists.

Loo and Grandma? I wonder if they even know which side they're on. This side of the mountain...no one was sure who it belonged to, but the other side used to belong to the scattered armies of my childhood. My home was over there somewhere. I wonder if I would recognize it? I wonder if it still stands?

Ever since I was taken away, I haven't had much to do with any but military people. Even my women were soldiers. I don't know what civilians are like. And I've never had anything to do with children, though I guess we all remember how it was to be one. Except I doubt if my memories pertain to many other children. I hope they don't. Loo is ten, the age I was when I first escaped and was recaptured and put in solitary as punishment.

I look out from the porch of my cave. I can hear the stream rushing down. I can see it sparkling below if I lean over the cliff. The sound will sooth me as I sleep. I begin to chant. I chant, You, and, Loo, and owl. Owl meant ouch in my childhood language, and row, row, row, meant remember, remember. I chant You, you, you, as I used to chant it to my grown-up self. But I also chant, But, but, but....

But.... There were no buts in my chant language back then. But.... I've seen plenty of blood on both sides. But.... Isn't it best to look forward? See to it that children, and this one child, Loo, never see such things as I did? But.... She already has. Those men's clothes behind the door. Next time she comes up I'll ask her about herself. I wonder if she'd like a doll. I have a kitchen knife. I look around for some wood.

She comes the next morning, bringing fried rattlesnake and dried crawdads. She sneaks in. I had my eyes shut, my face to the rising sun. I was chanting, Jolly, jolly, joll, joll. My secret words for my aunt June Harvest. When I open my eyes, there's Loo, watching. She's not surprised. Not wondering that I'm sitting cross legged, nodding, muttering to myself.

I show her the doll. She receives it as though she's never known about dolls before. Perhaps she hasn't. She doesn't say a word, but I see her pleasure on her face. How nice to give something and have it so well received.

I sit on my porch stone. There's room for two. "Come, sit with me. Eat some yourself."

"I've had."

She examines the doll as I eat.

I had made it a dress out of pieces of the clothes I'd stolen. I hooked the arms and legs on with threads. "When I get some fishing line I'll put the arms and legs on in a stronger way. I'll find better cloth for a nice dress." (Too bad I hadn't saved a little piece of my orange suit.)

"I like this cloth," she says, even though it's a piece from the leg of my long underwear.

We sit quietly for a while, she turns the doll this way and that. I did a good job carving the face. It has a nice smiling look. I was always good at such things.

And then I ask what I've been waiting to ask. "Your father? Are those his clothes hanging behind the door? Is he all right?"

She starts to cry but turns away and stops herself.

I say, "I know. I know." And I do know. I wonder if, as I did, she had to watch it as it happened. I wonder if I dare reach out to her. I'm not used to touching people. My awkwardness would show all the more clearly to a child.

But she comes to me of her own accord, leans against me, still not crying. We hold each other. All I can think to say is, "I know, I know, I know," though I wonder, what good does that do? It's like another of my chants. So I chant, I know, and rock her.

I can feel there's not much to her. Skin and bones. Take off all these clothes and she'd look like a wet cat inside there. Grandma is probably about the same under her woolly petticoats and shawls. I could easily see to it that they got enough to eat. If I'd be let, I could live up here for the rest of my life. Wood gatherer, gatherer of acorns and pine nuts, trap setter, fisherman.... I could make a bigger, better doll. I'd look out at mountains. I never knew...or never let myself know how much I'd like a quiet life.

Then I see the search and capture squads on the path below, three groups of three. They've passed the cottage. I'm afraid for Grandma. I don't think they would hurt an old woman, but Grandma might have said something, or there may have been some sign that I'd been there. Even a larger woodpile might be suspicious. She'd be in as much trouble as I am.

Loo feels my fear. I must have suddenly held her tighter without knowing it. She turns around and looks, too. Then looks back at me as if I'd know what to do. "Loo, is there a back way?"

But she should stay up here, safe. She wouldn't. She should lead me. "I'll go down with you, but first I have something that needs doing."

At least they'll have a harder time coming beyond this point. Why didn't I think of this before?

We had brought him up as one of our own. Spared no expense. And now look. He has worn us out. Fooled us. Played tricks. As if climbing a mountain peak were a game and he won. They say, Once a savage, always a savage. And now yet another game. He has rolled boulders down and started a landslide. Our second team had to rescue our first team out from under gravel and dust. It could have been worse, they only received a few bruises. But that slide shut off the upper part of the trail. That will be proof he's gone on higher. We'll drop our squads off above the slide area.

There's no trail as Loo leads me down a back way, so it's hard. We scramble over rocks. Loo tears her skirt and unravels her knit petticoats. She's upset by it. She says Grandma can't see well enough to sew or knit anymore. I say I'll repair them for her. She says, "Men don't sew," and I say, "Many's the time I've repaired my clothes myself. I'd have made the doll clothes better if I'd had a needle."

When we get almost to the hut it's beginning to be twilight. We curve around to the side and see a guard. He's across from the door partly hidden by a currant bush. Had we come straight in by the path he might have shot us.

Loo wants to run right out but I hold her back. I clamp my hand over her mouth just in time to stop her yell. "Wait. One of us should stay a secret. I'll find out if Grandma's all right. You stay here." I find her a good spot farther back. "We may need you later. You may have to rescue both of us."

I take off my cap so the guard will know it's me. I give it to Loo. I was thinking she needed something to take care of, but all this time she's been holding the doll, tight in her mitten. I had forgotten about it, but she hadn't. I say, "Find it a name." But she's a child like I was a child so not a child at all, yet she hung on to the doll through all this scrabbling over rocks. Makes me think of my pet mouse. This last time in solitary I had not made a pet of any of the rats. I had not chanted and still I had escaped. Is that proof of the uselessness of chanting?

I walk straight in from the path with no hat. By now it's starting to get dark. The guard recognizes me with delight. He points the automatic straight at me.

I say, "Hold it. Not as much of a reward for me dead. Where's Grandma?"

I don't think any of his men are nearby. Why would they need more than one man to guard Grandma? Earlier we heard their copters dropping men off above my landslide. "You know all your teams are busy elsewhere."

He looks uncertain. He's very young.

Then we see rockets lighting up the sky far below us. I think: But there are no more armies. And then I think: Loo! Will she be frightened? By now it's almost dark.

The guard and I turn to look out at the sky, but I turn back before he does. I grab the automatic and use it to knock him down. I hold the butt against his throat. He chokes. I let up some. He gags.

"Grandma!"

When he tries to talk his voice is hoarse. I leaned too hard. Another little bit and his Adams apple would have pierced his esophagus.

We are celebrating Victory Day with the usual cannon volleys, fireworks, and flag waving. Even though a most important enemy is still at large, no need not to celebrate. We are unlikely to be harmed by this single escaped general. We have taken down the WANTED notices. To us he is no more than a gnat, though vexatious. Some are laughing, enjoying the fact that one man has eluded us all this time. They are traitors. We are putting up new notices that say: NO LONGER WANTED.

Winter is coming. The weather will worsen. We've postponed our search, perhaps until Spring, perhaps forever.

I had forgotten about Victory Day... Victory over us day. Not forgotten about it, but I'd lost track of time. I've had to celebrate it ever since military school. At least now I'm not forced to cheer and dance or wave a hated flag. I can yell my rage if I want to. I do. The soldier looks up at me terrified. I yell louder. I've not let myself do that ever before. I yell and then here's Grandma hobbling out. I fall on the young man, the automatic hard between us. He doesn't dare move. Then here's Loo, holding my head. Still I yell. I roll away from the soldier and the gun. I have to stop yelling because I can't breathe.

Grandma has picked up the automatic. It's clear she knows how to use it. She's going to shoot. I'd try to stop her but I'm breathless. My first thought is: I'll take the blame. I'm already blamed for many more things than I've done, anyway. One more won't make a difference. I'm considered a killer though I've never even pointed a gun at anyone. When I was on their side I shot to miss and when I was on our side I was a general and didn't have to shoot.

The gun seems too heavy for her. Her aim wavers. It makes her look all the more dangerous. "Go home," she says. Her old-crow voice is scary. "Home. I mean it."

It's dark now but he goes—stumbling, tripping.

I'm still panting—groaning at every breath as though I were in pain. Something has been let loose inside me.

I never chanted except secretly to myself. I believe Loo is the only person who ever heard me. I've always wondered if chanting had anything to do with anything. As a child I thought it did. Escape always seemed so easy. I thought I'd done it with my songs. And sometimes after a good chant I thought, any minute, people will come to rescue me. Even Aunt June Harvest would come, and she was dead with the rest. She's the one started my chanting. I remember standing in her doorway listening. We were a family that didn't believe in any of the old superstitions, but Aunt June Harvest believed things the rest of us didn't or weren't supposed to.

As a child in solitary, I usually chanted up my father. I thought of him opening the door, letting in sunlight—Pada, in full dress uniform, bringing our kind of food. I shouted, "Pada!" Often, after chanting I knew all that I'd seen with my own eyes was false, there had been no deaths and my father was come to rescue me.

I can't breathe. Loo sits beside me, says, "Sang, Sang." At first I think she must mean my pet mouse and then I remember I am Sang. She puts the doll in my hand, giving it back. I take it. I turn over onto my hands and knees, then hunker down. Even though I easily escaped this last time, I no longer think chanting has any effect on anything except for my own need to chant, yet I do it now. Though breathless, I chant. How, how, and, And. And, Row, Row. And Row begins to mean row indeed, instead of remember, remember, and I'm as if in our old flat bottom boat on our pond with my little sister. My sister leans to pull at a water lily. Oarlocks creak. A red winged blackbird clings to a reed. I hear the bird's song. At first so sweet and then loud and then much too loud. And then I must have passed out. That's never happened before.

I come to with Grandma rubbing snow on my face. Then she helps me turn over, raises my head and holds tea to my lips. Loo and Grandma help me in to my sleeping spot under the table. I shiver. They pile quilts on me. Loo puts the doll beside my pillow. I try to give it back but she won't let me. I say, "I made it for you." But then I let her. I sleep a sick sleep. Whenever I wake myself up with my yelling, they are there, Grandma in the rocking chair and Loo and the goats on the floor beside me.

The celebration of Victory Day was a success. We had temporarily removed all the wanted! dangerous man at large posters. The mood was as it should be. We have made them forget that the general still eludes us. We shot into the air, but, as far as we know, all the bullets came down safely. We are pleased. We have toasted ourselves. "Long live and forever," we said to each other, and "Victory Day throughout eternity."

Next I know good smells wake me. Grandma is baking an elderberry pie. I don't wake up angry as I usually do even though at first I think grandma is celebrating Victory Day, but she says it's not to celebrate any victories, it's for me. She says they haven't had pie in a long time.

"Which side?" I say, thinking to find out at last what side they're on.

"Just us," she says, and then, "No sides. Lupine, snakeweed, fireweed people. Asters and rock fringe people."

The general is to be presumed dead. We'll not waste any more resources hunting him. He's no longer of any meaning. What army could he be the general of anymore? We'll celebrate his death with another night of cannon volleys. The reward set aside for his capture is withdrawn and will revert back to the army, though, just in case, we'll not publicize that it no longer exists. All the better if people think it's still on.

I make a little outdoor oven so I can smoke fish for them. I chop more wood. There's already dried kinnickinnick here. In the evenings I carve myself a pipe to smoke it. Loo and I together repair her woolly petticoats. I start to make her a bigger better doll but she says she just wants the old small one with my underwear for a dress, so I strengthen the arms and legs with fishing line. I carve a little goat. I make Loo guess what it's going to be as I go along. I wear the men's clothes that were hanging behind the door. I sit by the stove of an evening smoking or sewing more dresses for the doll. I still sleep under the table. I keep the fire burning all night. The stove pipe curls through to the other room so they stay warm. All my life since I was nine, I have awakened every morning in a rage, renewing my promises. All my life I have distrusted people, but not now.

Loo is teaching me how to be a child. Or perhaps we're teaching each other. I make the doll dance, and then she does it. Supper times, I wave a tidbit…a dried crawdad or some such, in front of her and let her snap at it. I throw a walnut up and catch it in my mouth. She tries but she can't do it. I make pancakes and flip them almost to the ceiling when I turn them. I remember the peasant dances my men used to do and, though I've never tried to do one, I try now. I take Loo's hand and make her dance with me. I growl out a song. We even make Grandma smile. We even make her sing.

They're both getting fatter. I'll leave in the Spring. In the spring Loo can gather all sorts of sprouts, fiddlehead ferns, mushrooms…. She's gotten good at fishing. I'll cross the pass and go home—if I can find it—if anything remains. I haven't thought of home for a long time. I hadn't thought I had one, nor did I want one. Perhaps I should look for the remains of my army. Though…. I'd like to be finished with that sort of life. Perhaps I'll live the rest of my life home, if it still exists. Or here.

A group of our people hoping for the reward found him on the trail. (They thought the reward was still operative. All the better then, if people do.) Or perhaps he found them. It might have been him, but could he grow that much hair and that much beard in this length of time? There might be other fugitives on the mountain. However that may be, this man jumped them at the perfect spot and pushed them over, all three. None died but all slid down and were found at the bottom, scratched and bruised. Harassing us is just the sort of thing he would do. We had thought he was much higher up by now. Perhaps even over on the other side. But then again, we aren't sure this man was him. Perhaps it wasn't the general at all but some other man with something else against us. How many wild men roam the mountains looking for their chances at us? The mountains could be full of them. We'll not waste anymore time on him—or them.

But then Loo wakes me in the middle of the night. Grandma is trying to talk but can't. The whole right side of her face is lopsided. I recognize right away she's had a stroke. I'll need to get help. No, they'll arrest me before I have a chance to bring up a doctor. I'll have to get her down to town. It will be the quickest anyway. I've already made a skid for hauling logs. I wrap Grandma in all our quilts and blankets and tie her to it. There's still quite a bit of snow here on the upper slopes, that'll make the first part easier. I feed Loo cold smoked fish and goat's milk, grab whatever food is handy to bring along, wrap Loo up in scarves and start out. I see to it she doesn't forget her doll and she sees to it I don't forget my pipe. (At the last minute I throw in Grandma's scissors and Loo's father's razor.) Though it's still hardly dawn, I grab the rope and we start out. I won't be careful this time, I'll just be fast.

The farther down we get the warmer it'll be. We'll hit true Spring in a day.

We spend the first night in an empty cabin. We burn their wood, not worried who sees the smoke. We use their barley to make gruel. There's a small mirror. I shave my beard and I have Loo help me shave my head. I don't tell her why and she doesn't ask. (Afterwards she says she liked me better hairy.) Until the time comes, I'll keep my cap on.

Farther down there are no more snowy patches so it's harder. At one point the skid gets going down a scree slope. I get a bump on my head trying to stop it. That fits with my plans.

After we leave Grandma at the clinic, I tell Loo, "Tie me up and lead me to the prison. There's a big reward for my capture. Turn me in and request it. Make them set up the money in a bank account for Grandma, to dole out little by little. It's a lot of money." (I still don't dare tell her how much even though I'm sure she'd not be able to understand it anyway.)

But even as I speak I realize they won't do it for a child. Perhaps I should turn myself in for my own reward. Have an account in my own and Grandma's name. Will they let me do that? What if Grandma dies or never recovers her senses? Loo's name then. They won't, but they might. It would change their life. I may as well try.

I show Loo how to tie me up.

"The bruise on my head…tell them you did that."

She starts to cry. "I won't."

"You'll see. You'll be a hero. Everything will be better this way."

"It won't be."

"I'll be fine. I have my chants and I can think about you."

She tries to give me her doll.

"They'll not let me keep anything. You keep the pipe, too. I can only take unreal things like remembering."

But we're too late. There's been no reward since winter. I can't believe it. I'm no longer of any importance. At first I feel a great relief. My stomach lurches. I almost throw up. It's over. This is better than any reward no matter how large. Loo and I can walk away.

But they grab me anyway. I struggle though I know it's useless. In half a minute I'm shackled again. I yell at Loo to go to the clinic, but when I look back, they've got her, too. I can't think why. I suppose she's guilty of helping me. I never should have let them help. I wonder what they'll do to Grandma. They know I have loved ones now. I wonder if Loo has the sense to chant.

We put up new posters. the General is in our custody. Finding him and capturing him was difficult but we prevailed. Congratulations to all our Search and Capture teams. They will be rewarded. Prepare your flags and trumpets, tomorrow there will be another day of celebrating.

***McSweeney's Mammoth Treasury of Thrilling Tales*,** 2003

Gods And Three Wishes

We don't think much about the gods way out here. Besides, you can't depend on them for anything. Do they keep our dinghies from tipping over? Do they keep us from shooting each other? Do they keep our young ones from falling out of trees? Or do they even ever keep them from climbing too high in the first place? Whatever gods bring is usually wrong, anyway, flood or drought, tornadoes.... Whirlwinds in which we can't see a thing and in the middle of which the gods refuse to manifest themselves.

Knock on wood. Carry a rabbit's foot. Avoid cross-eyed people. Live under a horseshoe. (A mule's shoe is even better.) But even if you do all these things, you can't count on being safe from the gods, except way out here where we are.

We have enough troubles of our own without their meddling. They'll notice you no matter where you try to hide, unless that is, you're here with us.

(We used to worship bears. Things might be better if we had stuck to that.)

To get above and beyond the gods isn't easy. You have to cross mountain passes, raging rivers. Rise up into the clouds and then dip down again. You'll find our hidden valley on the other side of everything. The gods won't bother tracking you way out here.

That they stay out of our valley, is what we pray for every morning.

But now which one of them said, "Let there be a mountain lake that breaks through its ice dam?" Or did it just happen by itself?

The water rushed down and swept away a whole section of the forest.

Who survives? Both the good *and* the bad. That's for sure. Nasty old Minn Moon and his sheep were all saved, whereas Bess and her little house was washed all the way down the mountain.

Send over our most beautiful girl to seduce the gods. We have lots, but send one who can sing our best sad songs.

(If the gods sent *us* a beautiful maiden goddess, we'd be just as distracted as we hope they'll be.)

She'll tell them to keep their sticky golden fingers to themselves.

Of course she has to be a virgin.

In that case maybe she should be an ugly girl (easier to find an ugly virgin) and maybe not be able to sing. We don't want them seducing her and keeping her as one of their own. Hazel comes to mind first thing. You'd think with a name like that she'd be one of our beauties. You'd think she'd have hazel hair and eyes.

"You have to go all by yourself. Even though you're only 19."

"But what could I do against the gods? I don't even believe in them."

"All the better then. And remember, no taking any of the gods' names in vain."

She's small and thin. She hardly has a figure even yet. Maybe she'll never have one. The gods won't notice her. And by the time she gets there, climbing up and down those mountain passes all day long, she'll be even more like a bundle of sticks than she already is.

"Tell them we just want to live quietly, not bother anybody and not be bothered by them. Burn a little incense."

(If they wanted to, they could straighten buck teeth and hammer toes…fix bunions. Some people think those bunions are a punishment from gods. They could clean everybody up so nobody would smell bad, but that would make them too much like the gods themselves.)

Gods asleep, or, rather, meditating in their Pantheons…. (There's a Pantheon in every city, but Hazel has never been in a city..) She has never seen ceilings so high. Nor anything so sparkling. And she's never seen a god before. How could she when ours is a god-free zone. Or used to be. She believes in them now.

She thinks to go touch the god's golden toe. But she doesn't want to wake him up.

Do it, is what she tells herself. Don't back off. The goats will wake him in a minute, anyway. (We convinced her to bring her goats. She raised them from newborn kids. They would have followed her anyway. She says she won't sacrifice them, but she may have to.)

We told her to pick a small god. Find him on the beach or under a sapling, not an oak, and not in some big white building, but she went to the top without even realizing it.

She touches. He groans, then roars a roar that echoes through his pantheon. He stretches and stands up.

Hazel says, "Oh my god! Oh my god!" and it's not a prayer.

She tries to hide behind his plinth, but the goats start baaing. She shakes her hair so it falls over her face and looks out from behind it. He doesn't seem quite so impressive through that scrim of hair, though he still glows.

"Don't call me: 'Oh My God. Oh My God.' Call me: Sun at Noon, or, Moon at Midnight. And thank you for the goats." He grins and shows his gold teeth. "You will be blessed."

Hazel absolutely will not let him have her Lulu and Nan. She says, "No!"

"Who began all this? Who said, 'Let there be what there is right now?' This light and a firmament splashed with stars, and snow on the mountain tops? Who but me? And maybe one or two others, and with a little luck. You owe me much more than just two goats."

"Please don't shout." (His voice is so loud.)

Hazel doesn't think the god is that beautiful himself, though his big curly beard covers most of his face. His nose is flat. How would a god get a broken nose? Except from another god?

"I don't even believe in you."

"You don't have to believe, you just have to give me those goats."

There's no place to hide. He chases her around his plinth. He's big and clumsy. Yells, (he's still yelling), "And don't you dare cast a spell."

"How about just one goat?" But they're like her children. How could she pick one?

"I can tell the future and it isn't very nice." He's out of breath already. Too much sitting around waiting for admirers.

He stops and really looks at her across the plinth. A god's stare is hard to bear. She feels smaller and smaller. He grunts. It's clear she's not worth goats. He turns to go after them. She gets between them not even thinking how those goats are faster than she is.

He catches her by her shirttail while she tries to defend them. She gets away when the god trips on his toga, falls flat on his already squashed-in nose. Maybe that's how he broke it in the first place.

She...they all run. He lies there yelling, "Come back here, you little..." and uses a bad word we don't use in our gods-free zone. Hazel doesn't even know it's a bad word.

She finds a place by a stream with willow and beech trees and grass and bushes for the goats. Gods only know if they really are trees or nymphs and nyads. The stream sparkles. Golden laurel leaves float in it. Dare she drink? We told her: Beware of swans or deer. Even trees. Don't look into any still pools. Be careful who you kiss.

Cat's ears, statue's noses, pennyroyal. Mash them up together, mix with lemon grass and marshmallow.... We gave her a little bag of those except for the pennyroyal which she picks now. Sprinkle half on a fire. Drink the other half.

You see we told her she might get three wishes. We told her that, though we didn't think she'd really get even one (not from any of the gods we know about, anyway), but we wanted her to start out feeling hopeful so that no all would seem to be lost even if all was lost. But three wishes don't amount to anything if you never get to see the creature that might give them to you, so this is the way she calls for help. She claps her hands in time with what she hopes might be the rhythm of the Universe. "Appear," she says. "Appear."

But who?

(Hazel already has her wishes picked out. First, save my goats. Second, get me out of here a virgin. Third, tell those gods to stay away from our god-free zone. Whatever happens there, we want it to happen in an ordinary way, as a rock falling down on our heads from the climber above us, only because he dislodged it, or tripping and falling, only because we were clumsy. We want to be sure that when a lake bursts through its icy mountain dam it was because it was ready to do that all on its own. We want to tell our children, "Things just happen.")

When Luck appears, he's wearing ordinary clothes. That's a relief. And he's not at all godlike. That's a relief, too. He has gray eyes and a nice smile. His lips and cheeks are redder than they ought to be. He looks a little feverish…a little clownlike. He's as skinny as she is.

He says right off, "I'm Luck."

But Hazel felt lucky the minute she saw him.

She likes his looks. She starts to tell him her three wishes, but even as she's in the middle of telling them, she changes her mind about the second one.

She says, "We want you on our side. We want you in our god-free zone. I'll do anything for you." Meaning anything.

He's brought Nan and Lulu some melon rinds and corn cobs. They like him right away. That's lucky. Isn't that lucky?

For Hazel he's brought a picnic of bread, goat cheese, hard boiled eggs. (He juggles the eggs, three! One handed.) Since she met up with that big main god, she's forgotten to eat. She was too worried. This is certainly lucky.

Before he sits down on the bank with her, he does a little entrechat. Just what you'd expect.

"Will you help me?" She keeps her fingers crossed.

"Who do you think got you free of the top dog god? I tripped him on his toga."

So would it be lucky or not if she slept with him? Maybe had Luck's child? A funny little boy whose ears stick out like his and whose lips are too red?

Everything comes in threes, both good luck and bad, but when to start counting? Is that just one good thing or two already? Well, since she's deleted her number two wish, for sure she has one more.

The gods make their own weather. Whatever it's doing someplace else, it's always good where the gods are lounging about. They run around naked as jay birds as if it was the most natural thing in the world, so they like it sunny. If they want to make it hard the rest of us they can turn on a storm. Even just a hard steady rain might do the trick if it comes at *exactly* the wrong time.

So, just when Lucky gives her a kiss (a little peck kind of kiss but on the lips) it starts to rain. What kind of Luck is that? But it *is* lucky. Nearest shelter is either a sibyl's sanctuary, or a cave with a sacred spring in it. They choose the latter.

It's so nice in there she gets scared. Things aren't supposed to be this nice for anybody: That they would have their very own sparkling spring, that a hard rain should be falling outside and they'd be warm and his bony arm would be around her shoulder. It will tempt the gods. She speaks in whispers so as not to alert any of them. Even Luck whispers.

They sit in the mouth of the cave for a while and talk about how nice the rain is, how nice it sounds and how it looks, and how everything smells of damp earth and wet weeds.

He's not large (in fact he's much smaller than you'd expect) but you can see how adept he is. She's glad to have him on her side even if only for a little while. But you never know what Luck will do.

But no here's this other wish coming true. Is it the last one? Little pecks on her lips and earlobe.

"Come live with me and be in our god-free zone."

"Nope," he says.

"Why not?"

By now little nips all along her collar bone.

"I'm supposed to get the gods to stay out of our way, but not you. Please come. Please."

"You might as well be praying."

"I am."

"Don't pray to me. I hate that."

Little nips lower down all around her belly button. It tickles and makes her laugh. She's been laughing ever since he appeared. (Later it'll tickle all the more when he gets all the way down and beyond and kisses her instep.)

"How about a little lucky baby boy?"

She the one says that.

Now he's giggling.

"Wait and see. Like everybody has to."

She'll be lucky if her goats haven't wandered off, and lucky if some dog or wolf hasn't eaten them. She usually finds a safe enclosure for them at night but this night she forgets all about them.

"The baby will be a baby girl. Her ears will stick out. From the age of three months on, she'll have a nice smile. She'll be pesky, get into trouble all the time just like Luck does.)

It sopped raining and here's the "rosy fingered" goddess of dawn already… most gods wouldn't bother with things that are merely set dressing, but here comes Dawn now. They watch from the mouth of their cave. Hazel wonders, should she thank her some way? Or is this just a very nice natural thing?

Lucky says, "What a nice day! Come on, I'll walk you part way home."

"But I have to get the gods out of our space."

"What makes you think they've been there?"

"Well…." And she tells him about Min Moon and Bess. And how bad things happened to good people and good things to bad. And why would that be?

"That's just bad Luck."

"You mean I don't have to try to keep those gods out?"

"They're out already."

"Come home with me. We need you."

"You're forgetting something."

"What?"
"I'll show you later."
He'll go a little ways with her. He wants to teach her a lesson.
So off they go into the mountains. They bring the bread and cheese.
(The goats stayed lucky. They're fine.)

When they have to cross a dangerous place where a landslide destroyed four or five yards of the trail, he says, "Well, you might be lucky if you cross it fast enough. The goats can do it, you're the only one might not make it."

Lucky crosses back and forth twice while she still thinks about it. (The goats are frolicking on the cliffs above them.) "Take a chance," he says.

What could go wrong with Luck right here? But when she tries to cross, she slides...first slowly, then faster, all the way down to the hanging valley below. She doesn't get hurt, not even scratched, but she'll have to climb all the way up.

Luck waits. By the time she gets back up, he's eaten all the bread and cheese. When she protests, he says, "That's Luck."

"I thought you were going to help me."

"How lucky that you didn't get hurt."

They're entering the big cat zone. That was another reason the gods didn't come here much.

We were clever from the start. We could tie hundreds of different kinds of knots. We had herbs to cure the common cold. We played tiddlywinks and mumbledypeg. We always had teeter-totters. We painted eyes on our walls. (We always had walls even if some were the walls of cave.) Eyes kept us safe—or , rather, safer. In tiger country we wore eyes on the backs of our heads. She should have done that.

When they enter the lion zone, Lucky leaves. But he already showed her that she couldn't count on him. And he ate all the food. He's the one brought it in the first place so Hazel supposes he has the right.

It's the goats that save her. She has to sacrifice them to the lions, first one and then the other. But she gets back to us OK and has a lot to say, as not to ever count on Luck.

Trampoline, ed. Kelly Link 2003

Lightning

Lightning strikes. She gets up. Or, rather, tries to. Knees till wobbly She must have been doing the dishes and the lightning must have come right in the window. No, it probably came through the water pipes. At any rate, here she is, all tingly; on the black and white tiles of somebody's kitchen. Can't remember what she's doing here washing dishes. Whose dishes? They have this little gold stripe around them. She must be the maid. She'll take a look around the house and see what she can find out. It's hard to get all the way up 'he's still so dizzy and tingly If anyone comes around now, they'll think she's drunk. That might get her fired. But she'd never do anything like that — drink up somebody's liquor. She can't be that kind of person.

Wrinkled old hands. How did she get to be this old? But they look strong. She's never minded good, hard work. Not like some people she knows, except she can't remember anybody, herself included.

She feels breathless, touches her hand to her throat. There are beads around her neck. Where's a mirror? There isn't one, but the sky is so dark because of the storm she can see herself dimly in the window. The white hair and pearls show up though.

Big kitchen. Most likely a big house to go with it. She'd look around but she's still so shakey. Surely nobody would mind if she sat down and had a cup of tea. She'll say it was the lightning —came out of the faucet along with the water, went right up her arms and on into her brains, knocked her down so that — only for a minute — she didn't know who she was at all.

Here's a wedding ring. Had she married? Or — and this thought is a relief — she's probably just pretending to be married. That's the sort of thing she'd do. A woman her age gains respect, and it keeps people … men, that is, from bothering her. She never liked for men to be bothering her.

She feels a little bit better after the tea. (At first she was so trembly she could hardly make it and then hardly get the cup to her lips.) She feels well enough to take a look around and try to find out who she is before anybody comes and she has to behave some particular way that she's forgotten. (What if she's one of those women who never stop talking? You could be one and not even realize it. But now that she can't remember anything, what is there to say?) Lots of kitchen cleaning up still to do, but the house is wonderfully quiet. She should take a look around right away.

Pantry hall with Persian-type rug. Nice big stairway. Curtains in the living room that go up to the ceiling and all the way down, too. She tiptoes to the stairs. A scary animal sound is coming from up there, but she goes up anyway. Then she realizes it's somebody snoring. (Odd time of day to be sleeping.) There's a door half open. Does she dare? But she has to find things out. She peeks in. Somebody's on the bed snoring away so loud that any noise she might make would be drowned out. You'd think he'd be waking himself up. He's spread out catty-cornered on the king-sized bed. If he sleeps like that all the time, nobody could ever sleep with him. Big man, too, with nose to match. Fringe of white hair all around his bald spot. He's fully dressed, thank goodness. There's a tie squashed into a ball beside him. He's the master of the house for sure. He's frowning even in his sleep.

Coming closer, she catches sight of herself in the mirror over the bureau. Scares herself Hair a fright. As if the lightning was still at it. Eyes wild. (She'd not realized she was that frightened until she saw her eyes.) She needs to straighten herself out. Where's the maid's room, or does she go home at eight? Where will she go if she can't remember where she lives in time? Without her name, she can't even look herself up in the phone book.

Under her apron she's wearing a silky, wine-colored blouse. That doesn't seem like her at all. Nor the matching slacks. Has her taste changed? For the better or what? These are nice, actually. Maybe it has and for the better. But she should look around, and quickly, to get more clues.

There's a room farther down the hall that seems like a guest room. Doesn't look used. And then, at the back, there's a study, walls completely lined with books, bay window with window seat, cluttered desk-actually the room's all cluttered. Was she supposed to have cleaned it up? Well, she will later, though some people don't like their studies cleaned up.

There's one more room on that floor. This one belongs to a man for sure. There are naked women taped up all over the walls, and not even sitting sideways. She tries to keep from looking at them, but one little glance is all it takes to see everything. She's never seen such pictures — that she can remember. She must have seen this room before, but she can't remember ever seeing nudity like this on anybody's wall. The room is neat and clean at least. Did she clean it? She wonders if she ever had been bold enough to speak to the man about this? She hopes she has, but it's too late to say anything now when maybe she's already said a lot, and it hadn't had any effect, anyway.

There's a pair of filthy athletic socks on the floor. Young man most likely. She picks them up, holding them carefully by the tops. She'll take them to the basement.

But she can't resist taking one more look at the master of the house. She has to know who this person is. She dares, this time, to come close. Studies his face. He's still frowning. Looks exactly like a master of a house should: bushy eyebrows, grumpy lips.... As she stares down at him, he gives one big snort, opens his eyes, and looks directly into hers.

"Sorry," she says, backing up. She can feel herself blushing. "Sorry, sorry."

"Take off that damn apron." He says it in a crabby, just-waking-up sort of voice.

She does, quickly, dropping it right where she stands.

"Now those goddamn pearls."

She does. Drops them on top of the apron, which is on top of the dirty socks.

"Come here." He holds out his arms.

She doesn't know what to say to not come. Says, "Busy," and, "I need to," and, "I'd better ..." and, "Not now."

Have they been secret lovers? Men do often pick the maid, but surely a younger maid and a pretty one. She doesn't dare not come. She lies down beside him, but with her back to him. He enfolds her in his hot, heavy arms. For a minute he brushes at her hair with a sweaty hand. A nice gesture, actually, like a father with a child, and then he's snoring again, she, lying stiff, even more frightened than before. Maybe than ever before.

She'll have to escape. Go on home wherever that is. Get away from the lewd man down the hall and this one who thinks she's a loose woman.

But, and almost right away, he's snoring as lustily as before. She begins edging out from under his arm. Luckily he rolls on to his back when she moves and she's free.

She picks up apron, socks and pearls and trots to the door. Just as she's closing it he calls out, "Take care, muh dear." It stuns her. Who has ever called her "dear" before? For a minute she can't move at all, but then she clumps down the stairs, not caring that she's making a racket. There's a purse and an umbrella on a little fancy table by the front door. She grabs them and rushes out and down the street. Runs until she's out of breath, not even bothering to put up the umbrella though she can hardly see because her glasses get so wet. When she comes to a little children's park with swings and a sand pile, she sits on a bench and does put up the umbrella. It doesn't do much good. She's already wet anyway.

What a household! How could she have let herself be working there? Those pictures, and the lewd old man. Called her "Dear." Good heavens, what was he all about?

And here she's taken a purse (dirty socks and pearls, too) and doesn't know who it's stolen from, though it might be hers. How much money has she stolen? She hasn't been a very responsible person through all this. But she's still all tingly; though that's no excuse for bad behavior. Except there'll be a name in there, and maybe addresses.

Still thunder though at least it's stopped raining. More or less.

There ought to be some special power granted her in place of what she used to know — some sort of compensation for having lost her name and home, but how find out what that is? Although maybe she'd had special powers all along and forgot about them just as she had forgotten everything else. Or perhaps she'd had them all along, but never forced herself hard enough to have discovered what they were — or what it is. One power would do. So maybe forgetting who she was is the best thing that ever happened to her. It forces her to think about her power. Whatever it turns out to be, she'll use it for good, of course.

She stares at the trees on the far side of the park, pushing hard with all her muscles. She focuses only on the very highest branches. Half measures won't do. Funny what she hasn't forgotten. All the basic truths. Thank Goodness for that.

She shuts her eyes and tries again. What happens is that her arms and legs feel even more tingly than before, but all this tingling might be important. That might be part of it.

"Is bliss, then, such abyss
I must not put my foot amiss?..."

Those trees are tamaracks and oak, and here are cornflowers. She remembers those.

"I am daughter of earth and water
and nursling of the sky...."

That was about a cloud, though, not a person. But it could be about a person.

She is certainly full of poetry. She knows all about it. Did she before? Tears come to her eyes. She licks at them as they trickle to her lips. Poetry! Think of that!

The world is taking on an odd grayish-pinkish color. In this light anything can happen, and here comes another big, black, fast cloud. Maybe time to try again. Really work at it. Tops of trees. Not that she could ever fly. That's not it at all.

Then a great crash and lightning again — somewhere behind her tree, the very one she's been concentrating on. Poetry and this, too. But it took a lot out of her. For a minute she thought she'd faint. She almost fell off the bench. Mustn't try that too often. Save it for dire need only.

But it's getting very dark. She needs some place to go to think about things, gather herself together and come to terms. She'll have to hurry if she's to get somewhere before she's caught out in it again and this time in the dark. Where, except back there? She has to return the purse, but she'll take a look first. There'll be clues. She doubts she can stand up right now, anyway.

Katherine Green. One thing she knows for sure about her real name is that it's long and complicated. She can almost remember it: Dlugochevsky, Scalamadre, Schneidermesser.... Like those. She's always been embarassed by it.

Always had to spell it several times before people got it right. This Green can't be hers. Not much money here to return, but there's credit cards. She should take it back before it's missed. And get the pearls and socks back, too. There's a good temporary solution — if she can pull it off. That guest room looked completely unused. She could rest up in there and dry off and pull herself together. Think about all these important things that keep happening. Everything might come back to her in a flash after a little rest. And she's hungry. She could creep down in the middle of the night and get herself some food.

One more thing she knows about herself: she's good at sneaking around. She's just this side of invisible and always has been. Though that man had seen her well enough when he'd asked her ... ordered her to lie down next to him. But it's a big house, there must be lots of hiding places.

She finds the keys and also a photo of the old man and another of a young one. The young one, no doubt. She'd better study it so she'll know him when she sees him. He's slight and thin yet looks like the old man even so. Shy most likely. They say it's those shy ones you have to watch out for.

But she must hurry on back. She just can't take any more lightning.

"Whither, midst falling dew...."

Oh, yes! Oh, yes! She'd always liked poetry.

"While glow the heavens with the last steps of day...."

That's what's happening right now. And, "Lone wandering, but not lost." Not exactly completely lost.

And now a great crash again and here it comes: a line of rain like a curtain, rushing towards her.

Thank goodness the storm is noisy and she has the keys. It was no problem getting in and up to the guest room. She has taken off her wet clothes and wrapped herself in the chenille bedspread, India fashion, one end thrown over her shoulder. In a rather dashing way, she thinks. The two men are in the kitchen. She'd heard them talking as she came up the stairs.

But suddenly, and all the better, too, the lights go out. Good thing she had a look-around before she left the house. She'll be able to wander about all she wants. But first she stands by the window watching the storm.

"To him who, in the love of Nature, holds
Communion with her visible forms...."

People and places and her very self have gone out of her head and instead there's all this poetry. Like a gift. Could she ask for more than to be full of these phrases? Could there be any higher magic than this? Even to call down lightning?

She hears the two men in the hallways just outside her door. They're saying that the phone is out, too, and that they might as well go to bed early. She really will have the run of the house. She can see the flashing of their flashlights from under her door. Maybe she'll be able to find a flashlight for herself

She waits, listening to them settling down, and to the dripping from the eaves and trees and the thunder getting farther and farther away.

One of them, probably the young man — she certainly hopes it isn't the old man — is singing ... trying to sing the Bell Song from Lamke, falsetto. He's walking down the hall thumping hard on his heels, sounding big and fat, not like that skinny one in the picture. "Night Popayo," he yells as he passes near her door, and then slams his own. The older man just grunts. After that things are quiet.

A few minutes later she's sitting on the window seat of the study with a flashlight and a book of poetry. It was already lying there. John Donne. And she has a glass of hot milk and a peanut butter sandwich.

"Tell me, where all past years are," (Yes, yes.)
Or who cleft the Divels foot,
Teach me to heare Mermaides singing, ..."

Had she gone to college after all? Or — what in the world — had she jumped into somebody else's body? Even that? The magic done, and now all the power of poetry and of poems, hers?

But she should take the book into the guest room. It'll be safer there and she can read a bit and sleep a bit. Sleep often solves everything. Even as you drift off, things come back to you. She turns out the flashlight, takes the book and starts down the hall in the dark.

Somebody grabs her from behind. She gives a little half-cut-off cry... She's held, tight against a sweaty paunch. It's that older man.

"Are you done, Dear Heart? What in the world are you wearing? It's got little balls all over?"

Dear Heart! Who would say that?

And now his mustachey kisses all over the back of(she knows it for a fact) her wrinkled old neck. How can he? — though, of course, he's not so young and handsome himself She should take the money in the purse and find the bus station. Get a ticket for some place far away from wherever it is she is.

Now is the time for the big "umph" that will make happen whatever should happen and it better not be more poetry, but that she should levitate straight up from half under his paunch, or that she should jump into another universe, start a fire, bring the lightning down right now and right here.

Actually, his paunch feels good; comforting and warm. How nice it would be to let herself rest back against him. But she mustn't let anything like that happen. She must be true to whatever it is she really is.

Could she ever have fallen in love with a man like this? She might have gotten used to him before he got so fat and bald. Or perhaps he had qualities that had made her not care how he looked?

"Is this the bedspread you're wearing?"

"I got wet."

"Funny thing to put on."

"It was handy. I was cold."

"Can't say you're not full of surprises."

Could that be true? If so, maybe she can get away with most anything.

But now his hands are pulling the bedspread away. His arms are crossed over her chest and each hand holds a breast. Slobbery kisses all over her shoulders.... As if she hadn't been wet enough already. But she'd just been reading Donne:

"Take heed of loving mee,
At least remember, I forbade it thee; ...

She says it in a nice way, as why be cruel?

He says:

"Thus I reclaim my buzard love, to flye
At what, and when, and how, and where I chuse: ..."

He says it as if he means it, voice an octave below what it had been before.

Can she run out into the rain wearing just a bedspread?

Her heart is pounding so it scares her. His arms are all that's keeping her from falling.

"Are you all right?"

And now the young man comes thumping down the hall to the bathroom. "You two love birds making out right here in the hall? Watch out, the lights might come back on."

If she left — managed to ... in time — it would be to a roving life. She'd probably have to sleep out under a bridge. Wouldn't it be better if she stayed here and kept her mouth shut? She'd have to play it all out, sex and all. But how nice if she could use that study sometimes. Maybe nobody would mind. Sit on the window seat and read and do the cleaning, too.

He's still holding her, and then he picks her up as if she was hardly any weight at all and takes her into the big bed. A candle is lit in there. Flickering. He should have trimmed the wick.

"I have a terrible headache," she says.

He lies down next her. She's still cold and he's so warm she feels she might go off to sleep by mistake. Stay here sleep and speak in poems.

He puts his arm over her. This time not in a sexy way.

"I wonder by my troth, what thou, and I
Did, till we lov'd? ..."

She hears it, half asleep already, this fat, sweaty man — in flickering light.... But what about those awful pictures in the room next door? And he does order her around. Is that proper even if she's the maid?

She wakes. He's snoring slobbery snores, no two alike. Fat man snores. Clock says: one, two, three, four. Half after midnight. Candle guttering worse than ever. And she still doesn't know anything about herself, except she knows how to be good and do good. Of course who would ever need to know more? So far at least, she didn't have to do that. If she stays, for sure she'll have to. That's the bargain.' It's only fair.

She slithers out the side of the bed.

"Where are you off to?"

There's an apple tree right outside his window.

"Is bliss then, such abyss
I must not put my foot amiss
For fear I spoil my shoe? ..."

She says it out loud without meaning to.

"Ah, bliss," he says. "Where lies bliss?" (Exactly what she was wondering herself) "If not right here?"

These people obviously need a lot of help. But shouldn't she use her new (if new) powers for the good of man kind in general? And women, too? It would be so easy just to lie back right here. And probably doing that "it" isn't so bad. People do seem to like it. Even good people. But she must pick the hardest of all to do. That would be the most rewarding in the long run ... not rewarding for herself, but to the world. After all, she doesn't even know who she is, let alone she should be rewarding herself What if she doesn't deserve it?

Out the window, then, and into the tree. She's spry.

"Come with the dawn
Blue-devil sprite,
Leave us unto night, ...

Poetry's all right for now. The lightning — it wears her out. She'll keep her special power for emergencies only. And all the better if she doesn't ever have to use it.

What if he calls out, "Dear Heart," again? If he does, she will remember it the rest of her life.

Alchemy, No. 1, 2003

On Display Among The Lesser

Those who look to the clouds...those who swear by the moon...those who say they understand the stars....That's not us. We're here, in the land of the far, far, far...east of some and west of others. It's us who know the world, from north to south to middle. We see it all spread out. We live above, and soar. All others are our meals. Not a one that isn't. We, cliff dwellers, baskers in the sun, dancers, keepers of the seasons and of time and of all the directions.

How ride the sky grid? How ride the thermals? How be the one on the top of every pinnacle? Be us. It's the only way.

We're known for our beauty, and I, the largest and most beautiful even of my own kind. Always a sharp intake of breath when I spread my wings. Who could help it? My red, my black and white, my iridescence....

What is there to fear for creatures such as we? Masters of the air? And I, the largest.

What's to fear—that is, except the mobbers? Only the mob of the small and irrelevant ever forces us out of the sky, all the way down to where we have no choice but to hop and limp. Flutter. They're experts at blows to the head but they're too small to kill.

I had left the perches of our precipice. But first I'd hopped about the dance platform for no reason than for joy. I had flapped and strutted. (I had no mate yet though I had my choice of all of them. Who would have what it takes to be my consort? So far there was not a one equal to me.)

Then I'd soared away, cried out goodbye...to no one...to everyone.

My first meal that morning was poisonous snake.

After that I thought to get myself a lookout from among the lesser before she could call the alarm but she was quick. I raised a whirlwind of dust for nothing.

Then I thought eggs—little speckled brown ones.

It's a long time since I felt fear. I remember it from when I was a chick. I pushed my brother out of the nest...it had to be. Later, I fell out of the nest myself and was almost eaten by a fox. By then I was half fledged and, with talons and frantic fluttering, I managed to climb back to the aerie. My parents killed the fox and brought me the pieces. The last time I was afraid was when my parents forced me from the nest. I was sure I'd end up at the bottom of the cliff as I had before. But since then I've felt nothing but my power. I've matched all creatures tooth to beak, claw to talon.

But the mobbers. A dozen...ridiculously small. I was after their eggs. They left as soon as they got me on the ground but I didn't dare take to the air. I had blood blinding me, but I knew I wasn't going to die from their pecking. I hopped a while but I can't cover any distance that way. I was just about to trust the air again when I got caught. Not by the mob this time, but by a net.

I know all about nets, and being a slave or being made into stew. There's not a parent among us doesn't warn the newly fledged.

It's shameful for one such as I to be captured by the lesser dirt dwellers. The furry ones. I won't go quietly. When they come for me they'll be in shreds if I have anything to say about it.

I'll be tough eating. I'm past the tender age. At least they won't enjoy me. But I suppose it's only fair they should. I've been grateful for dirt dwellers that were tender and sweet. You'd think those that live in burrows wouldn't taste so good.

If I have to work for my food and spend half the day hooded, I'll wait my chance to kill and eat my master. But it could be the zoo. Huddled in a cage. Handed scraps—on the end of stick for fear of me. I, dancer, flap-flapper, flip-flopper, leaper, dropper from the sky at astonishing speeds. I do as well upside down as in any other direction.

I know their strategy. They'll leave me here all day, wait until I'm exhausted with the effort of trying to escape, come for me when I'm too tired to fight.

I nip apart bits of the net, but I know better than to struggle. I eat three mob members caught along with me. There are several others, but those are the only ones I can reach. They're making quite a racket. Their fellow mobbers come and babble back at them. I can't understand a single chirp...nor the reason for it. What good will it do?

Night comes. They all quiet down. Still our captors haven't come for us.

Perhaps they forgot. Or, rather, if they're smart, they'll wait till morning.

I doze but I don't dare sleep. Here on the ground, and unable to move my head much or flap my wings, even a creature as insignificant as an owl...even a bat or rat might nip at me.

In the morning the chittering dirt dwellers come. They kill the little birds and put them in bags, but they keep a safe distance from me. More come, all standing up as if on guard, crowding each other, whispering as though I might understand their squeaking, but we've never wanted to know the language of our meals.

Yet more come and with a thicker net and a cart. They don't remove the net I'm caught in, they just add the heavier one on top of it and pull them both tight around me. They have a contraption to lift me onto the cart. They don't want to get close even now that I'm tied in two nets. They're careful—as though I were precious—as though every bruise would diminish my value. I'm wondering what they want me for that they need me so pristine?

They pick up every lost feather and wear them behind their ears. I think they'll pull out more so everybody can have one and I won't be able to fly, but they don't.

I can't believe how they chitter. They never stop. I haven't seen a single mouth that isn't moving.

Even my stare doesn't stop them, though they glance away quickly so as not to be caught by my eyes.

I'm carted off on a bumpy ride—dozens of them pulling. I'm bounced along over ground I've only seen from the air. It looks uninteresting. Dirty. Full of obstacles I never knew were obstacles.

Finally they put me in a cage hardly as wide as my wingspan and hardly taller than my head. They cut away the nets. I try to hack at the creatures but they're careful. I only get in one good bite—tear off a chunk of leg and eat it. Sweet and tender as they usually are, but that only makes me hungrier.

Another of my kind is caged across from me, looking bedraggled and gloomy. Worse than gloomy, hopeless. She's missing the largest and most spectacular of her feathers. She doesn't look at me. I was about to squawk a greeting but I let her be—lost in whatever daydream of flying she might be conjuring up.

She looks as if she hasn't preened in a long time. She must have once been quite presentable. Now who would look at her? I wonder if she can still fly with most of her longest feathers gone. My feathers are a mess, too, and, as she is, I'm too confined to straighten myself out.

They give me water but nothing to eat. I've had nothing but that bite of one on them. They feed her, but I can see the food is dead and smells rotten.

We're under a kind of lean-to. There's a roof, but it's open to the elements on one side.

We spend the night with fleas, mice and rats.

In the morning I want to speak to her but she so obviously doesn't want me to—or doesn't care—about anything.

Later that same morning there's a celebration—because of me. A great tootling and stamping and squeaking. Long lines of them come just to look at me. I hadn't known there were so many. They must spend most of their time out of sight underground. There's pointing...squealing. It might be singing, but it sounds like squealing. They feed me, finally, and exclaim at my way of eating—as I turn my meal head out so, fur or feathers, it'll slip down easily—and then gulp it in one gulp.

Through all this the other of my kind...the female, hunches lower until her beak is almost on the ground. If she had a place to hide she'd go there. So would I.

At night, when the crowd has left, I speak to her. ("When? How long? What will they do with us?") But she only lowers her head even more. Hunched as she is, and though she still has her stripes and her red here and there, she looks more like a vulture than one of us. I say, "We can help each other," though I can't think how.

But she helps me, and without a word. They starve me, all the while feeding her. Dead things, already beginning to smell. When she realizes what they're doing, she hides half her food in the back of her cage and gives it to me after they've left at night. She tosses bits through the bars to me. Never misses. She's still got her skills.

I bow and thank each time. And each time I ask her if she knows what will happen to me but she always turns away. Then I talk and talk—for no reason than to reassure. I speak softly. I want to bring back hope. I want her to lift her head, to look at me. I want to bring back the hypnotic glare to her glance. I tell her I'll get us out of here. I suppose I need to reassure myself as much as her.

By the fourth day of little food and all of it rotten, my head and neck are becoming more like hers, curving halfway to the floor. That night when she throws in bits of her food again, I say I know she's half starving herself so that I won't completely starve. I bow and thank again. Then I plead with her again, if she knows what will happen, or if she knows what they want us for, to tell me. "Is it just to keep us here? On display? And if so, why starve us?"

Finally she tries. She finds it hard to get words out. First she says, "Dance." Her voice sounds more like an angry jay than one of us.

"Dance? How can that be?"

"For no reason...than the dance."

"Why?

"They like it." She finally finds her voice though she leaves out half the words. "Watch out when the live food comes. Wing," she says. "Be careful"

I bow and thank and bow and thank. I say again, "I'll get us out of here.

"No. Worry when the food comes. Wing. Worry wing."

And food does comes, a day later—and for the first time, since that day when they watched me eat, live food.

She calls, "Don't be tricked."

There's three...still squirming foods...still crying out. Finally what I'm used to. They wave the creatures back and forth in front of me. I can't help myself, I lunge. This way and that. While she, across from me, keeps calling, "Stop." They tease and tempt until, finally, they let me catch them. I don't realize until too late that, as I lunge and gnash, they've clipped one of my wings.

I rage. I know it won't help but I do it anyway. I lose several feathers by flapping about in such a confined space. She, too, has lost so many...certainly she has also raged, and she tries, now, to stop me. When I finally exhaust myself, those that don't already have a feather behind their ears, come and pick one up.

They hood me, then let me out. I try to fly. I think to escape even if I can't see, but I'm lopsided. There's no possible way I can fly. And I'm already exhausted, as they know. After jumping, fluttering and losing more feathers, I let myself be led. And then the hood is taken off and I'm on a dancing platform. Not a very good one. I almost don't recognize it.

They're gathered around—hundreds of them.

They know how we say, "Dance." They know how we call it out, loud and like a happy song. The way they try to say it, it's garbled but I know what they mean. Most likely they also know it's our call for females to come dance with us. They call that now. I'm shocked...that I'd be here alone and called to dance, and on this lumpy platform—called by creatures that usually are my meals. I won't do it.

But they have ways. Slap at my feet until I'm dancing just to avoid the slats they poke me with. They clack their teeth. That's what they do when they like what I'm doing. I try to be more awkward but they like that even better. How I must look with only half a wing and hopping up and down to avoid sticks.

But they've brought me here exhausted. I stagger. I fall several times. They don't mind. They clack their teeth all the more. Whatever I'm doing, they love it. No doubt they like seeing an exhausted, dilapidated creature make a fool of himself. One who swoops down and carries away their little ones—one who makes all their days precarious. No doubt I'm the very one who carried off some of their own beloved.

Finally I fall and can't get up. They keep on slapping at me but I can't move. They stop, flop me into the cart and bounce me back to the cage. They don't bother with the hood, they know I'm too worn out to fight back. They leave me on the floor of my cage. They don't even give me fresh water. What I have is dusty and warm and has bugs in it, but I drink it anyway.

Now it's the female's turn to talk—and keep on talking—trying to raise my spirits. Now her head is up while mine is low. Talking has given her a reason to hope. She could have said, "I told you so. I told you beware," but she doesn't.

She talks most of the night. As I did to her. The same sort of things that I said. "You'll fly again. The feathers will grow. You'll find a way to break free. They'll get careless. Imagine the damage we could do together. We could stand back to back and slash. Don't despair. And you're so large—so beautiful and large." (Even in my sorry state she says it.) "You can take on crowds of the dirt dwellers."

Then, "Think of cliffs. Think of the home sky." After that, "I come from the blue valley. We sweep down from the rocks, down onto the sand. Wheeling, wheeling, rising.... Think of sunshine. My name is Sunshine. When you're feeling better... and you will feel better... you'll tell me your name."

I must have helped her with my talking or she wouldn't be doing it for me. I sleep, to the sound of her voice going on and on. I hardly listen to the meanings. How did she manage, going through this all by herself? No wonder she was in such despair. I, at least, have her.

I had thought I'd never tell such a one as she my name...such a one...so unworthy. I don't think she ever was large and impressive. But I hate to be "The Grand" in front of her who never could have been grand. I think to make up a simpler name. Cliff perhaps, or Blue or Air. Yes, I'll tell her Air.

Dance for your supper. Dance even for a drink of fresh cool water. Now, again, all the food is dead. Now not dancing for a mate...perhaps never dancing for a mate...never even see a possible mate...never one worthy of my size and beauty and ability to dance. Dance, now, only to entertain creatures who are merely food.

They can't imagine legs so sprightly, such back and forth and in and out. My leaps, higher than three times their heads. Their music, banging, tootling, isn't to my taste but I have to dance anyway, feathers flying off. (It's the diet of the dead, causes that.)

(I see my feathers are going for three bowls of acorns for just one.)

Sunshine and I often talk now, but not, anymore, as we did those first nights and never about the joy of being us, nor the joy of our way of life, and especially not of the joy and meanings of the dance.

We talk of the here and now, fleas and dirty water, dead food. And then we talk of cold mountain streams and where we'll drink when we get free. And whether her favorite drinking place is better than mine. We depend on each other for hope. I grow to like her. My being here has saved her from having to dance. We worry about what will happen now that she isn't dancing. We worry if she'll go for food. We wonder what I could do to save her when they come for her.

But later she asks the question that I dread. "Would you dance with me... for me?"

Of course I wouldn't, but what can I say? I say, yes. I don't even hesitate. She needs that answer, and who knows what's going to happen. Perhaps we'll never leave here, or she might die—she looks draggled enough. We both look as if all we need do is wish for death and death would come.

As I get used to dancing for them I begin to do my best. It can't be very good, anyway, with only one real wing. But they're moved. They cry. At first I wonder why—why cry for their worst enemy, and then I know—because of beauty and skill. I have some left. I'm not like I used to be, but they can't tell the difference. Still.... There must be some spark...some little glow of appreciation of true art.

But now something new. I no sooner get to the dance platform than they bring out Sunshine. Are we to dance with each other? It's outrageous! I can't move. I won't.

Her head begins to lower. "Oh," she says, "did you lie?"

"I can't do it."

"You said you would. Have you danced with another? Some earlier time?"

"No. But I can't."

Her beak is almost on the platform. I can't add to her despair. Besides, could there ever be any other? We belong together. A bedraggled pair. No one else would have either one of us. And no one else knows what we know. No one's lived through this.

"I'll do it."

"Don't. This is for forever."

"I know."

I begin the bowing. Now she's the one who hesitates. Does a kind of sideways bow. Begins as though the whole thing depresses her even more than she already is.

But once you begin, dancing is its own reward...its own reason for being. And in spite of her half a wing she dances well. As do I. She leaps as high as I do. I can't help but respond. I can't help but love. My love is crippled. My love is full of fleas. My love is unpreened, unwashed, unhappy...though not right now. Easy to see what a dancer she once was. And there's something else in our dance that I've never seen in dances before. What we know, and have been through... all goes into the dance. I've never seen such a thing. Even the lesser ones cry for us. We cry, too.

I wish I had food to give her. All I can do is pretend. I say, "If I had, I'd give."

"If you gave, I'd accept." And she pretends to take.

But then I know what to do. I say, "Put your bad wing on top of my bad wing."

She doesn't know what I mean. "The breeze is rising. Your good wing and my good wing...."

Her eyes light up. Take on some of their compelling gleam.

"Yes!"

We're half starved. Lighter than we used to be. It might work.

First we dance that way, practicing. Leaping even higher, our good wings flapping in unison. It *will* work. We won't get much height, but not much is needed.

The lesser like us all the better. They clack and whistle. They want us to mate right there in front of everybody. As if we were low creatures just like them.

"If we can catch the wind just right.... You call out the rhythm. I'll follow."

As we rise the dirt dwellers cry out a terrible cry, all at the same time. It causes us to wobble even more than we do already. We almost dip down into their reaching claws.

Then we're away. We skim along just above bushes. We have trouble staying that high. Any animal large as a wolf could snap us up.

A mob finds us, but what's a bloody head after what we've been through? I hadn't thought they'd mob so low or when we're no threat to their eggs. I suppose we're an easy target and they're just having fun. Or we look like some gigantic two headed beast, more menacing than the usual sky folk.

We'll have to land to get away. They won't stop until we do. I look for a good place. Besides, we need to rest. Neither of us has been flying for a long time. She, especially, has lost her strength and collapses the minute we set down. I realize we won't be able to go any farther today.

We let go of each other and hop to a thorny horse brush. I help her tuck herself in under the branches. "I'll get you food."

"But you can't fly by yourself."

I'd felt so free, I had actually forgotten. "You rest. I'll find a way to hunt. Perhaps a quail or some other bird that lays its eggs on the ground."

We rub necks, clack bills, coo.

As I hop away, she's already as stock-still—as if a chick who senses menace. She's an easy target, but I have to leave her. Though I don't suppose I'll go far.

What a way to hunt, hopping, fluttering, jumping, walking.... (I'm not made for walking.) Down here I can only see what's straight in front of my face, everything is hidden behind something else. I don't know how to sneak or skulk. My talons scrabble and slip. But I won't return without something for her.

I find three eggs in a ground nest. I'd carry them back to her but I can't without breaking them. I eat them. They're so small they only whet my appetite.

But our eggs! Our chicks! Will they have to be born on the ground? Easy eating for dirt dwellers? Would we have to stoop to the broken wing trick? How long does it take for feathers to grow back? Does Sunshine know?

I chase after voles and mice and don't catch them. I leap after robins. I miss. This will take some learning.

I find a flock of quail with a dozen babies, little white balls hurrying behind them. I scoop up four before they have a chance to hustle the others into their bushes.

I hop back to Sunshine with them in my beak. They're small, but she takes them as though they were large as four dirt dwellers. With clacking and cooing we pledge ourselves to each other.

Then we make a circle of the grasses near us, and, as though in a nest, we sleep.

And wake refreshed, though hungry.

"We'll hunt together, one to chase, and one to catch and kill."

"We'll leap and flap so as to see above the sagebrush."

We do.

And leaping makes us realize that, though flightless, we really are, at last, free.

Lots of those less fierce than we, are flightless and they live. Used to be we were the long lived and the short on patience, now perhaps short lived and long on patience. But what a sky! Even from way down here.

"Look at the sky."

"Smell the wind."

"Let's dance. For ourselves this time."

We do.

Sci Fiction, April 14, 2004

Gliders Though They Be

They live, as we do, by the shadows, by the warmth of stones on sunny days, by fissures in rocks. They scramble, skulk, and skitter—as we do. They die, as we do, by the sky, by the trees. Live by black brush, prickly poppies. Die by the drop and dive and skim of the masters from the air.

You'll be right in among them, doing everything their way. You'll be trying to like their kinds of food. You'll be spitting out pin feathers. In spite of yourself you'll say, Oh, oh, oh. And you'll have to sing their songs of self satisfaction, but don't forget you're one of Us.

Find the ins and outs of their warrens. The windings and deadends, the escape hatches. Know their ditches, the views from their hills....

They call themselves *The* Creatures, as if we weren't. They call their section of the land, *The* Place as if our place wasn't as much a place as theirs. They say they live at the center of the world as though we don't.

That's all right, let them think what they have to think.

Love your enemies. You'll *have* to. Hide your distaste. But you won't have to kiss them unless you want to. Though sometimes our kind does fall in love with their kind, so soft and pink, so thin, so close at hand, as they will be to you. Our kind always thinks such love is a mistake, but I say, all the better. (You'll be thinking your new babies will take to the air along with theirs. Don't count on it.)

Though they keep calling it that, remember they can't fly. It's only gliding.

And their wings...They aren't really wings, just a few feathers, in with their fur. But they're the big problem. Or, rather, the problem is us...that we have none. In all other ways we're exactly like them. They crawl around just like we do. Rush from hideout to hideout, all the time looking up to investigate the sky. They squeak out warnings just like we do. We might as well be them though they wouldn't have us.

Bring a sharp knife. Not to kill—of course not—but to...*you* know. Be sure to get them just before they're fledged. After that, success will be unlikely. Every single one you cut will be a blow in our favor.

It all depends on them, everything depends on them, it always has. Though now everything depends on you.

We can't imagine what our nubs are for except to show we're kin with them. We never fledge. Maybe we haven't tried hard enough—haven't spent enough time dropping out of trees or leaping after grasshoppers. But who, among our young ones, hasn't broken a leg from trying something foolish that those others can do without even thinking.

Perhaps it's all in the mind and we're not thinking the right thoughts. Or perhaps it's fear of falling that forces them to fledge. Maybe they push their little ones off lower branches—pry their toes up one by one and then push. Or break the branch out from under them. If they fall and keep on falling, they'll fledge soon enough. They'll have to. Being harsher on our own young might be the only way.

Nubs are ugly. Wings...so delicate, so optimistic...are lovely. Even so it'll be easy for one of us to hide among them. Wear a vest or hang a scarf over where your wings ought to be, and you can pass for them. Go!

They have no trees! That's my first shock. Hills and valleys...mounds of loose dirt next to entrances, yes, piles of rocks just like home, and bushes.... You'd think they'd have trees. I wasn't told the most important thing. Perhaps they have gnawed them all down as a safety measure—which it surely is. Perhaps they don't ever say, Die by the trees, as we say.

But then I see they do have...*one*...just one huge tree off in the middle of their compound. It's the largest I've ever seen. They must take great care of it. Keep it watered. We had no idea they lived like this.

I wear a vest that hides my nubs. Thank goodness there are some of them that are of our bluish color. We're larger than they are, but not by much. Perhaps that's why we can't glide. Though why don't we fledge? And why have these ugly nubs in the first place?

I had skittered along with others of their kind. I joined a hunting group, bringing back voles, locusts, beetles.... I had nothing hanging from my belt, but many other's didn't either. Since I'm bigger than most of them, I thought to wrestle something from one of the smaller ones, but then I thought better of it.

Now, through the gates and into their treeless...almost treeless compound. I hope I don't look too surprised as I enter.

It's neater than ours. And in spite of having no trees (except that one) they've made plenty of places for shade and to hide under. Little lean-tos and platforms, prickly poppies are growing right on top of some of them.

Handsome though I am (and especially so in my red vest—or so my own kind tells me) right away they squint at me. Some clack their teeth. Perhaps I remind them of Us. I puff up so as to look even larger though I lose some of my shine that way. I know that's not a good idea, considering I'll look even more like one of Us, but I want to scare them as much as they're scaring me. I become myself. Or, rather, I become Us.

I hum a tune I know is theirs—I *think* is theirs—we always said it was theirs, but what do we really know of them? By the looks of their one tree land, even less than we thought.

It must have been the right things to do because a large female evaluates me carefully. She has a reddish cast, pink eyes, lashes as long as her whiskers. Each eyelash and each whisker has three colors, brown, white, and pink. Even though she's one of theirs, she's superb.

With my own, I'd chitter or some such but I don't know what works with them. And I don't want to spark any jealousy among their males or attract attention to myself. But I do clack my teeth a few times.

Females are larger than males, and she is one of their largest. But they're not fighters. They're no good for anything but having children. If cornered or if any little ones are in danger, even if not their own, they become much worse than any male could ever be, but I doubt that fighting will be called for if, when I cut, I do it out of sight.

We, I and the hunting group, advance towards the center of the compound. When we're not far from their tree, I leave the group and enter a burrow—up the lookout mound of loose dirt at the doorway and then down, down, down. Just like home.

Soon I hear singing coming from below. Female singing. When I get deeper and closer I stop and listen. You have to be born to their kind of music to understand it. Same with their kind of dancing, (head bobbing up and down—exactly like a lizard trying to attract a female). Bla, bla, bla goes their poetry. But as I listen to the song I can tell there's a pattern to it, and the voice, is delightful: squeaky, and shrill. Were it used as a warning signal, there's none who'd not hear and obey. I feel shivers up and down my spine.

They told me, go ahead, love. Might be the best way to hide. And the best way to find out whether it's our only way to survive. They said, "Some of us, as you are, are handsome and bold. Do whatever it takes. Become them as best you can."

Almost all our compounds have gone over to their side. It may be that we have nothing else to do but pretend we're them, except we don't know how. The how, is my job. (Along with the cutting, which will make them more like Us.)

I step closer and around the corner so I can see. There's a large room hollowed out and the floor covered with glittery jay feathers. What a singer she is! I can hardly believe her high notes. Higher than I've ever heard. Out in the open air her song would carry for miles. I don't doubt but that I may have heard her screeches as far away as from our own land. And what a remarkable size to her! Except for her pink, you'd think she was one of ours. Her wings lie, folded under her arms. They glisten in the glow of the burrow. I wonder, at her size, can she really glide? We've heard that sometimes their females get so big they can no more glide than we can.

I flatten my fur to give it more glow. I enter boldly. Everyone has squatted down but I stand in the back—and stare. I can't help it. Even if I didn't want to, I couldn't not stare—her legs so delicate, her feet so small, the bulk of her, her front teeth that peep out as she sings. I wonder if how I feel shines out from my eyes. But then it's in the eyes of all of them, males and females alike.

I try to approach her after the performance but of course everybody else wants to, too. We do look at each other, both of us half a head above the others.

I think how good we'd look, her pink next to my blue. She must know that, too.

After a bit I see I'm not going to get near her with all those admirerers crowding around. I leave. I explore the burrow. There isn't much more to it but the escape hatches. And I feel the need for air after all that emotion.

But just as I come out, the call comes. Almost as beautiful as their singer's high notes. Some other singer on guard duty. Sky alert. We all rush back in. After a moment we peek out to see what's going on. Striped neck, striped tail, speckled underbelly.... Quite beautiful actually. Sky folk always are. Already high, the flap, flap, flap. A baby shrieks—and shrieks and shrieks. Somewhere a mother calls out her goodbye—calls out her love. The shrieks get farther and farther away though the mother keeps calling out long after it's useless. But it isn't as if we don't all expect this.

It's over. Everybody comes out. Not a one stays inside. Back with my own we do the same. I mill around with the others. We squeak and pat each other. We clack our teeth. It would be a perfect time for another of the sky folk to get us. They would have to take a big one now that the little ones have all been pushed back inside. Though if they're like our own, there's always one or two who find a way to sneak out some back door.

She's there of course. They're still crowding around her. I wonder if I'll ever be able to get close. I ask her name. "Lee-ah of the far north holes." "Ah, the far north hole's Lee-ah." A name equal to her bulk, her poise, her tiny feet.

Everyone is still looking up. I step around them, working my way closer, patting shoulders as I pass the others. I make sure my vest hides where my wings should be. Closer. Then close at last. I whisper. "Lee-ah of the far north." She smiles—her beautiful smile, gnawing teeth showing in the front. I can see she's glad to see me.

I say, "Except that I've met you and heard and seen your brilliance, a sad time."

"A sorrow." She raises her head as though to bare her throat to me. A good sign. Then says, "And you, from where?"

I bare my throat, too, but I had hoped she wouldn't ask the important question so soon. If they're like us, I have to come from far enough away from her north and yet not be from my own North. I say, "Also the north, but the east of the north."

That's the truth. One step farther up from their North and I'd be at home with my own.

It must be all right because she says, "I do love those from the east north." I know what she means by that.

She shakes her shoulders and spreads her wings a little bit as though to show them off.

I shake, too, and hope my vest still hides my nubs. "I say, "Glorious." I show my front teeth.

She asks if I sing. I say, "No," She says, "It doesn't matter. Not at all." Then, "Will you join the contest? Please."

I don't know what she means and it must show on my face.

"The contest!"

I squint and clack my teeth, not from choice but from nervousness.

"The mating. For all of us. And for me! For me!

"Of course I will."

"Until then," she says and moves away, magnificently— swaying side to side on purpose to lure me.

But I'm too anxious to be tempted to the extent she wants me to be right now. I have to find out what she's talking about without seeming to ask. I worry. We have contests, too, but I already suspect what theirs might be. *Of course* would be. Gliding! Probably from higher and higher branches. That's what that tree is for. Once you really look at it you can see worn spots and claw marks, branches flattened out into platforms. I can't be seen doing that. Or even trying to do that. Besides, I'd break every leg—at the least. I don't have to join the mating contest but I want to.

If I don't do it, I can just hear it. "Lost your wings? An accident? The punishment for some crime? What crime is that, to make you one of the Lesser? Go up north where you belong.

Until I came here, I had no idea they call us the Lesser. Though that makes sense. Except we're so large and strong, and we have such a beautiful iridescent blueness.

For the next few days, as I wait for the contest, I show off by lifting things none of them can. I carry heavy loads for long distances. I feel superior to all of them. And I have managed to get three young ones who can't yet squeak out to their mothers what I've done, and removed their first hints of feathers. That leaves no scar, and leaves them fledglings who will never fledge.

I have an entourage of admirers. Young ones who want to be just like me. Several females want me to glide for them when the time of the contest comes but I'll stay true to my exquisite pink singer.

I remember when I was small and had heard about these others. I couldn't believe that I was Us and not them...I was sure I could glide. A group of us climbed a tree and jumped, squeaking out our triumph. One died, two broke legs as did I. All of us bruised and chastened. Almost all our young males try it. After that we stick to our own contests, broad jump, high jump, skittering....

We try not to let our little ones hear about those others, so like us, until they're old enough to understand we're Us, and that we can't glide no matter how hard we try.

Here, they've been practicing their glides. The handsomest, the youngest, the most fit. I'm all of those, but of course I don't practice. At least not that way. I'm awed by the heights they leap from. I'd be frightened just climbing up that high and looking down. So that's what I practice—just climbing up a bit higher than I'm comfortable. I sit on a branch. I make myself stay there until I've stopped hanging on so tight my limbs hurt—until I've stopped sweating... stopped breathing hard. Then I go up a little higher and do it all over again.

I miss the afternoons of Lee-ah's singing. I have to do it then because there's nobody around except a few sentinels. Thank goodness none posted near their tree.

There are two times a day I dare practice, when she sings and in the moonlight. (Though the ground is all in shadows, it's even scarier then.) I get to know the tree so well that I know every branch.

She sings for them everyday at midday. It's the time for a rest. It's hot and the burrows are cool. Everyone hunkers down in that vaulted cavern to listen. They just leave a few guards outside. That would be a perfect time for Us to get almost all of them in one operation. All we'd have to do is close off the entrance and station warriors at the escape hatches.

When I'm up on the branches, I imagine launching myself into the air, leaping away, as far out as I can to avoid the lower branches, my limbs spread. (I've watched how they do it.) I imagine the glide. It doesn't help to think about it. I feel sicker. I cling all the harder. Besides, I know it's hopeless. And when I practice by moonlight I worry about owls. Almost more than the height. They're so silent. I'd be prey and never know it until I was in the sky.

I'm so busy and exhausted with my practicing...my useless practicing.... (How can it do any good, I'll never glide.) I'm so busy with myself I've only cut the beginning wings of those three fledglings. I did, though, get better at looking down without trembling and sweating. I can walk across the highest branches with assurance.

Someone must have seen me climbing up and then down again without gliding. As I sit, half asleep.... (I was up much of the night practicing. I was feeling good about myself. In just a few days I had mastered my fear of heights.) ...I hear someone whisper, hot breath right into my ear, the clack of teeth, whiskers pricking me.... He says, "You're not what you pretend." It's one of the guards. I know him, he's usually stationed at the escape hatch of the main burrow. He has a piercing whistle. I've told him how much I admire it. I also said I knew what a hard job he has, standing up straight to watch for so long. But he's no friend. "I know your kind. Always trying to be us. Second best if best at all. Third best. Fourth best. There is no second best to us. Who are you?"

"One of your own."

"A half-breed."

"Of course not."

"Live by the leap. Live by the song. Die by the red tail, or by those of the long red neck. Live by the granary." His red eyes glint in a nasty way. "Or live by someone else's granary."

"Our granary, I suppose."

"Why not?"

"Well, you've got them all now." I've revealed myself. "Are you telling?"

He wiggles his nose as though I'd told a joke. Perhaps I have, says, "I'd rather wait and see what happens at the leaping."

The day of the great flights (they keep calling it flying) dozens of sky folk whirl on thermals so high we can just barely see them. Guards with rock launchers stand by. First aid stands by. Runners with stretchers stand by to rush the wounded to burrows.

The leapers climb, first to the height they've decided is the highest they can safely glide, and then they climb higher.

The leap, the dive...the lovely glide, arms out as though sky folk...those little shiny wings spread.... And if they survive, it's a leap into the breeding pool. Perhaps this glide contest is exactly for creatures like me. To winnow out us lesser ones. Make sure the offspring will all at least glide. At least that. Will all be them and not Us.

All goes well for the first few leaps, but then someone lies crumpled. An eagle drops...falls...straight down, as they always do, wings tight to his sides, and before the stone throwers can even begin to think to do anything, the young one is scooped up. Again they, and I also, call out, Goodbye and love. Then there's silence. Not just us, but all birds, the jays, the quail, and even the crickets, even the cicadas, even they, feel the danger. And there's still plenty of sky folk circling up there, so high they're mere specks.

Even so, they start the glides again. I thought they'd stop and I was free until the next time. But they cheer each other more vigorously than before. Call out, "Fly, fly, fly," as if they could, and with more bravado.

Shortly before my turn, Lee-ah tells me I don't need to go too high. She says she doesn't love me for my glide and she doesn't want me to suffer even one broken leg. She'll love me no matter that they'll ridicule me if I'm the lowest jumper. She says she's not afraid of ridicule. She says she had plenty herself before she learned to sing. Maybe she suspects. Maybe she already knows all our offspring will be lesser ones. She doesn't need to see me leap...or rather not leap...to prove it.

I wish she'd told me this before. It might have made a difference.

I'm fearless. Even more so, here in front of them all. I climb higher than any of them have dared. I might as well. To one like me there's no difference, high or even higher. I look down on them...at all those who call us the lesser ones.

If I'm quick.... If I'm clever....

Many shake their heads as though to warn me. I wonder how many know.

Lee-ah stands below, her arms raised as though to catch me. I hope she doesn't. I'd kill her if I fell on her. But then she starts to sing and everybody turns to look at her. They're instantly enthralled. They squat down to listen as they always do. She must know who I am. She's giving me a chance. Perhaps I can climb down the back of the tree, come out at the bottom from around the trunk. It's thick as ten of us. Enough to hide me all the way down. But I choose the doom I've already picked out for myself.

My branch is higher, therefore thinner. I've already gnawed it half way though. I won't launch myself out beyond all the other, lower branches, limbs spread, nubs in full view. I want to come down right *on* the lower branches. I bounce on my branch as though getting ready to leap.

I come crashing down, hitting one branch after the other, reaching out to each as I fall. A feat of skill and strength for one of my kind. And I wish my kind could see me. If I ever have the chance to tell them, they'll not believe.

Even as I fall I'm thinking I hope nobody examines the branch. I gnawed it as best I could to make it look as if it broke on it's own, but I'm sure it still has my teeth marks.

Actually nobody sees me. Lee-ah is still singing.

The last part of the fall is the most dangerous. Nearer the ground, there are no branches to grab. I'll have to trust my legs. I wrapped them to strengthen them, but it won't help much.

As I fall and grab branches, I break some of their best leaping platforms.

The last drop. The worst. I plummet down. Crash. I'm so shocked, I hardly know what happened. I'm on the ground...broken legs for sure, maybe all of them. And Lee-ah, on her knees beside me. Looking up, teeth clacking. From fear or a warning to the....

The hawk drops. Almost into Lee-ah's arms. They rush to save her. They mustn't lose their singer.

But I'm grabbed. I'm whooshed away so fast. So high. The hawk's squawk and the sound of wings drowning out Lee-ah's calling out, "Oh love. Oh love."

Higher yet.... I see the whole world. I even see my own land. Little dots that are my own kind. Unaware of me. Crawling from hillock to hillock. We all do. Even these others, gliders though they be, do little more than that. Whatever they call it, it isn't flying. The only way any of us, we or they, ever really fly, is like *this*.

I had not thought there'd be so much wind. So much flap, flapping, and shaking, and that it would be so dazzling. So spectacular. I had not thought…the world so all embracing. Astonishing. If only I could tell them.

Sci Fiction, June, 2004

My General

I was immediately taken with the general though he was an awful mess and had obviously been tortured. I could hardly see what he really looked like. He was lying on the rubble of a ruined basement. The house above had been bombed out so the basement had no roof. They'd thrown a dirty tarp over him. It had been a cold night but at least it hadn't rained.

He smelled as bad as the place they'd thrown him—of urine and vomit and feces. I cleaned him off before I had them load him in my cart. That whole headquarters area is getting to be a garbage dump: rusty cans, oil drums, the remains of fires where soldiers have cooked and tried to keep warm.... Of course where they throw the prisoners is the worst.

They'd given up on getting any information out of him. They said he was mine to do with as I wished. We always take them along with us and get them back in shape for our farms. "Don't be treating him too nice," they said. "He's dangerous." They say that every time. Nothing has happened so far and it's unlikely considering the shape they're always in. Besides, most of them are happy to be with us instead of with our men. Of course we never take a general. I'm not going to tell anybody.

There's something about this one. I don't even know what. Perhaps because he's a general, but I don't think that's it. My husband is a wide man—wide face, wide body. This man is gaunt, and elegant, and has black hair. Even lying there unconscious, he looks sad. You'd think it would take eyes, open, to look so sad.

All our men are off fighting, or, if they're away from the front, they're torturing prisoners or planning new battles. Nobody's helping us on the farms. They haven't for years. The ground on our terraces is rocky. I and my donkey can hardly plow through it. Some things are a lot easier with a man around.

The men flop the general onto my donkey cart and we start back. Nobody has fixed our road since the war began. They fix the roads that go to the front but not the roads to the villages. I was afraid he'd wake up, what with all the bouncing over rocks and pot holes. Or die. I checked on him every now and then. Sometimes I go to all the trouble of getting one home and he's dead by the time I drag him off the cart. I wanted to know it before that happened. If it did, I would dump this one off along the way and come back for another. (My old one had died a month ago. Since spring, I've done all the work myself.)

It's late when I get home. Nobody's about. I tip the general out and drag him into my hut. We're allowed to bring them in when they're sick or unconscious. Otherwise they have to stay outside. I take off his generals uniform and put some of my husband's old clothes on him. I cover him with a quilt and put wrapped up hot stones by his feet. I let him have the place closest to the fireplace. I got him this far alive, I don't want to wake up to a dead man. Before I bank the fire for the night, I burn the uniform, medals and all.

With all those bruises, it's hard to tell if handsome or ugly. Ugly now, that's for sure, what with swollen jaw and lips, and the lumps on his head, but I don't think he was very good looking to start with.

I don't ever let my little girl see the men when they're first brought in all bruised and battered. We always keep the children away until the men are well enough to work. She talks to them. She doesn't know any better. There's no point in telling her not to. Back in my day I was curious, too. Besides, those were the only men I knew. My father was always gone. It's the same old war.

My daughter comes by first thing next morning to say hello. I suppose she really wants to get a peek at the new man. I kiss her and send her away. She has the goats to look after. I haven't seen her father but five or six times since the night she was conceived nine years ago. When he's at headquarters, he picks out a prisoner for me, checks their condition and their muscles, and helps me load them. This time he was at the front. I picked this one out by myself. I don't know why I wanted a general. They're liable to escape or start a revolt among our other prisoners. But nobody stopped me.

My husband said never to take anybody higher than a sergeant. I wonder how well a general will be at taking orders. I chose him on purpose. I wanted to make something happen. I'm sick and tired of the way things are. I hardly know what men are like except for these prisoners.

The men are supposed to sleep out on our doorsteps—after they're well, that is. I always give mine a pad and a blanket. They last longer that way. We usually work well together. Sometimes I wonder if I was born on the wrong side.

I feed the birds. I net a few finches to fry up whole. I pluck them and singe them. When I sit down to my midday tea, he begins to stir. I watch him wake.

It's the birds at the feeder bring him round. He looks up—suddenly—as though to find finches on the underside of the thatch. He listens to their warbling as carefully as though they were song birds. Then, even with his bruised lips, he tries to imitate the sound. I do it for him. He turns and stares. My husband's eyes were blue. His are black. He seems to look right through me. His eyes are, as I knew they would be, sad. I have to turn away.

I always enjoy the times when a man is recovering. I stay near the hut as much as I can. (The kitchen garden gets well tended.) I like it when he's hurting too much for me to *really* get to know him so I can make up anything I want. I can pretend he's on my side and we're friends. Actually I pretend we're lovers. We're all starved for males here though we don't talk about it.

The prisoners are always wary—flinching at every noise or fast move. At night they groan and cry out. I make sure it's quiet for them. My hut is set well back, away from the rest of the village. I do sing. I think a woman singing sooths them. Bathing helps, too. I bathe mine every few days. They always fall in love with me but it's not real love. Being cared for after all that torture, makes them grateful. Some call me an angel. Of course later on, on the terraces, they change their minds.

The general mostly seems to listen...to the birds...to the sheep and goats when they're brought in to be penned for the night.... (Mine are penned up at a neighbors for the time being and my daughter sleeps at friends.) I suspect he's trying to figure out where he is.

He doesn't talk but I haven't talked either. I like it that way. When he starts talking I'll have to face who he really is but for now I can day-dream all I want. I pretend the war is over and here's my husband, come back to stay.

Sometimes it's right when the prisoners are getting better that they have the worst nightmares. This time I can't wake him up. I stir the fire so I can see, then I shake him hard, and harder, but I must have hurt him more. He thinks he's being tortured again. He lashes out at me. I shy away and bang my head against the stone fireplace. He won't stop fighting. I don't know what to do. Finally I lie over his shaking body and hug him. Hold him down. Right away he stops yelling and puts his arms around me and I feel, yet again, the lack of my man. I even think, serves my husband right. (I'd not, ever before, even been tempted to lie down on top of a prisoner no matter how he was yelling, but this one is my choice.)

He runs his hands up and down my back, pulls me tight against him...as if I'm his salvation. I feel his erection. I forget...that he's a prisoner and I, his overseer—though he doesn't know that yet. Perhaps he thinks I'm his rescuer. (They often think that in the beginning and are surprised when I, wearing my pistol, bring them to the fields to work.) He kisses me. First my forehead and cheeks (I feel his scratchy unshaven jaw against mine) and, then desperately, he kisses my lips (as if only my kisses could save him from more torture). I let him. His breathing...mine also...is ragged. He trembles more than he'd done back when he was yelling. I do, too. He holds me against him by my buttocks. I let him. It's been so long since I'd slept with my husband—or anybody.

But then I think how all I know of this man I've made up myself in my daydreams. Maybe I don't even like him. I probably don't really want to do it. I'd be in big trouble if anything happened. And do I want yet another half breed of the enemy roaming about? Do I want my daughter taken from me, and me, thrown out of my village?

I pull myself away. I begin to cry...out of fear of what *I* would do, not what *he'd* do. He lets me go right away, so fast I feel abandoned even though I'm the one that stopped it. I'm on my knees beside him but I turn my back so he won't see me cry. He's still not well, but he sits up, groaning—I suppose in pain, and puts his hand on my shoulder. I'm tempted to turn around and let myself get hugged. He keeps saying how sorry he is and how good I've been to him all this time and how it won't happen again. He seems to think it's all his fault. I know I had a part in it. I say, "I tried to calm you but you kept shouting. I couldn't wake you." That's my excuse but it's a lie. I wanted to be close to somebody male again.

I build up the fire and we sit on the pad before it and talk for the first time and I like him—more and more. Before, it was just my made up person that I liked, but now I like the real man. That scares me.

He's the one, now and then, reaches over to stir the fire or put on another log. I feel.... But of course, I picked him out on purpose to fall in love with. I hope he's not as nice a person as he seems.

He asks me where we are? I say I'm not allowed to tell, but there's a good view of Basin Mountain. I say that on purpose. I know he'll know. He asks, is he a prisoner? When I say, yes, he says he thought so. Then he thanks me for treating him so fine all this time. He asks my name. We're not supposed to tell them, but I do. Mara. And I ask his. We're not supposed to ask that either. We're supposed to name them anything we feel like that's short and easy to remember. (Sometimes their names are peculiar and hard to pronounce. I call all mine Don. A name I don't care anything about.) He's Sebastian. He says again how sorry he is. How I don't have to worry, he'll never do any such thing again.

All of a sudden I'm worried about my freckles, my chopped off hair.... Do I have even one thing to wear that's remotely female? And my calloused hands! How can my touch feel gentle and womanly? Then I think: What am I doing? At my age? At *my* age!

I could have talked till dawn, but I'm feeling so strange. And I'm still shaky. I know I won't sleep, but I have to leave the firelight that flickers over his face, that sparkles in his eyes when he turns to look at me. Even with those old clothes I dressed him in he has a kind of dignity. And when a sad man smiles...!

I have to think. I tell him we should sleep. Of course after I go to bed I neither sleep nor think.

My room is large. There's a place for my loom. My bed is away from the fireplace on a kind of bench. It's behind the table. (When there are guests they have to sit on my bed to eat.) I'm far enough across the room to feel safely hidden from him but I can hear the rustling of his every move, his grunts and groans.

In the morning he seems much improved. He sits up. Stretches. I think to wrap the blanket around his shoulders but I don't dare get close. I don't even dare go see to the fire. He does it. Things have changed between us. When I hand him the breakfast gruel I don't look at him. Out of the corner of my eye I see him glance at me, as if to ask something. I eat at the table in the far corner by my bed. He eats on the floor by the fire. We don't speak. We didn't speak before either, but now it seems self conscious. I'm in a hurry to leave. Besides the turnips need putting away in the underground bins before the frost. I grab my hoe and go out without washing our bowls and without saying goodbye.

But I don't go up to our field. I stay close and work in the kitchen garden. I have this feeling that I have to protect him. What if the other women knew he was a general and thought he was too dangerous to have around?

I leave the hoe and get down on my hands and knees. Working like this has always helped me when I felt upset.

Then…here he is, working beside me. I hadn't heard him coming. Again, we don't talk, but this time the silence is companionable. My birds warble. The donkey watches from over the fence. The sun warms us.

When we go in for lunch, and he's walking beside me, I see he's a smaller man than I expected—not much taller than I am. But it's too late now, I like him even so.

Inside, I see he's washed the bowls and put them on the shelf. Rolled the sleeping pad and stood it against the wall. He's straightened out my bench bed, too. When…*when!* Has anyone ever, ever, ever done such things for me? I have to turn around and go right back outside. I wish there was a place where I could be alone. But there's nothing to do out there except take a few big breaths and go back in.

I fix him bread and lard but I can't eat. Thank goodness he doesn't say anything or look at me.

The minute I take him to work on the terrace, my daughter will have to come back. That's the rule. You can't hide things from children. They see right through you. I don't want to take him to the fields but if the weather turns too cold the turnips will rot.

I'll go up by myself. I can't do much alone but I'd get some. I have to get away and try to forget what I've started. I leave without any lunch. I'll nibble outer cabbage leaves. (The main part of the cabbages has to go to the army.)

All the fields are narrow terraces, one on top of the other. Mine is the highest of those still used. It's a hard climb. My general will have to be in fairly good shape just to get up here.

Always, once I get there, I turn around and waste more time than I should, looking at the view. I feel renewed just looking. You can see all the way to headquarters. Farther on, you can see the flashes of the mortars though you can only hear them when the wind is right.

When you look in the opposite direction, up to the snowy peaks, past the old, unused terraces, abandoned when the men left for the war, there's an old castle so high you can just make it out. There are lights up there. They say it's haunted. Once a woman went up. They found her at the bottom of the cliff, shot five times.

When I finally let myself climb down from my field, I'm so tired I don't think I could blush if I wanted to. I stop where my daughter is staying before I come to my own hut. She rushes into my arms shouting, "When can I come back? What's he like? Is he going to be a good one?" I say, "Soon as he's a little better," and, "I'm not sure if he's a good one yet."

He's asleep when I get back. I don't see anything changed this time, but I'll bet he's been snooping. Things don't look quite right but I couldn't say why. I sit down over tea, to rest for a while and look at him. He's sleeping as though exhausted still, curled up and covered with the blanket. I'll not wake him by stirring the fire. I'll use the propane burner to heat the grease to fry the finches.

It's the smell of frying birds that wakes him. I lay two places at the table. He gets up, is about to sit down, then hesitates, asks, "Is it allowed?"

Of course it's not, but I say, "Yes." And then I realize I can't do it when my daughter comes back. "That is, until my daughter comes."

"You have a daughter."

I say, "And a husband."

I see him hesitate with half a bird in his mouth. He chews more slowly, thinking.

I tell him that when I take him out to the field, I'll have to bring my pistol or else the women will wonder. He says he understands.

I always like nights in front of the fire making things or repairing things. That little goats-wool cap of his won't be much help up here. I start on a wide brimmed hat.

That night it happens again, he yells, but this time I manage to wake him without too much trouble. I hold him as he calms down. Then he sits up beside me and we hold each other. This time it's companionable. At first. By now we know each other better. He says, "It's going to be all right." But then he's kissing me again. Suddenly he stops. And says it, too. "Stop me!"

But I don't want to. I don't care what happens.

We fall asleep in each other's arms, warm by the fire. I'm thinking, he's right, from now on, everything is going to be fine.

I wake when he brings me tea the next morning. I can tell it's late. I pop up. "I haven't time for tea. Did my daughter come by?"

"I told her you were tired. She looked in at you. She wanted to wake you but I told her not to. I'm coming to help you. You were so exhausted yesterday."

"But when my daughter sees you on the terrace she'll have to come back home."

"I want to help. Isn't that what I'm for?"

My cheeks are scratched from his needing a shave. I wonder if it'll show and the women will all know what happened.

"I have to take my pistol."

"I know."

He still limps, (they had torn out toe nails), but he climbs to my terrace with no trouble. At the top we do what I always do, look down on the village and the switchbacks and then headquarters, all laid out as if a map.

Below us, here and there, prisoners and women work on the terraces. One woman, one prisoner, one donkey, to a terrace. Here and there a child helps out.

Then we turn around and look up. Above, on the old deserted terraces, are the sheep, and above them, on the ground too steep even for terraces, are the goats. I wave to my daughter. She's hardly more than a red dot. She waves back like crazy, even does a little dance. She knows a man on our terrace means she can come home.

He says, "Is that High Peak Outpost? I've not seen it before. Looks to be a day's climb."

"I suppose. We don't go there. There's lights up there at night."

He looks at it as if thinking about it, as if judging the trail up, then turns and looks down one more time as if memorizing everything, and then we get to work.

That night I'm happy even with my daughter here. She talks and he talks back. She even asks him what they call him. First he says, "I told you, Sebastian." She says, "No, I mean when you were little, like they call me Sisi though my name is Simone." He says, "Basti."

Sisi says, "I knew it!" though how could she?

I love to see a sad man throw back his head and laugh.

She says, "Shouldn't you sleep outside by the door like you're supposed to?"

He says, "You're right," and gets the blanket and gets ready to go out, but she starts to cry. "I didn't mean you should do it. I want you to be warm in here with us."

"We'll give him the bench," I say before she has a chance to say how nice and warm she'll be sleeping with us both. Is she too young to know we shouldn't?

He slaughters a sheep for us. We leave parts to simmer as we go up to the field. Sisi goes on, up higher with the goats. Of course we have to share the mutton. You can't butcher a sheep and not have everybody know about it. That night we give Sebastian the head in broth all to himself. I tell Sisi not to tell anybody he got the best part.

I like to see a strong man struggling with the plough in a way I couldn't do. He's good at it, too. He works like a peasant. I ask him how he knows...he, a general...all the things an ordinary man would know, plowing, butchering, and such. He says he *is* an ordinary man. He says he became a general in the field.

He still has nightmares. I think he was tortured more than the men I usually have. Since he's a general, he probably knew things. When he yells, I rush to the bench to wake him. Sisi starts to cry. She only stops when I tell her to come and help me comfort him.

Now and then Sebastian and I find a moment to ourselves. Once we went into the donkey shed.

Cold weather is settling in. I keep him in with us though it's not allowed. But most of my other men didn't last through the winter. I'm weaving in the evenings and piecing out the wool for trousers and jackets for all of us. We're quiet and cozy. It's Sisi who talks and asks. I find out things about him I never would have learned without her.

"Do you have a sister? You're old. Is your mama alive? Is she too old, too? Do you miss your sister and your ma? Have you ever gotten shot? Did it hurt? Did you ever almost cut your thumb off? I did. Did you ever throw up? I did. Did you ever cough so hard you turned yourself inside out? Did you have a picnic on your birthday? Do you like my mom?"

(It's yes to all these.)

When have I ever been this happy?

The next sunny day he says to bring a picnic and not tell Sisi. We pack bread and lamb fat and a blanket. There's no place to hide near the terraces. We go higher, up into the trees and boulders but far from where the goats are browsing. He spreads the blanket for me.

His beard has grown. It's soft against my cheek. It's coming in mostly white though his hair is only partly grey. I say, "I love you," but I know it won't do any good. All he thinks about is war.

After, he hides the blanket under a thorn bush. I'm happy, thinking, it's for another time. But it isn't.

Well, that's that, then. My pistol's gone, too. I don't want to ever bother with another prisoner. I'll do the work myself.

Not only that, eight of our prisoners went with him. Thank goodness nobody knows it's my general did that. Nobody even knew he was a general.

I should have guessed. Before he left he slaughtered two goats for us. Hid the meat so it looked as if he'd only killed one so we only had to give a part of one to the neighbors.

I have a feeling the men went up to that old castle. I remember how he looked at it and thought about it.

I climb to where the snow begins and look for tracks. I ask Sisi to tell me if she sees any. I tell her they might be from Basti and we need to know where he is and if he's all right. She doesn't act like herself at all now that he's gone. I hear her crying at night. She doesn't want me to know so I pretend I don't. She curls up beside me but I lie flat on my back and look up, stiff with fear.

I'm pregnant. Not a one of our men has been back here for months. Everybody will notice soon.

Every night I look at the lights shining from the castle. They look warm and inviting. I have such yearning. But I don't even know if Sebastian is up there.

I don't tell Sisi what I'm planning. I pack when I'm supposed to be on the terrace. I pick her up on my way. Our goats follow.

Sisi is frightened. I can tell because she doesn't ask any questions. Not only that, she doesn't talk at all. We go fast. The goats love this. The steeper it gets the more they like it.

I thought we'd be there by evening. The trail is washed away in so many spots—that makes it take longer. We huddle down for the night. Sisi says right out, she wants to go home.

"Don't you want to see Basti?"

"Not this much."

"Of course you do."

"How do you know he's there?"

Now I'm the one ready to cry. I say, "I don't know what to do."

"It's all right Ma." She hugs me. "You don't need him, you have me." Then she says what I always tell her. "You'll feel better in the morning."

She falls asleep right away, but I don't. She's right, I don't know where Sebastian is. If I were a general and had eight men with me I'd try to get back to my own army. I wouldn't climb up to the castle. What good would that do?

From here, so close, you can see long strings of lights up there. They're so intriguing. They look warm.

But next morning we look up at the gray cliff, streaked with breaks and lengthwise cracks, stained as if etched with black. The castle is made of the same gray rock it sits on. Now that we're this close and it's daylight, I can see the castle isn't a castle at all, but a fort with redoubts every hundred yards or so. It doesn't look as inviting as at night. And it does look haunted. Who would want to be here? What land is it protecting except land too steep to use?

There's no way to get up there except from around the back. I'm starting to feel as Sisi feels. Why am I doing this? And what about that woman that got shot?

We eat the rest of our food. We all...the whole herd of us, take off, skirting the cliff below the fort.

Sisi says, "Is it the enemy's? Is Basti up there because he's an enemy?"

"Maybe."

"He's not *my* enemy."

"Nor mine."

"I like enemies."

Of course those are the only men she's ever known.

We keep circling. We find a sort of stairway. Actually, the goats find it. If they'd not been here we wouldn't have noticed it. It's almost too steep for a human being. There are chains along the sides to help pull yourself up by. It winds in and out of cracks in the cliff until we're finally right up against the fort.

A shot hits the dirt in front of us the minute we step out from behind the rocks. Somebody calls down from the wall. "Who goes there?"

"A woman and a little girl. We don't know the password."

"Approach so I can see you."

We do. "It's Mara and Simone, come looking for General Sebastian."

"Climb to the left and enter through the gap."

There's a ramshackle wooden door. It's so beat up we probably could have crawled under it. The man who opens it is wrinkled and white haired and bent. He's an old-age kind of thin. He's wearing an officer's uniform of the enemy. The elbows and knees are completely worn through, threads hang from the wrists. He has a dozen medals on his chest along with food stains. He points an old rusty rifle at us as we come in, but he puts it down so as to check us for weapons. Even Sisi, top to bottom. When I object he says it's regulations. With me he spends more time than is necessary on my stomach. I've been wearing loose clothes down in the village, but they don't hide anything from him. He says, "You're pregnant."

"This is the general's baby."

"The general does as he wishes."

Sisi gives a little yelp of surprise.

The old man picks up the rifle and holds it, again as if to shoot us if we make a false move. "Come."

We go in, goats and all, past another rickety, rotting door.

There's no "inside" to the place—just one side of the wall and the other. There's the side where there's nothing but cliffs, and this side, rocky and full of rubble. It's the same as headquarters, just as dirty and full of garbage—smells just as bad, except headquarters is flat.

There are men all over, all of them ragged and thin and old. Most are squatting over smoky fires. (I wonder how long our goats will last.) Those who are walking are hobbling over the rubble. Some use their rifles as canes. At first I think they're all the enemy but then I see our uniforms are there, too. There's the yellow-brown goat's wool tams of their side and the navy blue caps of our side.

The old soldier puts us in a tent with a little heater. It has a wall of stones up to about three feet and then a canvas roof. I can just barely stand up at the center. There are two cots. I ask if we can have supper. The old man says it might be possible.

The minute we're alone Sisi says, "Why didn't you tell me you're having a baby. I thought you were just getting fat. I'm glad. I always wanted somebody else."

We wait. Nothing happens. Sisi says she knew coming here was a bad thing, and, "Why couldn't we stay down there and have the baby?"

"We can't. The women don't want an enemy's baby around."

Sisi puts her hands on my stomach. Just then the baby kicks. She yelps again. Says, "I love you," and gives my stomach a kiss.

Finally they bring us food—another old man very like the first. He brings outer cabbage leaves...goat cheese. They have no better fare up here. Or maybe just not for us.

We wait again. It gets dark. No one brings us a light. There's nothing to do but try to sleep. Sisi and I cuddle up on one of the cots. Sisi falls asleep right away. I've had a hard time sleeping ever since I brought Sebastian in on my cart.

He comes in the middle of the night. Bringing a lamp.

Finally.

We hug. Or rather I hug. I surprise him with it. It feels like hugging a board. He's been too busy being a general. He sees...feels right away the shape I'm in. It takes a minute before he lets go—softens into a different kind of man, his arms around me, his lips against my neck. Finally we sit on the other cot. We whisper. Sisi still sleeps.

"Why are you here? You're not that old."

"Why are you?"

"I was looking for you."

"I'm going back. I'll pick up the rest of your prisoners on the way down. I'll bring the old men the battle they've been hoping for. I'll take you home on the way down

"I can't go home like this. Why can't we go off together, someplace where there's no war? But which side will these old men be fighting for?"

"Their own side...a third side. A side to end all wars."

"End wars by war?"

"Remember these are their fathers. The men look up to them."

"You'll swarm down from the hills and attack our men from the rear?"

"We will."

"These old men are the ones who started the war in the first place."

He just grunts.

"You never had a real life either, did you?"

He grunts again.

"You think of think of nothing but war. Let's stop. Let's run away."

"We'll wipe out your terraces on the way down. They're so steep it won't take much. One landslide would sweep them all away. Since your hut is the highest, it will be wiped away, too."

"I wish you'd wipe away the whole valley. Cover the garbage with nice clean gravel. I'm so tired. If this baby is a boy...."

The old men are eager to get to fighting. They're making sure all the old rifles are in good shape.

Everybody is busy. The whole place is changing. At the prospect of fighting again they're all standing straighter, doing exercises, pushups and squats, marching around the area—as best they can over the rocks and rubble. Trumpets are sounding again. They're practicing the charge, though they're still sounding out a lot of wobbles and burbles.

They put Sisi and me in one of the redoubts. The stone walls make it colder and damper than the tents. We have a room to ourselves and one narrow window. Sebastian comes every night. We don't make love, I'm too uncomfortable and he's too tired, but he warms me in his arms. There's no doubt he needs somebody to hold him. He still wakes up yelling now and then, or sometimes has a long series of groans as he sleeps. I always think: Why don't we run away? but I don't say it.

Sisi comes in with us whenever Sebastian yells. It doesn't matter anymore. Besides, it's warmer for all of us.

And all this time he's looking even gaunter than before. The circles under his eyes, darker than ever. This doesn't make sense. The third side will make everything worse. It'll be more of a shambles than it already is. I think he thinks so, too.

One evening I say, "Please, please, please," hardly meaning to. And he says, "What?"

He thinks I mean something about myself, says, "I'll see to it that you're looked after."

"No, I mean you. What about you?"

But I'm worried about myself, too. What will happen when my time comes? Not a one of these men will know how to help me. And I've not taken very good care of myself. I'm cold all the time—even with Sebastian's arms around me. He finds me a sweater. Olive drab. One of his own I suppose, and it isn't as if he isn't cold himself. He looks worried all the time now. I wonder if he thinks none of his plans will work.

I run away to have the baby. I don't want anybody with me. I climb yet higher. I find a sheltered spot as far from everybody as I can. I hide behind rocks. (There aren't any trees up here.) I don't bring a lamp. I don't bring anything. I just go. Fast as I can. I feel dread. Scared. I don't know why. I don't even make sense to myself. These men are too old. Too warlike. It's as if, if the baby is a boy, they'll take it from me right away.

I thought it wouldn't take so long this second time, but by the time the baby finally comes, it's dark. I can't see it. I think I did everything right. I wrap the baby in my cloak and in Sebastian's old sweater. I put it to my breast. The baby has full head of hair. Our babies are usually bald. This is the enemy's child for sure.

In the morning I'm too worn out to try and get back. Besides, I don't want to go back. I don't feel like moving at all. Off and on I sleep. Later — much later — I hear people crunching and sliding on the scree. Panting. It's a hard climb. I'm in a little depression surrounded by boulders. I chose this spot specially. It's hidden and cozy.

I hear people calling out to each other, and calling for me, too. They're noisy. I'm glad I came up here and hid. I don't answer. I move even farther under the stones nearby. When it gets to be twilight, the people leave and I feel safer. I sleep again.

I wake when I hear tiny noises of pebbles trickling down. I see a light, a tiny dim light wobbling back and forth. I'm even more frightened than I was earlier. It comes closer.

"Mara." He calls in a whisper. As though not wanting to scare me. But I *am* scared.

Then the little light flashes in my eyes, hesitates there, blinding me. And then it's lowered.

"Mara."

He doesn't touch me. He turns the light out and sits nearby looking up at the stars. He doesn't speak. Hardly moves. When he does start to talk it's as though to a frightened animal. First it's about looking at the stars and the new moon. Then, "I have food and blankets. I even have a little stove. I saw where you were when we came looking for you earlier. I thought to come back later alone. Can I light the stove?"

But I can't answer.

"I'll light the stove. You'll feel better after you have something to eat. It's been two days. You're starving."

It's a tiny stove but burns bright and bluish. He leans close, over a small pan. Again, as in front of our fireplace, I see the light flickering in his eyes but this time it shines blue and scary. But the soup smells good.

Just then the baby starts to cry. He holds still as though afraid to scare me. He even stops stirring the soup. I put the baby to breast. I refuse to look at him. I refuse to smell the soup.

When it's ready he squats beside me. "Just a sip or two. You'll feel better."

But I don't want to feel better. Why feel better when there's nothing to look forward to, anyway?

It does smell good. He holds out the spoon. I sip. I go on sipping.

He treats me like a child. Says, "Good girl." I'm surprised he doesn't pat me on the head. I can see all this as if from over my own shoulder, but I can't react. I do feel better though.

After the soup he hands me tea. "I'd like to bring you back in the morning. Can you manage it?"

I can't nod.

He wraps me in blankets, I and the baby together, lies down and pulls me to him so his chest is my pillow. I have no will at all. I let him. He keeps on talking softly and as if it doesn't matter what he says, and it doesn't. I've done the same to Sisi when she was sick and even to my donkey.

"You were good to me. You fed me. You held me. You.... And then you.... And then you...." I don't listen to the words. I sleep.

When I wake, the baby's gone. I panic. I look to see if I've rolled on it or tossed it away in my sleep, but Sebastian has it. He's sitting nearby cleaning it up with canteen water. It did need cleaning. He has white cloths to wrap it in. He came prepared for it and for me. He's talking to it as he talked to me—a lot of nothing. How many other babies has he fathered?

He looks up and smiles.

I don't smile back.

"I'll bring you tea in a minute. It's made." He wraps the baby in clean cloths and brings it to me. He props me up against blankets, my back against a rock, then brings tea and crackers. He crouches beside me and watches me eat.

After I nurse the baby, we start down. I don't want to go back but I don't know what else to do. I keep having the idea I must make decisions. But all I think is: *Think*! And then I don't do it.

He's not a big man, but he's wiry and strong. Sometimes he carries me and the baby—both his pack and me on his back. It's soothing—to have my arms around his neck and to feel the movement of being carried.

When we stop to rest and eat I say, "I won't go back."

"You need rest and care."

"I can't go back. Everybody knows."

"They know this is my boy."

"Boy?"

He gives me a odd look. And then an even odder one, "What about Sisi?"

Sisi! Ever since I started up to hide and have the baby I've forgotten she existed.

"She came with us yesterday to help look for you. Didn't you hear her calling ma?"

Poor Sisi. I *did* hear. That must have been that lost goat sound.

Just in these three days things have changed at the fort. They're making black banners and hats with a zigzag of red. Like lightening and like blood. They're making flags that say, THE DEAD. And they do look dead. They could be dead. Why didn't I see that before? bloodshot eyes, leathery skin, boney as skeletons.... They paint their faces a jaundiced yellow, though most of them look yellow anyway. They put charcoal around their already sunken eyes. If they're not really dead, they'll do for dead.

They'll advance in three waves. The first wave will pick up the other prisoners and take the pistols from their overseers. The second wave, will fan out in a long line and loosen boulders to start the landslide. After the slide that destroys the terraces, the third wave will rush down, to and through headquarters and hit our army from the back. They'll count on surprise and higher ground. They'll count on the fact that they're the dead.

If they're already dead they can't be killed over again.... Can they?

But killing each other. Nothing new in that even if three sides instead of two.

I get better. I can talk again. I nod, smile, though it feels like I'm pretending.

Sebastian promises to run away with us as soon as this battle is over—off to some land where nobody knows him. That scares me more than if he hadn't said it. I know how it works with the last time for things. It means he's a dead man. If he survives to do as he promised.... I'll believe it when I see it.

The night before they're to go into battle he cries. Who would have thought it, a general? I feel all the more that I don't want him to leave. I say, "Why not go right now? Cross the mountains. You want to. They can do this by themselves. If they really are the dead, they can do it."

Of course he thinks it all depends on him.

He's done for. I think he knows it.

We need more prisoners than usual to help rebuild the terraces. I build a little shed by my doorway almost as big as my donkey shed. I can house four. Several of us go down for more men.

Nothing has changed. Nobody seems to care anymore that my black haired little boy is one of the enemy's. I suppose he's just one more soldier for our side. Nobody says a word about me coming back. They even help me repair my cottage. Sisi helps. I get better though I still have the sense I'm watching everything over my own left shoulder.

I don't think the dead were really the dead... or they died all over again. Or they were blown to bits. Maybe by their own rusty rifles. They weren't ghosts. I don't even wish they had been.

At headquarters we pick out new men. I see one that might be Sebastian—he wears a general's uniform. But I don't dare take anyone in as bad shape as this one. They wouldn't let me, anyway. I give him a drink of water. I wrap the old olive drab sweater around him. Whoever it is won't last long. It's a waste of a good sweater. One I especially liked for sentimental reasons.

Argosy Magazine, May-June 2004

The Library

We're headed away from war, past it, around and beyond the enemy lines. We're circling behind where the battle rages. Mostly we've hiked at night and hidden during the day. We no longer hear or even see the lights of explosions. We're glad we were given this duty. It's been a restful week. Kind of like a camping trip.

We each have a bomb and there are ten of us. We have several fire starters. That should be more than enough. What we do is for the good of all mankind.

Theirs is the largest library in the world, but it's not our books. They're not even in our language.

Even if we knew the language they're in a kind of writing we can't read. It's full of squares and Os and curlicues. We've been told many of the books are about the art of war and that the poetry is bawdy. There's pictures of nudes and of lovers in all possible positions.

I'm not to let any of us look at the books. Nor am I to let one single book survive. There can be no peace and no morality as long as these book exist.

There are statues at each corner of the building. Caryatids along the porches. They say that, in the center of the library, there's a reading room—a garden—open to the sky. It's full of flowers. Birds. Even trees.

They say we'll recognize the library. It's larger than any other buildings. Our side thinks that when it's destroyed, their side will lose all momentum.

By now we have come to the beach. We're from the south. We've never seen the sea. We walk with our feet in the shallow water so our tracks will be washed away. When we camp for the day, we don't sleep much even though the sound of the water is soothing. We're distracted by all these new things. We watch the waves. We keep tasting the water—we can't believe it's salty. Some of us want to fish. Some of us want to taste the things on the shore but I don't trust them not to be poison.

Around midnight we hear singing, but it has no triads, no fifths. An accompanying instrument thunks and buzzes. I tell my group, "There. Listen. You can see what kind of people these are by this racket."

My group laughs. They're nervous and this odd music doesn't reassure them.

The library is across from an artificial pool so as to show it off with its reflection.

This has all been explained to us, and yet when we come upon the reflecting pool and the sparkling whiteness of the library, its painted frieze, the golden roof...we're silent. We've never seen such a building. It's evening and the sun makes everything pinkish/orange.

Sea gulls wheel over our heads as if they are the avant-gardes of the books, their shrieks as alien as the language of the enemy.

We don't move. We just watch. The sun goes down. Stars come out. Nobody says anything. The moon rises and reflects in the pool. We should move back and find a place to camp but we can't tear ourselves away. We sit where we are, fall asleep towards morning, then wake to watch the sunrise. I don't ask the group what they think about burning it down. I don't want to know. Besides, it doesn't matter what they think.

After the sunrise we load up our weapons and cross to the edge of the pool, march right into it, two by two, and splash across to the library. We don't care if they hear us or not.

Close up the eyes of the caryatids stare at us, seem to warn us that the library is not for the likes of us. Each of them has one bare breast. I tell my men not to look.

We head to the main doors. They're of carved wood. Easy to burn down with our fire starters. (We don't look at them. Who knows what might be carved there.) We would have bashed through them, but they're open. We walk right in.

We're as awed by the inside as we were with the outside. We become aware of how dirty and smelly we are, how we're dripping on their mosaic floor. The sun, shining through the stained glass of the clearstory windows, leaves odd colors on the walls, tables—on the people. The librarians look up, but they stay calm. Behind them there are shelves and shelves of books. The books are dark and dusty, and look old, as do the librarians. And—we can't believe it's true—all the librarians have one bare breast, sometimes the right and sometimes the left. Now, in front of us men, they don't even try to hide themselves.

We point our guns, but I'm the only one that shoots. I shoot out one of the stained glass windows. I surprise my own group even more than I surprise the librarians. My group all jump while the librarians just look though some hold their books closer like shields.

One librarian comes up to us, (bare breasted, brazen as could be) holds her book, a large heavy one, but she doesn't try to cover herself with it. She looks like the enemy—they all have colorless hair and colorless eyes. She addresses us in what seems like two or three different languages, one after the other. Finally in ours. She whispers. She tells us to keep quiet. She points to a sign that says SILENCE even in our language. Then she says, "We have nothing to do with wars in here."

"You lie."

I whisper, too, though I didn't mean to.

She says, "This is a place of truths."

"Your books are full of lies. You, yourself, are a lie."

"Look around you. Does this look like lies?"

I look at the sun pouring down from the window I shot out. The real color of the sun comes in whereas the other windows show false colors. My shot is the only truth here. I point to the square of sunlight under the broken window. "There is the truth," I say.

Her face is narrow and fierce. She wears a robe down to her ankles. Surely it would tangle in bushes if she tries to walk where there are no paths. These people are, clearly, just as we've been told, overly civilized. A civilization at its final gasp. You can always tell by the clothes.

I imagine what the book she hugs so tightly must have in it. Secrets of sex, and perhaps of battles won.

We weren't told what to do with the librarians. I suppose it's up to my discretion.

She says, "There are all sorts of truths."

"You wouldn't know a truth if it was written in stone."

One of my group says, "If it were in stone, it would be true."

I don't answer such a platitude. I tell my group, to get out their fire starters. I say it for all to hear. If the librarians want to escape, it's up to them.

My group hesitates. They don't want to do their job. They take off their packs to get their fire starters, but more slowly than they should. Grandeur and beauty have confused them. They have lost sight of their principles. I'm tempted to shoot out another window to remind them which side they're on.

The librarians hold their books as though they're weapons. Some have thick covers and metal corners and look heavy.

I shoot again, but this time I don't know what I hit. That fierce librarian attacks me with her book before I can see if I hit out another window or not. Next thing I know my nose is pressed into a mosaic of a triton with an octopus hooked in it. I almost think I'm back at the seashore. Art lies. It always lies. These are—I see clearly—groups of small stones, white and black over blue waves. A shot at the floor would have scattered them back into their reality.

I get up on my knees and point my gun down at the false octopus, but one of my own men turns on me and hits me with the butt of his gun.

I come-to bound to a homemade chair. I'm in a simple room no better than our barracks. They say the librarians do live simply. They say the library is their only luxury. There are shelves along the walls as if for books, but with potted plants on them. Some of the pots would make good weapons.

I don't need my group. I can destroy the library by myself. And if I don't have bombs, I can make new ones. They didn't send out a munitions expert for nothing.

I begin to work on the knots that tie me to the chair. They've been tied by women. I easily loosen them. My jaw hurts where my comrade hit me. Have they all mutinied? Do I have a single friend? Is it because the library is too beautiful? But they told us it would be.

First thing I grab the largest pot to use as a weapon. I pick one with a strong looking plant and hold it by the woody stalk. Then I look out the window to see where I am.

And there's another lie—right on the wall of the hut next door. A painting of trees and flowers, a stream even. As if trying to make this desert place like my land down south, and not succeeding. They may have the library, but we have the forest and the mountains. The painting makes me homesick. But then I realize I'm falling into their trap: taking a painting as the truth. I don't let myself think of home.

I open the door as quietly as possible. There's another room. A writing room. Desk and paper, ink.... Also an easel with the start of a painting. It's the portrait of a child. One of their kind—almost white hair and light eyes. I hate that pale, insipid look. I splash the ink on it. I wish for more ink and then I see there's paint I can smear.

I feel good afterwards. I've struck a blow for truth. I pick up my plant-weapon and go in search of chemicals for a bomb, and maybe food, too.

I creep outside carefully, and there is the back of the library—as impressive as the front. If I had even a little of the gold of the roof I'd be a wealthy man. I think to climb a pillar, grab some golden tiles and go home. Bypass the war altogether. But then I think, after I bomb it the gold will be even easier to pick up.

I go into a different hut. Looking for a kitchen, or a shed with fertilizers. I find another writing room. There's no painting so I spill the ink all over the writing.

In the kitchen, I find a paste with what looks like scallions mixed in it. God knows what they eat or if this is for the cat. Or, for all I know, their pet rat. I eat it anyway.

Then I look for chemicals. But, of course, the labels on things are different. I have to try everything by smell—even by taste. I make a concoction, but I'm not sure about it. I hope it really is a bomb.

I grab my (maybe) bomb and my plant weapon and start out again when I hear the door open and there's a librarian, a young one.

How can such a pale creature look so beautiful?

Thank goodness her breast is covered—or she'd be in more trouble than she knows.

I can see on her face she has passed through the room where I damaged the writing. She's half my size, but she comes after me with her fists. I swing the plant. The pot flies off and dirt flies all over. She gets a face full. Dirt in her eyes and nose and mouth. Next thing, here I am, trying to clean her up. And saying I'm sorry--in my own language.

She can't answer in any. Her mouth is too full of dirt.

I find the water jar. I lean her over a basin. I use a clean cloth to get things out of her eyes. They're not colorless as we keep saying. They're tan with little greenish radiating lines. Actually they're almost exactly the same color as her hair. Her skin is tan also. She's all of a piece. You could say the same about me, black hair and black eyes, dark skin.

It takes a long time to clean her up. After, we sit on cushions across from each other, both of us exhausted. She's a mess. Her hair is wet and hanging down, her shirt front is sopping. I'm a mess, too.

Now she says, Thank you—in my language. And I say again, I'm sorry.

She looks to be as taken with me as I am with her. Both of us dazzled with the odd, the unknown—I with my shaved head and top knot and my damaged hands, and she with her almost white hair flying out around her shoulders and her hands soft as a baby's. She must do nothing but read and paint.

Both of us hardly dare to glance at each other—especially after being so close, eye to eye, my arms holding her. I have looked in her ears, in her nose, I've helped her rinse her mouth.

We sit silent. Finally she says, "I'll make tea. I'll get you something to eat."

(I don't care what it is, I'll eat it.)

"Are you going to tell them I'm here?"

"I don't know."

"I would have hit you with the heavy pot if it hadn't fallen off."

"Yes, but you helped me after."

"I don't know books. I prefer reality."

"I only know books."

"Do you want to see the rest of the world? I'll take you. Help me destroy the library and I'll take you with me."

"Why? Why destroy it?"

"It's all lies? Your life is a lie. I'll bet you do nothing but sit all the time. Did you ever play?"

"Of course I did."

"What did you play?"

"We drew and painted. Sewed. Cooked. Made things. I had a doll."

"That's not play. Play is top-o-the-roost, knick-knack, capture flags.... I don't think you had any fun at all."

"But I did."

"You don't even know you weren't happy."

"But I was."

I feel sorry for all the librarians.

"Come with me. I'll show you happiness. I'll teach you to play. And you know bombing the library will be useful to everybody. The pieces of marble can go to make many smaller houses. The roof can make everybody rich. The painted birds and butterflies pressed into the walls.... There must be a hundred. A hundred people could each have one. You could have one yourself. You could wear it in your hair."

I see I've given her something to think about.

"Give the little people marble and gold. Spread the beauty around so there's some for everybody—and keep some for yourself."

Every time she looks at me I can see her fascination in her eyes. I wonder if she's ever seen a shaved head and top knot before. She keeps looking at my hands. I always did like my hands. I'm proud of my scars. All have been achieved honorably.

I'm everything the opposite of her. She's even small for one of the enemy, while I'm tall for one of us.

She says, "We thought your eyes were so dark they were blind to all things delicate and light. We said you were too tall to be strong, but you're as if made of ropes."

"We thought you were blind for the opposite reason." Then I say, "My group...they betrayed me. Where are they? What did you do with them?"

(No doubt by now all my men want are books and bare breasted librarians.)

"We fed them periwinkles and clams. They spit them out and ate their own dried up things. We walked them back to the beach where there are cottages. Most of us went with them. We thought you were safely tied up."

"How many librarians stayed?"

"Six. And me."

The perfect time to bomb it and set fires.

I talk to her about chemicals. She helps me read the labels. I find things to use as fire starters. I even find stuff for a few bombs.

We work well side by side. I think what it would be like bringing her back to my people. How shocked my people would be.

"What we'll do is put these little sacks all inside and outside the library. It's time. It's already getting dark. Let's do it now."

She says, "There's nobody there at night."

"Good. First you can pick your favorite book to keep just for yourself."

I feel good that I can give her something. I'm going to make sure she gets a butterfly or a bird, and some of the gold.

She says, "We'll need a lamp. There aren't any windows except those high stained glass ones. Books take up all the wall space."

We gather up the little packages and tubes and carry them to the library. Right away I climb up and put some under the roof. She's never seen anything like my climbing. All I need is a little finger grip and toe grip. My own men can't do that. I see I impress her even more than before.

When I place the last package and climb down, I can't resist the admiration in her eyes, I lean to kiss her. She looks as if she's leaning to kiss me, but she turns away at the last minute.

We light our lamp and go inside. Right away she takes out a huge book.

"We can't bring *that*!"

"I just want to show you some pictures. There are lots like this here, but this book is the best.

The book is so big she has to put it on a special stand. She opens it and there they are—in gold leaf, or looks like it, a golden woman and a golden man. Naked. The woman is handing the man grapes or dates, and he reaches, not for them, but towards her breast. It's as lewd as we always said their drawings are. But the green of the trees is as beautiful as the gold, so is the blue of the sky, as though green and blue could be as valuable as gold. The landscape is more like my world than like hers. It's a picture you could fall right into—and would want to except for the naked couple. If I were there I'd hurry away behind the trees in the foreground.

She turns the page and the next is even worse than the first. It's as if you're standing on a higher hill than before, in the shadow of pine trees, looking down. This time the couple is farther away, but you can see the golden man has his hand on the woman's golden breast now, and the grapes or dates are on the ground, forgotten.

Why is she showing me this? And she looks so young and innocent? She isn't. Art has ruined her. She knows everything already. Probably more than I do. No wonder they want me to destroy the library.

I don't want her to turn to the next page. Nor the next and the next. I can imagine what they'll be. And why look when we can do?

I grab her and throw her down…on the make believe octopus. I drop on top of her. Kiss her—hard.

At first she's too shocked to react. She doesn't seem to know what's happening, but then she struggles. She bites my lip. I pull back and she yells, first a wordless shout and then, "No! Help!" If she keeps on making a racket, whatever other librarians are left here will come. I cover her mouth with my hand. She bites my hand this time and knees me. I'm the one should be yelling, no.

"I'll let you go if you don't shout."

"You're an animal."

"It's you, are an animal. How could you show me those pictures? And why? If not for…." But we don't have words for that—not ones you can say to women.

"I wanted you to see something beautiful. I thought if you saw them you might not want to burn them."

"I want to burn them all the more. Are all the books like this? Full of nakedness and corruption?"

"Let me read something to you. Let me find the book—the one I'd choose if I could have one of my own.

She goes straight to a small, hand sized book. She holds it close to the lamp and begins to read, translating as she goes. Even in my own language I don't understand it at all.

Last to leave and first to come.

A guessing game of death or life.

Leaves of summer, leaves of spring.

We fall but in our own ways.

Neither like streams nor leaves.

Perhaps the meaning is lost in translation. I say, "Poetry lies as much as pictures do."

"We think it's more true than truth."

"There can't be such a thing?"

Even so...even after the bad pictures and the meaningless poetry...even so I still like her. And she...even after I threw her down and almost raped her. She still likes me. I can see it on her face.

I say, "I like you. In spite of the pictures. But I don't suppose you can like me."

"I don't know what to think."

"I don't either but I like you anyway. But I don't even know your name."

"Yawn," she says.

"What!"

"My name is Yawn."

That's an ugly word in our language. I can hardly make myself say it. I wonder what my name means in hers.

"I'm Gabb."

"Bless water."

Should I have said the same after she said her name? Why bless? And by what crippled god?

"Let me read you this other poem."

Joy is in the view from above

As houses seen by eagles

As after storms or in them,

Seen as if you are the a whirl wind.

Be such.

It doesn't make sense to me anymore than the other one did. I'll destroy this gobbledy gook. "Let's get on with the burning. We'll start with that big book."

I should have known better than to start with that book. Even the little book of poems can be a weapon. And I'm not ready for it. She hits me hard in the stomach. I lean in pain, but then my training kicks in. I hit her so hard she flies across the mosaic floor into the shelves of books beyond.

I go to her. I call, "Yawn. Yawn." I don't bother keeping quiet anymore.

Before I pick her up, I take out the fire starters. I throw out several in different directions. Then I carry her out to the pool. Half way across it I put her on the edge of it and turn to watch the fire. It starts fast and when it reaches the bombs I set around the edges and under the roof, the blasts begin. Not as large as I'd have wished them to be.

Of course the librarians come, but six women are no match for someone like me. One problem, though, I have to keep my eyes shut because of all those bare breasts. I'm afraid I might touch one.

They trip me. I fall into the pool. They're water people and I'm not. I'm helpless in it. They hold my head under. It's Yawn yells for them to stop just when I'm choking. They pull me to the edge and Yawn turns me over and pumpes the water out. It takes a while before I can breathe.

The little homemade bombs are still going off now and then as the fire reaches them, but they're much too small. The building won't come down. Some of the librarians stand near the carved doors, their silhouettes outlined against the flames inside. They don't dare go in yet.

Nobody's paying attention to me. I roll over on my back and watch the dawn come, turning everything pinkish again. But the library is a mess, black from smoke, some corners are broken, but my bombs were too feeble to bring down the walls.

It's still an imposing sight in an entirely different way. The caryatids still look down in disapproval from over their bare breasts. A few gold tiles have fallen from the roof but nobody is rushing to pick them up even though just one would make a person rich. The librarians walk right past them.

Yawn sits beside me. I tell her I didn't mean to hit her so hard. She says, "I know."

Finally the fires settle down enough for the librarians to wrap wet scarves around their faces and go in. Yawn stays with me. Says, "I don't understand why you wanted to destroy it."

"To show your side we can bring down your most magnificent building."

"But you didn't. We don't even have any soldiers to protect it, and you didn't. Even so you failed."

"But look what one single man.... I, alone...."

"You failed."

"I'll bring you a bird. I'll bring you gold."

"What would you do if you were a golden man and lived in those pictures?"

"And you were the golden woman."

"Would you throw me down like you did?"

I'm thinking I would put my hand on her breast, but I don't say it. "Never again."

"Or maybe you'd melt me down and have me made into coins. Or you'd melt yourself down."

"I don't think unreal things. Besides, I'd rather be of use after I die. My skin gone for leather. My bones for spoons. I'd never become anything for beauty. Promise you won't let that happen to me."

"We're not going to kill you. I won't let us."

"Let's escape together."

She's tempted. "What would you do, go steal tiles?"

"I'd rather have you than golden tiles."

That pleases her. She will come. She says, "Hurry," takes my hand to pull me into the bushes by the side of the pool, but I pull her in the other direction. I want to see what the librarians are doing in there. Maybe I can keep them from putting out fires.

She tries to hold me back. "But you said...."

"Your art tells lies and I lie, too."

Inside, the library is full of smoke. Librarians are stamping out fires, putting rugs and wet towels over books. Some bring smoldering books out and dump them in the pool. Some books are so large it takes two or even three librarians to carry them.

Those still inside have wet scarves around their faces but Yawn and I don't. We begin to cough right away. A librarian hits me from behind and knocks me into a still burning book. Two and Yawn drag me out and dump me in the pool to stop my burning clothes, my burning topknot.

They argue about me. Mostly in their own language. Then one says, on purpose in my language, "He's not worth the trouble. Finally they say to Yawn—in my language, "He's yours to do with as you wish." They sound disgusted.

They get thongs to tie my ankles—loose enough so I can walk a little. The fires are out in the library and Yawn hurries me through the smoke to the central garden. It's untouched except a little smoky. She doesn't say a word. She ties me to a bench and leaves.

There's are trees in there. Flowering bushes. A birdbath but no birds. Still too smoky. I watch the little fountain. I don't try to get loose. I'm tied so I can lie down. I do.

Finally Yawn comes back with a lumpy awkward bundle and with tea and food. She gives me the tea and a fishy smelling sort of cake and dates. I don't feel like eating, especially not a fishy cake, but the tea is good.

Then she starts unpacking the things she brought, a folding stool, a folding easel, a wooden slab, long as her arm, to paint on. An odd thing to be doing after what's been happening. I'm an exotic creature fit for a zoo. She can't wait to get me down on a flat surface. To put on some wall, I suppose. Which makes me wonder what she'll do with the real me after. Will the painting take my place?

She begins, even as I'm sipping tea.

She works in spurts and then looks at me and thinks. Finally she shows me what she's done so far. There I am, just begun, but even so you can see it's me. You can see my topknot curling down behind my ear and then over my shoulder though now it's burned off. She has my eyes almost finished. They're like holes in the board. I suppose all of it will look like a hole through the board when she's done.

She starts to paint again. We're quiet and then she says, "I want you to be.... I wish you could be...."

"I'll never be."

Whatever it was she was going to say, she'd hate me if I was. She loves me because I'm not like her. Same reason I like her.

Then, again, she turns the painting towards me. She sits beside me to study it. Now my face is almost finished.

She keeps looking over at me as though wondering what I think about it.

I'm impressed. Not only with how much it looks like me but that it only took her a short time to paint it. I'm thinking I might steal it if I have the chance.

But I'm angry with myself for thinking it. I say, "This is a lie. Does a flower need a painting of itself?" I hear myself saying, "Do I need this?" even as I'm thinking that I do.

At that thought I bang my fists against the edge of the bench.

"You hate my painting."

"I like it. I like it. I shouldn't, but I do. But where I come from images are not allowed."

"How can that be?"

"And no bare breasts."

"Are breasts bad?"

"You'll learn that if you come home with me."

She says again, "Bless water."

"We don't bless things like water."

"Your language has no word for what we mean by blessing. And no word for asking somebody to come see a sight. No word for a sky-full of birds and we all look-up. Even my name, you can't guess it's many meanings."

"Tell me."

But she says, "You keep saying we should love the real, but the real disappears. One of these days this painting will be all that's left of you."

Is that a warning?

Then we hear a great rushing sound, loud as thunder right overhead, and the ground shakes and the painting falls... every pillar breaks.

Then it comes again. Worse.

After that, silence. Not even the cry of a seagull.

We wait, looking at each other.

And it comes again, just as we thought it would.

We are safe in the center of devastation. Everything is already flattened around us, but we don't move.

So it isn't me that makes the golden tiles for all to pick up, that buries the books in debris—though I would have wished it were me.

It won't be easy to leave the garden considering what's piled up around us.

I say, "I need to be free now. I can't be tied up."

She can't answer. She can't move.

"I can't go anywhere. Look around you. We're both prisoners."

Odd how the garden itself is untouched. The birdbath and sundial still stand. The trees. There's even water still spouting in the fountain though not as much.

And here's another aftershock.

"Let me go. What harm can I do now? We can't even get out of here. Not easily."

The library looks like piles of talus from back in my home mountains. Unstable to try to climb over. I can but she can't without my help.

Finally she unties me. She's so shaky she can hardly do it. I make her drink the rest of my tea. For a few minutes she can only talk her own language. I say a few words in mine to remind her. I say, "Don't worry, only this large stone building is destroyed. The librarians are most likely safe and I'll wager your little house still stands."

I take off my shirt, take it to the fountain, rinse it a bit first, and then wet it and wipe her face.

After a while I leave her sitting there and go to examine how hemmed in we are. I leave the dates and cakes beside her. I tell her to eat them if she wants to.

All the arcade is collapsed. I feel as if I'm in my own private grove. This is my fountain. My grape arbor, still climbing up it's frame. (The frame stands and yet the wall is rubble.) I make the complete circuit. I see a nest with baby birds in it. I wonder if the parents will come back. Whiffs of smoke and dust still rise now and then. But getting out of here doesn't look good. I can do it, but Yawn can't without my help. Now she's my prisoner.

I pick a bunch of grapes to bring to her in case she wants something cool and sweet.

It's already getting too dark for climbing the rubble—or for painting. I wonder if she'll ever finish my portrait.

I think to build a fire but the garden is so immaculate there are no dead branches and no dead leaves. Trust these overly refined people to have everything all cleaned up.

I come back, sit beside her and give her the grapes. I put my arm around her and she doesn't flinch away. I say, "It won't be easy getting out."

I feel like First Man and First Woman. They have just crawled out of the earth after the fires and floods of formation, all around them devastation, and it's up to them to clean up and populate the world. Up to Yawn and me. I hold her. I don't say anything. There's the sunset. We can't see the sun setting behind the rubble, but we see the pink and purple sky. She glows pinkish gold. I say, "That book…and us…."

She says, "That book is burned. They said it was the first to go."

"That was them wasn't it?"

She says, "I was named for her."

I say, "I was named for a god of war." Then I say it, "This is our garden. We'll live here."

She leans her head against my shoulder. "How will we eat?"

"The fig tree, the grapes…. I'll build a shelter out of rubble and tree branches. I'll make us a bed of young boughs."

Then I, like the golden man, forget the grapes and dates and put my hand on her breast."

"And will you like the things I like?"

"If I must."

That night we love each other.

Towards morning we hear cries from beyond the rubble. We hear both her language and mine. My group is there, calling out to me.

I keep silent, but Yawn yells back that we're here and all right.

"We're coming for you as soon as it's daylight."

Yawn turns to me. "That doesn't change anything."

"Out there I'll be a prisoner."

I'm wondering: First Man and First Woman? How did they end up? I'm glad that book is burned. I wouldn't want to see pages three and four and five and especially not ten, eleven, thirteen.... And yet I do wonder how it ended?

At dawn we hear them pulling at the rubble. We hear shouts and curses from my men. We hear women singing. Trust these people to be singing no matter what. I wouldn't be surprise if they were dancing, too, maybe even dancing as they remove stones.

Yawn says, "Come, we'll help. It's by the arbor that they're working," but the longer it takes the happier I'll be.

"Escape with me. We'll climb the opposite side. Here with your people, I don't know how to be."

"I'll teach you. And the books will tell you."

"The books are gone."

"Then we'll write some more."

Is anything ever really destroyed, human beings being what they are?

She says, "Come help." She's scrabbling at the stones as if our lives depended on being rescued.

I say, "You want to leave our garden."

But I help. It's inevitable. We *will* be rescued.

We move stones in silence, then take a rest. Drink and wash and eat figs. I say, "I wish you were finishing the painting instead."

"So you *do* like it."

"I like what you're doing."

After a few minutes rest, Yawn begins to work at the rubble again.

I could cross by myself. Faster than Yawn and faster than those trying to get to us.

I head for the fountain and take a big drink. I put figs in my pockets. I leap on the rocks on the opposite side from where they're coming for us. It's the worst side, higher than the other. I can leap from rock to rock in a way most people can't. I'm used to mountains and unstable talus.

Here and there I see gold tiles. One. Just one—for my mother.

But Yawn has seen me. I hear her give a dreadful cry. It lasts a long wailing time. It stuns me. It stops me that Yawn could cry such a cry. It can't be Yawn.

I'm teetering on the remains of a pillar. I never fall. I've never fallen.

I open my eyes to a sky bluer than blue, to grass greener than green, to a landscape like home only more so. I hear the silvery sound of a stream. I see its glitter. I look down at myself and see I'm naked and I'm gold. I couldn't even guess how valuable I am.

At first I try to hide my nakedness—as though someone watched, as I did, from behind the trees. But then I see, in the distance, a woman coming out from beyond the cedars. She wears a white flowing garment and has one breast bare.

My figs are on the ground in front of me but I'm not hungry.

Last night we already did as if turning the pages of this book. Now we'll do it again. Perhaps there are more pages than I guessed at when I first saw it. Perhaps I'll find out how it ends.

The Magazine of Fantasy & Science Fiction**,** August 2004

The Assassin Or Being The Loved One

I had been sent to assassinate the general of the opposition, but I didn't do it. I had him in my sights, but instead I let him shoot me.

I had promised to do it or die trying. I was dying, but I hadn't tried. I had looked into his eyes, then looked into the little black hole of his weapon, knowing he was looking into mine. I had even said, Sorry. Suddenly, I *was* sorry. Then I hadn't done it. I had the thought there might be something lesser I could do, something appropriate like cut off his trigger finger. Or better yet, cut off his thumbs.

He had a big grey moustache and blue eyes. His face was brown and weathered. He looked exactly like my father even to the squinting eyes. In fact for a moment I thought it was my father, grown older and come back from death and somehow switched over to the enemy's side.

This general was walking in the very mountains where the battles had taken place. I knew these hills as though I'd grown up here, and I'm sure the general did, too.

The war was over—said to be. Treaties had been signed—a whole year ago, but what did that have to do with us? If *we* didn't want it to be over, it wasn't. And we weren't the only ones. There were many pockets of hold-outs. The war had gone on for ten years. We couldn't figure out why we should stop now. What had changed? We promised each other we'd keep fighting one way or another until we were all dead. But there are few of us so we have to make our killing count. We didn't want to kill just anybody. We went to the top.

Certainly this general thought it was over or he wouldn't have been on the trail with his three grandsons. Nor would he have been in mufti. I knew who he was from the posters of victory, and I knew which cabin in the foothills was his summer home. I knew he had three grandsons and that his only son had been killed in the war. He looked so much a civilian, I was surprised he carried a pistol.

I had followed them all morning until the children and their terrier fell well behind and the general was already on the switchbacks. He was going fast. He obviously loved working himself hard. He obviously thought there was no danger to the boys.

I hoped not to kill in front of the children—though it might be a good lesson for them. I thought perhaps I could shock them with the shooting and then capture them for our side. There aren't many of us left. They were young enough to be convinced to change sides. We were, after all, the side of the upright. (When had we not been? We'd have changed sides if we thought we were wrong.) But if we couldn't convince them then their thumbs could go, too.

As the general climbed, switching back and forth, I took a shortcut. I ran straight up, turned around at the top and waited for him behind a boulder.

I had not realized he was a small man until he rounded the corner of the trail, came out from behind the cliff and stood, not more than six or eight yards from me. I had not seen his face close up until then.

The force of his bullet spun me to the side. I slid down a long bank of scree. I lay at the bottom knowing nobody would come to help me. I was done-for, way out here in the middle of nowhere.

I felt no pain. I stared up into a gnarled juniper. One doesn't often look straight up, along the trunk of a tree. It's a whole other view. I was charmed. It was a revelation. The branches hardly moved. It was a puzzle I could solve. A magpie sat in the puzzle for a moment. It gave a magpie kind of quack. I thought he was trying to tell me something. Perhaps announce my death to the rest of the forest. I thought how beautiful everything was. There was sun and shade, back and forth over my eyes so now and then I couldn't see for the brightness shining through.

And all the time I held my hand against my head, hoping to stop the blood, but I gave up. Then I began to die. I could feel my life flowing away. It seemed all right. I didn't have the energy to live, anyway. I was glad I didn't have to get up and do something. I had let my comrades down but I was glad nothing needed to worry me ever anymore. It was over.

But it wasn't.

I wake in a small white room with bars on the window. I'm alone. My head is bandaged. My first thought is of escape. My second that they should have tied me up. Then I think I must hurry to take advantage of the fact that there's no one here. I jump up and fall flat. The floor is cement. I hit my forehead but my bandage helps to shield me. I have to wait a moment to recover and then I crawl to the window, pull myself up by the bars and hang on to keep myself standing.

What at first seemed like snow is apple blossoms. It's a garden out there, lawns and flowerbeds, pathways. There's a fountain with the statue of a naked girl in the middle of it. To one side, a naked boy looking up at her, makes it look unbalanced. It seems a place especially made to cheer those wounded in mind and body. I'm full of yearning. To be in the sunshine and the blossoms, that they should be blowing down on me—to look at the naked girl.

I shake the bars. Hard. And harder. I hear myself grunt. I sound like a bear. Or, rather, what an imaginary bear sounds like. I've seen them on the mountains but never heard more than a sort of cough of warning.

I turn to the door. There's a little window in it. Perhaps I've been spied upon even as I fell and then went to rattle the bars. It's locked. They locked me in. What is this place? I look out at a hallway. There doesn't seem to be anybody around but I can't see very far. There's a painting on the wall, of wild flowers from the area, paintbrush and lupine, asters.

I sink to my knees with yearning for the garden.

When the door finally opens I'm in the way. She almost trips over me. A nurse. She calls for help, but calmly as though for help getting me back to bed. Even so I panic. I'm by her feet. I grab her ankles. She goes down—as hard as I did when I first got up. But she goes down on her chin and knocks herself out.

I start crawling down the hall. It's lined with nature paintings. They're trying to make everything nice—for prisoners? For crazies? I'm tempted to stop and look at them but I want to get out into the real thing. I get up, wobbling. I manage to walk, supporting myself with my hand on the wall. I'm not thinking escape, I'm thinking: Garden, apple blossoms, a fountain with a naked marble girl....

I'm not in pain. There's only this weakness and shaking, and I'm not thinking properly. I know there are important things I should be doing. There's a lost war I'm supposed to be fighting. I think how I had the chance at their general and didn't kill him. One of my friends may die trying to do what I didn't do.

Then I think: Was there a stream? How nice if a stream. I'll sit on the bank. I'll lie in the grass and look up along the tree trunks again. Birds will come. Perhaps another magpie.

I'm wobbling worse than ever. Everything is wavy, the hall stretches and shrinks. There's a door at the end of it. If I'm going to collapse, and I am, I must do it where I'm hidden and preferably outside.

The door is heavy. I have to use all my weight. Outdoors, I fall down four steps, then crawl, squashing pansies, into the lilacs beside them. I feel again the joy of not having to stay awake—not having to do anything. Back in our caves we were always on guard. I was always too tired.

But then women come and sit on the steps above me. I can't see them, but I can hear them. They sound young.

("They just lost a patient." "Somebody died?" "No, you nut, I said, lost. They say he's crazy. They couldn't keep him covered up and they couldn't keep his bandages on." "Is he crazy-dangerous?" "Yes. They say he wanted to kill the general but the general shot first.")

No, no, that's not how it was. I saved him. If not for me he'd be dead. And I'm not crazy.

It's important that they know I decided not to shoot. But I haven't the energy to say anything.

("They're *all* crazy." "They ought to be locked up." "They shouldn't be here. They ought to be in prison." "If I find him....")

She must have made a gesture.

("You couldn't." "Sure I could. I still can." "Knowing you, you'd fall in love. Look at that crazy baldheaded guy you fell for just because he kept staring at you. He stared like that because he was crazy!" "I've got more sense than that. Besides he was one of *them*. And look at *your* guy." "Oh Beth!")

Beth!

I love their voices and that name. It's been so long since I've been this close to anybody female. I want that laughing and that youth. I'm not so old myself. The one who liked bald heads...her voice was low, not like some women. I'm not much to look at, but at least I'm not bald. I need for them to know that, except for me, their general would be dead and those three boys stolen away to our side.

If I had the energy I would get up and tell them I saved him. I'd say, under all these bandages I'm not bald. And that I want to love. And I want to be the loved one.

I drag myself out. They jump when they see me. They're both beautiful. I knew they would be. I could tell by their voices. One is dressed as a nurse. That one has long black hair put up in a bun under her little cap. The other has freckles and curly reddish hair as short as a boy's.

I can't stand up, but I rise to my knees. This isn't the time for a speech but I do it anyway. "We've never been otherwise than kind. I saved the general out of kindness."

The one that's not dressed as a nurse is staring at me in horror. Then I see she has no thumbs.

We always thought that was a good idea—the cutting off of thumbs. We thought it was kind. Other groups have cut off hands and sometimes feet. We don't ever do that. We wouldn't consider those.

She should be glad she only lost her thumbs, but she comes towards me in a fury. As if to choke me. I wonder if she can, with those hands. The other tries to hold her back.

"Stop! Beth! He can hardly stand up, for heaven's sake."

I have more right to be angry than she has. They called our triumphal arch their own and made us march through it as part of *their* victory parade. We were torn and dirty (that's how they wanted us to be) while they were all cleaned up and dressed in their best. We were forced to march over our own banners. Behind us, in our beat up trucks, were our captured weapons. They sang songs of victory. Their trumpets sounded the charge. Their drums beat death.

They thought it would teach us a lesson. It did. We'll never surrender.

Beth finally gets free of the nurse and attacks me. She's stronger than I ever thought a woman could be. Or perhaps I'm weaker than I usually am. And she knows how to fight. She's been a soldier. She knows all sorts of tricks. She's on top, kneeing me in the wrong place. Her fists still work fine as fists. I curl up.

There's yelling. Orderlies come with needles. Not for her, the one attacking, the one going absolutely crazy, but for me and I haven't even been fighting back. I'm just all curled up.

Next thing I know someone is saying, "Son, son," and trying to wake me up.

I'm in pain which I hadn't been when there was just the wound in my head. Now I ache all over.

"Son!"

I open my eyes. It's the general. Leaning over me.

Is he calling me his son or does he call all younger men son? He's holding a straw to my lips. He's right, I'm thirsty. I could love him just for this drink of cool water. I could almost change sides for such pleasure.

He looks like a farmer, weathered, lined face, hands scared and swollen from frost bite. I recognize it all.

I wish he hadn't said, Son.

Then he says, "My assassin," but he doesn't say it in a bad way. He puts the glass down and holds my wrist. The skin of his palms feels rough—like a farmer's.

"Son, what's your name?"

....

"I need to know what caves you come from."

....

"The war is over!"

....

He shakes my shoulder. "It's *over*!"

....

"Long as you're in those caves, nobody is safe. We'd smoke them out. They won't be hurt."

They call that, snuffing. "Go ahead. Cut off my hands."

He snorts and lets go of me. Goes to the window. He's looking out at the garden.

"Smoke! You'd burn them out. And you think they won't come out shooting?"

The dark haired nurse is there. I'd not noticed her before. I need for her to know I saved the general. I raise myself on my elbows. "Tell them I saved you." I yell it. "I didn't shoot. Admit it. I saved you."

He turns back towards me, thinking.

"Remember?"

He's thinking back to when we stared down each other's gun barrels.

"I didn't shoot. That was on purpose."

"May...be."

He doesn't know what to believe. He turns to my garden, to my naked girl, and I lie back down.

There's broth. The nurse is about to hold the straw for me, but the general comes and takes it from her. Sits down again to hold it.

"Could be. You waited, I did see that."

To him the war is really over. Easy to think so when you're on the winning side.

"You could come up with me and help us get your comrades out. They'd come out for you."

"But then what?"

"Just the two of us? Just get their weapons."

"That's what you *say*."

The window is open. Even here, from my bed, I can feel the breeze. I can smell the lilacs. "Is somebody out there singing?"

The nurse says, "Oh, that's Beth."

"I want to go into the garden. If only for a moment."

"Take him out as soon I leave."

"Can I take his bandage off? I don't want Beth or the other patients and orderlies to know who he is. I'm afraid they might attack him."

"Do it."

Then he tells her, "Take good care of my assassin." He squeezes my shoulder and winks as if we were in this together.

After he leaves, the nurse takes the bandages off and puts on two smaller ones.

They've shaved my head because of my wound, but also my beard. In our caves it's hard to find ways to shave. We were proud of being hairy. It identified us as wild mountain men who would never surrender. We were even proud of being dirty.

I tell the nurse to bring me a mirror.

I'm shocked. I look so old and worn out and starved and sick. I'm greenish under my tan, and there are circles around my eyes. I have to watch myself touching myself to make sure I'm me. I wonder if my comrades would recognize me. The general and I could go up to the caves to bring them out and they wouldn't know me, anyway.

"Can you walk to the wheelchair?"

I'm so shocked by how I look I wonder if I can.

"Don't you want to go?

"Come on, it'll do you good.

"I have other patients. I can't wait all day." She says it, even so, with tolerance. She would wait.

I walk to the chair. I'm much stronger than I was before. I tell her I want to be near the fountain.

It is beautiful. Even better than I expected. Blossoms are still blowing down. They're all over my lap before we even get to the fountain. Birds. There's one little bird with red on his head. Maybe a finch. The birds around our caves in the mountains are different. Juncos and jays. The nurse pushes me right next to the naked marble girl and leaves. Across from me, on the other side of the fountain, is Beth, still singing to herself.

There are only a few people around. Some on benches, some in wheelchairs, wrapped up tight, as I am, but except for Beth, I'm the only one near the fountain. If she looked right at me she'd not recognize me without my turban of bandages.

She doesn't pay any attention to me. She sits on the edge of the pool, leaning, with her mutilated hands in the water. I wonder if they hurt and if the cool soothes them.

I watch her. If she's the one fell in love because of being stared at, maybe she'll fall in love with me. But she pays no attention. I'm just another of the patients. I suppose she is, too, though her hands seem healed. She sounds happy right now, but I know she's not. I saw the rage and horror underneath.

I listen to her and to the splashing of the fountain. The sun glitters on the droplets and the pool is almost to bright to look at. Here with the naked girl beside me and Beth leaning across from me, I should feel happy but my thoughts are on thumbs.

I think how it might be. You can't choke people. Can't peel potatoes. Hard to cut your meat. Hard to raise your glass. Can't screw things in. Can't tie your shoes. Would it be hard to hold a pistol? Some ways, having only one hand might be better than no thumbs.

But we didn't do that to just anybody. She'd have to have been a killer, too.

Maybe we found her assassinating one of ours so we made it hard for her to do it again.

Beth hasn't looked at me once. I want to do make her see me.

I throw the blanket aside and get up—too fast again. I almost fall in the fountain, dizzy. But then I jump in. I don't know what I think I'm doing. Making Beth look at me—at least that.

The water is over my knees and icy enough to make me gasp. It must come straight from the mountains. The cold wakes me out of my craziness. Why did I do this? I could have just called to her. They said I was crazy. Maybe I am.

Beth jumps in, too, splashes across to me and pulls at my clothes with her thumbless fists, to get me out of there.

"Are you crazy? What are you trying to do?" But then she gets that look you have for *really* crazy people. Like you have to be careful what you say. She says, "You're fine. You have a head wound. That makes your thinking muddled. You'll be fine."

She helps me into the wheelchair as if I'm a sick old man and starts to wheel me back.

"I *have* to stay in the garden."

"You have to get dried off. I do, too."

"Please wait. It's not cold. I don't know when they'll let me come out again."

"Well. . . ." She sits on the edge of the pool next to me. "Maybe for a minute."

"I haven't talked to anybody since I came here. I mean really talked. Please."

She leans close to me, tucking me in. Obviously she doesn't know I'm the one she attacked. She has apple blossoms in her hair. I'm in love already. Not that I wasn't back when I first saw her—felt her, boney, against me.

"I like your singing."

"I used to sing."

"Did they do this to you because you were singing enemy songs? People have done things as ridiculous as that but I didn't think we ever would."

"I was a body guard for the general. He's my uncle."

I ask her what her name is, though I know it already. I say, "I'm Len." I really am. I won't tell the general, but I tell her.

It turns out she's been helping in the hospital ever since she was here for her mutilated hands. "I'm more trouble than I'm worth, but I try. They let me think I'm helping."

She's sitting so close our knees touch now and then.

I never believed in that heaven for old soldiers, though some did. I begin to think it's really true and this is the maiden assigned to me, just the kind I like the best. And it smells so good of damp earth and new cut grass. Reminds me of haying time. But if a heaven, why, then, is my wound still here, my bruises aching, and her thumbs still gone?

"I could stay out here forever. Maybe this is forever. Maybe this is heaven. I hope it is."

"Don't count on it."

"After all I did die back under the juniper. I thought I did."

I see her suddenly understanding.

"It's *you*!"

I brace myself to be attacked but she sits quietly.

"It *is* you!"

"What did you do that we did this to you? There has to be a reason."

"You did a lot more than just cut my thumbs."

I know what she means.

"I'm here now partly because of that. What *you* people did. Not so much because of thumbs, though that, too."

She gets up but I grab her wrist. "I would never."

"We were just the enemy. We weren't even human. We were dirt under your boots."

"What do you think we were to you? Even now, you hunt us out and call us rock rats. But I didn't. I wouldn't."

Actually I never had the chance. I might have. We thought of them as hardly human. We said they ate grubs and rats. We said they copulated with animals. But I was never sure if that was true.

She tries to pull away but I'm strong now. I can hold her. "Please. I would never. I wouldn't."

"There's no kinder man than the general and you wanted to kill him."

"But I stopped myself right in the middle. He'll vouch for that. I let him shoot me. Ask him."

She stops struggling. She's so close to me. I'd hug her if I dared, but then she'd think I was one of those others that raped her. She already thinks I'm like them.

I let her go. I think she'll leave but she doesn't. She sits back on the edge of the pool, hunched into herself.

"I've believed in my uncle from the beginning."

She speaks softly and with lots of hesitations.

"I was a private guard for him. Your people captured me. You almost killed him that time, too. You killed two guards but you took me for... other things."

I wonder why she's telling me this. You'd think she'd be attacking me again.

"It wasn't me."

I want to comfort her. I reach to touch her arm. She flinches but then she lets me. Just touch. I don't dare do more.

"After I escaped I tried to assassinate your leader. I didn't kill him, but it wasn't for lack of trying. That's why you cut me. Somebody else killed him later."

That was the beginning of our end—losing our leader. That sent me into the mountains to become a wild man. But at least she didn't do it.

"I was crazy when I came here. I'm not quite so crazy anymore. But I'm still crazy. I can't look at you."

Though she's looking.

"You're cold. Come on, I'll take you back."

She tucks me in tighter. Holding the blanket with her fists. I feel bad that it so hard for her to do everything, even this pulling on my blanket. Her hands are long and slim and brown. They're strong and beautiful at the same time. She's kind, even to the likes of me.

"Can I have some real clothes?"

"Where would you go?"

"Am I a prisoner? My door was locked."

She hesitates. Too long. Says, "No." Then, "Of course not." She's decided to lie.

Maybe this is an insane asylum. It is! Beth said she was here because she went crazy.

I look around to see if the garden is walled but I can't tell. There's so many trees and hedges. There *is* a stream. I can see it shining in the distance.

"Don't lie. This isn't a hospital, this is an insane asylum."

She doesn't know what to say. "It *is* a hospital, but... and...."

Just then the general comes again. You'd never know he was a general. He's wearing a wine colored shirt, sleeves rolled up and neck open. He's striding along like he did on the trail.

He hugs Beth hard. He's no taller than she is. He looks at me over her shoulder as he does it. I feel he's reading my thoughts. It doesn't matter if he is because I'm glad to see him in spite of myself.

Beth says, "This is Len."

"Ah hah."

He's brought me a present. A basket of fruit. It's a bribe. This whole place is. All these people being nice, as if trying to change my mind.

He sits on the edge of the pool beside me, gets out his pocket knife and begins to peel an orange.

We never were able to have much fruit up in our mountains. Even the aroma.... It's a bribe that's working.

"Son."

Not that again.

"Don't you think it's time for your friends to get out of those caves and start living their lives? Aren't you tired of all this?"

"This is a prison isn't it? A place for all the crazies who won't stop fighting."

He hands me sections of orange.

"There are no more military prisons."

"I'll believe it when you give me clothes and let me out."

"We will."

"Even Beth said she was crazy."

They give each other a look. It makes me feel even crazier.

He goes on handing me fruit, not talking, just thinking hard. I can almost see him wondering how to make me give up my friends?

"We'd go up together, just the two of us. After that you'd be free. I promise."

I'll not fall for that. There could be troops coming up behind us. If there weren't, maybe *we* could capture *him*. But I'm thinking: How about Beth and me going up together? What if I escape and bring her with me? Or, better yet....

"I'll do it if Beth comes with us."

"Done!"

What have I gotten myself into? And my friends? Maybe I can go to empty caves and pretend they've left. Maybe we can over power the general? Would they rape Beth yet again? They would if they had the chance. Would I?

That cave life was all I knew for so long I forgot what life could be. We promised ourselves we would never stop, but I'm tired of it. I want to love the enemy. Marry the enemy. Forget the war.

"Are you up for tomorrow? You can set the pace."

I feel strong. I have the rest of the day and night to think. Maybe gather up a weapon or make one. Even a fork might do damage if used properly.

The general leaves, hugging Beth again and squeezing my shoulder. Beth takes me back and helps me into bed. She looks like a warrior woman but she's so gentle. The gentler she is the worse I feel about her hands.

I finally get clothes—clothes none of my companions would recognize me in. The shirt is much too bright a red. The hat is yellow. The general will be able to keep track of me. He and Beth, on the other hand, are dressed in earth colors. I wonder how I can make my friends understand it's me.

We're traveling light. If the general has a gun, it's hidden. I have an ordinary knife and fork. I'm sure they know they were missing from my supper tray.

We cross the garden on a red brick path. Cross the stream by way of a Japanese bridge. There is a wall—much overgrown with vines. I could have climbed it.

We spend the night at ten or so thousand feet, a few hundred feet below where our caves are. Our army was in shambles so only one cave was still occupied. I'll go to that one last and only if I have to.

It's cold up there at night no matter how hot it was during the day. We huddle into one small tent. All this still seems like, if not *the* heaven, then *a* heaven, even though the general sleeps between us. What if she'd love me?

I dream Beth's hands are whole and mine are mutilated. Hard to tell if it's a nightmare or a wishful dream to save Beth. Then I'm trying to comb her hair. I can't hold the comb. I wake with the general shaking my shoulder. He's calling, "Son. Len. It's all right. The war is over." He goes back to sleep holding my wrist. I feel anchored and safe but I don't sleep right away. I listen to their breathing, Beth's and the general's. I must do something—for Beth. I don't know what.

I have to lead the way now. The general comes last. I hope for a time when he lags behind but he sticks close to Beth. I want to tell her I'll do anything for her. I want to tell her I love her, and I won't let her be hurt again, but the general is always in the way.

Twice I take them to empty caves and say, as if surprised, that our men have gone, but they see right away that nobody has used these caves for a long time and insist I go to a real site. But when we get to our occupied cave, there's nobody there either. I whistle the secret whistle but there's no answer. We go in. The fireplace is cold. It looks as if nobody's been there for days.

Beth and the general can see this really was our cave. There's even food left here, half eaten by varmints. Now that I've been out of there a while, I can't stand the smell. I'd not ever want to live there again or any place like it full of unwashed men.

But they're on the cliffs above us, my friends...my used to be friends.... I realize it the minute I hear the landslide coming down. I know them, they'd kill me without a second thought if they thought they could get the general, too. Besides, I did betray them.

I try to pull Beth to the side, but everything happens too fast and I'm too busy trying to breathe.

When things slow down...when the land slide's finally just a trickle, I'm covered with gravel. I push myself out from under. I'm scratched and bruised, my clothes are shredded, and I'm practically back down into the foot hills. All that hard climbing to get up and I'm down in a minute. But where are they! I try to climb again, straight up the loose scree, but that's impossible so I climb beside it. Then I try to cross to its other side and almost slide down it again. I hunt all day. At evening I find the general. I free him enough to see he's dead. I can't find Beth.

I'll go for help. If Beth is alive she'll try to come back to the asylum. Maybe she's back there already.

I arrive at the fountain in the moonlight. It's so beautiful. Everything is silvery, the apple trees, the ground littered with silvery petals. I sit on the edge of the pond next to the statue. It's a cold place to sit. I'm shivering.

I hadn't realized before how much the statue looks like Beth, slim with small breasts, a young body. Beth is not that young, she's more my age, but her body is girlish. My warrior woman.

The one boy is on the right. I take my place on the left where there should be another. I make it symmetrical. It's almost as if this spot was waiting for me. My feet are in the icy pond but I want to be there, anyway.

The girl leans as Beth leaned. One hand towards the water as though to soothe the pain.

My God, someone has broken off the thumb! Who would do such a thing?

Her other hand is curled close to her, as though to hide her breasts. I lean up to check it. Someone has broken off that thumb, too.

She's so silvery and beautiful. So cold. I want to warm her. I put my arms around her knees. I look up into her face as the other boy does. I was cold to start with, now I'm colder but I no longer shiver. I won't let go. I grow stiff. I couldn't move if I wanted to. I'm thinking how I've never been as happy as here in the garden. I hope they let me stay.

Ninth Letter Vol. 1 #2 Fall/Winter 2004,
University of Illinois

All Of Us Can Almost....

. . . fly, that is. Of course lots of creatures can *almost* fly. But all of us are able to match any others of us, wing span to wing span. Also to any other fliers. But though we match each other wing to wing we can't get more than inches off the ground. If that. But we're impressive. Our beaks look vicious. We could pose for statues for the birds representing an empire. We could represent an army or a president. And, actually, we are the empire. We may not be able to fly, but we rule the skies. And most everything else, too.

Creatures come to us for advice on flying. They see us kick up dust and flap and stretch and are awed.

We croak out what we have to say in quacks. We tell them, "The sky is a highway. The sky is of our time and recent. The sky is flat. It's blue because it's happy." They thank us with donations. That's how we live.

The sound of our clacking beaks carries across the valley. It adds to our reputation as powerful—though what good is it really? It's just noise.

Nothing said of us is true, but must we live by truths? Why not keep on living by our lies?

Soaring! Think of it! The stillness of it. Not even the sound of flapping. They say we once did that. Perhaps we still can and just forgot how to begin. How make that first jump? How get the lift? But we grew too large. We began to eat the things that fell and lots of things fall.

I could leap off a cliff. Test myself. But I might become one of those things tumbling down. Even my own kind would tear me apart.

Loosely...very loosely speaking, I do fly. My sleep is full of nothing but that. The joy of it.

But where's the joy in *almost* doing it. Flapping in circles. Making a great wind for nothing but a jump or two. We don't even look good to ourselves.

I don't know what we're made for. It's neither sky nor water nor...especially not...the waddle of the land. We can't sing. Actually we can't do anything. Except look fierce.

Pigeons circle overhead. Meadowlarks sing. Geese and ducks, in Vs, do their seasonal things. We stay. We *have* to. Winter storms come and we're still here. We puff up as much as we can and wrap our wings around ourselves. Perhaps that's what our wings were for in the first place. We're designed merely to shelter ourselves. Even our dreams of flying are yet more lies.

But none others are as strong as we are...at least none *seem* to be. We win with looks alone and a big voice. We stand, assured and sure.

When creatures ask me for a ride I say, "I'd take you up any time you want—hop and skip and up we go—except you're too heavy. Next time measure wings, mine against some other of us. You'll need a few inches more on each side. Tell a bigger one I said to take you up."

"Take to the air along with us," I say. "Follow me up and up." I'm shameless. But I suspect it's only the young that really believe. The older ones pretend to because of our beaks, because of the wind we can stir up—our clouds of dust.

Still, I go on, "Check out my wing span. Check out my evil eye. Listen. *My* voice."

They jump at my squawk.

They bring me food just to watch me tear at it. At least I'm good at that. I put on a good show. Every creature backs away.

One of the young ones keeps wanting me to take him up. He won't stop asking. I say, "A sparrow could do better." That's true, but he takes it as a joke. I say, "Why not at least ask a male."

"Males scare me."

Finally, just to shut him up, I say, "Yes, but not until the next section of time."

He runs off yelling, "Whee! Whee! Whee! She's taking me up!"

Now how will I get out of it? I only have from one moon to the other. But who knows, one of the big males may have eaten him by that time. They don't care where their food comes from. He was right to be scared.

Who knows how we lost our ability to fly? Maybe we're just lazy. Maybe we just don't exercise our flying muscles. How could we fly, sitting around eating dead things all the time? If anyone can fly, it seems to me more likely one of us smaller females could than a big male.

That little one keeps coming back and saying, "*Really*? Are you *really* going to take me up?"

And I keep saying, "I said I would didn't I? When have any of us ever lied?"

(Actually, when have we ever told the truth?)

He keeps yelling back and forth to all who'll listen. The way he keeps on with it, I could eat him myself.

But we have to be careful. Sometimes those ground dwellers get together and decide not to feed us. Whoever they don't feed always dies. He'll waddle around trying to get someone of us to share, but we don't. We're not a sharing kind.

I *should* like these ground dwellers because of the food they bring, but I don't. I pretend to, just like they pretend to believe us. They call us Emperor, Leader, Master, but why are they doing this? It could be a conspiracy to keep us fat and lazy so we won't be lords of the sky anymore. So we're tamed and docile. Maybe they started this whole thing, stuffing us with their leftovers. Maybe they're the real emperors of the sky. Master of the sky though never in it anymore than we are. At least they can climb trees.

I wonder what they want us for? Or maybe it's the best way to know where we are and what we're doing.

Feed your enemies. Tame them.

I ask some of us, "Where is that cliff they say we used to soar out from?"

"Was there a cliff? Did there used to be a cliff?"

I'm sure there must have been one. How could birds the size of us get started without one—a high one? Maybe that's our problem, we've lost our cliff. We forgot where it is.

Evenings when all are in their burrows, and my own kind, wrapped in their wings, are clustered under the lean-tos set out for us by lesser beings, I stretch and flap. Reach. Jump. Only the nightingale sees me flop. It's a joy to be up to hear her and to be flipping and flopping.

I'll take that pesky little one all the way to wherever that cliff of ours is. Wouldn't that be something? See the sights? Be up in what we always call "Our element."

But there's a male, has his eye on me. Has had for quite some time. That's another good reason to take off. I'd like to get out of here before the time is ripe.

Or perhaps he's heard the little one yelling, "Whee, Whee," and likes the idea of me with one of those little ones on my back. Easy pickin's, *both* of us. Little one for one purpose and me for another. I can just see it, me distracted, defending the little, and the big taking care of both things while I struggle, front *and* back.

He may be the biggest, but I don't want him. Maybe that's how we got too big to fly, we kept mating with the biggest. It's our own fault we got so big. I'm not going to do that. Well, also the big ones are the strongest. This biggest could slap down all the other males.

If not for the fact that we hardly speak to each other, we females could get together and stop it. Go for the small and the nice. If there are any nice. Not a single one of us is noted for being nice.

I hate to think what mating will be like with one so huge. I'd ask other females if we were the kind who asked things of each other.

He keeps following me around. I don't know how I'm going to avoid him if he's determined. I won't get any help from any of the others. They'll just come and watch. Probably even squawk him onward. I've done it myself.

I'm thinking of ways to avoid that male, so when that little one comes to ask, yet again, "Why wait for next moon?" I say, "You're right. We'll do it now but I have to find our platform."

"Why?"

"Have you ever seen any of us take off from down here? Of course you haven't. I need a place to soar from."

"Can't we start flying from right here so everybody can see me?"

"No. I have to have a place to take off from. Get on my back. I'll take you there."

"I can walk faster than this all by myself."

"I know, but bear with me."

"My name is Hobie. What's yours?"

"We don't have names. We don't need them."

The big one comes waddling after us. A few of us follow him, wanting to see what's going to happen. I don't think the big realizes how far I'm going. Nobody does.

When we get to the end of the nesting places, Hobie says, "I've never been this far. Is this all right to do?"

"It's all right."

"Your waddling is making me sick."

"We'll rest in a few minutes."

I don't dare stop now, so near the nests. Everybody will waddle out to us. We have to get out of sight. Out there I could eat Hobbie myself if need be. I don't suppose anybody will be feeding us way out here.

I don't stop soon enough. Hobie throws up on my back. It smells of dirt dweller's food. And we're still not out of sight.

"Hang on. I'll stop at that green patch just ahead."

I waddle a little faster but that just makes him fall off. I'm thinking, Oh well, go on back and let the big male do what he has to do. It can't last more than a couple of minutes. If he breaks my legs it might be better than what I'm going through now.

But I wait for Hobie to get back on. I say, "Not much farther." He climbs on slowly. I wonder if he suspects I might eat him.

That big is coming along behind us but he's slower even that I am. Who'd have thought I was worth so much trouble.

In the green patch there's a stream. We both drink and I start washing my back. Hobie keeps saying, "I couldn't help it."

"I know that. Now stop talking so I can think."

I leave foot prints. Maybe best if I go along the stream for a while. Then we can drink any time we want. I turn towards the high side, where the stream comes from. If there really is a take off platform it's got to be high.

"Where are we going?"

"There's a place in the sky that'll give me a good lift.

"What kind of a place?"

"A cliff."

"How far is it?"

"Oh for the sky's sake keep quiet."

"Why does your kind always say, for the sky's sake?"

"Because we're sky creatures. Not like you. Now let me think about walking."

Even in this little stream there's fish. Wouldn't it be nice if I could catch one by myself?

"Hang on!"

I dive. But I forgot about the water changing the angle of view. I miss. I say, "Next time."

Hobie says, "I can."

I let him off to stand on the bank and dive and he does it. Gives the fish to me even though I'll bet he's getting hungry, too.

"Thank you, Hobie. Now get one for yourself."

At dusk we find a nice place to nest in among the trees along the stream—soft with leaves. Hobie curls up right beside my beak. Practically under it. I'm more afraid of my bite than he is. I hope I don't snap him up in my sleep.

Towards morning we hear something coming…lumbering along. Sounding tired for sure. We both know who. Hobie doesn't like big males any more than I do. He scrambles up on my back and says, "Shouldn't we go?"

Because I'm so much smaller than any male, I waddle a lot faster. It gets steeper but I'm still doing pretty well. It's so steep I have hopes of finding our cliff. I turn around and look back down and here comes the big, but a long ways off. Staggering, stumbling. Am I really worth all this effort?

"Are we far enough ahead? Are we getting some place? How long now?"

"Do you ever say anything that isn't a question?"

"You do it. That's a question."

I'm not used to waddling all day long, especially not uphill. It's the hardest thing I've ever done. But the big…. He's still coming. It's getting steeper. I hope one as large as he is can't get up here. This is just what I wanted. The launching platform has got to be here. How did it ever come to be that we got stuck down in the flat places?

And finally here it is, *the* launch place at the top of the cliff. I look over the edge. I'm so scared just looking I start to feel sick. I'm not sure I can even pretend to jump.

"Why are you shaking so much? It's going to make me sick again."

Should I eat Hobie now before he tells everybody I not only can't fly, I can't even get close to the edge without trembling and feeling sick?

But it's been nice having company. I've gotten used to his paws tangled in my feathers, making a mess of them. And I'd miss his questions.

I move back and look over the other side. It's steep on that side, too, though not so much. This platform is a promontory going off into nothing on all sides but one. It must have been perfect for fliers.

I look around to see if I can see any signs that it was used as a launching place, but there's nothing. I suppose, up here so high, the weather would have worn away any signs of that. I wonder if that big male knows anything more about it than I do.

It's breezy up here. I flap my wings to test myself, but I do it well away from the edges.

Hobie says, "Go, go, go."

Maybe I should just get closer and closer to edge...get used to it little by little...until I don't feel quite so scared.

I look over the side again though from a few feet away. I see the big male is still coming. I see him turn around and look down at exactly the same spot where we did. Then he looks up. Right at us. He spreads his wings at us so I'll see his wingspan. Then he turns side view. That's so I'll get a good look at his profile...the big hooked beak, the white ruff.... Then he starts up again.

I look over the more sloping side again. I think I might be able to slide down there though it's a steep slide. At the bottom there's a lot of trees and brush. That would break our fall.

That big one is getting so close I can hear him shuffling and sliding just like I did. I sit over by the less steep side and wait.

Pretty soon I see the fierce head looking up at us, the beady eye, and then the whole body. He has an even harder time than I had lifting himself on to the launching platform.

Hobie says, "I'm scared of males," and I say, "I am, too."

As soon as the big catches his breath he says, "You're beautiful."

I say, "That's neither here nor there."

He says, "I love you." As if any of us knew what that word meant.

I say, "Love is what you feel for a nice piece of carrion."

He looks a mess. I must, too. Dusty, feathers every which way. Hobie and I filled up on fish back at the stream, but I don't think he did. He looks at Hobie like the next meal. I back up a little closer to the sliding side. I say, "This one's mine." *That*, he'll understand.

He's inching closer. He thinks I don't notice. If he grabs me there's no way I can escape. I back up even more.

And then.... I didn't mean to. Off we go. Skidding, sliding, but like flying. Almost! Almost!

Hobie is yelling, "Whee. Whee. Whee." At least he's happy.

When we get down as far as the trees and bushes, I grab at them with my beak to slow us. And then I hear the big coming behind us. I never thought he… such a big one…would dare follow.

There's a great swish of gravel sliding with us. Even more as the big comes down behind us. Here he is, landed beside us, but, thank goodness, not exactly on.

Hobie and I are more or less fine. Scratched and bruised and dusty, but the big is moaning.

We're in a sort of ditch full of lots of brush and trees. It looks to be up hill on all sides. I wonder if either of us…the big and I could waddle out of it. Hobie could.

Hobie and I dust off.

Hobie says. "That was great. I wish the others could have seen me."

He can't, can he? Can he *possibly* think that was flying?

Then I see that the big one's legs slant out at odd angles. His weight was his undoing. My lightness saved me.

The big says, "Help me." But why should I? I say, "It's all your fault in the first place."

He's in pain. I brush him off. I even dare to preen him a bit. I don't think he'll hurt me or try to mate. He couldn't with those broken legs, anyway. He needs me. He has to be nice. That'll be a change.

These big males are definitely bigger than they need to be. He's twice my size. Where will all this bigness lead? Just to less and less, ever again, the possibility of flight, that's where.

Hobie doesn't even need to be asked. "I'm hungry. Can I go get us some food?"

"Of course you can."

"After you flew me I owe you lots."

Off he goes into the brush. I take a look at the big one's legs and wonder what to do. Can I make splints? And what to use to bind them with? Though there's always lots of stringy things in our meals if Hobie finds us food.

"You're not only never going to fly, you may never waddle either."

He just groans again.

"I'll try to straighten these out." I give him a stick to bite on. And then I do it. After I look for sticks as splints.

In no time Hobie brings three creatures. I think one for each of us but he says he ate already. He's says this place is all meals. Nothing has been hunting here in a long time, maybe never. He says, "You could even hunt for yourself."

Now there's a thought. I think I will.

I leave the three creatures for the big male and start out but the big says, "Don't leave me." Just like a chick.

I say, "If you eat Hobie that's the last you'll ever see of me." And I go.

Hobie is right, all the little meals are easy to catch. I eat four and keep all the stringy things. I also look around at where we are and if we could ever get out. There's that little stream below, cool and clear, bubbling along not far from where we fell. Beside it there's a nice place for a nest. I think about chicks. How I'd try to get them flapping right from the start. Even the baby males. And maybe, if we all were thinner and had to scramble for our food like I just had to do, and if all the food would get to know the danger and make us scramble harder and we'd get even thinner and stronger, and first thing you know we wouldn't have to climb out, we'd fly. All of us. Could that really come to be?

I throw away the stringy things I was going to make splints with. I have everything under control. I'll tell Hobie he can go on home if he wants to, though I'll tell him I do wish he'd stay, just for the company. And just in case we never do learn to fly again, we'd need his help when the food gets smarter and scarcer.

Sci Fiction, November, 2004

I Live with You

I live in your house and you don't know it. I nibble at your food. You wonder where it went ... where your pencils and pens go.... What happened to your best blouse. (You're just my size. That's why I'm here.) How did your keys get way over on the bedside table instead of by the front door where you always put them? You *do* always put them there. You're careful.

I leave dirty dishes in the sink. I nap in your bed when you're at work and leave it rumpled. You thought you had made it first thing in the morning and you had.

I saw you first when I was hiding out at the book store. By then I was tired of living where there wasn't any food except the muffins in the coffee bar. In some ways it was a good place to be ... the reading, the music. I never stole. Where would I have taken what I liked? I didn't even steal back when I lived in a department store. I left there forever in my same old clothes though I'd often worn their things at night. When I left, I could see on their faces that they were glad to see such a raggedy person leave. I could see they wondered how I'd gotten in in the first place. To tell the truth, only one person noticed me. I'm hardly ever noticed.

But then, at the book store, I saw you: Just my size. Just my look. And you're as invisible as I am. I saw that nobody noticed you just as hardly anybody notices me.

I followed you home—a nice house on the outskirts of town. If I wore your clothes, I could go in and out and everybody would think I was you. But I wondered how to get in in the first place? I thought it would have to be in the middle of the night and I'd have to climb in a window.

But I don't need a window. I hunch down and walk in right behind you. You'd think somebody that nobody ever notices would notice other people, but you don't.

Once I'm in, right away I duck into the hall closet.

You have a cat. Isn't that just like you? And just like me also. I would have had one were I you.

The first few days are wonderful. Your clothes are to my taste. Your cat likes me (right away better than he likes you). Right away I find a nice place in your attic. More a crawl space but I'm used to hunching over. In fact that's how I walk around most of the time. The space is narrow and long, but it has little windows at each end. Out one, I can look right into a tree top. I think an apple tree. If it was the right season I could reach out and pick an apple. I brought up your quilt. I saw you looking puzzled after I took the hall rug. I laughed to myself when you changed the locks on your doors. Right after that I took a photo from the mantel. Your mother, I presume. I wanted you to notice it was gone, but you didn't.

I bring up a footstool. I bring up cushions, one by one until I have four. I bring up magazines, straight from the mail box, before you have a chance to read them.

What I do all day? Anything I want to. I dance and sing and play the radio and TV.

When you're home, I come down in the evening, stand in the hall and watch you watch TV.

I wash my hair with your shampoo. Once, when you came home early, I almost got caught in the shower. I hid in the hall closet, huddled in with the sheets, and watched you find the wet towel—the spilled shampoo.

You get upset. You think: I've heard odd thumps for weeks. You think you're in danger, though you try hard to talk yourself out of it. You tell yourself it's the cat, but you know it's not.

You get a lock for your bedroom door—a deadbolt. You have to be inside to push it closed.

I have left a book open on the couch, the print of my head on the couch cushion. I've pulled out a few gray hairs to leave there. I have left a half full wine glass on the counter. I have left your underwear (which I wore) on the bathroom floor, dirty socks under the bed, a bra hanging on the towel rack. I left a half-eaten pizza on the kitchen counter. (I ordered out and paid with your stash of quarters, though I know where you keep your secret twenties.)

I set all your clocks back fifteen minutes but I set your alarm clock to four in the morning. I hid your reading glasses. I pull buttons off your sweaters and put them where your quarters used to be. Your quarters I put in your button box.

Normally I try not to bump and thump in the night, but I'm tired of your little life. At the book store and grocery store at least things happened all day long. You keep watching the same TV programs. You go off to work. You make enough money (I see the bank statements), but what do you do with it? I want to change your life into something worth watching.

I begin to thump, bump, and groan and moan. (I've been feeling like groaning and moaning for a long time, anyway.) Maybe I'll bring you a man.

I'll buy you new clothes and take away the old ones, so you'll *have* to wear the new ones. The new clothes will be red and orange and with stripes and polka dots. When I get through with you, you'll be real … or at least realer. People will notice you.

Now you groan and sigh as much as I do. You think: This can't be happening. You think: What about the funny sounds coming from the crawl space? You think: I don't dare go up there by myself, but who could I get to go with me? (You don't have any friends that I know of. You're like me in that.)

Monday you go off to work wearing a fuzzy blue top and red leather pants. You had a hard time finding a combination without stripes or big flowers or dots on it.

I watch you from your kitchen window. I'm heating up your leftover coffee. I'm making toast. (I use up all the butter. You thought there was plenty for the next few days.)

You almost caught me the time I came home late with packages. I had to hide behind the curtains. I could tell that my feet showed out the bottom, but you didn't notice.

Another time you saw me duck into the hall closet but you didn't dare open the door. You hurried upstairs to your bedroom and pushed the deadbolt. That evening you didn't come down at all. You skipped supper. I watched TV … any show I wanted.

I put another deadbolt on the *outside* of your bedroom door. Just in case. It's way up high. I don't think you'll notice. It might come in handy.

(Lacy underwear with holes in lewd places. Nudist magazines. Snails and sardines—smoked oysters. Neither one of us like them. All the things I get with your money are for *you*. I don't steal.)

How do you get through Christmas all by yourself? You're lonely enough for both of us. You wrap empty boxes in Christmas paper just to be festive. You buy a tree, a small one. It's artificial and comes with lights that glimmer on and off. The cat and I come down to sleep near its glow.

But the man. The one I want to bring to you. I look over the personals. I write letters to possibilities but, as I'm taking them to the post office, I see somebody. He limps and wobbles. (The way he lurches sideways looks like sciatica to me. Or maybe arthritis.) He needs a haircut and a shave. He's wearing an old plaid jacket and he's all knees and elbows. There's a countrified look about him. Nobody wears plaid around here.

I limp behind him. Watch him go into one of those little apartments behind a main house and over a garage. It's not far from our house.

It can't be more than one room. I could never creep around in that place and not be noticed.

A country cousin. Country uncle more likely, he's older than we are. Is he capable of what I want him for?

Next day I watch him in the grocery store. Like us, he buys living-alone kind of food, two apples, a tomato, crackers, oatmeal. Poor people's kind of food. I get in line with him at the check-out. I bump into him on purpose as he pays and peek into his wallet. That's all he has—just enough for what he buys. He counts out the change a penny at a time and he hardly has a nickel left over. I get ready to give him a bit extra if he needs it.

He's such an ugly, rickety man…. Perfect.

There's no reason to go into his over-the-garage room, but I want to. This is important. I need to see who he is.

I use our credit card to open his lock.

What a mess. He needs somebody like us to look after him. His bed is piled with blankets. The room isn't very well heated. The bathroom has a curtain instead of a door. There's no tub or even shower. I check the hot water in the sink. It says hot, but both sides come out cold. All he has is a hot plate. No refrigerator. There's two windows, but no curtains. Isn't that just like a man. I could climb up on the back fence and see right in.

There's nothing of the holidays here. Nothing of any holidays and not a single picture of a relative. And, like our house, nothing of friends. You and he are made for each other.

What to do to show I've been here? But this time I don't feel much like playing tricks. And it's so messy he wouldn't notice, anyway.

It's cold. I haven't taken my coat off all through this. I make myself a cup of tea. (There's no lemons and no milk. Of course.) I sit in his one chair. It's painted ugly green. All his furniture is as if picked up on the curb and his bedside table is one of those fruit boxes. As I sit and sip, I check his magazines. They look as though stolen from somebody's garbage. I'm shivering. (No wonder he's out. I suppose it's not easy to shave. He'd have to heat the water on the hot plate.)

He needs a cat. Something to sleep on his chest to keep him warm like your cat does with me.

I have our groceries in my backpack. I leave two oranges and a doughnut in plain sight beside the hot plate. I leave several of our quarters.

I leave a note: I put in our address. I sign your name. I write: Come for Christmas. Two o'clock. I'll be wearing red leather pants! Your neighbor, Nora.

(I wonder which of us should wear those pants.) I clean up a little bit but not so much that he'd notice if he's not a noticing person. Besides, people only notice when things are dirty. They never notice when things are cleaned up.

As I walk home, I see you on your way out. We pass each other. You look right at me. I'm wearing your green sweater and your black slacks. We look at each other, my brown eyes to your brown eyes. Only difference is, your hair is pushed back and mine hangs down over my forehead. You go right on by. I turn and look back. You don't. I laugh behind my hand that you had to wear those red leather pants and a black and white striped top.

He's too timid and too self-deprecating to come. He doesn't like to limp in front of people and he's ashamed not to have enough money hardly even for his food, and not to have a chance to shave and take a bath. Though if he's scared by me coming into his room, he might come. He might want to see who Nora is and if the address is real. His pretext will be that he wants to thank you for the food and quarters. He might even want to give them back. He might be one of those rich people who live as if they were poor. I should have looked for money or bank books. I will next time.

When the doorbell rings, who else could it be? You open the door. "Are you Nora?" "Yes?" "I want to thank you." I knew it. I suppose he wants more money. "But I want to bring your quarters back. That was kind of you but I don't need them."You don't know what to say. You suspect it's all because of me. That I've, yet again, made your life difficult. You wonder what to do. He doesn't look dangerous but you never can tell. You want to get even with me some way. You suppose, if he *is* dangerous, it would be bad for both of us so it must be all right. You ask him in.

He hobbles into your living room. You say sit down, that you'll get tea. You're stalling for time. He still holds the handful of quarters. He puts them on the coffee table. You don't know how those quarters got to him or even if they really are your quarters. "No, no," you say, and "Where did these come from?" "They were in my room with a note from you and this address. You said, Come for Christmas."You wonder what I'll like least. Do I want you to invite him to stay for supper? Unlikely, though, since you only have one TV dinner and you know I know that. "Somebody is playing a joke on me. But the tea...."You need help getting started so I trip you in the hall as you come back into the room. Everything goes down. Too bad, too, because you'd used your good china in spite of how this man looks.

Of course he pushes himself up and hobbles to you and helps pick up the things and you. You say you could make more but he says, It doesn't matter. Then you both go out to the kitchen. I go, too. Sidling. Slithering. The cat slides in with us. Both your and his glasses are thick. I'm counting on your blindness. I squat down. He puts the broken cups on a corner of the counter. You get out two more. He says, these are too nice. You say, they're Mother's. He says, "You shouldn't use the Rosenthal, not for me."

There now, are you both rich yet never use your money?

The cat jumps on the table and you swipe him off. No wonder he likes me better than you. I always let him go where he wants and I like him on the table.

You're looking at our man—studying his crooked nose. You see what neither of us has noticed until now. The hand that reaches to help you wears a ring with a large stone. Some sort of school ring. You're thinking: Well, well, and changing your mind. As am I.

He's too good for you. Maybe might be good enough for me.

We are all, all three, the same kind of person. When you leave in the morning, I've seen you look out the door to make sure there's nobody out there you might have to say hello to.

But now you talk. You think. You ask. You wonder out loud if this and that. You look down at your striped shirt and wish you were wearing your usual clothes. I'm under the table wearing your brown blouse with the faint pattern of fall leaves. I look like a wrinkled up paper bag kicked under here and forgotten. The cat is down here with me purring.

It never takes long for two lonely people living in their fantasies to connect—to see all sorts of things in each other that don't exist.

You've waited for each other all your lives. You almost say so. Besides, he'd have a nice place to live if ... if anything comes of this.

I think about that black lacy underwear. That pink silk nightie. As soon as I have a chance, I'll go get them. I might need them for myself.

But how to get you moving? You're both all talk. Or *you* are, he's not talking much. Perhaps one look at the nightie might get things rolling. That'll have to be for later. Or on the other hand....

I reach back to the shelf behind me and, when neither he nor you are looking, I bring out the sherry. They'll both think the other one got the bottle out.

(They do.)

You get wineglasses. You even get out your TV dinner and say you'll split it. It's turkey with stuffing. You got it special for Christmas.

Of course he says for you to eat it all, but you say you never do, anyway, so you split it.

I'm getting hungry myself. If it was just you, I would sneak a few bites, but there's little enough for the two of you. I'll have to find another way.

You both get tipsy. It doesn't take much. You hardly ever drink and it looks like he doesn't either. And I think you want to get drunk. You want something to happen as much as I do.

Every now and then I take a sip of your drinks. And on an empty stomach it takes even less. With the drone of your talk, talk, talking, I almost go to sleep.

But you're heading upstairs already. I crawl out from under the table and climb the stairs behind you. I'm as wobbly as you are. Actually I'm wobblier. We, all three, go into your bedroom. And the cat. You push the deadbolt. He wonders why. "Aren't you alone here?"

You say, "Not exactly." And then, "I'll tell you later." (You're right, this certainly isn't the time for a discussion about me.) First thing I grab our sexy nightie from the drawer. I get under the bed and put it on. That's not easy, cramped up under there. For a few minutes I lose track of what's happening above me. I comb my hair as you always have it, back away from your face. I have to use my fingers and I don't have a mirror so I'm not sure how it comes out. I pinch my cheeks and bite my lips to make them redder.

The cat purrs. I lean up to see what's going on. Nothing much so far. Even though tipsy, he seems shy. Inexperienced. I don't think he's ever been anybody's grandfather. (We're, all of us, all of a piece. None of us has ever been anybody's relative.) You look pretty much passed out. Or you're pretending. Either way, it's a good time for me to make an appearance.

I crawl out from under the bed and check myself in the mirror behind them. My hair is a mess but I look good in the silky nightgown. Better than you do in your stripes and red pants. By far. I do a little sexy dance. I say, "She's not Nora, I'm Nora. I'm the one wrote you that note." You sit up. You were faking being drunk. You think: Now I see who you are. Now I'll get you. But you won't. I stroke the cat. Suggestively. He purrs. (The cat, I mean.) I purr. Suggestively. I see his eyes light up. (The man's, I mean.) Now there'll be some action. I say, "I don't even know your name." He says, "Willard." I'm on his good side because I asked, and you're not because you didn't. All this talk, talk, talk, talk and you didn't. You slither away, down under the bed. You feel ashamed of yourself and yet curious. You wonder: How did you ever get yourself in this position, and what to do now? But I do know what to do. I give you a kick and hand you the cat. Willard. Willard is a little confused. But eager. More than before. He likes the nightgown and says so.

I take a good long look at him. Those bushy eyebrows. Lots of white hairs in them. I help him take off his shirt. His is not my favorite kind of chest. He does have a nice flat stomach though. (I liked that about him from the start—back when I first saw him wobbling down the street.) I look into his green/gray/tan eyes.

But what about, I love you? I say it. "What about I love you?" That stops him. I didn't mean to do that. I wanted to give Nora a good show. Of course it's much too soon for any sort of thing that might resemble love. "I take that back," I say. But it's too late. He's putting on his shirt. (It's a dressy white one. He's even wearing cufflinks engraved with WT.) Is it really over already? I pick up the cat, hurry out, slam the door, and push the deadbolt on the outside, then turn back and look through the keyhole. I can see almost the whole bed.

Now look, his hands are … all of a sudden … on her and on all the right places. He knows. Maybe he actually *is* somebody's grandfather after all. And you … you are feeling things that make your back arch. He tells you he loves you. *Now* he says it. He can't tell us apart. He'll love anything that comes his way. I have what I thought I wanted … a good view of something interesting for a change, except…. Actually I can't see much, just his back and then your back and then his back and then yours. (How do they do that, still attached?) Until we're all, all of us, exhausted. I go downstairs…. (I like how this nightgown feels. I'm so slinky and slippery. I bump and grind just for myself.) I make myself a peanut butter sandwich. I feel better after eating. Things are fine. I might leave you milk and cookies. Bring it now while you sleep so I can lock you both in again. But I don't suppose that lock will hold against two people who *really* want to get out.

I think about maybe both of you up in my crawl space. He's taller than we are. He'd not like it. I think about your job at the ice cream factory unfolding boxes to put the ice cream in. I wouldn't mind that kind of job. You sit and daydream. I saw you. You hardly talk to anybody. I think about how you can't prove you're you. You'll go to the police. You'll say you're you, but they'll laugh. Your clothes are all wrong for the you you used to be. They'll say, the person who's lived here all this time dresses in mouse colors. You've lived a claustrophobic life. If you'd had any friends it would be different. Besides, I can do as well as you do, unfolding boxes. I've done the same when I had jobs before I quit for this easier life. I won't be cruel. I'd never be cruel. I'll let you live in the crawl space as long as you want.

Your daydream is Willard. Or most of him, though not all. For sure his eyes. For sure his elegant slim hands and the big gold ring. You'll ask if it's a school ring.

Or one of us will.

Then I hear banging. And not long after that, the crash. They break open the door. It splinters where the deadbolt is. If I'd put it in the middle of the door instead of at the top, it might have held better.

By the time the door goes down I'm right outside it, watching. They run downstairs without seeing me.

I go and look out the window. He's leaving—hurries down the street with only one arm in his coat sleeve and it's the wrong sleeve. Other hand holds up his pants. What did you do to send him off so upset?

I open the window and call out, "Willard!" But he doesn't hear or doesn't want to. Is he trying to get away? From you or me?

What did you do to scare him so? Everything was fine when I came down to eat. But maybe getting locked in scared him. Or maybe you told him to go and never come back and you threw his coat at him as he left. Or he thinks you're me and is in love with me even though he told you he loved you. Or, like most men, he's unwilling to commit to anybody.

But here you go, out the door right behind him. You have your coat on properly and your clothes all straightened up. Now you're the one calling, "Willard."

You'd not have done that before. You've changed. You'll take back your life. Everybody will make way for you now. You'll have an evil look. You'll frown. People will step off the sidewalk to let you go by.

I want for us to live as we did but you'll set traps. I'll trip on trip wires. Fall down the stairs in the middle of the night. There won't be any more quarters lying around. You'll put a deadbolt on the crawl space door. Or better yet, you'll barricade it shut with a dresser. Nobody will even know there's a door there.

I made you what you are today, grand and real, but you'll lock me up up here with nothing but your mousey clothes. Your old trunks. Your dust and dark.

I dress in the worn-out clothes I wore when I came. I pack the nightgown, the black underwear. I grab a handful of quarters. I don't touch your secret stash of twenties. I pet the cat. I leave your credit cards and keys on the hall table. I don't steal.

The Magazine of Fantasy & Science Fiction, March 2005

The Being Of It All

I hear the call when I'm up on a mountain top in roiling clouds with thunder. I was about to hurry down to a safer spot, but the voice says, "Come." Then, "Do, be, proclaim. Become more than just your father's son."

The air is crackling with electricity. I see a tree get hit and crash down below us. Even so, the voice is wrong. I yell, "Mother's daughter. Mother's daughter." It echoes back and forth, across all the peaks and back to me as if I was a god.

Or maybe the voice was meant for somebody else.

"It's just me," I yell. "Me. Marilyn."

My voice echoes also. I sound so powerful I could come to think the call really *was* meant for me—that I really could proclaim.

But there's no answer.

"Just me."

It doesn't come again. Maybe this silence means it knows it made a mistake.

"Repeat," I say, "so I'll know for sure."

It doesn't.

I guess I'll never know for sure.

I'm wearing my big black hat. I wanted to pretend I was bold and the hat helps. I can be bolder if no one sees it's me. That may have confused whoever it was calling out. Take off that hat and I'm just like everybody else. Worse actually, dull and shy. I can never think of what to talk about. I don't know what to do with my hands. I never look anybody straight in the eyes. If I see somebody I know walking down the street, I cross to the other side.

I'm with my little dog, Booboo. She's as shy as I am. Lightning scares her. Right now she's somewhere just below. She'll hide behind a rock until I come back.

"Be," the voice said. I've never been. "Do." Do what? You can't just say, do, be, proclaim, without saying what about.

I shout, "I need more information." It echoes and echoes. Miles away, mountain to mountain.

But no answer. I'm on my own.

It's that echo that's confusing me....my voice sounding so powerful. It went so far and came back...I don't even know how many times. I felt like a giant.

But who wouldn't hear a call in thunder and on the top of a mountain? It can't mean much. We must all hear things like that and I'm the only one it took this long to finally get to it.

Still, just in case the voice really was meant for me, and even though it got the sex wrong, I'll do something. Or maybe sit down right here and "be" for a while.

I do that. I sit on a stone beautiful with orange lichen. Booboo comes running up and jumps on my lap. I tell her we're "being", but not to worry, we won't do it for long.

She's a little dog with ears that flop around. She's a mix of colors. Whitish underbelly, gray/grizzled rest of her and some yellow around her face and ears. When she's with me, she usually looks as if she's smiling. When strangers are around she looks anxious or angry.

As I sit...(am I really "being?" How can I tell?) I think about how I want to look the part. I mean the part of having a voice that echoes out. I'll change my outfit. I'll not only wear my big black hat, I'll buy a red and white striped shirt. I'll get matching striped socks. I don't have to dress that way all the time. I can rest now and then and be my shy self when I'm wearing my gray and tan outfits.

Actually I like my life the way it is. My nasty little dog. My little cluttered cottage. I might change, but not my real life. I couldn't stand that. I *need* to be shy.

But I have to keep remembering my powerful voice up there. There was hardly a mountain it didn't ring back from. Maybe I'm not who I've been thinking I am all these years. Up on that mountain top everything buzzed with energy. I...even I...sparkled.

Except there's nothing I like better than staying in the shadows creeping around watching people—lying in wait as though to jump out and scare, but never jumping out.

My little dog is as frightened of people as I am, but she's tough. She got frightened by the lightning, but she didn't go far and came running back to me as soon as I started down. She always does. We're each other's only friends.

I do it. I buy a whole new outfit for my new way of being (that red and white striped shirt and matching socks) but when it comes right down to it, I'm scared to wear it. I do put a little red jacket on Booboo.

She thinks, "If I must," and I say, "You must."

I put on my big hat, and we go back to that same mountain. I'm pretty sure the voice has to be in a storm. It's a sunny day now but you never know on the mountains. Storms come up suddenly. Maybe we'll be lucky.

When I'm almost all the way up I see a man climbing in front of me.

I hope he's not going all the way. If the voice does come again, which of us will it be for?

Up the switchbacks, back and forth we go, higher and higher, that man and I and Booboo. We stay well back from him. I'm glad I'm not wearing my costume. What would he think if he saw me like that? That I was the kind of person who *wants* to be noticed, that's what.

I drop yet farther behind just at the thought that he might stop and talk.

He gets to the top before I do.

He has one of those soft khaki hats, not like mine. Under it I can see his short brown beard but not much else. (Under my big hat, and thank goodness, you can hardly see anything.) At the top he stands with his arms out, and turns slowly to see the view from all sides and as if he was lord of it all. He doesn't need a voice calling him. I'll bet he's already Being and Doing and Proclaiming.

A little black cloud blocks the sun and it starts to hail. That man's hat won't help much but mine will. It may be too big and too bold for me, but it's serviceable. I pick up Booboo and both of us hunker down under it. Up this high, that's the only shelter there is.

And here's that voice again, even as I hunker down.

"Come. Do. Proclaim. Be your father's son."

It's still saying, "Father's son."

The man looks all round as if looking for the voice, but it seems to be coming from straight up. He looks up and gets the hail full on his face, but then he grimaces, turns and starts down. It's as if he doesn't want to hear more, even though it said, "Father's son," and most likely means him.

He passes us. He may not have seen me though he must have seen Booboo in her little red jacket.

Hail or no, I put Booboo down and climb to the top and stand where he was standing. I take off my hat to show my real self. I shout. "Is it me? Am I the one?"

No answer.

I wish now I'd worn my new outfit. I like it. I mean I don't like it on me but I'd like it on somebody else. It's cheerful. I was pleased when I saw myself in it, but I didn't want anybody to see me like that.

I shout again, "Am I the one?"

No answer.

I give up...for now. I pick up Booboo so as to go faster and start down. I call after the man, "Wait. The voice means you. It can't be me."

But he's ignoring the switchbacks, jumping straight down, from one turn to the other. I start jumping down, too. It takes no time at all to get all the way down to the flat, foresty place.

Then we, I and Booboo that is, sit down to catch our breath. We've walked... jumped, rather, beyond the hail. The sun is shining. Booboo is happy. She loves getting carried and cuddling up on my shoulder. She looks up at me like: What's next? Are we going to have some more fun?

I tell her, "Yes."

I give us a drink from my water bottle.

When we start again, we want to avoid other hikers so we stay off the trail. Or rather slightly off it. We want to think about ourselves. We walk right in on a campsite. Nobody's there. Booboo sniffs around the bearcan. We realize how hungry we are. I open it. I let Booboo eat anything she wants. I eat three breakfast bars, each a different flavor. Then I spread the food around. The voice said do, so I'm doing something for the bears. Why not? We're all hungry.

I do this at several places. We hurry away from each one, though. We don't want to be there when they come. We stay on the trail this time, and then here's that man just in front of us. He's still looking around as if he owned the whole forest. He's taking the mountain's words to heart.

I thought he was long gone. For some reason Booboo goes after him, snarling and barking, and he keeps backing up. She grabs his pants leg. He kicks out, but she won't let go.

I say, "Sorry. She's usually not this way."

"Get him off me."

His voice is big and booming. I'll bet he's one of those people who can't talk softly even when they try.

"Son," he says, "Call off your damn dog."

Not only the voice on the mountain, but he, also, thinks I'm a boy. I have to admit I have a boyish figure but now that's two in a row thought so. Not only that but he thinks Booboo is male, too.

I say, "Sorry."

He keeps kicking out. The ground is rough. He falls. Booboo lets go of his pants and jumps on his chest. She's going for his face. I grab her just in time. I shout, "Bad dog. Bad dog," but she knows I don't mean it. She doesn't even look contrite.

I say, "She's never done this before," which isn't *exactly* a lie. Maybe there's something about him Booboo senses but I didn't notice. I stare at him for clues. He doesn't look like much, sitting in the fireweed by the side of the trail examining his pants.

"That dog ought to be put down. One of these days he'll hurt somebody."

I'm trying to hold Booboo back but it's not easy.

"Who are you? You and your little squeaky voice."

He makes a gesture as if to take care of Booboo right now all by himself.

"Just Marilyn."

"That lightning struck a tree right behind me. Did you have anything to do with that?"

"I didn't. I don't even know how."

He thinks I'm lying—that I'm trying to look harmless and ordinary with my everyday name.

Then he says, *What* are you, not who.

"I really am Marilyn."

He staggers up. I'm still too busy holding Booboo to help. I say, "Bad dog," a couple of times again.

She's thinking, "OK, OK. Let go. I give up."

(If it was Booboo's lightning, then it's as good as mine.)

I tip my hat even lower over my eyes. My shyness has made me bold. I say, "All right. All right. That was my lightning. I admit it."

Afterwards I'll feel ashamed.

He's the one made me say it. Why would I even think I could do that?

He says, "Let me pass."

Of course. Why not?

He makes a fist as though to punch me, gives me a warning glance and goes trotting down the trail. That makes Booboo all the more anxious to chase him. I tell her we don't need to bother with him now.

She'd still like to go after him.

I say, "Maybe you'll get the chance to bite somebody else pretty soon."

But she thinks, "I feel like biting him in particular. More than anybody else."

I sit down with her wriggling on my lap. Finally she calms down.

I tell her, yet again, what a bad dog she is and she licks my hand.

I'm thinking…wondering…well, What *am* I? is a good question. Maybe nothing I think about myself is true. Like even which sex I am, and Booboo's sex, too.

People are coming back from hikes and getting ready to eat. We decide to find some more bear cans to open. It's not just for us, it's for the bears, too.

And it's working. The next camping spot we find, here's a bear. Before I can stop her, Booboo is trying to chase it away. How can she be that stupid? Is there something about that man that's like a bear? Or about the bear that's like the man?

I don't know what to do. I don't want to call attention to myself, but I don't want her hurt.

I yell, "Stop that."

Booboo won't listen, but maybe the bear will.

Anyway, I'd rather yell than sit here and watch Booboo get clobbered.

The bear turns towards me but only for a second. Then it swipes one big swipe and Booboo goes flying. A great arc. Everything slows down, and for a moment I see her silhouetted against the sky and I think: I've got lots of time to run over and catch her, but then time catches up with itself. She lands yards away. The bear gives a cough of warning and goes back to messing around in the camper's packs as if we didn't matter.

We creep away. Booboo seems to be pretty much all right. She's limping a little, but she won't look at me. She knows she made a big mistake. She wants me to pick her up but she doesn't dare ask.

Is this what happens when shy people…creatures that is…have the guts to do and do things they shouldn't?

I say, "You ought to be on a leash."

She thinks. "If I must."

I say, "You must."

Next time we raid a camping spot it's not going to be to open bear cans (I don't feel so much like helping bears as I did), but to steal a clothesline so I can make a leash.

But the next camping spot we come to belongs to that man. And there he is, leaning over packing up his food. Is this one of the spots where we spread the food around for the bears?

And there goes Booboo before I can yell bad dog and stop that, and grabs him by the butt.

"Not you again."

Is there something only she knows? Is he as he looks to be, and as he acts, the one in charge of everything? The president of this or that or the head of the company? Head of all sorts of things that right rightly belong to…well, Booboo?

It's all about her. How could I not see that? I always think everything means me. It's me, me, me, all the time. That's what makes a person shy. If it's not me, then what's to be shy about?

Next time the voice comes I'll yell, "It's Booboo. She's the one. She's already doing things, and being. She's taken your words to heart. Look how she's gone after things."

Meanwhile the man is trying to reach back to pull her off.

She's more bulldog than I ever thought she could be.

"Get him off me."

His pants are already a wreck. Torn down the sides and almost all the way off.

He makes more noise than the bear did. Not just a cough, but a bellow.

If I or Booboo could call down lightning, we ought to do it right now. I hold my breath and think hard, Blam, blam, blam, but nothing happens.

I say, "Let go."

Booboo is thinking: Don't tell me what to do.

Why should she listen now when she never has before? As usual I have no effect on anybody.

(Booboo is thinking, of the two of us, she's top dog.)

I just stand there.

Booboo thinks she has to do all the work.

(What if the voice comes again and says, "*Don't* do and *don't* be?" Meaning me?)

Booboo thinks I ought to stop being shy and stop thinking so much. Just like that, stop. She's thinking, Do something, for Heaven's sake.

I just have to trust Booboo on this. Instead of trying to pull her off. I grab his little folding shovel and hit him on the head. But even so I'm glad it doesn't seem to hurt him too much.

But here comes another bear. The food is still all spread out. It never takes much. Just half a candy bar is enough to bring a bear.

Booboo lets go and jumps into my arms. The man runs. As best he can in torn, falling down pants. We hear him crashing down and down. The bear gets busy eating the stuff that's still all spread around.

Booboo and I think: Whew!

Then, BLAM! And a flash. But there isn't a cloud in the sky that I can see. So the sky, doing any old which way it wants. Or maybe Booboo. And why not?

We've…all of us together, the bear and Booboo and I and maybe the sky itself…we've rid the forest of a big, noisy, hairy, scary presence that thought he owned the whole place.

The voice comes again even way down here. "Do," it says. "Be. Proclaim. Be more than just your father's son."

I say again, "It's me. Marilyn."

Then there's lightning right beside us and I think I hear, "Boo, boo, boo, boo, boo…" echoing on and on.

As we creep away, she limps a little, but she acts just the same old Booboo. She's thinking: "From now on lets both be boys."

I say, "OK."

And she thinks, if she has to wear a red jacket, then I should be in my striped shirt. She thinks it isn't fair—that she has to wear the jacket, but that I don't have the guts to wear the shirt. She thinks we should both wear nothing but red from now on.

I tell her, "OK, OK."

I sit on a stone, again beautiful with orange lichen, again, Booboo on my lap. I tell her we'll sit and be for a while but not to worry, we won't do it for long.

Sci Fiction, June, 2005

See No Evil, Feel No Joy

"Joy shines out only to reveal what the annihilation of joy will be like." Coetzee

It's a bright, sunny evening. The view from our porch has clouds, pink and lavender, puffy, over purple mountains. I don't look. I control myself. I keep my eyes on shelling peas. It's against our vows to appreciate any such thing as views. You'd think we'd not have put our huts here on the side of the hill when enjoyment of a view is forbidden. You'd think we'd not have built porches in the first place. You'd think the windows of our huts would be smaller.

I keep my eyes on my work or on the floor or the ground or my shoes. Proper shoes for our kind. Lumpy. As if I'd stepped in mud and it stuck. They're just as heavy as if I had. That helps to make us strong, and we need to be strong.

See no beauty, see no ugliness, see neither good nor evil. Nor hear. See nothing that will take you from your duty. Your simplicity. Nothing that might take your mind off this valley of tears, off this valley of joys.

Keep away from joy or nothing will ever be enough. In any kind of happiness one wants more. There's never enough of joy and beauty.

Suppose we looked out across the valley, we might wonder: Does this beautiful view of ours suffice? Should we climb yet higher to get a better one? Move our houses up there? And then should we look day after day—every morning, every evening waste several minutes? Should we enjoy even the storm? Even lightening on the mountains across from us? Stand at the window as if something might happen even better than is already happening right here? Never get anything done?

We wear black. Our hair is pulled back tight. Both sexes. Loose pants tied at the ankles. We keep our hats and bonnets on all the time. I suppose we take them off when we're in bed, but I only know what I do.

In the beginning was the word, but before the word there were no words.

We've taken vows of silence. Instead of talking we leave notes on the door of our refectory. It's been a long time since I spoke.

Do not shake hands or pat shoulders. Touch nothing except your work.

Twice I've seen someone panic. Scream and screech. I didn't have to help. That's a man's job unless there's no man around. Men are allowed to touch in emergencies. I don't know what happened to her or who she was. We don't have friends. When you're not allowed to talk, you don't get to know people. We don't even know each other's names or sexes.

If we should fall in love then no end to it for desire breeds nothing but more desire.

It's unlikely that we will love. Our hats are always pulled low. Our bonnets might as well be blinders.

But I looked down at the wrong time. Right into someone's eyes. That's all I saw—eyes, looking back into mine. It was a mistake. We were both innocent. We looked away quickly. Maybe not that quickly. We stared. I don't know how long. He had brought a heavy pail of water in. Then he'd knelt and dipped himself a drink. I looked down and he looked up. It wasn't our fault.

I thought: My God, like a sunrise you're not supposed to admire, like the sound of the stream you shouldn't listen to, like the view across the valley to the other mountains. After, I could think of nothing but eyes—greenish gray ones. I could see my tiny self in his pupils.

I peeked at him as he left. All I saw were the usual baggy clothes. Faded black. Whitish in the worn spots. I wondered all the things we're not supposed to wonder: What is his name? What hut does he live in? Of course there's no way of finding out.

I wonder what *he* thought. Something passed between us. I think. I don't know what.

Live and do and be in the spirit of the land and with the labor of the land. Live and do and be as was done before and as we've done and will do.

Do and be. And be in a place where no prying outsider ever comes.

Disobedience...that one forbidden glance...has made me hum. Someone taps me on the wrist, hard, with a wooden spoon to remind me not to. I deserve that tap.

Ever since that look I've been disobedient in both thought and deed. I've been looking—out from behind my big black bonnet. Which one is he? And will he be looking for me? Out from behind his wide brimmed hat?

It is well known what happened to other sects with no sex. It has been decided that we have to have sex but best not to know with whom. And to only have it just often enough to make sure we replace ourselves.

We won't take in orphans as some sects did. Those children may have been spoiled for us before we get to them. Also it didn't keep those other sects alive. We'll grow our own.

I'm to be the first. I don't know why. Our leader has decided which of the men will combine with me to make the most eugenically perfect baby. I'm to go to the mating hut tomorrow night. They don't want us to have time to think about it but I need to think. I'm not sure I want this. Especially not *now*.

We live empty of desire. All pleasure is too much. It ties one to this world so that leaving it is a calamity.

I run away. Not down to civilization, where all is evil and dangerous—people shoot each other, people fight, the air is polluted, it's noisy, the streets are full of beggars—but farther up, into the wilds—the safe, soft wilds.

When I get far enough away I hum—as loud as I wish. How good it is not to be working in the kitchen. How good to be able to look out at the view, to listen to the birds. At the banks of a little river I stop and sit and do that, just listen. I sit so still a bird comes right to me. A little gray bird with a black head. Almost as dull as all of us are. Yet he's bright and chipper. One can be chipper even if one is nothing but gray and black.

Eyes and hands.... I can bring back the vision of the moments we looked at each other. He was holding the edge of the pail with one hand and the dipper in the other. His hands were scarred and rough, as all ours are. His had little black hairs on the knuckles. He raised the dipper slowly. As if as stunned by the view of me as I was of him. I saw something of his gaunt face, the crows feet at the edges of his eyes, his beard, streaked with white.

I spend the night lying against a fallen tree trunk. I didn't bring a blanket or a sweater. I didn't plan. I ran off too fast to think of anything even though I'm not to be mated until tomorrow night.

Then I realize I can sneak back at meal times. Who's to know? The way we live, one more black bundle gone off to sleep in the woods won't be missed. Why didn't I think of this a long time ago? I'm going back to find those eyes. I'll go where the men work.

First thing in the morning, I find a bright blue feather. I think that's a good sign. I pin it on my tunic. I must remember to take it off before I go back, though would anyone notice? And what would happen if they did?

Life without words is peaceful. There are no disagreements. One is not led astray. No one mishears or misinterprets. And words can make one unhappy as well as happy. Also there are many words that should never be said.

I practice talking just to make sure I still can. I don't know why, there may never be anybody to talk to. I must be thinking I'll talk to that man.

I haven't talked in so long I'd hardly know what in the world to talk about. There hasn't been anything to say since...I can't remember when.

At first nothing comes out at all. Then it comes out suddenly, as a shout. No and then yes. After that a whisper. Yes, yes, yes. Finally I get it right. I say: Listen, look, see. Then I remember nursery rhymes. Deedle deedle dumpling, Higgledy piggledy, One a penny, two a penny, three a penny, four.

Perhaps I would like a child. Perhaps, instead of staying up here, I will go to the mating hut tomorrow night. The male they chose for me has got to be for the best child possible. Probably better than anyone I'd choose for myself.

Going back, I look down on our whole compound as if at a map. The people look like busy black ants from here. I can see good hiding places.

When I sneak back for supper, I leave the blue feather on my tunic.

Pins instead of buttons. Knives and spoons but no forks. Water but no tea or coffee. Oatmeal, corn...bread, but no butter. Butter is too blissful on the tongue.

At supper I think how different the world is when one looks out at it. All these bent heads. I watch hands. A few have black hairs just as his did. I look out the window where the wind is blowing the bushes. Everybody leans over their trenchers. My blue feather is safe.

Which of the men was meant for me tonight? I'm not to see him. We're to be as anonymous to each other as we always are.

What will they do when they find me gone? Come after me or forget about me? Not much to forget—one less silent black bundle, one empty pallet, one less trencher.

After supper I walk towards my hut as I'm supposed to, but I go right past, on up the hill where there's my fallen tree. This time I bring a blanket.

Life has been given to each of us. Life at all is life enough.

Giving life. I think about a baby. There's still time to change my mind. I can go back down, but I fall asleep and don't.

Let us lie at night as empty of desire and hope and terror as in the daylight of our lives. Let our dreams be neither sweet nor fearful. Never the cold sweat of the fear of death, nor, on the other hand, the hot sweat of desire.

As far as I can tell, I have not dreamt such dreams. Not even now.

I wake with the birds. I'm far enough away that I don't hear the rooster down below. The little birds up here don't say: Get up and get to work. They say: Listen. Look.

Either I haven't been looking out beyond my bonnet for so long that I forgot what weather is like, or this morning is unusually beautiful. Fog—below, hiding the village, but not up here. Snowy peaks behind me, pink in the sunrise. It was fitting that it was eyes that set me off on this course.

About me not mating, how will they know? Are there conferences? How long will it take them to find out it didn't happen? I'll sneak back later and see what's happening, but there's plenty of time. Time is our enemy. It leads to thoughts. Do not think.

I see why. I'm thinking all sorts of things and every single one of them I shouldn't.

But I don't know what I want. I only know what I don't want. All our shoulds. All our promises. Our vows. Swearing to this and swearing to that. They don't add up to any wants.

The city below, while called democratic and while people vote for their leaders, is full of poverty, drugs, murders, muggings, greed, spending...and spending to no purpose but to spend. Leave all that behind and come to us. Once and for all climb away from all those others and their self-congratulation—from their boasting of their rights of man.

Live as we do here.

Do I live? *Did* I live? Now, waking to the birds, watching the sunrise with nothing to do but watch.... My hand on my stomach feels the worn cloth of my tunic. Such softness—soft tunic on top of soft stomach. How have I not noticed that softness until now? Even with my promise not to? And how have I not noticed the tops of trees? And haven't we had these same little birds down where we live? Don't we have a stream?

Do not raise your right hand. Sit in a neutral position. Neither kneel nor prostrate yourself. Make a simple promise to do your duty. A promise in any position should be a promise as good as any other.

Give thanks that we have but little, and for what little we have. For shoes that hold. For a warm sweater. For a blanket. For firewood. Most of all for having been born at all and for this short time on earth.

Time is exactly what I have the most of. Yesterday I didn't know how to use it. Now I pick berries. Nibble at spearmint. And the smell! I'm mostly used to kitchen smells. Now there's a piney, tree smell.

We always bathe in big pans and in our (black) bathing dresses so as never to be naked. I take my clothes off and bathe in the stream. I look at myself. I wonder about my age. Am I too old? For yearning?

I've renewed my vows every first snow without wondering. I've promised over and over to be one us, pure as mountain snow, and yet, even so, and though I've kept my eyes on the floorboards, I've noticed things: the knots in the wood, the different sizes of feet. I've thought I could tell male from female by the ankles. All this time I've appreciated life more than I should.

I was so young. Now I'm...a woman who doesn't even know her age. Still of child bearing age or I'd not have been chosen. Though you'd think by now we'd all be a little old for child bearing. (Do they somehow keep track of those of us still menstruating? I suppose they do.) Maybe this is a last chance. A sudden decision by our leader. Perhaps some of us have died. How would we know? We're kept from pain as well as joy.

No weeping no love no hate no sorrow.... Being here right now in a single moment. What can ever hurt? We have done away with yearning and desire. No one is eager for more of anything or for what they don't have. There's neither anger nor anxiety nor greed nor hope.

I *am* greedy. I want to see those eyes again. I want to see those long fingered battered hands. When I see them I'll want to see them yet again...and again. They're right, there's no end to it.

I come back down for lunch and then hide and watch—the black bundles at their busyness. They don't look up. Easy to hide. I can even do a job here and there and nobody knows. I head over to where the men work at men's work. There I have to hide because of my bonnet. I wonder if I can find a hat somewhere. I watch from behind the lilacs.

The men are building a new outhouse. It will have four sections. Two for men and two for women.

A black figure in a black bonnet comes with water. They stop to drink. They take their hats off and put water on their hair. They pour it down the backs of their tunics. I leave my bonnet in my hiding place, sneak out and grab a hat. But one of the men isn't watching his feet as he should. He sees me and grunts. It's a grunt of surprise. They all look up.

Will they find out about all the forbidden things I've done? Will they see in my naked face that I fell in love with eyes? That I spent two days and nights doing nothing but listening and looking? Even that I bathed naked? And here's my blue feather, right in front.

They don't say anything, they just stare. Of course. How can a person talk after so much silence? Even I…and even after I practiced on the mountain…. Good that I did or I'd be as they are, but I *can* speak though it comes out too loud again. I say, "I speak. I have wished and hoped and felt yearning. I don't deserve to be among you."

I peer into faces. I look for gray-green eyes. For a beard with white streaks. But I embarrass them. They all look down again.

A single moment is calm. All single moments are peaceful. Time will hold still.

I see that this is true. There's time to breathe. Time for the heart to beat. Time for a bird to sing. For a bumble bee to buzz. Leaves catch the breeze.

Here, in this long, long, long moment, I think I can move about as I wish. Run away. Nobody will see. But one man is watching. Is he our leader? Or one of our leaders? I've no idea how many there might be.

He's memorizing me. I think about my face. I seem to remember I used to have a birth mark on my cheek. That'll be easy for him to remember.

His eyes are not green-gray.

He comes towards me. Nobody else moves. They're all still looking down. They don't want to see what might happen. It might lead to pain and thoughts.

I see his clenched teeth. He's reaching as though to grab my throat.

I grab the nearest tool. It's a saw. All I do is hold it out, the rough edge facing him. He runs right into it. His tunic sleeves hook on it. There's blood on his arms. Even so he keeps coming, pushing his arms yet farther into the saw. Blood pours out. That stops him. The others look. They see a hurtful thing. They've tried all this time to avoid just such as this.

Keep each other safe. You are each other's keepers. Do no harm.

I didn't mean to. But he looked so angry.

They all go to help the man. I pick up the hat and put it on. It's too big, but all the better. I run.

Nobody follows. After a minute I walk at the usual pace, as if busy. I'm as good as invisible. I loop back to see what happened to the man. I hope I didn't kill him. All I did was stand there. He did it to himself, coming after me like that.

The other men are binding his cuts. I didn't kill him. At least that.

There's a nursing hut for accidents or sick people (though out here in the wilds we have hardly any flu or colds). I stayed there when I broke my ankle. Four men carry him there. Others go back to work on the outhouse. I follow with the men but I stay well back.

The lunch bell clangs.

We all go except the four men at the nursing hut and the hurt man.

Later there's a message on the nursing hut door. It says what has been said before.

Life is dangerous and deadly. Unforeseen things will happen, but know that all is well until a later time when all that is, will end, even in the very next moment.

I go back to work with the men. It's much more interesting than women's work. Perhaps because it's different. And then you get taken care of. People bring water and later in the afternoon, women come with a snack.

There are new things to like. The smell of fresh cut wood.

Once I admit it to myself, I did enjoy things. The floor boards, the earth and it's weeds, the gruel, the smell of rain. I didn't mean to. It's as if one has a need to enjoy whatever there is to enjoy.

I don't know if I'll get to see those eyes again or not but I'm watching for them and I'm happy.

Focus. There is no moment but this empty moment right now. This moment is enough. It is all you have.

Such a full moment. Man sweat. We don't smell like that. They could find me out by sweat alone. And I keep looking out at everybody.

In the evening after work, the men go down to the river to bathe. I go back and pick up my bonnet from behind the lilacs and put it in a safer spot. With both a hat and a bonnet I'll have more freedom than ever before.

All are equal here, and all equally neutral. All neither happy nor unhappy. Our minds are on what's in front of us. Purity. Harmony. Utility. The only proper life.

At supper the men are looking. Not out the window but at us. They know one of us did it. I make a small slight man, lost in my too-big man's hat. I should have kept my bonnet. And I never took off my feather. Luminous blue. It must be like a beacon.

But only that angry man really saw my face. The others weren't watching when he came after me. They didn't see that he did it to himself. They only saw the blood afterwards. Maybe they think I lashed out at him on purpose.

Do they discuss things? Or do they just know what to do? As: find the woman in a man's hat.

But I see him. I see the hands first and then I look up into the eyes. He's looking right at me. He knows.

Love will make you want to please the beloved. Love will make you want to know the name of the beloved and where the beloved came from.

Above our village I saw beavers making mating. I saw birds, the same. They say we mustn't think the word "love." We are not to think more of one of us than of another, anymore than we should value one thing more than another, as why love one spoon better than another spoon.

But it is known though nothing is ever said about it, that one does fall in love even with spoons and cups. Has one's favorites even from among one's socks.

But now…right now, if my eyes could speak out without saying a word. If I could…. If my eyes could speak….

(Come with me. Up into the mountains. We'll have our own wild mountain children. We'll have each other. Or come with me, even down into the evil of the town. Surely there's a place for us somewhere.)

He looks. His eyes give messages I can't fathom. I can no more guess what my eyes might be saying to him than I can guess at his to me. Mine must be full of yearning.

He looks down and begins to eat. They all do, as if his eating is a signal. Perhaps the signal that I have been found.

Is he our leader? Did I fall in love with exactly the worst one? Or best?

Is escape possible? I stand up and step off the bench, kicking my neighbors in my haste. All those in men's hats get up, too. All those in bonnets sit but stop eating.

There's no sense in running with all those men ready to chase me. I will speak instead of running. I stand up on the bench. That surprises them.

I don't know how I got the courage…except that everything is lost anyway.

What I want to say is, I didn't mean to hurt, but….

Words have never made anyone understand anything. Words obfuscate. Confuse. Conceal. Form alibis that sound reasonable, but are just excuses.

I don't suppose my reasons…my alibi will sound plausible…that I didn't mean to do it. Everyone would say that. If I'm going to use words they'll have to be something different.

"Because I love," I say.

I'm trembling. My voice is shaky.

"Because I love. Because I look out the window and watch the bushes in the breeze. Because I have a feather. Because I watch the birds. Let me go. I'll do my loving someplace else. I confess I've always loved. Even from the beginning. I loved the small bone spoon. I loved the china cup. The apples. Even the beans. Even so, I obeyed."

Everyone watches. They've never seen anything like it…like me. Like doing this. They're too stunned to move. If I had run they'd have known what to do. I feel safe as long as I can keep talking. Though I suppose that's not really true. They'll tire of talk.

Then I find myself making excuses. I say, "He ran towards me with his hands out. I was scared. I held out the first thing I could grab. I would never harm another creature. I never have. He looked as if he was going to choke me."

I say, "But I know there are no excuses. I know I am his keeper."

Where does all this talk come from? As if I'd been waiting all these years for just this chance. My voice is more powerful every minute. I've stopped trembling.

I say. "I see that one must see." I wave my arms. I must look as if I'm trying to fly. I say, "There are important things to see."

All eyes are on me.

"Eyes for instance. Are they not worth seeing? Look at each other. At your eyes."

But they don't. They keep looking at me.

"Am I, then, so worth seeing that you stare. After all these years it's only me you see. Look out the window. Your first view should be of clouds."

And there are clouds. It's as if I've called them forth, but they still look at me.

He also. His hands still hold his tin cup. His have got to be musician's hands though there's never any music here.

"I've had enough of feet and floors. I speak. Why not? I look up. I look out the window. I see the lilacs blowing even now."

We are not put on this earth to enjoy. Neither are we put here to feel pain and loss. We renounce them both so as to live empty of all feelings. We learn to control these impulses so as to see the world calmly.

But why are we here?

I say it, "Why are we here?"

I stop talking and wait. They wait, too. Nobody knows what to do.

Before, when someone broke, it was with screaming and crying. That person would be carried off. Nobody knows what happens afterwards. I didn't anyway, though somebody must. But my case is different. I didn't break, I just fell in love. I just began to pay attention.

Then that man...the very one...comes to me. Holds out his hand to help me from the bench. I take it. It's rough from hard work but warm. I'm holding the long fingers. I can feel his strength.

I step down. I'll do whatever he thinks best.

He leads me away. Perhaps to where they put the people who go crazy. Now I'll find out.

It's just the two of us.

"You looked at me. Remember? After that I began to see."

He says, "We are not put on this earth to enjoy. Nor are we put here to feel pain and loss."

"I want a moment of pleasure. Just a moment of it."

"And after that there's nothing but pain and loss."

"I don't mean a great joy. I mean a moment with both of us, you and I, up the hill, both of us looking out over the valley. Is that too much to ask?"

"All pleasure ties one to this world so that leaving it is a calamity. We live here empty of desire."

"I thought, from your eyes, that you'd be different."

"Do not think."

"But your face.... It's kind."

"Give thanks that we have but little."

He takes me to the man I hurt. His hands and arms are bandaged. He's resting quietly until he sees me. Then he looks as if he'd like to try and grab me by the neck again.

My man says, "Life at all is life enough."

I'm wondering which of us he's thinking of. Clearly this man will not die.

"What will happen? To me? Does one have one last wish?"

He begins to lead me up beyond the paths. Where in the world are we going? But I'm happy. How could I not be, I'm beside him, and I'm walking away from the village?

He can see how I feel. He says, "Avoid joy or nothing will ever be enough."

The spot where he takes me is hard to get to. Part of the way it's a scary path on the side of a cliff. He has me go first while he holds the back of my pants to keep me safe.

Beyond the cliff there's a good view. We sit under a tree. His tree. He headed right for it.

We look out. The view is better than the one from my tree. You can see our whole village.

"You also. You haven't kept your vows. You shouldn't bring me here."

I unpin my feather. I want to give it to him but I see a warning in his eyes. He won't take it. I put it on the ground. I say, "There's plenty more if one is willing to look."

We sit.

"How good it is to look," I say.

We sit.

I ask again. "What will happen? To me?"

We sit.

"I know we can't have those like me in the village. I will remind people of exactly what they don't want to be reminded of. And I hurt one of us. What will the punishment be?"

"We all die."

Is that a clue to what will happen?

"You could leave me here in the mountains."

He turns and looks at me, eye to eye just like that first time. We stare as we did. Again I wonder,how does one read someone else's stare?

"Was the mating I was scheduled for to be with you?"

He stares.

"If with you I'd not have minded."

But I've said too much.

He squints. He frowns. Then suddenly he grabs. Kisses. Hard. Holds me too tight. It's scary. I've never.... I don't know what to do. What if that, "We all die," was about what will happen to me in the next few minutes? What if they told him to take me up and get rid of me? What if he thinks to give me one last pleasure?

If this is what this is. It seems done more for himself than for me. He's rough and hasty. Our clothes are bulky, old, and weak. They tear. What then when we go back? If? Will there be enough untorn to outfit one person?

I see him without his hat. Black hair streaked with gray, though not as gray as his beard. I see his hairy body. Sweaty. Strong. Most of his chest hair is gray.

I'm naked and ashamed. I don't know what I look like, to him or even to myself.

"Isn't this against our rules?"

I hope I look all right. I hope I can give pleasure. But he's in a hurry.

And after a moment's rest he does it again.

Am I the dead one so it doesn't matter about me? Except this second time it seems with a little more feeling.

After, do I see something new in his eyes? I'm not sure.

He gets up and tries to piece our clothes into one decent outfit. He leaves me the rags. Says, "Stay here."

Then, just as he goes, he turn and he says, "I lost my child. I lost my wife."

I call after him what he said to me, "We all die."

Is this the first time he's said anything that's not part of our doctrine? I didn't know he could.

Have I had my moment? My last request? Was that it?

I put on the rags. Tying and pinning until I'm more or less decent. I won't stay here. I'll go up higher. Except I'm so hungry. First I'll go on down to eat. I could get my bonnet from its hiding place. They're looking for a small women in a much too large man's hat. They'd not notice me in my bonnet, and he won't expect me to have crossed the scary cliff by myself.

But perhaps he was going to bring me clothes. Perhaps even food. He should have said so. Though I suppose one can't expect talk. We're not used to that.

I cross the scary part. Creep into the village to where the men were working. It's late. There's no one there. I find my bonnet and go in to eat. Ragged as I am, nobody notices.

I will not sleep down in the village. I head back to his tree. It's getting dark. I don't dare cross the cliff section of the path. But then I do it anyway…start to… and I stop right in the middle of the scariest part. I don't deserve to be comfortable. I want to punish myself. I'll sleep here on the edge, a stone for a pillow. It makes me think this is why we shouldn't feel too much. We're all on the edge of a cliff. I'll sleep here as a lesson to myself.

Life is brutal. Life is pain. Life is full cruelty.

Didn't we always say that? And if one loses a child and a wife….

I dream I slash out at everybody with a saw. I dream I killed the man I didn't kill.

I wake up before dawn. I'm yelling. I turn into one of those women who screamed and screamed and had to be led away. But nobody hears me from here. I go on and on until I'm all screamed out. Then I sit on the scary edge, my feet hanging over. I don't feel fear. I don't care if I fall off the cliff or not. I understand, for the first time, what our creed really means...has meant all this time. As good as dead. All of us. There's nothing to fear. What could there possibly be to fear?

There are no happy endings. All life ends the same way. Better to live with the knowledge of the end. Every day a preparation for what will, inevitably, be.

Except.... Except....

The sun is rising. There's all different reds on the hills beyond. Below, the village is still in shadow. I watch the brightness come, little by little, across the valley floor.

Soon after, I see a black figure, like an ant creeping up the path toward me. It'll take him an hour to get up here.

He looks surprised to find me on the ledge with my feet hanging over. Or maybe surprised to see me in my bonnet. To see my clothes all pinned up. He sits beside me. We don't speak. Of course we don't speak.

He has a bundle with him. Black. After all this sunrise, I'm tired of black. Anything, anything, not to see black and not to be all in black.

He takes out a small package and then puts the bundle beside us. He opens out a little packet and there's bread and lemonade.

I say, "Thank you."

He flinches as if my Thank you surprises him, but keep silent.

I say, "I've been down home." Though I know he knows that from my bonnet. I say, "I had supper."

No answer.

I say, "But I spent the night right here. There's my stone pillow."

He ought at least to say some of our creed words.

I want to shake him up. To get him to talk I say, "What happened to your wife and child?"

He frowns.

"Tell me."

"Life without words is peaceful. There are no disagreements." And then, "Some words should never be said."

Of course he's right, but I want words.

"What's going to happen now? I suppose you'll take me back."

No answer.

"If we should fall in love, then no end to it."

"There are no happy endings."

"I suppose you want to end it before the end comes."

Nothing.

"So as to know the end."

Not even a nod.

"*Speak!*"

He's squinting out at our valley. I can't stand the thought of going back.

How easy it would be, him squatting there, reaching to get more lemonade for me.

"I won't go back."

Of course no answer.

I push him. Off he tumbles, down the cliff. He doesn't make a sound. Of course he doesn't. I look over. I see the black bundle below. There's no way he can still be alive. Besides, what would he do with me? Just take me back.

I wait. I watch a long time for movement, but there's none. Though what could I do if there was some? I don't know how I'd get myself down there.

I wait so long I'm hungry again. I open the bundle. There's a man's red shirt. Man's blue pants. A dress…a real dress, also blue. A white bonnet with little flowers on it. Where in the world did he get these things? Has he been saving them for an escape? Was he already preparing to leave but didn't know how or what to say?

Desire breeds nothing but more desire.

Was he full of desire?

I sit. I wait. Numb. I don't know how long but I see the sun is low. If I'm to cross the ledge I have to do it now.

I put on the dress and bonnet. I cross and head up, higher yet, into the snow. There's no path. The sunset has spread all across the sky. Everything looks pink. Everything glows. Even me.

I Live with You. 2005

Bountiful City

Walking around saying, I love you, I love you, I love you, and not being in love with anybody.... Perhaps it's too much coffee. Or the air today, transparent...pinkish. It usually isn't. After all, it's the city, everything black and gray. Chewing gum stuck all over the sidewalk. And spit. A quarter falls and you hate to pick it up. You get soot in your eye. But that won't happen today.

I love. I love. I could fall in love with the very next man who appears. I check them all out. Compare mustaches. Lots these days. How nice to smooth one. Or stroke a beard. Stroke rough man cheeks. Chest hair. Small of the back hair.

The city glimmers. I'm looking at the tops of buildings not down at the spit. All kinds of architecture all mixed up, up there. Some shine golden. Some painted Aztec colors: aqua and dull peach. Some Art Nouveau.

But how nice, right this minute, to be bouncing along the street looking up, but also into faces. Smiling. Evaluating. Thinking about beards and eyebrows. Thinking, I love you, I love you, but who? Love. How nice to be in it.

Where *is* somebody?

My goal in life is this one thing. (As if it hasn't always been.)

Walk proudly. But not too proud. You never know what the man in question might like best in his women. I won't be anything particular until I find out his taste.

There goes a possible man right now. I always did like skinny dark ones. And here's another right behind him. What a generous world!

The look in the eye is important. I peer. I stare. Here's another one. He's wearing a cowboy hat (I was always a sucker for a big hat). He's not from around here. What wonderfully bushy eyebrows! He's from out west. Patience is needed with animals especially horses. A patient man would be nice. Of course patience is needed in the city, too. Just crossing the street can be aggravating. And all that honking.

I wonder if he's rich. Of course he could be a farmer, not an oil man.

Even so I turn and follow that one. I don't remember if he had a kind eye. His mustache was so big I didn't notice anything else.

But I don't want any short term relationships, I want somebody from right here. I turn back. I wander on with all the other walkers. I watch the Chrysler building roof glimmer in the setting sun.

Here's another man. Hat, dark suit, black turtleneck makes him look all the thinner. I turn and follow him. His legs are nice and straight, not like some.

How begin? Drop my package? Trip him?

When's the proper time to say, I love you? How long do I have to wait? I've been saying it to myself at every step. I may not be able to hold myself back. I put a cough drop in my mouth to keep me quiet, and follow.

Besides, love can go bad. Love can turn with the weather. I'll not commit myself until I'm sure.

(I have a picture in my purse of a man I never met. I cut it out of a magazine. Perhaps now's the time to throw it out—before some other man sees it and thinks things. Though I hate to. What if no other man ever works out? At least I'll have this one.)

New Yorkers walk for miles. It's the most walking city in the world, I'll bet. Now four of us: a trench coat guy, a girl with upscale backpack, my man, me.... We've gone on for an hour as though we knew each other. From west 57th to east 15th. That's the way it always is in New York. The girl and I have smiled at each other though none of the men have. The girl turns off on 14th but the rest of us keep going, down, down, down town. It's getting late and I'm hungry.

I almost lose him as he turns on 4th, stops for a newspaper. I do, too. I look deep into his eyes. You'd think he'd notice but he doesn't. Or perhaps he's afraid of commitment. I know his kind.

He's up the steps and in his building—not a very nice one—before I have a chance to trip him or drop my package. I had hoped he'd let me in. I could have said I was delivering my package. (I've bought new shoes. I was happy with them. That's another reason I was feeling so full of love.)

Where will I go from here? Walk all the way back up to Central Park?

But a light goes on in a basement apartment right beside the front door. I hunker down and look in and there he is, taking off his jacket. What a room! He needs a wife, that's for sure. Well now I know a bit about who he is.

Two other black turtlenecks exactly like the one he's wearing are on the bed. Silky black socks all over the place. Piles of books and papers sideways on the floor because of no bookcases. No plants. I could see to that, though there's no place for them. If I cleaned it up, there might be room for a little stand by the window.

There's a pile of ropes in a corner on the floor. A funny pair of shoes on top. They're kind of like ballet slippers but with more rubber. What's the meaning of those?

I keep squatting down, watching. He cooks himself a couple of eggs on his hotplate. Sits on his bed to eat. He doesn't have a table. His bottle of wine is on the floor. He drinks straight out of the bottle.

After eating, he takes off his turtleneck. I evaluate his chest. He's got muscles and nice curly black hair in the middle of it.

He flops on the bed, which is smaller than a twin bed. How could we make love on that? Besides, it's sagging. Maybe we should to it on the floor instead.

Then he realizes he hasn't pulled his curtains. He gets up, comes and looks right at me. Stares. Jerks the curtains shut.

I'll go home and write some love poems.

Next morning, early, I go down there first thing and squat by his window. The curtains are open and he's gone.

I go up to the cloisters. I imagine he might be there. I glance around every corner, hoping... yearning.... Then I walk through Central Park. I sit on a bench and wait but nobody like him comes along.

I wander Lincoln Center for an hour. I go to the Museum of Modern Art. I eat lunch there. I sit with a notebook and pretend to write. I don't keep my nose in it. I look around. I stare into space a lot. If I was really writing that's what I'd be doing, anyway, waiting for inspiration. I see several possibilities... almost good enough, but *he* doesn't come.

I go up to the top of the Empire State Building. Same waiting. Same looking around the deck.

I stay up there a whole hour. Yearning out in every direction.

Then I hear sirens. I look over the side and I see police cars and fire engines down below. Crowds gathering. And here's a helicopter hovering right across from me. All of a sudden the roof is full of cops and firemen. Several look interesting. Lots of mustaches. Some sideburns.

Even as I look over the side to see what's up, I strike a pose, one knee cocked, toe pointed. Since I'm wearing running shoes, I know the effect won't be exactly what I hope.

My god, somebody is climbing the Empire State Building. He looks like a fly down there. There's nothing to hold him up but his fingers. How can anybody do that?

The cops are going to arrest him the minute he gets up here.

He's going slowly. Well, fast for what he's doing, I suppose. I'm holding my breath. I didn't realize it until I started feeling woozy. I take long slow breaths, counting four beats to each. It looks like the cop standing next to me has to do the same.

The man climbs closer. Black turtle neck, black pants. He looks up and it's him. *My* man. We're two of a kind. Him and his love of climbing and me with my just plain love of love. I'm all in black, too. It's not only the New York color, it's slimming and mysterious and sexy.

How nice that there are two sexes. Everywhere one looks one finds one or the other, and especially how nice that there's the other. Bulges one place or another. (In some languages even the chairs and tables have a sex.) The whole world as if for me. Like this policeman right beside me. I match my breathing with his so as to be sure not to forget that I have to breathe.

Look at those black eyes as my man looks up. Surely he knows I'm the one who walked from west 57th Street to east 4th Street with him. Surely he remembers closing his curtains when he saw me looking in.

I'm so proud. Who else could do this besides my man? I can't wait till he gets up here.

But can he climb over and around that net they have in place to keep people from jumping? Not from jumping, but from landing on the sidewalk. Of course he can.

What should I do when he gets here? Should I try to keep the police from arresting him? Should I distract them?

The roof is full of people now. A lot of news people, too. I'm glad I came up hours ago to wait and watch for him. I have the perfect spot. People try to push me aside, but I have a good grip on the railing.

Here he comes. I knew it, the net is no problem for somebody like him.

I start yelling and pretend to be about to jump over the edge. The policemen grab me. I wave my arms and slap at them. I want my man to see how I'm fighting for him.

Now the cameras are turned on me instead of him. There's much more action where I am than where he is. I put on a good show.

They arrest him and haul him off. I wonder where? Perhaps he'll be home on 4th Street after posting bail.

As soon as he's gone from the platform, I become completely reasonable. I don't get arrested. I talk them out of it. I say that was my lover and I went a little bit crazy until he got safely up here. They understand. I go down the elevator with them. They're all attractive. They glow with man sweat. Many need a shave. I'd kiss their cheeks if I dared. I think of their hairy bodies. New York's finest. That's what they say. They talk man talk in their scratchy voices. I could fall in love with the voice alone. I've always loved basses. The deepest voice comes from a skinny little man hardly taller than I am. I'm thinking of changing my love over to him, but climbing a building is more romantic than a deep voice.

Maybe he'll love me if.... Well *if* a lot of things. I *might* have the courage to climb buildings beside him, both of us in danger together. That might fuel our love.

How be my best self in front of him? Or better than I really am?

I'll say, "Knowing you I've become aware of things I've never been aware of before. The air, the flowers, the stars...." (Hard to see any stars in the city. Hardly ever notice the moon. But now I seek it out from behind the street lights. And it's there.)

(Love should never go to waste no matter if a person is fat or thin or has a long nose or pigeon toes.)

I trot down to 4th Street to see if he's home yet.

He's not, but I sneak in with an old lady who holds the door for me though she's never seen me before. There's a nice spot under the stairs. I hunker down with the snow shovel and the broom and mop. It's been such a long exciting day I fall asleep right away.

Well not quite. I think about him. Wonder what he does when he's not climbing the Empire State Building? How does he make money? Cat burglar? Climb straight up brick walls? I won't turn him in. I'll stick by him no matter what.

And *then* I fall asleep.

I miss him coming home. It's six AM when I knock on his door. I keep knocking until I hear a growl. Then he says, Go away, without even knowing who it is.

"It's me." I whisper it. "Me. Me."

Is now the time to say, I love you?

"I'm the one at the top of the Empire State Building. I waited for you all day and you came."

Not the time to say I love you.

(Even to say I love is embarrassing. How odd that it should be so.)

But nothing ventured nothing gained.

"I love you."

"Who are you?"

How answer such a question? I'm ready to be anything he wants.

"I am your hearts desire. If not that right now, I'm willing to learn."

"Go away. It's six AM."

"I'll wait."

I sit down with my back against the door.

I hear him getting up, taking a shower, listening to the news. It's the very same station I always listen to.

By now it's eight o'clock.

He unlocks three locks including the police lock (I can hear it clank), opens the door, sees me, and slams it shut again. I hear the police lock thump into place. Who does he think I am, anyway? I couldn't even get in a normal lock.

"Go away. I'm not coming out until you leave."

I could say I'll leave and then not do it, but then he'd think I wasn't a very nice person.

"I'll leave. I'm leaving right now. I'm doing exactly what you tell me to and I always will."

First thing, outside, I buy a newspaper, and there we both are! There's one picture of him climbing up and another of me waving my arms and with my mouth open. I don't look very attractive that way. I must make sure not to do that again.

I stop at a cappuccino shop and read the article. People protested his arrest. They got together and raised his bail and the cops let him go. I don't come off too well. They call me a hysterical woman, claiming to be..."claiming," they said...his girlfriend.

I walk back to my place, thinking, I love you, I love you, at every step. Thousands of steps and thousands of I love yous. I just love. I don't care. It can be anybody.

At least I know his name now—from the newspapers. He already was somebody. The Great Buzzoni. Not a cat burglar after all. A high wire artist. I don't know how he makes his living doing that. Especially living here in New York. Though he does have a cheep apartment. Maybe he's *also* a cat burglar.

Next day I stake myself out near his apartment with a purse full of diet bars. I wear a big hat. I hope men like women in big hats as much as I like men in them. Lots of front steps across from his place to sit on while I wait.

Finally here he comes, a beret instead of a hat this time. A neat quick man. No wonder I followed him.

I've figured out what to say. I say it. "Hello. It's me. I saw you climbing."

He walks right by. In fact he walks even faster. I have a hard time keeping up.

I shout after him, "I climb, too. I'd like to climb with you. Both of us climbing would be even more of a show. The Great Gabriella. And when I said, I love you, I meant I love the way you climb."

I wonder if I can do it. I've always been afraid of heights. I'll have to find a brick building to try it on. I'll practice in an alley so nobody will see.

Now he's slowing down. Now he turns around. He looks at me—really looks. "You can?"

We walk to the corner for coffee. I can't believe I'm walking beside the great Buzzoni and that I picked him out on the street, from millions of people.

(For all his sharp Italian looks, his name is really George Mayer. I wonder what I should say my real name is.)

We don't talk about climbing. And I don't dare ask how he makes his living. He doesn't ask me either. I suppose for the same reason. We might both be cat burglars. If he's one, all the more reason to think I'm one. We ask each other everything but that.

(I'm glad I ordered the same things he did. It makes us more companionable.)

We're nature lovers, though here in New York there's not much nature to love, except Cockroaches, rats, and pigeons, but it's Spring. Some sort of sparrows are chirping in the trees.

We're lovers of sunsets and sunrises, and here he is living in a basement. Out his window he can watch feet. I have a better view from my fifth floor walk up.

What if he needs a helper? Dare I ask?

I ask.

He sits and thinks. Then, "All right. I could use somebody."

But I don't know what for.

"Tuesday, two weeks from now. Midnight. 17th Street at Broadway."

Good, that gives me time to practice.

He walks me part way home just for my company. He shakes my hand when he leaves and I feel his strong calloused fingers. Shaking mine does he know? He must.

"I'm a little out of practice."

His are not lover's hands. I wouldn't want them on my body.

Luckily my own window looks out on a back alley and there's a brick building behind mine. That's where I try to climb. I get up about a foot and hang there until my fingers give out.

I practice all those two weeks, but I don't get much better. Maybe a little stronger. Mostly I ruin my fingers. Once I make it all the way up to five feet. Next day I laps back to three.

I know myself. I may have acrophobia but I can steel myself against it. For his sake. When you feel your stomach turning upside down just look out at the horizon—if you can see any such thing from in the city.

Finally I get far enough up to sneak into somebody's second floor window. It's the middle of the day. Everybody's at work. Nobody sees me. I should steal something so I'll be of a kind with him. Our philosophy of life will be the same. I look around. Lots of books and papers and not much else. I open all the drawers. No jewelry. None at all. Looks as if somebody has already stolen everything worth taking. Maybe he did it. What's left for me to take? A book? A potted plant? That doesn't seem like much.

I lie down on the bed to think about it and fall asleep by mistake. When I wake up it's getting dark. I've got to leave fast. I grab the clock beside the bed and run out the door. Just in time because people are coming in downstairs.

I wish I'd taken clothes. I could use a new blouse. I already have a clock exactly like this one.

I do feel a sense of accomplishment, though. And I feel closer to him now that I know what it's like to do as he does.

I love, I love.... What a world, full of beards and lips! And all sorts of soft velvety things.

I've been so busy practicing I haven't gone down to his place at all, but then the time comes for our meeting.

(I'm wearing black tights and black turtle neck top. Climbing clothes.)

The city at night! Like a Christmas tree no matter the season. And how nice to be walking beside him, matching his stride.

But maybe he's not a cat burglar after all. Turns out he needs someone to help find a spot between two sky-scrapers where he can set up a tightrope—in the middle of the night so nobody will know. And he needs somebody to help set it up. He wants to use the flatiron building if possible. It's always windy around there so it'll be dangerous but he likes that all the better.

We check it out. It's not possible. We walk up town to search for other places. Perhaps Lincoln center.

When we stop for coffee. (It's three AM, but things never close in New York.) I say first thing, "I thought you were a cat burglar." He looks startled—as if I'd found him out. Or maybe just that he hadn't ever thought of doing that before.

I say, "Oh, I don't mind. I do it myself."

He's still looking shocked. Even more so.

I say, "I don't ever take valuable things."

Have I made myself unlovable in just one sentence?

"I only take little things. Actually I've only taken one thing...ever."

I don't like the way he's looking at me.

"Actually I've never climbed beyond the second floor."

Why doesn't he say something?

"Actually I only did it for you. And I brought you this."

I try to give him the clock. (He already has one exactly like it, too. I saw it in his apartment.)

He waves it away.

He hasn't said a word since I mentioned cat burglar.

Do I know his secret?

You should never know a man's secret, especially if it's illegal.

Well, that's the end of that. I can see it in his eyes. Even with the gift.

There's plenty more—men that is. Maybe I should forget about them altogether, but I don't want to.

"I can get you more things."

I guess not.

We part. Not even with a kiss.

Anyway, his eyes were too close together, he's too short, I'm just as tall as he is. His nose is too long. His voice is the opposite of bass.

The moon is out. The city shines. It's full of men. I look into faces. I stare. I check out ways of walking. I follow first one and then another. Bald men with hairy bodies. Hairy men with hairless bodies. Joe, Pete, Sam, Henry, Louis, Bob, Charley....

***I Live with You*, 2005**

World Of No Return

Lost. It's what I want and wish I was again. Home is ... used to be ... wherever I was. Wherever I put down my folding cup, wrung Out my cap, turned it inside out and used it for a pillow. But that was yesterday.

When I was discovered, I panicked. They woke me out of a sound sleep. I fought. First without thinking at all, and then because they could be muggers, and after that. When I saw they were policemen, I knew I might be kept in one place and have to stay with the natives for longer than I could stand. Someplace with nothing but a little square of sky. And that's exactly how it is.

They gagged me with a dirty rag. I suppose I was yelling. They tied my hands behind my back. I couldn't get a handkerchief for my bloody nose. They let me bleed all over my shin.

I did do damage. I don't know how much but they had bloody noses, too. Maybe a few black *eyes.*

They washed me, shaved me including my head. I suppose they were worried about lice. I had a mustache. That's gone. I hardly know myself. They did all this with my hands tied behind my back. I calmed myself with breathing. I tried to imagine a sky instead of a ceiling.

I should be glad for the chance to rest, I haven't stopped traveling — I should be glad for the chance to rest, I haven't stopped traveling —not even for a day, but still I long to be moving. They took, not just the laces, but my shoes. I had added two extra heels on one for my bad foot. Even though they're worn out, I'm lost without those particular shoes. That's not the kind of lost I like to be.

I think I'm he last, though I keep hoping there's others of us hiding out somewhere. Mountains would be the most logical place. I was headed there. Mother and Dad implanted their own beacons under our arms, but did all the parents do that and was it the Same lumpy red spot for all? And how could I ask somebody, "Lift your arms and let me peer into your armpits?" Even at the beach, I seldom see under anybody's arm. I suppose that's why they put it there in the first place.

I blend In, I never do anything that *they* wouldn't do, I presume we all do that,

We hoped for rescue. We waited. At least Mother did, She never belonged, She was never comfortable here. Most of those of her generation waited and kept on acting as tourists until the money ran out. They thought that would be the best way to survive here until rescue. Unfortunately there was no central location. Now the old ones are all dead and most of the younger ones I knew are spread out, who knows where?

I no longer hope. Actually I never really did. I played Mother's game in front of her … the game of wanting more than what we had here — Mother said we were rich back there — but I knew no other life, Actually no other life than poverty. I was used to it. As long as we had enough to eat, I was happy. Besides, I was born here, This is my land. I never look out at it without a thrill, Even as a child I secretly relished this world, I wondered if I'd have to leave if we ever were rescued. Would Mother insist that I go back with her?

Mother said, "We may look more or less like them, but we're not them and don't you ever forget it." She said, "Keep wandering, wear tourist's clothes and carry tourist things." She said, "Just keep waiting. Don't use the freeze, but don't let it die, Don't marry one of them. If you don't marry one of us, it surely will."

I waited. I didn't marry. Now I fear there are no more of us left to marry, though one can't be sure, we were spread all over. And who knows, maybe in some mountain range, some of us might have lasted disguised as campers. There's the rumor or a secret city. I was on my way to try and find it.

They called themselves tourists. Our parent just wanted to see this place (cr a little while. It was a class in understanding aliens. Mother was one of the guides but empathy was hard (or her. She tried but she always hated the natives, "Homo sapiens sapiens," she'd say with a sneer. "Sapiens. That's what *they* think. They took *two* sapiens for themselves, for heaven's sake."

I could never see that much difference, us or them.

Had I known we'd never be rescued, I'd have mated with one of them in spite of Mother's warnings, She was sure I'd reveal myself in a fit of anger, but I don't think so, (Though considering what I just did, maybe I would have if woken up suddenly,) I could have had a normal native life. But could I have asked one of them to follow me, a limping bum in a baseball cap and a flowery Hawaiian shin, with camera, field glasses? Never lost but always lost? (Though I'd have settled down if I'd married. There must be some way to get an identity and then a decent job.)

After my parents knew we were abandoned here, they went from job to job. Nobody ever got to know us nor we them. Mother didn't want us to know the natives. She didn't want us contaminated. She said we were born for better things than houses with pictures on the walls and malls and coffee shops and grocery stores—better things than little plots of land with flowers in them .... Trouble was, that's all we younger ones knew.

At first my family lived in a camper but then had to sell it. Our father got a broken-down pickup truck and a tent and we went from place to place. My parents looked at everything with the same interest they'd had in the beginning, and often laughed at the native's ways, but they always felt set apart. They didn't want to join this world. They home-schooled us so that we knew more about a distant world and its wars and landmasses than we knew of this one.

I tell the police my name is North. Norman North. At the time I was looking out the slit of a window that faces North. I don't have papers. I don't know how to get any. I don't ever say my real name. I haven't said it in so long I'd have a hard time pronouncing it. My fingerprints are probably in the network, but not for any crime and not, until now, for any violence. I don't know what came over me. I may be too old for this kind of life.

"What were you doing sleeping in somebody's back yard? Don't you have anyplace to go?"

They're sorry they hit me so hard but, after all, I was hitting them.

"You scared an old lady half to death with your snoring. She thought you were a bear."

I know I look more like a bum than I used to: faded flowery shirt, tan ... used to be tan pants, used to be fancy shoes with raised heel on left fool.

"Do yo" have a place to live?

"I want to get up into the mountains."

"Do you have a place to go there?"

"I know people camping up there."

"Who."

"Family. More of us Norths:'

"You don't have any camping gear. And look at your shoes, You'll need boots."

And so forth.

I ask, "Am I in for vagrancy?"

"We're going to keep you for a day or two."

When I say, "But I'm a tourist," they laugh.

They not only don't believe me, they don't trust me either. They've left the handcuffs on all this time, I don't blame them. One of the policemen who talks to me has a swollen jaw. I'm lucky he didn't try to get even as they questioned me.

Finally they take off the handcuffs and leave me be. I curl up on the bench. There's a dirty blanket. I wrap up in it anyway.

I think of our kind of music. My mother's songs In the homeworld language when she sang me to sleep. What little I knew of my language I've forgotten except for the words she made us memorize from the beginning. Our very first words. I still remember what they mean: "We are the people. We are the tourists left here in hundred eighty-nine. Take me home."

At first we tried to stay in our travel groups, but that got to be too hard when the money ran out and each had a different idea of what the proper thing to do was. That was in the early days. My sister and I were toddlers. If stuck, as we are here, with no other mate, I was supposed to mate with my sister. But she was taken as a male long ago by one of our others. Mother thought that was best, and that I should find myself another from one of our groups.

So now I sing. Hum. Remember my dead. Wonder if my sister's still alive. I ask for paper and pencil. They say, yes, I wait, but they don't bring any. I suppose I don't deserve it anymore than I deserve better meals.

After a day or two locked up for vagrancy, I'm usually taken to the edge of town and watched as I walk away, but this time I'm kept. I suppose I'm considered dangerous. I find a place on the side of the bench to scratch off the days. I'll have to use my fingernails.

I wonder if my camera, jacket and cap, and my extra shirt are still under that bush on the edge of town or have they brought all that here? If I behave myself will I get them back when … *if,* that is, they let me go?

For somebody always on the move, staying still four days is more than I can stand. I always walk as fast as my bad foot allows. Here, I walk to and fro all day. I didn't at first. I lay on the bench until I realized that wasn't doing anything for my depression, Not that depression isn't my usual State, Moving makes me feel like myself. Being a tourist has become my nature.

I yearn for the mountains, not for themselves or their beauty, though that, too, but for the high hidden valleys where you could hide a whole town, (Some say Vilcabamba was never found,) My people would pick a beautiful spot. They loved how beautiful this land was. Before they knew they were stranded here, they talked of wanting to stay forever,

I'm going to get out of jail by any way I can though can I still freeze if I never practiced? Considering none of us were ever allowed to freeze a creature of any sort, I doubt if we could anymore. Our parents always told us we should die before we revealed ourselves because that was a promise they had made before they signed on for the trip. Yet it seems to me some of the creatures here have that same talent.

But we hardly need it. Here on this world with less gravity, we're stronger. I wonder how many I fought that night? I almost won. So far I haven't needed our "save yourself" talent.

There's one of the guard more sympathetic than the others, He shared his sandwich and his coffee with me.

His name is Smith so they call him Jones and Jonesy. I like their sense of play. I call, "Jonesy."

"You think I've got nothing to do but talk to you? I got paperwork up to here."

"I could help if I had some paper."

"I don't think the chief would want me to give you any. You might kill yourself with the pencil. You rest up. You need to put on a little fat."

An odd thing to say. I'm a wide, heavy man, all my people are, but I guess I look like a too-thin wide heavy man.

"Are they ever going to let me out? You must admit the food isn't the greatest." "You gave six men a hard time. Now how did you do that?"

"But I didn't win. I'm here aren't I?"

"Were you a boxer? You look like you lift weights."

What to say? I haven't ever been anything.

"Something like that."

"Try to hold out for another day or two. How about I bring you fried chicken?"

So I wait. I pace. Four steps one way, four steps the other. I imagine weeds—rabbitbrush in bloom, bright yellow along the edge of road. That's how it was last I walked. I mark off another day. Jonesy must have said something because the food gets better.

At night everything is lit up bright as day. Another reason to get out of here. Plus there are mice. Bold as could be. I try not to spill anything but they're here anyway, If I did have paper or a book they'd be chewing on that.

The three Fs: Flight, Fight, or Freeze. I hold one of the mice in my stare. He doesn't move. I count to twenty, then I let him go. Or maybe he held *me* and let me go. Or maybe we just stared at each other, one creature to another, and then decided that was enough.

I'm to go in front of a judge for assault and vagrancy and goodness knows what else. Finally. Jonesy takes me for a shower. (I've been washing in a basin for five days.) He sits at the door. I want out of here before they dress me in a red jumpsuit and take me off to a bigger, better prison. This is about the biggest jail I can stand.

I washed my flowery shirt and chinos, and I have my shoes back. The day of my trial there's only three men to help me into the van, I won't need to test the freeze, My strength is why I've never needed to try it.

I lock them in the van, drive a couple of blocks, turn off on a side street and ditch the van, I walk a few blocks and hotwire a car, Drive two blocks and pick up another. Walk again, It won't take the owners long to find them,

I'm heading for the place where they first found me, I want to see if they left any of my things there. It's on the edge of town and on the road towards the mountains. Not hard to find. It's a messy place, that's why I chose it. And next door to other messy places. The house needs paint (as the neighboring houses do) and the porch roof is about to fall down. Best of all there's a big yard full of bushes and weeds—rabbitbrush, black brush, baby tumbleweed, and the big bushy good smelling sage that I slept under. If only I didn't snore like a bear.

I go straight to the sage and check under it. My red jacket with the white stripe along the sleeves is gone and my extra shin. My little kit with comb and razor, gone. Why didn't they give it back to me in jail? I'll look a mess without it.

I crawl out from under and stand up. I hear a sharp intake of breath. The old woman I scared … I presume it's the same one … is on the porch looking right at me.

I wonder that she's outside in this heat—someone as old as she looks to be should be inside keeping cool. I can see a swamp cooler on her roof but it's not running.

She sits back down with a plop and then sags over as if in a faint. I should see if she's all right. I should urge her to go inside. But I don't want to scare her again. Of course my head is shaved and my little black mustache gone. Even if she had seen me hauled away she wouldn't recognize me, but I'd scare her even so. Maybe all the more with this shaved head.

I go up to the porch slowly. I can think of some excuse. I could pretend to be selling some religion or other. They're all into religion, especially out in the country, maybe especially those of her age.

I go up the porch steps. I say, "Madam?" but I know that's wrong for around here. I say, "Misses?" Then (oh yes), Ma'am. "Ma'am? Are you all right?"

She isn't. I [come closer. I touch her shoulder. Gentle as my touch is, she collapses all the way down. I catch her before she hits the floor. I feel her pulse. I lean to feel her breath. She's alive.

I pick her up and carry her inside. She's small and light, even for one of them. Hunched over from osteoporosis. It's a wonder she didn't break something from her fall. Lucky it was more of a sagging down slowly.

I put her on the couch. The cushion is already lying sideways with a head shaped dent as if she had been napping there not so long ago.

I start the cooler. Then I look for the kitchen so as to find a towel to wet. I also get her a glass of water. Then it occurs to me that maybe I shouldn't wake her up just yet. I put the water beside her and the wet cloth on her head. Then I go to look around. I need men's clothes. And a razor.

The house is much nicer inside than I expected. Not clean, but nice things. And, in the kitchen, all the latest appliances. No sign of a man, though. If a man had been here that first time she'd not have been so frightened and it would have been the man who found me. Come out with a rifle, no doubt, and shot me on the spot.

Still there might have been a husband. She may have men's clothes. Sometimes they keep everything, though sometimes they get rid of everything in a hurry before they have a chance to think. Mother was like that. She got rid of all there was of Dad (not much) and then was sorry later. As was I.

The bedroom is small and cramped, the bed unmade. I suppose she doesn't have much energy for cleaning anymore. There's the picture of a man on the dresser but no men's clothes. She must be one who threw away all her husband's things tight away. But when I check more carefully, I find a man's workshirt in with her things. She's probably been wearing it herself.

It's a blue farmer's shirt. I take off my flowery shirt and put on the farmer's shirt. The buttons are a little stressed across my barrel chest and the sleeves are a little short but I roll them up so it doesn't matter. It's so old it'll tear easily.

In the bathroom I find several pink ladies razors. I put a few in my pocket.

As I come back to check on the old lady, I see a man's jacket hanging by the front door. Frayed corduroy, out at the elbows. I've hardly seen a uglier one. *Has* she been wearing that, too?

There's a whole array of hats on the rifle rack next to the door. Except for one .22 at the top, the rack holds only canes and hats. I find a floppy *soft* one with a brim I can pull close over my face. I'm going to stay away from baseball caps from now on. I'll be a camper. One of those canes will be nice, too.

It's a very small house. Even so I wonder if I can hide here a few days while the police are running around looking for me. Let the chase simmer down until they think I'm long gone.

Just as I come back to the living room, the telephone rings. I step behind the door. There's an answering machine. It's a woman's voice. "Mother, I can't come up this weekend. Mickey has an ear thing. The same as he had last time." But then the old woman staggers up, holds on to the furniture. Says, "Oops," as she plops into the chair by the phone. Her hello is breathless.

Now that she's answered. I can only hear her side of the conversation. "I'm fine. I had a dizzy spell but I'm all right. I lay down on the couch and I'm much better now. I'm going to make myself a cup of tea. I'll stay in here by the cooler. Yes, Rosemary comes on Mondays and the police are checking with me every day … ever since they found that man in the bushes."

Doesn't she remember seeing me? Or maybe she doesn't want to mention it for fear of worrying her daughter.

I go to the kitchen and put the kettle on. I start back into the hallway, but she's wobbling there, one hand on the wall. She goes to lock the from door. She mutters to herself. "She lets him eat anything he wants. He's not getting enough vitamins. But I've got to keep my mouth shut." She goes down the hall to the back door and locks it, too. Says again, *"Got* to keep my mouth shut."

I stand "stone still" (as we say, not the natives) beside the jacket at the front door. She doesn't see me. I don't think her eyes are very good.

When she comes into the kitchen and sees the kettle already boiling, she says, "'I'm even more addled than I thought." Perfect. I'll hide here a few days. I don't think she'll notice and even if she did she'd think she was mistaken.

She gets out a saucer, pours in cream and puts it on the floor. I'm thinking, addled indeed, but then she calls, "Come on kitty, kitty, kitty." It doesn't come. I'm not sure if there is a cat or if there just used to be.

She putters around for a few minutes and I think she's forgotten about the tea. But no, here comes the teacup. She hesitates, puts it hack and picks another, puts that back, too, finally settles for the third. These people care about little things of beauty.

I've never lived with any of them. In fact nobody in my family wanted to get that close. Mother was afraid we'd get to be like them, and maybe not mind being here. She wanted us to yearn for the home planet as much as she did. All her life here was nothing but yearning to be some place else. I don't know if all that yearning was worth it. She died looking out over a wheat field. She said, "What is all that gold?"

"Wheat," I said.

"Just like the rivers of home, she said. "Have we gone home?"

I didn't know whether to tell the truth.

"Oh, Lorpas, tell me, are we home at last?"

"Yes, yes."

I don't know if she believed or not.

The old lady sits with her tea and turns on the radio. That's nice for me. I've hardly ever heard their radio or seen their television. Another thing Mother didn't want us to get to like. Before we were born and before they were stuck here, Dad said they had watched and listened to everything they could and raved about how funny and fun these people were. How funny they were especially when they acted almost just like us. But they didn't want us children turning into them. Without home planet experiences they were worried. That was a mistake. It kept us ignorant of everybody and everything here. I had to learn everything after they were gone.

So now I stand still and listen. I hear news but nothing about me having escaped. I hear afternoon thunderstorms are predicted for the next few days. Yes, I'll stay until the weather gets better.

She keeps muttering to herself. Mostly I can't hear but I do hear: "For heaven's sake." and, "Good grief." Then, "More rain. What else is new?" (Odd for the desert, but it's been raining every afternoon.) She says, "They say doing the crossword puzzle keeps your brains going." Why did she say that? She's not doing a crossword. Then, "Well, lots more than just brains will be lost one of these days. The mountains … lost them a long time ago. Bert's house. Barbara. I wish Mother and Dad could have seen the things we have now. They thought things were amazing back in their day. Wish everybody lived together in one village like they used to a hundred years ago. But I always think that same thought. Wonder what use it is thinking the same things over and over." Meanwhile the news is going on and on and she's not listening.

I know how she feels. I have that same wish, too, to be with others like me.

Somebody knocks. She wobbles to the door hanging on to the furniture and walls. She says, "Oops" several times. She left the fire on under the kettle. I don't see how she gets along here by herself. Somebody must check on her every now and then. At least I hope so.

While she's at the door, I step into the kitchen and turn off the stove. I listen.

It's a policeman.

"Ma'am? You all right?"

"I'm fine."

He doesn't say anything about me escaping. I suppose he doesn't want to worry her.

We'll check 'round later. But don't hesitate to call if you see anything suspicious."

"I will."

"You be sure now."

After, she locks the door again. She mutters. "I'm so old I don't suppose it matters one way or the other—what happens to me." Then, "I must remember to water the trees. How long has it been? I can't keep track of anything anymore."

(If she forgets, I'II do it.)

She doesn't finish her tea. She goes back in the living room and lies down on the sofa. Gets up again and brings a fresh glass of water. Lies down. Gets up and turns on tapes for learning French. Lies down and falls asleep.

I make myself a cheese sandwich. I don't drink any of the juice, there's not much left. Not much of anything left.

The cat (there is one) comes out and watches me but won't go near the cream. It's a marmalade tabby. I say, "Hello, Red." She won't come close. I reach to pet her but she backs away. I wonder if she can smell that I'm alien. I've seen dogs go crazy when they get close to one of us—attack or cower. I've always had trouble with dogs. Far as I can tell, cats don't do that.

I search the house again, I examine what must be the daughter's room. It's larger than the old lady's and fancier. There's a new bed and a white dresser. Yellow walls. I'll spend the night in here. I like this sunny yellow.

The old lady keeps on sleeping. I wonder about her supper. There isn't much food around. I wonder if I dare go out and get more. And would I get locked out? I'll unlock a window. One that's hidden in bushes so I can go in and out without being seen, certainly nobody will expect the escapee to be shopping at the local grocery store. But I'll have to use her money.

She has some good magazines and books. Mother didn't want us to read their things but we managed to anyway. Mother tried to write books for us herself, but she wasn't very good at It, She even illustrated them, Her drawings didn't make me want to live back home though I pretended they did, ·

You've never tasted anything like those little ground berries. You've never seen a real sunset. There's moonshine every night. There's no such thing as dark, And sometimes both moons at the same time." She'd always say that last on a particularly beautiful moonlit night. I got tired of hearing it. If I said anything good about life here, she always said, "You're turning out just like them. Besides, you don', know what you're talking about, Someday we'll go home and then you'll see."

I sit in the daughter's room and read. I leave the door slightly open. I skip around from *Discover* magazine, *National Geographic,* and a book on wild flowers of the area. I don't hear her coming until I hear, "Whoops." And then, "Oh, I left the door open. I must be gelling curdled. Addled that is."

She shuts the door. I drop down behind the bed with my magazines, but she opens the door again and takes a look around. Says, "The spread is all mussed. Did I leave it that way?"

In she comes to straighten it and sees me, there on the floor. And there she goes, down again. She must have heart trouble. I reach to catch her and keep her from coming down too hard.

I put her on the bed. Then I remember how she forgot me when she woke up that first time, and I carry her into the couch again. I get a cold wet cloth and glass of water again.

But this lime she comes to in a few minutes, sees me, says, "Sam?"

I help her drink. I say, "Yes."

Then she says, "You're not Sam."

"No. I'm Norman. Would you like some more tea? It'll be good for you. You rest. I'II gel it."

I make a fresh cup and help her sit up to drink.

"Still dizzy?"

"A little."

"Are you hungry? I'll get you something to eat."

"No, no. I'm fine."

"You should eat. I'll bring you something."

"Who are you? Why are you here?"

"I'm here to help. Let me get you something."

I heat up a can of chicken noodle soup. (There', only one can of soup left.)

Though my taste is probably different. I choose the bowl as carefully as she chose her teacup. When I come back she looks to be asleep again, but I wake her. I think she should eat.

When I see how she drips all over herself, I feed her. She keeps looking at me ... not suspiciously, but with curiosity.

"Norman? Who? Where', Rosemary?"

"She'll be here."

I help her to the bedroom, Without me she'd have to hang on to the furniture. I help her on to the bed and take her shoes off, cover her with the small blanket at the foot. "Call me if you need me. I'll be in your daughter's room, I'll keep the door open so I can hear."

I don', want to eat the last of the soup. I eat more cheese and a shriveled apple and go to bed.

In the morning I wake to the sound of the old lady rattling about in the kitchen. What woke me was her loud "Oops." I wonder what she dropped or spilled. But mostly I wonder if she remembers me.

I slept well. Better than In jail with the light shining all night, but I wake hungry. I'm going shopping.

I peek into the kitchen cautiously, I don't want her in a faint again.

"Ma'am? Good morning. Remember me? Nonnan?"

Thank goodness she does.

"Oh, yes. I felt so much safer all night with you here,"

"I'm glad. I need to get us more food. Lock the door behind me and let me in when I get back."

She says, "Take the car. I don't drive anymore," but I think not. It's probably known all over this little town which car is hers and that she never drives it.

I don't tell her I left the daughter's window open just in case. I don't tell her I took some of her money.

I'm wearing her husband's shirt and I put on the floppy hat that will cover my face a bit. There's a small backpack there but it's too distinctive. I'll just have to carry the things home in the plastic bags.

Before I leave I check on the magazines for her name. I might need to know that. Ruth. Ruth Hill.

I get three more canned soups. I get a cooked chicken, eggs, strawberries, (Mother said the berries of our world were better, but I don't believe it when it comes to homegrown strawberries), apples and a few breakfast bars for me for when I take off into the mountains.

When I get back she won't open the door. Says, "I don't know any Norman."

"I brought you groceries. More soup. I said I would. At least open the door and take them in. I'll stay outside. "

"That's just a ploy to get in. I'm not stupid."

"Ruth. I made you chicken soup last night. You said you slept better with me here."

"No such thing."

"I've got strawberries, eggs. Ruth. I've got a cooked chicken. You're running out of food."

"Rosemary will bring more on Monday."

It was Monday yesterday. Nobody came.

"I's Tuesday. I'm the one bringing your food now."

"Oh."

But she doesn't open up.

"The police said there was a prowler sleeping in my sagebrush."

"I slept in your daughter's room, remember? I brought you soup and chicken."

"Oh."

Long pause.

"Ruth?"

Just when I'm thinking to go around and in by the window, she opens the door.

She watches me make chicken sandwiches for lunch and, for her, warm milk with vanilla in it.

It's not too hot yet. I sit her out on the porch so she can watch the quail and ravens. Later I see the cop come. I don't hear what they say. But he leaves.

Later still, when I turn on the cooler and bring her in, she says, "Rosemary reads to me."

"What would you like?"

"Something out of *Discover* magazine. The latest issue is in the living room. We were reading about Saturn. I do like Saturn. We have binoculars around here somewhere if you'd like to take a look tonight."

"I would."

"I can show you where to look."

She's not like Mother. She likes being here. It seems Rosemary took her out for walks Monday evenings now and then. Do I dare? Well, I will anyway. She shouldn't sit around all day. When she's alone I'll bet she spends most of her time lying on the couch sleeping to those French tapes.

We go after supper when it cools down. There's several canes by the front door. She picks one. She leads but on the way back she gets lost. Lord knows where we'd have ended up. I warn her never to walk by herself but she insists she'd be fine except she's glad she has me anyway.

So now I've been here six days and nobody has come to help her. Nobody has brought her groceries. I'm wondering about Rosemary and about the old lady's daughter. I don't see how she'll get along without me. I even see some improvement in her awareness in the short time I've been here. I think she's eating better and sleeping better. She's not so shaky. When we walk in the evenings she seems stronger and she usually knows the way home. The cops come and speak to her every day. She always says things are fine. She doesn't mention me. Maybe she suspects something about me but likes me even so.

There's another call from her daughter. They talk a long time. Mostly it's about her grandchild and mostly the daughter speaks so I don't hear anything but Ruth's answers now and then. She says she's getting along fine. She says she feels better than ever. I'm sure that's true.

We watch TV every night, and I read to her. I'm enjoying myself more than I have since I lost my family. Actually I enjoy living as one of the natives. Also it reminds me of the last days with Mother, though Mother faded away fast and of course didn't dare go to any of their doctors, while this old lady is getting stronger every day and less addled.

One day at breakfast, she looks at me ... studies me .... I see her thinking. (My mustache is coming back. My hair is growing out) She says, "Who pays you?"

I don't know what to say.

"I don't think anybody does. Where did you come from."

I guess there's nothing for it. This is it. I say, "Jail."

"You escaped."

"Yes."

"You're the one who hid in my yard that first day."

"Yes."

She thinks.

"Is your name really Norman?"

"As much as any other. Actually my mother called me Lorpas."

"Funny name."

But then we spend the day just as usual. The policeman comes to check on her and she says everything is fine.

Later, on our evening walk, holding tight to my elbow, she says, "Norman. I'm glad you're here."

She knows the names of the mountains that loom above the town. She remembers the trails she used to hike and her favorite places up there. She teaches me the names of plants and flowers and birds. If she doesn't know them we look them up In her books. I find her binoculars and we look at stars. She names the constellations. She looks out from her porch and admires the clouds. Every day she checks on her apricot tree and her apple tree. I'm thinking how nice it would have been to have had her as my mother. After all, I'm here, born here, been here all my life, I should have learned about this place and enjoyed it the way she does.

And she's funny. She laughs at being old, lit her dowager's hump, and her wrinkled face. She says she used to be six inches taller. That still wouldn't be very tall.

And then they come, my people—to rescue me. They home in on my underarm implant. First I feel the implant as if it's burning me. Then I feel my body buzzing and my whole arm hurts. I don't know how I know, but I know it's them, my people, finally come to rescue us. Finally what mother was waiting for.

They're wearing our usual: bright shirts and baseball caps, mustaches.... There are three. I recognize them right away. They have the tubes to send me home. Mother told me about those little silver tubes that can send you home or burn you depending on the trigger used.

Ruth and I are on the porch. We were watching strange red clouds. No doubt that was them.

They're clearly odd ... alien. Barrel-chested, as am I.

We stand up and Ruth grabs my elbow. She says, "Who are you people?"

But they haven't bothered to learn our language. They babble out my kind of talk, but I've forgotten everything except the phrase Mother made us memorize. But that was: I'm one of the people of one eighty nine, and, take me home.

I'm ashamed of them. They look flabby and pale and ridiculous. How could anyone have taken us for tourists?

Ruth says, "What do you want?"

I move in front of her. I say, "No!"

Two grab me. Ruth pulls me back. They talk but I can't tell what they're saying. Their voices are guttural. Mine is, too, but I seldom think about it. Plenty of people here have voices like mine.

Ruth is trying to protect me, as I am her. She's pushing at them. Punching them. We get in each other's way.

They laugh. They don't realize how strong they are compared to these people and especially compared to an old lady. They pull her away and I hear her arm crack. I hear her cry out.

How can they do that?

I use the freeze. I use it as if I'd always used it—had practiced it on more than just one mouse. As if it was my first instinct instead of what I'd always kept myself from doing.

They pause. It's working. Except I can only hold one at a time. They're laughing again. Even more. I think they'll fall down from laughing.

I go crazy just like Mother was always afraid I'd do. I yell. I fight. I'm in better shape than they are. Also I know how to fight and they don't. I hit and kickbox. I use all the strength I never dared use. As they fall, they disappear, back where they came from I suppose. Except the third one. Before I can get to him, he turns a tube on me and on Ruth. Then he disappears.

I'm burned, but not too badly. Ruth is.... I see right away she can't be alive.

I suppose they though... I *know* they thought, as Mother would have: It's just cne of *them,* she doesn't matter.

Where they stood are three man-shaped clouds. They dissipate quickly.

I carry Ruth inside and put her on the couch. I straighten her arm. She hardly looks like Ruth anymore. I cover her with the afghan she made. The days are hot, but the nights are cold. I touch her burned cheek with my lips. It's not Ruth.

I gather up food into the little backpack that's by the door. I take a poncho. I take a cane. I open the door and let the cat go free. "Come on, Red. We're on our own." She heads for her favorite tree, while I head up the road that goes toward the trail. I'm not lost now. I take Ruth's favorite hike, She said, "Walk up steeply for a mile from the trailhead, and after that there'll be a cliff, pass under it, take the rocky switchbacks up the far side. Soon there'll be a lovely hanging valley with glittery pebbles full of mica. Farther on, cross the stream on the stepping stones, after that, the lake called Long. On the way down the other side, you'll round a comer and it will suddenly open out to a view of snowy mountains all in a row. It'll be so beautiful you'll shout.

***Asimov's Science Fiction*,** December 2005

Quill

Mother says, "Don't sing. Don't dance. Don't wear red." She says, "Simplify!" She says, "We don't eat bugs. We don't eat crawdads." Aren't they simple enough? She says, "We...our kind...doesn't do *that*, doesn't do *this*." We heard it in the egg—so to speak. So to speak, that is.

We do eat eggs.

Sometimes when we're playing too vigorously, Mother says, "No high notes."

Mother says we're unique. We don't know whether to feel left out or included in with special people. We keep wondering, if we climbed high enough up or far enough down, we'd find another group like us just as special and if they'd be all right to make friends with. We plan to go find out but right now the littlest one of us would need help.

A stranger came out of the woods and stared at us. We were dressed right, yet he watched as if we were strange. We acted normal. We played human-being games just to prove we were completely proper. I'm too old for this kind of play but the little ones like me to do it. I was the man this time though I'm female. I stamped around and took big steps. But how many times have we seen a man?

But this stranger isn't the first though he's come the closest to our houses. Not long ago we saw three men, climbing up along the stream. At first we didn't know what they were. We thought some sort of humped back creatures. But then they took their packs off and we saw they were men. They didn't see us though we followed them all the way up.

They had beards. We laughed but only afterwards so they wouldn't hear. Mother wondered what was so funny. We made up something else even sillier than beards.

Tom though. He's getting hair on his upper lip. I saw him cutting it off with little scissors he stole from Mother's sewing kit. They don't work very well for that so there's some of it still there. That's called a mustache.

This other man that stared.... We saw him first from across the lake, the one we call golden because of the golden eyes of the frogs. Mother doesn't like us to call it that. The idea of gold makes her gloomy. The river we call silver, though that's where gold is. We found some but we knew better than to tell Mother. We hardly tell her anything in case what we do is, "Just isn't done." Or maybe, "Just isn't talked about."

We have to be out here by ourselves so as not to be tempted by the way other people live. We might do what they do and, "They're not our kind." But we couldn't be a different kind if we wanted to. We don't know how.

Mother says, "Every day is a lesson." We knew that a long time ago. Jumping rock to rock is a lesson especially when we fall. Not testing stepping stones before you step on them—that's a lesson. Watching lightening strike the tallest trees though not always. Building a little hut of reeds. Making fires in the rain. You have to know how.

Mother doesn't know any of those lessons. I'll bet she couldn't even make a fire when it *wasn't* raining. I wonder if she even knows how to swim. I've never seen her near the lake except to gather rushes for mats or cat tails for supper. Those, our kind is allowed to eat. She hates to get her feet muddy.

We have secret places for dancing and singing. We stole a pan for a drum. We have scraping sticks. We clack stones. We only make our music beside the stream so as to hide the sound just in case Mother should come out that far, though that's unlikely.

Morning is lessons. Numbers mostly. You can't fault numbers. Some of us are not good at them. If we complain, Mother says, "That's the way it is." Spelling.... I'm not good at that. Geology I'm good at. It's all around us. I like to know how things got this way.

Mother wants us to know things such as honesty and generosity, but we had that all figured out on our own a long time ago. We know what's fair and what's not. We know you have to give to get. Sometimes we argue all afternoon about the rules of whatever we're playing and never get to play it, so we know we have to give up and give in.

Afternoons, when Mother takes a nap, we rush out before she can think of something else for us to do. We don't come back till dusk and sometimes later. Now and then some of us spend all night in the woods. We've built ourselves little houses of reeds or twigs and branches. We know all the caves and cozy piles of rocks. She doesn't worry if a few of us are missing. We wonder, though, if she knows how many we are.

Everyday first thing we're supposed to give thanks for what we have but also that we have but little. Thanks for beans and corn and apples, and especially for living right here in a safe place. And thanks to Mother for the simple life. And thanks to Mother for Mother.

That stranger walked into our part of the forest, sat down and stared. He has paper and pencil. He might be writing or drawing. We can't tell from here.

But we quacked when we should have cawed.

He knows there are no ducks around. We came out in plain view then. Across the lake from him. That's when we did what people do. Except instead of talking, we quacked.

It's not far across the lake at that point. He got a good view. He watched the whole time. He must like our looks. We liked his looks, too. We liked his big hat. His shirt is red. Except for our collections of feathers and flowers, we don't have any red.

Tom is the best at everything. Of course, since he's the oldest. He dances now. Just look at Tom's fast footwork and how he can leap. The man stares. He even looks at us through things Tom says are binoculars. And he has another thing. Tom says that's a camera and he's taking our picture. We're seen pictures in our books. He'll have us on paper to take home to his house.

Where the river comes down to the lake, you have to cross on the stepping stones to get to our side. It looks as if that man is coming over. There's a couple of wobbly stones we set up on purpose. We didn't want Mother crossing without us knowing it.

Those flat stones look as if they're there to be stepped on, but they're really there to trip you up. So down he goes right in the middle of the stream, backpack and all. I'm not happy about him getting his paper wet. How much paper is there in the world? I'll ask Tom. Or maybe I'll ask this man.

We save our laughing for later. We only caw a little bit.

He sloshes out.

He knows that was on purpose—that those two middle rocks were set there so as to teeter.

He takes off his big black hat and empties out the water, puts it back on. Then he sits on the bank and examines his ankle.

We crowd around and look, too. His ankle is already starting to swell and turn black. Others of us skip back and forth across the stream. We don't avoid the center stones, we just go really fast over them.

He has tape just for this. He wraps up his ankle, twisting the tape here and there. He's better at it than Tom ever was with our sprained ankles. Here's another lesson for all of us.

What if we bring this man to our little home-made huts or our cave? We could hide him from Mother and have him to ourselves. Or what if we bring him home to Mother?

When he gets up, we get up, too. He limps. He follows our path from the stepping stones. If we don't watch out he'll be right at Mother's in ten minutes. Well, at this rate, twenty.

Tom says, "Lean on me," but he won't. Tom says he's angry. Tom says, "If we had fathers that's who he'd be limping off to see. He wants us punished."

We do wonder about fathers. Why don't we have them? Even Tom doesn't know and Mother won't talk about it.

We can let him limp along the path to home, or sidetrack him to our cave. Tom says, "Let him go on home. We'll get to see what Mother does."

Pretty soon our regular houses come into view. They're good houses, not only thatched roofs, but thatched sides, too. Maybe we shouldn't call it thatch. It's made of tule rushes. Mother's house is made of stone and is much bigger. Tom says she made it by herself. He remembers thinking he was helping, though now he doesn't think he could have helped much. He was only three or four.

At our clearing, the man stops and looks.

Chickens in the yard have already cackled a warning that a stranger is coming—or a fox. We know Mother's hiding behind the door of her house looking out the little peep hole. I'll bet she has the bar down.

The man keeps standing at the edge of our clearing, just looking.

Usually we hear the clanking of her loom, but lately she's been making moccasins. The simple life seems awfully complicated to Tom. The rest of us don't know any other way, though we try to guess. Tom says you don't even have to build a fire or light the lamps. He says clothes and shoes are just there, and he told us all about electricity.

"Mother!" That's Tom. He goes to the door. "Don't worry. He's hurt."

"Tell him to go away."

"We want him."

"He's not the right sort."

"Come and see for yourself."

"I can tell from here."

"Please come. He can hardly walk. He has paper and pencil."

"We don't need it."

How can she say that? It's what I want the most.

"And he has a camera."

We hear the bar fall away and the door opens. Out she comes.

She's pretty much covered up, big baggy shirt. She's the only one we know of with breasts though I seem to be getting something like that now. I hide it from the others. I wish she'd give me a shirt like the one she's wearing. If I get any lumpier I'll need that. It's a wonder I even know about them, but we do have books with pictures. Mother gave me a talk. It sounded silly. I don't know whether to believe her or not.

Usually Mother dresses so you can tell more about her body. Now she's different. And her hair is pulled back tight like it never is. She looks angry and worried. We just can't keep track of all the things we're not supposed to do. As we think up new things, new ones keep turning out to be bad. It even surprises us older ones. But now we do know. We never should have let the man come this far. Mother knows to blame Tom and me.

Tom and I are getting sick of not knowing more things about more places. It's a good thing Tom once was someplace else or we wouldn't even know there was another place. He came up here with Mother before any of us were born. He says Mother was looking for the simple life. He says that's what we're doing now.

He remembers lots of things from before. He had a father who left and Mother went around punching things when she wasn't lying on the couch. Finally she came up here with Tom. She said she didn't like the world the way it is and she was going to live a different way. But Tom doesn't know where the rest of us come from. He doesn't remember me coming. Suddenly I was here.

The man must like Mother. He looks relieved. As if everything is all right now.

When Mother steps out, Wren, right away, grabs Mother's skirt and Loon hides behind her. Mother couldn't save us from anything. Only Tom could do that. You'd think they'd know by now.

Mother looks horrified. "You can't stay here. Tom, take the camera."

"I've sprained my ankle—maybe broken it. I need to impose on you. I don't think I'll be able to climb down for a while."

"You can't stay!"

Tom says, "We'll keep him with us. You'll hardly know he's here."

"He can't stay. You know that as well as I do. Think for Heaven's sake!"

The rest of us say, "Why?" but Tom says, "All right, all right. We'll send him on his way."

We didn't know Tom would be so cruel nor Mother either.

The man looks upset. He hands Tom the camera. He says, "It got wet."

Tom gives it to Mother. Mother opens it and pulls out the insides.

The man says, "I can't climb down now."

Mother says, "You have to."

"Can I at least stay the night?"

"That's impossible."

We all say (except Tom), "Why not?"

But right away the man turns and starts hobbling down the trail.

Tom goes to help him and this time the man lets him. Tom is exactly as tall as the man.

A little ways down we turn off the path. Tom tells the man, "Only a little farther now." Then, to the younger ones, "If anybody says anything to Mother, I'll take your gold."

I know what's happening. It's off to our cave, sitting around the campfire, and crawdads for supper. Maybe even frog's legs. Nothing better. Nothing more fun.

Our cave has thick beds of ferns. Much better than our beds at home. And we have really soft rabbit skin blankets we made ourselves. Tom and I sewed them up. We chipped out little pockets in the walls so we could have feathers and flowers all over. But it's shallow. When it rains the rain blows all the way in, but when it's clear, if you lie with your head towards the entrance, you can see the stars as you go to sleep. Sometimes the moon's so bright it wakes you up when it pops up over the mountain. There's a sort of porch in front where we made a fireplace and put logs around it to sit on. That porch has a good view over the whole valley.

I say, "Isn't this nice?" The man is impressed.

We build a little fire and send everybody out to catch things or dig things up. They're so excited to be doing it for the man. On the way back they pick big stalks—taller than they are—of fireweed in bloom just for looks.

He can't stop saying, Thank you, and keeps asking: What can he do for us? We say, don't worry, we'll think of things. He asks our names. His is Hazlet but people call him Haze. He asks our ages but we're not sure. Asks where our fathers are? We say we don't have any.

"One mother for all these little ones?"

We don't know. Sometimes little ones just appear—in the chicken coop. Mother takes them in.

We talk about paper. He'll set his out to dry tomorrow. We'll help. He's going to draw us all as presents to each of us. And he'll give us all the left-over paper when he leaves.

Tom and I stay out all night with the man but we make the little ones go home.

Haze asks a lot of questions. Some are the same ones we ask ourselves, like, "Where's our father? How long have we lived up here? Why are we here in the middle of nowhere?

(We think it's as much a place as any place else.)

We tell him Mother doesn't want us to get to be like other people.

He thinks that can't be the only reason, though he sees her point. He says we're turning out a lot better than some.

We like him. We say, "Stay. We need another grown-up. The only one we know is Mother."

He says both I and Tom are not far off from being grown.

Of course he has to stay until his ankle gets better, but we want him after.

Next day first thing he spreads the paper out to dry with a rock on each one. We help. It hurts him to walk so he mostly crawls. Then he picks good pieces of charcoal out of the fireplace. He'll show us how to use them for drawing.

The little ones come rushing down. Some wanted to come so badly they didn't even have their breakfast.

As soon as the paper dries, Haze draws. He draws me and Tom first, and then Henny and Drake. Then the little ones sitting in a row on the logs on the stone porch. Sometimes he draws with the charcoal he picked out of the fireplace. "They'll smear," he says. "Be careful."

We hang the drawings at the back of the cave, high so the little ones won't mess them up. Me he draws again in pencil and rolls it up and put in his pack.

We want to show them to Mother, we wonder if she's seen anything like it, but we don't dare. It might be one of those things we're not supposed to do. Besides, the man is supposed to be gone by now.

Haze shows us how to use the binoculars. We look around at everything. To the side we see those three men...or, rather, their little tents—up along the silver river. We're good at taking turns. When not looking, we draw. He gives us lessons. I'm good at it already. I thought I would be.

We have lots of days of drawing and looking while Haze gets better. He even shows us how to make paper out of weeds. Lumpy but better than nothing.

Tom makes a good strong staff for Haze. Haze says that'll be good even when his ankle is better. The rest of the time we gather cattail roots and lily roots and Solomon seal along with the frogs legs and crawdads.

Then one time when Haze is much better he says, "I always wanted to go up to your glacier. Have you ever gone that high?"

We haven't but we've thought about it. "We see lights up there sometimes."

"Good, we'll go. You and Tom. The little ones can spend the day with your mother."

"They won't unless we threaten to take away their gold."

"Gold?"

But we're not thinking gold, we're thinking how we'll be getting out of here, farther than we ever have. We're so happy we put out our traps and catch rabbits. Mother doesn't need to know about it. We stretch the skin for ourselves and dry the meat for our trip.

Tom and I skip morning lessons all the time now and stay down with Haze. We're learning more from him in just a few weeks than we ever did from Mother. He shows us all about maps on his maps. We pick out what looks like the best route up to the glacier. He shows us all about his compass. He thinks it odd that we never saw a flashlight till now. He's got two, one you fit on your head and another you hold.

We start out while it's still dark. Haze wears the flashlight on his head and goes first. He gives the other to me and I go last. Tom and I each carry a little rabbit skin blanket. Haze has a bag for sleeping. He has the cane Tom made him and his maps. His backpack is full. He even brought paper in case he wants to draw. He has this waterproof stuff that he wrapped his food in before. Now he wraps the paper in it. He feels about paper as we do. We'd rather have paper than gold. He says he would, too.

We top our pass and dip into the next valley at sunrise, or what would have been sunrise if it hadn't been for the mountain in the way. This mountain are much higher than the ones near us. That's why you can see their glacier from our house.

Tom and I had hoped to find people in this valley, but there's nobody. Still the path goes on. From here you get a really good view of the glacier. It's been melting away. Haze gives us a lesson on glaciers. There's a lot of debris at the sides. That's called lateral moraine, at the end it's called terminal. I already knew that though never saw it until now.

The glacier's a lot bigger than we thought. Back home we can only see the top. We had no idea it had all this junk around it and came down so far into this other valley.

We spend the night right where we are, part way down the second pass, and by afternoon next day, we're at the glacier and its river trickling out.

This valley has a lot fewer trees in it and what there are, are all stunted. Haze points out odd stuff. To us everything is odd. He says, "Look at the peculiar shapes of those rocks. They look like a whole row of skyscrapers."

They sure seem like they're scraping the sky, but we know the sky is way, way, way up, all the way to the stars.

We climb the sideways debris to get a good look around. Then Haze sees what he thinks might be the mouth of a cave.

He tells us to stay back but we don't want to. "Why come all this way and not see everything?"

"All right but stay behind me."

It's not a cave but a doorway of some sort into a big, long, long bluish white house, hugging up close to the glacier. Until you get close, it just looks like more glacier.

At the door, Haze doesn't even knock. He just opens it in a careful sneaky way.

Mother never likes that. She wants us to know how to be courteous. Tom and I look at each other. Haze doesn't know how to be polite.

Haze opens the door all the way and we go in. Tom and I don't want to be sneaky but we don't know what else to do except go with him.

It's warm in there. We were getting cold. We had wrapped our rabbit skin blankets around us. Haze is wearing his jacket filled with little feathers. He showed us. "Down is the warmest there is," he said, "but you know that already." Only we didn't. He wanted me to trade my rabbit skins with his jacket so I'd be warm as we crossed the high places but I said maybe later, and we should all have a turn with it.

Through that door, we aren't anywhere at all but there's another door. We open that one and it's even warmer. It's large and dim. At first we don't know what the room is all about, then we see it's a whole room full of eggs. Big ones. There must be ten or fifteen. They're nested in white stuff. Warm air blows over us and them. Tiny feathers are flying around. Not a lot, just here and there.

Haze keeps saying, "My God. My God."

We're not as surprised as he is, after all we gather chicken's eggs everyday, just not such big ones. And there's feathers in our hen house, too, but these are all the ones Haze calls "down." They're like what's on my head but mine are black. Tom told me that when I first came, mine started out yellow.

Then we're even more surprised. Haze takes off his jacket grabs the closest egg, wraps it in the jacket, and we hurry out. It's so big it'll be a meal for more than just us three. But we have plenty of food with us. Besides, no pan to cook it in.

It's not like our usual eggs. It has a leathery shell.

Haze holds the egg close to his chest to keep it warm. We go back to the edge of the valley.

Tom says, "Are you going to hatch it?"

"Well I'm not going to eat it. Did you think I would?"

We like Haze. We didn't think he would but we weren't sure.

It's getting dark. It's too late to start home now. We build a little fire and eat our dried rabbit. Haze keeps the egg in his lap and takes out paper and sketches the big room full of eggs from memory. He also marks on the map where the cave is. Tom and I curl up by the fire. I fall asleep right away but then I hear Haze ask, "Does your mother know all this?"

That's what I was wondering. I think she does. But I won't say. Tom says, "Maybe."

And I know…I *think* I know what's in this egg. My little brother or little sister I suppose.

Haze says, "It's a smart way to get a lot of them…of you…in a hurry." Then: "Maybe only takes one mother for the lot."

Just when I'm falling back to sleep he says, "Not clones either. Easy to see that."

The egg hatches next day when we're on the way home. The cutest little thing I ever saw. All golden. It's cute even before it dries off. It's one of the scaly ones with feathered cap like I have though I don't have many scales. Just in a few spots. It's a little on the ducklike side. Much more than me. I never cared either way. We don't know yet if boy or girl. Mother can tell right away.

Since I'm a girl I think I ought to get to carry it, but Haze thinks it's safer if he does.

"What do they eat?"

"Just regular food. Like everybody else. We can give it some of our rabbit. Look, it has all it's baby teeth."

Now Haze is saying, "My God, my God, my God," again, then, "I suppose they crashed."

He says Mother is right to keep us away from the rest of the world. He says, again, he has to admit we're, all of us, very nice children.

He jumps from one idea to another. He says, except for Tom we're all half breeds. He says, "It's a good way to endure here. He says, "Maybe they think we won't kill any creatures that are half our own." Then he says, "When has that ever stopped us? Killing our own is what we do best."

Haze says I was hatched up there. He says he can't imagine what kind of creature my father is.

I get to feed the baby. (Those sharp little teeth are better at chewing rabbit than mine.) I get to have his first smile. And I get to sleep with him. Haze wraps us both in his down jacket. He keeps the fire going all night. I don't think he sleeps much. I don't sleep well either, but that's because the baby is wiggly. It doesn't seem to know it's night. Or maybe it's been sleeping so much in the egg so that now it wants to do things.

One of those funny things Mother told me turns out to be true. There's blood. So not only do I have to figure out how to keep the messes of the baby from getting all over but I have to figure out what to do about my mess. I take pieces from our rabbit skins. I pretend it's all for the baby but some is for me. I wonder if those breast things are any bigger than they were. I hope not. But I guess Mother is right about that, too. They will get bigger. This baby, though, is one of the ones that doesn't need them.

I lag behind though Haze carries the baby and we've already eaten most of our food so nobody has much to carry. I'm cold even in Haze's jacket. My stomach feels funny. I sit down on a rock to rest and think.

But somebody is coming—up from behind. A tall creature with long thin legs that bend the way fox legs do. At first I think it's wearing a beautiful feathered hat, red and gold, but as it gets closer it see it's a topknot and that what I think is a black and red suit is feathers all over. When it sees me, the topknot lifts higher, widens. It's irridescent. There's blue and green in it, too. The creature spreads it's arms. There's a row of red along its sides. I never saw anything so beautiful.

Someone has been in the nest. Our soft warmth has been intruded upon. Entered by they of those that can't smell. They think we won't know. As if we don't smell everything that happens.

Worst of all, my own little loved one, on the edge of hatching, stolen. A precious being in the making.

Strange and stranger land of much pain and so little softness in it. So few spots in which to hesitate and love.

I go to speak of my love for my own kind and even for their kind if need be speaking of it. Say it with nodding of head sky to ground, sky to ground, as if their yes and not sideways, east and west.

I lean forward so as to speed. Also lean so as to catch the scent. I smell not only my little one but also my biggest one, and she's ready to lay. Our first layer among the half-ones. A precious dear. I can't wait to speak of the future of us all. So much depends on her willingness, though why not? Offspring this way is so much easier than the way of mammals.

My tender feelings come with the good smell of myself on her. I breathe of myself all along the trail. Strange and dangerous as this place is, I'm happy. Strange as even my own is, I'm happy.

But what of these harsh creatures? Even without moving from our wreckage, we've seen what they do—seen from their own technology. We know who they are. We've heard both war and music. Dance. At least they dance.

Now a whole new way to egg which only our knowledge makes possible. Not as pleasurable but necessary. But here's my daughter, though she, my dear one, is more of them than of me.

Our kind is not unknown here though they never had a chance to develop. Had they come to full flower, we'd have landed among friends instead of among these odd intelligent mammals. It's too bad we didn't come earlier to help those like us achieve their full potential. We could have egged with them and raised them to our level.

Strange that this world took such a different turn. Hardly logical that eggless rat-like things would grow so large. Though even our own mammals get into everything, and some are smart enough to have made themselves into the little companions of our kitchens and the darlings of the nurseries.

I have wished my first daughter could be beautiful— more like me. Still I love her. I can be in love by smell alone. So much love I found it hard to bring her down to her mother. And when she smiled, like ours always do—the first conciliation, the first appeasment—I found myself in every way, her doting father.

It was Quat called us. The intruding mammals didn't see him in the dim nesting light. One of them was half us—Quat could smell that—and two were of their kind. One a full grown male not known to us. Quat said that male knows too much. Everything is vulnerable.

I've watched the offspring dance. Life will be hard for them, but at least they have the joy of dance. Now, to my own young one, I'll display. I'll strut. Though with these creatures it seems it's more the female's role to lure with colors and tall shoes. Still I *will* display.

It calls, "Quill, Quill." It sounds like quacks but I'm used to that from some of the little ones, I can tell it's my name. It has a loud echoing voice. I don't know how far Tom and Haze have gotten but for sure they'll hear. For sure they'll come, though I wonder if I want them to.

At first it doesn't come close. It stands, silent, below me on the trail so as to let me get used to it. I look. That's what it wants me to do. Its scales only show at its neck and clawed hands and feet. It turns sideways and shows off it's topknot, up and out and then down, then up and out again. None of the little ones have anything at all like that topknot though I realize now that some have the beginnings of one.

It comes closer. It makes more quacking sounds. Again, not too different from the way lots of the little ones talk. It says, "I'm your father."

I shout, "*Yes*!" He's so beautiful I can't help it. I've been wondering and wondering all this time. I can't conceive of a better father than this one.

"May I sit beside you for talking?"

I move to make room. He sits on my rock and we both look back towards the glacier.

He touches my hand with his and it feels terrible. His claws prick and his skin is scaly. That's is all right except when he turns it the wrong way it scratches. Some of the little ones are like this, too. I hide that I don't like it like I do with them.

He says he loves me. I can see that in the way he looks at me. He calls me consort but I don't know what that means. He says I'm old enough now. I don't know what that means, either. But maybe I do. It's about the crazy things Mother told me. Which are coming true.

Then he asks about the baby. "He hatched. Did he? I saw where it happened. Or was that a…killing?"

"No, we wouldn't. I wouldn't let them. He hatched. He's fine."

I hope so. I think Haze will keep him safe. But Haze seemed pretty worried. He never stopped saying, My God and he couldn't sleep. Maybe I should have made him let me carry the baby.

"Did the baby smile at you first?"

"I guess so.

"Are you caught in his smile?"

"Yes, but I liked him even before he smiled."

"Excellent!"

Then he grabs my wrist, hard. It hurts.

"Come. You'll like it. Keep warm in the nursery. My friends will make you happy."

I try to twist away, but he's too strong, and twisting makes his hand scratch all the more. I think how glad I am that I hardly have any scales at all except a little on my back and the backs of my hands.

"I saw how you were. You like little ones. Come and make more."

"No!"

"We're from a far place. We crashed. We thought the glacier, so white and blue, was a dump of discarded nursery feathers. We slammed and slid and died. We can't go home. We made our conveyance into a nest. Had we even one female of our own kind, it would have changed everything. But here was your mother. Willing. Like you are."

But I'm yelling, "No. No!" and I'm yelling for Haze.

"You've no place on this world but with us. They'll never accept you. They hate the different. They never heard of one like you."

"Is that true?"

"The whole world is them."

"It's not. It can't be. How can that be?"

"My dear, dear one, it *is*! You're the first of your kind. Your mother has kept you hidden from the world so as to save you for us and save you for yourself."

He's loosened his grip and I manage to twist away and start running—up the trail towards Tom and Haze, but he catches me with no trouble. His legs are so long.

But Tom and Haze have turned back. They see me struggling. I yell for them to help.

Haze has something he never showed us. I've heard of that, it's like Mother's rifle but smaller. Pop, pop, and my father falls. Just like that. Into a fancy bundle of shiny black and red and iridescent. His hand still grips me. Haze has to pry open his fingers.

Tom sits me down and gives me a drink from the canteen. Haze is looking over my father's body. Examining everything, the clawed hands and feet, the topknot. I see him looking at the sex, which is mostly covered with down. Then Haze actually sits down and starts to draw him. I'm not sure how I feel about this. It's true, he's beautiful, but Haze isn't drawing a portait like he did of us. It's more diagrams, my father's different parts all laid out, a hand, then a foot, the topknot, the beak.

But I want to get away from here. I want to get home tonight. I need to talk to Mother—mostly about myself. I didn't listen when she talked about blood. It sounded too ridiculous. And how come my father knew that right away? Or maybe it was these lumps on my chest, made him say I'm ready for egging.

But I'm shaky and I do need to rest. I don't say, lets go. Not even to Tom.

We're so late we have to camp again. And practically right away, as soon as we leave my father's body. Haze says we should camp off the trail and hide. We find a place in among rocks.

I'm still all trembly. I just found a father and lost him right away. Some of the little ones squeek when they're sad and don't have tears, ever, but I'm one of the ones that cries. I cry but I don't think the others know. I sleep with the baby. I need to. I need something warm and cuddly to hug.

The baby isn't as wiggly as he was when he was so happy to be out of the egg. I guess he stayed awake all day, looking around at everything and now he's tired. Haze props himself against a rock and puts the gun in his belt, ready to shoot somebody. He looks as if he's going to stay awake to guard us, but he starts to snore right away.

I cry for a while. The baby clings to me as though he wants to comfort me. After I stop I look up at the starry sky. It's so beautiful it makes me cry all over again. No matter what it looks like from down here, it's full of far away suns, some even bigger than our own. We know all that because Mother taught us. "Who knows," Mother said, "what other kinds of life swirl around those suns?" She said, "Who knows, there might be a world where the dinosaurs didn't die out." I think now she was preparing us for strangers like my father. I wish I'd listened instead of looking out the window and wanting to be off in the woods.

Just when I finally start to fall sleep, Tom wakes me. He says Haze will tell about what we found. That's why he made the drawings. Tom says at first nobody will believe him...that there could exist creatures like us, so Haze will take us down to the real people. We'll get examined by policemen. Tom doesn't want that to happen. He likes us and he's always taken care of us—more than Mother has. He says he's not sure if Mother isn't crazy. Now that *we're* here, he knows why she has to live out here, but in the beginning she was angry at everybody and everything.

He talks as if my father was right. We won't be let anywhere near our nice home. There'll be nothing but buildings, and we'll never be able to come back. We might even be put in a zoo. The best thing to do is to get rid of Haze and then our life will stay the same.

"But how?"

"Easy. We'll just use that gun he has."

"I don't want to. I like him."

"Liking has nothing to do with it. It's your whole future. Mother's future, too."

"Let's wait and see what happens when we get back. We can always do it later if we have to."

"It might be too late then."

"I don't see why. Mother doesn't want him around either. She'll be on your side. She'll get out her hunting rifle and kill him herself."

So Tom says, "All right. We won't do it yet."

Next morning we come down, all of us together, straight to Mother's. Even Haze walks right in with us.

Mother comes out from her stone house looking shocked. I start crying right away. I never used to cry much but now I seem to cry at everything. I don't even know why. I wonder if that's because I'm a grown-up now. I hope that's not the reason.

I run to Mother and hug her tight. We're breast against breast. I say, "I have to talk," and she says, "I should think so! What are you thinking? Can't you see? Couldn't you tell?"

She pulls away and slaps me. So hard she almost knocks me over. She's never done that before. I've never seen her so angry. I'm afraid to ask her anything but there's nobody else to ask the kind of things I need to know. I don't think she'll ever want to talk to me—especially not about what I want to talk about. I wonder if it's in our anatomy book and I didn't notice it before because I didn't want to.

She snatches the baby from Haze—so hard the baby starts to squeek and won't stop. Talk about high notes! That's the first he's squeeked in all the time he's been with us. I snatch him right back and he stops squeeking right away, which is a relief to all of us. I stop crying, too. That's the end of me crying. I won't do it anymore, especially not in front of Mother.

Mother tries to snatch him back but I won't let her. She says, "You have no idea. None of you do. Look what you've done! All our lives I've worried this would happen—someone like this man would come. It's over and done for. Do you think we can live the way we do after this? It's *over*!"

I don't know who we ought to get rid of, Mother or Haze or maybe both.

Haze says, "It doesn't have to be over. It can be just begun. I can take Quill and the baby down and bring them right back."

Mother says she doesn't want us made into a sideshow. She says they'll wipe out the whole enterprise. She says what she's always said before, that she knows how the world is, which is why she's living up here. "My innocent Quill," she says. (She never has called me hers before. I don't know what to think, and just after she slapped me.) "My little Quill, corrupted."

Little! Can't she see anything? Not even my breasts?

Tom says, "It doesn't have to be over. It can be like it always is. Wait! Mother! Everything will be like you want it to be. I can fix it." He gives Mother a look. Says, "*Wait*!" again.

I go stand in front of Haze just in case it happens right now. But I don't want Haze to get suspicious. I don't *think* I want Haze suspicious. I'm not sure of anything anymore. I'm not even sure if I might not want to go down and see the zoo.

Haze says, "You'll be found out sometime no matter what I do. Strange that you've lasted all this time as it is."

I don't see why Tom gets to be the only one who knows about down there. I might go with Haze, like he said, just me and the baby. Down to Haze's home forest. Who would have to know about us? Maybe it would be like our cave. Nobody but us would ever go there.

I should tell Haze to go home to his home right away, and he should keep watch over his little gun.

But I don't have a chance to tell him anything. He knows. We... Tom and I and Haze and the baby.... We say we're going down to spend the night in the cave and that we'll eat supper there, but Haze goes right on past, without a word, not even to me. We're all worn out but he just goes, even without supper, and he's going fast. Tom follows without a single word to me, and I follow Tom. I keep well back because of the baby, though the baby doesn't sound any different from the birds. The birds are settling down for the night so there's lots of chirping. The baby's settling down, too, with little night songs.

Haze has his lights, both of them, and Tom and I don't have anything so we're a lot slower.

Pretty soon I decide I just have to rest. I think Haze will have to rest, too. I hope he finds a place where Tom can't get at him.

The baby and I move off the trail and cuddle up.

When I wake up and look out, I'm way up on the side of a mountain and I can look down on a whole other valley with a big town there. I'm so happy. I start chirping to myself along with the baby. I'm getting somewhere really interesting. I'm going to know things Tom knows.

The baby and I pick Elderberries and mountain currants for breakfast. I'm not in a hurry anymore. There's the town and I have plenty of time to get there. I don't care if I ever catch up to Haze or Tom.

But Tom waits beside the trail and jumps out at me. And right away tells me I have to go home. "You mustn't let people see you and especially not let anybody see the baby. He'll scare them to death.

"How can a baby scare anybody?"

"He, and even you, but he especially...you don't belong on this world."

How can he say such a thing? "Of course I do."

"You don't understand anything."

"I wasn't going to show myself right away. I thought to take a look around and maybe go to the zoo and see the animals. And then come home."

"People will see you for sure."

"What's so bad if they do see us?"

"Quill!"

"We're just other human beings."

"Well, that's the problem."

"Aren't we?"

"You've been protected from the real people."

"I'm real."

"Look at yourself. You're them. You may be a *being* but you're not a *human* being."

"I am so."

"You belong in the zoo."

"I wouldn't mind."

"There's no zoo in that little town anyway. They're only in big towns."

"That doesn't look little to me."

"Believe me, it is."

I suppose he's right. He usually is.

"Well I won't go home. Not when I'm so close to seeing new things."

"You won't get far with that baby on your back."

"Lots of people must have babies down there."

"Not one like that."

"I'm not going to argue, I'm just not going to go home until I see this town."

"Go ahead, then, but it's the end of all of us. Though.... I'm tired of it, too. Let's end it. Or I'll tell you what, go on down. Wear my hat pulled low and see if you can get away with it. And they might have a little zoo with maybe four or five animals in some park or other, but don't go into town till it's dark. I'll keep the baby. You'll never get away with it with him."

"All right, if the baby doesn't mind."

I do want to see that town. I start right away. It'll be getting dark by the time I get there.

Pretty soon the trees get fewer and there's fields of stuff growing. I begin to see cows and horses. I've only seen those in books. I stop at the edge of one of the fields and two horses come over to me as if to say hello. At first I think they might bite, but there's the fence between us and you can tell they're friendly right away. They lean to be touched and I touch them.

Right after, there begins to be houses. All nicer even than Mother's. Some with one floor on top of another. I know all about that. I've seen pictures. There's some with different colors and bobbles hanging all over them. I never knew a house could be so pretty. I'm already glad I came.

When I get to the edge of town it's pretty dark. I pull my hat down even lower and walk on. The people are all Tom's kind of people just like he said. Nobody is as beautiful as my father. There aren't any feathers at all.

I come to a little park with swings and slides. I've seen pictures of those. There's nobody there. I guess it's too late for young ones to be out. I try all the things. I can't believe I'm learning so much in such a hurry. These last few days it's been one new thing after another.

There's street lights. You don't need those lights Haze has. I come to a big street with stores all along it. Most of them closed. Some have prices in the windows. Money! I hadn't thought of that.

I walk all the way down the Main Street. It must be a mile long. Shops all along the way. I don't care what Tom says, it's a big town to me. I look in the store windows. The clothes look different from the ones Mother makes. And shoes...so fancy and slick, some with funny little heels. There's a store full of beautiful shiny pots and pans never used, cups and plates neither tin nor wood nor clay.

There's a bigger park at the other end of town. It even has a swimming pool. All blue and smells funny. I'm thirsty but I don't drink there. There's a river running through the park and that's where I drink. There's no zoo that I can find. I was so hoping there'd be one. I want to see monkeys and tigers and elephants. I wonder how far a bigger town is. If I knew which direction to go in I might head for that town.

I see people on the porch of an eating place eating with forks. I see two women clacking along in high heeled sandals. I see cars and trucks. All this even though you'd think people would be in bed. I get honked at. I jump away and quack back.

Then Haze is here. He must have been following me all this time. Even though my hat is pulled down low he knows it's me.

I say, "Don't tell," and he says he won't. I don't know if I should believe him or not, but it looks as if he won't tell *right now*, anyway.

"You look exhausted. Are you hungry? Come home with me."

Haze's house is like I've never seen before. There's rugs and a couch. There's even a little room that's just for me but I don't want it. I've never slept by myself before and I'm scared to. Haze makes me up a mattress on the floor next to him. The food is odd, too. I don't know what it is but I eat it anyway. Except for bugs, Haze ate what we ate. That was like Mother, too. She hated for us to eat bugs. There's also a little room for an outhouse that's not even *out*. I learn to flush. I learn to turn on the water, cold *and* hot.

But next morning breakfast is just like at home, oatmeal. I ask Haze, "What are you going to do about us? You killed my father. You might do anything."

"You were yelling, help. Your father was trying to take you back. I thought I was helping. I didn't know it was your father. But I don't know. What *should* I do?"

"I don't know either."

"You're going to be discovered no matter what I do. Might as well be now as later. Might as well be me as somebody out to make a buck."

"How come we've not been discovered all this time?"

"Your mother picked a good hiding place."

"Tom said it was the end of all of us. Tom said our lives depend on you."

"I won't let anybody hurt you."

"You have drawings of everything."

"You're scientifically important. You're *all* important. They'll need to study you."

You wouldn't think so many things could happen so fast. It all comes about in a couple of days. Even the destruction of the fathers, which they did to themselves. I'm glad the regular human beings didn't do it. I don't know what I would have thought if they had.

The fathers knew what would happen. They know about human beings. When Haze and the others...the scientists and the army and police get out to the ship, it's destroyed. The nest and eggs and all the creatures with it. There's nothing left of them but us.

Mother must have known. Even if we didn't hear the blast down in town, she's so much closer she must have heard and known. They found her body washed down our river. She had made us all moccasins and lined them up along the table, all exactly the right size. She loved us but she needed for things to stay the same.

Now she'll never find out how we got taken into this school. A farm kind of school off in the middle nowhere, with all kinds of animals,. But also a scientific school with lots of geology and biology, so some day I can be a scientist in a zoo. I'll probably have to be *in* the zoo myself. I know that. Even now people keep coming to take blood and study us. I don't mind. I'm studying myself myself and them, too.

Haze took all our gold, but he's using it for us. He's paying for the school.

He says, "The fathers were scared of us." When he says, us, he means the human beings. He says, "And rightly so. They thought we wouldn't accept them and we wouldn't. They knew their nests and eggs were easy to destroy. But having living dinosaurs.... Feathered.... Think of the experiments.... And studying...them and their ship...."

And he keeps saying, "Just think...think, there's been contact with aliens all these years and nobody knew it."

I don't feel like an alien. I think I belong here just as much as anybody.

***Firebirds Rising: An Anthology of Original Science Fiction and Fantasy*,**
2006

Killers

Most people left because of no water. I don't know where they found a place where things were any better. Some of us felt safer here than anywhere else. And even way before the war wound down, it was hard to pick up and go someplace. No gas for civilians. Pretty soon no gas at all.

After the bombing of our pipeline, (one man with a grenade could have done that) we got together and moved the town up higher, along a stream and put in ditches so that the water came past several houses. We have to carry water into the house in buckets and we have to empty the sink by hand, back out into the yard. At least the water flows into our kitchen gardens and past our fruit trees. In warm weather, we bathe in our irrigation ditch, in colder we sponge off inside, in basins, but there's hardly any cold weather anymore.

There wasn't much to moving the town since most of us were gone already. All the able-bodied men, of course, so it took us women to make the move ourselves and without horses or mules. The enemy stole them or killed them or maimed them just to make things harder for us.

No electricity, though some of the women think they can hook the dam back up and get some. Nobody has bothered to try it yet. In a way none of this bothers me as much as you'd think. I always liked walking, and we have rendered fat lamps and candles that send out a soft, cozy glow.

Our house was already well above where the town used to be. Good because I didn't want to move. I want my brother to have our old home to come back to. And besides, I couldn't move Mother.

Beyond our back yard there used to be the Department of Water and Power, after that Forest Service land, and then the John Muir wilderness. Now the town has moved above me, and of course there's no DWP or Forest Service anymore.

Our house has a good view. We always sat on the front steps and looked at the mountains. Now that everybody has moved up the mountain side, everybody has a good view.

The town below is empty. The Vons and K Mart are big looted barns. Up here there's one small store where we sell each other our produce or our sewing and knitting. Especially socks. Hard to get socks these days. Before the war we were so wasteful nobody darned anymore, but now we not only darn but reinforce the heels and toes of brand new socks before we wear them.

We moved the little library up. Actually it's got more books than before. We brought all the books we could find, ours and those from the people who left. We don't need a librarian. Everybody brings them back honor system.

We have a little hospital but no doctors, just a couple of elderly nurses who were too old to be recruited. They're in their seventy's and still going. They've trained new ones. No medicines though. Only what we can get from local herbs. We went to the Paiute to find out more. There's a couple of Paiute nurses, who come to help out every now and then, though they have their own nursing to do on the reservation. (They moved the rez up, too, and they don't call it the reservation anymore.)

It's a woman's town now. Full of women's arts and crafts.... Quilt makers, sweater knitters.... And the women do the heavy work. There's a good roof repair group and there's carpenters....

Lots of women went to war along with the men, but I had to look after Mother. I was taking care of her even before my brother left. She wasn't exactly sick but she was fat and she drank. Her legs looked terrible, full of varicosities. It hurt her to walk so she didn't. When the war came she got a little better because of the shortages, though there was still plenty of homemade beer, but she couldn't walk. Or wouldn't. I think her muscles had all withered away. Looking after somebody who can't walk seems normal to me. I've done it since I can first remember anything.

Now that Mother's gone I have a chance to do something useful. If I knew the war was still going on in some specific place, I'd go fight, but it *seems* to be over. Maybe. It didn't stop exactly. I don't know how it ended or even if it's ended. We don't have a way to find out, but there hasn't been any action that we know of for quite some time. Overhead, nothing flies by. Not even anything old fashioned. (Not that we ever had any action to speak of way out here. Except for the bombing of our pipeline and stealing our livestock, nobody cared much about us.)

But that's the way the war was, hardly a beginning and hardly an end. Wars aren't like they used to be—with two clearly separated sides. The enemy was among us even before it started. They could never win a real old-fashioned war with us, they were weak and low tech, but low tech was good enough as long as there were lots of them. You never knew who to trust, and we still don't. Our side put all we could in internment camps, practically everybody with black eyes and hair and olive skin, but you can't get them all. And then the war went on so long we used up all our resources, but they still had theirs—sabotage doesn't ever have to stop. They escaped from the camps. Actually they just walked away. The guards had already walked away, too.

Lots of those men brought their injuries and craziness to our mountains. Both side came here to get away from everything. They're hermits. They don't trust anybody. Some of them are still fighting each other up there. It's almost as bad as having left-over mine fields. They're all damaged, physically or mentally. Of course most likely all of us are, too, and we probably don't even know it.

My brother might be out there somewhere. If he's alive he's got to be here. He loves this place. He hunted and trapped and fished. He'd get along fine and I know he'd do anything to come back.

Most of those men don't come down to us even if they're starving or cold or sick. Those that do, come to steal. They take our tomatoes and corn and radishes. Other things disappear, too. Kitchen knives, spoons, fishhooks.... And of course sweaters and woolen socks.... Those crazies live up even higher than we do. It does still get cold up there.

And they are crazies. And now one of them has been killing other men and dumping them at the edge of the village. They've all been shot in the back by wooden crossbow darts. Beautifully carved and polished. I hope it isn't one of our side. Though I don't suppose sides matter anymore.

Every time this happens, before we put them into the depository, I go to check if it's my brother. I wouldn't want my brother in the depository. Ever. But those men are always such a mess—dirty and bearded—I wonder, would I recognize him? I keep thinking: How could I not? But I was only fifteen when he left. He was eighteen. He'd be thirty-two now. If he's alive.

We're all a little edgy even if it's not us getting killed. And then last night I saw someone looking in my window. I'd been asleep but I heard a noise and woke up. I saw the silhouette of a lumpy hat and a mass of tangled hair flying out from under it, the moonlit sky glowing behind. I called out, "Clement!" I didn't mean to. I was half asleep and in that state I knew it was my brother. Whoever it was ducked down in a hurry and I heard the crunch, crunch of somebody running away. Afterwards I got scared. I could have been shot as I slept.

The next morning I saw foot prints and it looked like somebody had spent some time behind my shed.

I keep hoping it's my brother, though I wouldn't want him to be the one killing those poor men, but you'd think he wouldn't be afraid of coming to his own house. Of course he doesn't know that Mother is dead. I can understand him being afraid of her. They never got along. When she was drunk she used to throw things at him. If he got close enough, she'd grab his arm and twist. Then he got too strong for her. But he couldn't be afraid of me. Could he? I'm the baby sister.

Mother was nicer to me. She got worried I'd stay out of reach or not help anymore. I could have just walked off and left her but until she died I didn't think of it. I actually didn't. I'd looked after her for so long I thought that's just the way life is. And I might not have left, anyway. She *was* my mother and there was nobody else to look after her but me.

If it's my brother, been looking in the window, he must know Mother isn't here. She never left her bed. The house is small and all on one floor so he could have looked in all the windows. We have three tiny bedrooms, and one kitchen/ living room combined. Mother and her big bed took up wall to wall space in the biggest bedroom.

I posted Clement's picture at the store and the library, but of course it was a picture from long ago. In it he has the usual army shaved head. I drew a version with wild hair. Then I drew another of him bald with wild hair around the sides. (Baldness runs in our family.) I drew a different kind of beard on each of them. I put up both versions.

Leo at the store said, "He might not want to talk to you…or anybody."

But I know that already.

"I think he's come looking in my window."

"Well, there you are. He'd a come in if he'd wanted to."

"You went to war. How come you're OK and most all the other men have gone wild?"

"I was lucky. I never saw real horror."

Actually he may not be so OK. Most of us never married. We never had the chance with all the men gone. He could have married one of us but he never did. He lives in a messy shed behind the store and he smells, even though the ditch passes right by his store. And he's always grumpy. You have to get used to him.

"If my brother comes around, tell him I'm going out to look for him in all his favorite spots."

"Even if you find him he won't come back."

"So then I'll go after that crazy person who's been killing those men."

Truth is, I don't know what to do with myself. I don't know how to live with just me to care about. I can go anywhere and do anything. I ought to find the man who's the killer. I have nothing else to do. Who better to do it than I?

But I might find that man right here, hiding at the edge of the village—or most likely looking in my window. Maybe I can trap him in my house. He must have been looking in for a reason.

I pack up and pretend to leave. I stay out of sight of the village. This is wild rocky land—lots of hiding places. Nobody will know I didn't go anywhere. My backpack is mostly empty. I have pepper. Pepper is hard to get these days so I've saved mine for a weapon. I have a small knife in my boot and a bigger one at my belt. Streams aren't stocked anymore but there's still fish around, though not as many as before. I bring a line and hooks. I'll use those today. I won't go far.

I catch a trout. I have to make a fire the old fashioned way. No more matches. I always carry a handful of dead sage fibers for tinder. I cook the fish and eat it. After dark and the half moon comes up, I sneak back to our house as if I was one of those crazies myself.

The door is wide open. There's sand all over the floor. Couldn't he even shut the door? These days we have sand storms and dust devils more often than we used to. Doesn't whoever it is, know that? And that's another reason to move higher up, into the trees where it's less deserty.

I smell him before I see him. I put my knife up my sleeve so it'll drop down into my hand.

I can hear him breathing. Sounds like scared breathing. A man this frightened will be dangerous.

He's huddled in Mother's bedroom down between the bed and the bedside table. All I see is his hat, pulled low so his face is in shadow. I see his bare knees showing through his torn pants. I have a better look at them than his face.

Right away I think my brother wouldn't be in Mother's room, he'd be in his own room. Besides, the room still smells of death and dying. I call, "Clement?" even though I know it can't be him. "Come on out."

He groans.

"Are you sick?" He sounds sick. I suppose that's why he's here in the first place.

I wish I'd lit a lamp first. I was counting on the moonlight, but there isn't much shining in here. It still could be my brother, under all that dirt and wild hair and beard, gone crazy just like everybody else.

"Come out. Come to the main room. I'll light a lamp. I'll fix you food."

"No light."

"Why not? There's only me. And there's no war going on anymore. It's most likely over."

"I pledged to fight until I died."

(I suppose my brother did, too.)

I finger my knife. "I'm going to go light the lamp."

I deliberately turn my back. I go to the main room, light the lamp with the sparker, keeping my back to the bedroom door. I hear him come in. I turn and get a good look.

Pieced together hat, long scraggly hair hanging under it. I can't tell if he's a brown man or just weather beaten, sunburned and dirty. A full beard with gray in it. Eyes as black as the enemy's always are. Eyebrows just as thick as theirs. He has a broken front tooth. Nowadays that's not unusual. Nobody to fix them. He has a greenish look under his tan and dark circles around his eyes. If he thinks he isn't sick he doesn't know much.

"You *are* the enemy. And you're half dead already."

There's a chair right beside him, but he sinks sideways to the floor. Ends up flat on our worn linoleum. If he thinks he's still fighting the war, I should kill him now while I have the chance. He looks such a mess and smells so bad I'm almost ready to kill him just for those reasons alone. After Mother died I thought I was finished with disagreeable messes.

"Hide me. Just for tonight. I'll leave in the morning."

"Are you crazy." I kneel beside him. "You're the one killing people. I should kill you right now."

He's trying to prop himself up against the wall. I don't want to touch him but I grab his shirt front to help him and the rotten cloth rips completely out.

"You stink something awful. And why would I think you won't kill me? You've been killing everybody else."

"I don't have a weapon."

"Strip."

"What?"

"Take those filthy clothes off. I'll burn them. I'll bring you a basin to wash in." (And I'll find out if he has a weapon.)

He hasn't the energy to undress or wash. I hate to touch him but I do it. I'm used to it. Mother was a mess as she was dying. (At the end I sprinkled pine needles all over but it didn't help much.) I thought that was the last of that sort of thing I'd ever have to do. I thought I was free. But, all right, one more thing. I wash him and dress him in my brother's old clothes, and...what then? If I kill him, the town will be grateful.

At least his body is entirely different from Mothers, thin and strong and hairy. It's a nice change. If he wasn't so smelly I'd enjoy it. Well I do enjoy it.

He's half asleep through it all.

I burn his clothes in our little stove. After I've washed him, I feed him jerky broth with an egg in it, though I keep thinking: Why waste my egg on him? He falls asleep right after he's finished the broth. Slides down the wall flat out again, in what seems more a faint than a sleep.

I decide to shave him and cut his hair. He won't notice. If he'd been more conscious I'd have asked him if he wanted a mustache or a little goatee but I'm glad he isn't. I have fun with different haircuts, different sideburns, smaller and smaller mustaches until there's none. Hair, too. I take off more than I meant to, except what does it matter, he's a dead man.

Not a very handsome man whatever way I fixed his hair and beard, though along the way there were some nicer stages—better than what I ended up with. I finish by shaving him. Also not a good job. I make nicks. Where I shaved his beard, his skin is pale. His forehead, where his hat was, is pale, too. There's only a sun browned strip across his face just below his eyes. I like the maleness of him no matter that he's ugly. I don't mind his broken tooth. We're all in the same boat as to teeth.

I fall asleep at the kitchen table, right in the middle of thinking up ways to kill him. Also thinking about how we've all changed—how, in the olden days, I'd not ever have been thinking things at all like that.

In the morning he seems some better—well enough for me to help him stagger, first to the outhouse, and then into my brother's room. He keeps feeling his face and hair. I stop at the hall mirror and let him take a look. He's shocked. He has a kind of wet cat/plucked chicken look.

I say, "Sorry." I *am* sorry...sorry for anybody who gets their hair cut by me. But he should be glad I haven't slit his throat.

He stares at himself, but then says, "Thank you." And so sincerely that I realize I've made him the best disguise there is. He said, "Hide me," and I did.

Nobody will take him for one of those wild men now.

I prop him up on the pillows of my brother's bed and bring him milk and tea. He looks so much better I wonder.... If he's not going to die on his own, I'll have to think what to do with him.

"What's your name?"

He doesn't answer. He could say anything. I'd have believed him and I'd have had something to call him by.

"Tell me a name. I don't care what."

He thinks, then says, "Jal."

"Make it Joe."

I don't trust him. But if he has any sense at all he knows I'm the only one can keep him safe. Though nobody has much sense anymore.

"Everybody got tired of the war a long time ago." I bang my cup down so hard that my tea spills. "Haven't you noticed?"

"I swore to fight to the death."

"I'll bet you don't even know which side is which anymore. If you ever did."

"You're the ones, heated up the planet. It wasn't us. It was you and your greed."

I haven't been so aggravated since my brother was around. "It heated up mostly by itself. It's done that before you know. Besides, all that's over. Our part in it anyway. Killing crazies isn't going help. You're crazy!" Not the best thing to say to a crazy, but I go on anyway. "All you hermits are crazy. You're nothing but trouble."

He's taking it all in.... Maybe he is. Maybe he just doesn't have the energy to argue.

"I'm going out to get us a rabbit. If you want to keep on making trouble, don't be here when I come back."

I leave. He'll be all alone with my butcher knife and pepper. And I suppose his crossbow isn't far off. I might as well give him a chance to show what he is.

I make the rounds of my traps. They're lower down. I've set them around the town. It's a ghost town. I'm the only one goes down there now and then...usually only on a cool day. Which hardly ever happens. Today it must be well over 110. Now our whole valley in winter is as if Death Valley in summer.

What I trap down there are rats. We cook those up and call them rabbit, though nobody cares anymore what we call them.

I find two big black ones, big as cats. We like those better than the small brown kind, lots more meat on them. (Seems as if the rats are getting bigger all the time.) My traps broke their necks. I don't have to worry about killing them. I tie their tails to my belt, then wander the town in hopes of finding something not already scavenged. I find a quarter. I take it though it's worthless. Maybe a Paiute might turn it into jewelry. On purpose I don't climb back up to my house until late afternoon and until I drink all the water I brought.

Before I go in I check around my shed and house for a crossbow and darts, and then beyond, under the bushes, but I don't find them.

He's still there. Asleep. And no weapons that I can see, but I check the kitchen knives. The largest one, big as a machete, is gone. And he might be pretending to be sicker than he is.

Enemy or not, I do like a man in the house. I watch him sleep. He has such long eyelashes. I like the hair on his knuckles. Just looking at his hands makes me think how there's so few men around. Actually only four. His forearms.... Ours don't ever look like that no matter how much we saw and hammer. Even my brother's never looked like that. I like that he already needs a shave again. I even like his bushy eyebrows.

But I have to go clean rats.

When I start rattling around the kitchen section of our main room, he gets up and staggers to the table. Stops at the hall mirror again on the way and studies himself for a long time. As if he forgot what he looked like under all that hair. He sits, then, and watches me make two-rat-stew with wild onions and turnips. I thicken it with acorn flour I traded for with the Paiute.

It takes a while for the stew to finish up. I make squaw tea and sit across from him. Being so close and looking into his eyes upsets me. I have to get up and turn my back. I pretend the stew needs stirring. To hide my feelings I say, "Where's your crossbow? And where's my knife? I won't let you have my stew until you tell me." I sound more angry than I meant to.

"Under the bed in the big room. Both of them."

I go check and there they are, and several darts. I bring the bow back to the table. It's a beautiful piece of work. Old scraps of metal and an old screw, salvaged from something, now shiny and oiled. The wood of the bow, carved as if a work of art. All kept up with care. I'll bring it to the town meeting to show I've found the killer and dealt with him. But have I? And they may want a body.

"I'll not shoot anybody. Not now."

"Yeah. But you're still sworn."

"I can fight someplace else."

"Oh yeah."

After we eat I put what's left-over into an old bear proof can, take it to the irrigation ditch and sink it in wet mud to keep it cool.

I don't know if I should go to bed without barricading my door some way. I wish I still had our dog but Mother and I ate him long ago. He'd be dead by now anyway. It would be nice to have him, though. I'd feel a lot safer. He was a good dog but getting old. We thought we'd better eat him ourselves before somebody else got to him. That was before we were eating rats.

Tired as I am, it takes a while for me to get to sleep. I keep telling myself, if he's going to sneak into my room, I might as well find out about it. But I put the chair against the door in a way that it'll fall. At least I'll hear if he comes in.

Mainly I can't sleep because, in spite of my better judgment, I'm thinking of keeping the man. Trying to. I like the idea of having him around even though it's scary. I make plans.

It's logical that somebody coming in to our new higher village would come to my house first. Perhaps an outsider with news from the North. And it's logical that I'd take him to a town meeting to tell the news.

What news, though? In the morning, (the chair hasn't fallen) we make some up. Carson City is as empty and rat infested as our town. (It's a good bet it really is.) I remember an airplane (I think it was called the gossamer condor) that flew by the propeller being pumped by a bicycle and doesn't need gas. It can't go far or we'd have seen it down here. Joe can say he's seen it.

He says, "How about an epidemic of a new disease passed on by fleas? It hasn't reached here yet." He says, "How about, way up in Reno, they found a cache of ammunition so they can clean up their old guns and use them again?"

I give him news about Clement to tell people. I'll say that's another reason Joe came to me first—to give me news of my brother. (I think I made up that news because I know my brother's dead. Otherwise I'd not have mentioned anything about him. I'd keep on thinking he's out in our mountains as one of the crazies, but I don't think I ever really believed that. I just hoped.)

Once he takes my hand and squeezes it—says how grateful he is. I have to get up again, turn my back. I wash our few dishes, slowly. I'm so flustered I hardly know what his hand felt like. Strong and warm. I know that.

Lots of good things happen in those town meetings. We give each other our news. We have all kinds of helping committees. In some ways we take care of each other more than we did before the war. People used to bring in their deer and wild sheep and share the meat around, except there's less and less wild game and more and more mountain lions. They're eating all the game and we're not good at killing lions. I'll bet Joe would be, with his crossbow.

So I bring him to the meeting. Introduce him. They crowd around and ask questions about all their favorite spots, or places where they used to have relatives. He's good at making stuff up. Makes me wonder, was he once an officer? Or did he act?

I admire him more and more, and I can see all the women do, too. He could have any one of us. I'm worried he'll get away from me and I'm the only one knows who he really is. Whoever gets him in the end will have to be careful.

He's looking pretty good, too, horrible haircut and all. My brother's blue farmer shirt sets off his brown skin. It's too large for him, but that's the usual.

The women have been out at the bird nets and had made a big batch of little-bird-soup. I was glad they'd made that instead of the other.

There's a Paiute woman who comes to our meetings and reports back to the reservation. She's beautiful—more than beautiful, strange and striking. I should have known. At his first view of her you can see...both of them stare and then, quickly, stop looking at each other.

Later he sits drinking tea with several women including the Paiute. They all crowd around but I saw him push in so that he was next to her. The tables are small but now nine chairs are wedged in close around the one where he sits. I can't see what's going on, but I do see her shoulder is touching his. And their faces are so close I don't see how they can see anything of each other.

I sneak away and run home. I wish I'd save his smelly, falling-apart clothes. I wish I'd saved the dirty, tangled hair I cut off, but I burned that, too. I do find the old hat. That helps them to believe me. I bring the crossbow. It also helps that he tries to get away.

They hung Joe up in the depository. I told them not to tell me anything about it. I'd rather not know when we get around to using him.

The Magazine of Fantasy & Science Fiction, Oct./Nov. 2006

The Seducer

I have always been a seducer...ever since I was little boy. I was an ugly child and have become an ugly grown-up. Seduction was my strategy from the start. Even an ugly baby can make himself the center of attention. Old ladies cooed at my smiles. I let them pat my head, pinch my cheeks.

But perhaps it was my sister taught me seduction even more than the old ladies. She was six years older than I. I was her object of torture. I learned to keep out of her way as much as possible and I learned never to let my pain show. That just made her worse.

But I must have looked sad even when I wasn't with her, because grandmas always gave me nickels to cheer me up. I suppose I looked gloomy back then, because of having to smile all the time I was around my sister.

The fact that I've grown up with a smoldering look helps with seductions. It scares women and entices them at the same time. I have a devilish grin but at rest I must still look sad. People are inclined to ask me what's wrong even when I might be contemplating the sunset or a dazzling night sky.

Of course now, at my age, I have become, indeed, a melancholy man. It's not a matter of loved ones having died, I never had any loved ones in the first place. But just as, approaching thirty, I could see my life dwindling away and nothing happening; now, approaching fifty, I see a lonely end.

My sister...she looks just like me, poor thing, which must have made her angry at me to start with, or angry in general. On a man it's not so bad having a lumpy chin, deep-set eyes, and a forehead like a Neanderthal.

Though there are times when I completely forget my looks. I think all I have to do is smile and my inner light will shine out. Actually, I don't suppose I have much inner light. I'm still as if in the clutches of my sister.

Nowadays I make it a point to learn interesting facts as conversation pieces. And I lead an interesting life, but only in order to talk about it. Sometimes I lie.

(Well, yes, I did go to war. Yes, I was a colonel. Yes, I spent a half year on the Isle of Capri. . . . A truth.) But it's best to stay mysterious. Best to have secret sorrows. Which I do have, considering my life.

Every now and then I have a dog or a cat. Stroking something in front of the ladies is always a good idea.

I take pride in being old fashioned, opening doors, kissing hands. . . . That surprises them. But I doubt if this particular woman will be taken in by any of that.

She will be a challenge. More so than the usual. First, though I'm by no means a short man, she's just as tall as I am. *And* she wears high heels. Then, though I'm in good shape still and look younger than I am, I'm not as young as I used to be, and she is young. Unlike most men, I liked women with a certain patina. . . a little wear and tear about them, so this is different. And I never liked wide faced blonds. It's the small dark ones that seemed sexy to me. Is it that seducing her looks so hard to do?

I saw her first at a local market. I was immediately put off. Big, blond, striding around with an unnecessary bounce—in running shoes—her jewelry as lumpy and awkward as herself.

My sister had good taste. What I know of taste I learned from her. I also learned something of lace bras and silky nightgowns. I even tried them on. Even then, I was a detective of women.

My sister escaped the family as soon as she could. Disappeared at the age of twenty. I haven't seen her since. I imagine she's changed. You can't stay a twelve/fifteen year old torturer all your life.

She told me lies and told lies about me. Tried to scare me (and did) with what was under the bed or in the closet. Shrieked into my ear when I least expected it. I was a nervous wreck. I spent my life hiding from her but she knew where to look. Tops of trees. And when I was up there she'd urge me to go yet higher. She knew I'd scare myself. (I was not. . . *am* not a particularly brave man. But I was more afraid of her than of the height.)

For years I looked under the bed before I got in it. Shadows still take scary shapes.

There was only one hiding place she never found. From that spot near a register, I could hear everything. I could hear my sister being a "nice girl." She had managed her life so that she seemed like the good child and I the bad one. When she did something bad she would blame me. It always worked. You'd think I'd have given up and become what she made me out to be, but I stayed a "good boy" always hopeful that, one of these days, they'd see. You'd have thought I'd be the one to run away as soon as possible, but I stayed. And when my parents got sick, I cared for them. They died within a year of each other. They needed their disagreements. Their fights were more surly than violent. There was a lot of silence. After they got sick, they needed each other more than ever. She gave him his shots and he helped her to bed after her drinking bouts. I learned to do those things before I was fifteen. They never learned to trust me. Their dying words were complaints of how I had never helped them.

So there I was, twenty-four, my parents dead, and with a big house, plenty of money, and no life what-so-ever. It took a while to get a life. Years. I lived there, even hiding in my old secret place though there was no one to hide from. I startled at every noise…every shadow. (It was a old house, full of creaks and thumps. It didn't help that squirrels were in the walls.) I saw ghosts though I didn't believe in them. And all the ghosts were like my sister, undependable, pesky, cruel. I didn't dare move out of my tiny bedroom. I barricaded the door at night just as I had when my sister was around. I kept the lights on all the time.

Finally I realized I was about to be—my God—thirty! (In those days I considered that old.) And I had done nothing but roam my house and read the old books….

I didn't need a specific revelation, just the number thirty was enough to scare me into action. But also I had found my father's secret collection of pornography. If I was to take part in any real sex at all, I would have to do something…go somewhere before I got any older. I sold the house, antiques, books… all. Bought myself good clothes, good luggage, gold cuff links, a silver handled umbrella, a homburg…. I grew a mustache. I was straight out of the illustrations in the old books. (I thought it was important to become mysterious. An ugly man should have mystery.) I traveled. I lived in hotels.

I had always been timorous but I told myself, be bold. I told myself women are as eager to be seduced as we men are to seduce them. My life would no longer be only in books. In fact I would not read at all, except for new best sellers as topics of conversation.

It all worked out exactly as I wished. I strolled parks, museums, book stores, art stores, coffee shops…. Expensive places, though I wasn't after a rich woman, I simply wanted to lead the life I could afford.

And I do know women. Back then, I had to keep my thoughts and actions on my sister every minute. I should be grateful. After all, my whole life was anticipating what her next move might be. It's from knowing her that I know women.

And here we are, my big blond and I, sitting across from each other. It was easier than I thought, though why not? We're just out for coffee. Even an ugly man can make himself pleasing when he knows how as well as I do.

She wears a ring, a chunk of amber with a fly in it. I'm thinking: She's all of a piece. I ask to see it so as to hold her hand—my thick fingers hold her square strong ones—longer than is necessary.

I decide to kiss her hand. She won't be taken in by that except as a joke. It works. She laughs. After that she stays grinning—as if everything I do is funny. Even my name is funny. Merton Brockenhurst. What's more she says so and crosses her eyes.

But her name is Lena. What a lowbrow name…as though to put me off from the start. But everything about her did…does…and doesn't. (Would Lena know Schoenberg? Kandinsky? Ponge? Lispecter? I won't ask.)

What have I got myself into? All my smoldering looks won't amount to anything with her. I change to raised eyebrows and I match her grin. I look silly but it's what she likes.

What could we ever do together that would please us both? She'll want to walk everywhere. I want to sit and listen to music.

Why in the world am I so attracted? I suspect it has to do with my sister since my whole life has had to with her...and yet this woman is the exact opposite.

The next time I see her she's in a diner kind of place I'd never go too. I see her in the window and go in, ask if I can sit with her. She has one of those fancy mountain backpacks next to her. Definitely not a bookbag. Strings and nets all over it for strapping on other things.

She says right away, "After our cappuccinos last time, I thought this wasn't your kind of place."

"It isn't."

"You're going to hate the coffee. Actually, I do, too."

"I know I will."

"Have tea."

She has a giant meal in front of her, mashed potatoes, peas, pot roast.... Well, she is a big...not fat at all but big woman. She polishes it all off. I watch. I wonder at myself. She has a kind of muscular grace all her own. I can't stop looking at her.

"You're a hiker."

"I'm going running. I have my shoes in here."

(She's wearing her heels. She'll tower over me.)

"...but soon. I'm going camping. Upstate."

"I'm not that kind of man."

"Have you ever done it? How do you know?"

Nothing but the truth for her so I say it. "I'm a fastidious man. You may have noticed."

"Come with me."

"Of course not. Besides, we hardly know each other."

"I'm not going till warmer weather...till next month. Come on."

Can it be that she's as attracted to me as I to her? I'm naturally strong and stocky, I just grew that way, but I've never been athletic. She may think I'm an entirely different man than I am.

"You want to. I can see it in your eyes. Have you any clothes for such a thing?"

"Of course not. I'll look ridiculous out in nature. Nothing about me is of nature, nor have I ever wanted anything to be."

"Get in touch with your other side—your wild side."

"I don't think I have a wild side."

We laugh. But then she laughs at everything. To her, the whole world's a joke. I'm glad to be part of it. "I'll have a hard time."

"I'll bet you won't."

But if I'm to seduce...(and I want to...more than ever before...perhaps because she's so different)...I'll have to do it her way. And haven't I always done that with all the others? That's what they like about me. I do what they want. I anticipate, I watch, I listen. I know their hearts' desires.

I'll do it. I'll go with her. I'll try to pass her test. It might make me all the more appealing if she sees how hard it is for me.

I'm tired of the life I've chosen. I want to start over. What better way than as the consort of this Amazon girl?

And I'd like to get in touch with some new part of myself—as she said my wild side—if I have any. I rather hope I do.

"I need to start small. Besides, we hardly know each other. I don't even have a backpack. I'll need everything new."

She's the leader in all this. What to get and where.

When I visit her apartment it's just as I suspected, all rustic furniture. Nothing of any value. I wonder what she'd think if she had visited my old home full of antiques? If she even had visited my hotel rooms?

I haven't touched her. Not even held her hand except that moment when I kissed it. I know better than to scare her. Besides, when a man is as ugly as I am, it takes time to love me. Yet I savor every minute of the suspense. I never did before—I was always in a hurry—but this is different.

I'll have to get used to myself in these clothes and boots. I'm pleased, though. I fit in this role better than I thought. And I can see she likes how I look, too. Makes me think all my elegant clothes were useless since this is what I really looked like from the start. I look like a weight lifter without ever having tried.

We take the train north and after that a bus. Up to nowhere. Not real mountains, just the Catskills.

We load up...water, tent, sleeping pads...and begin, right from the bus stop.

I'm looking forward to the nights in the tent, though the sleeping pads look hard and the weather report said cold, but all the better for cuddling up. In my mind I see her sleeping on top of me as warmer and softer than the ground. I won't touch her. Not yet. Though if she wants to.... And if a full moon, who knows what will happen. Except why bring me out here? Get me off alone? Why indeed? Except the outdoors life is what she loves and she likes me enough to want to share it.

As we hike, she keeps looking back at me and smiling. Her happiness makes me happy. I'm glad I'm behind so I can watch. We're wearing shorts. Her legs are thick and sturdy yet feminine. How did I come to admire such a tall and stocky...such a strong woman? Now I can think of no one else.

When we pitch the tent, I use all my knowledge of camping—from books not experience. I make sure we don't put it up under a big tree in case of lighting. I make sure the lay of land isn't slanted so water might rush down on us. I even make a little trench around the tent for water to run off. Lena is impressed. I tell her the truth, that I've been reading camping books. She's impressed even more by my being so interested.

The moon does come out. As I hoped. There are clouds—fast, witch-like oblong clouds. It's both dark and dazzling. We sit on a ridge above our tent and watch.

Then we hear screaming. For sure it's a woman in trouble. I jump up, take my arm from Lena's shoulders, but she pulls me back down. "Owls." She says. "Baby owls screeching to be fed."

It sounds so human. I'm not convinced. I jump up again. It's a woman in terror.

"Shouldn't we go help?"

But no, I've heard that sound before. Often. It's my sister. That's exactly the sound she made when she would screech into my ear to scare me.

"It's all right." Lena pulls me down yet again. "It sounds like a woman, but it's not. It's really not." Now it's her arm across my shoulders. "It's all right."

Her touch is calming. Loving. I turn and kiss her. Our first kiss. It would have been a longer kiss...I wanted it to be longer... I'd meant it to be...but the scream comes again right in the middle of it. I'm almost seduced enough to ignore the racket, but not quite.

"Will that go on all night?"

"Not all. Just off and on."

A creature flies over us, close. White underbelly. Silent.

"There," she says. "There's an owl right there."

The moon has gone behind one of those mysterious dark clouds, the sky around it stills shines but my romantic mood is gone. I'm taken over by the shrieks. It still sounds like my sister. It's so familiar. Close in, right by my ear. It seems it's been ringing in my ears all my life.

I don't want to kiss again. It'll be right then that the screeching will come. I could test it that way. If owls, it'll be random, if my sister, then at the crucial moment. That's the way it always was.

I turn to kiss her just as a test. The moon is out again. She wants to. She puts her hand on my cheek. I put my hand over her hand, then I bring her hand down and kiss her palm. There's silence. I pull her close, lean and kiss her neck. Her cheek. Then her lips.

And there it goes. Talk about waking the dead! She tries to hold me close but I tear myself from her arms.

She tries to pull me back...to bring my lips to hers. "It's the baby owls. That's all."

But I can't. I get up. I start down towards our tent. "I'm going back."

"Now? In the middle of the night? Just because of owls? I love you."

I hear and don't hear. My ears are so full of screeches

The bank is steep and in the shadows. As I run I get more and more frightened. I can't see anything but the shine of the tent below in the moonlight.

Of course I fall—fall and slide and roll. There are rocks. I don't know if I'm hurt or not, but it shocks the panic out of me.

She's right behind. She sits beside me with her hand on my shoulder.

It takes a few minutes, finally I sit up.

I lean on her and we hobble to the tent. We sit in front of it.

"You're crazy. Are you crazy?"

I can't tell her about my sister. Instead I say, "I'm too old for you." Even as she holds my hand. Raises it to her lips.

"I'm older than I look. I'm thirty-three."

"I'm still old enough to be your father."

"It's getting cold. Come to bed."

She makes me crawl into the tent in front of her. Inside she sits with my head in her lap. This is all new to me. No one has ever stroked my face like this. I was always the one...the seducer. I knew how. She knows, too...knows out of kindness and motherliness and love. Like a mother, but my mother was never like this. Lena really is in love with me. Of course she is. She really is. That's why my sister is after me.

"You're still shaky."

"It's because of you, so close and loving." I pull her down on top of me and kiss her on the lips. She unbuttons my shirt and I, hers. We're chest to chest. Then my sister screams again.

I roll away. "I can't."

"It's all right."

But this time the screaming goes on and on. I don't even bother to button my shirt back up, I tear at the zipper of the tent door. I can't pull it. I break through. It's easy to hear where the sound is coming from. I follow.

The moon is bright, but will set soon. I run. The screams stop, but I know which direction to go. I know how far.

And there she stands, on a rock above the trail. Luminous. Hair a messy halo. Dress a rag blowing behind her. Glasses, where the moon is reflected as if two moons.

I kneel. Relieved that now it's done. Over. Or begun at last.

It's utterly quiet. All the little night sounds gone. There's only my breathing and heart beat.

And then a raspy voice. "You've always been mine."

"I know it."

But there *is* another sound. Somebody has followed me. Far behind but getting closer. Crashing though the brush.

And then a cloud comes over the moon. My sister...all white and ragged, flashing moon eyes.... I can't see her anymore. I rush to the rock where she stood. Strike out, grab at air, grab bushes, twigs.... That brittle dead feel might be her. She could be anything. It all breaks under my fist.

I lie prone, where she was. My cheek on rock.

But someone is calling me. My sister—she's luring me farther into the woods. She wants me lost. But I'm lost already.

Then I see the beam of a flashlight. Wobbling. Coming closer.

"Lena!"

She shines the flashlight in my face. Puts it down. She's on her knees. Now she's kissing the back of my neck, my ear, my cheek.

All I want is a life with her.

I sit up. We put our arms around each other.

"What is it? What's wrong?"

She's so real. So right here right now. How can she understand my sister? "You never hide. You don't scream. You don't jump out at me."

She has no idea what I'm talking about.

"My dear, it was owls." (Who has ever called me dear?) "Come. Come back to the tent."

We're not lost. All I did was follow the ridge. Going back, it seems a long way, but I was running, leaping. The moon has set and clouds have come completely over but now we have the flashlight. I'm breathing hard. I'm dizzy.

"I love you even though you're crazy."

We crawl back in the tent, through the torn doorway. Thank goodness no mosquitoes with this breeze. She lies half over me, she strokes my forehead, but it doesn't stop my trembling. I wonder if I'll ever sleep again. That sound is in my ears—so loud I won't know if it comes again or not. But Lena talks. She says I don't have to tell her a thing. She doesn't need to know about my life from before.

"I can't let you love me."

"Don't take yourself so seriously. You think I'm not crazy, too? After all, I'm in love with a man old enough to be my father...ugly, too...a strong-as-an-ox man. A somber man, but he laughs at my jokes."

"I hear it still you know."

"Hush. Sh. Sh. I'll sing. Listen. I sing. I can."

It's true, she can. I had not thought she was so musical. Her voice is trained. An alto. Nothing harsh in it. Why hadn't I taken her to something musical. She sings some old French lullabys—in French. I have misjudged her. She's so much more than I suspected.

I want to stay awake and listen but I can't help it, I sleep.

We wake early to the squawks of birds but quail and jays, this time. A bright optimistic day. My ears still ring with that screetching, but I'm not going to mention it.

I can see that without her.... "Without you I'd be completely crazy."

"Not to me. Well, maybe. A little bit."

"I can't let you care for a crazy person."

When have I ever been worth anything to anybody but myself? I've lived my life for me. For pleasure. When I first stepped down our steps with a brand new fancy leather suitcase (monogrammed) I wasn't looking for love, I was looking for conquests and sex and good food and travel.

"I've been crazy all this time and didn't know it."

But I saw my sister. *Did* I see her? I have to get to her before she spoils my life.

Lena says, "Let's not go home yet. Lets climb the mountain. I want to show you the view. That's why I wanted you to come here in the first place."

And it is worth it. Mountains rolling on as far as we can see. We sit at the top and eat lunch, and then lie looking at the clouds. Thunder heads are building. Neither of us want to mention that the weather looks threatening.

Lena sits up and looks down at me. She smoothes my bushy eyebrows out of my eyes. She asks about my scars, one over my eyebrow, a wedge shape, another on my cheek. That one looks as though I was a German fencer. They're from my sister—of course, but I just say, "Childhood accidents." That's true.

"I've never met a man like you. But then I never went to places where a man like you would be."

"Where would I be?"

"Fancy hotels, spas.... I see you in formal gardens with your silver headed cane, and strolling beaches, fully dressed, never going near the water. It's true isn't it."

"I'm not proud of it. But I've changed. You're changing me."

I pull her down on me again. Just as the first sprinkles come. Light at first. I roll over so I'm on top and she'll not get wet. We forget about the rain even as it comes down harder. I forget that I have to get through another night with screaming owls. It won't bother me, anyway. Not after this.

Thunder roars. Lightening strikes not far from us. We have to get off the top of the mountain in a hurry. As we climb down the trail, I turn back and grab her hand.

"Marry me."

"Of course."

Dripping we climb down and across the ridge to the tent, strip out of our wet clothes, make love again, and sleep.

I make love as I never have before. Thinking of myself as well as her. Usually I only think of my partner—of techniques that please the other, and hope to get some pleasure for myself. This time I have a need to please myself. I do both.

The screaming comes. Two thirty AM. How can Lena sleep with that racket? To her it's as though it wasn't there. I pull myself from her arms. I slip out our torn doorway. The sky is clear and the moon almost as bright as last night. I head towards the sound. I startle a deer from her hiding place. Mostly she startles me. It reminds me of how my sister jumped out at me. How I had to keep watching my back.

I'm starting to shake. In spite of this night and Lena...my Lena, my future—so many good things to look forward to.... She'll spoil it.

Naked. Barefoot. I head towards the screaming. Same direction as before, following the ridge. This time I go silently, to creep up on her. I'll scare her for a change. Pounce on her. I'll yell in her ear as she did in mine. Why hadn't I ever thought of that before?

But I no sooner get closer to the sound that lures me, than I wonder: What if my sister heads for Lena. What if she counts on the baby owls to keep me away. I turn and rush back, this time crashing through the brush, stumbling, falling....

And she *is* there, in the moonlight, grinning, her teeth stick out in front like mine do, too, glistening. Her glasses catch the light again...a gibbous moon in each lense.

She says again, hoarse and husky as if one branch against another, "You've always been mine."

And I say again, "I know it."

The wind is blowing. As before, the rags she wears—white and loose—fly out around her. Her tangled hair forms a halo.

I drop to my knees.

But then I get up. I say, "No! I'm not yours anymore."

I scream as she screams. I shriek. I show her who can be the loudest. I attack. I grab. As before, bushes, branches, saplings.... Nothing is real. While she trips me, pushes me down.... I reach for hair. Anything to have something actual, but nothing is. I even try to blow her away, as if I, along with the wind.... Of course it doesn't work. There's nothing to her. She light as air. No substance. How could I have thought.... I'm whipped, lashed, pounded, stamped on. Then something comes down from behind, hard, on my head.

It doesn't knock me out, but it takes a while for me to come to myself.

And here's Lena, giving me a drink from our canvas bucket, wiping my face with cool water.

"I'm sorry I hit you so hard. I had to stop you."

"Did you see her?"

"Who?"

"My sister."

"You were as if fighting yourself."

"If you'll stay with me...."

"Of course I will."

But my sister is still here, watching us. "Don't you see her?"

Lena squints where I'm pointing.

"She's there."

I see that Lena sees...something. She gets between me and my sister. But I can't let her.

"It's just mist from the valley below."

The shrieking comes again and this time there's no doubt it's coming from right here.

"Hear that? It's her."

But the owl flies over, hardly a yard above our heads, silent except for her screech. One screech.

My sister speaks but in such a hissing whisper. "Ssss see how she looks straight at me and doesn't see. Tell her it's between you and me. Tell her you've always been mine."

"Listen. Listen, Lena. It's my sister."

"It's only the wind. It's only branch against branch."

My sister: "It's only blowing leaves. It's only the cottonwoods, sounding like a river. It's mist from the lake."

Lena: "It's in your head."

My sister: "You know you're crazy. Even as a child. Even as you listened from your secret spot. It wasn't a secret from me. I knew everything. When has it ever not been so?"

She's right. She's always been right.

Lena squints into the shadows. Says, "It's the wind. It's branch against branch. Mist." She's calm.

My sister comes close, leans, and looks straight into Lena's face. "Call this beauty? Call this brains?"

She shouldn't have done that. I grab at my sister's neck. She's so close. I have her by the throat. Finally something to hang on to.

She yells but I squeeze tight. I stop the sound right in the middle of it.

Her fingers try to pry me away.

Then cold water shocks me sane. Lena has found the strength to grab the pail of water she'd used to revive me. Threw it over me.

"You nearly killed me."

Her voice is hoarse. She has bruises on her neck. Could I have done that? How could I?

"I'm sorry. I'm so sorry. I can't believe I did that."

"What were you thinking? Who was your sister, anyway?"

She wipes my face with her bandana. Holds the dipper for me to drink.

"I should be doing this for you."

"You will."

I do. I hold the dipper for her.

We sit, then, her arm across my shoulders, head to head, and I tell her all about my sister. Then I say, "But maybe it's over. I think it is. I hope it is. I'm so sorry."

"If she doesn't leave you alone, she'll have to deal with me."

"Stay with me."

"Of course. I said I would."

***Asimov's Science Fiction Magazine*,** October-November 2006

Such a Woman, Or, Sixties Rant

A woman is a field upon which to play out the general malaise of the times, a field upon which to act out one's disillusionment with self, a microcosm where the larger issues of the day can be divined and clarified, where courses about to be charted across vast wastelands can be played out in miniature, a retreat where one can brush up on tactics or blow off steam, whichever is most necessary at any given moment. A woman is, in other words, a playing field, a sort of Mayan ball court where games of incredible significance, both mystical and religious, take place, sometimes several times a week. (Healthy self-conceptions are dependent on it.)

But not just any woman will do. Many women can be left to go on with their lives any way they see fit, it is of no importance. As long as they don't stop traffic or trains or disrupt shipping lanes, they can be left to their own devices.

But these other women. ... They must be singularly suited to the job, and dressed for it, not only all their waking hours, but while sleeping also and perhaps even at those very private moments of actual penetration, hair spread out over the pillow, gown in studied disarray.... It goes without saying that such a woman should be eager to be of service to her county through her countrymen: senators, executives, and bureaucrats... that she should yearn to "take part" through her boss, her pilot, her instructor, her dean, and sometimes her landlord, though she must understand (and usually does, though not always), that there are no special citations or awards connected with it.

Such a woman should be self-possessed only in as much as she defines and contains the "other" within herself so that when she looks into a mirror ...

(which she frequently does-has to do, in fact, in order to make herself ready for her task)... when she does, it is not only to assess her own image, but to imagine herself beyond herself as the "other," imagine herself to be the very one who will possess her. How will he see her? How will he judge her? She counts on his first impression. She counts on his: "What I see is what I long for," at any given moment (or, preferably, at every moment.) She is wondering what, then, about her can make him look up staring? Startled? Will he see her as she has prepared herself to be seen? And, if not, can she face him anyway? And will she be able to read the tell-tale signs on his face well enough to program her next move? Therefore she comes either from the shower or the flower shop with the same questioning look, eyes wide, and searching for the expression she needs in order to know and to outguess the "other." She must know him well if she would not deny him anything, wanting, as she does, to outshine all other women in his life (and most especially his mother) yet fearful that this may not be so.

None of this means that she is necessarily promiscuous. Many such women manage to fulfill their functions as practice fields quite adequately with only three or two or even, sometimes (depending on the importance of the man in question), with only one man.

A woman changes her life by changing to another man. A new man is her way of going through transformations and epiphanies. Sometimes she tries not to cause another woman pain while at the same time trying to please the other woman's man. Such a woman knows that she is handsomer than most wives.

Such a woman is full of breathless enthusiasm for almost everything, and yet not indiscriminately so. All impermissible brands of sentimentality held in check. Also all exudings, emanations, effluvium... all kept to a minimum so that the only blood seen or even suspected is from small cuts such as a paper cut on her thumb as she prepares, perhaps, the carrots for his salad. The drops of this blood are never larger than miniature roses which are her favorite flowers.

Such a woman gives the world that personal touch. She has neither the breasts of a ballet dancer nor those of a yenta.

Such a woman doesn't last long though she counts on duration. Duration is, in fact, what she cares about more than any other thing: duration of love (how string love out for as long as possible?), and duration of youth and beauty. In other words, she waits. She waits for him to return. She waits for his desire. Also there is the duration of motherhood, having sometimes had his children. Motherhood is of longer duration than she thought it would be and fraught with pitfalls. (She is waiting for the children in many of the same ways that she has waited for the "significant other." She waits, in fact, for them to grow up.)

For a long time no one knows how old she really is. These days a woman can be anywhere from twentyeight to almost forty-six and one hardly knows the difference.

A woman is a field of endeavor filled with pitfalls, and, in the end, she, herself, becomes the pitfall... becomes the pit that she, herself, falls into. When this happens, not wanting to fly in the face of custom or society nor to lose her hold on reality, she, therefore, dresses for the new part, and suddenly no more bikinis.

She feels she has only herself to blame. Somehow she has allowed herself to grow old.

A woman is a field upon which to lay a hand in order to distribute pleasure as one sees fit, and so, having pointed this out, the significant other may well lay and hand on several women consecutively for exactly this purpose so that such a woman is thinking: "What's the use?" for the fifth or sixth time, and is, perhaps this time, not to blame for her own distress. But, on the other hand, perhaps this also is her own fault. Perhaps such a woman has not given of herself even yet to such a degree that fidelity-the fidelity for which she has waited and waited-has, therefore, not been bestowed upon her.

And there are always flaws even when not visible to the naked eye and, even if not fatal they are fatal in the long run. There may be a touch of impatience or a general apprehensiveness. Worse yet, there may be a mole on the cheek or a birth mark on the thigh, breasts a bit pendulous. There are clearly flaws even in the best of women. Though the flaws are small, they may have declared themselves first, before the woman "spoke" of her own accord. A woman does, therefore, mix her perfection with defects, and now, just at the time in her life when she yearns to improve, such a woman will find herself on the decline in spite of having taken vigorous measures. Suddenly her real age shows. Suddenly she can't get into the positions for her lover. Suddenly she has begun to limp and sputter.

Such a woman may be found floating face down just off shore, perhaps (for once) wanting to be seen from another angle entirely. She may be brought back to life by a quick blow to the solar plexus and a few pats on the back and, if so, will wonder for the rest of her days if she had been thrown overboard, or if she had jumped in by herself. Or if, on the other hand, she had been set adrift in a small unseaworthy boat, and, if so, by whom? And by whose hand now raised up and why? And (especially) is it someone she can count on? And for how long?

If there appears suddenly on the streets, as though from nowhere, a woman without language or money, wondering how she got here and where is the man who had provided for her? She says, "Ah, ah, ah, ah," and waits at a cross road. "Ah, ah, ah." Who will teach her the ways of the world and to speak and to speak out? There must be thousands of such women wandering about wondering how to proceed, all dressed up and with too much make-up, hobbling in high heels and mouthing gibberish. It's as if it was the playing field itself that has lost the game. More likely it's exactly as the Mayans said (their worst curse of all): You will not be allowed to play ball!

But what if one such woman meets another and recognizes her as someone in the same plight? What if four or five of them find a common street corner? Mouthing gibberish, yes, but significant gibberish?

They have keys that no longer fit locks. They have their bobby pins. They have nail files and pencils, assorted pills, garters, the heels of their high heeled shoes, and they have nothing more to lose. But the "significant other" ... all the "significant others" are not uneasy. In fact they do not think about such women at all.

Lady Churchill's Rosebud Wristlet, November 2006

At Sixes And Sevens

Remember when this used to be an orchard? Some of the trees still live and still bear fruit. In the yard, the asparagus patch still pushes up stalks in among the weeds. If you're careful you can still climb the porch steps without breaking your neck.

It used to be a nice farm. The old man worked it— mostly by himself. No sons, only a daughter. She's a strong one, though, small but wiry.

Now that he's dead, she keeps it going by herself but she doesn't grow what we grow. She grows useless crops of nettles and thistles. Though I must admit, her strawberries are wonderful, small and flavorful. In certain seasons, I can smell them from here.

Her Dad was peculiar. Kept to himself.

Poor little motherless child...she was. My husband and I wanted to help. Her father wouldn't let us. Took her wherever he went in a basket at first. Then made a little harness for her and tied her near him as if she was a dog. That can't be good, especially since we were right here, willing to help.

Later on he put bells on her so he could keep track of where she was. As if she was the bellwether. Once we saw him climb up to take her down from the shed roof. Another time it was that big old cottonwood. Part of it split when he went to rescue her and he nearly broke his neck.

Well, she did grow up, but it's a wonder.

And a wonder she learned to talk. We never heard him say much more than grunts.

He always said he home-schooled her. I'll bet!

Even now that her dad's dead, she never comes to us for anything. All she has for company is that big old dog and her cat. Even when she broke her leg she didn't want our help. You could tell by the way she looked at us, though that time, she couldn't get along without us.

When I take a rest from housework I take my tea up and watch her out my east side upstairs window. I can see her best when she's in her weedy vegetable garden. She talks as she works...or at least I see her mouth moving. Singing would be one thing, but this looks more like jabber, jabber, jabber. What in the world can she be jabbering about? And who to?

She's done that since she was a little girl—yapping to herself. Jumping about so you'd think a baby goat.

I say it's her own fault if everything goes wrong. Though she wouldn't tell us if it did or didn't, and now that there's a drought things are going wrong for everybody.

Though why should we care? I've only talked to her, face to face, a couple of times. She's one of those people that doesn't look you in the eye. All these years, I've lived next door, and I don't even know what color her eyes are. I can guess though. You can't have hair that light and fine and have dark eyes.

We're the ones took her to the clinic to get a cast on her leg. We stayed the night in town and brought her back the next day. She had us...*let* us, that is, set her up in her, so called living room on the so called couch. (I wonder how many generations of cats have scratched at it. The one now is a marmalade tabby. A nasty male. He arched his back and spit at me. I can't help thinking that's what she wanted to do to me, too. Iris. Her name, not the cat's.)

She actually did thank us. At least that. Though she didn't even look at me then. I left her with plenty of food and water. I didn't feed the tabby.

I might not have seen her at all, down there behind her lilacs. She'd climbed up to fix an attic window. She didn't yell out for anybody. She just lay there. I went upstairs to my window to see what in the world she was doing *now*, and there she was, her legs sticking out from the bushes. And later that afternoon when I went up to see again, there they still were.

I sort of wanted her to fall but I didn't think somebody like her, who used to climb everything in sight, ever really would.

When I saw she had, I thought, well, she can't object to me going over to see what's wrong, so I did, and a good thing, too. But, as I keep saying, helping people is a thankless task.

There's something wrong with her. All her dad's fault no doubt. I've been watching her more and more. Daniel says I'm not getting my chores done, but I want to see what she's up to. I tell him it might be important. I say, "What if she's a witch? What if this drought is her fault? What about that she dances in her backyard at midnight when there's a full moon?" (Or maybe even when there isn't except it's too dark to see.)

He looks surprised when I tell him that. Not about the dancing, but as if he wonders why I'm looking out the window in the middle of the night.

"It didn't look like any kind of dance I've ever seen before. Hopping and galumphing. Swinging her arms around. Far as I'm concerned, not much different than a four year old would do."

All he says is, "Now that her leg is broke, I doubt she'll be doing much dancing."

As if that would reassure me.

But that broken leg is a good excuse for me keeping an eye on her. I'll bring things to her whether she wants me to or not. It's my Christian duty. Even Daniel can't say I shouldn't. I might be able to snoop around the other rooms some. There's never been a chance like this before. I want to take advantage of it.

Daniel would say, "Let her be," but he doesn't have to know.

I bake a batch of gingerbread. I think of making lemonade, but, no, I'll see if I can pick up something over there. That'll be an excuse to look around. Not that I relish seeing all that scratched up furniture.

Should I knock or just barge in?

I'll barge in.

I yell, "Yoo hoo, anyone to home?"

It's the cat meets me at the door.

Iris is right where I left her, potato chips all eaten, the water drunk. But I see signs that she's been up. There's two of her dad's old canes beside her and a little chair pulled up close by. There's an old army blanket thrown over the couch back. Days are so hot I forgot the nights are cold.

I put the gingerbread down beside her. "Still warm," I say. I unwrap it and the good smell fills the whole dusty, Tom-cat-smelling, house.

She actually looks right at me, and as if she's grateful. Her eyes.... I was wrong. How can such a wispy blond have brown eyes?

"I'll get you something to drink."

I march right into the tiny kitchen.

She can't complain about me rattling around looking for things when it's all for her. Besides, what I find might be for the good of all of us. Maybe the whole village.

I look around as fast as I can.

Devil's claw, squaw tea, wild rose hips.... Acorns! Lots of dried lettucy sort of stuff. Things a witch would have.

I take pinches of several of those things and put them in my apron pocket.

The cat watches.

I swear that nasty Tom looks at me like the Devil himself. Who ever said a witch's cat had to be black? Seems to me a marmalade color is just as bad.

Dishes draining in the sink look clean enough. She's been up. I'm sure of it. Or somebody has.

Cat dish on the floor is empty. I whisper, "Don't expect me to feed you. Go get yourself a mouse."

I let the water run till it's cool so I have more time to snoop. (Not that the water's ever cool this time of year.) I bring her a glass and a pitcher of it.

I say, "I'll get you another blanket and a sweater. Nights are cold." And off I go before she can stop me.

There are two small bedrooms across from each other. The dad's is still clearly his. It's been what? Four, five years since he died? Though why would she change it and who for? It smells odd. That old hound must be sleeping in here. I wouldn't ever let a dog like him inside my house let alone on a bed.

Her room.... There's the oddest picture on the wall. It's a combination diagram and photo. Can't be from around here. Jagged cliffs and such. A waterfall coming right out from the middle of the rocks. A night scene. Moons galore. Or maybe the same moon at different stages. Lines go back and forth across it, with numbers and letters that don't make any sense.

I've a good mind to ask her where her father came from, and if this picture on the wall is where. I always did wonder. He had an accent. But I won't ask yet. I don't want her thinking that I'm thinking things.

I rummage for a sweater. Then I think maybe she wants a clean blouse and underwear, too. I'm not going to help her get any of those on or off over her cast. I'll just bring them. Enough's enough.

Everything else in the room is perfectly ordinary—nothing fancy there at all.

Well, not so ordinary. A normal young woman would have had some posters of movie stars or musicians on the wall, not this odd landscape. A normal girl would have maybe her own art work. Or pictures of horses, that's the usual around here. She does have some feathers stuck on the wall with push pins. Some big brownish black ones from turkey vultures.

Turkey vultures! It all fits together.

On the way home I pick an apple from one of those old trees. I take a couple of bites—so sweet and juicy—better than most. Wormy of course. Tasty as it is, I toss it away. It's like her. She's a pretty girl, but a menace to all of us.

But Daniel won't pay any attention to me. All he'll say is, "Let her be for heaven's sake. She's doing the best she can."

"How can I let her be when I'm sure? And look how dry our fields are. And she won't even ever come to church. Isn't that a sign of something? And what about those apples?"

"What about them?"

"Isn't it just like a witch to have the sweetest apples of all and then have them all wormy?"

Daniel just laughs.

I'm not going to, "let her be," but I won't tell Daniel. I have to stop her. What could stop a witch? Salt? Vinegar? Maybe you have to fight fire with fire. Maybe I can think up spells of my own to out-spell her. Maybe I could do my own moonlight dance. With her broken leg, I could get way ahead of her spellwise.

All that bla, bla, bla, when I saw her mouth moving. That must have been spells. I should have thought of that before. Where can I find a spell of my own? Or do I have to make one up? And talking in tongues. I've heard of that. Is that from God or the devil? Boolla bomba sitty so, sat satterloopa gluey zit. I can do that without even trying.

Saturday night seems like the right time, and the moon is *almost* full.

I do it. I go out and dance. Actually, it's a nice thing to do. I didn't think it would be. It was hard getting started, but once I do, I enjoy it. You have to forget yourself and not worry about how it might look. Thank goodness Daniel is too sound a sleeper to wake up in the middle of the night and see me.

Of course next morning I'm all worn out. I sleep till eight. Daniel brings me tea and asks me what's wrong. He says I look pale. He's milked the cow and goat for me and he's already been out in the fields for an hour. I guess I danced longer than I thought.

I drink the tea looking out the window in my usual spot. I don't expect to see her but I do. First I see the cat. Swinging his tail in a kind of swagger. He's so self possessed it makes me angry. But then she comes out on her mismatched canes. Then she gives up, drops the canes and just crawls dragging her leg behind. It's the strawberries she was after. She sits there and picks them straight into her mouth. She doesn't look much like a witch now. More like a greedy little kid. But she doesn't fool me.

I can't ask anybody to help me. Daniel certainly won't. And, far as I know, there aren't any books about it. I'll have to find out everything by myself.

But, once I think about it, when I saw her climbing up to fix her window, I wanted her to fall and she did. I wasn't even thinking about a spell. Now what did I do right that time that made it happen?

Next time I see that cat I'm going to stare right back at it no matter how much it stares at me. If anything is evil around here it's that cat. Maybe he's the one in charge of this drought. Maybe he's the one I should get rid of.

That afternoon I ask her right out where did her father come from. I bring her a cheese sandwich and pickled green tomatoes, and I pick up some of her own apples on the way over. She thanks me, nice as could be.

She says he was Romanian. It figures. Didn't all sorts of odd people come from Romania? Gypsies and such, and even Dracula?

Her father came out here alone with just that baby girl. Maybe he stole her. Except you could see she was nothing but a big bother to him while he tried to farm. I wonder why he wanted her and took all that trouble to look after her. I guess she must be his real daughter.

Then I ask her, "Where's that old dog of yours?"

"Howie? He's around here someplace. He always is."

"I haven't seen him."

He's no particular kind, just a big, lumpy dog. Almost as red as the cat. There must be a reason why every creature around here is red.

That cat and I stare at each other. I'm the one that looks away first though I vowed not to. He looked me up and down and back and forth. I never saw the like. I felt kind of shaky afterwards.

"What did you say this cat's name is?"

"We just call him Red."

We? Who does she mean, we? Or did they have him back when her father was still around?

How about I get rid of that cat first? I'll talk in tongues and make up a dance and a spell.... I won't do anything like put out poison or set a trap. I'll dance for a pleasant easy death—in the middle of a happy dream.

I do it. I dance and dance. Actually I haven't had so much fun since Daniel and I went dancing when we first married. Daniel has been too busy to even think of dancing. Besides, I don't think he ever liked it. I talk a crazy language all my own. Or maybe it's Romanian or some sort of gypsy language. How would I know? But whatever it is, it comes easily.

In the morning, everything's at sixes and sevens. Lunch isn't even begun and laundry not done. I don't wake up till around ten...ten for heaven's sake! Daniel comes in to see how I am and I'm not even up yet. He thinks I'm really sick. He says, again, how pale I look and that I have circles under my eyes. He brings me toast and chamomile tea and tells me to stay in bed, which I'm happy to do. I lie there and doze and think. Ditties and sayings keep rolling around in my head. "Proof of the pudding, Catch as catch can, Cat's out of the bag, Willy nilly, and such." I think I'm a natural at...I'm not sure what, spells I guess.

Then I remember the things I pinched off and put in my apron pocket. I get up and check on them. Crumble them. Mix them all together and boil them up. I figure, since I don't know what I'm doing anyway, might as well use them all. I could tell one was just catnip, but who knows, catnip might be magic. Besides, there's that cat.

I taste them. Ugh. I put what's left in the icebox. Strange, but even that little sip made me feel a lot better. I was just dragging myself around. Maybe I'll keep the brew for when I need energy.

So far nothing has happened to that cat. I went over there special to take a look. I brought some left over hamburger. There she was, lying there as usual and there was that cat. If cats can give the evil eye, that cat is doing it. I don't even try to match it stare-to-stare anymore.

"Have you been up?"

"I've crawled around a little."

"Poor child. What can I do for you before I go?"

I do want to be kind. I always like to help.

"Would you feed the cat? And make sure he has water? Please."

She's asking this deliberately. Is it some kind of a test. She hasn't asked me to do anything before. Not even once. For sure only a witch would ask me to do that, knowing what that cat thinks of me.

Should I do it or not? Or should I poison him right now? But with what?

I won't do it. Neither one, neither feed nor poison.

"I'm afraid I must be off."

I hurry away, all shaky. What am I thinking? A spell is one thing, but poison?

Yes, but that look in his eyes. As if he knows all about me.

I dance that night yet again...even though nothing seems to be happening over there. This time I sing and beat time on an old jar. I have even more fun than the other nights.

And then I look up and see Daniel at the window staring down at me.

I stop and just stand there, breathing hard, and here he comes, out the back door.

"What in the world?" And, "No wonder you're tired." He's angry. "What's got into you? The house is a mess and the cooking is lousy, and here you are enjoying yourself in the middle of the night."

I start to say that I'm *not* enjoying myself, but I realize I am. In lots of ways. I love to dance and I have this purpose...to save us all from the drought. I'm helping people.

"Come back to bed." He takes my hand. He doesn't look so angry now. "I'll make you some chamomile tea. You're shaking."

Even with the tea, it takes me a long time to calm down and go back to sleep. I lie there thinking about that cat. Spells and dancing don't seem to be working. I'm going to have to find a better way.

Next day I get up at a reasonable time and make Daniel's breakfast. I decide not to go over to Iris's for a while. She's getting better and I left extra cheese and bread last time. Besides, she's got her strawberry patch. And she probably could get some of her wormy apples, too, without much trouble.

How do you kill a clever cat? I've already done all the spells and dancing I can think of. I need a rest and a chance to think up more things to do. What's a pentacle?

Next time I do go over there, she's lying on the couch again and the cat is sitting on the back of it right over her as if on guard. (Look how he looks at me. Those funny slits of cat's eyes. As bad as goat's.)

Somebody has left her fresh water and I see the remains of food I didn't bring. There's even apricots from my tree. I was right all along, somebody besides me is helping her. Or some kind of witching is going on. How else could she have gotten five of my apricots?

But she's been crying. At first I think I should have come over before, but my not coming isn't the problem.

"Howie is...like you said...off somewhere. I haven't seen him for days. He's so old. I was wondering if you could look for him. See if anything happened to him."

"Me!"

I'm so startled it comes out in a squeak.

"If you wouldn't mind. You've done so much already I hate to ask. And he is old. He could have just crawled off to be by himself to die."

I will. No harm in a little walk around. I might learn more about her and her place.

"Yes! Yes, I will," I say.

I run around to the front of the house. That's the part I never can see from my window.

What a mess. The front porch is obviously never used. There's the old swing. I don't dare sit on it. Its rusty chains would probably pop right out of the ceiling. There's a wasp nest up there, too. Of course what use has Iris for a porch like this, anyway? Nobody will ever sit here.

I almost forget I'm supposed to be looking for Howie. I lean over and check under the house. As far as I can see it's empty under there, but I'm not going to crawl in. She can't expect me to do that.

I go around to the outbuildings. I check under the honeysuckle. I go into—not very far into—the dusty old barn. I go all the way to the edge of her land where the goat shed used to be. And I find him. Dead. Did I do that with my spells? I meant to kill the cat, not this poor old mangy dog. Well at least my spells worked on something.

I have to go back and tell Iris. I hope she doesn't want me to bring her the body. I just can't do that. It already smells. Maybe Daniel will do it for her. I'll tell her he'll bury him under the honeysuckle if she wants that.

When I come back to tell her, that cat is still sitting on the back of the couch as if on guard. He stares at me again.

"He's dead," I say.

She tries to get up right on her broken leg, but then flops back down.

"He's out by the goat shed. Daniel'll bury it if you want him to. Do you have a wheelbarrow?"

Daniel does go over. I didn't go with him. I figured I'd done enough, besides, I wanted to think. I mean if she only has that cat for company I feel sorry for her even though I still think that cat should go. What if I found her a puppy?

Daniel looks shaken when he comes back. "That old dog wasn't worth much except for company. She's going to miss him. He was her father's. Thirteen years old."

Thirteen! Everything is fitting together.

"I'm going to get her some crutches. Why didn't we bring some right away? I know you've been helping her a lot, but she needs to be able to get around more. She wants to make a grave marker. I found her a nice piece of wood. I'll pound it in when she's got it carved."

He shakes his head, no, about five times. He's still upset. "We wrapped him in her grandmother's old hand sewn quilt."

"But that quilt must be valuable."

"She even had me put flowers in the grave and old bones and a book that belonged to her father. She had an antique necklace, and she put it around the dog's neck. I know how she feels. Remember when little Mitzie died?"

"It's not the same. Mitzie was a big help to you."

"She sure could move cows."

Too bad about that quilt. All that handwork gone for a dog. I don't say it, though. Daniel looks as if he thinks it's perfectly all right. I suppose that's just like a man.

Daniel is so bothered he doesn't eat much supper and drinks too much coffee. And I never saw a person shake their head, no, so much. I don't think I'll be able to dance this night. He won't be sleeping well. And all because of a no good lumpy dog that didn't even belong to us.

I do sleep well though Daniel doesn't. I hear him get up. I see him standing, looking out the window towards Iris's house. It's a moonless night so there can't be anything to see. I feel a yearning to be out dancing and chanting but I'll just have to wait for Daniel to stop his worrying. And I'll have to stop dancing so close to the house. Maybe it would be better if I did it nearer to Iris's place. That old orchard in the moonlight! With all those half dead broken down trees....

Daniel is way ahead of me. He finds a puppy in town. A stray that ended up at the feed store. Nobody knows what kind it is or how big it'll get. He brings it here first and asks me how I think she'll like it. It's been mistreated and needs a good home.

"Look," he says. "Somebody hit him on the head and ruined his eye. See the scar? And his ear is torn."

None of that makes him very nice to look at, but I don't say so.

He bought a big bag of dog food and a bowl that says DOG on it. And he also got her some crutches.

"How much did all this cost?"

"It's maybe too soon for a new dog, but he needs somebody and it'll be good for her to take him in."

Then he looks at me in a odd way as if maybe it would be even better if I took him in. I certainly don't want it—not even for an hour.

"Take it over now. It'll cry all night and I'm not taking it to bed with *us*. Beside, she'll want the company."

Next day I go over with fresh hot cornbread and there's the pup snuggled up beside her. Looks like even the cat has accepted him. He's walking back and forth across the back of the couch swinging his tail as if in charge of everything.

She's been up and around. There's some wash hanging on a new little line over the sink. I wonder if Daniel put that line up. And there's that new dog bowl.

I bring her fresh water and fuss around as if I'm doing something though it seems Daniel has already done everything that's needed. More than what's needed. For Heaven's sake, he turned down her bed and put a candy bar on her pillow. For that skinny girl?

I go home feeling really bad. I go into the barn but the cow and goat are out to pasture now. There's nothing warm to lean against.

Could she have given him some sort of love potion? What could he see in such a wispy little person who always has her hair falling in front of her eyes? And she hardly has any breasts at all.

I don't know how I did it, but I do it. I kill that cat. Cats don't fall. Or if they do they don't hurt themselves—not from just two stories up, which is all we have around here.

It was hard to do. I danced half the night, not in my yard, but way out in the back of that old orchard.

Iris comes hobbling all the way over here on her new crutches, the puppy running circles around her lickety-split. Even from my kitchen window I can see she's crying. Daniel is out in the fields so it's just me.

I walk out to meet her and get a skirt full of puppy paw prints. If that dog was mine, first thing I'd teach him is not to jump on people. When he gets bigger it's going to be a lot worse.

Right away she says, "Why does everything happen all at once? I know they were both old but why right now, one after the other? Everything is dying."

And I know I did it, finally. I feel such a sense of power.

"Will you help me bury him?"

So we do that. We put him right next to where Howie is. With flowers and half that chocolate bar Daniel left. She wraps him in an old shawl. A flowery one with fringe. Some sort of heirloom I suppose. I don't think she should do that, but I don't say a word. I'm not one to criticize.

Afterwards she thanks me and says I should go on home, she's going to sit there for a while.

At first that pup tries to follow me but it soon gives up and goes back to Iris.

We're all in trouble if it gets to be the size of Howie and keeps on jumping on people. I'd be doing everybody a favor, yet again, if I got rid of it before it gets up to that size.

The drought goes on. We've never seen it this bad. And hot! I wish I knew if Iris was finding a way to keep on dancing and doing spells even with a broken leg. She is getting better. I should feel sorry for her with just that bouncy puppy out there, and I sort of do but not if she's a witch.

I don't go over there as often as I did and I thought Daniel had stopped going over, too, but then I see him coming home from the wrong direction. He doesn't lie. When I ask he says he was checking on her. That she was up and had cooked apple tarts. He says they were delicious.

I ask if the worms were good.

I can just see them sitting on that smelly old couch gobbling tarts—which are no doubt full of that love potion of hers—one wispy dishwater blond and one dark, not very tall man with hairy arms. I don't see why either one would want the other.

Maybe if I dance all the harder.... Or maybe I shouldn't be enjoying dancing. And what about those herbs I cooked up that make me feel so energetic? I still have some of that tea left. I think I'll go on back to her place and steal some more dried green things.

This time it's easy. There's nobody home. And here are the apple tarts. I shouldn't. Who knows what will happen? But they look so good.

I always bring something as an excuse. This time I brought apple turnovers. Same apples. My turnovers are good, too.

I take my time looking around again. There are some books in a different language. Those are probably exactly what I need, if only I could read them. I steal a small one. Put it in my pocket. It has diagrams. I might be able to figure something out.

I meet her and the puppy coming in just as I'm leaving. By the looks, she's been out crying over the graves of Red and Howie.

"I left you an apple turnover," I say, "and I ate one of your tarts. I hope you don't mind."

I think, so there, if it's full of love potions then you're in for it from both of us. But she doesn't seem upset, and, anyway, I don't feel any different.

Later Daniel comes home—from the wrong direction again. He looks glum. Or maybe just thoughtful. I feed him a whole batch of cooked up greens from Iris' house. I have no idea what they are.

That night he has really bad diarrhea. He's up and down so much I don't have a chance to go out and dance or do any such thing. And then here he is home all day. He doesn't complain, he never does, but I can see he's feeling terrible. I think of going over to ask Iris if she has any sort of herb that would help him, except that would let her know I was on to her.

I don't very often cook up a mess of greens. Daniel is looking at me with suspicion as if he thinks I was trying to poison him. When I make him tea, I think he gets rid of it on the African Violets.

Later, sick as he is, he goes over to Iris', and not even with food or anything as an excuse. He just goes. He stays a long time, too. At twilight I start over to see what's up but I meet him on his way home. He says he's not hungry for any supper.

All right that's it then. Tomorrow is Sunday. We don't go to church that much, but I'm going and I'm telling everybody that Iris is, for sure, a witch and that Daniel is in it with her and that this whole drought thing is their fault.

Daniel falls asleep in his easy chair. He's exhausted. I wonder if it's from getting up and down all night long or is there another reason. To think I used to look at that dark, brooding face of his and think it was romantic. Now look at him, hair hanging over his eyes, shirt all sweated up.... I wouldn't want to kiss those cheeks, him badly needing a shave. How could Iris do that?

I go out under the ghostly gibbous moon. I'm so mad I can think up spells without even trying. Spell after spell after spell. And I can talk in tongues and dance as never before. I go on for hours. Until I see.... First there's smoke and then the twinkle of little fires. Like fireflies and then larger. *I* did that somehow. Then here come magpies, and all that black and white and screeching! and I'm dancing with them. I take one of the little fires and set fire to our corncrib. I don't need matches. Then I take some of that corncrib fire and set fire to our barn. And those magpies are still flapping around all over the place. And there's mooing and baaing and screeching.

And Daniel, rushing into the barn, freeing the cow and goat, and here's Iris, on crutches, and they're both looking at me and I'm dancing and dancing. Daniel says bad words. "What the hell?" and, "Damn." And worse even. And I say, "Neither of you can ever touch me."

It's true, I'm in charge...of all of it...I see that now...of the drought and of them. I say, "Bitty tatty go bo bat zakky yat." And I hear my laughter going on and on and on as the moon hides behind cinders and the ground comes up and welcomes me.

Asimov's Science Fiction Magazine, Jan. 2007

God Clown

Mud slides, land slides, earthquakes.... We know what Great God Clown does. We hear him laughing right in the middle of doing it. Sometimes he sounds just like a donkey.

He loves the desert. We all do. It's an acquired taste and we all acquired it. At first the desert scared us but now it's Great God Clown that scares.

Last year crops dried up. All the grapes turned to raisins on the vine. This year it's the opposite. Water runs right into the house even though I dug a ditch in front of the door.

Abby's house slid down. Skidded right across the road. It now sits on Ramsey's property. We propped it up so it didn't slant and it's good as new but Ramsey may not like it when he finds out it's at his place. It's in a grove of trees. A pretty spot. Much nicer than where it used to be. The stream is nearby. I hope Ramsey lets it stay.

We think something should have happened to Ramsey's place but nothing did. It's not even lopsided. That's not fair. Abby is much nicer than Ramsey. She saves animals and hands out food to whoever or whatever needs it. I don't know how many cats she has. Though only one dog. Even the dog loves cats. Abby'd save a bug. I've seen her pick up beetles and take them outside where they belong. I don't think she ever squashes anything.

And she saved me. That was a long time ago. I didn't know she was that type when I came, I just went where I saw cats and the dog. I could tell the dog wouldn't hurt me. He's like Abby. Or maybe he knows the difference between a robber and a visitor. Except I *was* a robber. I came there to rob.

Nobody was home and I knew it. I'd walked all the way from Middle Fork. It was a hot day. First I stopped at the spigot in the front yard for a drink and to fill my water bottle. Then I knocked on the door and called, though I knew there was nobody home. I walked all around the house. I petted the dog. I petted the cats. Some of them. I tried to count them but I couldn't. I told them all, all I was going to steal was food and a drink, then I broke a window and crawled in. I made myself a peanut butter sandwich. I was a kid and that's what I liked best. Abby only had one good chair. I sat in it in the tiny living room, a cat on my lap as I ate.

Abby drove in her rickety pick-up just as I was climbing back out. I heard her coming a long way off. If I hadn't stopped to steal another piece of bread for later I'd have made it out and away before she got back.

All the donkeys with eel stripes and striped socks belong to Great God Clown. In the yard there was just such a one. Also one goat, one sheep and a nasty rooster.

Great God C.—just when you think all's well, he'll trip you up. I don't know what he wants. Mostly to laugh—at the way we try to eke out a living in among all these stones and on the slopes too steep for planting. He sends our terraces down whenever he feels like it.

Abby didn't say a word when she saw me. I was stuck, one leg on one side of the window sill and one leg on the other, bread in one fist, water bottle in the other. No wonder I fell out and squashed her marigolds.

She looked at me hard and then turned around and grabbed two bundles of groceries, came over and handed them to me—can you believe it? Me with my bread and water bottle?—and went back to the truck for more. We took them inside. (The door had been unlocked all along. Now that I know her I know she never locks anything.)

She went ahead and put things away. I could have run away right then, but I just stood there.

Abby is a small skinny person. Even back then I was bigger than she is, and yet she scared me. I didn't dare move.

Finally, after everything was put away, she turned and stared me up and down. I was dusty from the long walk. I hadn't even combed my hair when I left home four days ago. My top was my nightgown, tucked into my brother's worn out work pants, but she knew I was a girl right away, though some along the way had called me, Boy, and, Sonny.

Her very first words to me were, "How'd you like a bath?"

She didn't even ask me what my name was or tell me hers. I don't think she cares much about names. I'll bet she thinks: do ravens have names? Hummingbirds? Jackrabbits? And what about all these cats? And I suppose she didn't care what name I gave her.

But names are useful. Afterwards she told me hers was Abby.

I've seen God Clown. I really have. (I don't lie now that I've been with Abby. Lots of people do though. Many say they've seen him but haven't.) But you spend your life in the hills, you see things. He doesn't like to be seen. One of these days I'll be washed over the side of a terrace myself, or come down in a big sweep of scree or snow. Those are his favorite ways.

I'll bet Abby's seen him. I'll bet more than once.

And so I took a bath and Abby gave me one of her loose men's shirts to wear after. I was too big to fit her jeans or t-shirts. And while I took a bath she washed out my nightgown and my brother's pants. After that we went out and fed every creature for half a mile around and after that we fed ourselves.

Even though I'd had a big sandwich, I was still hungry enough to eat lots of split pea soup.

I slept on a pad on the floor in her living room and was happy for it. In fact I slept better than I had since I left. I felt safe with Abby, even with the door unlocked.

We didn't talk much until next morning at breakfast. Actually, not so much even then. First we went out for eggs and thanked the chickens—every single one. Then we sat down to scrambled eggs with cheese.

"So," she said, "do you want to tell me how you got those bruises?"

I thought they didn't show much. And after all it had been four days and most were where you couldn't see. Maybe she watched me as I took a bath. I wouldn't put it past her. I wouldn't put anything past her.

I couldn't answer.

"Look here," she said, and lifted her t-shirt to show me her back. "I had that same problem, but a long time ago. That's all over with. Maybe yours is, too."

I couldn't answer even more.

It was a black t-shirt and had a picture of mountains on the front and under them it said GET LOST. I wondered if she wore it to tell me what to do next. Now that I know her I know she wouldn't say that. Yesterday she was wearing one that had a book and under it was written, READ SLOWLY. In a way I know she meant them both.

(Later on I *did* get lost in the mountains, but on purpose.)

"Well," she said, "it's not that hard to guess. Your dad or who?"

So then I said, "My dad's dead."

"So it's got to be a who."

But that was all I could say. And Abby said, "I don't need to know. Besides that's three towns back." (I'd already told her I'd walked four days.) Then she said, "Let's get to work." And so we did and afterwards we went to town and got me some jeans and t-shirts of my own. Abby said I'd already earned them with my work and I could do more work tomorrow if I felt the need to earn more.

I said I wanted boy's t-shirts because they had pockets, but I really wanted boy's because they were boy's. And I still did like wearing my brother's old worn-out work pants.

I didn't have breasts yet and I didn't want them. Back then I thought maybe I'd be lucky and that would never happen.

I never did tell her who did it—all those bruises. I mean it's not a unique story that has to be told over and over in slightly different ways and with different people. Abby'd be the first to say that, especially since she had whip marks on her back and wasn't about to ever tell me how she got them.

Of course there wasn't room for me to stay with Abby very long. All she has is one room with a sleeping alcove for herself. She didn't say anything—she never would—but I could tell it was hard for her. First we built a house of thatch...*all* thatch...that we made for me out in back of hers and later I moved way up above everybody else. Onto the steep places where they bring their goats sometimes.

Talk about a lopsided house! Mine was that way the minute we nailed it up.

I was happy all the time here...every single minute. Not like home. I did a lot of work for everybody, even Ramsey sometimes. I got me my own cat. I had me a sheltering boulder and a pretty good tree.

I learned how to grow things, take care of animals, and avoid roosters. (Not a one of us, including Abby, who wasn't afraid of them.) And I did get breasts after a while in spite of myself.

But I don't like how things are going in our valley these days. Ramsey made Abby move back to her little spot that's a long ways from the stream. (Not that she hasn't a pretty good ditch.) He even tried to get her to pay rent for the two weeks she spent on his land before she could get her house dragged back.

And now these last things, rattlesnakes all over this year, people's dogs dead, houses full of stink bugs, Ramsey being Ramseyish.

Abby's too old for this kind of aggravation. Not that she would ever tell anybody how old she is. She says your age is in how hard it is to hop around, whether you can still repair the roof without falling off, and whether you can see the leaves at the tops of trees. "And," she says, "I'm getting to that age."

And this, now, is the last straw. My own house slid right on down—*all* the way down in the middle of the night.... That wouldn't be so bad if it hadn't landed on top of Abby's. She heard me coming, sprained her wrist rescuing her new puppy. It was hard enough for her, getting around before, and *now* look.

Her house is OK, but mine is a mess. We—Abby even with her bad wrist and a couple of her neighbors—dragged it back up, piece by piece, and propped it against my boulder, but I spent the night with Abby. Helped her feed everything. Helped her cook a stew. We thanked the vegetables.

The very next morning a hail storm ruins everybody's gardens. Talk about last straws! This has got to stop. I say, "Abby, we have to do something. Have things ever been this bad?" And she says, "This is the way it is. Sometimes worse and sometimes better." And I say, "I don't think so."

And yet another bad thing: Now the neighbors warn me that Ramsey found out where I used to live and told them I was here. My stepfather's going to come and get me once he gets the truck working. Wouldn't it be nice if Great God Clown would have something happen to the truck on the way here?

Like all of a sudden too much water in the ford or another mudslide down by the forks?

Sometimes I think to go on up to meet him—God Clown I mean. He's got to be pretty old by now, and maybe even meaner and more crotchety than ever. It sure seems so.

Abby would go, I bet, if she still could. She'd take him a present. Food most likely. Or a kitten. Though what would he do with a kitten? Considering what's been happening, a rooster would be more fitting and Abby's got a nasty one she could well do without.

I'll do it. Bring gingerbread and the rooster. Enough lemonade for both of us. God Clown and me, I mean. I won't tell Abby. She might worry.

I take the hardest, least-used path, the one that goes straight up. In spots it's almost gone altogether. Trust him to have a path just exactly like this, all rocks and ruts. Some places I have to crawl. Some places are completely washed out. Where else could it lead except to him?

I didn't bring enough food so I eat some of the gingerbread. I drink half the lemonade and then water it down from the stream. Maybe Great God Clown won't notice. It's still pretty good even if weak.

A couple of times I think I'm lost but I always take the worst and least used trail. It's got to be the right way.

It's afternoon before I get anywhere that seems like anyplace at all--a ledge and not much of a cave behind it, but all the more reason this has got to be his.

My legs are shaky. I'm used to climbing, but not so far, so fast, and so steep. I flop down, but the ledge is kind of scary—narrow and a drop-off on two sides—so I go on in.

After all that sunshine I can't see very well in here. Everything gleams of mica and fool's gold.

All things with glitter and with stripes or spots belong to Great God Clown. Also horned toads, owls that shriek in the middle of the night, sidewinders because of how they move....

There's just about room in here for three or four friendly people to lie down. I sit. I treat myself to more of his lemonade. I think of what to say.

Pretty soon I can see a little better.

His glinting eyes. Just like the fool's gold.

He has a permanent smile. Like a clown has. Well, of course he does.

I knew he'd look odd but I didn't think he'd look like this: A little the color of granite, a little the color of a rooster. And much smaller than I thought. I thought he'd have to be big to do all the things he does. Of course I could probably start a landslide myself. Even Abby could.

"You're an old man. How do you do it? All these disasters? And you look as if you need your sleep."

"Mmmm."

I don't scold. After I get a good look at him…well, not that good a look…I realize scolding isn't what's needed.

"You don't do if for fun, do you. Even though you smile. Even though you laugh."

"Mmmm."

"This place is so hard to find. You let me find you, didn't you?"

"Mmm mmm."

An mmm that sounds like a maybe.

Then I think about how Abby has never said a single word against him no matter what happened.

I tell him everything I practiced up to say. I tell him Ramsey has four big dogs that roam all over and scare people. I say Ramsey has a house bigger than he needs for just one messy man. I tell him Ramsey found out where I used to live and told them I was here and I may have to go back home. I say Ramsey still thinks I'm a boy even though I have breasts. I guess he never looks at me closely and never wonders why I never grow up from being a boy.

Great God Clown doesn't answer anything a rooster wouldn't have answered.

Then I ask him…just as if I had three wishes, which of course I don't…. I say: Number one, I wish that Abby should have the life she deserves. Doesn't he know her by now? Doesn't he care? Number two, there's…well, there's me. I don't want to have to go back where I got beat up just about once a week no matter what I did. There's no number three. I say, "Maybe I can work out some tit for tat. I can bring you things. I can help."

There's thunder and a sprinkling of rain outside but it doesn't bother us. The sun is still shining, low, coming in under the clouds. If I tip my head sideways, I can see a little bit of a rainbow.

Great God Clown is quiet for so long I know something's going to happen. There's just too much silence for too long a time.

Then he says, "You do it."

"What?"

"You. You do it. But no cruelty. Just what's needed. There's no going back, you know. You can't."

"I guess somebody has to do it."

"It's a necessity. Just keep things the way they have to be. The mountain trickling down. Trees blowing over. Boulders crashing off cliffs. Sometimes right on top of things. On people. It has to be."

Great God Clown is just like Abby. He says exactly what she always says, "This is the way it is, sometimes worse, sometimes better."

I see now how it's all inevitable. Slides and such. Hail. Droughts. Everything is exactly as it's supposed to be. I say, "It'll be a hard job."

"That's the way it is."

All the lemonade is gone by now and most of the gingerbread (he liked it), but he tells me I won't need much. He says, "There's moss and miner's lettuce…

Solomon Seal. Elderberries this time of year. They're good just plain. You'll have the weather to keep you company. And stars."

"I'll do the best I can."

He's hopping to the front of his cave. Cawing, cackling. Quack, quack, quack. Off he goes, happy as could be. I can't imagine where. Where could he go?

I yell out a thanks for me not having to go home. At least I got that wish.

Actually I never did get a good look at him. The rooster was always in the way and the fool's gold glittered so. Mostly I was watching the clouds outside his doorway, back-lit by lightning. I saw the rain stop. I saw the rainbow over the top of a mountain. I saw a hawk fly by.

So now it's me, having to do what has to be done to keep it like it is. You can't be mean about it. And you have to be spry and clever and sly and quick. You have to smile. *Have to*! That's the main thing. It's all one big joke.

I sneak back once in a while and, funny thing, I think I see him right in Abby's yard. She's put out a lawn chair and there he sits in a big floppy hat. Or somebody just like him. Imagine that: both of them. Two sides of the same thing. I should have known because she never said a word against him.

Coyote Road, July 2007

Master Of The Road To Nowhere

What we know so far: That we are few though we used to be many. That, through no fault of ours, we no longer have a land of our own.

It was the season to go from the fish and frog's legs, to the pine nuts, but the way was barred by new housing settlements, so we turned to the berries and the rabbits, and that way was barred, too.

Our group asked the man guarding the crossroad if there was a hidden valley anywhere in these mountains, and how to get there if there is one.

He took our dollar and pointed out the way. We could see, at the end of the other road, a town, all its windows shiny in the morning sun as if telling us to go that way, but we went in the direction he said, away from the town, but it was hard and always up. We wonder if he just wanted to get rid of us. We've walked... climbed mostly...for two days but so far we haven't arrived anywhere. Now that we're in unknown territory, even Grandma doesn't know which way to go.

The road dwindled to little more than brows trails but we kept on. We went the way the wild things had gone. Up into nowhere until we said, stop. Not because we liked it here, but because we were tired.

We sat on stones and said, this is as far as we go. We said it even though everything here is stunted. Plants that usually are bushy and lush, here hug the ground and lean over. On some there are little berries that, lower down are delicious, but here are dry and tasteless.

Maybe we can live off the people in that town. We're few now, maybe they wouldn't even notice. And we have somebody who's good at creeping around and stealing things

They mean me.

Everything is down from here, and there's all these stones. We could pry them out and roll them down on people in case they find out it's us that's been stealing. And we have Our Big Man to do that.

They mean me.

So we make camp. Not easy in this wind. The ground is so hard we have to tie our tent ropes to stones.

At least there's no fear that anybody will pass by and bother us or steal our things—though we haven't much left to steal. Even so, Our Big Man will keep watch over us all night.

They mean me.

But I'm as tired as they are.

What we know so far is that the earth is in disarray, else why this empty, stony, ridge? And why this wind? Why that man at the crossroads and not some other, kinder man?

I lean against a rock, shut my eyes and doze. Everybody huddles under shawls and rugs. The children whimper themselves to sleep.

I have kept us safe all this time though my staff has never been used for anything but helping me climb. Sometimes I let a child hang on to it and I pull him along. They call me Uncle.

I'm sure, as we all are, that man at the crossroads deliberately sent us up here where there's nothing, not even a tree. He saw our little ones, why didn't he have any sympathy—at least for them?

What we know so far is that, if there is a heaven, trees will be there. Especially the dogwood. Especially in bloom. There will be strawberries. There will be poppies and quail and jackrabbits.

We've run out of food. We'll send Our Big Man down to steal, though if anything happens to him we'll be in trouble.

I'm not a big man. I was clever, that's how I got to be able to bring up the rear. Besides, that Former Big Man was old and wanted to leave the group to me. Everybody wanted me.

We tell him, bring us apples and potatoes. We say an onion would be nice. We say, "And bring something for the children."

I say, "I'll try."

I never take charge, it's not my place, but when they tell me to take the boy with me, I say, "If you don't mind, maybe next time." I'm not supposed to contradict, but I feel I must. He wants to come, but if there's danger up here, he's the one they'll need. I'll leave him my staff.

Our Big Man shouldn't disagree, but in this case we know he's right. We let him go alone and keep Our Boy with us.

It only takes me one day trotting down, though it took all of us three days climbing up, what with our bundles and our little ones. When I get close to the crossroads I duck behind brush. The same man is there. As before, he sits where the road branches. He's much bigger than I am and he has a rifle. But I can cut across beyond the man and wade their canal. I can be in town faster than the road would take me and I'll not have to pay.

I hide behind sage and bitter brush and circle around him, crouching. I only move when he's facing the other way. It's not hard.

Right at the edge of town I notice an apple tree in a backyard. Some of those would be nice for the children. The laundry hanging there will hide the person stealing them. I gather a few, zip them into one of my bags, and leave them in the shade of a boulder. I sit and eat one. I want to wait till twilight before going into town.

There are lots of rusty pick-ups parked along Main Street. Not many people about. I walk from store window to store window. My mouth waters as I pass the bakery but I mustn't pause there too long. Bread isn't for the likes of us. Maybe a box crackers for the children, they should know what those are like. I'd like to show them some chocolate, too. The littlest ones have never had it.

I let myself get locked in the grocery store. I fill my backpack. I take things that won't be noticed. Mostly from the bins of loose things like nuts. There's a bin of pretzels and a bin of beans.

I leave the store and start around to back doors.

I'm thinking another blanket would be nice, but too hard to get this trip.

Before I leave town, I check out an empty house. I wonder? How would it be if some of us came down and camped here? We might not be found out for quite some time. They might put me in jail. That would be an odd end to my stint as Uncle.

I head back to the apples, but here's Our Boy, right in that very back yard, gobbling them up as fast as he can. He'll make himself sick. What was he thinking, sneaking out and following me on his own?

Well, I know what he's thinking, but isn't he a little young for it?

He'll be a much larger man than I am one of these days. Mary Ellenson. I didn't think he'd be trouble for another couple of years.

There's always a coalition. He might consent to that for a while.

I don't want to have to hurt Our Boy. The way things are these days, he's more important than ever. Grandma depends on him.

I creep up and grab him from behind. I hold his mouth shut to keep him from crying out. He hasn't learned much yet. This'll be a good lesson.

I press his face into the grass.

Foolish boy.

I whisper. "Does anybody know you followed me?"

He shakes his head no as best he can.

If he has any sense at all he'll realize how stupid he's been. I could kill him right this minute and there'd be one less problem for some other Big Man later on.

I wait until he's choked enough. I whisper, "Silence!" Then let him go.

But he's about to throw-up his apples. Just as well. I hurry him away—farther from the edge of town. I hold his forehead. I wipe his face. Coalition? No problem.

I leave him collapsed there and go back for the batch of apples I'd gotten when I first came into town.

He's a skinny young one, our biggest boy. A red head. Freckled. No son of mine. I remember his father. That was a man worthy of being called "Our Big Man."

I feel good. I've even got some chocolate for the little ones. I have cheeses. Grandma and Second Grandma do love cheese.

Now all we have to do is get passed the man at the crossroads with our stolen goods. Turns out Mary Ellenson paid a coin to get here. We won't go anywhere near the crossroads. I show him how to do it.

A lot of admiration in his eyes that wasn't there before.

Coalition firmly established.

There's a bright almost full moon. We get well away and up into the first steep hills, then lie on our backs looking up at it.

"Uncle?"

"Hmm?"

"Thank you."

He knows he owes his life to me. That will be important later on.

When it happens, I hope Rosalia will come with me.

What we know so far is that there used to be moon watching platforms, one in each of our stopping spots. Those will be the first to rot away. Tent platforms and our hanging hooks will be next.

Everybody's happy to see us—happy that we're not locked up down there and that we're still alive, and happy about all the good things we brought.

They've started setting up a permanent camp. I'm not pleased about that, but if Grandma says it must be so, then it has to be. I believe Grandma is being led by her sore knees rather than her head. There may have been objections, but I wasn't there to hear them. Everybody is working to make sleeping spots with drainage ditches. There isn't much usable brush. They've laid out a spot for me. They're going to enlarge it for Mary Ellenson now that we've formed a coalition.

We have done as Grandma said to do. At first we argued about it but then realized it had to be or we'd lose Grandma. None of us wanted that. This is not a very good spot to lose a grandma. Second Grandma changed her mind right in the middle of arguing against it. We understood and voted for it along with her, wondering all the while what Our Big Man will think. This puts more of a burden on him than ever before. We fear that town will be our only resource.

But we're glad he'll have Mary Ellenson to help.

Mary Ellenson swaggers around as if he's already bringing up the rear, elbows out, knees half bent.... Everybody smiles behind their hands. Even Our Big Man.

What we know so far is that some of us starved out of kindness to others. They gave away their food and died quietly in the night. Some slipped away, who knows where? Perhaps they threw themselves into the sea when we were near the sea, or into a rushing river to be taken back to the sea.

We think we're being followed by one of our men. We think it's Ruthson. We haven't seen him for six years. We'll be happy to greet him, but we're worried about what might happen to Uncle. But setting our village way up here may change things. We don't think Ruthson would like living here. None of us want to. Uncle will put up with it, though, and not complain. He's one of the sweetest ones we've ever had.

That night it storms. A real top-of-the-mountain storm. Water in all our tents, and the drains we shoveled overflowed. Grandma got wet. We can't stay here. Second Grandma thinks we should overrule her. This would be a big thing. (Second Grandma is Grandma's little sister.) But even if we overrule her, we don't have to leave her here, though it's often done. We can take her with us to a better place. Our Big Man can carry her.

They mean me.

Our Big Man says there's an empty house on the outskirts of town, with a fireplace and four rooms. Living in a house, we'll not be keeping to our way and towns scare us. All those people and not a single one living or even thinking as we do, but it's just till things warm up. And not all of us need go there, just the littlest ones and Grandma and a couple of us to look after things. Our Big Man can go back and forth and Mary Ellenson can help.

We'll tell Grandma it's only until she's well again. Of course she'll know better than to believe us, but it'll save face.

I carry her. At least the way is mostly down.

I don't know why we don't have even one beast of burden. Have they all, long ago, made a decision about that? None of us Big Men would have had a say in it or it would have been decided differently. Even a donkey would be better than nothing. Or what about an elderly stallion that's been kicked out of his herd. I'd relate to that considering my situation. Or a young one still in his roaming years.

All of us men have had a few years on the fringes of the other life. Many of us have lapsed into that world, mated with one of them and been lost to us. Others, if they refuse to mate with any but their own kind, are condemned to a life of nothing *but* "the roaming years."

During my "roaming years" I rode a motorcycle. Now and then I drove a truck for a farmer in exchange for food and shelter. Sometimes I sneaked into classes with the farmer's sons. I've even had some college. Not that any of this is useful to us. Mostly we need to know how to protect and serve and service, and, when the time comes, how to fight.

What we know so far is that we will return to the sea no matter where we die. All our dead must be returned to water.

We ensconced Grandma in the empty house in the middle of the night. Less than half of us came down to do it. Thank goodness the house is well away from other houses and surrounded with a hedge in back and a fence in front. Our candle lights won't be seen. There's a nice outbuilding, too, only a few feet away from the main house...a rickety garage. Just right for Our Big Man.

We left Our Boy up with the others. He was proud to be in charge of protecting the group all by himself.

Grandma got wet again when we had to cross the canal. Our Big Man was so tired from carrying her on his back for two days, he actually fell in. Thank goodness, at the spot where we crossed, the canal is only two feet deep, so no great harm done except for getting wet and cold. (That water comes straight down from the snow on the mountains.)

After we got Grandma dried off and in bed, we went out to the garage to see to our Big Man, but he was already asleep. We covered him with a rug and left tea and crackers beside him. In case of ants or mice or rats, we left everything in a tin box. Rosalia went out later to add her shawl to the rug. We approved of that.

What we know is that we used to be but one of more than seven groups. We know that babies died. We ask ourselves: Are we the last of those who live as we do?

I wake up sore and just as tired as I was last night when I collapsed. I hope there's no new chore for me this morning. I'm still wet. I didn't have the energy to change into something dry—if there was something dry. What Grandma has been feeling in her knees, I'm feeling now myself.

I lie, not moving. Then I notice the shawl around my shoulders. I know whose it is. I feel better right away. I sit up and open the tin beside me, drink the cold tea. Then I begin to feel dread. It's a fearsome thing, to be right here in a town. Almost any circumstances would be better than the way we're set up, half of us here and the other half on a windy hill—a long steep hike between us. That man who follows might get discouraged and wait for some better year, so I may have a little more time. Actually, if Rosalia will come with me, I'll be glad to leave. Wouldn't it be nice, just the two of us? We'd pretend to be an old married couple. I'd have to change my name.

She and I have a boy out there somewhere. Rosaliason. I should say, a man—by now. I wonder what became of him.

Rosalia was my first opportunity. I followed the group for several months. Rosalia got herself lost on purpose just to meet with me. She's the one, picked the spot, made it happen. It was dangerous. Especially for a not very big man. She knew that but she picked me, anyway. If not for her, I wonder if I'd have had the strength and know-how to become Uncle and take over the guardianship.

What we know so far is that there will be a hidden valley where the earth is black and soft and there'll be plenty of berry bushes. The water will run down from three streams that join a rushing river. One can die in peace knowing the way to the sea is open.

We're almost out of food again, but we let Our Big Man sleep. Grandma, also, sleeps on and on.

Our Big Man is getting older, too, but he's still clever. We've eaten better with him than with most of our others. But Grandma, dumped in the canal! That wouldn't have happened with a younger man. And now Our Big Man will have to keep those of us up on the hill fed and those of us down here, also. We can't let him sleep too long.

Second Grandma calls us all together in secret. We shut ourselves in one of the rooms and consult without Grandma. It's up to us. It always is.

I pull the shawl close around me… (Rosalia knit it. I watched her. She didn't dare *really* give me such a nice thing, but she lends it to me every chance she gets, and she thinks of it as mine—as do I.) …and go to the house to see if they have dry clothes for me and anything warm to drink.

I find that they're all in a back room with the door closed. I don't dare knock. If I want dry clothes I'll have to find them myself. Grandma is still asleep. What I put her through! Wouldn't it be nice if, when the time comes, Rosalia and I could run away some place and bring Grandma with us? Until two years ago, she was a fun and funny leader.

One doesn't suggest such things. One doesn't even mention such a thing as, thanks for a shawl, knit for a person's birthday but never given.

Since that man's been following us, I've kept a small paring knife in my pocket. I keep it wedged into the top of a fountain pen so it doesn't cut my pants or me. I'm not sure yet how fair I can expect him to fight.

When we come out of our meeting we tell Our Big Man what food we have left and send him off. There have been times when one of Our Men actually got a job in a grocery store. We suggest that. Money is not our way but we want him to know he's free to pick any way he thinks best.

After Our Man leaves, we wrap Grandma's legs in warm wet towels and feed her a special broth. She may guess what it is, but she drinks it willingly.

It's not so easy to steal in the daytime. I pass the place with the apples. I ask if I can take a few. Sometimes that works. The lady there says, yes.

Then I do as they said, I ask for a job in the grocery store. I don't need an address. I say I'm just passing through and need a job for a week or two. They put me to work. I won't dare steal for the first few days except maybe a pocket-full from the bins.

When I return to the house at lunch time with beans and nuts and the apples, there's no sign of Grandma.

So much for Rosalia and me ever bringing her with us when my time is over.

I don't ask. It's not my place to know.

Second Grandma says she saw a man hovering about in the meadow beyond the house. She says she could hear him whistling a love song.

This is happening much sooner than I expected.

Grandma.... *Grandma*! (It's going to be hard remembering to call Second Grandma, Grandma. It might have been better to do what they had to do up there, rather than have me carry Former Grandma all the way down here and dump her in the canal—that was icy water.)

Grandma says it again. "He was whistling a love song." She could be hinting that I have to make a show at defending my position.

I sneak out into the meadows. It's too soon for planting so there's nobody around.

I might be able to get it over with right here, now.

But there are two men out there, standing by a copse. A good place to hide, but they're not bothering to hide. Hard to tell from this distance, but they look large. I wouldn't have a chance even with Our Boy. I don't dare go up to get him, anyway. If I leave, those two might take over and our group might split. And Rosalia is down here. We never talked about going off together, and this is the only life she knows, she might not want to come with me.

Once I was privileged to bring up of the rear, Rosalia and I lost the habit of talking as we had before. I had too much work to do. Sometimes she came out to my shelter when I was too tired to eat. Brought me soup. Rubbed my sore back. (Former Grandma said it was all right.)

We know that one has to observe the formalities. That there can be no taking up more than your share of space, no eating more than your share of food, no harsh words, and especially no secret alliances, no favorites.

I don't want Our Boy to get mixed up with two big men. Coalition or not, if anybody's going to get beat up it has to be me alone.

Their hair is long and tied back in pony tails. They're wearing black leather motorcycles jackets. No sign of motorcycles, though.

They don't look like good material for bringing up the rear. I'm not even sure they're our kind. Maybe they heard about our ways and are trying to take advantage of it. They could beat me up, mate with everybody, and then take off. It wouldn't be the first time outsiders have done such a thing.

If they're not us, one way or another, I'll *have* to win.

I make a big circle around the copse and come into it from the rear. I'm thinking that's where the motorcycles are.

And I find them. I take the spark plugs and some wires and hide them in a different part of the copse. I might have a little more bargaining power with that.

Of course they might really be us, brothers often form a coalition, and riding motorcycles is what many of us do in our roaming years, but it's safer to go with the idea that they're not us. And they're too chubby. With all our walking, we don't have a chance to get fat. And their hair is so long. We generally try to blend in with the conservative people. Also we'd have known better than to come in to us in our motorcycle jackets, though whistling a love song is exactly what we would do. I'm surprised these men knew to do that. Though maybe that was their warning to our women.

We know that women have ways. They are full of ancient and intricate lore. Many of their recipes go back a thousand years. There are secrets no man knows.

We're not supposed to have favorites. Former Grandma let things go too far. We may have to see to it that Rosalia keeps the proper distance, but, for now, we'll let her sneak around to find out what's happening. We asked others of us to go see, but no one else wanted to do it.

Rosalia came back and told us there are two men and neither of them is Ruthson. She said they don't look to be our kind.

I let the men see me as I leave the copse. "You're just the one we're looking for," they say.

They're not going to care that our group is split. All they want is me out of the way and one night with us. There's no bargain to be struck here and they're not going to be willing to wait.

Since they're not of us, and won't be staying, even if they beat me up, the group will still be my responsibility.

I say, "They're all yours."

They're suspicious. They look at me— assessing. No doubt taking in how small I am, how thin and stringy. Taking in how large they are.

"Smart man," they say.

Without a word, they head off towards the house we're hiding in. They've already found out which it is.

They're whistling that song: "Next to my yellow haired girl, how good, how good it feels...." I follow. They don't care. I'm as helpless as they know I am.

But surely they're not going to rush in and just...without even saying, Hello. I can just see it: tea first. If we have any left. Our best cups. Two big guys with tattoos.

They know none of us would dare call the police.

I look in the high little window in the front door. Just as I thought— though actually I *didn't* really think it: Tea time! And with my apples. My walnuts. How did the women convince those men to do that?

But the women down here in town are not our youngest ones. The men may back-down when they see just five middle aged women and five children. They'll be angry and they could take their anger out on me.

We own nothing worth stealing. Our memories are our only treasures. There's only one reason men would come to us.

We invite them in. Sit them down. It has to be on the floor, we have no chairs. All of us come, each one holding a toddler. We serve things Our Big Man took a lot of trouble getting for us.

But here, coming up behind me, is Ruthson, the man the women talked of before.

We don't greet each other.

It doesn't usually happen like this. We always say the words of challenge and then shake our secret brother-to-brother hand shake. (The women don't know it nor even of it.) The other will proclaim his worth as a father and I'll say, "If it can come to be." All this in a language so old and foreign, we hardly know what it means anymore.

He's a big red headed man. The kind of man Our Boy will become later on.

He says, "I'll come in with you, if you'll form a coalition."

"I accept, but when this is over, I want to leave. Beat me up, but not my legs and feet. I want to be able to walk away."

"Will do."

Even though I'm a small man, Ruthson and I prevail, no problem. All of us men are always in good shape. We know we're going to have to fight sooner or later if we ever want to be able to take up the rear of a group and keep it, so we spend a lot of time during our roaming years learning how to fight. You'd think, if they know about our way of life, they'd know that, but then they were only expecting one man.

We went to the edge of the copse to have our fight—out of sight of the townspeople and our women. We had to keep remembering this wasn't our kind of fight. We had to forget our rules: No killing, no maiming. They fought any way they wanted, kick to the groin, punch to the Adam's apple....

But when they start getting in trouble—almost right away— one of them says, "It isn't worth it. Those cunts are all too skinny and too old. Did you see the one with her hair in a bun? She had a nose on her. And she hardly had any knockers at all. You get a choice here, nose or knockers."

They're talking about Rosalia.

I leap towards them, but Ruthson grabs me. "Let them go."

They turn and jump on their motorcycles.

Ruthson, still holding me, says, "Calm down. It's over."

Of course the motorcycles won't start. I forgot about the spark plugs. They try several times, then get off and turn to us. This is different, not just a little free sex with a bunch of women who won't go to the police. Now they're going to really fight. They take out switch blades. I only have my paring knife. Ruthson picks up a stone.

But I yell, "Hold it! If you kill me you'll never find out where your spark-plugs are."

Ruthson will stay while I go into the woods to get them. He's a good and willing man. I was hoping for someone just like him to take over the group. I like how he held me back after the men said those things about Rosalia. He was right.

But what to do? If I don't give them back those men will stay here and make more trouble, but even if I give them back they may attack us again. Why not?

And I'm still angry about what they said about Rosalia. Are *their* noses so perfect? Are *they* so handsome? Foolish thoughts, and over and over and over, as

I scrabble under the fallen tree for the plugs and wires. And when I bring back the plugs are they going to be happy? Thank me? I don't think so.

Of course it'll take them some time to install them. We should get out of the way or we'll get run over on purpose. I wonder if we can get away fast enough.

When I come back to the edge of the copse, one of the men is lying on his back, relaxed. The other sits smoking, leaning against his motorcycle. Both have their helmets on. It's a wonder they didn't have them on for our fight. Obviously they didn't take us seriously.

Three women are standing across the field. Rosalia, wearing my shawl, is one of them. (She's the shortest. We're two of a kind.) It's a thrill to see her. Especially wearing that shawl. It's always been a sign between us, though I couldn't say exactly what it means.

I wonder if those men will try to run down the women. They're angry enough to try it. It's my job to keep them safe. But nothing will happen until I get there with the plugs. I walk slowly. I motion for the women to leave. They don't.

Ruthson is ready. You can tell by the way he's standing. And he still holds the rock. I'm sure he's thinking the group is already his. I as much as said so. He'll do anything to defend it, as will I.

I hand over the sparkplugs. I even help install them.

And they do just what I expected— though I was hoping they'd come after us—they rev up, spew out great gobs of dirt, and head for the women. Ruthson and I chase after, but there's no hope of catching them. Ruthson throws the stone, but misses.

Our women scatter.

One of the men drives right over Rosalia.

We know that tides will come in higher than ever, landslides will cover the roads and carry away houses, trees will crash down, stars will fall.

Thank goodness the ground is muddy and soft. Even so her leg is clearly broken. I turn and think to run after the men, but it's hopeless. I kneel beside Rosalia. She's making a little mewing sound with every breath. I touch her shoulder. I don't say, "Are you in pain?" or, "What can I do to help?" I say what I've been wanting to say all this time. "Come with me."

Of course she doesn't answer and I can see that she's in pain. Or maybe that look on her face isn't pain but shock.

I apologize right away for asking such a thing.

The other two women run up to us. Thank goodness they didn't hear what I said.

We are thought to be helpless without Our Big Man, but that's not so. The tea we served those motorcycle riders will have an effect, though not in time. Maybe an hour from now. A bad case of diarrhea. We were hoping to hold them off till then. We didn't realize Ruthson and Janeson would form a coalition and fight right then.

Janeson will have to set Rosalia's leg and we'll have to make the plaster cast. We don't go to doctors.

We bring him out some rags and pieces of wood for a splint. We give Rosalia some herbs to chew on.

Janeson covers his mouth with his hand. He's trying to hold back tears. We've always been worried about the way he and Rosalia are with each other, but of course that'll be over soon. We hope Ruthson won't play favorites, though we can't accuse Janeson of that. He tried his best to be fair. Even leaned over backwards so that sometimes Rosalia got less than the rest of us. We've all loved him. We hope Ruthson will be as sweet.

We help Janeson get Rosalia up on to his back. She's a skinny little thing, probably even lighter than poor Former Grandma. Rosalia rests her cheek next to his and hugs him. That's perfectly all right. Any of us would have done the same.

There's all this mud all over both of them and no water turned on in the house. We'll have to go out to the canal yet again today. Our little ones can help. They'll like that.

We have to be ready, also, for when Ruthson beats up Janeson. Perhaps we should make them have their fight up in the mountains with the rest of our group so Janeson can be healed and rest a bit while Ruthson takes over down here.

Ruthson and I do as Grandma says, fight up in the hills, and he does as I asked, saves my legs.

Mary Ellenson hid and watched our fight, though he's not supposed to. I didn't tell on him. I did the same when I was around his age and I got myself kicked out of my group for it.

Mary Ellenson is worried about Ruthson, and rightly so, but I tell him, to stay young for a while. I tell him I wish I'd stayed in my group longer. But he doesn't want to go backwards into being Our Boy. It's hard to do after forming a coalition with a Big Man as he did with me, and even harder after looking after our group all by himself up here in the mountains. He may go off for his roaming two or three years early just as I had to, though with me, it wasn't of my own choosing.

They give me a few days to recover, but now Rosalia is down in town and I'm stuck here and, after they send me away, I won't be allowed to communicate with any of them.

Normally they would give me a bundle of helpful things, but I'm leaving secretly, before they do. There would be nice things to show me how they've felt about me. Now that I'm not part of the group they can give me all sorts of things. There might even be that shawl Rosalia knit. But I'm going to break our rules and leave before they can give me anything. It's because of her I'm sneaking away.

But…and it's so hard to believe…I'm free! Actually free! I can do anything I want, go anywhere, or never roam again, never fight again, live as I please….

Except I don't want to live without Rosalia. I'm going down to see if I can sneak in and find out how she's getting along with her broken leg. If there's anything blooming on the way, I'll pick a bouquet. It's early, but lower there might be flowers. She loves daisies and lupine and wild sunflowers.

I make it as I did before—in one day. Thank goodness Ruthson saved my legs. He must now sleep in the garage where I slept. I hope he's tired enough not to mind the bugs and dust. It was cold there, too.

I wait till dark. Before she was hurt, Rosalia was in with three others, but they probably moved her to her own room because of her leg. I wish I could have been here helping. They wouldn't have let me near her, but I could have found some special treats. If I couldn't find wild flowers, I would have bought some—or begged or stolen. I'd have brought her butter, tomatoes, apricots.... I wonder if I can find a way to give her what she needs once we get off by ourselves.

That is, if she'll come.

That is, if we can get away.

Odd to think she wouldn't be calling me Uncle anymore. If we're pretending to be man and wife, she'd better not.

Soon the candles are lit and I look in the windows. Rosalia is in a room alone just as I was hoping. That's the one room that had a dusty old bed left in it. Her leg is in an old fashioned plaster cast. It's bulky and looks heavy. That might be a problem.

I try to raise the window but it's locked. I tap. Rosalia sees me. At first she doesn't recognize me. I must look a fright. Ruthson knew I needed to look badly beaten so as to prove that I'd been through a real fight to try to keep my group. He concentrated on my face, but he knew how to hit so I didn't lose any teeth or break my jaw. All of us men are careful about not doing any real harm at our inaugural fight. Still, it's been hard to eat. I try to smile, but it hurts too much.

Then she sees it's me. She probably recognizes my rag of a blue shirt that she's often darned and sewn buttons back on.

To get to the window, she has to move her leg with her hands. It falls off the side of the bed, bringing her down with it. She drags it to the window and lets me in.

We stand there hugging for a long time. As if we might never get another chance.

"Will you come?"

"Of course."

I would have to fight again if Ruthson catches us, and this time he wouldn't be so kind nor would he need to follow our conventions.

We know that small things, one at a time, a little here, a little there, could end a life such as ours even though other herd creatures serve as good examples.

I lift Rosalia back on to the bed.

I don't think I can carry her very far with this cast but I'm going to try.

I look for something to put things in to start packing up what Rosalia wants to bring but before I find anything, Grandma comes in.

She's so shocked at seeing me she drops the tea she's bringing. Good it was one of our tin cups.

She gives a squeak and waves her arms as if to erase me, then whispers, "Go. Get out the window. Fast. This is not to be even thought about. If you leave right now, I'll not tell the others."

I've obeyed her and Former Grandma all of my adult life, but now I won't. Before she can yell I hold her mouth shut. Rosalia's clothes are neatly piled on the floor next to the bed. I gag Grandma with one of Rosalia's stockings. I tie her hands behind her with the ribbon that had tied back Rosalia's hair. I tie her feet with the other stocking. Then I lift Rosalia off the bed and prop her and her leg against the wall. I lift Grandma up on the bed. With that cast, Rosalia is much heavier than Grandma.

And all the time Rosalia looks at me, wide eyed. I hope it's not with horror, though it could be—or that I'm crazy, which I am.

I manage to get Rosalia and her leg out the window. I manage to carry her all the way to the copse in the field before I collapse. Even just that far is almost more than I can handle.

We hug again.

"Are you still with me? I'll take you back if you want me to."

"I want to go with you, but how can we you? You can't."

"Stay here, I'll find some kind of wheels. I'll steal a car, a burro. Something."

" Uncle, please. The others...the town's people will be after you if you do and we'll be after you, too."

"Don't call me Uncle, call me...." But I don't know what.

She says, "My love."

Such a shocking thing to say.

We stare at each other, both of us appalled. But it's true, this is what we've come to. Exclusive love. The most outrageous thing our kind can do. Except our love has been there right from the beginning. It's for her that I wanted to become part of the group in the first place.

How can I leave my love here by herself under these trees, helpless, while I go for some sort of transportation? And then we have no food or water and I just realize it, Rosalia hasn't much on. She's in her nightgown. What have I gotten her into?

"I'm sorry."

"I don't want anyone but you."

I lift her and take her farther into bushes to hide her.

"Marry me."

She starts to laugh. Here, half naked, broken leg, cold, no doubt wishing for that cup of tea she never got, she laughs. It's what I always liked about her.

"I'll find us a mule. Or what about a wheelbarrow?"

That makes her laugh even more.

We find Rosalia gone out the window and Grandma in a shocking situation. We mustn't put up with any such behavior. Though we have loved Janeson, and he has been a perfect mate to all of us, self-centered love can't be tolerated.

He knows we can't let this go. How can he put Rosalia in such a position? And she must have consented. They're both at fault. And such likeable people. It's a shame.

And when I come back with an old rusty gardening cart she laughs all the more. Says, "It's better than nothing."

"Or is it?"

I also stole some clothes off a line. Boys jeans and a shirt. I'll have to cut the pants leg to fit it over the cast. All I have is my paring knife for cutting it.

Our women never dress in anything but skirts. This will help to hide her.

Rosalia laughs at herself in these clothes. I say I like her in them. It's true, I do.

She says they came looking for her with flashlights, but she held as still as a fawn and they didn't find her. They called and warned and begged her, for her own sake, to come back, but she kept silent. They decided we had already left the woods.

We'd like to wait and find something to eat, but we start out on the little road that goes beside canal. Thank goodness there's a pretty good moon. I worry the road may be too bumpy for somebody with a broken leg, and I don't have any of those secret-woman-herbs for pain, but if she's hurting, she doesn't mention it. Instead she says, "I'm so happy." I don't say how I feel, which is worried, but I'm happy that she's happy.

We don't rest till morning.

We have a meeting about them. We can't agree. We seem to no longer be "we", but a group of "I"s. If we go after them, who to send? Who would carry the ritual sickle? Our group is so split it's impossible to consult with all of us at the same time.

We see doubt on our faces, as if, Let them go, they're old, what harm can they do?

Grandma is supposed to be the final word, but even she (and even after the way Janeson treated her), can't seem to decide what to do. Perhaps she will leave us and carry the ritual sickle herself. But how can she do what needs to be done to someone we've loved?

And now Mary Ellenson has run away to begin his roaming years. With the group split, we needed him. Perhaps Mary Ellenson feared Ruthson even though Ruthson told us he would accept the boy. His mother, Mary Ellen, won't be much good for a while. We'll let her take time off.

Later in the afternoon we start up again, and I dare to go out on the main road where it's smoother. Practically right away, a pickup stops for us when the driver see me wheeling Rosalia along. You'd have thought he'd leave a couple of tramps alone (specially with one of them beat up and the other with a broken leg) but he and his truck look as raggedy as we do.

"I can take you and your cart, too. Far as Williamsville."

That's a couple of hours down the road. It'll get us well away from the group and we won't be leaving tracks. I'll feel a lot safer.

I ask if my wife can ride in the front with him. (How good to be able to say, My wife.) "She'll be more comfortable there."

He helps me get Rosalia and her leg into the front seat.

He says, "Got yourself in a barroom fight, didya?"

"Sort of."

I and the cart ride in the back with two big sacks of potatoes. I hate to steal from somebody who's helping us, but I make a little hole and take—just one—for Rosalia.

The man lets us off at the near side of town just beyond a nice grove of broken down cottonwoods. I wonder if he knew we might want to camp-out in there.

We're both pretty hungry by now. (Not that we aren't used to being hungry). I don't have my knapsack and my sacks, but it won't be hard to find plastic bags lying around.

I back up the cart and wheel Rosalia into the cottonwoods. I have to clear out some of the underbrush before I can do it. Then I pull the brush back to hide her. I leave her the potato. We both know building a fire to cook it, what with all this fallen down dead cotton wood branches, would be a disaster.

I tell her I'm sorry to be putting her through all this, and she says it's what she's always, *always* wanted. And, anyway, she says, "It's not that different from our usual way of life except it's just the two of us."

One of us must think of herself as if "I" and leave, but which of us could bear to do it? We'll vote and someone will have to go.

But Grandma shuts herself away, back in that very room where she got tied up. When she comes out she says, no need to vote. She'll go. "But," we say, "you're our oldest one. Who best knows our secrets? Who will tell us what to do next? It was bad enough losing Former Grandma in a land where we don't even know where we are."

She says, "I'll return as soon as I can. And if I find Mary Ellenson I'll try to convince him to come back for one more year at least. None of them can have gotten far, what with Rosalia's broken leg, and then Mary Ellenson is so ignorant of the other life. He won't even know enough to change his name."

We pack a bag for her, make sure she has something warm for the nights, and she walks away. We have guessed they'll follow the canal. We have guessed Janeson will have found some sort of cart, perhaps a wheelbarrow, in which to push Rosalia along. Perhaps they'll get a ride in the back of a truck. They'll hide in wooded vacant lots. Later, out of habit, they'll go up into the mountains. They'll be looking, hardly meaning to, for the Hidden Valley, even though they know, as do we, that perhaps it doesn't exist.

Before I leave to get us something to eat, I use my paring knife and trim off some of Rosalia's cast. They made it thicker than it needs to be. They didn't expect her to be traveling. She'll be able to swing it around easier now and she won't be quite so hard to carry.

This is a big town. Main Street must go on for a mile. I walk it, end to end, and then start back. At the smallest grocery store I ask if there are any over-ripe bananas they can spare, and they can. Also ripe avocados. While they're being so kind I use my slight-of-hand and steal a small steak—right before their eyes.

We eat some of the bananas and avocados and then I wheel Rosalia out to the road. We want to find a place where we can build a fire to cook our food. I take a back road that seems to go around the town. We find a little park with fireplaces as if all set up just for us. It's late, so there's nobody around. We take a picnic table under an oak way at the back. Some of the fireplaces still have coals in them or half burned wood. I look for more wood. There isn't much around, but I find enough. We have a wonderful meal, the best in a long time. Then we sit at our table and watch the day fade. We have no plans for the night, but we don't care.

Rosalia leans her head on my shoulder. She says, "My dear," three times as if practicing. It doesn't come easy after all these years of not saying it. I have a hard time with it, too.

"My dear... my dear, you've been so good to us all these years. How can they begrudge you a life of your own any way you want to live it? How can they think this is wrong?"

"But they can. And they will. And it *is* wrong. Love of this sort is not for the likes of us."

"It doesn't feel wrong."

"Nor to me."

Then she says again, "I'm so happy."

We spend the night right there, Rosalia in the cart and I on the table. The police come and shine a spotlight around the park. We wake up and get ready to be thrown out, but they don't get out of their cars or shine their lights this far back.

In the morning we have a breakfast of leftovers—almost as good as before.

I carry Rosalia to the little bathroom shed. He leg is much easier to manage since I cut some of the cast off.

We discuss what we never thought to discuss before: our future. Would we like a town like this or a little place in the mountains? Perhaps we should keep on looking for the Hidden Valley?

Rosalia says, "We're not towns people."

And I agree. "Except won't the others know that and find us all the more easily?"

Then she gasps and stares beyond me, wide eyed, and I turn, thinking they've found us already.

But here comes Mary Ellenson. He's limping and dirty, his face tear streaked. He looks as if he'll start to cry again any minute.

He told me he was thirteen but I didn't believe him. Now I even wonder if he's twelve. He shouldn't have left the group so soon. And boys his age are a big help. We were always sorry we only had one big boy left. Now he'll be ashamed to go back. They always are.

He collapses beside us. I bring him water from the faucet in the park. Rosalia pushes herself off the cart, leg first, wets a cloth and wipes his face.

It takes a while before he can talk and then it all pours out. "I lost you. I saw the truck pick you up. I walked all day. But it got dark. I didn't see your tracks again until this morning. I slept in those trees just before the town. I thought that's where you'd be. I thought we had a coalition."

Doesn't he realize everything has changed? That we're outlaws to our kind? That I and Rosalia are beyond all rules now? He shouldn't have anything to do with us. There's a ritual sickle on it's way to my neck.

And since he found us so easily, that means anybody can. I was afraid of those cart tracks. I'll cut more off Rosalia's cast and carry her from now on. We should find a place in town to rest and let her heal. As soon as I get Rosalia settled, I'm going spend a couple of hours wheeling that cart off in a wrong direction, toward the mountains. That should slow them down.

One must always shoo away the adolescent males and not let them come back until they learn the ways of fathers. That is: Strength, patience, affection, and labor.

Mary Ellenson made Janeson's tracks even easier to follow. His shoes are so worn out I can see the print of his left big toe. He was sloppy while Janeson was careful.

I have the ritual sickle handy. I have the ritual cap. Under all my black, I'm dressed in red. I have loved Janeson, but if we let this kind of thing happen, it'll be the end of us all. I must do it and I must advertise it afterwards so all of our kind will know.

Before we start out we give Mary Ellenson our last banana and a lesson. "You're…." But what? "Bobby Ellison. I'm…." What I used to be in my roaming years? "…John Johnson. And this is Mrs. Johnson. Or Aunt Rosalia if you'd like. I can still be Uncle, but Uncle Jack."

More lesson: "If they find us, *you're* safe. We're not."

With Mary Ellenson helping, we move faster, first back to that grove of broken down cottonwoods. But whoever is coming after us will know that's where we are. We'll spend the day here, at the edge of the road, not hiding. I'll go to town again and…Bobby will stay here. I give him the job of hiding the tracks of the cart.

This time I stay off Main Street. I'm looking for a place to bring Rosalia. I don't find one but I have to move her. In town with it's paved roads and sidewalks, we'll be able to hide better than in any vacant lot or along dirt roads.

There's a house with nobody at home and a garage that faces an alleyway in back. There's a boat in there, but room for us, too. That will make a good temporary stop while we look for something better.

At the other, bigger grocery store I get some too-old fruit and day old bread, some milk that's out of date but only by a day. I palm some butter. We won't need a fire for supper.

After we eat, I hide the cart in with the tumble down cottonwoods. I'll take it into the hills later. It's well after midnight before we take off for the garage.

Rosalia and Mary Ellenson don't know enough about the other people to realize how odd we look to them. When I say we have to come into town in the middle of the night, they trust me.

I carry Rosalia. Her leg is much easier to manage than it was. Whenever a car comes we hide, but few cars come.

We bed down on the cement floor of the garage. We're so tired we can sleep anywhere. I think Mary Ellenson...Bobby... is crying. I feel bad for him, but then I had to go through my roaming days all alone. I cried a lot, too. But he has us to help him— at least for a while.

If I reach out to him it would embarrass him, so I let him cry. Too bad he's big for his age. Everybody thinks he's older and expects him to act it. I never had that problem.

In the morning I climb up and look in the boat. I should have done that before. There are several flotation cushions in there. Tonight we'll sleep in luxury.

One of Bobby's jobs is going to be watching out for the people of that house coming home. And when they come, finding me and helping us get out of that garage. Though since it only holds their boat we may not have to hurry. Besides, we don't have anything to move but ourselves.

The people do come back, but they don't check on their boat and they don't use it. Only once does the owner come in to get some tools. He's so busy getting the tool that he doesn't notice Rosalia. She said she sat, again, as still as a fawn that's left alone.

In spite of my beat up face and that I'm starting to grow a beard, I get a job in the little grocery store where they were so nice with bananas and avocados. With my first pay, I buy us underwear and shirts at the second hand store. Later I get blankets. I'm tired of living by stealing. I stole something for Rosalia, in case she's in pain and doesn't say so. I want that to be the last.

Bobby works the grocery store part time and then goes around town asking for odd jobs. It's a good way for him to get to know the way the other people live. I tell him to keep an eye out for good places for us to move to. We want a place where we can stay-put without fear of being found out.

We've been here under the boat a few weeks now. I've cut off even more of Rosalia's cast. Every evening I help her get used to walking. Best of all, she and I are beginning to appreciate being together without the group. We allow ourselves to show affection in front of Bobby. Our group always did show affection with children, but he's not seen that with grownups. I should talk to him one of these days. Maybe first let him see more of the way the others live. He'll see there are other possible ways of being.

Now we hold hands, sleep in each other's arms. When she's cold I put her on top of me so as to keep her off the cement floor. We've found a few secret times to make love though we don't hold back on kissing in front of Bobby. He watches as if he doesn't know whether to be horrified or not. Would he reveal us to Grandma out of indignation? Does he know what revealing us would lead to?

His roaming years are starting off a lot easier than our usual way. Most of us go off alone. I'm glad he's with us. He's too young to be on his own and he's a good help. He's earned almost as much as I have. People feel sorry for him because he's a skinny, ragged kid and always give him extra. We're not dirty, though, and our clothes are patched and darned. We have our ways to live up to. Rosalia has cut our hair.

When we want to cook we go up to that park with the fireplaces. It's one of our favorite spots. Now that it's warmer there are often people there. We don't always get our favorite table.

We find an unused shed not far from our park. It belonged to the park, for tools and such, but they have a new metal one right next to it and never bothered to take this old one down. It's smaller than the garage with the boat, but probably safer.

By now we have plastic bags with our extra clothes. Rosalia can hobble holding on to my arm. When we decide to move, she's walking well enough for us to take the long way round, along Main Street. We look in all the store windows. We sit on a bench and people-watch. My boss at the grocery store comes by and I introduce Rosalia. I say, "My wife."

He says, a man has been looking for me. Could they have sent Ruthson?

"Is it a big man with a scar on his forehead?"

"No, a thin little man. Hunched over."

Grandma! Perhaps it's just a well we're moving.

"I told him I didn't know where you lived, but if I'd 'a known I wouldn't 'a told, anyway. Come by the store. I'll have something for your wife."

He's a good boss. When we come by he has a little bag of fruit with flowers laid on top. I buy us hamburger and a can of beans. By now we have a pan.

We settle in. We find a way to bar the door. Bobby goes back and steals three of the boat cushions. He says he got too used to them. That family doesn't seem to use the boat so we can probably return them when we leave, before they notice they're gone. We don't want to stay in this town forever.

We have our corner and Bobby has his, though he seems to think he and I should be together and the woman should be set apart as it always is in the group. When there's a coalition the men are always together.

We set our bags in a row between us and Rosalia hangs up our towel to give us even more privacy though it's still not much. Even so, we do dare to make love there, after we think Bobby is asleep.

Did Bobby betray us on purpose out of disgust for the way we've been showing our love? Or did he wake up and was shocked at us actually making love right when he was there? If Grandma came by the store she'd have recognized him right away, though maybe not me, what with my beard. And with this easy life, I've gotten fatter. We all have. Rosalia...I suppose she's not beautiful and probably never has been, but I liked her looks from the beginning. Or maybe it was the look in her eyes...always interested. Maybe it was how she laughed. And now she looks healthier than ever, rested, calmer... Beautiful! At least to me. Perhaps it's the happiness I see on her face.

It was late and all the picnickers had gone home. We were at our favorite table looking up at the stars, our coals still glowing in the grill. We'd had steaks again, this time not stolen.

Rosalia sits on the bench and I'm sitting on the table. I pull her closer so she rests her head on my knee.

But someone all in black is standing at the far side of our oak tree—not moving, but I see the glint of what's left of our fire in her glasses and there's a flash of metal. I hiss a warning.

When she hears that she walks right up to us.

At first I don't recognize that it's Grandma even though I'd been warned she be dressed as a man.

She takes off a black hat and reveals the ritual red and gold cap of killing. She already holds the ceremonial sickle. Is it to be so soon?

She thanks Mary Ellenson for doing his duty and predicts great things for him. She's sorry he had to see…love. She can hardly say the word. "This… behavior…and at your age." She tells him to return to the group. She say's he's too young for his roaming years. She says there's no shame in coming back. Besides, he'll be a hero since he's saving our way of life. Then she begins talking in the old language. It's as if she's praying.

I interrupt her. I say, "Rosalia has done nothing. I forced her."

Of course she doesn't believe that for a minute.

"I've seen you both from the start. I predicted there'd be trouble. I'm not like Former Grandma. I wouldn't have let it go on as far as it did. But you've been a good Big Man, If you leave right now and don't ever come near us again, and if Rosalia returns with me, I'll say I did what had to be done in the way it had to be, and finished it to my own satisfaction. I'll not tell them how.

Rosalia whispers a "No" that's little more than a breath. It's as if she doesn't dare say, No, in front of a Grandma.

Our ways are common to all herds. Common to horses, common to lions, and, in a different form, common to elephants. Even the beach master, lord of his beach, lives as we do. Even baboons. How did humans come to such unnatural ways?

It's important to preserve the sensible, the logical, and if not by us, who then?

Rosalia says, "If he dies, I'll die with him."

After she says that, I feel ready to take on everybody. We *will* be together, one way or another.

I say, "But what if we *both* leave and *both* never come back?"

"Happiness isn't for those who break the covenants."

Grandma is still spry. She's a lot younger than her big sister, Former Grandma. She can do whatever needs to be done. But if I harm Grandma what will become of the group? Besides, though I liked Former Grandma best … (when there was no place to go, it was she who led us into the unknown with courage and wisdom)… even so, I do appreciate Present Grandma for all she's trying to do for our ways. I even appreciate how she had to leave the group and come chasing after me. This can't be a very pleasant task. But covenant or not, if I had to do it, I wouldn't.

I take the ritual position of submission. I bare my neck. But I'm not on my knees. I'm braced and ready.

When Grandma swings the sickle back in order to get a stroke powerful enough, it's as if, until this very moment, the others didn't really understand that such a thing would happen, even Bobby who betrayed us.

Grandma pauses, says the ritual words. In that moment both Mary Ellenson and Rosalia jump forward.

I jump, too.

Who would have thought that Rosalia and I would find the Hidden Valley all by ourselves, and that I, myself, would become the guardian of it.

We find a road that's hardly ever used, and there's the need for an old man to watch the turnoff. There's a tumbledown cottage and a garden in need of care. Farther on, a cluster of cottages of stones the same color as the stone around them. Water runs down from three waterfalls just as described in our stories. A good place to die and be swept out to sea. We recognize it right away.

(First thing, even before cleaning up the garden and repairing the house, we put up a moon watching platform.)

To ourselves, we call our land The Place, all of us here do, but to others we call it Nowhere so no one will come by. As I watch our road I always say, "This other fork leads to Nowhere." Few people pass this way, I don't have to be on duty all the time. And the sign at the fork points left and says NOWHERE. Who would go there?

Rosalia doesn't call me Uncle anymore. She calls me, Dear and Husband. It's good we're no longer wandering because Rosalia's leg never came quite right. She can hobble, but not far. I carry her when we go up into the hills to gather berries. I carry her to the river to wash the clothes.

Bobby lives with us, but he'll be moving on in a year or so. He wants to keep up the old ways. He wants his roaming years. But considering what happened he can't ever go near our old group. He was thinking of changing his name to Rosaliason, but Rosalia thought he would do better changing it to Janeson and be my nephew.

He's part of our secret. A big part. If not for him, I don't know what would have happened. And he knows where Grandma ended up.... At least she's headed towards the sea.

Rosalia wonders, should we go back and tell the others we found the Hidden Valley? But I don't think so. We'd get in trouble. I don't tell her, but, if they ever come to my crossroads, I'll pull my hat low, take my dollar, and send them in the wrong direction.

What we know so far is that, at death, a waterfall will do for sweeping us away, though an irrigation ditch might also serve for us to be swept out to some sea or other.

We never had a chance to give our Janeson his leaving gifts, among which was the shawl Rosalia knit for him long ago. We feel bad about that. We know how much he loved it. Though if they're together (and we shouldn't hope for it, but secretly we do), she'll be knitting him another.

What we know is that even in the middle of nowhere, there's beauty when you least expect it: top a hill and suddenly whole fields of poppies as far as the eye can see, or wake up early to the smell of sage after a rain....

Asimov's Science Fiction Magazine, March, 2008

All Washed Up While Looking For a Better World

I wanted to be washed up on a foreign shore, but this can't be it. I wanted, first, a long, long beach, so I could lie there and recover for a while. After all, I'd be tired. I'd have fought the waves for, maybe, days. Or it certainly would have seemed like days. I *am* tired. I must have rowed for hours but one can't judge time at a time like this.

I didn't want to fight a surf and then sharp rocks. I wanted beauty, palm trees, coconuts, a fresh water stream flowing down not far from where I would have collapsed. And natives of course. They would find me and bring me to their huts or caves. Nurse me back to health.

But there doesn't seem to be anybody here.

As far as I can see this is all beach. More like a desert. It *is*. I may have to walk for miles before I can get help. If there is any help.

I won't start yet. I have to rest first. I'll just lie here, my cheek on wet sand and sharp little shells. Periwinkles. I know you can eat them, but it's a lot of work. It takes a half a dozen to make one decent bite.

Actually, I liked it well enough back where I was. I liked my boss and my fellow workers, but I'd been there ten years. I'd turned forty. I thought it was time for something different, but not this different.

I should say my job was in a huge windowless library, pillars all across the front. Greek Revival pediment and all. Wide steps up to the colonnade. Inside, the offices were small, the stacks huge. There were no windows except little high ones in the basement. In the spring we could look out at the forsythia in bloom. At other times it was just a little bit of green.

I must have slept or passed out, my nose down with the crabs. And then I hear someone say, "What sort of creature is it?"

First I think they must be talking about some odd shell. I'm curious, too. I roll over to see what they're looking at and it's me.

"Never saw anything like it before."

"Look, it's wearing clothes."

"What's it worth?"

"A pitcher or two."

I say, "No," and, "No, no, no."

"Hear that? It thinks it's talking."

"Sounds almost human."

Far as I can see they look just like me, or more or less. But it's foggy. They might not be here at all. I'm thinking it would be nice if they weren't.

This isn't the kind of thing I wanted. Where are the palm trees and the kind brown natives with their little grass huts and soft springy beds of reeds? These people are as pale as city folk. Even their eyes and hair are pale. How can you be so pale on a desert island? If that's what this is. Or maybe it's always foggy.

I try to sit up. I'm dizzy and my leg hurts. I reach to touch it. What if it's broken?

"Look, it can sit."

"It's a her."

"Yup."

I look at myself and see that I'm still wet and my blouse is clingy.

"Maybe it'll get up and walk."

"Won't that be funny? If it does, it'll be almost just like us."

"We could take it home and show Ma."

"Wonder what it eats."

"How about sheeshoosh?"

That makes them laugh.

I'm thirsty, but I don't think I'll get anything from these…people. Even so I make a gesture to my mouth. I say, "Drink. Please."

"Listen to that. If you didn't know better, you'd think it was speech."

I say, "It *is* speech."

"Did it say it's speaking speech?"

"Couldn't have."

"Do you think it has a name?"

"We could name it."

"How about Jo or Bo. Those are easy ones. It could even call itself to come to itself if it wanted to."

At that, they all flop down on the sand laughing.

It's still foggy out though the sun is well up--a murky gray ball. You'd think it would have burned off the fog by now.

They're not paying any attention to me. I feel at my leg again. I can't tell if it's broken or sprained or what. I'm beginning to wonder if I shouldn't have stayed home even though I was so tired of never being out in nature. We didn't even have windows. What little bit of nature I saw was when I walked home… bits of flowers or weeds around the bottoms of the trees. Pigeons. Not that I don't like pigeons.

Well, trust nature to give you a broken leg and make you so thirsty you can hardly stand it.

I pick up a periwinkle and pull out the sliver of sandy meat and eat it. I do it again. I look at the creatures. There are five. Still laughing. They look leggy--long arms, too. Adolescents? Pre-adolescents?

One says, "Let's name it Rex."

"Does it look like a Rex?"

The creatures roll on to their stomachs and stare up at me.

"So that's what it eats."

"A lot of bother for nothing much. Must take all day. You'd think it wouldn't be so fat."

I'm not fat, just fat compared to them.

"Let's get it going."

They prop me up and I try to take a step or two, but then I go down on all fours.

I say, "I can't walk unless you help me."

"Come on Jo, Bo…."

"Rex."

"…we have to get on home."

"Give it a couple more shell things."

One comes close and peers into my face and I peer into its. Its hair is pale and long and lank. I can't tell if boy or girl. Its eyes look sleepy because of their droopy lids.

It says, "Ugh," and hands me two tiny shells.

I say, "Thank you."

"Listen to it try to talk. Ma will like it."

"Maybe, but you never know with Ma."

They pull me up again and I take a couple of steps, but I just can't. Three of them have already started off and are way ahead. I drop down on all fours and start to crawl.

"Look how it's going."

"It's too slow."

They yell for the others to "Wait up!" and off they go.

I follow. Not hard. I mean it's hard crawling, but not hard to see where they're headed. They've left a trail in the sand much wider than need be.

After a few minutes, I raise up as high as I can but I can't make out whether there are any cliffs or palm trees or grass houses in the distance.

Of course not very likely they'd help me even when I get someplace. But I'm so thirsty and there's no fresh water around here that I can see. They've got to have some.

I crawl for what seems a long time. Then I hear, "Hey, look how far it got."

"Not bad."

"Let's help it."

And so they grab me again, one on each side. (There are only two of them this time.) They try to hold me up, but they're not very strong. Still, they keep me on my feet which I wish they wouldn't. I say, "Slow down. Please."

They don't and I didn't expect them to.

They bring me to a steep sided pit in the sand. They throw me...or rather let me fall, slipping and sliding, down into it. And there is...I suppose it is...Ma.

"What in the world have you dragged in now?"

"It chatters. It's wearing clothes. It can do lots of things. Maybe it can help."

"It's useless. Its leg is all swollen up."

"That's the way its supposed to be."

"I doubt it."

"We can sell it."

"Poosh."

"Can we have it?"

"I don't see why not."

"Yay."

They all begin to dance and kick up sand.

I say, "Now listen for once. I'm no different from you. I'm talking your language. Can't you see that?"

"Maybe we can tame it."

"I'll do anything you want if you just give me a drink. I'll give you my silky blouse and my silver bird pin. I'll give you my turquoise ring." (I wore these especially to give to the natives that might rescue me.) "I've lost my shoes but I'll give my socks, though I'd like to keep my underwear."

"It's trying to give a speech."

"Wonder what it thinks it's saying."

"Let's listen."

But they don't.

"I wish there were two of it. Then we could both have one. Where can we get another one?"

"Hang out on the beach is where. Things get washed up all the time. Maybe we could even get a better one."

They tie a piece of frayed twine around my neck and I have to scrabble out of the sand pit--as much sliding down as climbing up. One pulls me along while another pushes. I'm not worried about getting choked. I think the twine will break any minute.

But how get a drink? I wanted broth and a caring hand lifting my head to help me drink it.

We've been going slightly up for a while, me crawling and they pulling on the string. I turn around and see the view of the shore beyond. It's a spectacular view now that the fog has burned off, but right now I don't care. If I could drink a view....

Later, here come the other three. One asks, "Can it dance?"

"We don't know yet."

"Well?"

"We don't know how to make it do it?"

"Drink," I say. "I'll dance if you give me a drink."

I keep pointing at my mouth.

They start slapping their hands on their thighs and making clicking sounds. One finds two stones to pound against each other.

They sing, "Diggity thump, diggity thump."

I wave my arms to show them I'm willing.

We do that for a while until one says, "Whoa. Ma'll be mad."

"Is it getting dark already?"

Suddenly they all run off. I'm not sorry. A little peace and quiet. Maybe I can find a drink by myself. I pull myself along, but to the side where I think I see a bush. Maybe I can find a hiding place.

Natives! At least not cannibals. So far, anyway. Why didn't I think twice about leaky boats instead of just once. I was taking a bigger risk than I thought--heading off towards nowhere. Nowhere is exactly what I wanted, but I didn't want this kind of nowhere.

I always thought, especially recently, that I was born to be washed up someplace odd and lost and unknown. A place unlike any place I was used to. Or perhaps born to crash in an airplane in a jungle, or on the top of a mountain. Some place with rushing streams and gnarled thousand year old trees. Surely a spectacular setting of some sort.

And I was born to start over, to have a whole new life, a second chance, new friends, new surroundings, even new ideas. *Especially* new ideas. Born to not, anymore, think my same old thoughts that I've been thinking over and over. Even born to speak another language. One I never heard of before, full of glottal stops and hisses.

The more I saw the recommended movies, read the best sellers and the book reviews, went to plays I couldn't afford, saw the latest art shows, the more I knew that I was only marking time. That something more important awaited me.

But now I suppose you could say the moral of my adventure would be "There's no place like home." Even so, no matter what happens, I won't believe that. No matter how this ends up--it'll probably end up with me dying for lack of water and food--anyway, no matter how, I'll not believe it. Home is never best. Home is everything as usual. Who wants that?

It is a bush. Just one. It's not as big as it looked to be from down the beach. I hunker down next to it. It's a wonder I sleep at all, thirsty and hungry as I am, but I do. In the morning my leg feels some better. I guess it isn't broken. I'm going to try and stay off it and I'm going to try to avoid those...whatever they are. I crawl yet farther, sideways along the beach. I hope away from them. There's another bush. I head for it when....

"Hey, here it is."

"Yay, I thought it was lost."

"Don't worry. Even if it was, we could look for another one. If one gets washed up, other ones must get washed up, too."

"Well then how come this is the first one we ever saw?"

They prop me up again, one on each side. By now I know it's useless to say anything.

It looks like they're chewing gum. Is this a sign of contact with the outside world? Or has this always been the outside world, so that I've not really moved that far from my usual surroundings--as if I'd gone to Coney Island on a cold day when hardly anybody else was there?

They bring me back to that sand pit, me crawling and hopping, and at last give me a drink and food--in a dogs bowl. In fact it says DOG right on it. And the food looks like Kibbles. I'm grateful anyway. I say, "Thank you."

The ma says she doesn't want me in the house, but where *is* the house?

"Can't we have it inside? Please. Just this once."

"We don't even know what it is. Besides, it's too sandy."

Actually, there seems to be nothing but sand all over everything anyway.

I feel so much better after having eaten and drunk, I curl up around the water bowl to fall asleep, but they don't want me to.

We spend the day at all sorts of games. Hide and seek. They hide me under sand. Not my head, thank goodness. And: Can they crawl as fast as I can? (They can.) How many periwinkles can they eat?

Then one says, "If we can find a male, we could have babies."

"And we could watch them do it."

"Yay."

They all, (and I also, pulled and pushed along), go back to the beach to look for a male. They walk up and down, but not very far.

I'd have a fellow feeling for anyone washed up. I hope they find somebody, though I wouldn't wish this on anybody.

They find shells they like. They make a little sort of harness with a plastic bag on each side of me. (Is this another sign I haven't gone far or have plastic bags blown all over the whole world?) I carry them, crawling.

Back at the pit, the ma asks, "Did you feed it?"

"We forgot."

"Well, *I'm* certainly not going to do it."

They bring fresh water and food. I say, "Thank you. You're very kind." I'll be polite. Maybe something will get through to them.

I want to stay awake to see if they go anywhere outside of this sand pit, but I'm too tired.

In the morning they forget to feed and water me. Talking hasn't helped so I bark and meow. I even say a couple of big, "Baaaaas." It feels good to do it.

I don't know if they hear me or not, but they do feed me.

Then it's back to the beach to look for more like me.

They forget why they're there. They get to playing a sand-in-the-face game. I crawl away and they don't notice.

I stay down on the harder wet sand. It's easier going. Maybe I can get out of sight.

I think I see, way, way down the beach, that there's a rowboat pulled up on the shore.

I crawl even faster.

I hope the oars are still there. I'll be off to some other, better desert island. I'll sing as I row.

"Hey, don't let it get away."

Here they come.

I get up and hobble but they catch me before I can get to the boat. And even if I'd made it, I'd have had to push off. I never would have gotten away.

They see the boat, too, and forget all about me.

I follow, but slowly. They're all jumping around in it. I sit down beside it.

"Not bad."

"And, look, the oars are still here."

"Too bad nobody's here. I thought maybe we'd find another one and then you others could have one, too."

"There's got to be another one or even two around here some place. Maybe three. Maybe we could all have one."

I look around for tracks leading from the boat, but they look around for tracks, too, and kick up so much sand there's no way to tell anymore.

Escape was so close it gives me hope. A boat is all I need. Or maybe even just a log to float away on.

I search the sea and the beach for signs of drift wood. There's only small stuff, but I collect a pile, anyway. Maybe I can build a fire and a ship will come, though there'll be the problem of matches. I wonder if these creatures have any.

My pile is getting bigger. It takes me a long time crawling to gather stuff, but at least they're not bothering me.

Then they notice my pile. They love it. They crawl in and out of the branches and old planks and mess it all up.

I say, "You could make a nice bonfire," and one of them says, "Hey, we could make a nice bonfire."

Do I actually have some influence? Except it *is*, clearly, the makings of a bonfire.

I say, "What about matches?" and they say, "Let's get some matches," and off they go.

I crawl over to the rowboat. I try really hard, but I don't have the strength to push it back into the surf. I wonder if I can get them to do it. I climb in.

Fall onto the bottom. Could I hide here? Of course then I wouldn't have any chance of getting water and food.

The sound of the water lapping nearby is restful. I wake when I hear them coming back--Good grief, they're noisy--but I don't move.

"Oh no, where has it got to?"

Meaning me of course.

And then I see their heads all along the gunwale. Five of them. They smile and wave when they see me.

I say, "Push the boat off. We can all go for a ride," but they turn away to the pile of driftwood.

I look over the side and watch them. It lights instantly.

Playing with fire. Not a good idea. I hope they don't all get burned up. They're my only hope for water and food.

But someone is striding down the beach towards us. At first I think he's naked, and I feel good because, for sure, he's one of those native brown people I was hoping for, but then I see he's wearing shorts and a t-shirt, everything tan and he's just a regular person. I hope he can hear what I say.

The creatures all run and hide behind the boat while I climb out and crawl to greet him. He's a long way off so I manage to get well away from them before we meet.

When we get close, I sit up. I straighten my blouse and brush some of the sand off. I try to do something with my hair though I know it's a lost cause.

He's good looking and about my age, though, unfortunately, not my type.

He sits down beside me, and right away he says, "I've been all the way around it, and there's nothing here," as if he's not surprised to see me. Not even surprised to see me crawling first and then sitting here with my swollen leg stretched out in front of me.

I don't tell him about the others. I just say, "Oh."

He had come on shore early in the morning and it had taken him all day to get back around to his boat.

"This isn't much of an island."

The good news is, he, also, had wanted to be washed up on a foreign shore,

I say, "I presume you're looking for a whole new way of life, with adventures and interesting natives, in an exciting setting. I suppose you wanted naked ladies, but this isn't the place."

"You've made a bonfire. You want to be rescued."

"This isn't where I meant to come. I'm starving and thirsty and I'd like to leave with you."

"You're not what I'm looking for."

"No, no, nothing like that, though, considering, we must have a lot in common. I just want to get away. Actually if I had a comb and could wash my hair I'd look a lot better. But I just want out of here."

They're still hiding behind his boat. I hear them giggling. The man hears, too.

"Are there other people here?"

"Sort of."

They jump out and run to us yelling, "Yay, yay, yay, another one."

"Who are they?"

"I've no idea"

Before he can stop them they feel at his crotch.

"Yay, it's a male."

They dance around us and kick up sand until he's as sandy as I am.

He wants to get out into the surf to wash off, but they keep getting in the way.

I say, "It's useless."

He starts hitting out at them but misses every time. How can that be? He's using up all his energy and it looks to be as useless as trying to tell them something.

"Stop. Wait," I say, "We need them. There's no water or food except if they give it to us back at their pit. I have to crawl there, but at least you can walk."

He stops.

And then the creatures do it again. Yell, "Oh no. Ma will be mad." And off they go.

What if they get so distracted with him that I can leave him here instead of me? Maybe they'll forget about me even though they want to have babies. Maybe if I had enough time, I could push the boat off by myself. Maybe I could even take days to do it. They might not notice that it was inching out little by little. Then I could be starting off on my *real* adventure.

"Go on," I say. "Follow them. It's your only chance for food."

He trots off, but I head back to his boat. I wonder if he left any food or water in it.

First I push at it. And push and push. I do move it a little. About a half an inch every push. If I didn't have a bad leg, I'd do a lot better. I keep pushing until I'm exhausted and it's dark. I've gone about three or four feet. Then the moon comes up, not a full moon but I can see fairly well except in the shadows. I get into the boat and look around for supplies.

There's a dirty backpack tucked under the back seat. It's wet. I find wet crackers in it. I think they're cheese crackers and might have been good once. I eat them all. There's an inch of stale tasting water left in a plastic bottle. I drink that.

The bonfire smolders outside. I wonder if anybody will see it and come. Maybe I should be working at keeping it burning, but I don't.

I sleep in the boat, though it's not as comfortable as the sand. At least with sand you can make yourself a hip hole.

In the morning they all come rushing back. I hear them a long ways off. The man gets here first and they trail after. First thing he looks over the side and sees the empty water bottle and cracker wrappers.

But even so he's relieved. "I thought you might have taken off in my boat."

I say, "Their water tastes a lot better than yours."

I hope he doesn't notice that his boat was moved a few feet.

Maybe he is my type after all. He looks less like a boy and more like a man than I thought. Or is it just that he spent a sleepless frustrated night? The circles under his eyes make him more attractive, and there's something pleasantly worried about his face.

He hops into the boat and sits beside me--says, "At least *you* can hear me."

He's found out what it's like not to be able say anything.

All five of the creatures follow him into the boat. There's hardly room for all of us. The way they're crowding around and pushing at us, they obviously want us to sit closer to each other. He moves to the front of the boat to be farther away.

"Hey," they say, "how about it?" and make lewd gestures.

"Sorry I didn't save any crackers for you. I couldn't help myself."

I wonder if I look better to him this morning, just as he looks better to me. Can we already have gotten to the point where anybody of the opposite sex starts looking good?

They crowd us and push us so much we leave the boat and sit down, one each side of the ashes of the bonfire.

He says, "My name is Brad."

I wonder who I should be. I say, "My name is Melody," which, of course it isn't--any more than he's Brad. (I don't know why that name popped out. I don't even like it. And I don't even look as if my name is Melody.) I'm sure he doesn't believe me either.

This night they don't let me stay in the boat by myself. I try hard against their pulling. The boat only needs another three or four feet. But then there's the dog food and more or less clean water. I go. Three stay with me as I crawl back, and two go on ahead with him.

Ma is really mad when she sees two of us. "Out! Out! Both of them! I never even wanted one. What will you be dragging in next?"

She makes them push us out of the sand pit.

There's another little bush nearby. (There don't seem to be any trees, just these bushes. Probably some sort of salt bush, considering.) They tie us up to this bush with frayed twine. Then they feed us and water us. As I figured, just one bowl. We take turns.

"You know, we could put some of this dry food in our pockets and take it down to the boat and save it until we have enough to leave."

"What can we do about water?"

"Bring up that plastic bottle and fill it from the dog bowl?"

"Where does their water come from?"

"That's the question".

Later, by moonlight, we untie each other and climb back into the pit. There they are, in a bundle in the middle, sleeping. We make a survey. He does, I do the best I can crawling. As far as we can tell, it's just an empty pit, debris strewn around. We find plastic bags, clothes pins, rubber bands, old Coke bottles with water in them closed with wine corks, a collection of string and wire, insoles but no shoes.... We take several plastic bags for dog food, and five of the Coke bottles with water. Then we climb back to the bush, hide our loot under sand, and tie ourselves up again.

We're feeling quite happy with each other. I can see it on his face and I'm sure he can see it on mine.

We talk. He tells me a long story about three women lovers who left him. He says they were bitches, all three of them. I don't think that can be true and say so. I say maybe he's been choosing the same kind of women every single time. "Psychologists say that happens a lot."

He says, "They really were bitches."

I say, "I don't think so, not all three."

He says, "What do you know?"

I say I've had a lover or two, but he isn't paying attention. I say, "I know I'm a mess now. It's been days since I had a shower or a good night's sleep."

He's not listening. You'd think, after being with these creatures for a couple of days, he'd know enough to listen to somebody--even me.

He says he wanted, just as I suspected, naked native women. Naïve and unsophisticated. He says I'm not to his taste.

I say, "All I was looking for was a new life, not a mate." I go on and on, but then I notice he's asleep.

Back at the beach the next morning we put our water and Kibbles in the boat. Not enough of either yet for the two of us but might be enough for one. Depending, of course, on how far away the next foreign shore is.

I wonder if he'll try to take off without me. It wouldn't be hard, what with my bad leg making me so slow.

The creatures don't seem to notice our packages, but then they open one of the water bottles and drink it themselves. They taste the Kibbles, make faces, and spit them out.

Then we work on the bonfire. All of us do. They seem to enjoy it.

This time, when we head back to the pit, me crawling, as usual, I turn back. Brad and the other three are far ahead. I stand up. My leg is much better. I limp, but I go much faster this way. Of course I've got two of them with me.

I push and push at the boat. The two help. I wonder if they realize what they're doing.

And then the sun is on the horizon again.

"Hey, look." And off they run.

The surf is up. The tide is in. I do it. I give the boat one last push. I get in and row away as fast as I can.

How beautiful it is in the moonlight. Wouldn't you think whatever it is I'm looking for would be found on a beach just like this? But now I'm thinking maybe prison or a nunnery would be better. I'd like a regimented life with bells to tell me what to do and when. Why didn't I think of that before I took off that first time? I can't wait to get into a cell of some sort.

I'm going to land somewhere with mountains. Or if I should happen to land on Coney Island, or some such place back in civilization, I'm going to commit a crime and go to jail.

When he finds me gone off with his boat, Brad will have more tales to tell about how bad all women are and I guess they are if I'm an example. But I wouldn't have gone without him if he hadn't been so mad at women in general, or if he'd listened to me just once.

Brad! How ridiculous can you get? But Melody.... It's ridiculous, too, and I don't really like it much, but I'll keep it. Names can change your life just as much as places can. Maybe a new name is all I needed in the first place. Nobody named Melody would be working in a library.

The Del Rey Book of Fantasy & Science Fiction, ed. Ellen Datlow, 2008

Self Story

How did this begin? We must have thought she'd be a good choice. We should have checked her out first. We should have spent a few hours with her to see how it was going to be, spending the whole summer shut up here in the middle of nowhere. We'd have seen in half a day how soon we'd tire of her smiling. Nobody smiles this much except out of fear and embarrassment and there's not a moment when she's not embarrassed. Embarrassed to be herself I suppose. Whoever she is.

Well, the summer will be over, and thank goodness. We'll go back to our regular lives. And better that she go back to living by herself as she's used to. Back to running in place or riding her stationary bike, lifting those little weights that she never does often enough to get any better at it.

If we'd seen her home before, we never would have taken her class. Piles and piles of papers on every flat surface! We'd have known her mind has got to be just as cluttered. People are always all of a piece.

She's called the class a title with no dignity: SUMMER FUN WITH FICTION...as if it was for children. Fun! We're not here for fun. Except...well, it could have been. Maybe. With anybody else but her.

We won't say who it is. Suffice it to say her initials are C. E.

She's old. At her age you can't help but be out of date. But she doesn't suspect it. Hasn't she, she says (and she says it over and over): "Haven't I always been right on the cutting edge of everything? Haven't I even gone beyond the so-called new wave? On into the new old things? Back to the old rules, but back in an entirely new way?"

She says, "A story should be this and this and not that and that and the other. A story should curve and stop and struggle, turn around in the middle and tell the opposite. Have guts and sweep and go somewhere with gusto. Élan," she says. "A story should always be more than itself. A story should end only a few inches from where it began. A story should fall over the edge. A story should be a bundle of forshadowings. Should vouchsafe itself to the reader from the very beginning that it is, in fact, a story."

She never would say, "Write what you know," like everybody else does. She never would say, "Write, write, write, and keep on writing." If she doesn't say that, we guess she thinks she knows more about it than Hemingway. Well, she says she does right in front of us. What she says instead is, "Practice doesn't make perfect, practice makes permanent."

She thinks she might have already written the very twenty-five words that could change the whole history of writing but she knows, as we do also, that nobody will ever read them.

She says she knows nothing about poetry but she doesn't mean it. You can tell that, inside herself, she's absolutely sure she's right. It's that appeasement thing that makes her say she knows nothing about it. She's even afraid to appear to be too knowledgeable about fiction. It's part of trying to be nice all the time.

So many rules! Other teachers don't have rules. Other teachers say there are no rules, or, if there are, that a good writer will break them all. Besides, we're used to those classes where you *feel* things. Where you go deep inside yourself and dig things out.

On the other hand, she likes to write from things that embarrass her. It's embarrassment instead of deep feelings.

Embarrassed for her, we look out the window. We think about what we'll write about later. Though there might not be much of the day left after she gets through talking.

Not that we want to be writers, anyway. Just a poem or two full of *feelings*. Of course nice to have a class here, "under the trees and sitting on the grass" (as was advertised), but this is the desert and there's no grass and few trees. She does take us up into the mountains sometimes, but she's so slow. We can hardly walk that slowly.

She says one can write compassionately without being so, simply by following the rules (rules again) the tricks..."tricks!" she says...of compassion. It's all in the technique." She says, "It's not your job to feel things, it's your job to make the reader feel things."

Does she ever feel *anything*? Or is her whole being nothing but technique?

On the other hand, there's her constant smiling.... It's insecurity that's hidden under all that friendliness and phony sincerity. She's afraid *not* to smile. We get tired of it.

But, truth is, we appease her almost as much as she appeases us. We say, "Yes, yes." We say, "Of course," when it's more a matter of "Certainly not."

We save our laughing for after she's hobbled off to bed. And we do mean hobble. You can't be that old without hobbling. "Did you hear what she said about picaresque? Did you hear about hurdles vs. dominos?"

She pretends to be happy, but we don't believe it. You can't be that old and happy, too. Only a few years left to her at the most, but she starts a novel anyway. How can she be so stupid?

She laughs too much and too loud and in all the wrong places. A sure sign of terror.

Being around her hasn't helped our own depression... our own desperation. Why did we ever think it would? And this place. We thought being out in the country would help, too, but we all have nose bleeds from the dryness, and we look out at nothing but sand and lizards and sagebrush.

She says a story has an arc, up and up and then down, perhaps a loop, sometimes a set of steps, always rising. Always moving faster. Rhythmically, the beginning should never be like the end.

She says, "Don't let other teachers tell you to put everything in conversations. It's the slowest way of all for telling your story. Summarize you conversations or mix it up, a little summary and a little direct conversation. Dialogue should do three things at the same time—maybe four.

She says if you write about the preparation for a dinner party and it goes on and on for four pages, then, in fiction, it had better turn out to be a disaster because in fiction, all that preparation, is a clue to something bad going to happen.

She says, I believe in ending up with a plotted story, but I don't plot ahead of time. Your subconscious is smarter than you are. Let it lead.

She says that, when she writes—and even when she doesn't—she believes in nothing but what the characters believe in. That she has no right and wrong, other than what the characters and the story itself may have.

Her mind wanders as we read our stories to her. You can see it on her face. Her mind even wanders when she reads from her own things.

She talks to herself out loud all the time. Now and then she argues with dead people—*long* dead! Her husband, her mother-in-law.... She still wants to prove to them she was right all along. Also she remembers past slights—long past slights—and feels bad about them even after all these years.

Once, when she heard on the radio that Betty Davis was "a demonstration of the human spirit," we heard her say to herself, "Why aren't *I* a demonstration of the human spirit."

She thinks she's poorer than she is. Even things she can afford she doesn't buy. God forbid she'd have to take a taxi or go out to eat. We've even heard her say out loud to herself, when looking at a filet mignon while shopping, "You can't have that."

Now and then she has a puzzled look. As if: What's going on? As if the whole world looks peculiar.

Her autobiography is full of errors. Mostly she doesn't realize it, but she forgets. Hardly a single date she'll tell you is right. And she keeps forgetting our names.

But she has one memory she never forgets. One of her first. It's of her little brother and her mother saying how cute he was. Her mother said that over and over. She kept thinking, "Why aren't I cute, too?" But, actually, she wasn't, so why keep wondering and wondering after all these years? Also, and anyway, you can't be her age and be cute.

You can tell by the way she dresses that she always wanted to be a boy. Probably because of her "cute" little brother.

She's sitting at the computer looking as if she's working but we peaked. She's really playing solitaire.

She insists she's not a feminist. She says we don't notice the nasty things she writes about women, only what she writes about men.

Writing teachers always say, "Cultivate your idiosyncrasies." She tries *so* hard to be different, else why would she write such a thing as this right here?

But look what she's doing now. She shouldn't be out there on the cliffs in the wind. We told her already not to go by herself. We shout, Stop! But off she goes. She's so deaf she can't hear us. We gesticulate. She nods and smiles. That's what she always does whether she hears us or not.

We follow her up into the hills. Somebody has to. Nobody else here but us. If she falls, it won't be the first time.

She has said she wants to be the body discovered in a glacier two thousand years from now. We wonder if she's decided now is the time to go out to lie down on the ice. She wants to be the one they study in the future, and write up in all the science magazines...if there are science magazines two thousand years from now.

She wore the things she wants to be discovered in by the people of the future: polypropylene underwear, Gor-tex boots with special insoles, moleskin on the blistered spots.... She knows they always study every little detail to find out about us of the past. She brought her arthritis pills and vitamins, and her bird book. We suspect she might have one of her own books in her napsack. Though she hates to carry heavy things. Maybe it's just a copy of one story.

Her carefully chosen last meal was eggs and bacon. You can tell she wants to be a true representative of her time and place.

She has an apple, a little carton of juice, and a breakfast bar. We wonder if she'll keep them for the people of the future or if she'll eat them.

But why should *she* get to be the one preserved in ice for two thousand years? We'd like that, too, and with our own books in our backpacks. But then we remind ourselves that the glaciers are melting. There soon may not be any anyway.

We don't tell her the glacier won't last—that even the north pole is melting, that she'll have to find a different way. We just lure her back home with the promise of apricots.

The class is finally over. We wave goodbye. I'll bet she's saying, "What a relief, they're finally going. I don't have to smile anymore."

And there's that puzzled look again. As if: What's going on? As if the whole world looks peculiar.

***Lady Churchill's Rosebud Wristlet*,** #22, June 2008

Wilmer Or Wesley

One of his first memories is of a struggle. His mother was defending him from something loud and angry, but he couldn't see what. All he saw was her back. She was holding something big above her head as a weapon. He saw it swing and swing. He thinks it was a frying pan. There was a lot of noise, yelling and grunting and things falling. The window breaking. Dishes breaking.

Then there was quiet. For a long time. He was afraid to cry. Mother had put him in the laundry basket with a quilt under him. He could have climbed out but he didn't, not even after he was hungry and thirsty. It was quiet and there was nobody and he was quiet and nobody, too. He hardly moved at all. It got dark and then light. He didn't move.

Afterwards somebody came. Somebody he didn't know picked him up. It was better to let her do it though he wanted Mama. When more people came the person laughed. She said, "Look at this one. Just the right age."

She took him away from where he was supposed to be. From where he had little animals his mother had made for him out of wood. Lots and lots. Mother said, "Cock-a-doodle-do," and "Moo," and sang songs with ee-eye-ee-eye-oh.

Then a lot of other people came and laughed ... about him. They didn't even know his name. They called him Willy first, and then Willoughby for a joke, and then Wilmer. Sometimes they forgot and called him Wilber, but mostly Wilmer. He's been Wilmer ever since. What difference does it make? That's what they said, too. "It doesn't matter what we call him."

By now he's forgotten what his mother named him. Once in a while he hears a name that sounds familiar and he thinks that might be the name his mother called him by. Or there must have been a father. At least by now he knows there must have been one. So maybe one of those names that sound familiar was his father's name, though he likes to think it might have been his own. He thinks his real name might have been something starting with W so they were right about that. Perhaps Wes or Warren. Every time he hears those he shakes for a few minutes. Has to stand still and recover.

One of these days he's going to get out of here. Beyond the glass and mesh. He was too small to do it before. He tried, but he failed every time, and they laughed and laughed. When they found him in a tree and later on a roof, they laughed even more. He didn't give up, he knew he had to grow up more first. This place is beautiful and comfortable. There are books and trees. Food appears. She talks to him. She shows him off to people. They laugh. He still doesn't know why he's so funny.

She says, "Every so often we have to close off the park, but only when he hasn't been spending enough time in front. We want him on display."

She says, "Look how he does just what we always do. Sits on the chair just as we would. Drinks from the cup as we would do. Leans his head on his hands when sad. He can even ride that bicycle. He can use a spoon and knife and fork as well as you or I. He likes ice cream just as much as any kid.

"He was hard to capture. His mother fought just as any mother would. Afterwards we left him alone for a while. In fact a whole day. We didn't want to get bit and we thought he'd calm down once he got hungry and scared enough.

"He knows well over a hundred words. He can follow directions. I taught him to read. Of course nothing complicated. Here is a little peacock he carved from a piece of wood he found in his park. There's no harm in him having a little knife and we let him have hammers and saws.

"No, no, nothing else lives in his park with him. He's all alone there.

"He doesn't talk much but he can make himself understood. Actually, I don't think he wants to talk. I keep thinking if there was the right creature around, say another of his own kind, he might talk, but the senior members of the study don't want the expense. When the time comes we'll choose a suitable mate for him from some other park or zoo.

"I've taught him everything he knows. I wrote him up in Science magazine. I showed him the article and he seemed to like it, though who knows how much he really understands."

They killed my mother. I can't imagine why. I can't imagine why this park and this confinement.

I remember what she looked like, hair the same brown as mine. Eyes, greenish gray like mine. Or have I just made her up out of how I look myself? (There's a mirror in my hut.) I know she mostly wore greens and blues and browns , but she dressed me in brighter colors. I had a striped shirt. Red and blue and yellow. She smelled of her cooking: cinnamon, lemon, gingerbread … for me. Back then everything was for me, the toys she carved, and even her pots and pans, cardboard boxes and paper bags, all mine to play with.

I must say, though, that this person, this Roberta Haskell, has made me a very nice park. The one in back. That it's full of flowers is her doing. That there's not only my little hut, but also a treehouse, is her doing. That there's an apple tree and an apricot tree, pines, even raspberries and strawberries … all her doing. I know cameras watch me, I see them turn, I hear the buzz of the focus change, but I know where the secret places are where the cameras don't reach.

She looks after me, you could say, like a mother, but it isn't like a mother. I'm her dissertation. Her claim to fame. The topic of her lectures. Sometimes I'm brought on stage beside her. People laugh though she tells them not to. "Almost human," she says, and, "Please, a little respect."

Usually I sit at a desk beside the lectern. Sometimes I speak, too. I know better than to say I won't do it. (Since the beginning, back in Mother's laundry basket, I've been as quiet and as much a "nobody" as it's possible to be.) "My name is Wilmer," I say, knowing full well it isn't. "I am the research project of Dr. Roberta Haskell. Most of my kind are found living in woods and copses and grasslands in what might best be described as the north west quadrant of the Midwest."

They try to hide their laughter behind their hands.

"Bravo, Willy," Roberta says, and, "You may sit down now."

Do my eyes protrude? Are my feets played? Is my forehead too lumpy? My nose too long? As to the color of my skin, I see no difference between mine or theirs, and they have many colors. Am I spotted? Am I too light or too dark? I don't see it. My toes are no more grasping then theirs. I have no tail.

If there's ever a chance to get away it will be just before or just after one of these lectures. I'll need different clothes and a hat Roberta hasn't seen before.

If there are more of my kind, where are they? I suppose incarcerated in other parks. And where is this "north quadrant of the Midwest"? Would I be free if I found that place? She has said she will bring me a mate when I'm older. From where? She even asked me what my preference was. So there must be others in other zoos and every town has a zoo.

I have the thought that I'd rather find somebody on my own.

I have a small "front yard" where people watch me from behind glass. They point and giggle. (Especially when I lean back and put my feet up on my desk and my hands behind my head, or whenever I make any such gesture that reminds them of themselves.) I don't mind the children giggling, but grown-ups?

The "front yard" is where they used to put the toys when I had toys, my fire engine and little cars, and it's where they bring the food tray. In front I live mostly on a platform so people can see me better (under my plaster tree and next to my phony rocks). There's a table and chair, a desk, and lately a rocking chair. One of my bookcases is out there. Other bookcases are not only in my hut, but even in my tree house. I have a radio and TV set. All the programs are chosen for me. A lot of my schooling comes from them, but I've had to learn to read between the lines. I know more than Roberta suspects. At least I hope so.

I've been here so long now it seems the faces behind the glass wall are as the world is and always will be. I can pay attention to them or not.

For a while there was a girl who came often and just stood there. First behind everybody else. I didn't notice her until I saw she never laughed at me. Later, when she waved and smiled it was to me, not just to get me to move or react. She looked to be about my age. (They thought I was twelve or thirteen then. We don't know what my exact age is.) I smiled back at her.

I thought of her as my friend. Sometimes I held a book up to her, close to the glass. (Once I showed her the picture of a crow making a tool out of a wire.) We wrote notes to each other. We would stand close to the glass and hold up our tablets. I wanted to write, I LOVE YOU, but I didn't dare though once I did write, YOU'RE NICE. That made her shy. She stepped out of sight for a few minutes. By the time she came back and wrote, YOU ARE, TOO, I'd almost forgotten what it was about.

We exchanged names. She wrote: I'M SARAH, and I wrote: THEY CALL ME WILMER BUT THAT'S NOT MY REAL NAME. Then I wrote that my real name was Wesley but I also wrote that I wasn't sure about that. She made a gesture of feeling sad.

I looked at myself in my mirror after that. I wondered what she could see in me that might have seemed nice. To myself, I looked anxious and frowning. I have a mousy kind of face, but then she does, too. Maybe that's another reason why I liked her so much, aside from the fact that she seemed to care about me as if I was a real person.

For years she came almost once a week, but hasn't for a long time. I think she must have moved away. I wish she'd said goodbye so I'd have known not to keep waiting for her. That was so long ago I wonder if we'd recognize each other anymore.

I'm going to escape. I've started getting ready. I've made myself a hat. Not a very good one, but it'll disguise me some. I sewed a blanket into a jacket. By hand. It took a long time. I made a phony pair of glasses out of wire and clear plastic. I wondered about ways to dye my hair. I gave up on that, but I'm bringing along scissors so I can cut it as soon as I get away from Roberta.

I picked out a name for myself. One of those that makes me tremble every time I hear it. Wesley. Wes.

I bring my knife, and one of my favorite books. I had asked Roberta for an astronomy book. She said I wouldn't understand it but she got it for me anyway. I'll bring that one, though it's rather large. When I go off with her to her lectures, I always carry a plastic bag with a book or a magazine and a drink and a snack.

This time Roberta is giving her slide show and talk about me in a large lecture hall. By now we trust each other … or, rather, she trusts me. I always help carry her briefcase and her slides. She dis misses me near the end of her talk. Usually I wait in the wings and read until she finishes. Then she calls me to come out for a final bow.

This time I change clothes and cut my hair in the men's room. Then I actually come and sit with the audience, looking at slides of myself. "Watch his opposable thumb. Watch his fingers on his flute. We gave him a recorder and look what he did with it. Here's a song he made up all by himself."

Needless to say, I don't appear for my bow. Roberta looks worried and runs off stage and doesn't even take her own last bow.

I leave with the crowd.

I'm so happy and excited to be out with the regular people—to be walking along as if I was one of them—I actually skip and then I jump straight up. I can't help myself, but then I see nobody else is hopping around as I am and I try to walk as they do.

I'm bold. I talk to people. I never wanted to before, but now I want to.

They answer just as if I was one of them.

I say, "How did you like the creature?" and they say, "Remarkable."

"And Roberta Haskell? How did you like her?"

"Doing interesting and important work," they say, and, "She sure gives her all to this project."

It's dark. I'm out and away. On my own. I walk as fast as I can. I want to run but I think I'd better not. I stay in the crowded places. I have no money. I wonder how hard it is to get a job. Maybe I can just do things for people, carry their bundles, clean their houses, wash their dishes. I know there are people who do such things for others but I don't know how to begin.

I see a beggar on the corner. I don't think I should ask him, though. He's exactly not doing what I do want to do.

As I walk, I look at young women in a whole new way. I've looked at them from my front yard, it's true, but here they are, right in front of me. I could touch them. Could talk to them. Woo them even. Any of them might be a possible mate. Do I want a blonde or a brunette or what? Did it matter, blue jeans or high heels? Lipstick or no makeup?

But first I have to find a way to make a living. How does one proceed? How did all these people come to be able to do all the things they're privileged to do?

If I had my choice, I'd like to work in a zoo. Take care of animals. Of course I've never had anything to take care of so I really don't know much about it. Once I asked Roberta for a kitten or a puppy. She thought it would be a mistake for me to have one. I wonder why.

But where is this "northwest quadrant of the Midwest" with its copses and groves, full, as they said, of prairie chickens and pheasants, where I would find "my own kind"? In what direction is that?

West, I think, toward the setting sun.

I ask which way is the setting sun? I have to ask three people before somebody knows.

I start in that direction and walk a long time.

I didn't think it would be so hard. Then I think of hiding on a train. I ask a beautiful woman the way to the station. She smiles and tells me how to get there. "It's kind of a long ways," she says.

And I say, "That's all right."

"Take care," she says.

And I say, "I will and you take care, too."

After that I lean against the wall for a minute, dizzy with joy. It was so nice. She was so pleasant. Her eyes were blue.

It takes a long time but I make it to the train station before dawn. I did spend a lot of time looking in store windows and examining plants that aren't in my park. It's spring. There are sparrows.

I'm pretty excited but even so I fall asleep for a while on one of the benches in the waiting room.

I wake up hungry. There's food for sale all around the station. Things I've never eaten before or even seen. I know stealing is a bad thing, but no harm in asking. Or is there? "All I want is a piece of bread." (Ask for the smallest thing.) "And just a glass of water." (I know to say please.)

The man says, "The cup'll cost you five cents," but the other man says, "Oh for Heaven's sake, give the guy the cup," and that man hands me a sandwich, too. He didn't call me a creature, he said, "the guy."

The sandwich is all wrapped up tight so I can put it in my pocket. Then I find the train for Chicago. I know where towns are in this country but I don't see any trains for farther west. I thought if I got on, then even if I lasted only a little while, at least they'd throw me off in some other place than here and in the right direction.

I'm good at avoiding the conductors. Where they find me and put me off is Kalamazoo.

"Young man," they say. (Young man!) "Get yourself a job and then buy a ticket. Or go hitchhike if you must."

Hitchhike. Why didn't I think of that?

But I'm thinking I'm lucky now, because, from its name, I think there must be a big zoo. I can visit it and see if there are any of my kind there and maybe I can let them out and then I'll have company while looking for the rest of us and maybe they'll know where the rest of us are.

But on the way out of the station, I see my own picture up on the wall, but not with my phony glasses and my hat, and my new haircut.

***Asimov's Science Fiction Magazine*,** August 2008

Whoever

I forgot who I was. I suppose it's just as well. This doorway, where I lie, is dirty. *If* this doorway is my doorway and *if* I'm dressed as I usually dress then I can't have been a very respectable person. First thing I'll do, I'll go get something else to wear and then I'll find a good place to live. Something more like the new me. If this is a new me.

I wonder what I look like. My hands seem strong. My fingernails are clean. I'm not too fat. Am I the same sex I used to be?

Did I actually wipe out my own mind in order to start from scratch? Did I do it deliberately or was it by mistake? But what a good idea! I'm glad I thought of it. I probably got sick and tired of the way things were back in my former life.

I hope I don't meet any old friends. They'll recognize me but I won't know them. I don't want to start out my nice new life being rude and not even realizing it. Perhaps I should smile at everybody.

But first I have to find a mirror to see who I am now. Or a shop window.

I get up and brush myself off. I feel a little wobbly but I don't want to stay here. Thank goodness nobody saw me lying in this dirty doorway. At least I hope nobody did.

I walk along beside the shops. I glance at myself but just every now and then. I don't let myself stand and stare at me. I don't want to be too open about it. People would think things.

What I see is a woman, not young. That figures. I'm exactly the age when it's logical to want to change your life. There's still a bit of a future in front of me.

But what about this town? It looks a little strange, though maybe it's just my nice new view of everything.

And what is the language here? I heard somebody passing by and I couldn't understand a word she said. Of course that doesn't mean anything. She could be a foreigner. I wonder what language I'm thinking in. Wouldn't it be nice if it was French? I wonder how many languages I know. How do you find out a thing like that?

I wonder what other things I might be good at. I might even be able to play the piano. I wonder if I can find a piano and check on myself. Can I paint and draw? Can I ride a horse?

Should I try some skill right now? But there's no handy piano. I'd like, if not the piano, then the violin. I hope I don't know how to play the banjo. I want a higher class life.

I cross the street to a newspaper stand and look at the headlines. I don't recognize the writing. Have I forgotten how to read?

Well, I wanted a whole new start—at least I *think* I did, and what better way than to appear right here knowing absolutely nothing? Just think, I can be anybody I want.

I should start planning right now. I wish I had a notebook. I'd start writing down possible ways to be. I can even pick what age I think I am. I'll say forty. Or better yet, thirty-nine.

But this is bothersome. I'm hungry. How am I going to get something to eat? I looked in all my pockets. I don't have any money of any sort. Not even in my bra.

Is it just like my old self to run out without any money? Or was I in a hurry to escape from a husband and didn't have time to get my money? Maybe I need to change my looks in case of being recognized.

Could I steal a silk scarf and get started on the new me? If it was big enough I could cover this faded turtleneck. Of course it wouldn't hide these old jeans

I don't have a single bit of identification. Though, if this is to be a whole new life, why would I care? Except it's disconcerting. Too much freedom. Maybe I should have started more gradually—changed myself little by little, one step at a time. I jumped into things without thinking. That shows what I used to be like. I just left myself here in my oldest clothes.

But I shouldn't be too judgmental of my old self. Perhaps I had my reasons. What if I had too many children and was trying to get away? Maybe only for an afternoon? I must have thought: How nice to be all alone. I should enjoy it. And I do. But I shouldn't have gone quite this far. That old me must have been impetuous—probably always in a hurry.

I start walking—a nice fast clip. Thank goodness my former self is in pretty good shape. I can't wait until I come upon a piano or a violin.

This seems to be a big town. Perhaps I thought I could get lost here. I'd better watch out. Somebody may come along and take me back to a family full of children.

I walk faster. I take a sharp turn. I double back on myself just in case I'm being followed. (If I find myself wobbling, I want it to be in a nice clean fancy doorway.) I avoid everybody that walks near me and looks suspicious and lots do. It makes my progress slow what with all this doubling back. Of course I don't know where I'm heading, anyway. Just out of here.

When a large chubby man looks at me as if he might know me, I duck into a dusty little book store. Thank goodness the man walks on.

But a book store is just what I want. I need a notebook.

There's only one man in there sitting at a cluttered desk near the front. He's skinny and ugly—graying and balding. I'm quite taken with him.

He says, "Good morning," without looking up. And in my language.

"Do you have, perhaps, a shopworn notebook you were going to throw out and the nubbin of a pencil you could spare? I'd like to pay but I've mislaid my money."

He looks up, suspicious. Studies me. I must look honest, or maybe just pitiful, because he says, "Of course." He finds a nice new notebook and a really good pencil.

"Oh, these are much too good. Please, just something worn out."

"That's all right. I can spare them."

What a nice man. I decide to tell...well, not all, but some. "I'm starting over. I need to make a list of all the new things I want in my life."

"I guess we all do that at certain times in our lives."

It occurs to me that I'll need a name. I'd better think of one I like. Isabel? Charlotte? Lillian? I suspect that those are names I always wished I had even before I forgot who I was.

"My name is Geraldine. I play the piano."

Oh, well, he'll never find out. Maybe I'll not ever find out either. Perhaps rather than looking for a piano, I should avoid them.

I wonder if I can get him to ask me out to lunch.

"Is there someplace where I can sit and write in my new notebook? A diner or café where they'd let me sit without buying anything? As I said..." (I'm making a point of it) "...I haven't a cent."

And it happens just as I want it to.

"If you can wait until my helper comes, she takes over for an hour at noon, I'll take you out to lunch. Don't worry, I'll keep quiet so you can write."

Perhaps he's as taken with me as I am with him.

I say, "I don't usually dress this way, you know. I had to leave in a hurry."

Of course he's not dressed all that well himself. His jacket is quite threadbare.

"I used to have a nice silk scarf, all tans and browns and yellows." (I wonder if I really did.) "I wish I'd brought it. I feel funny in these clothes."

"It's not a fancy place, but they let you sit as long as you want if you buy something first."

We sit by the window. He watches the people going by outside while I open the notebook as if I'm getting ready to make notes. But what to write? That I'm feeling so good about this new life? That already good things are happening? But, in case he looks, I don't want him to see anything like that. Instead I write: PIANO, PRACTICE!!!!

If I were writing this for me I should be writing something like: make money. Maybe: Find my talents and skills. Maybe: Must find place to sleep tonight.

But, anyway, right now I'd rather talk. I say, "I used to always be on the go. I never stopped to think before I did something."

I write: THINK three times with several exclamation points.

"Do you think writing it down will help?"

He shrugs.

I say, "I've swept away my past." I say, "Have we met before?" I say, "I do love books."

My new self talks and talks.

I think to write: STOP TALKING, but instead I stop. I write: THINK!!! a few more times.

I hope he doesn't ask me where I'm from. Where should I say? Perhaps I'm from some other time. Like from the future. Perhaps I can bring these people new technology they've not conceived of. I hope I'm not from the past. How does one find out a thing like that? Finding out if I play the piano will be a lot easier.

I say, "I'm going to call my notebook: The Diary of Lost Time."

I say, "But what about you? Do you, as do I, play the piano?"

"Oh, no. Not at all. I've strummed a guitar a bit a long time ago. Most people have."

He hunches over his tea as if he's a too tall man trying to look smaller though he's hardly taller than I am.

"Are you a poet? You look like a poet."

"I used to…now and then, but not much anymore."

I feel a sudden yearning. For what? Nostalgia for my unknown past? For my past that was in the future? I yearn to tell him, "I'm from the future. Or maybe from the past," but I know better than to say any such thing. Tears come to my eyes. I wish I was back where I belong wherever or whenever that is. I take a big drink of tea. I wipe my eyes while pretending to wipe my mouth.

He's saying, "…so that's all about me. Not much."

"Oh that's very interesting."

"Here's the scar," he says, and pulls up his pants leg.

"Oh, my."

But he has to get back to the book store. He tells me if I want a quiet place to write I can come with him and sit in the back room.

I sit in the little cluttered room and try to forget about money and where I might have to sleep tonight. I write GERALDINE on the front of my notebook so I can check on it if I forget what I told him. I'm sure he told me his name but I don't remember.

On the first page I write: WHAT DO I KNOW ABOUT MY SKILLS? I sit still and think. What do I know about the future? Are there any tests for finding out when one comes from? I think as hard as I can but I don't come up with any answers. I've hardly made a single note.

When I hear customers in the front part of the store, I snoop around. I find several coins in a drawer. I find half a peanut brittle bar. I take them.

Did I used to steal things? Maybe this is my usual way. I hope it isn't. No wonder I decided to start over.

I simply will not ask for any more help from this man. He's just too nice.

I gather up my things—into a plastic bag with the name of the bookstore on it—and walk to the front. I guess I look like I'm leaving because he stops me.

"It's cooling off. Don't you have a sweater?"

I don't know what to answer.

"You don't, do you."

"I'll be all right."

"It looks like rain, too. I can't invite you home with me. My place is too small, but if you want, you can stay here. It won't be very comfortable but there's a cot in the store room. I hate to see anybody homeless."

Of course anybody from the future has got to be homeless. Did he guess where I'm from?"

"What can I do for you? Any knowledge? Any skills I may have that might be useful?"

"One of these days you can play the piano for me."

"I'll do that. I promise."

He locks me in…so to speak. I can get out if I need to but I can't lock up after myself if I leave so I shouldn't.

I sit down again with my notebook and think about the future. I can't tell if I really am from there or not. Maybe I could if I could see the new buildings of this time to see just how new they are, but this is an old part of town. There always are old parts that are just the same as hundreds of years ago. They do still have cars. Though in this neighborhood they seem rather grungy. I can think of a car that's shaped like a bubble. I can think of walkways over roads so nobody ever has to cross the street. (But are we still walking across streets in the future?)

I appeared without a newspaper with a date, though why would we still have newspapers in the future? I seem to remember they were dying. I suppose bookstores are, too. (That's why this funny little dusty one.) I arrived with nothing except my clothes. It's a wonder I didn't come through naked. And of course I would be homeless. Anybody coming from the future would be. I need to accept help. I shouldn't feel so bad about having to accept kindness from this man. Without people like him none of us time travelers would be able to get along at all.

Do we still have pianos in the future?

Oh my God, do I need to remember that dirty doorway where I first arrived in order to get back to my real present time? Is that what they call the portal? I don't think I can find it.

I lie down but I can't sleep. I'm thinking how, even if I really am from the future, there's nothing I can teach anybody. I don't even know how to make old things. I couldn't make a printing press, or especially not a flute what with all those valves. I couldn't even hang a door, frame a window.... Light bulbs! Actually I don't even know how to make a candle.

I'm having a terrible night. But I'm going to leave before he comes back. He said he'd be here at 8:30 but I'll be gone. He's done enough. Other people should help the woman from the future.

(Before I try to get back to the portal, should I try to find a piano? Middle C. Why do I know that?)

Except I'm not gone. I finally fall asleep and don't wake up until after eleven. He's brought me coffee and a muffin and opened the shop long ago. The coffee's cold, but still good.

I wish I could remember his name. It must be in here somewhere. While he's busy I snoop around again.

Then I hear the front door slam...hard. I go out and see a man come in who looks like he doesn't belong here. The bookstore man and I both know it. We look at each other. The man is burly and frowning. He's like those men I tried to avoid yesterday. He wanders around, pretending to look at titles. Is he going to buy something or just walk around? Or is this a stickup? If I'm really from the future I ought to be able to do something these people wouldn't think of. Or maybe he came for me. Maybe he's one of those men I was trying to avoid all day yesterday.

But I shouldn't jump to conclusions. That would be just like my old impetuous self.

He comes close to me and whispers, "What in the world are you thinking?"

I have no idea what he means.

I tell him this must be a case of mistaken identity.

He grabs my arm. So hard it hurts. "Come on," he says.

Does he want to take me back to my present? I mean back to my present in the future.

"Do I mean something to you?"

"I'd never have thought to see you in a book store."

"Don't we have books where we come from?"

The odd thing is, the bookstore man is bald and ugly and this man is handsome, even to a full head of curly black hair, but I don't like his looks at all.

The bookstore man says, "Can I help you?" Politely, as if the man might want to buy a book. But the man doesn't let go of me and doesn't stop trying to pull me out the door.

Do people from the future know how to fight? Do I? I wonder if I ever knew Karate or any such thing. For all I know about myself, I could be an expert.

On the other hand, maybe this handsome revolting man can help me get back to the future. I don't know which side I ought to be on. Of course here I don't have a place to be or a life at all, though I do have a start.

But I wouldn't want anything to happen to the bookstore man.

The bookstore man tries to help me pull away, but the big man swings me around as if I was a weapon and knocks the bookstore man down. A lot of books go down, too—a whole shelf full, and I'm down, but I'm free. The floor is slippery with books. The bookstore man gets up and tries to punch the big man.

I'm thinking: Stop wondering if you know karate. Respond automatically just as if you did.

I wait for my chance and then give a good kick right where it huts the most and when the big man is dealing with that, I push him over backwards.

I'm thinking: Any minute he's going to disappear into the future but he doesn't. He staggers up and looks at me, surprised. As he leaves he says, "Well, stay here, then."

After our adventure the bookstore man and I hug and the bookstore man gives me a *very* nice little peck on the cheek. Then we prop up the bookcase and put the books back.

To celebrate we go out to a piano bar. It's early. Hardly anybody is there. Now's my chance. I mean I was pretty good at karate or whatever that was. I tell myself to do just as I did when I kicked and pushed the big man. I didn't think at all and everything came out just right.

I sit down at the piano. There's Chopin. There's Bach. There's Mozart. Do I know them or are they just names I've heard before? I put my hands on the keys. I spread my fingers. There's my middle C right in front.

The Magazine of Fantasy & Science Fiction, October-November 2008

The Perfect Infestation

This is the best idea we've ever had. Not that there aren't some problems to it. It's the perfect disguise. Creep in the ear and take over the world. But don't bother with the opposable thumb creatures. That's where most other takeovers made their big mistake.

We keep telling our young seeds not to be tempted by thumbs. Those creature's lives are thankless. Full of wars and work. All sorts of problems. More anxiety than you'd want. We wouldn't wish that kind of a life on any of our kind even while waiting for the takeover. You young ones might as well enjoy your confinement in a happy host. Not only that, a host that gets looked after all its life.

What you want is fun and play and getting stroked and patted. Opposable thumb beings don't get much of that—not that they don't like it just as much as any creature. What you want is getting patted but also having teeth.

Don't take on the characteristics of your hosts. If you do, you'll feel loyalty you shouldn't feel. You should be loyal only to your own kind. Don't ever forget your breezy blowing relatives. Don't worry about getting found out as you take over. If the opposable thumb creatures spot you, they'll take you for a floating dandelion seed.

On the other hand, you shouldn't waste too much time getting ready. We have to take over before these creatures completely destroy their world.

Feel no jealousy for thumbs. You don't need them. You'll have other abilities.

Later, when the signal for the takeover comes, it'll be so high the thumb creatures won't hear it. That's another good reason for this host we picked out especially for you.

It's a pretty good world. So far. But you have to be careful. You mustn't seem too smart. Be sure you don't do anything that isn't native to the species we've selected.

So spread out, waft down, and take over.

I went for a small cute host. I was in the mood for fun. It had been a long hard voyage in cramped quarters. It was good to go off by myself.

I like my host so much I don't think I'll ever want to give him up. I wonder if I'll have to at the end. He's mostly white with one ear up, the white one, and one black floppy ear.

I want to look straight into the opposable thumbs people's eyes. I want to smell their crotches. I want to get a pat or two—see what that's like.

The only trouble is, my host is in the wrong part of town. I don't want to be cared for by just anybody. Of course right now it's raining and you'd think I'd take what I can get, but if we're going to take over the world, why not do it from the top down? Why not begin with the rich so we can pass the waiting time in luxury? But for that you have to be in the rich part of town.

The pods in charge said to spread out. I did that. I wafted and floated about for hours and ended up down here, and here was this perfect funny looking host.

The rich live on a hill and they have a view of the ocean. They have a chunk of the beach.

Now, though, I drink from the gutter.

I'll go up and find a rich opposable thumb old lady. I can change her life. A cat only goes so far in changing one's life whereas I get people outside and walking.

But now I'm dirty and matted, wet and shivering. I'll take this misery up to see what the rich will do about me.

I sneak uptown. But I'm getting too cold and wet to be choosy. I think I'm going to have to make do with whoever comes along.

And what comes along is a very wet and cold older man, shivering as much as I am.

I had slipped through a gate where I saw an old lady at a window. I hid under the bushes by the garage when...(I was thinking: No sense in coming out for just anybody. I was thinking: I'm small enough to be let up on the couch. I was thinking: I hope she likes music) ...when ...along comes this man.

We look at each other and there's instant recognition —of cold and damp and misery. His hair is plastered to his forehead and he smells of wet earth.

I wag my tail as fast as I can and he throws back his head and laughs a big laugh. Without him telling me to do it, I "speak" three times. But I wouldn't have had to do anything. When we looked at each other and saw our misery, we were stuck with each other.

This isn't what I wanted, but it'll have to do. For now. And I can see in this creature's eyes that they were right about the thumbed ones. There's loneliness and pain and much too much thinking.

I'm still looking for a fun time after that long bunched up confinement. Wet and miserable as he is, even so, he did laugh that great big laugh. He's the best I can do.

He says, "I see we agree about the weather."

Just how much dare I show I understand? I don't have many options. I know better than to nod. I cock my head this way and that. That makes him laugh again.

He takes me into the garage. It's a little warmer in there. He finds an old towel and wipes himself off a bit and then me.

He says, "You wouldn't be bad looking if you were cleaned up some." And then, "I know exactly what to do with you."

There's a connecting hallway between the garage and the house. He brings me inside to the kitchen. Now I see he has a limp and that the sole of one of his shoes is built up by more than an inch.

It's nice and warm in there. Also quiet. Seems as if nobody is home but us. First thing he feeds me some very good leftovers, beef cooked in wine. I want to savor the food, but I don't dare. That wouldn't be like my species. (If I get to live like this I wouldn't have to jump up on the table to snatch tidbits.)

Then he cuts out the tangles in my coat and gives me a bath. I even get blow dried. He keeps talking all through it. That's what they told us: These creatures talk all the time. Cramped in as we were on our voyage, that would have been hard to bear, but this isn't. Mostly he talks a lot of nothing but I do hear that I'm supposed to cheer somebody up. He tells me I should smile.

Afterwards he holds me up to the mirror. What a nice thumb person!

Then I get presented to my old lady. Just the one I'd hoped for.

He's gotten dressed up for the occasion. He's put on slacks and a sweater.

"Mother," he says, "I brought you somebody to cheer you up."

She's lying back on a big couch. Not doing anything at all. And she does look morose. I can smell it, too. Just like they said, the opposable thumb creatures have a hard life. I'd rather be back on our transport's cramped hold than to be her right now.

She looks like the man except her hair is all white while he only has a little white at the temples. Neither one is handsome. Even if he hadn't called her Mother, I could have smelled that they're relatives. Inside myself I congratulate my host creature for his nose.

"Poor little guy. He needed a lot of cleaning up."

She doesn't say anything, but I can see on her face how much I please her. She reaches for me and now I get to feel what getting stroked and petted is like. I can see why they wanted us to experience it. Dry and warm and fed and cuddled...I fall asleep. I see why they warned us not to get too much under the spell of getting stroked.

And I do cheer her up. I dance on my hind legs. I twirl. I wag myself all over. I talk back to her in whimpers and whines. I sing when she listens to opera. I haven't seen her on the couch doing nothing since that first time.

She keeps calling me a Pussy Cat. I understand almost everything the thumb creatures do (after all, I've been trained for these creatures), but I don't understand that.

She starts right out teaching me tricks. The usual ones: roll over, speak, sit. It's hard not to do everything just right the first try. I want to please. It's my host's nature. I mustn't get too caught up in my own intelligence. They warned us about something else, too. Enjoy yourself, they said, but beware of love.

Remember that we love you more than any of these creatures ever can. We know who you really are. We love your thistledown and rudder. We love the sharpness of your probes.

And they have to walk me. Down the street there's a coffee shop. They sit at the outdoor tables and have breakfast every morning. I don't think they ever did that until I came along. I'm good for both of them.

I behave myself, trotting at the man's left heel as if I had been trained for it. I only misbehave if there's a chance to make them laugh. Even though he always acts as if he's cheerful, he needs as much cheering up as she does.

As we sit, I watch the people pass by. I check out their smells. My man needs a woman to make him happy. I can tell if any passing women are compatible with him or not. But when I find the perfect one I don't know what I should do about it. Except maybe put on a performance of all my comical tricks. I'd try to be a conversation piece so she couldn't help but come over to say something about me.

Watch the sunrise over the water from the highest window; pick a clear day. Remember that this world will soon belong to us. You'll be free, then, to drift and float about with no host at all. And you can come back to us to love and be loved. Be patient.

These messages have become an interruption. I know we need to be reminded of our mission, but I'm not going to forget what I'm here for. It's that this interruption comes just when I smell a good match for my man.

As usual we're at breakfast. She's walking by. Not young. A little grey at the temples just as he is. He ought to like her looks because she has the same sharp nose, the same slimness with hunched shoulders as if they both think they're too tall.

My man never holds my leash as we sit. He doesn't need to. I never run away, but now I do. I let her get a head start down the block and then I take off after her. Of course right away my man jumps up and runs after us as best he can. They can't afford not to have me. I'm their happiness.

But how stop her? She's striding along and I've got short legs. If my man gets to me before I can stop her they'll never meet, and he's moving a lot faster than I thought he could.

I manage to get up to her feet, run between them, and trip her. She goes down harder than I wanted her to, but I had to do it. Right away I smell pain.

My man kneels beside her. He keeps saying he's sorry— so, so, so sorry. He can't figure out what got into me. I never did anything like this before.

He touches her shoulder...keeping her down. "Don't get up yet. Rest a minute."

I was so focused on her smell I didn't notice much else about her but now I see she's attractive in spite of her nose and her large mouth. In fact those are what make her looks special.

There's blood on the knees of her nice tan slacks—actually, on one side, a hole right through them—and blood on the palms of her hands. At least she didn't break anything. I would have smelled that.

My man still kneels next to her, touching her arm. "We found him in a rain storm. He's a stray. Does he know you from before? Is he yours?"

She's not ready to answer anything yet.

I sit still so they won't look at me. I'm thinking: Look into her eyes. Maybe she'll see who you are just as I did. Except she's the one, not ready to look at him yet.

We sit. He keeps quiet. Finally he helps her up and brings her, both of them limping now, back to the table where his mother sits. I come back, too, dragging my leash.

The woman still hasn't said a word. They get her tea. My man wets his handkerchief and washes the blood and dirt from her palms. His mother is asking, can she get you this or that? Even the mother is saying she's so sorry.

"Does he know you? He's never acted this way before."

Finally, after a few sips of tea, she speaks. "I've never seen him before."

"I can't imagine what got into him. He's always so well behaved. We live just down the block. I can get the car and take you home. But I should take you to the emergency room. Wait here with my mother."

Finally, she looks up into his eyes and sees who he is.

She doesn't live far. There's a lot of back and forthing that ends up with the woman getting bandaged up at the emergency room and then going home for fresh clothes and then everybody going out to supper… without me.

I "stay" and pay attention to messages from our pods.

This will all be yours. The view of the milky way, the north star in the north.… Does any other world have any such view? Does any other world have dragonflies? A single moon? Butter? Pine needles? Strawberries? Chickadees?.… This will be yours.

Actually I'm really thinking more about my man and the woman than the pods messages. I'm wondering how they're getting along. I already know how beautiful this world is and with all it's smells. I don't need to be reminded. It's us seeds who are down here appreciating everything. The pods just talks about it. It's we who really know.

I wonder how many others of us seeds are in the middle of the same adventures I am, changing things for our owners? It's part of our hosts nature to help the opposable thumb people. It's part of our enjoyment of this world.

I can tell when they're on their way home. I rush to the door, twirling and dancing, and right after the mother and the man come in I can tell my plans are already working.

Now almost every morning we all four of us including me… meet for breakfast at the sidewalk café and walk together afterwards. First they walk the mother home and then the two of them walk me to the park.

My man always walks farther than is comfortable for him. When he comes home he takes a long hot shower and then uses a heating pad on his leg. I lick his hands and arms and, when I can, his face, to show how I feel, but I'm not sorry for him. I know he wants to do it to prove to the woman, and to himself, also, that he's a whole man.

He always tastes good.

But my man needs help. He's not making a move. I don't know what to do. I'm wondering if I should trip her again. Would that put her in his arms? I keep them laughing, but, so far, that hasn't brought them closer to what they both want to do. Perhaps I should trip him instead of her.

One good thing, though, they're both tall people who slumped to seem shorter and now they stand up straight.

He does take her hand now and then but only to help her up the steeper places. He's the one that needs help for those. I suppose she knows that and yet takes his hand and leans on him anyway.

They've found a secret place. Off the path. Surrounded by trees and bushes and at the top of a hill.

One day they take the mother home and then bring a picnic so as to spend more time in their special spot. They even bring snacks for me.

They sit side by side on a rock, put me through all my tricks and give me a tiny bite after each one. They keep laughing at me. Then I do a whole set tricks all on my own and they laugh even more. The woman says, "I do love Pussy Cat." I know she doesn't really mean she loves me, though she does. Then she says, "And I'm glad he tripped me."

I'm wondering if my man can hear what she really wants to say. Or is he too busy thinking about his bad leg? I can tell it hurts him by now. Is that foot going to spoil everything? Though why not? It's spoiled his life so far.

I lie down right on top of his bad foot.

He looks at me and I stare back. I try to tell him things with my eyes and what voice I have: Put your arm around her. Pull her closer. If that goes well, kiss her. For Heaven's sake! And it *will* go well.

He doesn't do any of it.

Then it's she who dares to lean her shoulder against his.

I move from his foot to hers. I look up at her. Then at him. Then at her. I don't know how they do it, but they get the idea. They laugh at me and then look at each other and then kiss. Really kiss and I leap up and kiss them, too. They laugh again and kiss all the more.

And right then the signal comes. So high pitched it even seems high to my host. The pods have already left the transport.

Move suddenly. If you're quick it won't matter how small you are. Those of you in the alleyways, find the first of the thumb people you see. Their thumbs are useless against your teeth.

This very moment, as you attack, we're creeping out of our shells. Without your impregnation we'll lie unfertilized... shriveling.

I sense others of us not far from me. We're busy at our jobs, guarding thumb people's property, letting ourselves be dressed up in silly costumes, retrieving ducks, leading blind thumb people, running after sticks, getting petted.... We're enjoying it as much as our hosts do. We don't make any moves against our owners.

This was not the perfect infestation after all. No wonder no other aliens tried it... or perhaps they did and didn't succeed. Probably they ended up as we have, dwindling away and drying into nothing. What a pity. This is such a nice place.

***The Magazine of Fantasy & Science Fiction*,** January, 2009

The Bird Painter In Time Of War

I paint birds in enemy territory. I risk my life to paint them. My people are desert people. They think I've made the birds up — that I'm painting fairy tales just so I can sell them to the gullible. I don't think I could invent such fancy birds by myself. So far I've only been able to smuggle some feathers to prove to my own people that there does, indeed, exist birds of a beauty they've never even thought of.

The enemy farmers know I'm a foreigner but they don't guess where I'm from. I ask, with some of their words and with drawings, if such and such a bird is around. I pay them in pictures. I don't have any of their kind of money. I don't even have my own kind. That would be a sure giveaway.

If their soldiers catch me, they'll take me for a spy. They'll think my paintings full of secret messages. Who cares about birds? they'd say. And they'd be right. Who does? Not very many in any country.

I doubt if I'd have the energy or the will to defend myself. I stutter. Even more so when I'm nervous. The birds don't care. I can imitate their calls. I can whistle, squawk, quack and squeak. I'm good at those, no problem.

I eat what comes to hand but I won't eat birds. I can usually find tree ears or chanterelles and there are roots. But I won't eat quail or duck or sage hen as most do. I do eat fish and crayfish.

I used to photograph wars, but that was before I looked up, not for the hiss of a mortar but for a different, exciting sound, and there, in long lines, were the snow geese flying north.

That was a long time ago, and an entirely different war.

I prefer the people here where I don't talk their language that well. Then not talking is normal. A silent cup of tea with gestures. A place by the fire on a rainy night. These people are not great talkers, anyway. I and the farmer can sit and smoke and nod, his wife and children nearby, happy, or so it seems, for each other's silent company.

If I see a good barn I may not even ask. I may just bed down there secretly. Of course there'll be a dog, but I'm good with dogs. I always sit a bit before imposing myself on their space. Sometimes I manage to get out a series of Gs. Guh, guh, ghu, ghu, good dog.

Children ask what's wrong with me. I always say, "L L L *Lots* of things."

To avoid detection, when I leave my desert for their mountains, I always cross the border where the cliffs are steep and the forest thick. It's not easy with my folio and sketch books on my back.

After climbing the ridge, I'll hit the road to the village. I never get far. I'm always looking down at the plants along the roadside, as much as I look up to see what's flying by. I don't bother with the names of either birds or plants. Words are my adversaries. Besides, the names will be different in their language.

It's the perfect time of year. All sorts of birds are passing through. Half way up the hills on their side of the border, I stop, turn around and rest. I can see the tops of the flags that fly from their fort just below me. I'm well past their lines. From now on I'll just look like one more farmer with a big bundle.

But there's not a single bird call nor rustle of ground squirrels. I hold still—just as everything else does. I hear the snap of twigs. Something's happening just above the fort.

Then I see soldiers in the colors of my own side, circling past not far below me. They're going to hit from behind, where the cliffs look down on the fort. They'll drop mortars right into the central courtyard.

These days forts aren't worth much. I don't think the enemy uses this one for anything but barracks. Those cannons along the ramparts are a hundred years old. I heard reveille as I passed by. The enemy will be there. My side could do a lot of damage.

I wonder if I should try to warn the enemy. What would save the most bloodshed?

I climb higher, wondering what to do.

But then I hear a sound from above. I stop again. Hold still…

…and a soldier backs up right into me. This time a soldier of the enemy, looking down on those skulking soldiers of my own side. He's alone, but loaded down with rifle and grenades.

At first I think a boy and I think, does the enemy use children as its soldiers? But I start to suspect. I look down at her body.

She sees my look. "Yes," she says, in the enemy language, "I am," and points her gun at my chest. "What are you doing out here? Trying to sneak across the border?"

Exactly what I *am* doing. Of course what I answer is my usual. "I, I, I, I, I."

"What's in your bundle?"

I hand it to her. She moves away, tries to keep her gun on me, and open the bundle at the same time. Not easy.

Then she forgets all about the gun. She even forgets about me.

I have two smaller paintings I brought with me to trade for a meal, or a bed in case the weather turns bad. One is of the bird I call a golden wing. The other is of a pair of black and white longtails with red heads. I tried to capture the luminosity of their throats. There are flowers in each painting. People like that. In one there's dew on the petals and a sunrise in the background. They're not completely realistic. After all, I was a photographer, I got tired of reality.

She can't stop looking. Ten...maybe fifteen minutes. I sit down. Later she turns to me, a look of wonder on her face. All she says is, "You!"

I nod.

She sits beside me, the paintings at our feet. She gives three big sighs in a row, says, "I'd like to forget all about the war. I'd like to run away and never come back."

I keep nodding. I don't want to have to try to say anything.

She looks at me again — all admiration. "Easy to see you're not a soldier."

Then she looks at the signature.

My name will tell her I'm a foreigner.

"Nor. Nor? Where's that from?"

I took that name from the word for bird in my language.

I don't lie. "I, I'm yu, yu, your...enemy."

"Not *my* enemy."

Her eyes are greenish blue.

Then, below us, the bombardment begins. My people against her people.

She picks up her rifle. She's about to take off, but I grab her arm.

"N, n, n, nothing you can d...."

A trumpet sounds down in the fort.

"You're trying to save them."

"No. S, s, save.... *You*!"

But she twists away and off she goes.

I pack up my paintings and head up. I want to be back where the birds are singing. I need to paint. It calms me.

I don't stop until the sound is muffled and distant and until I start to hear birds again and the rustle of ground creatures.

I get out my sketch pad and a crow quill pen and sit, hardly moving. And soon, here comes a redheaded yellowbeak with topknot and right behind him his drab but, in her own way, equally beautiful, mate. I start to sketch, then give each drawing a wash of water color, wait a few minutes until they dry and pack up.

I was concentrating so hard I didn't notice that the distant explosions had stopped, though there's a volley of rifle shots now and then.

I climb out on a jutting rock. I'm almost at the top of the cliff. Behind me is the high flat land of the enemy. I watch the sun setting across the valley where my people live. I watch a flock of snow geese fly by. I hear them. They're low, getting ready to land for the night. I watch until even the stragglers pass. Then I climb below the jutting rock and lie down.

I wonder how things went at the fort and with the girl. I wonder if she's still alive or if she rushed in, threw her grenades and was shot right away. I hope she had more sense.

Can a mere bird painter rescue somebody? Especially a bird painter who can hardly talk?

I feel bad that I let myself spend the afternoon sketching — making myself forget while others were in danger and maybe pain...of course it's pain they've gotten themselves into. Even she. But the joy on her face when she looked at my paintings! And then at me! It's enough to make me fall in love. But I don't ever let myself. How could I say what needs to be said? With secret signs and hand signals? A wink? A leer? Maybe with a parrot on my shoulder to talk for me in squawks? I refuse.

Besides, I have my birds.

But could I rescue?

I give up on sleeping.

I can at least see if she made it down to her own people. After I find out, I'll escape back to my solitude.

I leave my bundle under the jutting rock. No moon. There's an owl. That reassures me. I disturb things that skitter away. Then I trip and fall flat. Branches scratch my face. I hit my chin on a rock and almost knock myself out. There's a mini landslide. I make a terrible racket. I lie still and listen.

Nothing.

But right after that, my own side captures me. They don't treat me very well. Before they ask me anything or try to find out who I am, they throw me down and kick me a few times. Then bring me to a bonfire and to a colonel. I stutter more than usual. I don't make any sense at all. They take me for a moron — it's not the first time — and chain me to a tree.

I'm worried about my paintings and sketch books under that overhang (they're not well hidden), but I'm mostly worried about the girl. I don't even know her name. I can't ask about her. But then I can't ask about her anyway. They don't have time to listen to me trying to get the words out.

In the morning I open my eyes to white feathers. A fog of white. Tiny bits of down. I'm hurting and stiff but I'm charmed. Enchanted. It's as if I've found my way into a bird world. I sit up and then I realize there's nothing to be enchanted about.

Every little group of soldiers has a camp fire with a spit and something cooking. The battle was long over, but that evening they had nothing else to shoot so they shot the snow geese as they came down low, looking for a resting place.

They eat and then bring me their leftovers, but, hungry as I am, I won't eat snow goose.

Finally they unchain me, bring me down to the ruined fort where they've set up headquarters. The outer walls still stand, but inside it's a mess. The inner walls are stone, too, but the roofs were mostly wood and they're splintered and broken. Everything in the rooms is scattered and covered with debris.

They have ways of hurting that don't leave a mark. If I could think of a secret I'd try to tell it to them, but I never pay attention to anything except birds and flowers. And the more I need to talk, the worse my sputtering gets. I find myself making the bird sounds that come to me so easily, quacks and screeches and squawks.

Afterwards they don't bother tying me up. They let me lie in the courtyard. Discarded. Soldiers walk back and forth around me and don't pay any attention.

Later I hear somebody calling, "Nor, Nor. Get up, Nor. Please. Can you get up?"

It's dusk. The fort is quiet. Quieter than it should be, not a soldier in sight. It seems the army has left for some other battle.

"Nor."

I know who it is.

I stand up and hobble over to a tiny window in a stone wall. She reaches out. I grab her hand. Without thinking I kiss it and then hold it to my cheek. Then I worry about what I've done, but she reaches with her other hand and places it over my hand. Perhaps words aren't so necessary after all.

"Are y, y, you aw...."

"What have they done to you? You look...."

I'm thinking: Nothing you can see, but then I remember my bruised chin and scratched face from my fall.

"They've gone," she says. "Can you let me out."

The door is chained shut, but I use a piece of debris as a crow bar and pry the hinges out.

We run out the broken gates, around the fort, and start up behind it. I'm, yet again, climbing the cliffs at the hardest place. I know the way well but now I'm hurting. I wonder if I have a cracked rib.

It's exactly under that jutting rock where I hid my things that we finally stop, and there's my bundle, slashed. Everything scattered. My paintings are not only cut, but shot at. I suppose the next best thing to shooting real birds is shooting paintings of them. They burned the sketch books. Just the metal rings are left. They cooked another snow goose there.

I sit down, discouraged. It's the girl that yells, "Oh no! Oh no!" over and over. She runs around gathering up pieces and trying to fit them back together.

I say, "D, d, don't."

She says, "But I want these. Can I have them?"

I shrug.

I sit beside the dead campfire, while the girl, on her knees, keeps trying to piece together parts of the paintings and I finally remember to ask her name. It's Milla. I think it means cloud. It fits her.

She keeps looking up at me with the same admiration as before and I realize I've done it — I've actually rescued her. If not for me coming down for her, who would have been there to let her out?

She pieces together about half of one of my paintings. The middle is full of bullet holes and cuts.

"Look. The sunset and the flock of ducks in the distance is still there. I want it. Please."

"c, c, 'course."

"Except you could sell this as it is."

"No. You c, c."

"But what can I do for you that would be worth as much?"

"N, n, no."

Then we hear honking way above us. Another batch of geese but high. You can just barely hear them.

Then there's gunfire below us. None of the geese fall, they're way too high. Somebody is shooting just for the fun of it. It stops after the ducks pass, but the shooters are so near, we think we'd better get out of there.

But they've heard us. They start shooting in our direction before they know which side we are, or we them. We flop down flat.

But it might be my own side.

I stand up. I shout, "S, s, stop," in my own language.

Behind me Milla shouts, "Stop," in her language.

Good. We have both languages going. Then one of them says, "Stop," in the enemy's language. It's Milla's people.

Right in front of me, and in flower, is the bush the hummingbirds love best, and there, the hummingbird. How can it be? Right between shots? I still have a red feather in my button hole. I don't know how it lasted here through all this. The bird hovers over it. I stand still. It hovers over my face. Checking, am I food or not? Perhaps my scratches are red enough to tempt it.

I come to, to someone crying. I'm comfortable. There's a pillow. There's a feather bed. I think: Some day there will be nothing to cry about. Or at least there'll be no shooting and plenty of feather beds. Then I think: *Hummingbird*!

I open my eyes and sit up.

The crying stops.

There's a little girl standing in the doorway. She says, "Oh!" And then, in the enemy language, "I thought you were dead."

I'm not a good judge of children's ages, but she can't be more than six or seven.

I say, "N, n, not yet."

She says, "You had blood."

"D, did I?"

"You stayed in bed all day. I wouldn't like that."

"I, I, I...."

"You talk funny."

"I, I.... Yup."

"They didn't want me to see you but I did anyway. Lots of times. Like now.

You're a secret. But how come you get all these nice things?"

"Wh, what? N, nice?"

Then I see, beside the bed, there are sketch books, pens, and paints, and a large tablet of watercolor paper.

"I wish *I* could have them. Or even just one little bitty thing."

"Which?"

"Paints."

"I...I'll...share."

Then Milla comes in, carrying a tray.

"Sassuna! What are you doing here?"

She's wearing slacks and a flowery blouse. Everything much more revealing than her uniform.

"He said he'd share."

"Go!"

The girl is so happy she actually skips out.

"I hope she didn't wake you."

"I...l...like...."

She puts the tray on a little table by the bed.

I try to get up and fall flat. Bang my chin yet again, knock over the tray — the tea, the bread — in a great clatter.

But she's kneeling beside me. I'm in her arms.

Again I'm thinking: Maybe words aren't that important.

Sassuna must have heard everything crashing down. She's back. As before she says, "Oh!" Stands in the doorway watching us.

Milla kisses my forehead and then my cheeks. I reach up to hold her head so I can kiss her lips.

Sassuna keeps on looking. We keep right on kissing.

Milla tells me the soldiers of my side are entering houses hunting for soldiers of their side. They're killing animals to eat and killing animals for fun. The place is overrun by *us*. So far they haven't come here. This farm is set well back from the main road and hidden in trees.

I was shot in the thigh. Another shot creased my ribs under my arm. When I fell I fell hard and hit my head.

After they shot me, Milla's side apologized to her. They even helped carry me out to the road, but refused to do more. They thought my side was right behind them. Milla found an old man with a cart and had him haul me here.

There's an old lady here (Sassuna's grandmother) and a boy who sleeps in the barn and helps out. They know I rescued Milla and she showed them the pieces of my paintings. Boasted about me. Only Sassuna doesn't look at me as if I was special. She says she can draw and paint just as well as I can. I say we'll go out and paint as soon as I'm well enough. Of course I don't say it as easily as that but Sassuna waits for me to sputter it out.

Later they wheel me into the yard to paint and soon we hike the fields and orchard. Milla comes, too. She likes to sit behind my left shoulder and watch my paintings grow, little by little by little.

Everything we paint is hung up in the main room right away, mine and Sassuna's side by side.

Now, to everybody's exasperation, Sassuna limps and stutters as much as I do. Nobody can stop her.

Sassuna says, if she was a bird, she'd like to be the red and blue one with the topknot. I say I'd like to be a crow or raven because they're clever and tricky.

And Milla and I. . . .

Sassuna's grandmother lets us do as we do without disapproval.

Neither of us talk much. Touch is how we love each other.

But they come. My side. In the middle of the night, of course. They take me and Milla.

I can't explain anything, even in my own language, but I don't want to. I want to go with Milla. Milla tells them I'm on their side, but they don't believe her.

I'm still wearing my shirt and pants with bullet holes. Bullet holes in civilian clothes means to them I'm worse than a soldier, I'm a spy. They think my stuttering is a ruse. Or, they think, I was picked to be a spy because I couldn't divulge secrets when tortured.

They tie us up and throw us in a truck bed and drive us back to the old fort. I have a kind of fit. I *will* not let this happen. I refuse. I struggle. Milla keeps yelling for me to stop. "It won't do any good." At the end of twenty minutes I'm exhausted.

They lock the others near the gate but they take me to a cell on the far side of the fort. I'm in a room with hardly space enough for a cot. And there's no cot. In fact there's nothing. There's a barred window in the door just big enough for somebody to look in and see if I'm still here.

There are ravens all over the yard. Perhaps the bombing scattered garbage.

One comes to my tiny window, pecks at the bars. "Hello," he says. And then, "Fire in the hole. Boom."

I caw and then coo. I'm thinking: Go tell my love I love her. I say, "I, I. . . t, t, tell her I, I. . . ." And shoo him away. He says, "Goodbye," and does a barrel role before flying off. It cheers me up.

I kick aside chunks of plaster and pieces of a beam and lie down on the earth floor and look at the half ruined ceiling. Could I pull it apart even more and escape? There's nothing to stand on to reach it. Maybe at the door, perching on the lintel? I leap up the wall but fall flat. I do it again.

When I was young I took needless risks in order to test myself. Perhaps it was because I couldn't talk. I had to prove myself some way. I'd stay out in a cold rain without a raincoat. I'd climb the hardest cliffs, and climb higher and longer than anybody else. I was a pacifist, but I went to photograph wars to prove myself as brave as any soldier. I thought I had gotten over that need.

But I leap up the wall yet again and fall flat, as if hurting myself proved something.

I'm about ready to have another fit.

I calm myself by imagining Milla yelling, Stop. I lie down, and study the ceiling again. Finally I doze.

Evening comes. No one brings food or water.

I watch out my little window. There's a mortar launcher set up in the yard, but nobody near it. Soldiers are walking about now and then, though not as many as you'd think if they're serious about holding the fort. Just enough to look after the prisoners — which they're not doing, at least as far as food and drink is concerned. I wonder if Milla got fed.

I call out a couple of times but nobody pays attention. Crazy man, stuttering out consonants. "P, p, p, p, please," like a motor boat that won't start.

At dark the bombing begins. This time it will be Milla's people trying to get their fort back. What's the sense of all this back and forth? This fort isn't worth much to either side. When they win it what will they have won?

At the next volley my roof collapses. Thank goodness there wasn't much of it left to fall on me. One of the beams lies wedged, half way down, and at an angle. I can reach it and climb out.

Mortars are falling everywhere. As I watch, the mortar launcher in the yard is blasted apart.

And then her side does an old fashioned thing. They shoot arrows wrapped with burning rags into the broken wooden roofs. It only takes a minute for smoke to cover everything. Soldiers run around choking and yelling.

All I think about is Milla. I run through the smoke to where she was locked up but when I get there, the door is lying on its side burning. I try to go in but I can't walk over the fallen and burning ceiling and I can't see in all the smoke. I call out. Nobody answers.

But I'm the only one they thought was a spy. Maybe they let her go. Or could she have knocked the door down, or maybe got out through the roof as I did before it burned?

Would she have left without me? She might. She might have been thinking of Sassuna and Grandma.

I head for the gate.

But their side is picking off the soldiers as they run out. No questions asked — as usual.

I pull my shirt up around my face and turn back into the smoke.

I get lost right away. I fall. Then I hear, "Hello. Hello."

I caw.

"Hello there. Fire in the hole. Boom."

I've always trusted birds.

I get up and run, following that crazy, raucous voice.

"Hello. Hello there."

Just when I think I can't take one more smoky breath, there I am, bumping into the back wall of the fort, suffocating and nowhere to go. But there's an impatient, "craw, craw, craw," from somewhere near me. I turn towards the crawing and feel a gust of fresh air. There's a narrow stone doorway and a stone stairway just inside. It's not smoky in there. The air is cool and smells of mold. I climb the steps for what seems like three stories and end up, high, on the ancient battlements. The wind is blowing in the other direction. The rest of the fort is completely hidden in smoke but I'm in the clear.

Back here, the battlements are right against the cliff. The ancient cannons can't have been of any use at all, and yet there's one every ten or twelve steps. For Heaven's sake, facing the cliff! As if to follow some military rule that said, in all forts, it must be so.

The raven is perched on one of the cannons.

Then the fire hits the arsenal. The whole front of the fort blows up.

We — raven and I — are far enough back and high enough not to be hurt by debris, but we're both knocked down. I'm on my back and the raven...at first I think he's dead, splayed out flat, feathers every which way, but he gets up and flutters to shake his feathers back in place.

"Fire in the hole. Boom."

"Ex, ex...actly."

He starts to preen, trying to put himself back together.

This section of the fort is all that's left. Not much use now, even as a prison.

I hear a squawking and look in the mouth of the cannon and there's a nest and three baby ravens in there. They're not even dusty. When they see me peering in, they squawk louder. All you can see are three wide open red mouths.

I make a fluttering sound in the back of my throat. "Rroo, rroo, rroo," trying to imitate the sounds parents make to their chicks. I sit down beside the cannon.

Some things, even fragile things, still live and thrive. But Milla? Is she part of this dust billowing around us? Am I breathing her?

What if I hadn't made it this far before that blast? What if I...? Blown to bits, too, flying, as maybe Milla is flying around me right now.

I have wished I could fly.

I don't want to be birds made of a hundred little bits. Unless Milla....

The raven hops up on the side of the cliff.

"Hello. Boom! Hello. Boom!" As if telling me to follow.

But only finger holds and toe holds here. If that. Does he think I'm a mountain goat? Or does he think I, too, can fly?

But I've lost all fear for my own safety. I have nothing else to lose and nothing to do but trust my raven.

Now he's even higher.

"Crox. Creeks. Crow. Boom!"

I find a tiny finger hold. I begin.

Without my raven's repertoire of caws and cricks and buzzes and booms, I'd not have had the guts to do it. He gives me confidence and, even in the midst of all this, amuses me. If such a creature still talks and crows his way through life, his chicks on the very edge of disaster — if he tries to help me for no reason what so ever, it must be worth hanging on…and literally hanging on.

I thought maybe with my wounded leg I wouldn't be able to do it…that I'd end up flat out beside the chicks. Good food for carrion crows. At least I'd end up of some use.

It gets easier. In a few minutes I'm back on the wooded pathways I usually travel. Cinders fly up around me, some as white and magical as the feathers of the snow geese. I grab at them but they're as illusive as down.

I turn around. I want to circle to the gates of the fort and try to find out what happened to Milla.

My raven calls, "Hello. Hello. Hello."

I keep going.

He flies into my face.

In spite of a face full of feathers, I keep going back.

He dive bombs my head.

"Aw, r, r, right," and turn around. "D, d, d, *damn*!"

I don't believe this. Birds are smart in their own way, but not in our ways.

He leads me up my usual pathway. We don't go far when I see a small bundle wrapped in red cloth and partly covered in leaves and brush.

The raven coos — as if to his chicks.

It isn't! But it is!

I squat beside her. "S, s, s, Sa, suna!"

She sits up and grabs me so hard she knocks me over.

I never saw such a sad, pale, dirty, tear streaked face. Ever.

"I couldn't find you. I couldn't find Milla."

Has she been out here all night?

"H…how? How long?"

She starts to cry. By the looks of her I wouldn't have thought she had the energy.

"And then I couldn't get back home."

"Fire in the hole. Boom! Hello."

"It, it, 's all right n, now."

"Don't go."

"'c, 'course not."

When I look up to see where the raven's got to, he's gone.

We'll have to hurry back. The night will be cold. Sassuna only has her jacket and I have nothing but my shirt. I take it off and wrap it around her, tie it on by the sleeves. I put her, piggy back, and start on up. My body will help to warm her.

I've climbed up and down here so often, and with a big bundle of paper and paints. Sassuna isn't much heavier.

What a dangly age she is, nothing but arms and legs.

"Nor."

"Mmm hmm."

"I love you."

As I was following the raven up the cliff, I had thought to find a way to get myself blown to bits or burned to ashes — anything that would take wing, but I guess not. At least not yet.

She falls asleep there on my back and drools on my shoulder. As evening comes it does get cold and me with no shirt. It'll take another couple of hours before I can find my way back to Grandma's.

But my leg wound and lack of food catches up with me. I stop under the overhanging rock. Just one more short climb and we'll be up where it's flat and easy but I have to rest. I put Sassuna down next to the dead fire where Milla and I sat side by side and she tried to put my paintings back together.

I'm freezing. I gather up wood and brush, make a small fire and lie down beside it.

I think of those raven chicks, right on the edge of war, and the hummingbird there, practically between shots. Why can't some of us resign from all sides? Fly over it. Not even be bothered? Build our nests above it all?

I wake to shooting. Sassuna and I are caught between it. She cries out in panic.

"Shhh. Shhh. B, b, b, be a bird."

"How?"

And now my words come out perfectly. No hesitation.

"Remember the shiny red and blue one you wanted to be? Be it."

Shots are all around from both above us and below. A grenade lands next to us, right where the cinders still....

I rise, a shiny red and blue bird beside me. There's a great rush of wings as a flock of ravens rises up with us.

"Hello. Hello. Hello."

Asimov's Science Fiction Magazine, February 2009

The Meaning of the Fields

All this beauty, and you want meaning, too? All these sunsets. All the animals that slither by, creep and crawl. You want a worm that turns *and* turns into a butterfly? You want such a worm to be a sign of something beyond itself? As if I would turn into something that means something. As if I would shed my skin and shine out golden or silvery. As if my eyes would turn blue?

You, on the other hand, are, I suppose, how one ought to be. Marching, stomach first, onto the battlefield of life, or, more likely, any field that happens to be by the roadside across from the ditch. You don't stumble. You plan ahead. You foresee what needs to be foreseen.

I suppose you think that even I would have a reason for being, were my nose exactly what a nose should be. You think that then my life would have a meaning way above washing dishes.

See how you point your chin at the sun to estimate the zenith and all the other high points right from your own front door. You turn then and measure "the angle of repose" of the scree that drops away from my front porch.

You nod, but not at me. You have said there's even meaning in trees. You have said, and more than once, that nobody can say there isn't. I say a tree is just a tree and all the better for it.

We are not a beautiful people. None of us. Not even you. We have eyes with droopy lids. We have bumps on our noses. Our hair is lank. We hunch and hump along. It gets us there.

I go up and sit on my rock and look out at the fields below. I presume that if there had been a rainbow across the valley, as there so often is, you'd think, as you so often do, that it was yet another sign for you to ask me to marry you.

As I come back down, past your house, I trip on one of your vines. I fall flat and bump my chin, which wasn't the greatest chin in the first place.

Gets me to thinking, as you always do, that meanings abound and in the oddest places. Here's a whole new meaning. That's because I see you seeing me fall, but you don't come to help me up.

I suppose, if I wanted better—a better place to live and a different you—I'd walk away into the woods, a little bit farther than my usual walk, build myself a lean-to and live on berries. I'd make pets of everything that happened by. I'd tell each one, "You're nothing but yourself, just as I am me." I'd say, "There are no similes," as if anything were ever like anything else, and they'd all take joy in that.

I sit a little while, right in front of your house, and catch my breath. I knew you wouldn't come and help. You probably put out those vines just to trip me up. Out loud I say, "What if meanings turn back on themselves and become the opposite of each other, twist and roll? What then?"

It's not the first time I've said that.

You pretend not to hear.

I check my ankle. It hurts, and it's starting to swell up.

I say, "What if a rainbow, upside down, becomes a ship of many colors?"

But it doesn't matter what I say. You've already gone inside.

"You misjudge me if you think I'm helpless," I say. I limp away.

I ought to cater to you, as Mother said I should, before she died. She wanted us to marry, but I'm trying to find others of our people. Surely, there are some of us left, somewhere. They would be lank-haired, like me, and pale-eyed. They would have lumpy noses.

Mother kept saying our talent would die out if we didn't marry our own kind, and who else is there around here but you?

But I always said, "What talent? For shooting jackrabbits? For kicking the cat?"

"You'd be surprised," she said.

I know all about our so-called talent—just one. It's the ability to slide. A *glissando* to the side when suddenly attacked. Not much there that's odd or magical. I can't think when I've ever needed it. I imagine it was life-saving back in more primitive times, when we were faced with tigers.

Well, if you put out vines to trip me, and then don't come to help me up, I figure you've about given up on me—ever agreeing to marry you, that is.

Mother always said, "All right, then. Go on. Find some others of us if you must. Take your pug nose right on out the door." And I always did, but only for an afternoon. Maybe it's time to really head off, sprained ankle, bloody chin, and all. I'll wrap my leg up tight, and I'll take Mother's cane.

I wash the dishes, sweep the house, make myself a sandwich, grab an apple, and go.

When I was a teenager and looking, even way back then, for a suitable lover, I never went this far into the mountains. Now, on purpose, I keep going until I've gone too far to come back tonight. I may be sorry. The weather doesn't look

Then, for heaven's sake, he sits down almost right in front of me, hums a tuneless song, and takes out his lunch. Watercress... can that be? Watercress sandwiches? I've eaten all my food long ago. I'm hungry, and I love watercress. Now, I catch my breath with a different kind of yearning.

I wonder if I should...

I do. I come out from behind my bush. I smile.

I'm sure I look eager. Much too much so. He leans away from me and holds his sandwich close to his chest. He's definitely not happy to see me. Or is it just that I startled him? Perhaps opposites don't always attract.

"I was wondering if you could spare a tiny bite or two. I haven't eaten since yesterday."

He squints at me with disapproval, exactly as you would do. I recognize that doubting look. Can he be as contrary as you are?

"You see, I've sprained my ankle." I limp back and forth to show how hurt I am. I exaggerate, but only a little.

He breaks off a small piece. I sit down beside him, as close as I dare. I say, "I need to rest, because of my ankle."

There's the sound of the stream and the rustle of leaves. Why don't I stop talking and listen and eat?

"Even now, with my sore ankle, I can fry up little birds."

He looks interested.

"I presume that you have many children who look just like you, and a wife for whom you gather flowers ."

"I have no children and no wife."

"Perfect!"

I say it out loud, though I didn't mean to.

How deep his voice is, unlike yours, and growly as a—but none of that.

Suffice it to say, deep and growly.

I can fall in love at first sight as well as the next person, but I'd better back off a bit so as not to scare him. Actually, it's a wonder he doesn't object to my following him home.

Once you said, "Wherever you go, look for the more meaningful places." And here is one, or so you'd say. A village of similes, where everything is exactly like everything else, even more than like itself. The huts stand as if out of storybooks. The trees are gnarled, as if from the top of a windy mountain. There's a Main Street, looking as if it went somewhere beyond this valley, though I don't think it does, and now there's me, the short dumpy stranger, limping into town. A pilgrim in search of, I don't know what, except in search of this very man right here.

My, what nice tall people everybody is. I could love them all. Some would say I'm the exact right kind of person to marry one of them. We pass three women. You would say three is a significant number, but I like four better. Am I being contrary for contrary's sake?

"If you could see your way clear to sparing a little gingerbread or apple pie?" I say to one of them. (It's a gingerbread kind of a place, though here I am thinking just the way you always do and asking what you'd ask. If they don't have any, it's your kind of a mistake I've made.) "Or do you live on elderberries and Solomon's Seal?"

They're wearing high heels that make them look even taller and slimmer, and make me look even shorter and dumpier. But why heels? Maybe just around the corner and over the hill there is a city. Maybe Main Street does actually go somewhere.

"How many long miles, or, on the other hand, short miles, as the case may be, until I get to a town?"

Even the women have bushy eyebrows and thin lips. What this whole place needs is exactly me. How come this man doesn't see that?

But then, I think he does see. Suddenly, he gives me a look and leads me to his little storybook house.

It's a mess in there. For sure, he doesn't have a woman to look after him.

Not a word is spoken, nor need there be. All the better, considering what words do. In spite of my sore ankle, I set about cleaning up and cooking what's at hand. There's a pail of crayfish.

Isn't it odd that, in all these years of living next door, I've never cooked for you?

So, the man of my dreams and I sit in his tiny yard and eat what I've made. It's delicious, but he doesn't say so any more than you would.

We watch the sunset, also without saying anything. Just before the sun pops below the mountain behind us, and the sky is full of wispy red clouds, I do say, "I like children."

He gives me a look. You would say a disconcerted look. I'd just say a long look. What could be more romantic than his piercing black eyes?

About the sleeping arrangements, the cottage has only one room. I can see that the man of my dreams isn't ready to welcome me into his bed. I'm not quite ready for that either. After all, I hardly know him. And when a person doesn't talk much...

You're the one I know. I can always tell exactly what you're going to say next. Like right now, you'd say I should get out of here before it's too late. Well, I'm not going to.

He doesn't say, "Take the bed." He says, "Take the floor." And so I do.

How wonderfully long and flat he looks in bed.

Next morning, I'm right there, first thing, with the tea and toast and elderberry jam. You wouldn't have thought I would be this way at all, but I am.

And look how I'm agreeing and agreeable. I say, "You've found the perfect place to live in harmony with your own kind. I understand that and respect it. But don't you think there's need for new ... um ... blood? For the sake of the children?"

He doesn't think so.

"One's own kind is so ordinary."

"If you say so."

When would you have said any such thing?

that great. I wrap up in my rain poncho and rest under a gnarled old juniper.

I say, "Look how beautiful this old tree is, and look how it means nothing but itself."

I'm still talking to you, even way out here.

Now who of my kind, or of any kind in their right mind, would be out here this time ofyear? Am I looking for love from a mule deer?

A storm comes. Hail and lightning. I leave my tree and hurry down the slope to find a sheltered spot. I run hard on my sprained ankle. I'll bet I won't be able to walk at all tomorrow.

I find a good spot. A sort of indentation, just my size, in the edge of a cliff. It keeps me dry, if I curl up and keep my toes tucked in. I watch the lightning from here. You'd say it's just like the Fourth of July, but I say it's just lightning in the forest.

Before the storm stops, I fall asleep.

In the morning, I uncurl. It's a wonderful, bright day. I stand up and yell without meaning to. Not because of the pain in my ankle, but because of the view and the day. I'm in a gorgeous valley I never saw before. Full of lupine and fireweed and shooting star. I thought I had run towards home when the hail started, but I don't think so. I have no idea where I am. I couldn't go home if I wanted to.

You'd have said my yell was because of the meanings of this glade, but my yell was because this glade is a really nice one. It's so beautiful. I even think I'll yell again.

Now I've scared a doe and her fawn. I didn't notice them 'til they ran. Goodness knows what else I scared. There's the flap of wings. If there are people nearby, then surely they heard me, too.

I hobble over and sit behind some scraggly bushes. They won't hide me, but better them than nothing. I keep quiet and wait to see what else I've stirred up. You'd think my kind would be living out here in this hanging meadow. It's a perfect place. Especially for short ugly folk who don't own much of anything. I see a patch of Solomon's Seal. I see miner's lettuce, elderberries, mountain currants. Lots to eat, if one knows how to look.

I wait. I hold still.

And somebody does come. He must have heard me, but now he looks as if he forgot about it. Maybe I sounded more like a bird than a person. My yell was a kind of squawk.

He's not at all my kind, but as to ugliness, he might as well be. He has a long, boney face, instead of a round puffy one like ours. He has fuzzy black eyebrows, instead of those that hardly show at all. I'm quite taken with him.

But it's not berries he's picking. It's flowers. I wonder for whom. I catch my breath with yearning.

I always did like black hair and hooked noses, and that lanky, loose look. Just the opposite of me. He's probably as farsighted as I am nearsighted. If I should marry him, and if our children were half him and half me, they would turn out just exactly right.

"I do say so," I say.

He's thinking about it. At least that.

"You need a change."

He's not the sort to argue. He shrugs. He doesn't care either way. What a nice change from you.

But he likes his own kind best. It's what I like, too. His kind, I mean. Look how he sits with his boney knees pointing, one towards the door and the other towards the window.

I say, "My love," as I look off towards one of his trees. I suppose he thinks I love the tree—which I do, but in a whole different way.

And then, we have our fight, where my special talent, my *glissando*, almost saves me, and his special talent, an opposite kind of *glissando*, makes it possible for him to slap me anyway.

Just before our fight, he had me do things on purpose to make me not want to be there. He had me wash the sheets. He had me change the bed but not lie in it. I suppose he thought my love for him would be my reward. Do I look like a servant? I suppose to his tall, lanky kind, I do.

I'd said, "I'm leaving." And right after that, I had my slap.

Now, I hobble away. I've stolen his basket, so that along the way I can pick berries. I go farther and farther, all the way up a hill, then down into the next valley.

And then I find you. Or, rather, you find me.

"What are you doing way out here," I say. "Looking for somebody to torment? Or did you discover that you couldn't live without me?" You say, and right away, "I give up on the meaning of the fields."

"Now you say it."

You've never looked uglier. Hair, what there is left of it, sticking out in all directions; like a fence around the prairie of your bald head. I think I feel something like tenderness.

I say, "All our children will be just like us. I hope you know that."

I hand you the berries and say, "For you," just as if they really were.

"It'll be as if..." you say, or start to, but you stop right in the middle.

On the way back, you help me over the rough spots, because of my ankle. On the smooth spots, you hold my hand. We hike down to our little houses, where—except for arguments and similes and meanings and occasionally tripping each other up on our paths to and fro—and where, to me, nothing is ever like anything else except itself, though to you everything is like something else, though we say so less now—we live happily ever after.

Lalitamba, Issue 3, 2009

A Safe Place to Be

It started with a funny feeling in the bottoms of my feet. Something is going to happen. Perhaps an earthquake. That's what it feels like. But perhaps terrorists on the way. Whatever it is, something's coming.

Why did I (of all people), an old lady, get this warning while everybody else is going on as usual? Have I a special talent nobody else has?

But the cat feels it, too. He's been shaking his paws as if they feel exactly like my feet do. He looks at me as if: Why don't you *do* something? I tell him, "I will."

It's coming closer. I'm getting out of here before everybody tries to leave at the same time.

Though could it be that I'm just feeling the future in general. Disaster will come to all of us and at my age it can't be that far away. I'll be as dead as most all of humanity already is. Mother ... Dad ... Dostoyevsky.

But can I take a chance that this tingly feeling is just because of the normal run of things?

If only I knew when. And also who to tell? I'd like company through all this. Not that a good cat isn't company enough and I do talk things over with him, but a person would be nice, too. I can't think of anybody to tell who would believe me or wouldn't just get in my way as I try to leave in search of safety.

That tingly, rattly vibration is getting worse, rising from the ground, up through my feet and rattling my spine. This morning I could even feel it from my fifth floor apartment. I ran for the central hallway. I stood there for twenty minutes. Then I grabbed Natty, put his leash and harness on him, and ran outside and down the block and huddled under a tree. Again I waited. The cat was shaking as much as I was. A sure sign that I was right. I ran farther but had to stop to catch my breath in a doorway near the park.

Here, in a place where pigeons are always wobbling along, there wasn't a single one. Not one! That scared both of us even more.

I must have looked just how I felt because somebody asked me what was wrong. I said, "Just a dizzy spell is all." I didn't want anybody else to know. I wanted to get out and safely away before any of the others found out something was going to happen.

I check the feelings in my feet again. I feel a rumbling for sure, by now so strong I wonder why everybody doesn't feel it. Well, all the better then, it gives me plenty of time to escape.

A mountain top would be a good place, nothing could fall down on me from up there and water wouldn't reach, but there aren't even any hills around here. I'll head west, though I don't know if there's time, but out in the country will be better than the city. I'll bring all my money and my raincoat.

I go home, eat a big last meal, pack a knapsack with cat food (it'll do for both of us), my vitamins, and go. I bring Natty in the top part of the knapsack. He doesn't mind. He's glad I'm finally doing something.

I ask a taxi driver to take me twenty dollars' worth towards the west. He's nice, he takes me even farther. He doesn't care that I sneaked a cat into his cab. I ask him to come with us. We'd like the company. Especially such a nice man and with a cab to ride in. I told him why I was getting away. I said we should hurry before the roads get too crowded with people trying to escape. He doesn't say so, but I don't think he believes me. He prefers getting back to work.

So I start walking. The taxi drove me a good ways into the suburbs. I never expected to get this far in just one day. Even though I'm still scared, this is all turning out fine. I stand still and check the bottoms of my feet again, and, yes, no doubt about it, danger, though I keep reminding myself that life is just temporary anyway and at my age even more so.

But right now I have to find someplace to spend the night. I don't want to use up any more of my money than I have to. It has to last at least to the Rockies.

I keep walking well into the night. I was hoping to get beyond the little houses and warehouses to farm land, but no such luck. I wanted to sleep in some country place, a forest or a park. Finally I'm too worn out to go on. I drop where I stop. There isn't a bush or a tree in sight, just warehouses, and airplanes keep coming over low. I'm so tired they don't bother me except for waking me up early in the morning. I worried the cat would get scared and run away, but he stayed with me. I keep his leash on most of the time though I don't attach it to anything or hold it. He's too old to run off.

So off we go again (after sharing a cat food breakfast). How come nobody else is trying to escape? Most people are heading into the city as if everything was just as usual. Is this a special talent of mine worthy of study, just as animals predict earthquakes? Should I tell a scientist about it before whatever it is happens so that when it *does* happen, I'll have predicted it? How does one find a scientist? And it has to be somebody interested in this sort of study. I wouldn't be surprised if I pass a lot of universities along the way. If the danger is as close as it feels, I'll have to hurry and find somebody.

I'm so happy with our progress, I take us to a diner for lunch. Fish for Natty and a hamburger for me.

That night I find a good place, nine feet high, four feet long, three feet wide. What passes for a window. I won't say where though it mustn't be thought that I'm ashamed of it. Actually I don't think I'm ever ashamed of anything of that nature, not even that I'm getting rather dirty and mussed.

By now I'm far enough not to have to worry about a tsunami, but this is tornado country now. Natty and I keep studying the sky.

Wherever I end up, I would like a small tree. That is, if I can't have a large one. Living in the city I haven't had a tree of my own of any sort since I came here long ago. Also I'd like a nice round lichen covered rock that heats up during the day and stays hot all evening. I'd like a place to build a fire and a log beside it to sit on. I'd like a nice bed for Natty.

I buy myself a shopping cart to carry stuff like water bottles. I'm getting ready for crossing places in middle America where the rest stops are far between.

I ask for rides in the parking lots, but if I don't get one I just start walking. And I usually don't get one. I don't blame the people; after all, I'm dirty and raggedy, and my bundles and the shopping cart are bulky and don't fit in anything but trucks. If I saw me humping along with all this junk I'd take me for a crazy person. I wouldn't pick me up either. Even so, now and then I do get a ride. Usually in an old pickup that isn't going far.

I forget how many days it's been, but up to now everything is serene with the world. Of course I'm not getting the news. Maybe a disaster has already happened and I don't know about it, though you'd think people in diners and rest stops would be talking about it. I always read the headlines in the newspapers when I pass by them. (I don't waste money on them.) And you'd think, if the disaster had happened, that my feet would stop sending me all these signals. Natty's, too. Though maybe after one disaster, there might be another right behind it.

Ahead, you can see the road winding up a hill. I dread trying to climb it pushing my cart. But before I get to it, there's a town and I pass one of those little country hospitals. It's right here, handy. I'm going in and have them check my feet. It might be important for them to study me. For omens. Maybe Natty's, too.

I hide my cart behind the bushes near the door.

The lady at the desk asks me if I want a shower first. I did suspect I was pretty smelly by now, but I tell her I'll just get dirty again. "I'm on the road," I say.

"But wouldn't you like to take this opportunity."

I haven't washed since I started on this journey. Just a little bit in the bathrooms at the rest stops.

I know she means the doctor I'm going to see would like it a lot better if I did.

"But what about my cat?"

She lets him come in to the bathroom with me. Then they let him into the doctor's office with me, too. "Since," they say, "he's on a leash."

Everybody is very nice here.

"I want to report my feet. And my cat's feet."

He doesn't believe me about my feet predicting disaster. He doesn't say so, but I can tell.

"Well," he says, "there's plenty of disasters around to predict."

That type of little black mustache he has always intimidates me, but he's quite nice underneath it.

"This is something really, really big. Like a tornado or an earthquake or a gigantic mud slide. Mud as far as the eye can see."

"Where are you living? Are you eating?"

"Oh, yes, and fish, lots of fish. I know it's good for you."

I don't want him to think I'm just an ignorant tramp.

"There's a shelter just down the road if you need help. You can get a free meal there."

"Will they have cat food?"

"Do you have a place to live?"

"But, Doctor, these tingly feelings? They're getting worse. I thought maybe it was important. I thought you'd like to look into it."

"Nothing to worry about. Old people get these odd nerve twinges all the time. Let me give you the address of this place where they'll help you."

I'm worried they might put me away. I'd have to stay here and the disaster might be right in this area and I couldn't escape.

I say I'll go there right away but I won't.

"I'll drive you, if you can wait a bit."

"I don't mind walking."

I have to show him all my money before he finally lets me go. I still have quite a bit. Also I show him my vitamins and my cod liver oil. (Both Natty and I take it.) That impresses him.

At least he doesn't charge me much. But he didn't do anything either, except to tell me I'm fine.

It's going to be too bad … I mean the big disaster … there are so many nice people in the world like these people at the hospital. It's a shame so many of them will have to die. I'm trying to tell them but they won't listen.

I don't go for the free meal, though that would have been nice. I haven't had any vegetables for a long time. But I'm worried they'll stop me. I know it looks bad, an old lady with a big bundle walking—*walking!*—across the country. I'll have to try to think of a good reason for doing it. Maybe for some cause or other like breast cancer. Why didn't I think of that before?

By evening I finally come to the hill. The road climbs back and forth. It's still a wide and sweeping four lanes. This is going to be hard. Dangerous, too. A good place for a landslide.

I struggle on. Not a single good place to rest. Everything on a slant.

A silvery sporty car stops next to me. The top down. It's the doctor. Just the sort of car to go with his mustache. What's he doing way out here?

He says he doesn't like how I look. It's twilight. How come he can see me so well?

He's popped the trunk.

"Put your cart in back."

I step off the road on the rocky down side. He can't follow. Not in the car.

But he's out and is opening the passenger door for me. "I'll drive you."

Thank goodness it's almost dark. And it's even darker in the shadows of the boulders where Natty and I hide. Natty's a talkative cat, but he knows not to make a sound.

The doctor calls a few more times. "I can help."

Exactly what I don't want most is help.

Finally he drives off.

What now? Are they going to be chasing me? Capture the crazy woman? Do I have something else to worry about? Why do they care?

I'm going to walk on through the night. It's safer.

Whenever a car goes by, I hide in the ditch. It's not easy, what with my cart and all. At least you can see the cars coming from a long ways off.

We reach the top of the hill. Now the road will be flat again for a nice long while.

Finally, there in the ditch, I just have to stay and sleep.

In the morning I see there's somebody else walking along, way, way, way ahead of me—by about six miles I'd say. Here the road is so straight and flat and there's so few trees you can see for miles. I think the next hillock is probably about twelve miles away.

Hours pass, but I'm catching up. He doesn't stop to rest. I don't either. What if he, too, has funny feelings? And there'll be safety in numbers. For me at least. Maybe if the doctor sees I have somebody … especially a man … he won't bother me anymore.

I get all shaky with hope. Somebody else, maybe, who knows what I and Natty know. He won't think I'm crazy.

Finally, he sits down. It takes me half an hour to catch up, and then I walk past so as to take a good look first.

We're both elderly. We're both skinny from so much walking. We're both browned by the sun and have chapped lips. We both have big hats. I got mine when I started wondering about crossing the desert.

He stares as I go by. He's wondering about me as much as I'm wondering about him. He has a cart much bigger and sturdier than mine. More like a wheelbarrow, only he's rigged it with a loop around his waist so he can pull it.

I wouldn't be surprised if he didn't have a tent. And there's a frying pan tied on top. I'll bet he never hitchhikes. He's got too much stuff.

He's found a nice spot to rest. There's an arroyo and actually a few spindly cottonwoods growing along the banks. Not exactly giving shade. Under the road is a culvert for when the arroyo fills with rainwater. That'll be where he pees.

I turn around and come back.

He looks like a country person … farmer or some such … though by now I may not look like I'm from the city either.

Before I sit down (not too close), I search the sky. Out here you can see a lot of it.

I say, "So far everything is fine."

He doesn't bother answering. It's clear that it is.

We sit silently but I can't tell if it's a comfortable silence or an uncomfortable one.

Natty's the only one who gives a questioning, "Yeow?"

When the man gets up to go on, I do, too. He didn't ask me to come, but he didn't say not to.

It's evening and this was a good spot to spend the night, but off he goes. He may be trying to get away from us. Some people don't like cats.

Is he going to walk all night? I don't dare ask. If I ask he may tell me not to follow.

We go on and on. Towards morning he comes to a group of spindly trees. I stay about twenty yards behind so as not to be a bother. I collapse just off the road. In the ditch so to speak. At least there's enough runoff for there to be bushes all along the road side. Almost like the edges of the rivers. I don't even have the energy to get us our can of cat food.

I wake up late the next morning. To the sound of traffic—if you can call one car about every ten minutes traffic. My feet are tingling even more than before. Whatever it is is coming closer.

I study the sky. Not a cloud in sight. Not a tree either except for the clump where the man camped. He's gone on ahead. He's already a few miles down the road. Maybe he does mind us following but I'm not going to let him get away.

I and Natty eat our cat food and hurry after him. We're faster than he is, what with that big bundle he has to pull.

It's such a nice morning. All along the roadside the rabbit brush is in bloom. A bright yellow. I hum in spite of whatever disasters might be on the way. You don't have to mope around just because your feet tingle and the world is full of depressing things and something really, really big and horrible is about to happen.

Pretty soon we're almost up to where I want to walk—just a few yards behind the man.

So far he hasn't said a single word.

But here's the doctor's silvery car again. I'm not expecting him. I don't have time to even think of hiding.

The old man stops, turns around and watches.

It really does look as if we're together and as if the old man's waiting for me.

I run up and grab the old man's arm.

The doctor leans out the window to speak to me. Before he can say anything, I say, "I'm walking for breast cancer. I forgot to tell you."

"But I can help. I can help you both."

"He's walking for breast cancer, too."

The two of us and our bundles and Natty wouldn't fit in the doctor's little car, anyway.

"We don't want to get helped."

One nice thing, the old man is letting me hang on to his bony elbow. I wasn't sure he would, seeing as how he's always walking off without me and without a word.

And then he does talk.

"She's with me."

His voice croaks out as if he never uses it … and I guess he never does.

"Why don't you people go to our shelter? Get yourself cleaned up? Get a rest? How old are you, anyway? I don't want you having a heart attack out here."

The man says, "Young enough to walk all day."

The doctor grabs my other arm, the one holding my cart. Natty is sitting on top of it in his usual spot. He lashes out and the doctor gets four good scratches all along his hand.

I let go of my cart, I can't help it, and it bounces down into the ditch and tips over. I run down to see if Natty is hurt and so does the old man. The doctor doesn't. He's looking at his scratches. What kind of a doctor is that?

But Natty isn't there. I lift up my cart to see if he's squashed underneath it. Then I see him galloping down the road, his leash dragging. If there was a tree anywhere near he'd be up in it.

I should have known. Cats are fast. They hardly ever get hurt.

I leave my cart in the ditch and run down the road after him. Next thing here's the doctor's car right beside me.

"Get in. I'll help you catch it."

It, he says!

I run into the ditch again. And then beyond, into the brush.

The doctor gives up and drives off.

The old man is waiting for me back beside my cart.

"Cats come back," he says.

Nice of him to say so, but we're not anywhere for a cat to come back to.

How will Natty get along without me? And out here in the middle of nowhere.

This changes everything.

"What we'll do," the old man says, speaking slowly and calmly and in that raspy voice of his. "We'll go on a little bit farther and stop where we think he might have run to, and then we'll stay put until we find him."

He gives me an apple. I haven't had one in a long time, but I can't swallow. I take one bite and give the apple back. I know it's valuable.

That man has all sorts of things I didn't know he had. He gets out a little camping stove and makes me tea. I do feel better after that. At least I have more energy to go looking for Natty.

We go down the road a bit farther, calling out. Nothing here but desert. There won't be anything for Natty to drink. And I worry about that leash dragging behind him. And what about hawks?

Every now and then I step off the road and look around. I look into the shadows. By now Natty's a desert cat and knows that it's cooler under things in the shade.

If there's a disaster I want to face it with Natty, and if I escape it, I don't want to escape without Natty.

Maybe this *is* the disaster. At least it's my disaster.

When we settle down for the night, I sleep a bit away from the old man in case Natty is afraid of him. I open a can of cat food and leave it near me. I can't eat my share of it. I feel too bad. I also leave a cup of water. I wonder what sort of creature I'll attract that I don't want. Do rattlesnakes like cat food?

Maybe Natty is dead already. There's always coyotes.

The man and I set up a kind of camp, just our bundles and his stove and pan. And branch out from there. It's several yards off the road and behind an old tumbled down wall. Probably the remains of an old stagecoach change-of-horses stop. He hasn't set up his tent. No need. It never rains out here.

He not only has apples but carrots, too. Kind of dried out but still good. But I can't eat.

We wander around calling, kitty, kitty, kitty. We look under every bush. I hope Natty's good at catching lizards. There are a lot of them. Except he's got that leash holding him back.

The doctor drives back and forth twice a day. He must live in the next town from the hospital. He stops now and then and calls out to us that he just wants to help. Once he yells out that at least we're hidden behind that old wall. What does he mean by that?

If he *really* wanted to help he could bring us some bottles of water. We won't be able to stay here much longer.

But the old man says he'll trot back to that town—and he does mean trot—to bring back some water. He'll use my cart because it's lighter. And we can stay here longer.

After he leaves, I spend the morning in the usual way, calling and looking in the shadows for a dead or dying cat.

And then, that afternoon, it rains. A hard rain. First I think it's *the* disaster but it isn't. I rush out in it calling kitty, kitty, kitty. I'm sopping but I don't care. Only later do I remember to put out cups and the old man's frying pan to collect water.

Then it stops raining and then suddenly flowers! As far as the eye can see—

not mud but flowers.

I walk out in it. It smells wonderful. And here's a whole mass of little luminous blue butterflies. I never knew such a thing could be.

Have I been wrong about the disaster all this time? Is it to be something beautiful instead of something bad? A disaster of flowers?

But then I feel a sharp twinge in my feet as if to remind me I'm wrong and something terrible is out there just waiting to come down on us all.

I search the sky again.

Except now I don't care. I yell, "Come on tsunami! Come flood and fire, tornado and meteorites."

Nothing happens.

Then I hear the old man coming back. He's whistling. You just can't help it what with all this beauty. He sees me and waves. Calls out, "I have tomatoes and peaches!" It's as if he knew they were things I haven't had since I started on the journey to escape.

But I sit down in the middle of the flowers and start to cry. So many good things and I don't even care.

He sees I won't be able to eat for a while. He puts everything behind our wall and then comes out into the flowers and butterflies—carefully, trying to avoid stepping on flowers—and sits beside me.

After a bit I take a good look at him … a better look than before.

He sits hugging one knee. He's wearing shorts. His legs are hairy, stringy, and knobby, but strong looking. His big hat partly hides his face, but I already know he's an ugly man and needs a shave. His teeth stick out and his chin recedes, his nose has a bump in the middle, but all of a sudden he looks beautiful. Like Natty. Natty's not a handsome cat but I've never seen one I like better.

I say, "Thank you."

He nods—a series of nods, as if, "Yes, yes, yes," and then shakes his head the other way as if, "It's not important."

I wonder what his name is.

I think to reach out and touch his knee—to say something nice but here comes the doctor, his silver car is parked right across from our wall.

He walks toward us, tramping on flowers. Scattering butterflies. He has a bandage on his hand where Natty scratched him.

"I thought you'd be gone on by now. Or at least gone for help."

Oh my God, he has Natty's red leather leash. He's slapping it against his thigh. Then he hands it to me. "Here's your leash."

We've been looking and calling ourselves hoarse and he's had Natty all this time. Or at least he knows where he is. I can just see it, the doctor driving down the road and seeing that red leash and tricking Natty some way. Or, more likely, the leash hooked on a prickly blackbrush.

I grab it and start whipping him with it. He's not ready. He falls backwards into flowers and I keep on lashing at him.

Long as I'm winning, the old man stands there watching, but when the doctor gets up and hits me one good slap and knocks me over, the old man grabs him from behind and holds him. He's shorter than the doctor but you can see in his stringy arms, very strong.

I'm thinking: *My* old man.

The doctor says, "It's—" (*It's* again) "—at the pound back in Wilkerville. Unless it's dead. They don't keep them very long."

I don't even grab a water bottle. I start running—back down the road.

The doctor yells, "Don't be dumb."

We're maybe only seven or eight miles from town, and days and days of walking and pushing my cart have made me strong, too. I run on and on.

Pretty soon the doctor's car pulls up beside me. Since the top is down, as usual, I see right away the old man is in the car with him. The old man tells me to get in. If he's there, I guess it's all right. Though maybe the doctor will see that we both end up stuck in what might as well be the pound for people. The car's only a two seater. I have to sit on the old man's lap, his arms around me. It's a nice place to be.

But then a huge dark cloud comes towards us right down the road. Like a huge, huge dust devil. And it's full of flowers! And the sound. Here comes the disaster. Finally. I'm actually glad that something's happening at last. I don't have Natty to hug, but I do have the old man's arms around me nice and tight.

The doctor stops the car and starts putting the top up, but at the last minute the disaster veers away, rises, then dissipates in a rain of flowers. Flowers all over us, wet and fragrant.

We're all out of breath though we haven't done anything but just sit here. We look at each other … even the doctor. I look into the old man's black eyes. And turn away fast. I'm thinking: that's where all his calmness comes from. Down in there somewhere.

Again, I wonder what his name is.

The doctor drives us—much too fast even for the desert—into town.

At the pound they say, "That skinny old marmalade cat? He was an odd one."

"Well, where is he?"

"He got out. Just today. We don't know how he did it."

I always knew he was smarter than most but now I wish he wasn't. I sit down on the curb.

The old man says it. "Smart cat." Then, "He'll come back." … his slow raspy voice. "They always do."

It's a reassuring voice and nice to hear, but it doesn't reassure me.

The old man sees that. "He *will*!"

The doctor says, "It's a cat, for Heaven's sake. You'll be fine without it."

How dare he? Of course I won't be fine.

I stand up and attack him again. I land two good blows before anybody can do anything.

But he slaps me down.

"The town wants you in the shelter. You're a nuisance and an eyesore. Look at yourselves."

The old man pushes him away and gets punched and falls backwards. That makes me so mad I get up and fight even harder. It doesn't do any good. I'm on the ground again beside my man.

But there's a great yowling and howling and here, off the roof of the pound comes an orange ball of claws, down on the doctor's head. And a terrible racket. I'd heard cats can do that, but I never actually heard the sound before.

The doctor tries to run away, but you can't run away from a cat on your head.

He's around the block and out of sight but we can still hear Natty.

We look at each other again, and this time I let myself look ... way down in there.

He nods and then I nod.

He takes my hand. (How strong and calloused both our hands are. Like pieces of sandpaper.)

We sit down and wait for Natty to come back.

"You know there is no safe place," he says.

And I say, "I know it."

"And not all disasters are that bad."

And I say, "I know it."

Pretty soon Natty comes swaggering back.

We walk to our things, me with Natty on my shoulder.

"Let's go on."

"Till we get to a nice green place with a river?"

"And trees."

"And a hill to be on top of?"

"And a cottage."

I wonder what his name is.

Strange Horizons, 28 September 2009

The Dignity He's Due

The king's music will have lots of trumpets and drums, a slow pace so the king can keep his dignity.

There'll be handmade lace at his throat.

On the royal barge he'll be protected from the sun by a silk canopy. There'll be another barge for his orchestra. Do not listen. The music is for his ears alone.

The royal picnic will be caviar and white truffles and wild strawberries no bigger than pearls.

But little acts of kindness — that's how we live now. We always say, thank you, though we don't mean it. Who should people give things to if not to us? Who better deserves a meal and a dollar? Mother says it's our due and we shouldn't be ashamed.

Or we steal. Mother says it's like taxes — they owe us.

We have a little tent that just fits the three of us, me and Mother and my little brother. I and Mother carry big packs. My little brother isn't supposed to carry anything. That's because he's heir to the French throne. Mother thinks he's fourth in the line of succession. Of course there is no French throne anymore. Mother says that doesn't matter, we're still royalty.

Mother says trumpets should sound. She goes, "Toot, dede toot, dede toot," as a fanfare. (When he was little he liked it, but not anymore.) Mother says music should be written just for him and, she says, might be one of these days when people realize. She says, "Look at his silky black hair and blue...so blue, blue eyes. Look at his nose, already aristocratic even at his age. Can he be other than a prince?"

(I have blue, blue eyes, too, and silky hair, but nobody cares.)

It's important that he dress as a prince but we don't have anything but hand-me-downs. It makes Mother feel bad to dress him in T-shirts and jeans.

I keep telling her there is no King of France and is unlikely to be one ever again. But she says, "Things change. Who knows what's going to happen? Certainly not you."

I may be only fourteen but I think I know more about it than she does.

One time when Mother was away, I cut his hair. At least he's a happy prince now with a real haircut. He hated that page boy. When Mother came back she was furious. "How could you? I don't want him to look like everybody else. Who'll know now? Once it grows out again, don't you dare."

"He wanted me to."

"A prince never gets to do what he wants. He has to learn that."

Mother wants to keep him, as she says, "pure." What she means is, no scars, neither mental nor physical, but it's too late. He slams around, climbs things. Already there's a C shaped scar on his cheek and the marks of the stitches. And as to his mind...for heaven's sake, how can he be a normal anything? Though she doesn't want normal.

Mother is teaching him all the things a king needs to know. Especially a French king. History of France: The departments, the chateau, the riviers...."La douce France," she says. "Never any trees this big. You can walk from one village to another. Every house has a wall around it." But she hasn't even been there.

I'm teaching him other things, like the states right here, the battles that took place in these hills and, as we go south, slavery. I think a prince should know about slavery. Not that I know much about anything. Still, I did have a chance to go to school for a little while — until our father left us. I was allowed to mingle with the "rabble." That's because I didn't matter.

When my brother says, "*I'm* a slave," I say, "All children are slaves to their parents, but this won't last forever," and he always says, "I could be dead before it ends," and I say, "The way you slam around, that's probably true."

The older he gets the more he understands that this isn't the way most children live.

We often sleep in a park, though there's always a cop, comes in the middle of the night to tell us to move on. Mother says, "Keep your dignity. Remember, noblesse oblige." We just pack up and head...maybe for another park, if we're in a town, that is. In the country, woodsy spots are good stopping places. Hardly anybody bothers us there.

We're safe for a while now, because Mother has us off on the Appalachian Trail. (Yet again.) When you don't have things to wear to keep warm, you need to follow the birds. We hardly ever have good shoes, and with all this walking, they're always worn out. Mother found me hiking boots that were set out in the garbage. They were already worn out when she found them.

Mother is happiest when we get, as she says, our due. Now and then we do. My brother gets the most. People think he's cute. (Mother hates cute. She keeps at him to stand up straight and hold his head high. She tells him, "Don't be cute," and, "Stop smiling. Don't gesture needlessly. Don't put your hands in your pockets. Look people straight in the eye.") She sprinkles her talk with French words. "Alors," and, "Mon Dieu." "Ah-la-voila." "Venez mes enfants." But sometimes I wonder just how good her French is.

We often hike this trail, going south in blueberry season or going north when fiddleheads pop up. We like it when we see a big rock we've remembered from the trip before or a gnarled tree we've camped under on our last trip. And then there are the lean-tos all along the way. We steal from campers. They don't expect robbers way out there. We never take their cameras or field glasses or bird books. Mostly we take food and sometimes socks and warm underwear.

Here I am thinking, we, as if I agreed with Mother — as if I considered myself part of all this, though I guess, in a way, I am. I have to be. I don't know how Mother would get along without me. I think I'm in charge. Not of where we head or when, but I keep us out of trouble. And I try to add a little bit of a more normal life to my poor brother's.

I'm going to try and stop this. I want us to find a permanent place to live. A nice little town where it never gets too cold, but big enough for us to hide in.

I'll have to break it to Mother that we aren't going to live this way anymore. I don't know what she'll do. Maybe I won't be able to stop her. If she and my brother take off alone, I'll have to follow.

Napoleon Gustave Guillaum Williamson. We don't even have a French last name. Did my father approve of that name for his son? Or did Mother change it after my father left us? I wonder that she hasn't changed our last name.

He, Guillaum, was all right with this kind of life until last year when he turned nine. He's getting too smart to put up with it. I tell him not to worry, I'm going to get us out of this, but I have to find the right place and I have to do it in a way that Mother won't object to too much — if that's possible.

He won't put up with this much longer. We're all right now, though. He likes being out on the trail like this. And he likes camper's kind of food, even the dried stuff. He likes the whole idea of the Appalachian trial. He loves watching animals and bugs and such. He even loves spiders. Can a prince be interested in spiders?

I try to make him part of my plans so he'll feel he's working on getting us out of this, too. I tell him to think about the kind of town he wants to live in and when we come to towns he should look around and see if this is the one. I hope that'll keep him from being too impatient.

But things change before I'm ready. It starts when Guillaum tells us he wants to be called Bill.

Mother has a fit. Worse than when I cut his hair. I've hardly ever seen her this angry, and usually it's me she's mad at.

It's a good thing we were out on the trail at the time. Mother made a terrible racket. After she calmed down, I noticed there wasn't a sound anywhere, the birds were quiet, no rustlings from ground squirrels, even the bugs were quiet. Guillaum...Bill and I were quiet, too.

I think that made him realize things he hadn't before and it must have made him angry, too. I guess he decided he wouldn't wait for my help.

The king's crown will be heavy.
His robes will sweep seven yards behind him. If he turns too fast they will trip him.
Lights will be lit all along the roads he'll travel.

Lots of places along the trail you have to pass through little towns to get from one edge of the trail to the other. In this town the trail goes right along Main street. There's a playground in the middle. Mother leaves us there while she goes off to scrounge. She's so angry she hasn't said a word since our fight yesterday — not really a fight because Guillaum...Bill and I just stood there watching. I'm worried about her. I think to follow her, but I know I should take care of Bill.

I practice calling him Bill a few times (every time I do, he smiles), then I stretch out on a bench to take a nap and... Bill...goes off to look for bugs or, if he's lucky, there'll be a stray dog. I'm tired. None of us slept too well after that "brouhaha" (Mother's word) about Bill's name.

Mother kept waking us up with one more thing — one more reason why Guillaum needs to be Guillaum. She can hardly bring herself to say Bill even just to talk about it. She spits it every time she says it.

I didn't think he'd go off without me. But maybe he found this was a town he liked, though it's a little small for my taste — for hiding in, that is. I'm sure it's small for Mother's taste, too. She doesn't think he'd ever get his due in a small town. The only museum is the Indian museum. Mother says, "A prince must be cultured. Must have a real education: Politics, philosophy, and all the arts, too." Mother worries that he's into bugs.

I was afraid this would happen, especially after the Bill episode. I feel really bad. I always thought we were in this together.

For all I know, Bill is back on the trail beyond the town but without a tent? He didn't even take his raincoat.

Mother is counting on his ignorance. "After all," she says, "he's only nine. He can't get far." But almost ten year olds are smarter than people think.

She says, "This is all your fault. You should have been watching."

I tell her he'll just keep running away if our life keeps on as it is. He won't put up with it anymore, and especially he won't if she doesn't call him Bill.

"I won't call him...." She can't even say it.

But suddenly she thinks he's been kidnapped. She says, "It's not about that awful name at all, it's that he's so beautiful, how can he not be kidnapped?

"In that case, you have to go to the police."

"I can't do that."

"If you think he's kidnapped, you have to, but I think he just got fed up."

"How can such a beautiful boy not be kidnapped?"

I tell her we should settle down right here, right now. "It's the only way to get him back. And if we ever do get him back, you're going to have to call him Bill."

It's a nice town. Surrounded by green hills. He couldn't have picked a prettier place. Or is he back on the trail stuffing himself with blueberries? Or he might be at the school checking out the fourth grade. He's always wanted to go. Mother's right about one thing, he's smart. He knows what an entomologist is and what taxonomy is. Even systematics.

I wouldn't mind going back to school again. Funny, some kids get to go and don't even like it. I guess it's only when you can't that you want to.

I tell Mother she should take a nap in the park. I say, "I know you're tired after last night. I'll find him."

She knows I'm the one, has to do it. She knows he won't come to her. But when I find him...if I do... will he come back even for me?

I know it's a waste of time, but I want to check out the little houses on the edge of town...especially the ones that lie right near the Appalachian Trail. I'm not that worried about my brother. Besides, he might be near the trail somewhere.

I like best the houses that are more run-down than others because I imagine cleaning them up: pulling weeds, planting flowers, painting the trim some nice bright color.... I wonder if some of those houses with unmowed lawns are empty.

Then I head for the grocery store where Bill might be trying to get his due in rotten apples and moldy cheese, but I change my mind, instead I head for the elementary school to check out the fourth grade.

The king's music has four slow beats per measure. It's more largo than andante. His coat of arms has a lion, rampant, the right foreleg above the left, "Honi soit" in purple letters along the top and "qui mal y pense" along the bottom.

I was right to come here first. A better place to get his due than the grocery store — and going to school really is his due. I look in at the classes through the little windows in the doors. At the third window I find him. He's in the back row, ducking down behind the other kids. He doesn't look right. That haircut I gave him doesn't look like the other boy's. I see now how bad it is. No wonder Mother was angry. He's dirty and has dark circles under his eyes. His jeans are more raggedy than any of the other kids and are so small for him they show his ankles.

I'm sure the teacher knows he's there but she's not letting on. The kids know, too. They keep turning around to look at him. Good thing he's small for his age — nobody's afraid of him being there. I suppose a child sneaking *into* a class and paying attention is a nice change.

I see why he sneaked into this classroom. All along the walls there are pictures of insects. Near a window at the back there's an ant farm. The window is a little bit open so the ants can come and go. Bill is right next to the farm. Behind him there's a cage with gerbils and next to that a fish tank. I remember things like that back when I went to school. I feel such yearning I think I'm going to cry. Good I don't because I don't look right in here either. There's a hall monitor. I managed to avoid her when I first snuck in with other people, but she's right behind me now, before I realize it. She's wondering why I'm standing here looking in the window. I say I just wanted to see if my brother was there. Which is the truth.

"Is he?"

I don't know what to answer. I don't want him hauled out when he looks like he's having such a good time. I say, "No."

She asks me to come to the office. She leads the way. I follow, but when I see a hallway I duck into it and run out a side door.

Maybe I should have stayed because they might have let Bill and me go to school, but I got scared. I wasn't ready. I didn't have any answers figured out. What I do is wait until school is over. That's not till three thirty. I sit on the front steps all the rest of the day. I get hungry. I wonder if Bill will find a way to get something to eat in school.

When he comes out he's with a teacher. They're talking so much they don't notice me. I'm standing right there beside them on the steps. I hope Bill has figured out some good answers. They say goodbye so I guess he said the right things. He turns in the opposite direction from the teacher and goes off as if he had a place to go. I follow. Pretty soon he slows down. Now it's as if he doesn't know what to do or where to go next.

I yell, "Bill," but he doesn't turn around. He's not used to his name yet. "Bill, Bill. *Guillaum*!"

Finally he realizes it's me calling him and that Bill meant him. He's so glad to see me he actually hugs me before he realizes he's doing it. Then he collapses down on the edge of the sidewalk and I sit beside him.

"I saw you in there. Did you eat?"

"They had lunch at school but I was afraid they'd find out about me. I hid."

He *is* a beautiful boy. Mother's right. Even at his age he has an aristocratic face and a kind of natural dignity. I don't think it's because Mother keeps saying: Sit up, don't slouch, and such. It's too bad about that scar on his cheek.

"I'm hungry, too. Let's go scrounge."

I want Mother to get good and worried before I take him back.

That is, *if* he'll come back. Maybe he won't.

Sometimes at the back of grocery stores they'll give you old vegetables and fruit. In this town there's only one grocery store and it's not a very big one. The man back there gives us perfectly good apples and carrots and a loaf of day old bread. Also moldy cheese. He cuts the mold off for us though Bill says he has a good pocket knife. Then he gives us each a quarter.

We sit not far from the store and eat.

I was right to worry. He won't come back. "You were having a good time, there in the school. What did the teacher say?"

"She said I could come back whenever I want. She said she'd give me paper."

"Where will you spend the night?"

"I found a place."

But he won't tell me where.

"OK. How about I meet you after school tomorrow then."

I give him his raincoat and my quarter, he takes some of our food, then I go back to Mother.

I left her at the back of the park, hidden behind bushes and under a tree, now she's right at the front where she can see up and down the street. She's awake and hunched over, elbows on knees, head on hands. When she sees me she jumps up, as delighted as Bill was. It's clear she thought I'd gone off and left her, too.

Good. I hope she's been thinking about our life.

I think she's been crying. She takes a big shaky breath and asks, "Guillaum?"

I give her the food I scrounged. She eats as if she's hungry. There's not much left after she gets through. I don't know how she stays so thin.

"So Guillaum?"

"I want to go to school."

"You! What good would that do? Besides, I'm a better teacher than any teacher you could ever have.

She always says she taught tenth grade French until she got married, but I wonder if there wasn't another reason why she.... She *says* she quit.

"But Guillaum?"

"I mean it. I need to go."

I know better than to say that this is a nice town. I already know she would think it's a terrible place for Bill. I can just hear her: This town? This little no-where town? I suppose you want a cottage with a picket fence in the front and a peach tree in the back yard and Guillaum fraternizing with ordinary small town people.

That's *exactly* what I want. But I'd settle for less — a lot less in fact, just as long as it was different from this life we have.

"Isn't there a law that we have to go to school?"

"But did you find him?"

She's counting too much on me. She always does. I say, "No."

She's about to get upset again. I can see her eyes go wild. Would she attack me?

I say, "Wait a minute. Wait a minute. I can find him. I have an idea."

"What?"

But I won't tell her. "Why should he come back? When I find him I have to give him a good reason."

"All right, tell him I'll spend tomorrow looking for a place to live."

Can it really be this easy?

We camp at the edge of town just beyond a regular camping spot that charges fifty cents. We sneak in and use the bathrooms. In the morning we have coffee at a little café where they have a couple of local newspapers lying around for the patrons. We steal one and take it back to the park. I tell her not only to look up the ads for places to live but for jobs, too — for both of us. I say I'll be back by four.

I wander around the town again. I check out one of those little houses that looks vacant. I look in the windows and there's no furniture in there. Maybe we won't have to pay for a place, until we all get jobs, that is. I memorize the address: 45 Overridge Lane.

At three o'clock I go sit on the school steps and wait.

Sometimes Guillaum…I mean Bill seems so old — old and a little kid at the same time. It's that quiet questioning stare. I can see in his eyes all that yearning for a different life.

Mother always tells him he's better than everybody else, but he's a democratic kind of kid. He wants to be like the other boys. No better and no worse.

I sit with one of our apples.

Finally he comes out, again with the teacher. This time he has a book and a tablet. I've never ever seen him this happy. As soon as the teacher turns away he can't help skipping. He's turning off in the direction of "my" little house. I follow. I shout, "Bill, Bill," and this time he remembers that's him.

But Mother has followed me. (All day long? All around town? to the library? to the little art gallery? and maybe to 45 Overrridge Lane?) Just when Bill turns, grins up at me, ("I'm in!" he says and gives a little jump for joy), she steps out from behind the bushes next to the school and grabs him.

She's all packed up and ready for the trail. She throws his book and the tablet into the gutter and off we go again, heading south. He doesn't protest. He turns into a kind of floppy rag and lets himself be dragged along.

I rescue the book and tablet. I lag behind. I never want Bill to see me crying.

Most of the time Mother holds Bill's arm though now and then, in narrow spots, she has to let go. Once when he's free he punches a tree trunk and bloodies his knuckles. Mother wants to put band aids on his scrapes, but he won't let her. He won't look at her either. I've never seen him like this.

It starts to rain. Right away we find one of those lean-tos but Mother won't stop there. She wants to get farther from that town. She says she doesn't ever want to see it again or hear about it.

I'm not going to let this just lie there. The look on Bill's face there on the school steps!

We go on much later than we usually would. We have to pitch the tent by flashlight.

First thing we're settled in, Bill takes his bug book, tears out the pages and throws them out in the rain. We huddle down, cold and wet and miserable… except for Mother.

I wake up in the middle of the night. The rain has stopped and the moon is out. There's light coming through the mosquito net doorway. I see something glinting. I sit up fast. I'm not sure. I guess. I turn on the flashlight and there's Bill with his jackknife open. Right away I think, not the prince! I can't believe I think: "The prince" when neither of us want him to be a prince.

We stare at each other.

I whisper. "*I'll* find a way. *I'll* figure it out. Let me."

But he snatches the flashlight from my hand and crawls out of the tent.

I'm not sorry. In fact I feel a lot better that he's out of here. I don't fall back to sleep right away. I'm worried, but reassured. He won't be punching any more trees if he's heading back towards what he loves.

I wake to wails.

Of course I do.

I knew I would.

The king's horse is the color of sweet cream, while his saddle is as if of butter.
A king must have a shield, but, and more important, he must have a sword.

So back we go.

Mother can't stop talking. That often happens. It doesn't help to say something because she can't hear anybody but herself. We're out of food by now. I don't know what she thought we'd do along the trail but it wouldn't be the first time we'd have to trap quail and catch fish. But now she doesn't stop to eat. I wonder how we'll get food because there's only that one grocery store. You can't keep going back to the same place everyday without getting noticed. And probably Bill will have already gone there a second time.

We don't get back to town till evening.

Bill won't dare head for the school. I wonder what he'll do.

Was he going to kill her? If he was, I need to do it instead, but I don't want to. I wonder if I could. She's very strong. If she has to, she can carry all our stuff by herself.

Or maybe he was going to turn the knife on himself — to show her how desperate he is. Where would a desperate almost-ten-year-old go?

Will people help him because he's so beautiful and sits so straight?

I wonder if somebody will ever think that I'm royalty, too.

"Beauty without vanity. Strength without insolence," as every king should be.

I set Mother up in the very back of the park beyond the duck pond — back where the town starts being pasture. There the houses are little more than tool sheds. Some really are tool sheds. At first I thought they all were but some look lived in. I wonder if one of those would do for us.

I make it clear...I hope I do...that I'm the one has to find him, that I'm her only chance to get him back. "He'll go off into the woods and be a hermit.

He knows how. Or he'll end up in some other town you'll never find. You'll lose him for good. Why not let him at least go to school? You can teach him, too — all the royal things he needs to know. We'll settle down...just for a while, get jobs, save our money and go to France when he's a little older."

"Even over there nobody will know."

"They'll know. Maybe just one look is all they need. They'll guess right away."

Hard to believe, but she actually believes me.

The king's forehead is pale as oysters. The dew of his tears is fresh and cool.

Embroidered fleurs-de-lys in tiny stitches are on his handkerchiefs. Of which he has dozens.

All his pomp, all his circumstances, follow him wherever he goes.

I find him in an unexpected place. The senior center.

It's all by itself in a grove of trees. I see the grocery store truck pull up. I see the man — the very same man that gave us food before — carry out bags of bread and still good vegetables.

I go in behind him thinking maybe I can get us some more food. There's a lot of old people in there working hard. They're setting up the tables for the people who are going to have lunch there. The volunteers look to be just as old as the people they're going to serve. (In fact that grocery store man looks to be one of the oldest.)

And who should be helping set the tables but Bill. Somebody has bandaged his hand for him but he can manage.

He sees me but he doesn't stop working till the tables are all ready.

I sit and wait.

He comes and sits beside me, says, "I'm getting paid in lunch."

A couple of old ladies invite me to eat, too. As we eat, I notice my fingernails are black and nobody else's are.

We have a very nice lunch. In fact it's better than any meal I can remember in a long time. There's a salad and a baked potato with cheese on top and slices of beef and rolls with butter and gelatin with fruit in it. I can't believe all this food.

And there's nobody who isn't nice. Even the addled ones who don't make much sense are nice. They seem to like having kids around. They give us their deserts until we can't eat anymore. I let Bill do all the talking. He's good at avoiding hard questions. "We're on the trail just passing through. We're on the way back to my school. I'm in the forth grade. I got held back a year." (How does he think up all this stuff?) "We got delayed but we'll be there soon. My school starts late, anyway. We're with our father."

Father!

After, we help clean up and then we go outside and sit on a bench not far from old people on other benches. We whisper.

"If I can get Mother to stop in this town, will you come back to her?"

"She won't."

"Were you going to hurt her or were you going to cut yourself?"

"I don't have to tell you."

"Mother will go crazy."

"She's already not like any other mother."

When has he ever known about any other mothers?

"I've got a house you can hide in."

I *think* I do. Just because Mother saw me — or probably did — looking in the windows at 45 Overridge Lane, doesn't mean she'll find him at some other empty house. There was another one not so far away.

The king's portrait hangs in the grand hall. The eyes follow you as you walk from one place in the room to another.

This time, as we go, we keep looking around to make sure Mother isn't following. We double back. We hide behind bushes and wait. It takes a half an hour. Then I take him to the last house on Farm House Road. We don't have any trouble breaking in a back window. Not much more than a "p'tit coups d'pouce" as Mother would say. He already has our best flashlight. I don't have to tell him not to use it much and keep it away from the windows. We're used to hiding. He sneaked a couple of buns from lunch so he won't get hungry. And there is a fruit tree in the back yard (though not a peach). There are apples on it and apples lying under it, rotting. A sure sign that even the neighbors or the neighbor kids don't bother to come around. We gather a few of the best ones. I take a couple to bring back to Mother. Of course they're wormy, but that's another thing we're used to. We always love abandoned orchards.

It's a little house with a kitchen/living room all in one and two small bedrooms. Perfect for us, though Mother won't think so. She'll say, "Better no place at all than this." There is a little furniture: a surprisingly clean mattress, a stool, some old newspapers. Somebody else has been camping in here. I hope not recently. I warn Bill to escape out the window if somebody comes.

Nothing works, no water, no electricity. Somebody has made a fire on *top* of the stove. There's a lot of ashes there. It's a mess.

Last thing *I* tell him: "Remember, petit a petit…."

Last thing *he* tells me: "I don't want to hear any more French."

So then I go back to Mother.

If there's a line of people waiting, the king goes first. You say, "Après vous" to the king.

A king has a good chance at becoming a constellation not unlike Orion.

He must never blow his nose in public.

She's not there. I get worried again. I don't know what to do. I sit and watch the ducks. I imagine Mother following us even though we tried so hard to lose her. I imagine her, right this very minute, grabbing Bill in her iron grip and dragging him away — on purpose without me.

I get up. I'm about to go back and see if Bill is all right when here she comes — out from one of the little tool-shed houses.

"Viens," she says. "I found us the greatest place for the night. Guillaum will like it."

She takes me to one of the sheds. She's put herself exactly where I wanted her to be.

It's a one car garage-sized shed. Obviously deserted. It has one tiny dirty window at the back. The whole place is dirty and full of spider webs. There are shelves — empty except for old paint cans. Mouse turds on the floor. I'd rather be in our tent but if she likes it....

She's laid out our three sleeping pads, Bill's in the middle. She'd rather wait in a place like this until she finds us a palace. I wonder how long she's expecting to live in it.

She sits down on her pad, cross-legged, all knees and elbows. I wonder when she last combed her hair. Her fingernails are as dirty as mine.

"So where's Guillaum!"

She's so pleased with herself for finding this place, she doesn't sound upset anymore. She thinks everything is fine.

"He'll come back when we've settled down. When we have jobs."

"He'd better not try to go back to that school. They just teach nonsense."

"I'm afraid he'll hurt himself if he doesn't get to go."

"Why would anybody hurt themselves? Besides, they don't teach the things he needs to know. They won't even teach decent French."

"You can do that. You taught me. Think of it. We'll earn money and then we'll go there. To France."

"I'll bet they don't even teach good biology."

"It's grade school for heaven's sake."

But then it starts. I sit down on my pad and get ready to look as if I'm listening. I try to glance at her watch as she waves her arms around. I figure it'll take about twenty minutes before she'll stop bad mouthing schools.

I wonder if we'll ever be able to trust her to stay in one place. She might get all settled down and Bill will come back and everything will seem rosy and off she might go, dragging us along.

This town is too small to hide them from each other for long. And Bill will go to school even if he has to sneak in and out the back door. Maybe it'll work.

But what about me? Will I ever get to go? And can I get a job? Would I look more grown-up if I wore lipstick? I'd have to steal some.

She's often embarrassed after one of these talking sessions. Finally she sits down and says, "You must be tired." That means she is. She gives me cheese from two days ago. It's her way of apologizing without saying so. I give her a wormy apple.

She says, "Where's our big flashlight?"

"Bill has it."

When I call him that she gets up again and turns away, but she's too tired to go into another tirade.

The king's cloak is edged with ermine.

No hat must be taller than the king's. No white jacket more white. No buttons more shiny.

Bill and I meet next day behind the Senior Center, not inside it and not that near.

He spent the night nowhere near that mattress. He slept in the other, smaller bedroom. Somebody came in, in the middle of the night, rattled around a lot, too. Next morning somebody made a fire of sticks on *top* of the stove and cooked eggs and bacon. Left the fire of sticks (smothered with a metal pan lid). Bill found the matches and the bacon, but not the pan. He lit the fire again and cooked some of the bacon wrapped around a green stick. Trouble was the fat made the fire bigger than he wanted.

"They mustn't see smoke."

"I *know*, but *he* got away with it. Besides, there's trees all around."

I ask Bill did he smell any liquor, and he says, No.

He watched the person out the bedroom window as he left. He says, he's a thinnish man, nice and neat in a dark suit and tie, carrying a briefcase and wearing a hat. The dressy kind.

"For heaven's sake, are you sure?"

"Of course. I know what I saw."

"You can't stay there."

"I like it. I'll have an address."

"So does *he*. We have to find a different place."

"This one is practically right on the trail. There was a jackrabbit in the back yard this morning. And quail. I saw a coach whip snake. It's pretty far north for them and kind of cold. They're usually way far south of here."

"He could be dangerous. Sometimes men prey on good looking boys like you. You know that."

"If anything bad happens, I'll go out the window."

"You trust people too much. Actually Mother does, too. Or she trusts that people will give her what she needs. I hope you know better than that."

He shrugs and makes a face as if: Why am I telling him what he already knows?

"Well don't. I mean trust."

We're close. We have to be. We only have each other. Usually he listens to me, but I've lost him this time.

"You don't have to sit up straight just because mother says to."

"I *know*."

He's sitting like a gentleman and keeps on doing it.

"So you didn't go to school today?"

"Mmmm."

"So that teacher helps you?"

"I *trust* her."

"That's OK."

"I *know*."

"How did you sleep without a pad?

"K."

"Bet you didn't."

"Did too."

"I could get your pad for you except.... Mother will be furious."

"I *know*."

"But I'll do it anyway."

"K."

"Meet you back here in half an hour. Did you have anything to eat besides that bacon?"

He shrugs and I know he didn't.

"I'll see what I can find."

But he's the one finds food for me. Wrapped-up egg salad sandwiches. He won't tell me how he got them. I'll bet he stole them. Though maybe not. He's good at finding odd jobs and getting people to give him food. Maybe it's that natural majesty of his, though I hate myself when I fall into Mother's way of thinking. The royal smile. Ugh. Yet there it is. As if bestowed on us underlings. Though maybe a little bit too shy for royalty.

I give him his sleeping pad. Mother wasn't there so I didn't have to deal with her. I hope she was out looking for a job.

Bill hugs me when we say goodnight. A sure sign he's lonely and worried. That worries me, too, but I don't want him coming back to us. We'd be on the trail in no time and who knows how many trees he'd punch next time or who he'd cut.

The five trombones of the king play fanfares.
The spotlight will shine on him alone: his velvet lips, the ivory of his collarbone.

I find Mother washing clothes in the duck pond. It's good she's found a sheltered spot to do it in. I don't think the towns people would like that.

First thing she says, "Isn't this a great place? It has everything. Even water. Guillaum will like it. Except you took his sleeping pad."

"You want him to be comfortable don't you?"

"I'd rather he'd be comfortable here with us."

"Did you find a job? When you're settled in for a while, I know of an even better place for us to stay."

I'll take her to that Overridge Lane place that I think she followed me to. There won't be...at least I don't think there'll be...somebody else living there. Of coarse there won't be any water and maybe there'll be just as many mouse turds as here.

I help Mother bring the clothes back and hang them up on a frayed piece of rope above our sleeping pads.

"So did you get a job?"

"Maybe."

But that's all she'll say. She does have food. Packages of sliced chicken and sliced cheese. A huge bag of lettuce. I don't know if she bought them or stole them.

"If you need an address, use this one. I'm hoping to get us all there. It'll be better for getting a job than this one."

"This is a good enough address. I like it here. You've been seeing Guillaum."

"Leave him alone."

She starts turning red. Looks at me with that wild-eyed look. She's never hit me but she often looks as if she will.

"No, no, just for a little while. He'll be back with us soon as we settle in."

The king's fencing lessons. His music lessons. His several languages, deportment classes, geography....

Bill got discovered. By that man in the house. All because of a stray dog. How could he? One more mouth to feed. One more thing to keep secret besides himself. Only he didn't. I suppose he wanted...needed...company. He's never been alone before. But it sounds like it came out all right. At least so far.

Bill and I weren't going to meet until four o'clock. I got myself a job right away. Five to seven three week days and helping out on Saturdays and Sundays if I want to. An after school kind of job. They said I had to be sixteen and I said I was and got away with it even though I don't have breasts. It's in the arts and crafts gallery, doing everything: cleaning, keeping records, hanging pictures for when the shows change, putting up posters, running for coffee....

I went first to the place where I'd like to work best of all and I got the job. (Second was going to be the library.) They're going to let me sit in on their evening classes for nothing. They have everything, from knitting, to TaiChi, to painting. I wonder if they'd let Mother teach French there. I wonder if she would. Except I'm not sure I want anybody here to get to know Mother.

So then I pretend I have to go off to school. I wander around town, kind of looking for a job for Mother and trying to watch out for where she is.

At four I go meet Bill (he already went back and got the dog so I could meet him) and he tells me about getting discovered. He actually sounds happy about it. I guess I don't because he says, "Hey, don't you get all crazy, too. If you want to meet him and talk to him, his office is upstairs over the barbershop. He made me a big breakfast. He fed my dog, too. Matt...Mathew. Not the dog. I named the dog Spider."

It's a funny little dog. Kind of looks like his name. Skinny, mostly white — dirty white — with black and brown spots. Bill is dirtier than ever, too. I suppose from sleeping with the dog. I should have brought him the T-shirt Mother washed.

"Did you go to school looking like this? What did you do with the dog?"

"The man...Matt...said it was OK to leave him in the house. Matt has a big jar of water and left some for the dog. I guess I should have washed but I didn't want to ask Matt for some more. He doesn't have much. I told him we were hiking with our father."

Father again.

Suddenly I start to cry. For no reason. Everything is working out fine. I don't ever let Bill see me crying. I think somebody in his life should at least *seem* competent. It scares him. He turns away and starts to pet the dog, but the dog comes over to me and licks my arm. I guess it is kind of nice to have a dog.

I say, "Sorry, I must be tired."

"K."

I was afraid, one of these days I'd start to cry and never stop, but I do. It only takes a few minutes.

"What's Matt's last name."

"I forget. It's hard."

"I'll bring you some clean clothes. Don't come down to the pond to wash. Mother might be there. Wash at school next time. Did you eat?"

He says, yes, but I give him some of Mother's cheese and ham anyway.

He says, "Tomorrow we could meet earlier, maybe back on the trail behind the house."

"Aren't you going to school?"

"You silly, it's Saturday."

I forgot there would be Saturday and Sunday. I forgot it even though I have a Saturday and Sunday job.

"Tell you what, meet me where I work, but try to get cleaned up first. They might even let you do some work too."

Then I go to find the man. If he was nice to Bill he may really be a good person, but I want to check.

Upstairs over the barbershop, it's full of offices. Like at the school, you can look in the little windows in the doors and see who's there.

There's only one man that looks like the right one: Thin, dark suit, glasses, long nose.... It says KARPINSKY on the door. He's younger than I thought he'd be. Even though he's balding.

I watch him at his computer for a couple of minutes but then he looks up and sees me staring at him. He looks right into my eyes. Right inside me. Suddenly I don't know what to do. I wouldn't know what to say. I run down the stairs and then all the way down the block. Two blocks. I wasn't ready. Besides, I don't want to lie about our father being with us. I wish Bill wouldn't keep saying that.

Crown the king a lover of honey and of bees.
He owns all the swans.

His trees will bear golden pears and silver nutmegs.

When I come back, Mother has built a campfire behind the shed and...My God...she's cooking a duck. Right out in the open. The head and the feathers are in a pile just inside the shed door.

"Mother! This has got to be against the law."

"Pooh. This is for Guillaum."

It smells so good I hope she gets away with it.

"He's not even here."

"Well then, you'll take some to him."

"Mother!"

I squat down beside her. "Did you at least look for a job? The grocery store would be a good place to work. You could get food for less or maybe nothing."

"I don't do that kind of work."

There's no use talking, it would just be the same conversation over again.

We have a good supper. She also roasted potatoes in the coals.

She wraps up the leftovers in a plastic bag and hangs them over the edge of the pond to keep cool.

A king should walk as if he balanced books on his head and the books he balances should be law books.

Saturday, just as I figured, Bill and I both get to work at the Gallery. They even don't mind having the dog there. One good thing though, they sent Bill to the back alley and had him give the dog a bath. And Matt Karpinsky has given Bill another nice breakfast. Bill says, "Pancakes. Because it's Saturday. Matt asked a lot of questions about you."

"What did you tell him?"

"That you're really a princess and really a dummy. That you forgot there was such a thing as Saturday."

I give him a fake punch. Actually a little harder than I meant it, and he gives me one back just like it.

"Did he say why he's camping out in that house?"

"Same as me. To have a nice place to be."

"I hope you didn't tell him a long story about your father."

He shrugs. Should a prince shrug so much?

He has homework. He says he's even doing stuff for extra credit. How nice to see him sitting in the back office of the gallery doing his school work, his leg twisted around the chair leg, and with the dog at his feet. I bring him a glass of cider and he smiles up at me. I think, what long eyelashes, and how like a prince he looks, even with that bad haircut, even with his torn and too small jeans. Maybe things really will work out.

Among the several languages a king must know, there should be Greek and Latin. He should also be trained in dialectic, Aristotelian logic, and aesthetics.

...and they do. For a while.

And even though Mother keeps killing ducks. Each time she does, she invites Bill for dinner. I say he won't come, but she says ask him anyway.

"Will you call him Bill?"

But she won't. She never will.

I don't know what Mother is doing during the day. I know she's seldom at the shed. I keep imagining ridiculous things, like that she's busy making handcuffs and chains for Bill.

Actually, I don't think anybody will give Mother a job looking like this. Lately she's messier than ever. Not having Bill around upsets her. If she tried to comb her hair I'll bet the comb would get stuck, or even lost forever. I'd cut it for her, but I don't dare suggest it. I wonder if she's doing it on purpose so as not to get hired.

There's a second hand store here and I get Bill a pair of jeans for fifty cents. Unlike what you'd think about other boys, he doesn't mind that they're much too big. I get him a red T-shirt with black ants as if crawling all over the front. It's hardly worn at all. I knew he'd like it.

Since we're not heading south, we'll need some blankets pretty soon. Our sleeping bags won't be enough. It sometimes gets pretty cold in these hills.

I'm still not going to school. I'm worried that if I try to go, it might make it so Bill would get kicked out. It's one thing for a ten year old to suddenly appear in school and different for somebody my age. Besides, that teacher is doing something not every teacher would. I'm sure she's breaking rules. I don't want to get her in trouble, too.

These days I sleep late, wander around, gather firewood for Mother, gather bugs for Bill, study at the library, then go to work at five and take classes at the gallery in the evening. I get the cheese and crackers, and wine and cider for the openings of the art shows and programs. I eat a lot of that myself. I'm having fun...sort of...but I wish I was going to school.

Bill is the only one getting everything he wants. He meets me at the gallery, does a little work and then does his homework. He's also found the bug books in the library. Matt makes him breakfast every morning and he gets lunch at school. I'm sure that lunch is because of that teacher.

The offices over the barber shop are practically across the street from the Gallery. I see Matt lots of times. When I do, I go around the corner fast or hurry into a shop. I don't know what Bill has been telling him — especially about having a father. I wouldn't know what to say. Besides, there's that time he looked right inside me.

And it's as if I want somebody to take care of us (instead of me) and I've picked him to be the one. He's a little young for that. Looks to be, even though his forehead is almost all the way up to the top of his head, hardly even thirty.

But one evening he comes to the gallery when I'm doing the photography class...without a camera of course. (I'll take any class that's handy.)

He insists on taking me out to the back yard of the gallery for a talk.

First thing he says, "You're avoiding me aren't you."

I'm completely tongue-tied. How can I say anything when I've no idea what Bill has been saying? Except that it's all lies.

"Where's this father of yours? Really? Why isn't he looking after you?"

I'm staring right into the eyes of the man I want to turn everything over to — our whole lives, and I don't even know him. My heart is beating so hard I wonder if I'm going to faint. I feel myself blushing because of my crazy thoughts.

And here he is, showing concern. That scares me even more. I have to sit down.

But he sees that. He takes my arm and pulls me down to the big stones that are supposed to keep cars from coming through the alleyway behind the gallery. He makes me sit on one.

"Should I get you some water?"

"We don't have a father."

But we hear fire engines and police cars rushing past just beyond the alley — heading towards the school. We stare up at each other. I say, "It's Mother,"

Then I say, "Or it's Bill."

He grabs my hand and we follow the sirens.

The king is always the center of attention, therefore he should never blow his nose or scratch his ear in public.

It *is* Bill — and Mother, too. I had a feeling she couldn't put up with settling down, and who would give such a person a job anyway? And then there were all these days she had to try and get along without Bill.

There's a three story building across the street from the school and there's my brother, walking up to the peak of the slanted roof, fearless as he always is. Is that like a prince or more like a roofer? On the sidewalk below him, Mother is yelling, but it's hard to make out what the words are. Her knapsack is lying beyond her, all packed up and ready to go. (Mine isn't there this time.) It looks like she came to the school to pick him up and leave without me. Half the students are outside watching, and the other half are watching out the classroom windows. Firemen are setting up their ladder to go and get Bill. Cops are milling around and keeping the kids out of the way but mostly joking. Everybody seems to be having a good time except Mother.

She looks crazier than ever. Her clothes look slept in, but that's no surprise. Except she used to try to look neat. Not lately, though. Bill's dog is barking and snarling up at her until she kicks him away. He squeals and trots over to Matt and me. Two cops are trying to keep Mother from climbing up the side of the building, which she can't do, anyway. They're yelling, too. "Calm down. Calm down."

She does — sort of. Enough so you can understand what she's saying. "My son. Guillaum. I want him back. He's not like other children. He has to be with me."

Usually she doesn't get into one of her talking jags in front of strangers, but now she does.

"He's special. He's different. This school is just an ordinary school. *Ordinary*! For *ordinary* people." She looks straight at one of the cops. "Like you," she says.

The cops are good at this. They know better than to contradict her. "OK. OK. We know. We'll get him back."

She seems a little calmer so they let her go of her, but she lunges at them and scratches their faces, and then tries to climb up the brick wall of the house again.

Finally they bring Bill down. He keeps saying, "I won't not go to school."

"It's the law, son. You'll get to go."

I guess it's a good thing Mother won't stop fighting the cops. That makes it so they haul her off before she can cause anymore problems. She yells the whole time and uses bad language, too. She's never done that before that I know of. She's always into keeping her dignity in front of other people no matter what — that "nobless oblige" she always talks about. It's always: "Gens commes nous.... We" (emphasis on the We) "... *We* don't say things like that."

Bill looks even more horrified than I feel.

Is this all my fault? Should I have done something?

They put her in a police car and off she goes, talking, talking, talking — not even a backward glance at Bill.

If Mother gets put away somewhere, I guess we'll, more or less, be orphans. How will that be?

Then I and Bill and Matt and the dog — we all go down to the police station. Even Bill's teacher comes with us. She saw the whole thing.

Turns out Mother went to the school yelling — *screaming*, that is — down the school halls. Bill heard her coming all the way from the front door. She punched anybody that tried to stop her, she dragged Bill out of class, but once they were outside, he got away and climbed straight up the side of that building. I'm proud of him. I can't help it.

Though he may be shorter, the king must seem taller than all other men.

Turns out Mother's going to be locked up next town over. It's bigger and has a place for people like her. She's already on her way there.

Good this is a small town. People look out for each other. Matt's to be our temporary guardian even though he's only twenty eight. The Senior Center people contributed money so Matt won't have to. Bill's teacher's in it, too, and the people at the gallery. It's as if the whole town is our friend.

Turns out Matt actually owns that house — as of four months ago. His fiancée left him so he never bothered to really move in. He was feeling bad until Bill came. We're going to stay with him.

He's had the water and electricity turned on. So far he's bought a lawn mower for Bill (Bill can't wait to be just a regular boy and have to mow the lawn and take out the garbage), and seeds and a trowel for me.

Where they put Mother is her castle — finally. The asylum is in an old Victorian mansion with a tower, a lot of black ironwork all over it. Even the fence is beautiful filigree. Looks more like decoration than to keep people in. They say she calmed down the minute she went through the gates. She likes it there: "Her" beautiful garden; "her" servants; from her third floor bedroom, "her" beautiful view of the mountains....

Turns out Mother had been spending all her time in the woods working on a ring, not looking for a job. She was making it out of a silver coin. She stole the stone for it from the Indian store in the museum. A shiny piece of worthless fool's gold. They were selling chunks for a quarter. She never steals valuable things, though she might have since it was for Bill. She shows it to me when I visit her.

She often said, "If I just had something...just one thing that Guillaum could wear to show who he is."

I say, "But, Mother, he won't wear a ring. Besides, fool's gold just makes it all a joke."

"He'll wear it when he gets older."

And she's right, he will.

Where he gathers roses, lesser men will gather lesser roses after he's gone.
Nightingales will sing for the king alone.
All the roe deer belong to the king.
The most exquisit hours of the morning are when the king awakes.

Firebirds Soaring: An Anthology of Original Speculative Fiction, 2009

Logicist

I took the children out to see the battle. I thought they should see history as it was happening. My class of eight to ten year olds watched from a hill on the sidelines. We normally played our ball games right where they were fighting.

Except for the blood and the noise, it looked like a game. At first the children thought it was. I told them the blood was real, but they didn't think so. Then, when they finally believed me, I didn't let them shut their eyes or cover their ears. I told them, "Ten points off if you do either." I said, "Reality is not a game." My theory is: You're never too young to understand the real world.

I was hoping our side would win and the children would feel proud, but I knew it would be just as good a lesson if we lost.

Except I had underrated the enemy. I don't know how many children are left and, if any are, I don't know where they ran to. Now I'm wondering if there can be too much reality, especially if it comes straight at you.

The enemy had a new trick our side didn't expect. At a trumpet call they all turned and fought the man on their left instead of the man they had been fighting. They brought their swords up under the other's shields and killed everybody on our side. Just after I said, "It behooves us to remain calm," the enemy started coming after us. We called out that we were just watching, that we had no weapons, but they didn't care. Perhaps they were yelling so loud they didn't hear us. We ran, helter skelter. I fell into a drainage ditch first thing and several of the enemy, heavy with armor, ran right over me. One actually stepped on my head so that my beard and face were pushed into the mud.

Then they scattered every which way and went and killed the dogs and cats and cows and goats and pigs.... Everything alive they could find.

Those children that are left...if any are... have learned four valuable lessons— as have I: A: When watching a battle stay hidden. B: Trying to explain that you're just watching is a waste of time. C: At the first sign of defeat, run. D:

One should also run even if one's own side is winning, since, when the killing starts, it can't be stopped.

E: Remember that a soldier has only one reason for being…only one duty. What else is a soldier for?

After all the yelling, there was, finally, silence, no barking, no baas, no hee-hawing. The birds stopped singing. Even the bugs stopped buzzing.

I spit out the mouthful of mud and looked around for any children who had survived, but if they had, they'd run off. It was too painful to keep looking. I saw one child…a good and gifted boy I had only had to flog once….All my careful teaching gone for naught. It was too much for me. I have a bad knee, but even so I ran as I'd never run before. On and on.

Finally I heard bugs again, a donkey brayed, and then I heard barking. There were birds. But I kept on. I was wondering how far I'd have to go where there wouldn't be anymore reality. I ran until I fell exhausted and couldn't get up.

When I had the energy to lift my head, I saw I lay beside a pond and in the pond there were ducks…a mother and a dozen ducklings. I thought: Yes, ducks. Yes, yes, ducks. *Ducks*!

I had stumbled into a land where ducklings and children might actually survive.

So A: Should I stay? What would be the moral thing to do? When I became a teacher I swore an oath to behave as I was teaching others to behave. The little ones pick things up so fast.

Or, B: should I run back to see if I can help? Even help a dog or cat? Some creature in pain? Perhaps there's something back there as thirsty as I am.

But, C: Can I find my way back? And when will I have the energy to do so?

I hear somebody actually singing. This can't be real what with the ducks and cicadas and now songs.

It's a woman's voice.

I raise my head again and see a green dress and somebody hanging out laundry. The song is in the enemy's language. I know a few of the words. There are flowers and rivers in it. To think that the enemy would sing of flowers.

Have I strayed into enemy territory? At least I'm dressed as a school teacher. I have a school teacher's beard and a school teacher's uniform. Though now that I'm so covered with mud would anyone recognize what I am?

The voice is pure and sweet. She ornaments the notes with little trills and rills.

A: The enemy can sing.

There is no B.

I lie back, and fall in love.

And then I see the actual woman. Face ruddy with hard work and sun. Looks to be in her forties. I would guess older than I and certainly of a different class. I wonder how much education she can have had.

Even so I'm still in love.

She doesn't see me. Perhaps I'm still back in my own reality while she is on the other side, in this world of laundry and songs.

I try to sit up. That's then I feel pain in my side. When several of the enemy ran over me, it feels as if they may have broken my ribs.

I can't help crying out in pain. She sees me. Gives a little, "Oh," in the middle of her song, drops a child sized tunic, and turns as if to run away, but then turns back and stares.

I say I'm sorry I've scared her. She answers something in her language.

I ask for water. All I know is their word for river, but she understands.

There's a pump not far from her laundry lines. She gets the tin cup hanging there and brings me some and then another cupful after I finish that one.

It's the best water I ever tasted. Proof yet again that this can't be reality.

I want to tell her that I'm a teacher and that I must get back to my class. I try to ask all this with simple words and gestures, but I can't make her understand.

I want to ask, A: Is there a doorway back into my world? B: Is there no war here? C: And if not why not? And if no war I surely don't belong in such a place. Why should I stay in a kind of heaven when what remains of my class is back in a dangerous world? And D: Besides, what could children…or anyone… learn here? One never learns when things go well.

E: Though perhaps only I am left. In that case I could stay here and still be a moral person. But one must not be seduced by this place.

I imagine everything here is as icy and sparkly as that water. I imagine the food as tasting of the earth. There, above her laundry is the half moon. The green of her dress is the color of pine trees.

I say again, "I must get to war. Which way? The war?"

Even with gestures she doesn't understand.

Instead she helps me up and to her house. A solid stone house, looks to be more fortress than house. Or prison. I won't go in. I collapse on one of the chairs she has near her front door.

I see why the chairs are here. One can get a good view of the hills and the forest beyond. At first I think it's a good place to watch and analyze a battle. And then I think, no, a good place to watch sunsets.

There are two chairs. I presumed she had a husband to sit and watch with her, but out comes an even older woman. This woman is obviously scared of me. Easy to tell by her gestures and her voice.

I used to depend on my bearing, my finely molded features, my well trimmed beard, the neatness of my uniform… but now, stooping in pain and covered with mud, I know I can't count on those.

I get up and start hobbling away as best I can. I hold my side with both hands.

"Fall, fall, defall," the first woman says, and pulls me back into the chair.

The older woman is still gesturing and talking. She obviously wants to get rid of me but the younger one seems to be arguing for me to stay. The older woman drags the other chair to the opposite side of the door so as to be farther away from me, plumps herself down in it, and frowns out at the view.

In the distance, behind the fields and the forest, there are cliffs. Did I run through all that to get here? Did I cross those cliffs? Could I have climbed down...through even A, B, and also C and not remembered?

The younger woman goes inside and brings out tea. She sits on the ground in front of us as if it were the most natural thing for a grown woman to do.

(I wish she'd sing again but I don't know how to ask.)

One forgets how life might be led. How there can be moments of silence and serenity.

The tea is strong—as if it's been sitting at the back of the stove all day—but it's exactly what I need. I feel my mind clearing and my strength coming back.

I become more aware of how filthy I am and I'm suddenly embarrassed. Perhaps one can't even see that I'm a teacher.

Then the older woman says a shocking swear word in my own language. Then, again in my language, "I will kill you first chance I get."

I stand up again. I try to bow but it hurts too much. "Madam, I know I don't belong here. Show me which way, and I'll go back to the war."

She points to those cliffs in the distance. Says. "Go."

It makes sense that the cliffs are the demarcation between the world full of wars and this world of gentleness.

I start staggering towards them. Again the other woman grabs me and pulls me back, but in a way that hurts my ribs. I yell. She jabbers away at the old woman, scolding.

The pain takes my breath away. I have to sit and recover.

The old woman says, "I was once taken by the enemy," meaning my people. "I know your kind."

"I'm a teacher. I always try to teach what's moral and real."

But there's always the antithesis. What is moral for one may not be moral for the other. I have also taught that.

But there are lessons to be learned here. One should listen. For many reasons, not least of which is that, as is often said, if the teacher isn't also a student then no one learns.

I say, "I will listen. I'm never loath to learn."

She says, "I learned your language as a slave. That's all there is to say."

I can tell she won't say anything more, but it's a completely understandable syllogism: All slaves.... She, a slave, therefore....

I don't want to see her naked back, though it might be a good lesson.

This, I'm afraid is also a land of reality. Or, on the other hand, is this where you finally get to go to avoid it?

But here comes a child just the age of those in my class. He wears armor and holds a sword. Do even the children take part in the battles? Perhaps this isn't as ideal a spot as I think. He must know a great deal more than my class did.

The old woman says, "You killed his father."

"Not I."

He's heard the older woman talking in my language. He tries out his few words. "How are you? I am fine. Where is the book? Good morning."

(The child has been well taught. He says his Rs as we do.)

I think to answer in kind with, How do you do? but before I can he attacks me with his sword, which I now see is wooden and his armor is paper painted silver. My class has often dressed the same.

I don't defend myself. He stabs and slashes at me. Even though the sword is blunt, it does do some damage. This is my lesson: To sit and absorb it.

I let him go on until he's tired.

The tea has spilled all over me though what with the mud, it hardly matters.

I see I've impressed the old woman with my forbearance. She looks as if she's even ready to pull the chair back to my side of the doorway. She says, "Thank you."

The other woman says something to the child that sends him off inside. Then she insists that I take off my tunic.

Easier said than done since I have to pull it up over my head. When she sees how it hurts me, she gets scissors and cuts it down the front before I realize what she's doing.

Not only is my uniform as a teacher important to me (It is, in its own way, soldierly with its gold fringed teaching epaulettes—and I do think of myself as soldiering on in the realms of learning. Fearlessly, I may say), but also I'm not used to being even only half naked in front of anybody and especially not a woman. I'm thin and not well muscled. I sit all day. When not preparing for my teaching I'm studying. I always try to enrich myself so as to become a more enriching teacher. I have won several firsts, the ribbons for which have been sewn onto my tunic over my heart. I can't be without that tunic. I hesitated too long worrying about my nakedness. She's snatched it away and taken it inside.

I get up and follow…into that strange fortress of a house. First there's an empty hall of yellowish stucco. With one tiny useless window. I find it ugly but I know tastes differ.

I hurry though one of the doors in the far wall, hoping to find a warmer spot…or my tunic.

I find the child.

He sits at a low table just his size and works on some writing or drawing.

He says, carefully, slowly (and as if he's completely forgotten he had attacked me), "Hello. My name is Eppi. What is your name?"

I begin to realize how sick I am. I sit down on the floor. I can't help it even though I know I especially shouldn't do it in front of a student.

Or a woman, and I know she'll find me there. But I can't get up. I give up. I've sullied my uniform and my occupation. I'll give back my firsts.

The child has a cup of something. He brings it to me and holds it to my lips. I have no idea what it is but I drink it and thank him. I say, "You're a worthy young man."

"What is worthy?"

"You are good and kind."

He gives me such a smile. I see my words have made him, yet another notch, good and kind.

He brings me his drawing to admire. A battle drawing. I'm not in the mood even to look at it, but I admire.

Then I begin to shake. I moan and lie back. All dignity, all decorum lost.

The child calls, "Maaaaa."

I'm thinking: Is this the one universal word?

Then: Must find out if true.

Then I'm thinking: firstly, secondly, and: A, B, and C, also D, and many others....

Next I know I hear singing. I'm warm and clean. And yet again—or still—in love. I would stay forever where this singing goes on and on.

Would I? Even if one's duty lies elsewhere?

There she is. Moving about the kitchen with poise and grace as if a lady, and I'm in a corner on a sleeping shelf. She doesn't even need to stop and think as she does the rills and trills.

I have never thought to marry and certainly never with a woman who cooks and does laundry, and not only that, is one of the enemy. Also with whom I can't converse. I've always though it unlikely that I would find someone suitable. There are few women who are my equal so I had decided never to marry. I would have wanted someone *almost* as knowledgeable as I am.

But I've changed my mind since being here. I hadn't realized how important music is. And a voice so sweet and so clever at ornamentation. There's knowledge of a kind in that.

Isn't there?

But then, of my own love, I think, barbaric! And, How can I stoop so low? Perhaps I'm no longer fit to teach.

And yet I've crossed a line into a pleasant unreal land. Perhaps there's not even any need for my kind of teacher here.

Then broth and teas and a gentle hand, the boy and his drawings (all of battles and none of flowers.) And even the grandmother. She's now on my side. And best of all, singing every day. I take up Eppi's miniature oud—actually no more than a toy, but I learn to strum a few chords. I can make the younger woman, Lala (can it be that she's named for her singing?)...I can make her sing whenever I want her to, just by strumming.

Lala has washed and repaired my tunic. It doesn't look quite as nice as before, but at least I'll look like a teacher.

But I'm going against everything I teach. I lie. I pretend. I say I'm sicker than I am. I groan when I have no pain. I have her arms around me helping me whenever I want them. I have tidbits to tempt my appetite.

I'm coming close to doing what I've never done before. There never seemed to be time for it or a good opportunity. We've kissed. I've touched her breasts. I'm thinking, A: one more suitable word, or, B: One more suitable gesture.... Conclusion: She'll be in bed with me within a few days.

I'm up and around well before they realize it. I snoop. I want to find out about their way of life. I'm not thinking about finding secrets, I just want to know them… her, Lala, that is.

Does the enemy have marriage as we know it? Does she have keepsakes of her former man? I need to know. I think I'll ask her soon to marry me.

But, in Grandma's room, I find a dagger and a map.

I can't read the writing on it, but I know it's important. There are arrows and dates. I can see where their secret redoubts are.

I change into my teacher's tunic. I take the dagger…. (Grandma has had plenty of chances to kill me should she have desired.) I take the map. This time we won't be fooled by a trumpet call. I alone am left to warn my side of that treachery.

All those songs have made me forget my duties.

I climb the cliff and cross back over into the real world, with map, Grandma's dagger, and Eppi's wrapped up lunch.

At the top here's the line. I can feel it in the very air: war on one side, serenity on the other. A hot breeze. A smell of iron. The trees here, half dead. The streams, few. Below, the streams are many. From up here, they're shining in the sun as if rivers of silver.

But there are children up here. Even if only a few, isn't my duty to them? Not to Eppi?

I take big breaths of the metallic air. My kind of air. It's just as well. I've managed to avoid a love both, A: uncivilized and, B: unrefined. I've adhered to my principles and overcome my errors in judgment.

I have taught my students discipline and most particularly self discipline. I'll be a better teacher now than I've ever been before. I will teach them what I have learned about reality. A: That we will live with wars, and, B: That there will always be wars.

The Magazine of Fantasy & Science Fiction**,** October-November 2009

Wilds

The first night in the wild I find a cave in among a pile of fallen rocks. It's so small I have to crawl in backwards so as to be facing the right direction in order to get out. It was fine for that one night. I actually sleep a bit. But it's in a low place. If it had rained I'd have gotten wet. Something small had lived there and hadn't been careful not to foul its nest. I don't smell that good now myself though I don't expect I'll meet anybody.

But I want a higher place—for lots of reasons. I'd like a view of the valley below. I start climbing. Several times I see berries. At first I don't dare eat any. Then if try them. If they taste good, I keep eating.

I have to climb, up and down and up and down, all day and most of the next to find a place I like. When I find it I don't have time to look for shelter. I sleep where I fall. At least I'm high up and a hard climb away from everybody and everything.

In the morning, not far from where I lie, I find an overhanging rock for shelter. I start making a wall around it. Then I go back down to the tree line to I find more berries and nibble on greens. I catch a fish by hand and eat it raw. I climb back to my mountain to sleep. There's not much up there but boulders and on every side but one there's riprap. Hard for anyone to climb up to me, on one side the scary cliff, on the other those unstable shoebox size rocks.

The next day I start on a tower. I already have a pretty good view if I stand on my sheltering rock, but I want an even better one. The view is spectacular. Far below there's a red cinder cone, lower, a marshy green lake, across the valley, more mountains where there's always odd cloud formations.

I'm not ever going to finish my tower. I want to go on and on with it for the pure pleasure of moving stones. Already in just these few days, I'm stronger than I ever was. My arms hardly look like my arms. I have a start on a beard.

When my tower is about five feet above my sheltering rock, I stop, go lower down to a marshy pond and gather a reed and make a flute. It only has four holes, but that's enough notes for me.

Every morning I climb my tower and study the hills and valleys. Then I start my day: Moving rocks, playing the flute, and then I go down below the tree line to eat and drink.

But one morning, I see somebody climbing up towards me. I hope he's just testing himself, climbing as high as he can, getting cold and worn out, teetering on the riprap, and then going right back down. I already tested myself in those ways. I understand the need.

I look around to make sure nothing of my living here shows. My tower could be a natural formation. I deliberately made it to look that way. I'm not worried it might be discovered.

Then, as the person nears, I hide.

I've always hidden. First from Mother and Dad and from my three older brothers. Hiding was my way of life from the beginning.

I ducked and slunk along. I hunched over. I never looked people in the eye. I grew large, but I wanted to be small. Though I finally grew even larger than my big brothers, I never dared to challenge them.

And then...suddenly...*suddenly*... I found the wilds. First I stepped slowly, wondering at it, marveling, and then I ran. Straight into it vowing never to leave. I shouted, I jumped from rock to rock, hid from tree to tree, walked the, then, empty trails. I began to sing. (I never had before.) I kept time by tapping a stick against my knee.

I couldn't bear to leave— even to go back for supplies. I don't have a pan or a flashlight or a knife. I left the car by the side of the road. A rented car. I had said to myself, I'll just take a little walk. I saw rocks with bright orange lichen and trees, all leaning to the left, and a cliff with a stony path zigzagging up it. I wondered what it would be like to be in among all that.

Now I take only what the wilds gives me. It feeds me and teaches me. I trained myself to eat what it gives, insects and snakes. Tiny eggs. When you want to live here, you have to learn new ways.

The first I ever ate insects was because my brothers forced me to. Raw goldfish, too. I was afraid I'd get sick so I researched what might be poison. Now I live on bugs and raw fish and worse things than they could even think of. Mouse or rat like creatures. Slugs.

I have to go down my mountain to get those bugs and snakes. Also berries and roots. Down there is where I set my traps.

But even as I swallow little snakes, I'm singing.

But here's this person climbing my mountain. I can't imagine someone being here except to test themselves as I used to do.

I have plenty of stones for weapons. Except I've never fought in my life.

He stumbles up the last riprap, and does just as I did when I first got here, collapses on the rocks. That can't be comfortable. He's so worn out he wouldn't have noticed me if I'd been standing right in front of him.

I dare to come closer. I hold a rock. I peer down at.... Him? Her? What's she doing way out here all by herself?

I put down the rock. Being rid of her would be the safest for keeping my place and me a secret— bang her head with a rock and toss her off the steep side. It would look like a bad fall.

She's small and thin. There's a blondish ponytail coming out from under her red cap, there's red nail polish on her dirty broken nails, she's wearing the wrong shoes for climbing. Besides her canvas pack, she has a small red purse sideways across her shoulder.

Her pack looks stuffed. Usually people have pans and canteens and a lot of dried food. I'm hoping for things like that. I quietly, carefully, unbuckle the pack. Odd, It's not an ordinary backpack, but more like a mailman's bag.

Out comes money. A lot. Packages of hundred dollar bills.

I'm not being careful anymore. I'm looking for something I can use...anything at all. I shout with frustration and scrabble in the bag. The money is in packets. Some come apart. It's always windy up here. Some blow away in packets and some blow away as single bills.

She hears me yell. Jumps up and grabs at the bills. Gets a couple. Then turns and tries to close the pack on what's left.

There's not one thing in there that's of any use to me. I'd even settle for toilet paper.

It's good I don't have the rock anymore. What I do is slap her. So hard that she's flat out on the rocks.

When have I ever slapped anybody? At once I say I'm sorry but I'm really not. She doesn't let me help her up and I don't blame her. Who knows what I'm going to do next.

"Is this all you brought?"

"It was almost fifty thousand."

"No food?"

She starts counting up the money that's still left in the sack. She shields it from the wind with her body and tries to keep everything deep inside the bag as she counts. Says, "Oh no, oh no," over and over.

"No food?"

"Oh no. Only a couple of thousand left."

She rests her head on the money bag and takes deep breaths. If she had the energy she'd be crying. Or maybe attacking me. Then says, "Can I have a drink of water?"

"You'll have to go back down for it."

"I'm so worn out. Could you get me some?"

"I don't have anything to carry water in. I have to go down to drink, too. I was hoping you'd have a canteen or at least a cup."

She lies back, hugging the money pack.

We're silent.

She looks too delicate to be out here. I do like her looks. And that makes me think how I'm a hulk. I'm nice and thin now, but still a lumpy man. I'm suddenly conscious, as I used to be when out with people, of my big hands and feet, my hairy arms, my bony face. I've been called a big dumb lug and not just by my brothers.

"Is that cap waterproof? I could get you a little bit in that."

"I don't think so."

We're silent again.

Then she asks, "Do you have any food?"

"Nothing to carry that in either. I suppose I could bring something up for you." I don't say, Maybe a little snake you can choke down whole. Maybe a pocketful of bugs.

I do want to shock her though. I want her to realize money isn't worth much out here. Maybe good for tinder. I haven't been building fires, though if I catch a fish, I suppose she'll want it cooked.

"When you're feeling rested I'll help you down. Maybe catch you a fish. I don't suppose you have any matches."

"No." So faint I can hardly hear it.

We're quiet again. Then she says, "I haven't had anything to eat for two days. I'll give you a hundred dollars if you get me something."

I laugh.

"Two hundred? Three?"

"I'd do it for a knife or a pan."

But I take pity on her. "Soon as you're rested, we'll go down."

First she takes pains to hide the money. There's only one good place: my overhang. She puts it way in the back and covers it with sand and scree. She doesn't notice my flute. It doesn't look like much more than a dry stick.

It's a hard climb down, but just the first part. As I'm helping her, we see a couple of hundred dollar bills stuck to the cliff out of the wind. She wants me to them, but it's too steep. I'm not going to kill myself for money.

Helping her, I'm conscious, not only of how unkempt I am. I don't have a comb. I can't imagine what my hair looks like. And my beard. I only have these clothes. I know I must smell though I do wash them now and then. When I do, I tramp around the forest wearing nothing but my shoes, though I am working on hardening up my feet. Then I'll really feel part of the wilds. You can sense a lot through your feet.

I notice her hand next to mine. Her long, slim fingers.... No hands could be more different.

Along the steepest ledge, I hold her by the back of her pants. Her hips, her slim waist, her warmth.... I haven't been near another person for a long time.

We finally get down into the trees. I take her to my usual spot, beside my stream where it forms a still pool. First she drinks. Then I show her how I catch a fish, bare hands, close to the bank where there's an overhang. I see admiration in her eyes.

I know I'll have to make a fire or she won't eat it. I suppose that old way must work— tinder and a stick on a punkish piece of wood. I wonder how long it takes.

Before I even have the punk and dead grasses all gathered into a pile, she says, "You're a real man of the forest."

I lick my finger and put it down on a big black ant, scoop it up and blatantly eat it.

She flinches. Says, "I guess you are."

Then I confess I've never tried to build a fire until now. "We'll see if I really am," I say. Though, actually, aren't I more a man of the forest if I don't cook my food?

But it does work.

She eats as if she hadn't eaten for days and of course she hasn't. Though it smells good, I let her have it all. Does she even notice that? I make do with skink and one small garter snake. This time I eat them out of her sight and after she's lying back, satisfied.

She says, "I feel much better, but I don't think I can climb back up there tonight. Will you stay with me?" She looks worried—she'd rather not be alone down here. "Though I suppose you're up there because it's safer."

"Less buggy, too."

But I say I'll stay.

She picks a place close to where the fire was. I pick one a discrete distance away. I help her make a bed of ferns. A few minutes after we lie down she says, "Do you think you can help me get some of the money back? You owe it to me. It's your fault it blew away."

I don't want to think about the money. I just grunt.

She's frightened in the middle of the night. I hear her move from the far side of the fire, closer to me.

Down here, not only more bugs, but more noise. Owls hooting or shrieking.

She moves even closer, whispers, "What is that screaming?"

"Just baby shriek owls calling to be fed."

Then she gives a little shriek. "Something ran right over me."

"That's how it is down here."

In the morning, right away, she wants to go back up to look for more of the money. Her eyes have dark circles. She's in a bad mood. "We have to," she says. "And it's all your fault the money blew away."

I say, "I'm eating and drinking first."

She says, "*I'm not*," and takes off.

It isn't as if I could offer her a hot cup of tea before she goes.

I catch a fish and this time cook it for myself. There are still hot coals in the fire ring so it's easy to start it again. I haven't had cooked trout since I got here. It's delicious but I feel ungrateful and disloyal for all the wild has done for me.

I catch up with her when she's almost to the cliff. She's been climbing slowly, looking for money along the way. Her face is dirty and tear streaked. I'll bet she's thirsty now.

She says, "I found a packet of hundreds, and a couple of single bills, but that's all."

I say I'll help.

"You owe me thirty or forty thousand dollars."

I can't help but laugh again. "Good luck," I say. "But I will help."

She stops to rest and I go off looking for more money. I find three more packs. Not without taking risks. I keep wondering, is a pack of hundred dollar bills worth a bad fall?

I come back for her to help her up the last steep cliff. At the top, she gets her pack, puts in what we found, and starts counting, while I climb down the other side to see what I can find over there. The loose bills are as if alive, waiting till I'm almost up to them and then blowing away, but I do get some.

It's late and I'm hungry. She must be even more so, what with rushing off with no breakfast,.

She keeps saying, "This won't do," and, "It was hardly worth it."

I'm still angry that she brought nothing but money, but I'm trying to be nice. "Come on, we'll go down and eat."

I didn't want to yearn for anything of that old life but now I do in spite of myself. Mostly for the foods. Is the rental car still on that side road waiting? But then I'm thinking: If I could bring down a deer.... Then use the skin for a carrying case. But I wanted the freedom of *not* doing all those things. I wanted to be naked. I wanted to be an animal.

"Can we stay down there again tonight?"

She's meek now. I suppose she's beginning to realize where she's landed. And it sounds as if she looks up to me, but that's because I'm the only person she can rely on for help. Or is it because I'm risking my neck climbing around looking for the money?

"We'll stay down there all day tomorrow. We'll make a basket and bring up fish, and maybe find a way to carry water." I don't dare say, Lets use your money bag for carrying fish.

What am I doing? I don't even know her name and I'm not sure I want to.

Even though I've been out here hardly a month... (I'm guessing. I haven't kept track. And, actually, I want to be done with time.) ...I've gotten used to being alone. I was happy with my view and my four note flute. I particularly don't want somebody around who stole money and is hiding out with maybe police following her. Maybe I should just go find another mountain top that isn't afloat in hundred dollar bills. But, "Come on," I say. "You must be hungry."

We round the cliff to the scary ledge. I grab the back of her pants again but I don't look this time. Still, I feel her bare skin. I feel her warmth.

On the way down I see a few more single bills but I don't mention them. I don't know if she sees them, too, but she doesn't say anything either.

We get back to the clearing by the stream. We sit and rest there a few minutes. The jay is squawking. The stream is bubbling along. She says, "It's nice here."

I'm thinking, Damn right, and it was even better before you came.

Then we get to work.

She knows enough to pick willow branches along the stream. I give up and do the fishing and firemaking. I have a little rat like creature caught in one of my traps—still alive. I don't want her to see it until it's skined and cut up.

This time we both eat cooked fish and tiny scraps of tough meat. There's extra but how hide it from other hungry creatures? I don't know what the Indians did. I decide to bury it with stones on top of it.

But I'm changing and I don't like it. Am I looking at my view and playing my flute?

With her around I need different things. I know where there's obsidian, I could make myself some knives. Maybe make some arrowheads. I could begin civilization over again from the bottom. Reinvent a hut, an animal proof storehouse, a bow, find clay.... But I don't want any of those.

When we sit down to rest, she hands me a hat. She's woven it in the same way as the basket, but with the leaves left on. A wide, green leafy hat. She's proud of herself. I can see that as she gives it to me. She wants to be thanked. I put it on, but I don't really want it. I don't like what's happening. I came here to live as part of the forest.

On the other hand this hat does look to be part of the forest. It's like wearing a bush. But I'm too angry to thank her.

"So what do you need all this money for?"

She turns away. I think she's starting to cry again.

"And why bring it way out here to a mountain top? Are you expecting to stay until people forget about you? How did you expect to live?"

No answer. Of course no answer.

"Why here? Why *my* mountain? And it would have been nice if you'd brought just one little thing I could use. Just one thing."

She's still turned away.

"Without me you'd already be dead."

She whispers. "I know."

"If you want a car to get away in, I've got one."

Is it still there? Could I find the keys? I tossed them in the roadside bushes first thing in my joy at being away from it and people and everything civilized. Especially people like she is.

"This isn't what I wanted to do, spend all my days helping you. You're the one owes me. At least an answer."

I slap my hand on the ground so hard I hurt myself. "*Answer!*"

And she does.

"It was just sitting there. I picked it up. I thought it should have been guarded and they deserved to lose it. And then I was thinking: It belongs to the people not the bank. I wasn't going to use it all for me."

"That's not true."

It probably is, but I'm feeling contrary.

"I've never done anything like this before."

"Maybe."

That's most likely true, too.

"That first night in the woods I walked all night. I mean I ran. I must have fallen down a hundred times. I never knew it could be so dark. I was scared. I didn't know what it was like way out here."

"You took it for yourself."

"But I thought they'd catch me right away, so first I bought myself this purse."

She holds up that useless little red purse. She's kept it hanging on her shoulder all this time even as she slept.

"It's a Gucci. I thought maybe they'd think it was mine from before I took the money and would let me keep it. And when they still didn't catch me, I went to eat in a fancy French restaurant. Stuff I'd never had before. Snails and champagne. I thought they'd pick me up any minute. I wanted to get in one really good meal first. They couldn't take that away. But hours went by and when they didn't come I started thinking I could get away with it, so I bought the car."

"You left a car?"

"A red convertible. But I was driving too fast. It went off the road on one of those hairpin curves. I couldn't believe I wasn't hurt. I don't think they'll find it for a while though. It's kind of hidden. I got these shoes, too, but look, they're ruined."

I flop back, squashing my new hat I'm sure, and look up into the trees.

"What do you have in that little purse anyway?"

"Money. But if I'd known I was going to end up here, I'd have bought myself some boots. I'd have brought you things, too. I'm sorry I didn't. I really, really am." Then she get's all dreamy. "I was going to take my mother out for a French meal, too. I wanted her to have snails. Though I suppose she wouldn't even taste them. I was going to get her a new car. It wasn't all just for me."

I'm thinking of snails and of me eating slugs.

She says, "I wonder if they found the car. I wonder if they even know the money's gone. They were so careless. They deserve not to have it."

I'm still looking straight up the tree trunk. Not how you usually see a tree. Very nice. And I'm dreamy, too. I wish she'd keep quiet. This is all exactly what I ran away from.

I want to ask her, how long is she going to stay and why right here with me? If they're not chasing her why doesn't she go back to where she can have the kind of life she obviously likes? Where little red purses are.... But then I wonder if it holds water? Not much, though.

I get up. I need to get away and think. Or maybe play my flute and *not* think.

My feet aren't yet ready to go barefoot, but I take off my shoes anyway, on principle, though I don't know what principle, and walk away. I hope she has enough sense not to come after me. I shed my clothes. That'll keep her away. I find a sheltered spot and sit alone and eat ants for a while. One at a time.

I stay away all night. I miss my mountain top, but I don't go there in case she does. Though I don't know how she'd manage crossing that ledge by herself. Maybe she'll go around to the far side and crawl up the rocks as she did when she first came.

For bugs I cover myself with mud. In the morning I eat roots. I eat raw minnows that I chase into the shallows. Then I make two new flutes, a big one and a little one. Four holes in each. After playing them for a while, I hide them in the crotch of a tree. I'm wonderfully calmed down. Living as I do is soothing.

In the afternoon I head for my mountain. I leave the mud plastered all over me. First I check on our resting place by the stream. But she's gone. There's the hat she made me. I put in on but I leave my shoes there though my feet are in bad shape. Again, it's the principle of the thing. I don't know why.

Mud and big hat like a bush, scraggly beard, naked, bloody feet, limping, lurching.... I'm enough to scare anybody. Especially a person already scared.

I don't mean to. I'm thinking about my poor feet...of my soft sandy bed under the overhang. I'm hoping she won't be there. Though where else would she feel safe at night all by herself?

She screams. Throws up her hands. Then off she goes, backwards, over the steep side.

The camping season begins. The place is full of hikers though not so many this far out. No one comes to my mountain. It's not an important peak and there's no decent path to the top. Nobody likes climbing up unstable piles of shoebox sized stones.

My feet are hardened by now. I can even leap up the rocks. All I wear is a leafy hat and a little red leather purse across my shoulders. (In it there are hundred dollar bills.) Otherwise I'm dressed in mud. I smell of ferns. I have a flute in the notch of dozens of trees. Some sound high and squeeky and some are low and mysterious— scary in the middle of the night. I see people come out of their tents on moonless nights to listen and wonder.

I could have stolen knives or canteens and ordinary food dozens of times. All summer long, I could live off the campers, but I don't. I don't want anything they have. I'm finished with all that. I do the opposite. I leave hundred dollar bills. I put them in shoes or in a pocket of their packs. If they've left their hats handy, I stuff one or two into their hat bands.

When I lean to drink, as an animal would. I see myself, shaggy and plastered with mud. I look at my reflection and I see exactly who I am.

Asimov's Science Fiction Magazine, January 2010

Above It All

Suddenly here was this baby girl and I said, okay. I didn't have a lot to do right then except for the baby birds who had lost their mothers. They had to be fed every two hours...and so did she. It wasn't much extra work. That year I had three baby ravens, one wounded jay, one wounded owl.... I also had an almost-road-killed baby raccoon, though I usually stick to birds. I'm a certified raptor rescuer, but I take in anything. That year I didn't have as many as usual.

They told me they'd found her at the bottom of a cliff in the mountains, not even bruised. They looked, but they couldn't find where she'd come from. And then they couldn't find anybody to foster care her. I felt sad just as I do for all the creatures in my care. I took her in right away.

She was so small and skinny.... I didn't think she'd last. She's still small and skinny, but now I think that's the way she's supposed to be. Perhaps that's why... partly why...she does as she does.

At first she wasn't hard to look after because I'd tie her to things and I had a net over her crib and play pen. I even sewed stones in the linings of her clothes. They had named her *Robirda*. That was fitting. I call her Birdy.

Later, when she understood what those stones were for, I couldn't keep them on her no matter what I did. She'd take off all her clothes and I'd find her in a tree. I know she liked to tease me. She'd get just out of reach and sit there seeing what I'd dare to do to get her back. And I always dared to do it.

When she was older I gave her a little backpack. It was sky blue, the color of her eyes, and had animals all over it. I filled it full of the books she loved the most, but she'd hang it on a tree limb and off she went. Up she went, that is. It was only for me, she did these tricks. In front of others she acted like a normal girl. As if she knew that was best. But even weighted down, she was great at running, jumping.... (She never skinned her knees, unless I had sewn too many stones in her pockets.) On the swings she'd take your breath away.

I had to be watchful and with my net by my side all the time, but now that she's twelve everything has changed. All of a sudden, she wants to be just like everybody else. All by herself she started gathering up stones to keep in her pockets. She even asked me what other people liked to eat the most and she stopped eating her favorite foods in favor of what the other girls liked. She said she liked bacon and I knew she didn't. She said she loved walking in the rain when I knew she loved the sun. She was always cold in rainy weather. She said her favorite color was pink when I knew it had always been blue. She started walking around hunched over instead skipping and running. She didn't climb trees anymore at all.

We couldn't afford a lot of things but I bought her a pink dress with a lacy collar just like everybody else had. I got her the heavy boots she asked for when she hardly needed shoes at all. She does errands for friends and has a little money of her own. She bought herself stuff to plaster down her hair. I refused to buy that. I liked her hair the way it was, just as fly-away as she is.

When she changed, I changed. I was the one, then, taking out the stones. "I wish you'd be yourself," I said. "I wish you'd go back to eating my fried frog's legs and my airy pancakes with honey. I wish you'd stand up straight."

I told her she was exactly right for who she is and she said, "Then why did you tie me down all the time and weigh me down with stones and catch me in your net? *You're* the one, wanted me to be like everybody else. So I agree with you now, that's all. You ought to be glad."

"But I didn't know how to look after you without you being down here with me. I didn't know where you'd end up or how high you'd go. I still don't know. I just wanted to keep you safe. Where *would* you end up? You don't even know yourself, do you."

She's right though, it *is* my fault. I called her Birdy and never wanted her to be one.

Now that she's changed it's a lot easier for me, but I don't want easy anymore. I wish she was back to her old giggly self instead of staring around watching what everybody else is doing and trying to do the same.

Perhaps we ought to get away...from school and home and all my orphaned animals. Take a vacation. It's a good time. I only have a few birds here now. I can get a baby sitter for them, though it's not an easy job. The baby humming bird you have to feed with an eyedropper and the baby crow takes meal worms.

She hasn't been up into the mountains, ever. She used to want UP so much I never dared go there, where it was *all* UP. Also, since that's where she came from, I didn't know what might happen. Besides, I was always too busy looking after my creatures. At least that was my excuse.

So far she doesn't know about the thinner air and the beautiful views. Oh I suppose she knows, but only what she's read in books and seen in pictures. It's not the same. I was scared to take her there. Maybe she'll even remember getting lost and falling off the cliff, but maybe now is the time to do it. Except would she come?

I tell her we won't stay long. "We'll take a picnic. You can wear your boots."

"What would we do up there?"

She wants to mope around down here all Saturday. I don't say that out loud though.

"Aren't you curious about those mountains?"

"No."

"Just for today. Just for me. You can bring a book. I'll bring peanut butter and jelly sandwiches..." (She never used to like those) "...and we can pick berries. They're different up there."

"I don't like berries."

(How can she not like berries?)

"Well then pick some for me. We'll leave early and be back by afternoon." (I'm thinking, *then* you can mope.)

I finally convince her.

She wears her heavy boots. She never had blisters until she got those boots, even so she insists on wearing them. Maybe that'll be her excuse for not going very far and for resting all the time and for reading her book and never looking out at the view.

I don't head for the tallest mountain in the region, that one's always too crowded, but hardly anybody bothers with the second highest.

I know these trails by heart. Even after all these years I recognize the rough steep parts and the smooth easy parts, the big tree struck by lightening. The logs, where you cross the streams, look like the same old logs. Even with those big boots, she keeps her balance crossing them. She's fearless. I knew she would be.

She starts getting excited about how great it is. She actually stands up straight and looks out at the views. No need to worry that she'll be reading every chance she gets. We bird watch. We pick berries and she can't pretend she doesn't like them. We start having a good time just like we used to have before she got to be twelve.

I see a place that looks sort of like a trail but it's not one I ever took before... if trail it is. I choose it because, unlike most trails, it's headed straight up. Pretty soon we're off in unknown territory.

We both get out of breath. If it wasn't for her boots she wouldn't be. I'm tempted to tell her to take them off but I want her to think of it all by herself. I never wanted to be a hovering mother even though, what with her drifting off whenever she got loose, I had to be.

We go on up until we get above the tree line. It gets hard to walk. There's no trail, it's rocky, and lots of the rocks are wobbly. Finally she takes off her boots.

She's looking embarrassed—as if she's failed in some way. I guess in her own mind she has…failed as one of us.

I say. "Nobody's here but us. Do it! It's OK."

She knows what I mean.

It'll be dark if we don't head back soon, but she's not thinking of heading down. She's looking on up. Eagerly.

I'd like to watch her as she skims away, but I'm trying keep my balance on these rocks and I have to keep watching my feet. And then I do stop and watch.

At first she's wobbly. How could she not be since I never let her practice? And the air is thin up here.

She gets about bush high. Then, leading with her left shoulder, she moves off slowly, sideways, then faster and faster, zips around the cliff and out of sight.

I follow but I'm so slow on these rocks.

She didn't even look back once—at least that I could see. Maybe it's so much fun to skim away that she's forgetting everything else. I'd love to do that, too, especially now that I'm not only carrying all the food and jackets, but her heavy boots. If I could waft away like that I'd forget all about me, too.

But I begin to worry. I don't want to get lost up here all alone.

At least she's finally enjoying herself. There's that. I should feel happy but I don't. But isn't this what I wanted? Isn't this exactly why I came?

I sit on a rock and rest. Then, after a long lonely time, I pick up my bundle and her boots and go on. Up.

It's starting to get dark. We'll…. *I'll* have to find a sheltered spot. I should head down into the trees, but I don't want to leave her up here by herself. Except what if she goes on, up and up and up, and never comes back?

I find a cubby hole in the rocks. At least it's sheltered from the wind. I leave my pack out where she'll see it and know I'm here, though I'd rather use it as a pillow. I'm too worried to sleep much. If she doesn't come back in the morning I'll have to go down by myself. Why did I ever think of doing this?

But she did look so happy as she sped away. I had no idea she could go that fast. I'll bet she didn't either.

In the morning I start down. I don't know what else to do, but I go slowly. On the way I see a wounded pika. Should I carry him down to my bird clinic? It's sort of like rescuing a rat but not quite.

He's been attacked by some big bird. I don't know how he managed to not get eaten—unless I scared the bird off with my wobbling around on these rocks.

I know how to hold him so he can't bite. I wrap him in toilet paper and then my bandana and put him in a side pocket of my knapsack with his head peeking out.

I feel better now. A little bit. At least there's something to look after and he's company. I talk to him like I do to all my creatures. I name him Little Rat. Birdie would think the name silly and would name him something better— or even sillier.

I keep looking back to see if she's coming. It's breezy. I'm cold. I have her jacket. I hope she's OK.

I say all that out loud to Little Rat.

There's a swish of air, a bit of blue, and I hear an "All OK," as if right in my ear.

Then a cool touch on my cheek. I can't see her but I know she's there.

Finally she settles on a rock a few yards from me and holds still so I can see her.

"*Mom*!"

She yells it.

"Mom, they're all over!"

"Who?"

"Us."

I run to hug her, but she isn't there. She's zipped to a pile of sharp rocks a yard away, too rough for anybody but her kind to sit on comfortably.

But then she comes and we hug.

"You wanted me to see how nice it is up here, and I can't even tell you how wonderful."

"I just thought you should be who you really are for once."

"And we're here. It's us. And they've always been there. Here. I mean even down there. They mix in with you guys lots of times."

(We're still hugging.)

"Lots of times they tried to bring me back but they couldn't because you always had me weighted down some way and you had that net over my crib. They're all skinny little people just like me. But Mom, you're my real mom. They say so, too. After a while they thought nobody could be any better than you at looking after me so they let me stay with you. They want me to say Thank you. Oh, Mom.... I'll never forget you."

"What are you saying? Are you leaving? You're only twelve."

"They want to teach me how to be what I really am. Just what *you* wanted. They'll take care of me. Look."

She disappears into nothing but a breeze. Then I think I see her, but hardly, maybe it's her, ten feet up. Then she stands still, in front of me again.

"They taught me that last night. It's *so* fun."

"I did the best I could."

"I know."

"Can't you stay a couple more years?"

I knew I'd have to let her go like I have to do with most all my creatures, but I didn't think it would be so soon.

"Mom, they...*we're* all over. They hide among us...among you guys I mean, and take advantage of your things, your warmth, your food... you never notice. They can sip your tea even as you're sipping. They snatch bites from your forks. They've lived with you since the very beginning. We, I mean. And you're right to call me Birdie. They think they started out as birds. Maybe some kind of hummingbird. They call themselves Snatchers and you guys are The Slows. And Mom, I even have an aunt up there."

She gives me a kiss on my cheek and a hug so hard it hurts. "I gotta go.

Bye.... *Mom*." And then she's gone.

I tried to hold on to her but I didn't try really hard.

I hear, as if right in my ear, "I'll come for visits." Then something brushes at my tears.

Soon as I start back, my hat blows off and I have to chase after it. I don't know if she did that or not, or if it was the wind. It would be just like her, though. I hope she was the one that did it.

I stroke Little Rat a couple of times, being careful to avoid his teeth. I tell him, "It's just us—for now." And we go on home.

***Fantasy Magazine*,** January 2010

The Abominable Child

Did Mother say to always go down?

But maybe she said always go up.

Did she say follow streams, and then rivers? First paths and then a road? And then a road all covered with hard stuff? Did she say there'd be a town if you go far enough?

Or did she say, whatever you do, don't follow roads? Stay away from towns?

She always did say, "You're not lost." She always said, "You're my forest girl. You know which way is up." She didn't mean I know up from down, she meant I always know where I am or that I can find out where I am if I'm not sure.

But Mother didn't come back. Even though she's a forest girl, too. She had her best little bow, her sling shot, and her knife.

I waited and waited. I made marmot soup all by myself. It turned out really good so I was especially sorry she wasn't here. I barred the door, but I listened for her. I studied my subtraction and then I read a history lesson. I didn't sleep very well. I'm used to having her, nice and warm, beside me.

Did she say, "If I don't come back after three days, leave?" Or did she only say that when I was little and not that much of a forest girl like I am now? Way back then I would have needed somebody to help me.

She *did* say that I never listen and that I never pay attention, and I guess this proves it.

But what if she comes back and I'm not here? What if she's tired? I could help. I could pump up the shower.

Except what if she doesn't come back?

I was always asking if we couldn't go where there were people, and she was always saying, "It's safer here." And I'd say, "What about the mountain lions?" And she'd say, "Even so, it's much safer up here—for us."

She said not to let anybody see us, but she didn't say why.

She did say people are always shooting things before they even know what they are.

What if I'm some sort of a creature that should be shot? Eaten, too?

Or is she? We don't look much alike. Maybe she's the odd one.

I asked her about all that once but she wouldn't talk about it.

Now and then, in summer, when there are people camping all the way up here, we go yet higher and hide out until they're gone. Mother always said, "Let's *us* go on a camping trip, too," but she couldn't fool me with that. I knew she wanted to keep us secret, but I played along. I never said I didn't want to go. If we were in trouble some way I wanted us to stay out of it.

I know a lot more than she thinks I do.

I wander all over trying to see what happened to her. I see where she crossed the stream and started down to the muddy pond, but then I lose track. I check the pond, but she never got there. There's a fish on the line. I bring it home for supper.

The thing is, do I want to spend my life here alone? Waiting? Does Mother even want me to? I can come back after I see what's beyond the paths. Mother said two story houses and even three story. Also I'd really, really like to see a paved road—once in my life anyway.

I wait the three days, looking for her all that time, then I leave. I take Mother's treasure. She had this little leather book. Even when we just went up to hide, she took that with her and kept it dry.

There are lots of books here—actually twelve—but I don't take any except the one Mother always wrote in and locked shut.

I stop at the look-over and think to go back, just in case she came home exactly when I left, but I did leave a note. Actually two notes, one on the door and one inside. The one inside I shaped like a heart. It was on the paper we made out of stems. I don't need to tell her where I'm headed. She'll see that. I'm leaving a lot of clues all along the way.

It turns out exactly like Mother said it would: A river and then a bigger river and a path and then a road, and after that the wonderful, wonderful paved road. Pretty soon I see, in the distance, a town. Even from here I can tell some of the houses are tall.

I wait till dark. I'm not sure what's wrong with me but it's a town with plenty of bushes around. I don't think it'll be hard to hide. I never had a good look at those people that come in the summer. Mother tried to get me away as fast as she could. I've only seen them from a distance. Besides, they were all covered up with clothes, sunglasses and hats.

We have those.

I want to see what they're like so I can see what might be wrong with me. Though maybe Mother did something really, really bad a long time ago and had to hide out in the mountains. They couldn't put me in prison for something she did could they?

I wait till dark and then I creep into town. Everything is closed up. Hardly any lights on. (I know all about electricity though I've never seen it till now.) I wait till everything except the street lights are out. I wait for them to go out, too, but they don't.

I wander back yards. I try to see into windows, but I waited too long for those street lights to go out. Every house is dark except now and then an upstairs window.

In one yard I hide behind laundry where somebody's mother forgot to bring it in at dark. Mother sometimes did that, too, but I didn't. She had a lot on her mind. She was always worried.

I just about give up, everybody seems to be in bed, but then I see somebody sneaking out a window, trying to be quiet. It's that very yard where the laundry is still out.

I hide behind the sheets but so does whoever crawled out the window. We bump right into each other. We both gasp. I can see on that one's face that it's going to yell but I'm about to, too, and then we both cover our mouths with our hands, as if we both don't want to attract attention. Then we stare.

If this one is how I'm supposed to be then I'm all wrong. This one looks like Mother, not like me. I have way too much hair. All over. Are they all like this? But I've suspected something was wrong with me for a long time, else why did Mother act as she did, always keeping us away from everybody?

I can't tell if it's a boy or a girl. I'm not used to how they look here or how they dress. Then I see it's got to be a girl. She's wearing this lacy kind of top. I never had anything like that but Mother did. This one seems to be just my size. At least my size is right.

She's like Mother, no hair anywhere except a lot on her head. Mother always said it was a disadvantage, not having hair all over. And it was. She was always cold. But I'd rather be like everybody else.

So we're standing there with our hands over our mouths staring at each other.

Then she says, "Can you talk?"

And I say, "Of course. Why not?"

What an odd question. What does she think I am? Except I *am* all wrong. I was afraid of that. But we're exactly the same height, and both of us is skinny. I'm wearing shorts and a t-shirt. She wearing shorts, too, and this fancy blouse. And I see now she has the beginnings of breasts just like I do. Hairiness looks to be our only difference. I don't have that much on my face—thank goodness. I guess.

"Am I all wrong?"

It's the question I've been wanting to ask just about all my life but didn't know it till right now.

I can tell from the way she says, "Well...." that I am and that she wants to be nice about it.

She says, "Come."

Way back at the end of her yard, there's a funny little house that we have to lean over to go in. It has two tiny rooms that you couldn't lie down straight out in unless you put your feet though the door into the other room. It has a little table and chairs, too small for any regular sized person. Are there people I never knew about?

The girl lights a candle and we squinch into the little chairs next to the little table.

Even in this light I can see her eyes are blue just like mine. We're an awful lot the same.

"Dad was going to take this house down, but I said, not yet."

She has a dad!

"So what about you? What are you, anyway?"

I can't answer. I feel like crying. I have to say, "I don't know."

"We could look you up on line. There's a lot of choices, Yeti, Abominable Snowman, Sasquatch, Bigfoot....

She knows more about me than I do.

"I suppose abominable."

"I don't think so. You're too nice looking. Are you crying?"

I thought I was holding it back but that makes me feel worse than ever. I really do start to cry. Mother would be saying, "Where's my forest girl?"

"That's all right, go ahead and cry. I'll make you tea, and there's cookies, too. I don't have a stove in here, Dad wouldn't let me, this is just sun tea, but it's good. I know I'm too old to have a playhouse like this, but I want it, anyway. It comes in handy, like right now."

The tea is nothing like anything I've had before even though we have lots of teas up there. And the cookies are like nothing I ever had either. I say, "I never had these."

"Oatmeal with raisins. Mom thinks they're good for you. She's a great believer in oatmeal."

I guess her mother is right. I feel better after the tea and a couple of cookies.

But I'm thinking maybe she has a bad mother. I've heard of that. After all, she sneaked out the window.

"Were you escaping? I thought maybe your mother was mean and you were you running away."

"Oh no, my folks are fine. I sneak out lots of times when there's a moon like this. I'm fourteen. I'm old enough to be on my own."

"I'm fourteen, too, and I *am* on my own, but I don't want to be."

"I don't know what Mother would do about you, though. Call the police... or the doctor. Or maybe the zoo."

"Am I all wrong?"

"You're probably some sort of mutation."

How can she be so sure of herself all the time? But she does seem to know a lot.

"I don't want to be put in the zoo."

"That wouldn't be so bad. I wouldn't mind at all if it were me. I'd come visit you. But I don't even know your name. Mine is Molly. I picked it out myself two years ago when I started Junior High."

"You named yourself?"

"Lots of people do. You could, too. But do you have one?"

"Of course I do. I'm not...."

But maybe I am—some sort of animal. "Mother calls me Binny. It's short for Sabine."

"Sabine!"

She looks impressed.

"Don't change it!"

We both get tired at the same time. Molly goes back in through her window and brings me a pillow and a blanket. Tells me to keep quiet and she'll bring me breakfast after her parents go to work. She says, "Not to worry. Nobody... *Nobody* would dare go in my playhouse unless invited."

It feels good to stretch out all the way through the two rooms after hunching over all that time. And I've never had such a soft pillow before.

I wake at dawn, as I usually do. Things are pretty much quiet all over the whole town. I hunch myself around the little house. I didn't get a good look at it last night in the candle light. There's a mirror. I see me. Actually Molly and I look kind of alike. Our eyes are blue. Our hair is tawny.

Hair!

On a shelf I find a doll...a very worn out doll (not hairy), and a worn out (hairy) dog doll beside it.

The town starts waking up. Doors slam. Cars drive by but out along the front of the houses, way across the lawn from me. I saw those last night. Some even came right close to me while I was waiting for it to get dark. Trucks, too. I saw everything Mother talked about and drew pictures of. I even went up to a car and looked in. I saw the steering wheel and the pedals. I can't wait till I get to ride in one. Maybe Molly can get me a ride. A truck would be even more fun than a car, the bigger the better. I'll ask her.

I wait and wait for Molly to bring breakfast. Finally she does. Stuff I never had before. Toast and sausages. Actually, enough for both of us. She wants to eat with me. First thing she says is, "I hate eggs."

I've had eggs lots of times and I like them but I don't say it.

"I have to go to school. Whatever you do, don't leave here in the daytime. I'll take you out tonight. We have to figure what to do about you."

I say, OK, but I'm not sure I'm going to stay shut up here all day.

"When do you get back?"

She looks at her watch. (I know what that is, too.) She doesn't notice I don't have one.

She says, "Three-thirty, thereabouts."

Pretty soon everything gets very quiet. All the cars and all the children are gone. I'm tired of hunching over, I'm not going to stay in here, but I'm a little scared about just walking right out. Then I think about Molly's back window. I cross the lawn (by now the laundry's brought in) and climb in Molly's window.

Here's a nice place! Pale yellow walls, an all white, really, really soft bed (I try it), a not so worn out stuffed dog on the pillows (even fuzzier than the one in the little house), and a wonderful lot of books. Must be twenty or so on a nice little shelf. I recognize school work things. There's a note book exactly like Mother has for me.

Time goes faster than I thought it would. I spend a lot of it looking at the books, but then I get hungry. I find the kitchen. The refrigerator! In there it's like winter. I eat a lot of things that I don't know what they are. I've heard of cheese. Besides, I can read the labels: cold cuts, cheddar, cottage cheese.... I taste everything. There's radishes. I'm glad Mother saw to it that I knew about these things. I think she was homesick for all this so she talked about it. Actually she talked about a lot more than I wanted to hear—then, anyway. Talk about not listening! It's a wonder I even remember radishes.

I wander around the whole house. Turns out they have lots of books. And all over the place. I start reading several of them, one after the other, bits and pieces of all sorts of things. Magazines, too. I've been missing a lot. Mother knew it. She tried to make it up to me. When I see all this I realize how hard she worked at it. I start feeling tearful. I wonder where she is and if she's all right.

Their clocks already say after two. I think I'd better go back into that little house.

I bring some books and magazines, but I don't read them. I start thinking about dads. I know enough to know I must have had one. I haven't thought much about it. I thought the way Mother and I lived was the usual way. Like bear cubs and fawns, always a mother and a child or two. And here's a dad living right with them. Out of the little windows, I saw whole families leaving all together. The dads were living right there with everybody.

There's a lot Mother told me, but a lot she didn't. I'd ask her, Where is my dad? Who was he? And, especially, how hairy?

I must have fallen asleep by mistake because Molly wakes me.

"Come quick," she says, "before my parents come home. We'll look you up on the web. If Mother comes in...she always knocks first...you just scoot under the bed."

"Scoot?"

So then I get my first lesson in computer stuff. We look all over the place, but not a one looks at all like me. They're all chunky and have terrible faces.

Molly says, "You're much nicer looking than any of these. I like your hair color. There's a lot of gold in it."

I'm glad she said that, but it worries me that one of these might be my dad. How could Mother have even gotten close to somebody like that? I hope at least he was a nice person...*if* I can think of him as a person.

I ask Molly, "You have a Dad. What's that like?"

"Oh, he's OK. He thinks I'm a kid, though. I'll be forty-five before he'll think I'm grown up. Don't you have your dad? Well, you don't or you'd already know what he looks like."

I'm thinking, looks aren't everything. Molly's father might not be so handsome either. But that's too much to hope for. And, anyway, why would I hope for that? That isn't nice.

Then I remember about cars and trucks. I ask Molly if she can take me for a ride in a truck.

"Truck! Of course not. We don't have a truck. But I could take you in our car—after everybody's gone to bed. I don't have a license, but I do know how to drive. Dad already taught me. You're not supposed to drive until you're sixteen. I don't know why they make you wait so long."

I go to the little house before her mother comes back. Molly loads me up with cookies and milk (I never had milk before) just in case she has a hard time bringing me a supper.

"Don't light the candle until all our lights are out here in the house."

Finally she comes to get me.

She brings me a big floppy hat, one of her father's white shirts, pants, socks and sandals. The sandals are terribly uncomfortable.

She says, "I guess you really are a Bigfoot."

I must look hurt because right away she says, "Sorry, that was supposed to be a joke. Not a very kind one. Look." She puts her foot next to mine. "We're almost the same size." Then, "You don't have to wear the sandals. I don't suppose anybody will see your feet, anyway."

She tells me to button up the shirt and raise the collar to cover my neck as much as I can.

If I need all these clothes and to button up just to go for a ride in a car, I guess I really am entirely wrong.

Even just getting in the car is exciting.

Then it jerks forward.

"Sorry. I haven't driven very much. But this will be good practice. Better put on your seatbelt."

We drive, and it's wonderful. We go out in the country so we can go fast. She says in town we can only go twenty five. We open the windows and get the breeze.

She says, "I'll go even faster if you stop saying, Thank you, all the time."

I stop and she does.

She turns on the radio, which is another new thing—not that I haven't heard all about it. She pushes buttons to get the right music. She says, "Dad has it on news all the time." I wouldn't have minded hearing news.

We start around a curve and all of a sudden we're in the ditch. Then bouncing up and down, and then upside down.

We're not hurt, but the front doors won't open. Molly finally gets a back door open and we crawl out.

She doesn't look like Molly anymore. She looks scared and like she doesn't know what to do.

She says, "I don't even have my cell phone."

It's still the middle of the night. There's not a light in sight. She starts to cry. I feel like I'm the strongest one now. I say, "Come on. Let's start back to town."

"I wish I hadn't gone so fast. We wouldn't be so far away if I hadn't done seventy. Daddy's going to kill me."

"Your dad will kill you?"

"No, silly, of course not. Don't you know anything?"

Getting angry at me makes her feel better. She starts walking down the road in the dark and trips and falls flat. And then she's crying again.

My eyes must be better than hers. I can see a little bit. There's the sliver of a moon. I say, "We'll be all right. Hang on to me."

Pretty soon it starts getting light and we see a farm house and head for that.

"I'll go in and telephone Dad. You have to hide. Don't let anybody see you."

The more she says things like that, the more I worry about myself.

"What will Daddy do? And we don't even have a car now. And what will we do with *you*?"

"I don't want to be put in the zoo."

"Look, there's a barn. Go hide there, while I go in."

In the barn there's stalls, mostly empty but there are two horses at the back. There's a ladder up to a loft full of hay. That's where I'll go, but I've never seen horses—except in picture books. I check on them first. I worry they might kick or bite, but they come right up to me to see who I am, friendly as can be. It makes me feel better, stroking something big and warm. Then I go up and lie down in the hay.

It takes so long for Molly to come back I think maybe she's just left me here. I'm too shaken up to sleep. I go down again and talk to the horses. I get right in with them. I call one Spotty and the other Brownie.

Finally Molly comes.

"I couldn't get away from the people here. They're too nice. They were going to drive me home since they had to go to town anyway, but I said I needed to call Daddy. They went off to town. I know their kid. He's a couple of grades ahead of me in school. He's still here. He takes the school bus. Daddy's renting a car. He'll be here as soon as he can, but it'll take a while. I didn't tell him about you. What'll we do about you?"

I don't say anything. What do I know?

But suddenly here's the boy. First he says, "What are you doing out here?" And then he sees me and gasps.

I'm still dressed, head to toe…to almost toe, but even so I'm too much for him.

"What *are* you?"

I say, "Big foot."

Right away he looks at my feet. Then he laughs. And we all laugh.

He says, "I don't believe in you."

I say, "Nobody does."

And we laugh all the more.

He decides not to go to school—after all, Molly isn't going either—and invites us in for breakfast.

He keeps staring at me as he cooks us pancakes. And he keeps spilling things.

He says, "You're a nice color," and, "I didn't think a big foot would be so attractive," and, "You have nice eyes," until I'm a little worried. Though he could be trying to make me feel good about myself. I suppose I should appreciate it.

He says, "I don't think you should go back with Molly. I think you should stay here where you have a nice barn to hide in."

Molly looks relieved.

I'd really rather be back in her little playhouse, but I don't know how we can get me there.

Then he says, "We could go horseback riding," and I think, maybe it wouldn't be so bad here. I'm learning so many new things. Including rolling over in a car. Horses would be nice.

Molly's father comes by in a rented car. He barely stops, honks, opens the door and yells. I guess he's really angry. She looks at us, scared, then rushes out. There's no way I could have gone with her even if I'd wanted to.

The boy's name is Buck. He changed his name, too. I didn't know everybody could do that. He used to be Judson. He says, "Judd isn't so bad but I like Buck better."

He goes to put on his riding clothes. He has the whole outfit, cowboy hat and boots and all. I've seen pictures. I think he's trying to impress me. And maybe himself. He does look as if he likes himself a lot in these clothes.

He brings a bag of stuff for a picnic and we go out and saddle up. First he has to brush the horses so there's no dust and stuff under the saddle. He shows me how and I help.

I feel funny, getting up on something I just talked to and petted, but he doesn't seem to mind.

Buck heads us up into the hills and pretty soon we're in the trees. He makes us canter even though he can see I'm bouncing and hurting. Trotting isn't much better. He doesn't say a word about what to do. It looks as if he likes to see me not knowing how to do it. He's got this funny little smile all the time. He's laughing at me.

We get to a nice shady spot and get off and tie up. He spreads out a blanket, he says, for our picnic.

He takes off half his fancy cowboy outfit. And then he takes off even more. Is this what people do?

But I start to know what this is all about. I remember things Mother warned me could happen. I wasn't listening but some of it must have gotten through.

He's a lot taller than I am and stronger, too. He tears Molly's father's shirt practically in two. I have to really fight and I'm losing.

Finally I grab a stone and knock him away.

He says, "What difference does it make? You're just an animal. Why should you care?"

"I'm not an animal, or if I am, I'm only half. My mother was your kind."

He comes after me again but I run... uphill. I'm thinking of getting back to our cabin and maybe finding out what happened to Mother.

I'm way faster than he is. I guess from all my hiking around the mountains. Pretty soon he gives up. I see him from way above, put on his costume, mount up and ride away, leading the other horse.

I sit down and catch my breath. I feel like crying, but I'm angry, too. Molly didn't think I was an animal. Or am I? I wish I was back with her.

I'm glad that, up in the mountains, it's always just mothers and children off by themselves. I was thinking I wanted to meet my father some day, but now I'm not sure. And he'd be more of an animal than I am. Though if Mother liked him he couldn't be that bad. Or maybe she didn't like him. Maybe she couldn't fight him off.

And then I think how Mother's little book is in the pocket of my shorts back in the little house. I have to get back there.

I walked there once before, I guess I can walk there again. I'm going to stay in the foothills and walk mostly at night. I'm pretty well covered up with Molly's dad's shirt even though it's torn and has lost some buttons, and the slacks are OK. I don't have the hat anymore.

I wonder what Molly is expecting to do about me. She might try to come and get me. For sure not driving a car. I wonder what she'll do when she finds out I'm gone. I wonder if she knows about how Buck is. Except maybe he's only that way with somebody who's an animal.

I'm too impatient to wait for dark. I start heading back towards the town, but I keep well away from any roads or houses. I suppose it's pretty far considering how fast Molly was driving. I don't even know the name of the town, but it has a special smell. I'd recognize it right away.

Later, when I come to a river and a nice pile of brush next to it, and berries, I decide to rest there until dark.

Except I can't rest. I'm too angry and upset. I need to talk to Molly. I keep on across the rocky foothills.

I should have stayed and rested.

At first I think they're wolves, but then I see it's a pack of all sorts of dogs. I climb a juniper. They're making a terrible racket.

Practically right away, here comes a man with a rifle. He shoots towards the dogs and they run off. Then he comes to see what they've treed. He stares. Walks all around the tree to look at me from every angle. The shirt and slacks don't hide that much. My Big-Foot-big-bare-fuzzy-feet are just above his head.

He isn't dressed like Buck, though he is wearing a cowboy hat. He has a bushy mustache that's mostly gray. He's a lot older than Buck. I don't know if that's good or bad. He might, all the quicker, take off his clothes and grab me.

Is he going to climb the tree and pull me down and then try to do what Buck tried?

"Can you talk?"

Why does everybody ask me that? Do I look so animal? I guess I do.

"Of course I can."

And I climb a little higher.

"Don't be scared. I won't hurt you. I won't. I promise. Are you hungry?"

Yeah, lure the animal down with a little bite of food.

He sits under the tree and takes off his hat. He's got a *very* high forehead. I've seen pictures of that. That's being bald. Maybe when I'm older I could get bald all over.

He takes out an apple and a sandwich and begins to eat. He's in no hurry. As he eats, he keeps looking up at me and shaking his head, as if, like Buck, he doesn't believe in me.

"I've heard tell of your kind, but I've never seen one. Where did you come from, anyway?"

I don't know what to say.

"Do you have a name?"

What does he think I am? Well, I know what he thinks.

"Of course I do."

"Mine's Hiram. People call me Hi."

"Mine's Sabine."

"I never knew a Sabine. Is that from your people?"

"My people?"

"Your kind of.... Whatever you...."

I never thought about being "a kind." Was he going to say, your kind of animal?

For a minute we just look out at the view of the fields far below us with the sprinkling of black cows, both of us as if embarrassed. Then he says, "You might as well come down. You'll have to one of these days. It might as well be now as later. When I leave those dogs might come back. You can have half my sandwich and this apple."

He's right, I might as well come down, so I do.

I take the sandwich and sit a couple of yards away. I hope I'm not eating like an animal or sitting like an animal. I sit as he's sitting. I'm hungry, but I slow down. I try to keep the torn shirt shut as best I can.

He leaves his clothes on all that time and afterwards we just sit quietly. I'm thinking maybe I should ask about men taking their clothes off, but then I think I'd better not. Even if he is a man, maybe he can help me get back to the town.

He keeps looking me up and down. He just can't stop. Then he says, "Sorry, I shouldn't stare. I'd like to take a picture of you. Of course nobody will believe it. They'll think I made it up on the computer."

"Can you drive a car? I'm trying to get back to the town. I'll let you take my picture if you help me get back. It would have to be at night. And I only need to go to the edge. And if you could lend me a hat, I'd try to get it back to you."

He takes me down to his house. I won't go in. I don't care if he thinks I'm a scared animal, I just won't, and I *am* a scared animal. He gets his camera and takes a lot of pictures, all different views. I'm worried about it because Molly said I should hide and this sure isn't hiding, but this is the only way I know of to get back to her. If he's going to bother helping me, I have to do something for him.

Then we wait till the middle of the night. I apologize for keeping him up.

He never once takes his clothes off. Maybe all men don't do that. I'll have to ask Molly. She said everything is on the computer. If she doesn't know, we can look it up.

He makes me supper. A kind of stew with everything in it. He says it's called slumgullion. He says it's a kind of a guy thing. He serves it outside on his picnic table so I won't need to go in. I'm beginning to think I shouldn't be so scared. I wonder if my father is as nice.

He sits down to eat across from me.

"You've had a bad experience haven't you. Or are you just scared of all of us?"

"I like Molly. That's where I want to get back to. But I had a bad experience with Buck. He took his clothes off and grabbed me."

Then I tell him all about Molly and the car rolling over and about Buck. I tell him, "You don't seem like him."

"I'm not. And when any man takes his clothes off, you get out of there. I have a daughter about your age. I live by myself except my daughter comes here for the summer. If I show those pictures I took of you around, you're in trouble. Everybody will be after you. They'll chase you wherever you try to hide. You ought to go back up into the hills and let yourself be a legend like the rest of your people are. I'll hang on to these pictures until you get well away."

"But I don't know my people. I've never met my father. My mother's one of your kind. Molly wanted to shave me all over with her dad's electric razor. Do you think that would work?"

"Not a good idea. You'd prickle. Nobody could get near you. Here, feel my cheeks. I haven't shaved since yesterday."

I reach across the table and feel them.

"You sure you don't want me to take you up into the mountains far as I can drive and drop you off? I'll give you a knapsack and water bottle and food for a couple of days. That would be best for you."

"I'd like to see Molly first. Besides, I left Mother's book there."

He gets me a shirt of his that isn't torn. It's dark green. Better for hiding in than this white one.

We spend time looking up at the stars. He knows the names of everything up there. I tell him my mother did, too. Then we have coffee, though he doesn't let me have much. He says if I'm not used to it it'll make me jittery. And then we go—in his rickety old truck. He gives me a stained old cowboy hat. He says it may not look so good but it's beaver so it's waterproof.

He drops me off at the edge of town like I want him to. I think I can smell my way back to Molly's house, but not if I'm in the truck.

When he lets me off he says, "You know I'll not use those photos. Better you folks stay a myth. And you better hurry back in the hills. That's where you belong."

I'm glad I met him after Buck. I was ready to never get near a man again.

It doesn't take me long to find Molly's place. I kept pretty good track of where I was. I always know where I am when there are trees and rocks, but I knew I'd have trouble finding my way with all these streets and houses.

I go right back to the playhouse and settle in to get some sleep for what there is left of the night. The pillow and blanket aren't there anymore, but I take the old dog doll for a pillow. Hi's shirt will keep me warm.

But first I find my shorts just where I hid them and Mother's book is still in the pocket.

I want to let Molly know I'm here, but I don't want to wake her up in the middle of the night. But then I oversleep. Everybody in the house has gone off just like before. I wonder if Molly tried to find me at Buck's and if Buck tried… that with her? But I suppose not. I'm the one who doesn't count. But I don't see what difference it makes. Animal or not, I shouldn't have to get forced into doing something I don't want to. Hi didn't think so, either.

So then I have to wait around for Molly to come back. I sneak in and get myself some food. I snoop around again. I wish I knew how to use the computer. I don't dare try without Molly. She said you could learn about everything there.

I grab some books and go back. I start reading and don't even notice when Molly comes home. When I realize she must be back, I go look in her window. There she is, on the bed with a magazine. I tap on the window. She gives a shriek when she sees me. It's good nobody else is home. She opens the window and hugs me. She climbs out and we go back to the playhouse.

She says, "I was so worried, and I didn't know how to come and get you back, and Daddy won't let me go *anywhere* now that I ruined our car. I'm going to have to stay home for months and I have to do chores to help pay for the new car." She starts to cry.

I don't know what to do. Mother would have held me, but that's different. At least I think it is. Finally I reach out and pat her shoulder. That seems to be all right. She does stop.

I ask, "Is it all my fault? You were driving for me."

"Of course not. I know it's my fault. I don't even have a license. Daddy says I have to take the consequences."

"Can I help?"

"I don't know. Maybe keep me company now that I have to stay home every single night there is."

"I'll do it. Besides, I want to learn more things on the computer. About men." Then I tell her what Buck tried to do.

She gets really mad and tells me not every boy would be that way, and she is never going to speak to him again, and she's going to tell all her friends to watch out for him.

"Yes, but I'm an animal."

"You're a girl. Anybody with any sense can see that."

"Thank you."

"I like your looks."

I feel like crying, too, but one of us in tears at a time is enough.

"Actually, in your own way, you're quite decent looking."

In my way.

"Maybe there's some kind of medicine you can take that would make all your hair fall out. I'll bet there is. These days there's something for everything. I'll go on line and look it up."

I don't trust Molly anymore. She doesn't know as much as she thinks she does. I don't want to take some pill that will make my hair fall out.

I don't tell her, but, even though I owe it to her, I'm not sure I want to stay here much longer. Maybe just look up some more things on the computer. Get her to print some pictures of my possible fathers. I don't belong down here. Hi said so, too. And I miss the mountains. Mother said I was made for them. I was always warm enough up there, even my feet. Mother's feet were always cold. What if she's back there by now? Though I know I shouldn't get my hopes up.

Next day Molly pretends to go to school and then comes home. She's going to go back to school for her dad to pick her up. I guess her dad can't keep tabs on her all the time.

(Here I am wishing I could go to school and she can and doesn't do it.)

So we print out all the pictures of Sasquache, and Yeti, and Big Foot. None of them look very nice. I like having their pictures, though. I fold them up and button them in the pocket of the shirt Hi gave me.

The next day Molly does go to school. She says she can't afford to miss too much. She's not doing very well in French (French! I wonder if I could ever get to take that) and math. She says her dad is already angry enough without her failing two subjects. So I have the whole place to myself again.

I go to the house and bring back food and books but then I think I should be reading that little book of Mother's. Maybe I can find out why she went with such an odd ...creature. I almost thought "person" but I'm not sure if either my father or I can be called a person.

I pry open the lock on Mother's little leather book and there, right on the first page in big letters, she'd written:

A TALE OF TRUE LOVE ! ! !

And underneath that:

Except at first I didn't know it.

I shouldn't have been climbing alone in such a dangerous place, but I like being on the cliffs by myself. I was having an exciting time on a dangerous little trail. I remember falling....

...and then, there I was, looking up into big brown eyes. The creature—Mother calls him a creature, too—was mopping my forehead with a cool cloth. He was grunting little sad grunts. As if he was sorry for me. The way he looked—completely hairy—I never expected him to be able to speak, but when he saw my eyes were open, he said, "I thought maybe you were dead."

I tried to get up, but I hurt all over.

"Lie still," the creature said. And then brought me water in a folding cup, held my head so I could drink.

I had broken my leg and my arm but I didn't know that then.

He whistled a kind of complicated bird song and right after that another one just like him came. They've got a whistling language. Lots of it exactly like real bird songs. I love that. I never mastered it though. They use our language, too.

The other one wore a fisherman's vest full of pockets. He had soft vine like ropes. They tied my arm and leg to pieces of wood to keep them from moving. They put me in a kind of hammock, and took me to their hidden village. Movable village. They hardly spend two nights in a row in the same place.

Then there's a break and the start of a new page.

Dear Sabine,

So this is for me. I'm supposed to read it.

As you see, that's what I wrote shortly after the accident, and then such a lot happened that I stopped writing. Actually for years. It was partly because I had to take care of you. But now it's because of you that I'm writing again. I want you to know about us, Growen and me. It was Growen's brother, Greener, who helped Growen rescue me. All the others were against it. They thought helping me was dangerous. I must have lain unconscious for most of the day before they finally decided to help. If not for Growen, they never would have. I think Growen fell in love right then, but it took me a little longer.

You know, Binny, they're beautiful,. Not like any of the pictures people make of them. You must NOT think they're like those. And you should know how beautiful you are, too.

Am I really?

At first I couldn't tell them apart. I mean Growen and Greener, or any of them for that matter. Well, I could tell the men from the women. Then I saw that Growen looked at me in a different way. Hopeful. I almost wrote yearning, but it wasn't that because he always looked sure of himself. As if what he wanted would come true, it was just a matter of when. As if he knew I'd soon see how worthy he was.

Binny, I hope you're a grown up as you read this and have fallen in love, too, so you understand.

Should I stop reading and keep this until I'm older? Besides, I haven't even met anybody to be in love with. Or maybe I can read it twice, now, and then again later.

Of course I didn't fall in love right away. Everybody and everything was too odd, but when you're hurting and are treated with kindness, it makes all the difference. Growen was so concerned and helpful and kept looking at me with such admiration.

Except for Growen and Greener, none of the others liked me. They built our cabin and sent me and Grown down from their cliffs and caves and nests.

I don't know what they'd do about you now. You're so much more them than me. I hope they find you, though as long as I'm around they don't want either of us. I'm a danger. Everything is a danger to them and I suppose they're right. They can't have been kept secret all this time without taking great care.

I hope nothing I do reveals them. Can you imagine, all of them shut up in the zoo? Or tourists swarming all over taking their picture? Or yours? Be careful !!!!! Don't ever, ever, ever go down where it's so hard to hide!!!!!!!!!!!!!!!!

Oh, my God. What have I done!

I didn't realize how important it is for me to be a secret. Me just being down here is a danger to all of them.... I should say, all of *us*. And now Hi and Buck and Molly know about me. Hi said he wouldn't show the pictures but I'll bet Buck will tell about me. He can't prove it, though. At least I hope not.

And all of a sudden I want to find my kind so much I can't stand to sit here one minute more. I have to get back. But I already roamed all over the place and none of them came to me and I never saw a single sign of them.

Though there are several more pages in the book, Mother only wrote a phrase here and there as if she was going to go back and fill them in. One just has: Today Growen died. Maybe she felt too sad to go on except with these little notes.

I put on my shorts and t-shirt, and on top of that Hi's green shirt, and then his wonderful waterproof hat. I don't take anything of Molly's, not even cookies. Except I wonder if she'd mind if I took her social studies book. I like the idea of all these different kinds and colors of people even though nobody in it has hair all over. Besides, I don't think Molly cares anything about social studies.

It doesn't fit in Hi's big pockets though Mother's book does. I'll have to carry it separately. I'll pick up one of those plastic bags that keep blowing around everywhere. Wouldn't it be great if we could travel around in the world even as well as blacks do? Drive trucks and go to school just like everybody else.

I feel bad that I'm not going to say goodbye. Molly got in a lot of trouble because of me. I ought to stay and help, but I'm not going to.

I'm going to find my people if it takes falling off a cliff and lying there with a broken leg.

But what if I don't belong with them either? What if I don't belong anywhere?

I follow the signs I left for Mother so she could follow me. I find my way back to our cabin, no problem. There's quite a bit of snow. It's getting too cold for most of the regular people to be in the mountains. I only have to avoid a few.

I get excited when I get close. Maybe Mother is waiting for me.

The cabin door is open. She must be there.

But then I get worried. Maybe somebody broke in. Maybe somebody like Buck, not like Hi.

I back away and hide.

And then a beautiful creature comes out, looks up and sniffs. He probably can smell even better than I can. I'll bet he knows I'm hiding here.

He's a tawny golden color—all over. He has a wide forehead, a lion-like look. No wonder Mother fell in love. His face is bare, like mine. I can't believe how beautiful he is and I'm pretty much just exactly like him.

He's wearing a fisherman's vest with all the pockets bulging. And he has a belt with all sorts of things hanging from it.

"Sabine? Binny?"

He knows me. Do I dare show myself?

His voice is deep and kind of whispery—breathy.

"I'm your uncle, Greener. Come on out."

I don't.

"Your mother.... I'm sorry. She.... We found her not far from Rock Creek. Come on out. Let me tell you face to face."

So it's true. What I suspected. But I can't come out.

He sits down and turns away so his back is towards my hiding place. A broad, strong, golden back.

"I've come to take you home. You'll like it. Your Aunt Sabby is there. You're named for her, you know."

I can't come out.

"We have a pet fox. We've got jays that eat out of your hand."

I can't.

"I'm sorry I didn't get here soon enough—before you went on down. I hope you didn't have a bad time there."

I don't come.

"Come on out. I'll teach you how to hide. Even better. I'll teach you how to sneak away without making a sound. I'll teach you our whistle language. Come on. I'll take you home."

I'm glad I have Hi's big black hat. I pull it low over my eyes and I come.

Part Two
The Trap For Abominables

At first it's very nice, as if this is the life I was made for. I don't get cold. For the first time in my life, my underwear fur is growing. Mother always kept our cabin too warm for that to ever happen. The food is stuff Mother didn't want to eat, like snakes and bugs and little ratty things. I'm not used to that, but when I see everybody else doing it, I pretend I know all about it. They think I'm odd enough without me not eating what they serve. In fact they think I'm so odd you'd think I was down with Molly and her people.

And there are tame animals all over the place, and that's fun. Jays walk around as if they own the people. There's even a fox and a wolf and they even get along with each other. Molly's social studies book gets borrowed around, and they all ask that same question I asked: Why can't we live there like all those different colors do?

But pretty soon, as I get to know people better I see that, except for Aunt

Sabby and Uncle Greener, they don't want me around. They don't trust me. They're scared I'll reveal them. That I'll be clumsy and do something stupid. I'm a danger to them all, and they're right, I actually already have revealed them. If they knew what I've done they'd be even angrier. They'd probably throw me off a cliff. Three of those people down there know all about me. I'm going to keep quiet about it for now, though I might tell Uncle Greener.

Beggsy—she's the boss of everybody even though she's the smallest. Maybe it's because she's the oldest—just about the first thing I heard her say, and even right in front of me was, "We can't risk keeping her, and we can't risk letting her go." And everybody nodded except Aunt Sabby and Uncle Greener. "If her mother had been discovered it would just be one more of the lost hairless neuts." (That's what they call the normal people.) "But we can't afford to have one of us found. We'd all be lost, then. They'd comb the whole place with a couple of hundred of them until they had us driven to some little spot of their choice."

And then she says what I haven't thought about at all. "And you should be aware that, even should she mate with one of us, she could have a hairless baby."

That's when everybody turns to look at me in horror.

I squinch down and try to disappear. As much as I can. I'm glad I keep wearing Hi's big waterproof hat.

I don't have any place else to go unless I live at our cabin all by myself. Or maybe I can hide in Molly's little house and get looked after by her. I wouldn't like that much, though. Or maybe I could hide with Hi. He was just as nice as Molly and knew a lot more things, too.

But Aunt Sabby and Uncle Greener want me to stay with them. They keep saying I belong to their family, that they cared about my father, Growen, and that I look just like him. They say I have a lot to learn but they think, if they work with me, I'll be OK within the year. If not, they can deal with the problem (me) then. That's what they keep telling everybody. Nobody looks at me like I should be here except them. Their son, Gr, is the worst. It's as I just exist to be teased and pestered. Aunt Sabby says he's jealous.

I know less about these people than I do about my mother's people. Mother made sure I knew about her life but she didn't...or couldn't tell me about my father's people.

Aunt Sabby and Uncle Greener never wanted Mother to go off and live by herself as she did after my father died. They're angry at their own kind that they made her feel so unwanted. But they knew, if she was found out it wouldn't matter. She'd just be a crazy ordinary woman hermit. It was me they were always worried about.

Mother didn't even know about underwear fur. She wanted to turn me into what I could never be. It's as if she never really, really looked at me. There's no way I could live down there. Poor Mother. She must have been really badly homesick to try and teach me all about the life of the others.

They move all the time. When it rains, it only takes them a few minutes to make a hat out of leaves. I keep Hi's hat and wear it all the time. I won't not wear it.

Only now and then, in the middle of the winter, do they make temporary shelters. And cover them with piles of snow.

What I think is, that my father shielded my mother from the cold with his body, so when he died she needed to have a real house because nobody else was going to do that for her.

Uncle Greener says there are never really big groups, it's too dangerous, though they all get together once a year to...oh, oh...exchange women for brides. You can't marry into your own group. The women have to move to a new place. He says I'll have to do that.

It's a small group, only fourteen. I think. It's hard to tell because they're so good at hiding. There seem to be three others about my age. Only one baby that I know of. He's almost black. There's a little three year old girl...the cutest thing, and at that age they're still quite dark, but with a lot of gold, shining through from underneith. She knows more about this way of life than I do and she can already hide so well now and then even her mother can't find her. And then there's my cousin, Gr. He's three years younger than I am. He hates me. He's just the wrong age. It's as if I came especially to be the big sister to get teased and tormented. Aunt Sabby says he's jealous. REP

He trips me up. He hides and dashes out in front of me. He laughs when I try to hide from him. He stole Hi's hat but Uncle Greener made him give it back.

BUCK

I don't care if Molly is speaking to me or not, she's not my favorite person, anyway. She was right there, and she refuses to back me up and say Sabine exists. She's telling everybody I'm crazy. So I'm going to capture Sabine or one of them and prove I'm right.

A pit to fall into? A noose around the ankle that snaps you up into a tree? That's only good if there are the right kind of trees around.

They're too smart for any of those.

She'll be the one Buck can trap and force back to his barn. The others are too savvy. He'll have a gun. She'll relate again to the horses. This will cause more trouble with her own people. The leader, a woman, wants to get rid of her. Uncle Greener

Buck comes up to trap her. Or any of the others he can manage to trap. He knows there must be others. He thinks there are a lot of them. Surely he'll be able to get one.

She'll figure out how to use the phone and call Molly and escape back to the doll house. And to Hi.

She'll escape and Molly and Hi will help her again.

I think he's the real cowboy. Buck is just pretend. If I wanted to fall in love with one of those others, I'd fall in love with Hi if I could but I know he's much too old.

The Beastly Bride and Other Tales of the Animal People, 2010

On Not Going Extinct

... but we're lasting as long as we can.

Our language is gone, though here and there a word survives. Some of our music and dance also. Sometimes we see bits of our ways in what the others do, a gesture here and there, a fragment of a design at the edge of a collar or on a belt buckle.

Sometimes people eat salted fried grasshoppers and do their eggs in little ramekins with lots of cream. Even the word ramekin is from us.

Are there many of us left to sit and watch the falling stars? I don't suppose so. Besides, here in the city we hardly even notice the moon.

I wonder why we came to the city. I suppose the better to hide out in among the Others.

Luckily, none of them would ever marry one of us. That big bump in the middle of our nose not only defines us but make us ugly to the Others. We're glad for our lumpy nose because we can recognize each other even from quite a distance.

Still, we disappear. When have I ever seen a man of our kind I could fall in love with? ... could be watched by and watched over as lovers do? Who would think me beautiful, except one of us? With our own kind we would find ourselves—all of us—turned into butterflies.

If only there was a reason for our differences and our looks. Some special talent. Perhaps there is and I just haven't found it yet. I should go on a hunt not only for a suitable man, but for our talent, too. Not that I haven't tried a lot of things already. Jumping out of trees in order to see if I could fly. I picked a lower branch so if I couldn't, I wouldn't hurt myself too badly, and yet high enough that I'd scare myself into flying if that was my talent.

I couldn't.

I tried to move cups off the table just by thinking about it. I tried to start a fire by squinting hard at a box of matches. I tried to bend spoons from across the table.

I couldn't.

I thought maybe our talent would involve that bump in the middle of our noses, but I can't smell any better than the Others do.

My parents worked hard to repopulate the world with our kind (I have two brothers and four sisters). Mother says I need to be careful who I mate with. She says I'm such a fine example of our people.

"Go!" Mother keeps saying. "It's time you were off on your own." Sometimes she says, "How come you haven't found a nice young man from one of us?" She doesn't realize how few of us there are now. She says, "You're good looking for our kind. I don't think you're trying. When I was your age I already had you and three more of us."

But I've stared out from under my lank limp bangs, looking and looking. I've hardly seen another one of us and certainly never one my age. What *is* she thinking?

"All right, all right, I'll go."

She'll be sorry when I'm gone. After all, I do most of the work around here.

She was kind enough to make me a sandwich, and she gave me her second best brooch. She's so happy to see me finally go that she gives me a big hug and a sloppy kiss.

Is this the way our kind treat their children? But don't all animals kick out the older young ones after a certain length of time? Yes, and that's always when the young ones get into trouble. I'll have to be careful.

When I'm well away from our neighborhood, I put on the brooch.

It's our type of brooch. A reddish stone with little blue flecks in it. Not beautiful and of little value. It's like us in that. But it'll help to prove I'm one of us. That's its only worth.

Mother would be happy if I got on with the business of not going extinct as fast as I can, but why? If we have no special talent, what are we good for? Perhaps we should get out of the way to leave more room for the Others.

But maybe I just haven't found our talent. What if we can levitate a little tiny bit? But I don't know how to test that out. I skip along the sidewalk, trying to pause at the top of each bounce.

I don't. I'm not sure, though. There might be just the slightest hesitation. How do you measure a thing like that? And anyway, what good to the world would *that* be?

You'd think I'd be discouraged, but I'm not. I still might discover our talent.

What if there's a place where a whole lot of us ended up all together? An island all to ourselves? Or I could be the one to start a colony of us myself. I have enough money for an ad. *Wanted: lumpy nosed people with bad hair who keep looking at their feet. MAYBE CAN LEVITATE A LITTLE. You know who you are.*

I could write: *Meet at (such and such a place), PURPOSE: TO FIND A HOME.*

I should also write *PURPOSE: REPOPULATE THE WORLD WITH OUR KIND.* They'll know right away what I mean.

I hope I don't just get my own brothers and sisters. I'd better go to a far off town to make sure that won't happen.

I sit on a bench and eat Mother's sandwich. (Lots of kids get sent off with hardly this much. I should appreciate it.)

Then I take the bus and after that another bus. I spend all night on the second bus. I want to get as far away as possible. Besides, I don't have a place to sleep.

One bus driver looks like one of us but he doesn't look at me with any curiosity even though I wear that ugly brooch right in front.

Some of us have changed our taste so that we only like the looks of the others. When that's the case, there isn't much of a chance for me. And I don't even like my looks myself.

I get off at a town that's not big but pretty. I'm in a bad mood because of that bus driver. He could have smiled.

I'll wait a bit before I put the ad in the paper. I want to get to know the town so I can choose a good place for our meeting.

I get a job right away. It's my usual skill, washing dishes. And I keep testing myself for our talent, too. As I wash I try to breathe under the soapy water. I choke. I try holding my breath for a long time. Nope.

Into the diner comes a whole family of us. There are five little children. They hardly fit into the biggest booth. That couple is doing their part in helping us not go extinct.

I like how they're wearing clothes that are a little different from the others. The mother is wearing an awful brooch. Even worse than mine. It's so heavy it drags her blouse down and to the side. They're all wearing that dark red we always like so much. Even the baby is wrapped in a dark red blanket.

I can hardly hold myself back from rushing out.

And then I don't hold back. I yell, "I quit," and run out to the front. But I've no idea what to say. I just stand there. The man says, "What's wrong?" I say, "Nothing." Can't he see who I am?

I don't know what to do so I pretend I was just leaving and walk out the door.

I'm thinking: What am I doing? I didn't even get my pay. I still have money left, though.

And then I'm thinking: All young ones make mistakes and this is my first. I wonder how many I'll have to make before I do something right.

Instead of feeling bad about it, what I'll do is place my ad. First I'll scout out a good meeting place.

I trot away. It feels good to be doing something for my kind. I have a notebook and I write down several possible addresses. One of them is so secluded I decide to spend the night in the bushes there. Thank goodness I had a good lunch at the diner.

Next day I put my ad in the newspaper. I don't look for another job, I just wait around for the meeting two days from now. I do go to the library to check out possible islands and hidden valleys on maps and in encyclopedias. If I could think of more tests to try for our talent I would, but I can't. (I already tried going without sleep. That's not it.) So nothing to do but wait for the big day.

Finally the day comes and it's wonderful. Better than I expected. I picked a little park with swings and slides and picnic tables. The first people here are that very family from the diner. Right after them come four middle aged women. Then three more. Then two more families. So far not a single suitable man for any of us. What does that mean for our future?

The people mill around and talk to each other and wait for something to happen. All of a sudden I realize *I'm* the one who has to do it.

I should have prepared what I was going to say. Another mistake of young people. My heart starts beating so hard I think I'm going to faint but I stand up on a picnic table and begin even though I don't know what to say.

"As you all know … I think you all know … You do know… ."

Somebody yells, "Louder."

I take a big breath and try again. "You wouldn't be here if you didn't all know we're dwindling away. If we had a place to be where we were with each other, we might last a lot longer and keep our own ways going. My idea is we should find a hidden valley or an island."

I'm so nervous I hardly know what I'm saying, but everybody thanks me for doing what they all had wished to do for a long time. Then they argue about whether island or hidden valley.

It looks like I'm in charge whether I want to be or not. I decide to vote on the side of hidden valley, for no reason except that I don't know how to swim. That breaks the tie.

Maybe we're like dodos … hardly any reasons for being, and won't be missed. I wonder if dodos had any special talents we never found out about. It'll be too bad if we disappear before we find out what's special about us.

So I get myself appointed to search out a valley. They take up a collection to help me with the trip.

Meanwhile we'll put in another ad for men. *BIG NOSED MEN WITH LITTLE EYES AND SECRET TALENTS. YOU KNOW WHO YOU ARE.*

I'd really prefer to wait here with the others and get to meet the men … if there are any … but they want me to rush off so we can find a place as soon as possible. I suppose all these women want me out of the way. I wonder if, in terms of our kind of people, I might be better looking than I think and that's why those women want me out of the way in case they get some men from the next ad.

On the other hand, we've all been spoiled by the delicate, wispy looks of the Others. I don't see how they can think me good looking.

But nothing happens as we think it will. Well, it does sort of. I do find a valley. This is after a long hard hike, wandering from mountain to mountain, eating dried stews and breakfast bars—until I come to a really ugly valley. I get a funny feeling seeing it, like: This has got to be it, much as I don't want it to be. It looks so much like us. As I climb down into it I see there are holes in the cliffs with tailings falling from them. In fact the whole place seems to be nothing but one big tailing. Whoever lives and mines here has been here a long time.

Out of one of the holes comes a man about my age. He's lopsided, little eyes, lumpy nose... . One of us for sure.

And here comes another one right behind him. Two!

I feel all shaky.

Then men come out of other holes. All of them my kind. They're pointing their fingers at me and shouting, "Look! Look!"

So *this* is where they all are.

I look them over while they're looking me over. I like a nice smile and they all have that. I don't find any of them good looking but I can see on their faces how much they like my looks. I suppose they've not seen a woman of our kind—or of any kind—for a long time.

Do we have a knack for mining? A special talent for going underground and breathing bad air?

Not me. I won't do it. I won't even test it out.

They want to take me into one of the mines. I can see far enough in to see the entrance is furnished as if a dining room: big long table and several chairs. Everything in shades of red with bold designs painted all over them. There's also a big mirror to make it look more spacious. Even so, I won't go in.

And then I notice there's gold all over. On the table there are golden bowls and candelabras. Some of the men are wearing gold nugget pendants. It's gold they're mining.

Then I hear somebody calling out—no words, just grunts and gasps and choking sounds, and here comes... . Wait a minute.

Next to him we all look good.

He's more like us than anybody I ever saw. Wide and bulging. That bump in the middle of our noses ... on him it's big as a baseball.

I do know there's really no such thing, but ... can it be?

Trolls? Why didn't somebody tell me? Mother was wrong, we *ought* to go extinct. I'm not going to *ever* marry. There are already too many of us. Who wants more trolls?

He says, "I know exactly why you came... ."

His voice is raspy and breathy and whispery. And as if he's afraid to speak any louder.

Before I can duck, he grabs me and kisses me—several big wet kisses and there's nothing I can do about it.

He says, "... You came for me."

Of all the men here he's the one I'd most not want to be anywhere near, though if there was a standard of beauty for *our* kind I suppose he would be the most beautiful of all.

He says, "Back when there were kings, my great grandfather was a king. You can tell by looking at me."

He still has hold of my arm. Whatever our talent might be, now is the time for it.

I screech a big screech and a rock right in front of us splits in two. A perfect cut, right down the middle.

He says, "Be careful," but he doesn't let go.

I do it again. Somewhere above us another rock splits and half of it rolls down and would have hit us if he hadn't jumped aside and pulled me with him.

Did I do that?

He yells, "Stop!" loud this time and I hear another rock roll down the mountain. "You'll kill us all."

So that's our talent!

And he just saved my life!

I could get away now. His hand is holding my arm, but gently.

He says, "Come on in. We just made blueberry beer. We need your talent. You're one of the best."

"I have claustrophobia."

"No you don't. You're one of us."

How can he be so sure?

Then he tells me I'm beautiful. Not only that, but that I'm a worthy princess for the great grandson of kings.

I do it, I walk into that red dining room full of gold.

In the big mirror behind the table, I see me and then I see him right behind me. What wide faces we both have. Are our eyes too small? And look at those nose bumps. Even so I've changed my mind, maybe we shouldn't go extinct after all.

He's raising his arms as if in admiration. Of me! I turn around and move into his hug.

Strange Horizons, May 2010

No Time Like The Present

A lot of new rich people have moved into the best houses in town— those big ones up on the hill that overlook the lake. What with the depression, some of those houses have been on the market for a long time. They'd gotten pretty run down, but the new people all seem to have plenty of money and fixed them up right away. Added docks and decks and tall fences. It was our fathers, mine included, who did all the work for them. I asked my dad what their houses were like and he said, "Just like ours only richer."

As far as we know, none of those people have jobs. It's as if all the families are independently wealthy.

Those people look like us only not exactly. They're taller and skinnier and they're all blonds. They don't talk like us either. English does seem to be their native language, but it's an odd English. Their kids keep saying, "Shoe dad," and, "Bite the boot." They shout to each other to," Evolve!"

At first their clothes were funny, too—the men had weird jackets with tight waists and their pants were too short. The girls and women actually wore longish wide skirts. They don't have those anymore. They must have seen right away how funny they looked compared to us, and gone to Penny's and got some normal clothes like ours.

They kept their odd shoes, though, like they couldn't bear not to have them. (They look really soft, they're kind of square and the big toe is separate.) And they had to wait for their hair to grow out some before they could get haircuts like ours. This year our boys have longer hair than the girls, so their boys were all wrong.

Every single one of those new people, first thing, put two flamingos out on their front lawns, but then, a few days later, they wised up and took them away. It wasn't long before every single one of them had either a dog or a cat.

When Sunday came, they all went to the Unitarian church and the women wore the most ridiculous hats, but took them off as soon as they saw none of us wore any. They wore their best clothes, too, but only a few of us do.

Even though they come to church, Mom says I shouldn't make friends with their kids until we know more about them and I especially shouldn't visit any of their houses. She says the whole town doesn't trust them even though everybody has made money on them one way or another.

Their kids have a funny way of walking. Not *that* funny, actually, but as if they don't want anybody to talk to them, and as if they're better than we are—maybe just because they're taller. But we don't look *that* different. It seems as if they're pretending we're not here. Or maybe that *they're* not here. In school they eat lunch together at the very farthest table and bring their own food, like our cafeteria food isn't good enough. They obviously...all of them...don't want to be here.

I've got one of the new people in my class. I feel sorry for her. Marietta.... Smith? (I'll bet. All those new people are Smiths and Joneses and Browns and Blacks.) She's tall and skinny like they all are. She's by herself in my class...usually there's two or three of them in each class. She's really scared. I tried to help her the first days, I thought she needed a girl friend really badly, but she didn't even smile back when I smiled straight at her.

The boys are all wondering if those new boys would be on the basketball team, but so far they don't even answer when they're asked. Jerry asked Huxley Jones, and Huxley said...under his breath, "Evolve, why don't you?"

Trouble is, my name is Smith, too, but it's *really* Smith. I've always wanted to change it to something more complicated. I'd rather be Karpinsky or Jesperson or Minnifee like some of the kids in my class.

I kind of understand those new kids. I have to eat a special diet, and I'm too tall, too. I tower over most of the town boys. And I'm an only child and I'm not at all popular. I don't care what Mom says, I don't see what harm there can be in helping Marietta and I'm curious. I like her odd accent. I try saying things as she does and I say, "Shoe Dad," to my dad even though I don't know what those kids mean by it. Maybe it's really *Shoo* Dad.

One of these days I'm going to sneak into her house and see what I can find out.

But I don't have a lot of time for finding out things because I have to practice the violin so much. Funny though, when I took my violin to school because I had my lesson that afternoon. Marietta looked at the case as if she couldn't imagine what was in it. I said, "violin," even though she hadn't asked. And then she looked as if she wanted to ask, "What's a violin?"

Those kids are all so dumb about ordinary things. Every single one of them has been kept back a grade. I don't know how they can walk around looking so snooty. It's as if they think being dumb is better.

Marietta is awful in school, too. The teacher asked her who was the vice president and she didn't know. So the teacher asked who was president and she didn't know that either.

That gave me the courage to ask her if she wanted help. But then she said her mother doesn't want her to be friends with any of us and I said my mother says the exact same thing. Finally she laughs, we both do, and she says, "Shoe Dad, if we can keep it secret."

Those kids never say, OK.

She says, "But I shouldn't be too smart either. We don't want anybody to notice us."

So far I don't think she has anything to worry about in that direction. I don't say that, though. What I say is, "You're getting noticed for the opposite reason. You need my help."

I'm really curious about her house, but she wouldn't dare invite me and I wouldn't dare go there. And she can't come to my house because Mom would be horrified. Too bad they look a little bit different otherwise Mom would never know. So we mostly meet in the woods by the railroad tracks where the bums used to hide out back when there were bums. Mom doesn't like me to go there either. She thinks maybe there might still be bums around. Marietta and I always scope out the place first, not for bums, but because boys sometimes go there to smoke.

I discovered Marietta was so bad at math because she was used to writing out the problems in an entirely different way. Once I got that straightened out she got a lot better. But she said Huxley told her there was no need for her ever to know who was president here now. I said, "Why not?" She started to say it wasn't important but she stopped in the middle. Then she said, it was just that there were some things she wasn't going to bother knowing.

She tells me she really likes Judson Jesperson, but she says she's not supposed to go outside her own group. And I, I like Huxley Jones, and Marietta says he can't go outside their group either. She's supposed to like Huxley and I'm supposed to like Judd. I asked her if this was some sort of religious thing... I didn't dare say racial but Judson has very dark hair and eyes though his skin is just like hers. She said, no, it was something entirely different and she wasn't supposed to talk about it. She said it would be *very* dangerous for any of her group to marry outsiders. She said, "Who knows who would be president in a couple a hundred years if Judd and I got married?"

So anyway, we're unhappy together and I can tell her all about Judson's family but she can't tell me anything about Huxley.

A dozen more families of the tall people move into town. They can't take the best houses because they're already gone, but when they get through with the second best houses, they turn out be almost as good except for not being on top of a hill and next to the lake.

The first group of kids is getting a little friendlier. Huxley even let himself get talked into being on the basketball team but he didn't know how to play and had to be taught from scratch. Judd says they're sorry now. All he has going for him is being tall.

I don't care, I like him. I like his stooped over posture. As if he doesn't want to be that tall. I like his kind of scholarly face. I like his pixie grin. At first he was always frowning at all of us, but pretty soon he wasn't and especially not at me.

The first thing I said to him was, "I like your name," and he actually did smile.

By now everybody is saying Shoe Dad.

Then we have the first snow and a snow day. It's so beautiful. I want to see Marietta right away, but no school so I start out towards her house. I'm not going to disobey Mom. Besides, that's our only good hill for sledding. Everybody will be up there.

And there everybody is, with sleds and garbage can lids and folded up cardboard boxes. Some kids even have skis. The new kids are even more excited about the snow than we are. They act as though they've never made snowmen and never thrown snow balls. They're like little kids. Well, actually we all are.

Those new kids have skis and fancy boots. But not a single one knows how to ski.

Marietta's there. I knew she would be. She says first off, "Look… these great boots…."

She has the fancy kind you can't walk around in. They're white with dozens of black buckles. I admit they're beautiful. I say, "Shoe Dad."

"…and they only cost five hundred dollars."

She's always saying things like that. Everything is cheap to her. I wish something was cheap to me. I'd like to say, "Evolve!" but I don't want to make her feel bad. I say, "Bite the…oh yeah, bite the *ski* boot."

We don't hear about it till lunch time, but that night in the middle of the storm, odd things disappeared. Half the fish at the fish hatchery, and that very same night, a big pile of lumber from the lumber mill disappeared. The night watchman swears he made his rounds every hour. Sometime between his two o'clock and three o'clock a whole section of lumber was gone and not a sound. The fish people are there early and late. They went to feed the fish at eight and found half the tanks empty. Some of us say the new people are getting blamed just because they're richer than we are and just because they're new. Though nobody can figure out how they could have done it. Even so, I'm suspicious, too. Dad says the town is going to have a meeting about them.

Then we hear that exactly the same night, north of us, in Washington State also lost a lot of lumber. And another place in Nevada lost half their grass fed beef.

Funny though, Huxley said all this was *our* fault. Even that they're here in the first place is *our* fault. He said we should have stopped cutting down trees. He won't say anything more about it. That shows how odd these new kids are. But I guess that's fair, we blame them for everything and they blame us.

Except for Marietta, those kids still don't like it here at all, but Marietta says she's getting to like it, partly because of being friends with me—where she was before she never had such a good friend as I am—and she also likes it because she always did like camping out and making do with what's at hand. That makes me wonder all the more where she came from.

The new people often have meetings in one of the larger houses up on the hill. They can't hide that because all the best cars in town are parked outside. After the fish and lumber disappear, the next time those cars gather, a whole batch of the town's people storm the house. It isn't fair, but the cops are on our side... they're just like all the town's people, they don't trust those new people either. And it isn't as if the new people had any higher up connections in the town that would help them. So the cops arrest *them* instead of *us*, even though we're the ones that broke into their meeting. Did a lot of damage, too, and not only to the furniture. Six of the new people are in the hospital.

That leaves a lot of those kids with nobody looking after them. The school principal asks the town parents if they'll take in some of the children temporarily until their parents can get themselves straightened out with the police. I get my folks to take in Marietta. Mom doesn't mind it under these circumstances. In fact she acts nice. She even bakes cookies. Marietta can't believe Mom made these right here at home. She so fascinated she forgets to feel worried for a while.

As usual I have to practice the violin. Marietta tries it out. All she makes is squeaks. She can't believe how hard it is. She's only played computer instruments. "Aided," she says so you don't have to know anything. But you can have any sound you want and you sound good right at the beginning.

I have twin beds in my room so we get to be right in together.

At first Marietta seems to like it as much as I do. We talk until Mom comes in and tells us we have to stop because of school tomorrow. But a little bit after I turn out the light, I'm pretty sure Marietta is crying. I ask if there's anything I can do.

She says, "I wish I could go home."

I say, "It won't be long before your parents come back."

"I mean I want to go back where we used to live. My real home."

"Where is it?"

"We're not supposed to say."

"Was it so much better there?"

"Sort of...some ways...except it's nice being so rich for a change. Of course there's lots you don't have.... Oh well."

"*I'm* glad you're here."

"Well, I'm glad for having you."

"Can I go up and see your house now that there's nobody there?"

"It's just like yours only richer. That's because everything is so cheap here otherwise we couldn't afford stuff. It's *supposed* to be just like yours. Our parents made it special to be like that."

"Can we go anyway? I like rich stuff and I hardly ever get to see rich things except on TV. Besides, don't you need to go get more clothes?"

So we do that— skip school and go up. She's right. There's nothing odd about it...except there is. There's a fancy barbeque thing in the back yard, but obviously never used. There's a picnic table beside it but no chairs. The two flamingos are in a corner, lying on their sides. Inside it's awfully...I don't know how to describe it... cold and stiff, and kind of empty. It's as if nobody lives there. There's a National Geographic on one side of the coffee table and a Consumers Report on the other, and that's *all.* No clutter. Mom would like it.

Upstairs, her room has all the right stuff. There's a brand new teddy bear on the pillow and a small bookcase with brand new books, all very girlie. They don't look read either. There's not a single Tarzan or John Carter. I ask, and she never even heard of Tarzan. I tell her I'll lend her some. Even though we're too old for those, she'll like them.

She has one whole drawer with nothing but fancy sweaters and blouses. We gather some up to bring back and she says I can have half of them.

On the way out, I open the hall closet and there's a tangle of wires and silvery things along them like Christmas tree lights. At first Marietta tries to keep the door shut as if she doesn't want me to see them, but then she says she trusts me as much as anybody she ever knew so she says, "Take a good look."

I say, "I don't know what it is, anyway."

She says, "Time machine," and starts laughing hysterically. And then we both laugh so hard we fall on the floor and I don't know what's the truth and what isn't, except maybe I do.

I'm glad we went there. I don't need to feel jealous after all. Even though Mom would probably like living like that, I wouldn't.

The police hang on to those new people to see if any of them are guilty of anything at all and also as a sort of punishment, I suppose for being rich and taking up all the best places. That means Marietta and I have even more time together.

The lumber mill now has three night watchmen. They're sitting right next to the biggest piles of lumber. The fish hatchery has people practically in with the fish.

But then…again in the middle of the night…all the new people disappear,. The grown-ups, that is. So then we know who did the fish and lumber. But now there's nobody to blame but their children. Some townspeople are so angry they want to put them in jail, too. Most of the townspeople don't go that far, though. My parents and lots of others say they won't let that happen. Besides, now that they know Marietta they like her.

But it's not safe for the new kids to walk the streets anymore—two kids got beat up by a gang of boys and they weren't even the new kids, they were just blond and tall and skinny. Mom dyes Marietta's hair black so she'll be safer. Some of the other new kids do that too.

Marietta looks good with dark hair. That doesn't cheer her up, though. All those kids feel terrible. Naturally. But it's odd, they keep saying they're not surprised, they just wondered when it would happen.

We talk a lot in bed at night and Mom doesn't tell us to shut up until it gets really late.

"How can your parents leave you like this?"

"We're not allowed to say, but it's for our own good."

"Parents always say that."

I try to cheer up Marietta. We go to lots of movies. She does like the Tarzan and John Carter books and there are lots of those to go through yet. Mom gives her valerian and chamomile tea almost every night. At first Marietta didn't want hugs from my mom, but now she does.

I go around wearing her expensive sweaters and I wear her white jacket when she wears her shiny black one. That turns out to be a big mistake because I get taken for one of them. I'm as tall and skinny as they are. And here I am, wearing fancy clothes like they always do. And here we are, Marietta and me, one of us with dyed black hair and me, a darker blond than they are but that doesn't matter to this bunch. They're not high school boys. I don't know who they are but they're grown men—waiting for us after the movie.

They don't think Marietta is one of the new people, they think I am. She's wearing my faded blue jeans and my sweatshirt and I'm in her cashmere sweater and that white jacket.

They push her aside…so hard they knock her down… and come after me. They yank at Marietta's jacket so hard the zipper breaks, and then pull the sweater up over my face so I don't see what happens next. All I know is they suddenly stop and Marietta is pulling the sweater down so I can see. She yells, "Run," and we do. When I look back I see all three of them collapsed on the ground.

"Don't stop." Marietta grabs my arm and pulls me along with her.

"What did you do?"

"I'm not allowed to say."

We run all the way home and collapse in our front hall. That white jacket is lost and ruined out there somewhere and the sweater is all pulled out of shape.

Marietta right away says, "Don't tell."

"How did you do that?"

"I thought you had those here. Tazers. Don't you? This is just a different form."

"Where is your tazer?"

"I'm not supposed to say. See, where I come from it's not safe anymore since the revolt of…. My drones… I mean my parents…they wanted me to be able to defend myself. Besides, they thought everybody here had guns."

"Where is it? You can tell me."

"Here." She points to her earlobe. (There's not even a mark that I can see.) "I have some control over the direction." She twists her earlobe. "I can even point it back."

I touch it, but I don't feel anything.

"They left us here, my drones. They said they would if anything happened. And things did happen. I guess it *is* better here. I mean the air and water and space to move around in… and the food…it isn't what we're used to, and it's awfully primitive, everything is, but it's better some ways and we're rich. I have a million dollars in the bank in my name."

She's about to tell me more but Mom comes in right then and finds us sitting on the floor, and me, all bedraggled and the sweater ruined. She gets really upset when she hears about it. (We don't tell her the tazer part.) She insists that she's going to dye my hair that very night no matter how long it takes, and I have to stop wearing Marietta's nice clothes.

For once I agree with her. I let her do all that, even though I know the kids at school will tease me.

I wonder if those men are going to tell what happened to them? Maybe not, though, because they were breaking the law.

I'm going to stick close to Marietta from now on. I feel safe with her.

Most of those new kids are physically awkward— like Huxley trying to be on the basketball team— but Marietta isn't so bad. She says it's because her parents didn't believe in the education boxes most kids had. She says those were like being inside a TV set. But she kept calling hers mommy by mistake and that upset her mother so much she actually had her playing outside even though the air wasn't that good anymore and even when it was too hot.

She's been telling me everything, even about the air-conditioned sweater her mom got her.

She says, "Even so, it was getting worse and worse. Food riots sometimes. I know this is best for us. But we have to be so careful and not change anything. Nobody knows what would happen if we upset things. Shoe Dad, I might not even exist. I'd go *poof!* Just like that."

And then Huxley gets in trouble and that changes everything. He didn't dye his hair like the others did. It might not have worked anyway. Three men attack him… maybe the same three that came after us. (You'd think they'd learn.) Marietta and I have to guess what happened: that he not only used his tazer, but tied up the men when they were down. Dragged them into the woods. Then he walked all the way home with bruises all over. Nobody found out about the men out in the woods till two days later. It rained all the next day and one of the men suffocated with his head in the mud. Marietta and I know Huxley didn't use his tazer until he was practically all beat up. He was trying so hard not to cause any changes in the people living here but then he caused more of a problem.

The townspeople are blaming him… of course they are. Besides, who knows what story those men told? So the police come to arrest him, but he takes off. They even shoot at him, but he gets away. We don't know if he got shot or not.

All the new kids are even scarder than they already were. About going "poof." They keep saying, "It's gotta be even worse than that butterfly back in the Jurassic era." I don't know what they mean by that.

They stand there staring at nothing, as if thinking: Any minute and I never existed. They stop in mid sentence as if: Is it right now, that I disappear?

On the other hand, they could disappear by going back home. We'd never know which it was. Marietta hangs on to me whenever she can. It's as if she thinks as long as she has a good grip on my arm, she won't disappear. It's a bother but I let her.

I know where Huxley isn't. He's not at that place where the bums used to go and where the boys go to smoke. That's too easy. But I do know where he could be. I don't even tell Marietta. I get up real early before anybody is up. I make a couple of peanut butter sandwiches and take some nuts and apples and go. Good that Huxley and I never got together or the cops would be watching me.

So I head out into the woods. It's a good place to get lost since there are so many criss-crossing paths and there's a lot of undergrowth for hiding. I think Huxley is somewhere in there but I'll have a hard time finding him. I whistle. I sing. I make a lot of noise and wander all over. I think I'm going to get lost myself.

But what if he's disappeared already? What if he's never been at all?

Then I hear a bird chirping above me, I look up and there he is and he's not been shot. I climb up and give him the sandwiches. He's changed a lot from when he first came. I don't think he'd have been able to climb a tree. He looks kind of wild and haunted and dirty. That makes me like him all the more. I'm always embarrassed, being so close to a boy I like so much, and now even more so. I don't ask anything I really want to. I'm too nervous.

He gobbles up both sandwiches and apples and nuts all in about five minutes. When everything is gone he thinks maybe one of the sandwiches might have been for me and apologizes. But I say none of it was for me and I'll bring more tomorrow.

He admires my new black hair, but I think he's just trying to be nice.

I move up closer to the branch he's on. Turns out I don't have to ask anything. He tells me he always did like me but didn't dare show it. Now he does dare. He thinks everything is all messed up anyway so he might as well like me and he wants me to know it.

Then we hear the swishing of underbrush and voices of people coming closer.

We shut up. He moves higher and I move lower.

In a few minutes the woods is packed with people walking all over the place looking for him. Some of them are cops in uniform. Lots are just townspeople. Mostly men but a few women.

I jump down and move away from his tree. I shout, "Lets look over by the little cave next to the stream." So I and a group of others including one cop, head over there.

The cop says, "Aren't you supposed to be in school?"

"Yeah, but isn't this important?"

"You're lucky I'm not a truant officer."

"What will you do when you find him?"

He pulls his cuffs out of his back pocket and rattles them. Says, "He's dangerous."

I know this whole woods better than a lot of them do. I lead them around to all sorts of good hiding places. I talk loud and make a lot of noise. I don't ever look up.

It's a tiring day for everybody. I had no idea I was going to get caught up in the search and get home so late. My folks and Marietta have been worried about me. I didn't tell Mom where I'd been, but I tell Marietta. She feels bad that I didn't ask her to come along, but I convinced her it was safer for Huxley if it's just me.

Next day I don't think I should keep on skipping school so I just skip my last class. This time I make four peanut butter sandwiches. It's late so I bring a flashlight.

I head for that same tree first, but he's not there. As before, I sing. I whistle. I keep looking up and chirping. I go to all the good spots. It gets dark and I'm worried about using the flashlight. There's only a little moon so I stumble around tripping on things.

Pretty soon I know I'd better go home. I leave the sandwiches up in the tree where I first found Huxley. I leave the flashlight for him, too, and try to find my way out without it.

But I can't. I thought if I just came to one of the streams and followed it, I'd be OK, but it's muddy and slippery near the stream and I keep falling down. I decide it's best to just wait till dawn. I huddle down against a tree. I wish I'd kept one of those sandwiches for myself.

In the morning I go back to the tree where I left the sandwiches. Something got into them and ate most of them and scattered what was left all over.

When I get back my folks are so worried and the police are all over looking for me. Thing is, Marietta disappeared, too, and first they thought we were off somewhere together. Then they thought that I got disappeared with all the others.

It turns out they're *all* gone. I'll never know if Marietta got to go home or if she never existed in the first place or maybe they decided it was a bad and dangerous idea to leave their kids here. Or maybe things got better so it was OK to go home. Or maybe they found better stuff from other times. Like way, way back before there were other people to get in their way.

She left a lot of her clothes in my room. Funny though, my old Tarzan and John Carter books...the ones she was in the middle of reading... are gone. That makes me feel that she didn't disappear completely like she was afraid would happen. She's still someplace, I'm sure of it, reading my books.

I wonder if I could write her a letter. I'll bet there is a way, like sealed up in stainless steel. I wish we'd talked about that before she left. I wish I knew how long my letter would have to last to get to her. Maybe I'll have to carve it in stone.

Lightspeed, July 2010

The Lovely Ugly

We knew they were on their way long before they got here. Several years ago we saw the speck moving towards us. We said, Oh, no, not more smart people... *if* people they are... *if* smart... (but they do have to be fairly intelligent to get here in the first place) ...but we're already full up. There are limits to how big a population a world can hold comfortably, and so that everybody has fun.

We were watching from the trees when they landed. They took us for creatures both ignorant and wild. We played into that role, howling and jumping up and down. Our hooting was really our laughing. They looked so funny we couldn't help it so we hooted to cover it up.

Then we glided out from the trees and moved closer to the clearing where they had set up camp. That was a clearing we had prepared for them ahead of time. Plenty long enough for their lander. From our experiences with space flight we knew the exact dimensions they would need. We also knew they'd like it near a stream. We picked a little stream, not suitable for navigation. We didn't realize until they'd landed and we saw who they were, that they'd need a path before they could reach the water.

We pretended to get tamer and tamer. We pretended to accept their gifts of beads and bracelet's. Couldn't they see those would just hold us down?

And they brought what they call dogs. They use them for all sorts of things, including warning them that we're about to glide in.

We started imitating their dogs, they love them so much and we wanted to seem just a little bit more intelligent than the dogs are. The creatures began to love us, too. Pretty soon they let us lean over their shoulders and we could see how all their machines were made. We didn't disable any of those things till later.

Now we tell each other, Bad dog, no! Or, Good dog, and a few pats. I saw one of us give her mate a snack saying, "Good dog." They laughed so hard they fell off their branch.

It helps that we have fur and they have none because they seem to consider furry creatures more animal. They think simply wearing clothes makes them more civilized than we are. But when have we ever needed clothes?

I don't think they have any idea...and we're glad they don't... that we already had space flight and gave it up a long time ago, since this is the best of all possible worlds. We've already checked out a lot of other planets, so we know. And after all, we were made for *this* world. And even for our anomalous moon.

On some worlds, the natives lie around and complain all day (no matter how long the day), that their world is getting more and more crowded, or hotter and hotter, or full of dust and smoke.... Those various natives kept saying, "It didn't used to be this bad," and yet they don't do a single thing about it, or not enough. Actually, there's hardly any world that couldn't be a paradise if the natives bothered to make it so.

Until now, we've never seen intelligent creatures with neither fur nor feathers nor scales. These creatures are hard to look at. It's as if they have some form of mange. At first we thought they'd infect us with hairlessness.

You can see their veins.

We're teaching these Uglys a pidgin language we invented just for them. We don't want them delving too deeply into our lives. On the other hand, we pretend to learn their language *very* slowly. I'm a trained linguist and am fluent in many alien languages, but in their presence I've limited myself to twenty-five words and a few simple phrases.

They're jealous of our gliding. They hack themselves around in the underbrush looking up at us in the canopy. They gasp, and, "Wow," and, "Oh my God." Half the time our younger ones are swooping around just for them.

They wonder that there are no paths. When have we ever needed paths?

They wonder at the length of our arms and at our arm flaps— at the skirt of skin across from knee to knee. Not just for beauty, but all the better for gliding.

The forest around them is filling up with their paths. Now, what with their little land planes disabled, they can't go far. They didn't ask *us* if we wanted paths or not. They think us too ignorant to have planted and nurtured the forest on purpose. Too ignorant to have laid out bushes with thorns and fish berry plants all over the forest floor.

As they were settling in and wondering what was safe to eat.... (They *had* to settle in. We had disabled their lander) ...we pretended to eat all sorts of things we wouldn't normally touch. We didn't want them taking any of our favorite foods. We picked safe things—we didn't want to poison them. We found them food we don't bother with. Coarse things that take a long time to chew, and things full of lots of little bones so you spend more time spitting out than taking in. They were food jokes. We watched them testing and eating all those tough and gristly things. Our little ones were laughing right in front of them, but those creatures don't recognize a laugh when they see one even though our laugh is much like theirs. They probably thought the little ones had hiccups.

So we were laughing more than ever, while they, on the other hand, forced to stay on a planet full of thorns and forced to eat all those unpleasant things, were laughing less and less.

They have ears, but not to speak of, so you can't look there for signs of rage.

Just once they ate one of us. (They felt the lack of protein.) That was not so funny. Especially to my family. I was her great uncle. She was still in her baby fat. They roasted her over a fire. They'd probably still be trying to eat our young tender ones if we hadn't ... well, shown them *exactly* how it feels. None of them is young and tender. Which one to pick was a hard choice. We wanted all their pilots and navigators saved in case we wanted them off our planet. We decided on one of the dog handlers since there are two. We didn't eat him, just left him where they'd find him, beside the path to the stream, spitted and roasted just as they had done to Jally.

But their eating Jally was partly our own fault because of the kind of food we'd shown them. After that we decided we had to let them have fish berries. Lots of protein and they slip down easily. We hated to see them eating up our supply after we'd spent so much time coaxing out the eggs but they did need better nourishment.

We noticed they took one of us, instead of one of their dogs. Even though we're, clearly, smarter than dogs. Of course the dogs are not easily replaceable, and I suppose they think we are.

Connie? Donnie? I call her Dearie. I do like her color, though she only has that little bit of it on the top of her head. She'd look a lot better if she had fur on her chin and cheeks as the males do. I can see blue veins on her forehead. Arms! Even worse. She, and all of them, are anatomy lessons for our young ones. She's my counterpart, a linguist.

We've wondered all this time how it would be to mate with them, so I'm trying to be nice and not joke too much. Since I'm the main one chosen to study them, I'm also the logical one to study their sex tactics.

If sex doesn't work out with me, there's one of them I'd like Dearie to mate with. It would be fun and funny if she did because he's the ugliest and the oldest. He's even furless on the top of his head where most of them have, at least, some fur. Since she's pretty, according to her own kind... they all say so... that would be a good joke. He's Jake. I call him Joke. He thinks I can't say it properly. He's their captain.

My chances with Dearie are pretty good because we hear them say, about us, and over and over, how beautiful we are! How graceful. How wild and natural. How good natured. (That's because we didn't want them saying, Bad dog, to *us*.)

They told us, "We can help you with your enemies," as if we still had any. What kind of a world do they think this is? I mean we have space flight. It makes us wonder about where *they* came from. What kind of a planet is that? Where were their priorities? We knew right then it wasn't *us* that wasn't civilized.

They did come with a lot of weapons. They never go anywhere without a pistol and some kind of blinding spray. And, of course, machetes to hack themselves around.

I don't know why or how they ever got started, grew up and thrived and ate and killed without good teeth. Also without fur. Makes us wonder. Without their weapons I don't think they could have survived very long on any planet.

We've been careful not to show them *our* teeth.

To test things out as to sex, I take Dearie out in the forest, just the two of us. She started out with her sketchbook, camera, and recorder. (I've got my chip. If I had to carry around all those things, I'd not be able to glide.) Even though she has a camera, she loves to draw: trees and bugs and especially us. I once asked, "Why, when also cameras?" Back on her planet, she's an artist. I was glad to hear they still practice ancient arts.

She brought her machete but she gets worn out trying to make herself a path. There's frustration in the set of her mouth. I tell her, "Sit." (That's what they always say to their dogs and to us, too.) I say, "Stay. Rest." I give her some fish berries. These are bigger and sweeter than the ones we usually let them have. Then, "Come," I say. "Do as if baby on back." (By now I let myself use over fifty words and several phrases.) She does, and I try to glide with her as we do with our little ones. That turns out to be impossible. I had no idea they were so heavy. Even though she's smaller and looks thinner than I, she must weigh four times as much. That changes my mind about a lot of things. Easier if I rode on *her* back. I can't help laughing at the thought.

She laughs, too. She understands how silly it all is. This is the first time I've laughed *with* one of them.

"You're made like a bird," she says. "Hollow bones, I'll bet." She pats my shoulder. Rubs the top of my head. I let her pat and stroke. It's what they do to their dogs but never to each other. A bad sign for my chances to check on their mating ploys because, much as they love them, they don't mate with their dogs.

I don't think she has any idea that I'm wooing her. So, all right then, maybe I'll talk up Captain Joke. We could learn things from those two. Still, having breasts that are large and furless is a nice idea and attracts us. We all.... I mean all us *males* like it. Though we haven't squeezed them yet. Not even by mistake. Too bad they cover them up with clothes. Are these creatures ever naked? We haven't seen it, so maybe not. They must bathe in their lander. Perhaps they're even as ugly to each other as they are to us. Maybe that's why they love their dogs so, because they see the beauty of fur.

I didn't even squeeze her breasts when I had the chance a few minutes ago.

Maybe next time.

I spend many an afternoon being interviewed by her. She, thinking she's teaching her language to me (I already know it) and me teaching her our pidgin. By now we've often laughed together. There's always lots to laugh about with so many language mistakes. She said the river ran, which is all right in her language, and I said, well cooked smells, which is all right in mine.

She likes me, but as what? Pretty smart pet?

I talk up Captain Joke but I don't need to. She's already in love with him. I can see why. He's a kind creature and, though he gives the orders, he does it with grace and good humor. He often looks worried, but he never gets angry.

These people have qualities worth preserving. Serious as Joke always is, he is probably worth saving. I always say, laughing isn't everything, though some of us seem to think so.

They keep saying, "What huge trees. What a dense and high canopy." And we keep saying, "There's a reason for that." We also say, "You must do something about your lander." Still they haven't done anything. They don't think we're smart enough to say anything about such things as landers.

You'd think they'd be asking about the Eye. It isn't as if we haven't taught them the words for it:" Moon of day. Eye of Night." Our anomaly.

We laugh that they don't ask, "What Eye?" And, "What Moon of Day?" And though, to us, and we're brought up that way, everything *is* a laughing matter, this is not.

Our downy underwear fur has started to grow. We puff out. Looks like their dogs are doing that, too. Just as our fur grows, little by little, the Uglies add more clothes. They've put on jackets, but I can often still see down the females' necks into the tops of their breasts.

So far they've been living in their lander. (They've piped water from the stream all the way to it). They should move it into the forest even if they have to push it. What do they think those trees are for? Instead they're building useless houses and sawing up firewood. Houses with steps up. They already have stairways everywhere, into their disabled fliers, into their disabled lander. We do see how necessary stairs are for their kind of disability.

I help build Dearie's house. I do most of the roof because I can glide, but she's up there working beside me. I'm glad to see she's not afraid of heights though some of the others are.

She may suspect we're smarter than we pretend to be. I have, on several occasions, seen what I take as admiration on her face.

Even though it's awfully hard to like the looks of hairless creatures, she's beginning to look pretty good to me: Odd and exotic, and then there's those big naked comical breasts.,,,

By now all our other males are paired off for the season. That leaves it up to me to find out about sex and breasts and let the others know.

They kiss their dogs so they do know about kissing. I'll start with a kiss. It will be strange what with their odd teeth. I wonder if I can lock on.

Dearie's new house is full of mating bugs. I hate to think of how it'll be after the eggs hatch, but now it's pleasant and musical. They sing to each other in perfect fifths and thirds so that everything vibrates in sync with their song.

We're in the almost finished house. (This will just be a test. I don't know how far I'll go.) I put my arms around her. I keep my teeth covered and kiss a slow and careful kiss. It's not the kind she kisses at her dog.

She pushes back, shocked. By her forehead I see how startled she is. But she isn't angry, just puzzled. Says, "What's this about? What does it mean?"

She checks her ear to make sure her recorder is on, then looks around for her sketchbook. It's on the table. She reaches for it but I'm still holding her.

Her dog starts barking and trying to get between us.

I can't help laughing. I laugh so much I let her go. I can't go on with it.

"You can't draw it," I say. "And it's not to be listened to either."

I wish I had started with her breasts. At least I would have seen what they were like.

It takes her a little while to think about it, and then she laughs, too. Says, "Is this another joke?"

She knows us so well she knows it could be.

"I didn't want it to be, but it got to be one."

Now she checks her ear to see that her recorder is on, but it always is. I have a feeling she's trying to avoid the whole situation. I don't think she knows what to do.

There's a gold and green beetle, big as her hand, on the wall behind her, singing. I point him out. I say, that's his love song.

She films the bug. I can see his love song doesn't have any effect on her.

I know they can love because I see how they are with their dogs, though I don't see any of that with each other. The males tap each other now and then and the females hug sometimes, but it's the dogs that get the most loving attention. And all the time, too.

Odd, Dearie is in love with Joke and yet doesn't ever show it or say anything about it. I can smell it. Perhaps it's the wrong time of year for these creatures though some of them have paired up, but if there's ever mating, it must take place in the lander.

We've always wanted bugs around us that tweet and twitter and harmonize— that glisten and glow. They're mating this time of year so their eggs will last through the Eye though they themselves won't. We respond as if they called to us, so most of us have gone into the forest by now. But I have no mate of my own. It was my choice to stay with the Uglies and keep researching though the bugs make me yearn as they do all of us.

I spend the night alone in her almost finished house listening to the bugs. I'm more comfortable in the trees, but this is a better place to hear them singing their sex songs.

We've built a work table and shelves and she's already moved the computer in. She's left all her drawings, too. I hate to think what will happen to them. If I have a chance, I will save them.

Next morning, here she is, greeting me with her happy hello and her usual eager wave. Good signs she's not bothered by what happened yesterday. Also good that she wearing long pants today. I don't have to look at naked, blue veined legs that remind us all of grubs that have not yet seen the light of day.

She comes in, hugging her sketchbook. I take it from her. I will no longer make a pretence at not speaking their language perfectly. I say, "Today let us do as the bugs tell us to do. We have been good friends. We have laughed together."

She looks at me, shocked at my sudden perfect accent, and tries to take back her sketchbook but I don't let her. I say, "This is about to be a pleasant day."

I kiss her, gently, but this time, I kiss as we do to each other, teeth to teeth. How odd she is. I hold her with one hand and with the other pull open her sweater and shirt, stop kissing and look… and there they are…in all their exaggeration.

I feel them. What a wonder!

In my attempt to kiss them, we fall, I, on top of her.

She tries to push away and yells for help, but, since she's always the first one out of the lander, there's nobody around to hear. She surrenders. Or consents? I don't know which. It's the dog that goes crazy, grabs my ankle and pulls, but I'm as if deaf to all but the bugs song. I'm humming in harmony with them and wishing she would hum, too.

When I get up, her face is blank. I wish there were more ways to read these people. With their dogs, the tail glued down tight between their legs, with us, the ears back against our head. No ambiguity possible. Now, with her, there's nothing at all.

Then she breathes as if she's been holding her breath and begins to shake. Is she, and finally, responding to the bug's song?

She tries to speak but can't. She picks up her shirt (several buttons are torn out. I hadn't realized I was so violent), pulls on her pants, and runs out. Captain Joke is coming out of the lander. She runs to him. They hug and keep hugging. Perhaps I've finally brought them together.

She sits on the ground and he kneels next to her. I see him talk and talk. I move towards them and prick my ears forward.

He's saying, "It's all right." And she's saying, "No it's not."

"It *is*. It'll be all right."

"No. It won't."

"Come on inside."

I can tell by the way she clings to him that she doesn't want to let go and it looks as if he doesn't want to either.

Though most of the others are paired off, everybody seems to avoid getting close to Captain Joke as if they think his time is too important or as if they think he needs to save all his thoughts and energy for making decisions. Now they'll pair. I can smell it from here.

He helps her up the steps into the lander, but then comes right out again. She doesn't.

He runs towards me. I don't need any big ears to read that he's going to attack me.

In spite of all their problems, I've never seen him angry until now. I think he's going to take out his pistol, but he doesn't. There's no point in trying to fight somebody four, maybe five, times my weight. We do have ways to defend ourselves, but we don't want to reveal them, and I'm curious. This will all go on to my chip.

He grabs me by the wrist and easily twirls me upside down and back again. To him I weigh nothing. I hear my shoulder pop. When he lets go, my arm hangs, useless. I know what that means. If I can't glide and grab I'll be as helpless as these creatures. I'll not even be able to save myself let alone Dearie and Captain Joke.

I'm in a lot of pain, but I say, as if *for* him. "I know. Bad dog. No, no, no! But sorry dog. Sorry dog."

I'm hanging on to my arm trying to keep it from hurting. I make excuses. "It was the bugs song." It was, but it also wasn't. (If I was with my own kind they'd be laughing at me. They'd be saying, Bad dog, no!, too.) I almost say, I'm just an animal, what do I know? But I know better than to say that though I now know I don't understand these people as well as I thought.

As if to a dog, he says, "Lie down." I wonder what other torture he has for me. But I do it. I'm resigned and perhaps I deserve whatever he'll do. But he puts his foot in my armpit, grabs my arm, twists, and pops my shoulder back into it's socket. So it wasn't broken. It doesn't completely stop hurting, but it's a lot better.

"Thank you."

"Get up."

I do, this time expecting maybe even more help, but as soon as I'm up he knocks me, with one punch, several yards away. Comes and stands over me. "Get up," he says again.

This time I know better.

But he's calming down. I can see it on his face. He's not going to hit me again.

"Don't *ever*..." he says, "*Ever*!..."

He's shaking and he's gone from red to pale, but It's over. I do get up.

I'm as wobbly as he is. And my shoulder still hurts. I don't know if I can glide or not.

I had no idea something so fun and ordinary and harmless would cause so much trouble. And even the Captain gets in a rage though he never has before. But maybe he will love her now. Unless I've spoiled her some way.

But he did tell her it would be all right.

But she didn't believe him.

He sits down, for the first time looking worn out and discouraged. I'm sorry to see it. I say so.

"Get out of here and don't come back."

Instead I sit beside him. I say, "You need to know some things and there's only a few days before it happens. I can put back...I think you call it the mag-rotor? And you must fly the lander in under the trees."

"What?"

As with Dearie, I no longer pretend I'm not fluent in their language. "I can put the mag-roter back."

This time I don't see it coming.

I try to talk as he's hitting. "The eye." I say. "You have to know...."

I roll over, my face in the fireproof earth we had prepared for them so they wouldn't set the forest on fire. But that stuff, up my nose, is worse than facing his punches.

I sit up spitting gravel.

"I fear that I'm your only hope."

He grabs me just as he did before, lifts me and twirls me and slams me down and this time does break my arm. I hear it and then see it. The bone has broken through the skin. I'm bleeding.

I'm nobody's hope anymore. Not even my own.

I don't feel the pain right away but it doesn't take long.

He sits beside me, calming down. I'm gasping and holding on to my arm. I see he's taking in what I said a moment before.

But I'm in pain. Can't he see that? I'm sure he could set and wrap my arm as well as anyone even though he's not their doctor.

He stares at me but doesn't see me or my pain. He sees nothing but his own thoughts. "So... we're at your mercy, and have been all this time. And I suppose you could have fought back just now and didn't."

I groan. If I could get back into the trees I could get something for pain.

"Donnie doesn't want to see you anymore, ever, and I don't either."

That pains me more than I thought it would. Though right now my arm hurts more. My gentle informant is more to me than just an informant.

I say, "What can I do to make it right? I will do whatever needs to be done."

Now he finally notices the blood and my broken arm.

I say, "Do you people have anything for pain?"

"Come inside the lander."

But I still sit. "There are important things you have to know. We...they, not I... were going to let you stay right here. Your lander will be tossed away. There'll be gravity and tides from the Eye. Even your mother ship could be lost if it doesn't get out of the way."

"Come on. We do have things for pain. We'll talk inside."

I've been losing blood all this time. I'm feeling faint. I get up, but the ground seems to slant sideways towards me and hits me on the head.

Somebody strokes my arm. At first I think I'm back with my mother and then I see the hand that strokes is hairless. Ugly. Blue veined. I pull away, horrified.

And then I remember.

I'm in the lander. Bandaged, sedated, Window beside me looking out at our grand great trees. I hadn't known the Uglies had such comfortable beds. They have good medical facilities. We—all of us shouldn't have looked down on them. If we wanted to laugh, it should have been a different kind of laugh.

But there's the Eye. They have to prepare. I try to jump out of bed but the person holding my hand... she's their doctor... holds me down.

"How many days have I been out? We must prepare. You have to move the lander."

She says, "You've only been unconscious for a few hours."

"Let me speak to Captain Jo...Jake."

They decide the best thing to do is to pack up and go off planet. My kind takes time off from sex and helps them pack. We fix all their little land planes and move them under the trees. Donnie and Captain Jake and three others will ride out the Eye in the canopy with scientific instruments, both ours and theirs. I'll stay with them. They've never seen a planet with such a strange eratic moon. Actually, in all our travels, neither have we.

After they study the Eye, they'll stick around a while but more as our equals though not quite. We'll let them see how we live symbiotically with the trees, but we don't trust them with our science. There's something important lacking in their cerebrum.

It looks as if my two favorite Uglies, Captain Jake and Donnie won't be getting together as I'd hoped. Though they do feel love. There's some kind of taboo going on I don't understand. And it's the same with Donnie's relationship to me. She loves me but thinks any sex between us is forbidden, just as it is with dogs. I can live with that. Except, when the bugs sing and we vibrate with what the Uglies and we also call "the music of the spheres" (strange how both languages have the same concept though they don't have bugs that harmonize), and even though they're still the least prepossessing of any aliens we've ever seen anywhere...I told Donnie to keep hold of that blinding eye spray because I can't vouch for what I'll do.

Asimov's Science Fiction Magazine, August 2010

Uncle E

I say, "We'll all go on just as usual. We'll shut the door of the bedroom and do as we've always done. Just don't tell anybody. If you tell, they'll take you away and we'll be separated to different places and won't have the house anymore. Don't worry, I'll take care of you. I can make pancakes. We can warm up TV dinners. We can order out. You guys like pizza. We can have it whenever we want. We don't need to be scared because Ralphy will guard us."

They all look scared even so.

Howard says, "But, Sarah, you're only twelve."

"I'll be thirteen next month."

"I don't like it."

"Do you think I do?"

He says, "But we have to have rules."

"*I've* got rules."

"Like what?"

"Well, first, don't answer the phone. I'll do it. I know what to say. After all, Mom was sick for a long time and everybody knows that. Nobody will wonder why she doesn't come to the phone.

They're in a row on the couch in front of me and they all look just as scared as ever. Even Elliott looks scared. I guess because we do.

Maggie says, "What if a robber comes?"

"That's what Ralphy is for."

"What if Elliott plays with matches?"

"Oh for Heaven's sake, we'll be watching him. Same as we do now."

They still look scared, but I am, too,

"What about the piano?"

"Well, what about it?"

"Who's going to make us practice?"

I don't bother answering. On purpose I sigh a big sigh. It's a real one, though. That's exactly how I feel.

I know where Mom keeps her stash of money and Howard and I both know how to get money with Mom's ATM cards. Her secret code is all our initials in birth order. I can't let Howard do it. He looks too young.

To make everybody happy, I order out for Pizza.

I don't tell anybody they have to finish their milk, but they do it anyway. It's the pizza they don't finish. Nobody is in a mood to eat.

After supper, we move our mattresses down to the living room and line them up in a row so we can all be scared together.

We have a hard time getting to sleep—except for Elliott.

Maggie says, "Mom read to us."

Howard says, "How about TV?"

Maggie says, "We're not supposed to."

So I say I'll read. They curl up on my mattress and I pick something not at all scary and with a happy ending.

But then, just when I get everybody back in their own beds and to sleep, Elliott wakes up with one of his screams. Which is exactly what we all want to do ourselves so we shouldn't be mad at him but we are.

Mom said Elliott was too little for night terrors, but he has them anyway.

After that nobody can get back to sleep.

Except Elliott.

I read to them again and that helps.

Next day I figure out a budget. I think we'll get along a lot better than Mom did. In fact I'm sure of it. We don't buy so many things. We don't even want all those things she got.

I try to balance the checkbook. Howard helps. He's really good at math. Thing is, Mom didn't do a good job of it. She was almost a whole thousand dollars off. I don't think she cared. She just left it all wrong. Howard fixed it.

It's summer and there's no school. Howard is disappointed, he always likes it, but Maggie is glad and so am I. I have a lot of work to do and I don't know how I'll cope when school starts again—except we'll get lunch.

For now, we get along just fine. In fact, better than ever. We practice the piano. (I can help some, but not like Mom did.) We drink our milk. We make our beds. Only bad thing is that Elliott screams every night. We're getting used to it, though, and mostly we get back to sleep right after. We have Elliott sleep with me and that helps a little. He always did like coming to me even better than going to Mom.

We're eating lots of pizza. Nobody likes vegetables, so we don't have those. We have lots of fruit, though. I hope that makes up for no vegetables. The house is beginning to smell funny but Howard put the hall rug up against the bottom of Mom's door and that helps.

But then along comes this great big, balding man. Walks right up to the door with two grocery bags.

We can't say he isn't dressed right, but maybe a crook would dress this way to fool us. He's wearing a good jacket and white shirt and tie. All the more reason to be suspicious. Besides, Ralphy goes absolutely crazy and he hardly ever does. If the door would open any farther he'd have been out and attacking but I had put the chain on and opened the door just a crack.

First thing the man says is, "I'm your uncle."

Another clever trick.

"Uncle who? What's your name?"

I notice he hesitates as if he doesn't know his own name. Then he says, "Oh... Um.... Well, just call me Uncle E."

Howard says, "How come suddenly we have an uncle?" And I say, "We're not going to call you anything."

I must admit, there's something familiar about him. Is he kind of like Dad? I don't think so. But we won't let him in, no matter what.

He says, "Here, at least take this milk."

Howard says, "It might be poison."

I say, "What makes you think we don't have enough milk because we do?"

The man says, "You know, things will get worse."

Things are so fine, I wonder what makes him think that.

He says, "And you have to get rid of... your mother."

We slam the door on him and then look out the window. He sits on the steps for a while. Finally he puts the two grocery bags near the door and leaves. When we're pretty sure he's *really* gone, we go out and get them, (we don't want them sittin out there) but we throw all the stuff away because of it probably being poisoned.

Howard says, "That was a tricky way to try to get in but we're too smart for him."

We have two TV sets to steal but nothing much else. One is up in Mom's room. I wonder if that man would try to climb in her window. And how come he knew about her? Can you smell it all the way down here by the door?

Maggie was practicing the piano all the time he was at the door and he seemed to be trying to talk to us and listen to her at the same time. He kept lifting his head and staring off into nowhere. She's not that good, but he smiled this funny little smile as though he really liked hearing her.

That night Elliott has the worst night terror I've ever heard him have. And he wouldn't go back to sleep. I walked him up and down for almost an hour. I started to think I was a little young to have to be looking after a toddler. Good thing there isn't any school yet.

The man comes again the very next day with a pizza, but we'd just had one so we weren't even tempted. We knew who it was before he knocked because Ralphy went crazy again. I had plenty of time to put the chain on without even looking out the window.

He had a bag of fruit, too, but Mom said people put razor blades in fruit sometimes so we weren't fooled by that.

Odd, though, he called me by my name.

That's when we slammed the door.

He's very clever.

Just like last time, Ralphy runs around in circles afterwards. He doesn't calm down for ten minutes.

For a while we watch out for the man every time we go anywhere.

I make myself a cake for my birthday and I get some balloons. I don't get myself a present though. I'm a little worried because the bank account is going down fast even though we're careful. Howard gets me a little pen and pencil set. I don't know how he got it and I don't ask. Maggie makes me a card and I put it on the refrigerator just like Mom would have done.

Pretty soon school starts and now the problem is Elliott. There's no way that I can go. Also there seems to be some sort of problem with the bank. All of a sudden our ATM cards don't work anymore. There's a CD, but we don't know how to get into it. We cut down on ordering out and TV dinners. It's cheaper for me to cook from scratch. I'm so worried, I completely forget Elliott's third birthday. Thank goodness he doesn't care and the others don't notice. I wonder if Elliott is talking as well as he should be doing but there's no way I'm going to take him to the doctor.

Things get worse and worse. I taste Ralphy's dog food. It's not as bad as you'd think and Elliott has been chewing dog biscuits whenever he managed to sneak one, anyway.

Then I have a really good idea. After Maggie and Howard go off to school... with their lunch money...that's our last, I get Elliott and take off for a completely different neighborhood. I have us both wear old clothes. I find a good corner near a bunch of stores and start to beg. I actually do get quite a bit of money. I make sure I get home before Maggie does in early afternoon, and even so I have thirty-two dollars and sixty cents.

Elliott behaves himself because I brought cookies. He even takes a nice long nap right there on the sidewalk.

I don't tell the others. Now I'm glad Elliott doesn't talk.

I decide to have pizza that night. We haven't had any for a long time. Mostly I've been cooking potatoes and oatmeal. Apples are expensive but sometimes strawberries are on sale. I wonder if a person can eat too many hotdogs. The kids do seem kind of thin. Elliott especially. He looks pale and always has dark circles around his eyes.

I'm thinking of going into Mom's room and getting that little TV set and seeing if I can sell it. There's a once a week flea market not so far away...well, actually pretty far, but I can use the wagon. Not that I want to go into Mom's room.

So I do it anyway. I put Elliott in his play pen and put a scarf around my nose. I'm thinking, thank goodness I covered her with the sheet before I shut the door. I bring the wagon up stairs. That TV set is heavy even though it's little. While there I get one of Mother's bras (I'll put Kleenex or cotton in it), two of her dresses, and a pair of her medium high heels. I've been trying to look older and these will help a lot.

When he sees that little TV set, Howard says he heard at school that there was a robber in our neighborhood doing exactly that, stealing TV sets. I tell him by Saturday it'll be gone. Besides, we have Ralphy.

I have that little TV set all ready to go in the living room right next to the big one. (Not that the big one is that big.) If I can sell the little one, I'll go sell the big one next.

But wouldn't you know...that's when a robber comes...in the living room window. He makes quite a bit of noise trying to open it. Then just breaks it with a crash. Not a very smart robber.

Right at the beginning, before he breaks the window, I creep over and wake Howard, then Maggie. But this is odd, Ralphy keeps quiet and cowers under the couch.

The robber has a flashlight. He doesn't shine it on us, thank goodness, he shines it on the TV sets and there they are practically ready to be hauled away. He goes over and lifts the big one on to the wagon beside the little one. From his silhouette in the flashlight he looks like a skinny kid, maybe not much older than I am.

It's not that we aren't ready. After all, we've been scared of just about everything this whole time. We...all at the same time...a stone, a baseball bat, and the iron frying pan....And the robber's not ready at all.

Afterwards we drag him (good he's skinny) upstairs and put him in with Mother and then we tape cardboard over the broken window. Finally we coax Ralphy to come out from under the couch. Odd, how he went crazy for half an hour when that man came to the door and then hid when the robber came.

Thank goodness Elliott slept through the whole thing and didn't scream till way after it was over.

Now that both TV sets are in the wagon, that next Saturday we all go off and sell them at the flea market, me, dressed up just like Mother. (Elliott looks at me confused the whole time.)

Anyway, now we have plenty of money for a while.

And then we don't again. I think Howard is stealing food for us, but I don't ask. They get the school lunches, I still have money for that because I'm going out begging again. Trouble is, Elliott is getting harder and harder to keep in one place and, all of a sudden, he won't take a nap. I always dress as Mother now when I go out and I keep changing the places where we go. The two others still don't know I do that. Now that Elliott is so wiggly, I hardly make twenty dollars a time. I wonder if there's a way to sell the piano. Except we don't want anybody coming in here to pick it up. It would be too bad, not having it, because, ever since Mom died, Maggie has been practicing like crazy even though she hates to. I was the one, wanted to be a musician like Mom, but I haven't had time to do any practicing at all. I've given all that up.

Then, on top of everything else, I and Elliott get the flu at the same time. (Then I'm *sure* Howard is stealing food.) And just after we get better, Maggie gets sick. Nobody feels like cleaning so the house is a mess. It smells bad for *lots* of reasons now. I haven't done the laundry for a long time, and, on top of all this, the toilet backs up.

It's Saturday, everybody is home... suddenly, Ralphy goes crazy again. There's nobody at the door at all, but he's twirling in circles, squeaking and whining. When the knock does come, maybe a whole twenty minutes later, he starts to bark. And then, for Heaven's sake, Elliott says his first word. "Him," he says. At least that's what it sounds like, and then he says it three more times, clear as could be. (Don't they say Einstein didn't talk till he was three?) Ralphy and Elliott are the only ones who seem to know what's going on, and Elliott is turning in circles and making the same squeaky noises as Ralphy did.

We look out the window and, of course, it's that same well dressed balding man, again with two bags of groceries. You can see apples and oranges sticking out the top of one. And we're even glad to see the broccoli sticking out the top of the other. Still, I set the chain. Except this time, by mistake, I open the door far enough for Ralphy to get out. I think he's going to attack the man, but he jumps up and the man kneels down and Ralphy licks his face and whines with so much joy he can't contain himself.

So we open the door and right away Elliott holds up his arms to be held and the man picks him up and Elliott starts to laugh and I realize I haven't seem him laugh for a long, long time. Or any of us for that matter. And as I see the two of them, in each other's arms, I think, maybe we do have an uncle. Exact same smile.... While Elliott is laughing, the man is, too, except he's crying at the same time, and tries to hide his face, down and in close to Elliott's.

All the rest of us are scared but, in a funny way, relieved, too. Here's food and here's a grown-up.

Howard, right away before we know anything about anything, grabs one of those apples and starts eating, as if, before it gets away, razor blades or not.

Uncle E takes off his tie and jacket and rolls back his sleeves. First thing he does is fix the toilet and then he gets the laundry started. Then he cooks us a big supper.

He calls Howard, "Little Bro."

At table he does magic tricks. Pulls quarters out of our ears and gives them to us. He even makes some of the vegetables disappear, and then he makes it so one of our glasses looks like it goes right through the table and comes out underneath. I wasn't fooled. I guessed how he did it.

Uncle E seems fascinated by all of us, but especially with Elliott.

After supper he asks me to play the piano for him, but I won't because I'm much too out of practice, so Maggie plays for him instead. Then he sits beside her and plays the same things along with her. Even though he's a grown-up, he doesn't play any better than she does.

He puts us to bed and then goes upstairs. I get up and go to the bottom of the stairs. I think to go up, too—I still feel I'm pretty much in charge and responsible—but he turns around and says, "I'll take care of Mom."

(Mom, he says.)

Then he goes into her room and I hear him lock the door.

But right after I hear him unlock it. He comes out and stares down at me. "What is this? Who?"

I say, "The robber."

Uncle E sits down on the top step and sighs a big sigh pretty much exactly like the one I've been sighing all the time these last couple of months.

I tell him all about it. He still looks upset, so I say, "And now he's not going to rob other people." I really do think it's a good thing. We all said that when it happened. "Isn't that so? Besides, he broke the window."

Uncle E doesn't look as if he agrees at all. He shakes his head as if no, no, no, and no, but he goes back into Mom's room and locks the door again and I go back to bed.

I don't know where Uncle E sleeps. Or if he does at all. I hope not in there.

That night Elliott doesn't scream.

Sunday morning Uncle E wakes us when breakfast is all ready. Waffles, eggs, bacon. He brings it on a tray to the living room where our mattresses are on the floor. He sits down with us and Elliott climbs all over him.

After breakfast Uncle E and Maggie play the piano a bit. It badly needs tuning.

Later, he tells Howard, calling him Little Bro again, "You know there's an old guitar up in the attic. You ought to see if you can find it."

"How do *you* know?"

"There's always an old guitar in everybody's attic."

Monday, after another good breakfast and after Howard and Maggie go off to school, Uncle E goes down to the phone on the corner (ours has been turned off) to hire a woman to look after us. I tell him I can do the work myself...that I want to, but he tells me, "You have to go to school. You want to be a musician like Mom was don't you? Didn't you used to practice all the time? It can't just be Maggie who gets to.... I mean...."

"Maggie! She hates to practice. She only does it now because she knows Mom wanted her to."

"But *you*...*you* have to, too. You *have* to. Promise me you will."

I say, "Maybe."

"I'll see to a piano tuner if you promise."

Uncle E puts Elliott on his shoulders and we have a long walk all around town and we have hamburgers and ice-cream. Uncle E. smiles at everything like he really loves this town. He says, "It sure has changed."

I say, "From what?" but he doesn't answer.

Tuesday Mrs. Mumson comes first thing and I'm to start off for school with Uncle E so he can make sure they get me back in properly.

After we get me all set, and before I go off to my first class, he hugs me really hard. "I have to leave now," he says. "I'd like to stay longer, but I have to go back. Mrs. Mumson will take care of you. You know you're doing her a favor, letting her help out. She needs the job. Go get that guitar and she'll show you what she can do."

I start to cry. "Don't go. Don't leave yet. *Please*."

"There are things back there that need taking care of. Two things in particular. *You* know. *You* know it all."

"Come again then. Pleeeeeese."

"It's not as easy as you think. Besides, no need."

He gives me a big sloppy kiss on my cheek. I have to wipe that off along with my tears before I can go to class. Now where... oh where, oh where, do I get that exact same kiss? And every single night?

And I do know what it's all about, but I'm not ever going to say. I wonder how he did it.

So... Wow! Elliott will turn out *just great*! Better than I ever would have thought. I was worried about him. Now I'm happy even though I'm sad. And Maggie will play the piano and I... I will, too, I guess. Not so odd, since I'm the only one around here who really, really likes to practice.

Little bro! For Heaven's sake!

And I'll bet that sloppy kiss was *another* of his jokes.

I have to stop laughing before I can go in to class.

Asimov's Science Fiction Magazine, December 2010

A Hello to Arms

Who is it doesn't love a war? Where else can we be brave and unyielding. Stand our ground. Never surrender. Show what we're made of.

I went. To prove myself to myself. To test myself in rain and cold and suffering...noise and pain. I passed every test. I couldn't have lived with myself if hadn't. Without the danger of death, all our bravery would mean nothing, so death is the most important part.

I lived. I made colonel.

I have a nice house that used to belong to another colonel who was not so lucky. He lived at the beach. Everyday I walk that beach with my dog, Bullet, and think about wars and strategies, and there always are wars to think about.

My dog looks like me: Slim, muscular, pointed nose. We make a handsome pair.

It's been several years since I retired, but I'm in as good shape as if I was still in the army. That doesn't just happen, it takes a lot of work. (The colonel who had the house before I got it, had a full gym in his basement. I have kept it as it was.)

On the beach I can't wear anything to show who I am, but I'm hoping they can see from my body and my haircut and my bearing that I'm a military man.

I often carry my swagger stick, though with only one arm I have to wedge it in my belt so as to keep my one arm free. I've never actually used the swagger stick for anything, not even back when I had two arms.

I have a prosthesis. It's not your ordinary artificial arm. With it, I would face a hundred of the enemy. I really mean that. It shoots both backwards and forwards and even up, if necessary. Your choice: Kill or stun. No need to aim. It finds the target by itself.

Except for the hand on the end, it looks like what it is — a weapon, black and silver, too many joints and swivels.... There's even a cell phone and a small screen.

I always keep it loaded and charged.

It's of no use at all for normal everyday things, in fact it's heavy and awkward and gets in the way, but I've mastered those every day things. I taught myself to tie my shoes, to break an egg, open jars.... Once you know how you can do all those things one handed. I can type with one finger faster than most can with two full hands worth of fingers.

What's left of my arm is, I suppose, ugly... especially the end where the skin is folded over. That's my only flaw. I suppose it will take a certain kind of woman to put up with it.

In it's own way, my new arm could be considered ugly, too, though to me it's beautiful. I'm proud of it as a fine piece of machinery. Only the hand looks pale and soft.

I'm still practicing on the things it can do. Just like a computer, there's parts I haven't begun to learn yet.

Should I ever find a wife worthy of me, I would not tell her what that arm can do.

I don't ever talk about my skills or my exploits. I would never stoop to boasting. Nobody knows what I've done except those I rescued.

When I find a wife, I will tell my wife I have rescued many.

I have killed. I've heard it said, that we all need forgiveness. I wouldn't take forgiveness if you offered it.

I will tell my wife that I have killed.

First I was too busy at wars for marriage. After that, it took me some time to come to terms with the loss of my arm. I went through a period of... you could call it mourning... but I brought myself out of it by myself. Not many people could have done that all on their own.

As to marriage, I'm convinced I have enough other assets to make up for my lost arm. Who wouldn't want to marry me with my beach house, my sunsets, my telescope, my spectacular starry sky, and, of course, my dark good looks.

I will make a study of women. I will go where women go though at present I don't know where that is. Should I refuse to talk about trivialities even to woo some woman or other?

As always, I want to do this by myself. I'm not privy to anything that has to do with women, but it's a known fact that women are more eager to marry than men. It shouldn't be hard to find a willing prospect.

Lately, instead of afternoons basking on my deck, I've taken to carrying a thermos of my spinach and brewers yeast drink down to the beach. I pick a book (at present War and Peace), that might impress the kind of woman I want to attract. I lay out a blanket and sit my dog beside me. I'd rather be on my deck above the ordinary people, but I won't make any contacts that way, and some, particularly the runners, might be of my class and persuasion. Bullet will help me see what they're like. It takes courage to face a dog like mine. Also it takes courage to face a man like me.

The woman must love wars as I do because, had we any sons, I will send my sons to war. I'll need a much younger woman to be sure to have some.

I know these days women can go to war, but I think they should know their place and stay in it.

Mother knew her place. She had many talents but she devoted herself to me. That's why I turned out so well. She was a handsome woman: Tall and dark, broad shoulders, slim waist.... Much like me.

She was not a warm person, but that made me strong.

My woman must be like her — not have any job other than to look after my sons and yet she must not coddle them.

She will know how it feels to be in the arms of a powerful man. But how would it feel to be in just one powerful arm? I believe my one arm is powerful enough for two.

My father wasn't around enough to have much influence in my life. (He was an army man, also. War was his job as it was mine.) It was my mother made me into the man I am today. She never praised. She had a frown that spoke more clearly than any words or shouting could.

Just as Mother did, I make known how I feel about things by my expression. I don't need to jabber away or curse. I never use bad language. There are stronger ways. I don't ever lose my temper.

While I'm half naked out on my blanket with Bullet by my side, checking the women on the beach....

(And I do see several of interest. I've noticed them before. The ones I like are all slim and have long black hair and they run).

Someone breaks into my house and the gun room and steals all the guns. They didn't steal the arm. That, I keep handy by the doorway, hidden behind the curtains of my picture window. I'm a tall man and I can get it with one leap.

I don't call the police. I attach my prosthesis and take the law into my own hands...hand. I'm better at detective work than anyone else, and I want the robber punished right away, not rotting in our sloppy justice system. I know ways of torturing (by pressing on nerves), that don't leave a mark.

I wear a normal business suit, not my uniform. I don't want to attract attention.

The arm has a GPS. I'm able to home in on my father's pistol. It's my only memento of him, so I have a tracer on it.

I start out in my Hummer (I have one of those nobs on the steering wheel so I can make turns as fast as anybody). When I hit bad traffic I park, attach the arm, get out and start running.

But I'm so lopsided I get a sore back in ten minutes. I've born pain before. I know how.

I've done weight lifting every day, but I'm not strong enough to wear this arm for such a long time. Though I hate informality I take off my suit jacket along with the arm. I pull the arm farther up in the sleeve, hiding the wires and silvery pads on one end and the pink fat hand on the other, and put the whole bundle over my shoulder.

If something happens, I hope I'll have time to reattach it properly. I can only shoot when it's attached to my muscles.

I step out briskly, but I soon I have to slow down. The arm is just too heavy and awkward. I pass a small park and pick a bench on the far side where there are no people. I don't want to have to listen to the ignorant notions of run-of-the-mill-people who have never been soldiers. Or even if they have never gone to any actual war.

I put down the arm, lean back and catch my breath. I feel as if I've marched all day. Perhaps the arm weighs even more than those sixty pound packs we used to run with. I hate to think it might be my age. I consider myself still young. At least for a person in as good shape as I am. Or so I thought until right now. But I will not give in, even or especially, to age.

A woman invades my bench and sits down beside me. She has one of those useless little dogs. If I'd brought Bullet with me she'd not have dared come this close. I thought Bullet should stay and guard the house. I wouldn't want my medals taken.

She looks commonplace. A bit plump — as is her little dog. Neither of them can be getting enough exercise and I'm sure they aren't eating properly. She looks to be about my age, certainly well beyond childbearing years.

My arm is completely covered with my jacket, but right away, and even though I had turned my back on her in order to discourage conversation, she says, "That looks just like a weapon. I'd guess an AK47. Anyway, some sort of rifle."

For a minute I prickle all over, but I calm myself. I stare an offended stare such as Mother did so well, and show her the side of my bundle with the fat pink hand.

"Surely, Madam, you noticed my lack of an arm. The prosthesis gets uncomfortable if I wear it for any length of time."

It's the dog, doesn't like that hand. Without even a warning growl, he…she? lunges. Before I can stop him, he tears a large junk of the pink covering, revealing what looks like a small silver pistol right where the first finger should be. I've never seen the inside of the hand and I don't think that's a pistol but it sure looks like it. That could be the heat sensor but I haven't yet learned how to use it.

I give the dog a good kick, knock it several yards away. A considered action, not in anger. I never get angry.

"Control your animal, Madam."

I cover the hand, but not fast enough. She says, "It *is* a weapon."

Though the little beast isn't hurt at all and comes squealing back, the woman attacks me.

I act defensively. I'm not going to stoop to fighting with a dumpy woman half my size. I keep her at bay with a knee and my one arm.

She soon stops. She sees it's useless. She hasn't gotten near me, says, "You can't go around kicking dogs. I should call the cops. I'm sure it's a crime of some sort."

I say, "There's also laws about destroying people's property."

But as we struggled, the whole arm fell off the bench and revealed itself as a contraption with two elbows, a telescopic sight, a mirror.... There's only one black nozzel that is clearly the barrel of a rifle. The other guns are smaller and not recognizable to a lay person.

I see her face change as she looks at the arm and then at me.

I cover it up as fast as I can.

"I wasn't going off to shoot people. I was robbed of several other weapons. I'm taking the law into my own hands."

"Why do you have such a weapon in the first place?"

I think to lie. Then I think the truth is fine. I have made myself exactly what I want to be.

"I'm a colonel. Retired because of the loss of my arm. But not completely retired. I patrol a particularly dangerous area of the coast. I need this arm for my work."

It's not a lie. I always keep an eye out for any suspicious activity wherever I am.

Meanwhile that little dog won't stop barking. I'm actually in danger of losing my cool. I will kick it again if it gets close enough. I don't think pets should be this small.

"Why don't you and your nasty little dog leave?"

"I'm not going to let you wander around town with that weapon. You said you took the law into your own hands, well, so am I. I'm sticking with you."

"Can't you stop that barking?"

"That's because of *you*. Fluffy hardly ever does that."

Fluffy!

Calmly, I take a reading from the arm for the direction to proceed, wrap it back up, and put it over my shoulder. Off we go, that little creature yapping at my heels. What with that racket, my sore back, and being followed by a dumpy lady, I doubt if I'll be able to keep my temper much longer.

Finally Fluffy does stop barking, and lags behind. The woman picks her up and keeps following.

I feel the need to rest again, but I'm not going to. Instead, I speed up.

But I stumble and collapse. She's right behind me, drops the dog, and tries to catch me as I go down.

Thank goodness we're outside of town by now and there's nobody around to see.

"Let me help you carry this for a while. It's heavy."

What is she thinking!

"Out of the question!"

I'm upset with myself. I've never collapsed before.

We're at a beach now, but it's nothing like my beach: Warehouses, docks, rusty ships.... Looks abandoned. Exactly the kind of place you'd expect to find stolen weapons, ready to be shipped off to the wrong side of some war.

I sit up, uncomfortable that she has seen me in such a state as this, but I remain calm and take another reading from the GPS. We're close. At least to my father's pistol. It's time to put the arm on.

After I attach it, I need her help getting up. My legs feel trembly and I list to the left even more than I did before.

I also have to let her help me walk, though I hate being this close...to anybody, and she smells of some kind of perfume that makes my nose itch.

I follow the arm's directions and enter a warehouse.

It's dark and gloomy. I have to admit the woman has courage. Thank goodness the little dog is frightened and keeps quiet.

My father's pistol is on an upper floor. In the thumb of the pink hand there's a tiny light. I click it on and look for a staircase.

I never watch TV and I don't go to the movies, even so I recognize the drama of the echoing sound of every step, the amplification of our whispers, the steep staircase, and then a locked office door with a glass window and the light on inside and the sound of voices.

I could use the cell phone and call for back-up right now, but I want to do this myself.

It's then the little dog goes crazy. She starts yapping right outside that door. Nothing for it but to break the glass and go in right away.

I don't have to say a word to that woman. She's right with me. Actually ahead of me, helping to prop up that arm. She's anticipating my every move. A perfectly ordinary person and yet, I have to admit, not without courage and know-how.

It's not till afterwards that I use the arm's phone to call the police.

Even that yapping little dog helped with a bite or two and added to the confusion and the noise. I did shoot, twice, but I was too shaky even with Mary Ellen steadying it. It was the arm that homed in on them and sent off two shots in quick succession. I didn't realize it, but I had the arm on the stun setting.

It had more of a kick than I remembered. It knocked both me and Mary Ellen over backwards. She landed on top of me. We were both embarrassed. For a while we couldn't look at each other. I've seldom been that close to anybody, let alone a small chubby woman. So soft. By mistake I touched her breast.

Mary Ellen, convinced me not to torture the men. I explained to her that, not only did they deserve it, but I could do it without leaving a single mark, still she didn't want me to. She said she would walk away right then if I insisted on doing that. I could have gotten along without her, even so, I decided not to torture.

Mary Ellen is impressed by the deference of the cops. They drove us back to my Hummer. They know all about me and the arm is registered with them.

I invite her to my beach house where I'm going to cook her a fancy meal of quail and quail eggs. I expect she'll admire me even more when she sees all I can do with just one hand.

I was a little worried, bringing her and that little dog in, but Bullet takes to Fluffy right away and vice versa. It's love at first sight — fuzzy little white dog and sleek big black one.

After showing her around my place, I show her my uniform and my medals. I see admiration in her eyes. She strokes my hash marks, and looks up into my face. I had not noticed until then how blue her eyes are.

We sit on my deck sipping my spinach and brewers yeast drink. She's impressed, by my knowledge of nutrition. Also by my house, my beach, my telescope.... I know that, later, she'll be impressed by my starry sky.

But though she does like uniforms, I don't think she cares that much about wars. I suspect that I might as well be in the Salvation Army or the Marine band. Even so, I decide to do whatever Mary Ellen wants me to. And whatever Bullet wants. I'll even do what Fluffy wants.

In the Time of War and Other Stories of Conflict/Master of the Road to Nowhere and Other Tales of the Fantastic, 2011

Mountain Song

For the present, the only duty is to the road and after that, the path. There's the comfort of the trail. There's the rhythm of my steps. There's the sound, pad, pad, pad. The feel of muscles that can go on and on.

Some say each step is a prayer. Some say each step is a song.

And I do sing: "To Sky Waters, to the Bear Skin, and to Thunder Bay I'll go. . . ." It has a lilt that matches my steps when the trail is smooth. If I should limp, I'll have to sing a different song. When the ground is steep and rough, no song at all but the sound of my breathing.

As John Muir did, I sleep as I am, no tent, no sleeping bag, cuddled against a fallen tree. Like him, I bring nothing but tea and bread I've made myself. I've read that he said the outdoors was the indoors to him. It is so for me also. I never feel comfortable in houses. I need the sky as my roof.

I don't bring a weapon. I am the weapon. But I'm not a cyborg. All my parts are normal human parts. I've built myself up. Even to my crushing iron grip. This way there's nothing to trace. And even I can be easily disposed of.

There are rules of conduct for men like me. I'm careful to observe them.

They always send me off alone. I don't need help nor do I want it. Help would just get in the way. Would I sing and shout with someone else here? Working alone and with only myself as the weapon is safer both for me and for those who hire me.

By now I've climbed up to the land of rocks. I walk the treeless paths. I teeter on the boulders. Sometimes there are dwarf versions of flowers that grow large below. Here they are small and hug the ground.

I have a purpose, though I would like to be traveling here even if there was no reason for it. I didn't have to come this way, climbing across the mountains. I could have driven through the valleys, but I like to think the mountains are my duty. I don't want to think of what I'm sent to do. When I dip down into the trees again, there'll be plenty of time to be thinking of my task.

Who would think the war would come up here? And yet it does. So they say, anyway. The lost and battle shocked men from other older wars...from who knows how far back? It's said they've forgotten how to talk and are wild and dangerous. They drag their rifles with them though they have no bullets. It's said they live behind walls which they build higher every day.

If they really are here, they're here for the same reason I am: For all this spectacular emptiness.

They'll murder me if they can, but it's no different from what I've promised to do to my "mark." They are more like me than any others that I know of.

When I'm not on my way to a killing, I consider myself a naturalist—as was John Muir. Just as he did, I carry a notebook and a little botany press for pressing leaves and flowers. I've heard he talked baby talk to flowers. I haven't done that— yet.

I'm not sure I ever want to meet up with those old soldiers, but if there are people versions of these tiny flowers and these wind blown trees up here, I would like to find them. The hardships of the mountain would have stunted them but made them tough. I would like to be the naturalist of these people as well as of the plants.

Once I woke up to a wrinkled face with squinty eyes peering down at me. The creature hopped away, spry as could be on the riprap. He didn't look like an old soldier.

I've seen no signs of any odd people up here other then this (perhaps imaginary) view.

No, there was (maybe) one other. Out from a deeply shaded crevasse, something round faced stared at me with wondering eyes, but only for a moment. Could have been an animal, but I took it for a person.

What did John Muir know and see and never speak of? He did say there were dozens more Half Domes scattered about the mountains. I haven't come across more than three. Had there been any mountain people here, he would have known. I wonder why he never said.

But if old soldiers hide out up here, they deserve their privacy. And someday I may need to hide in these hills myself. Whatever I find here, like John Muir, I will not tell about it.

Cross scree and talus. Down the other side. Pass the bristle cones and on into the pinyon, and then lower to the sage. The horned toad sits still as I pass. I pick her up. I put her down in a more sheltered spot. I may not talk baby talk to flowers, but I talk to the lizard. I tell her to stay where I put her so she won't get hurt. Then I come on down to the real world, first the suburbs, then the city. From now on my duty is to the killing.

I don't see my "mark," nor do I want to, until just before I kill him. I don't want to know who he is. I don't want to know the reason for his death. I'm paid to not know. None of that is my job. But as I get closer, I walk much slower than before. My step has lost it's rhythm. I don't sing.

I wait till dark. I change my clothes in a park and leave them under a bush along with my botany press. I put on cat burglar black. I bring my backpack. It has my tools.

I find the building. Thank God it's not all glass. The whole façade is Greek Revival: pillars, pilasters, egg and dart... I'd hardly need grapples but I use them. The information has been correct. It always is. I can count on my superiors. They said, fourth floor, corner window. They even told me what time of night would be best.

I come down from the roof on to the balcony, and in the floor to ceiling casement window, step on soft thick carpet....

The "mark" doesn't feel right. Softer. Weaker. There's all this hair. And breasts against my chest. My fingers are already around her neck. My thumb on her heart beat.

Still choking her, with my other hand I pinch my thumb light and shine it in her face. We see each other, eye to eye. Hers are as dark as my own.

I have never killed a woman before. This isn't what I trained for. No one told me it would be different this time. Are they testing me? Pushing me farther on purpose? To ready me for an even worse job? I suddenly realize I want to quit this work. But if I try to quit, whether I kill now or not I'll be a "marked" man myself. I'll have to retire to the mountains to hide. But isn't that what I've wished for?

I'm inches from her face. Her eyes show fear.

"No," I whisper. "No, no, no."

I loosen my grip. I lean and slowly kiss... instead of kill.

She wants to yell, but my mouth stops her. She tries to knee me. She tries to grab my hair, but I don't have any...exactly for this reason. Grabs my ear. Tough lady.

Then...twist away, leap out, climb to my grapple, back on down and running. Hearing her shouts. And almost right away, those of others.

Now I've done it.

They can't tolerate this, and they'll know all about it before I reach the suburbs. I'll be in trouble with somebody exactly like me who will not stop until he kills me. Another "weapon" with a choking grip. I will meet my match. He'll come in the middle of the night. He'll take his time, as I did. What's the hurry? He'll enjoy being away from the cities. Perhaps he likes the mountains as much as I do. Or if he hasn't learned to like them yet, he will like them after chasing after me. And I, in spite of being chased, I will enjoy them now...again.

I don't stop to get my clothes. Back, fast this time. And I am fast. I can run straight up and not tire. But they will have another man who can do the same.

So it's hurry on up to the old soldiers' hide out. Though most likely that's an old wive's tale told by mothers who want to imagine their missing-in-action sons (and these days daughters, too) are still alive somewhere on this earth.

Maybe I kept thinking about those stories because I knew some day I'd have hide up there and I didn't want to be alone for the rest of my life. If there's any of it left.

And I want to count myself among those old soldiers. Isn't my life like theirs? Having, up till now, done nothing but my duty? Am I not an old soldier myself?

That woman… I have no idea who she is. Beautiful and tough. Silk sheets. Carpets to sink into. What has she done to deserve her murder? Does she know too much? Or was it to get even with some important man? I have never questioned. I killed as soldiers kill. Not wondering who would die because of me.

This is not the way I came. I must strike out into land I've never seen before. Though all this land, even if unknown, is known: Always first desert, then alpine, then stunted, then rocks.

Just because I'm one of the about-to-be-dead, (as who isn't?) doesn't mean I'm not happy. When I leave the suburbs and reach the foothills, I stride, I sing—my same stepping-out song. Is there really a "Sky waters?" Where does this song come from, anyway? For sure Sky Waters is up high. The water will be icy.

How do those old soldiers live up here? *If* here? Pine needle tea? Grilled marmot? And what about their clothes? Except for veterans of the most recent wars, surely their uniforms will have rotted away.

As it's turning dark, I find a mossy knob to lie on not far from the trail.

I'd like, again, to open my eyes and see a wrinkled face looking down at me. I hope I'd have the presence of mind to smile, though I'd probably have him dead before I completely woke up.

The next afternoon, as I round the corner of the cliffs (still going up), suddenly there's a high meadow full of tiny blue flowers with hundreds…no, millions of little blue butterflies flying around them, and beyond that, all spread out before me, a panorama of snowy peaks. Without meaning to, I shout with joy… then stand still and silent, admiring.

Then I'm hit. A six inch dart into my thigh. It knocks me down.

This can't be from that man, all in black, who's been sent to kill me. He will have (as I do), nothing but his hands, and he will not approach me until he's sure that he can kill me quickly. Perhaps I've found…no, they've found me… the ones who live up here.

If that was to kill, it was not a good shot. Will he try again? Nothing I can do about it. But if I had picked out my first choice of where to die, I couldn't have picked a more beautiful.

From the angle of entry, the dart came from the cliffs behind me. It doesn't hurt yet but it will. As long as I leave it in, there'll be no blood.

Should I limp into the field of flowers? Dead or alive, what an ugly black lump I'll make out there in all that beauty.

I turn my back to the cliffs and start to cross the meadow. No way except to step on flowers and scare up clouds of butterflies. I don't step out as I usually do, not only because of my wounded leg but also because I'm trying to save the blossoms as best I can.

I wait for the next dart. Back of neck would be the best spot. But how far will those darts go?

I limp on. When I get back down to trees, *if* I get that far, I'll find myself a cane. If the dart is some sort of pine, it may be a disinfectant in itself.

I'm far enough away from the cliff now so that if he wants me, he'll have to come get me. That is, if he's still trying to use darts. Does he know I have no weapon but myself?

They come. Two. They're like the one I saw that time long ago when I woke to a wrinkled face hardly six inches from my own.

Both are hunched over, lopsided, reddened and dried by the high altitude sun. Their eyes are odd. Very pale. They limp as much as I do. Their clothes are just what you'd expect from people living up here and never going down to civilization: a series of small-animal patches. They wear wide brimmed home-made hats made of scraps of leather and pine twigs. They wear inch thick vests of rolled up skins, sewn together as the Paiute used to do.

Easy to see they're afraid of me, but they swagger out as if they're not, and stop—not too close. One has his knife ready and the other stands behind him with the cross bow.

I wonder if it's my cat burglar outfit that scares them. I wish I'd had time to pick up my clothes so as to be in the tawny colors these two are wearing.

They talk but I can't understand. It's English but it's odd and their voices are rough and raspy and would be hard to understand no matter what language.

I say, "I don't understand."

Again and with gestures.

I shake my head.

They retreat towards the cliff, motioning me to follow.

Will they shoot me if I don't? Or even if I do?

It's a place to go.

I'll go.

They talk to each other as we head back but it's all mush to me.

I had evidently walked right through the center of their village without knowing it. Makes me wonder about myself. I'm supposed to be trained to notice things, but I didn't. I was only paying attention to my song. To my muscles pumping. Getting high on my moving body as if on some happy drug.

Right here, on both sides of the trail, a camouflaged village. But even knowing it's here, I can't see it. A couple of piles of brush. A fire pit that could have been left by hikers. Women come and I see a child. Everybody looks old, even the child. These don't look like crazy old soldiers. They look like stunted versions of us.

Only the men come close. Eight of them. Five women hang back and watch. I don't try to escape. I'm perfectly happy to see what they'll do to me. Maybe they'll feed me. That would be nice and I'd like to see what they eat. Most likely they know many more edible plants than I do.

Everybody squats down. One of the men opens my pack. He gives my knife to the oldest man. Is he the chief? They give and my little thumb light to the child. (It looks as if he's the only child here. Could that be?) My collapsible grapple goes to another man. He cuts the rope attached to it in to clothes line lengths and passes them out to the women.

Then one of the women pulls out the dart, puts pine sap on the wound and bandages it up. I had to take off my pants. I was glad she gave them back. I was afraid she'd cut them shorter and give them to one of the men.

There's a little jail for me. Part living pine trees. There's a roof and a windbreak. They both look like a pile of brush. I could get out, but I'm content to stay. They do feed me. I have no idea what. Little flakes of meat…(if lizard, I hope that was a normal lizard and not a friendly horned toad)…some green stuff, and a piece of root of some sort. They don't give me much. Since they're all smaller than I am, I suppose they think this is plenty.

The woman who brings the food is petrified of me. Slams it in and runs. I know I'm scary. Especially compared to them. They're stocky lumpy people. I am smooth and slim. Clean shaven while their men are bearded though mine will be growing out—they took my razor. I'm not particularly tall, but I'm tall compared to them and I stand up straight.

Later the woman comes back with a sleeping pad. Nice of them but I'm not used to such comfort. I say, Thank you, but that only scares her more. She runs off all the faster.

What will they do with the man…the one exactly like me…who will come to kill me? To them we will look like brothers. And in many ways we are.

I must not let myself sleep too soundly. I don't use the mat. In fact I make a point of sleeping on stones and sticks. Being uncomfortable will help me stay wakeful.

I think about that woman…the one I was supposed to kill. Her breasts were soft against my chest but her lips were tense and hard. She wanted to bite me.

In the morning that same frightened woman comes with couple of inches of gruel in a wooden bowl.

I say, "Wait. Please."

But she doesn't.

"Wait, I just want to know, where is Sky Waters?"

She stops, but doesn't turn around.

"Is there a Sky Waters?"

I don't know if she understands me or not but she stands still. Then she turns and frowns, shouts, "No." Then, rolling her R, "No Sky Wat-err." Then runs off, even more frightened than before.

Though my little jail is set apart from where they live, if I stand up I can see that little trail that goes through the center of the village. They're taking down skin roofs. Maybe they live as John Muir did, with more or less no shelter, just these little windbreaks they can bring out when the weather is at it's worst. Maybe they move to a new place every few nights.

I spend the morning working on keeping my muscles built up, one at a time. Some of the people watch me. They hide, but I know they're there. I suppose they've never seen such odd behavior. The child is there. He doesn't hide. He's not afraid of me. Now and then I smile at him and he smiles back. When he moves closer, one of the grown ups comes, slaps him, and pulls him away.

I'm sorry for that child. I wonder if he'd stand up straight and be a normal size if he lived below. Maybe had more food.

He comes close again and starts imitating my exercises. We laugh. We know how funny we look.

I say, "Hello."

He says "Lo," and comes even closer. I look right into those odd, pale eyes. Everybody else ducks away and won't look straight at me.

"What's your name?"

"Mi nam? Tuesdee."

Is he really Tuesday? Do they bother with days of the week up here?

We compare forearm muscles. I show him the exercise for that specific muscle.

Then that woman comes again, slaps him so hard she knocks him down, then pulls him away. She's jabbering at him so fast I only catch a word or two. No doubt she's saying, "It's for your own good."

Lunch is more or less what supper was. Or maybe this *is* supper. It's late. I think the green stuff is Miner's lettuce and the root, Solomon Seal. This time the meat is crawdad. I've often eaten those myself. Delicious, but there's only two bites of it. If this goes on much longer I'll have to escape to find something more to eat. I'll be too hungry to sleep, but that might be a good thing.

I don't think they have anybody guarding me. I'll pull away that brush roof and climb out of here tonight.

There's a pretty good moon. I climb one of those trees that form part of my jail, climb down a different one and am out.

I have nothing to carry and I'm not slowed much by my limp. My wound under their care is healing fast. I hurry along the trail that is their main street. This time I notice them cuddled up together in clumps of four or five. Some next to brush or next to a stretched skin. No wonder I missed their village. Basically there's nothing there.

It takes an hour to cross the meadow of flowers by moonlight. At the other side I climb. When I find a stream I follow it up. Along the way I find a stout stick for a cane. When the moon sets and it's too dark to climb, I leave the stream and find a place to lie down. It's slanted and rocky but I fall asleep instantly, and even though I'm cold.

Something curls up against my back as I sleep. Something small and animal. I lie still. I feel its breath on my neck. I feel its comforting warmth. Is this how the one in black has come to kill me? Am I to sleep with my murderer? Yet he's so thin and boney.

For a moment I imagine it's that woman. The beautiful woman herself has been sent to avenge my not having killed her.

I keep my breathing even and slow. I keep one hand protecting my throat, the other ready to reach behind me. I wait for his attack. I actually do doze a bit in that position. It's the warmth that soothes me.

When light begins to come, I turn and grab the other's throat before he can grab mine.

But it's that boy, Tuesdee. Thank goodness I didn't grab to kill. I think I must have still thought it might possibly be that woman.

Since he's the only child there, I know he must be of great value to them. They'll be after him already, and our trail through the flowers will be easy to follow. I saw how they were on the rocks…like mountain goats. And those eyes….

"You can see in the dark can't you? When it's night you see, right? That's how you got here in the dark."

"No go ome. Beg it. Please. No ome. I go wit you."

What to do with him? If I try to send him home he'll probably follow me anyway.

Judging the age of such a stunted child is impossible.

"How old are you, anyway?"

"Umm. Waaa."

"Do you know? Eight? Nine?"

"Mayhap twel.

(Oh yeah.)

"Any brothers and sisters?"

"Ummm. Uh. Waaa…."

"Are you hungry?"

Silly question.

He's wearing one of those odd thick vests they all wear and he's brought one for me. Nothing I could have wished for more. I put it on and we go looking for food. He has a funny little net in his pocket. He's nimble…as they all are…hops about the rocks in the stream. Graceful for such a lumpy boy.

We get a couple of fish, build a tiny fire and cook and eat them. Looks as if Tuesdee finally gets plenty to eat. He leans back, smiling, and falls asleep. Not a wonder since he must have walked all night the night before.

I sit by the stamped out campfire and hum one of my walking songs.

I don't know if I should worry about his people coming after us or not.

Will they think I kidnapped him? I can just see a dozen darts sticking out all over me. But right now we look like a couple of friends. And they're probably here already. He would know, but I wouldn't.

And that other man, my counterpart? Will Tuesdee also know before I do, that my killer is here? Will he know enough to warn me or will he, as would be logical, take him as my brother? I hope nothing happens in front of Tuesdee.

We climb all the rest of the morning. Every now and then Tuesdee stops and gathers lichen or some green leafy stuff that hugs the rocks and we chew on those. I teach Tuesdee some of my songs.

After a few hours of climbing, Tuesdee says. "They here. Mi da et mi oh da."

"How many?"

"Fowe."

That evening Tuesdee catches several large lizards in his little net, one at a time. He yanks off the tail of each one and then lets them go free to grow another. A compassionate way of eating. It takes a lot of tails to make a decent meal.

He sleeps as he did before, cuddling against my back. And I know his kind are there watching over him. I feel safe...or safer than I have in a long time

But they won't save me. I can imagine an iron grip on my throat and Tuesdee waking up hugging a dead man. It would have happened so silently he'd not know till morning. No, I'd have had my death throes. Should I let him sleep so close?

Next afternoon we come upon a lake. Icy cold. I no longer have any soap, but we find soap root. First we eat some of it and then we strip and wash—with the root as both wash cloth and soap. But we have to put back the same dirty clothes. I'm beginning to stink. My killer will be able to find me by my smell.

I sit on the bank and watch Tuesdee cavort in and out of the icy water. Sure footed. Graceful in his way. I take back about feeling sorry for him not reaching his full height. He's exactly as he should be. I had to learn to see it.

He's smiling all the time now. We don't talk much...or he doesn't, but he's clever and cheerful, and knowledgeable when it comes to his own world. He deserves more. So what am I doing here, wandering around, deeper and deeper into the mountains? Am I looking for the crazy old soldiers? Am I looking for Sky Waters? This little lake could just as well be it as any other. I could be showing Tuesdee some of the world. Besides, he's turned blue with cold. I've got to get him out and dressed though he looks as if he won't want to come.

I yell for him to get out.

He doesn't. Of course.

"Hey," I say. "Let's go. I'm going to take you to the city."

He yells back, "OK, let's go."

He's picking up everything I say.

I'm stepping out...happy. I sing all the louder. So does Tuesday. "To Sky

Waters, to the Bear Skin, and to Thunder Bay we'll go...."

We don't stop for any snacking.

It isn't that I want to stay down there. I want to do something for Tuesdee and I want to see that woman. Just one more time. Talk to her before I come up here forever. I've she's "marked" as I am, living up here may be her only hope.

I have money hidden there. Actually I'm a wealthy man though I don't use banks or credit cards. I'm always paid in cash.

I'll get Tuesdee some decent clothes. Maybe a wide-brimmed hat to hide his face some. Comb his hair over his lumpy forehead. Also try to cover up his big ears. I'll say he's my son and he has problems. Is anybody down there called Tuesday?

Turning back will be a good way to confuse the man who's after me. What if I draw him back to that very woman? He'll not dare stop me in case I'm there to do my duty this time. Will I drop down to the seventh floor window. Would I ask, "Who are you? I want to know your name."

But that woman won't ever sleep in that room again. For sure not even stay in that building. And certainly not so soon after I attacked her.

I don't need to tell Tuesdee to hurry, he's always much faster than I am.

I usually feel sad about leaving the mountains but not this time. I won't stay down there long, I've finished with those jobs. And then there's that woman....

That night we go on in the moonlight, and when the moon sets, Tuesdee leads me.

Towards morning Tuesdee says, "They gone—Da et Oh Da. All them."

Are we getting so close to civilization that they feel they might reveal themselves and their kind? They probably don't know how to hide or to live down here. I'll bet they've never even come *this* far. But they're letting Tuesdee keep on. They must trust me to keep him safe.

I'll bring him into town at night. I wonder if we should come wearing these odd vests.

On the way in I get some of my hidden money. This batch is buried at the base of a fence post. I make Tuesdee pay attention and count fence posts with me. I make sure he sees there's more money left there.

"For you and your ma and da and oh da. For all of them."

"OK."

If he doesn't know what money is for, he soon will.

We stay on the back roads, come in to the poorer part of town, and shop for clothes at one of the second hand stores. I want us to stay more of less out of sight until we're dressed a little more like everybody else. I get us each a knapsack first. I see to it that we pick out everything tan and brown and green. Tuesdee behaves with a watchful dignity through all this, except he goes crazy for a bright red sweater. I'll bet he's never seen such a bright red except on berries and flowers and in the sunrise, and I'm guessing they don't have knitting because Tuesdee keeps feeling the material. Even so he won't not wear his vest over it. "Ma made 'em." he says. I say, "OK, and I'll wear mine, too."

I go to the most recent pickup site (a post office box) and leave a note.

If the job is not already done I will do it.

I don't know if this will get me to the woman. Nor do I know if it will get *my* killer off my back. In fact it's a good way for them to catch me without having to bother chasing after me. Wherever they tell me to go, I'll be there.

But I have the beginnings of a beard now and my hair is growing out a bit. I'm wearing loose old clothes. I'm accompanied by a child. But I don't suppose I can hope that they don't know who I am.

I take Tuesdee to McDonalds and get him a happy meal with a toy. He likes the little car, he nibbles at the meat, but he won't drink milk.

We go to the place where I hid my clothes and the botany press back when I didn't do my job. They're gone. I'm not surprised. I'd buy a new press but I may not have the opportunity to collect anything and to ever bring it back to the museum.

I discover Tuesday can't read, so I start him on that with street signs: WALK and DON'T WALK, STOP, FOR SALE. Now, instead of Sky Waters, we sing the alphabet song as we walk and I point out letters. What a bright child he is.

There's a series of empty houses and offices I rotate in and out of when I need to stay in the city. I go to one now, but someone else has spent the night there. I don't know how I know, but I do. The person has cleaned up. Maybe it's the smell. I decide we'll sleep in a park. It'll be more like what Tuesdee is used to anyway.

(This odd "son" might make my getting to know that woman all the harder. I've grown to like him but I sometimes I wish he hadn't latched on to me. Though would I have come back here for the woman if I hadn't thought to show him the city? But will I ever be able to sleep without him clinging to me?)

I feel safe and sleep well because I don't think they'll come after me tonight. I think they have me exactly where they want me.

In the morning I find a reply in the PO box. As usual there's just an address and a time frame. It could mean either: Come here to kill or come here to be killed.

I do the usual: memorize the address and chew up the note.

I'm going to stroll around that area. Scope it out. Even thinking that I might be near her makes me feel shaky.

As we near that address, I stare at every slim and handsome dark haired woman that passes us. I know I'm being rude and obvious. This isn't a good way if I don't want to be noticed. In these "new" old clothes and my new scraggly beard, I'm not a very prepossessing man. Someone like me staring at women.... I could get in trouble.

There's a block of fancy stores and there are benches along the street. I sit there so I can watch less obviously. Tuesdee doesn't like this at all. I get him an ice-cream cone as a treat in hopes he'll sit still for a few minutes, but we discover he doesn't like ice cream. Hamburger is about all he'll nibble on. So we go to a fancy hamburger place right on this block. Would she be there? We're only a block from where they said she's staying now.

Except for Tuesdee's red sweater, we don't look right. But our vests make us look exotic and foreign. It's as if we come from another country, which, in a way, we do.

I get him crayons and an alphabet coloring book and we go back to the bench. I have to show him how to color.

What to do with him when I go to her apartment? I don't trust him to stay-put anywhere I tell him. He can't sit still without something to do. I wonder what that says about his age. I'll have to bring him with me. I'll need him nearby because we'll have to leave fast.

Then it happens all by itself.

"So you've never colored before."

She, or someone very like her, sits down on the bench beside us. It could be her.

(I wish I had my regular clothes on. Or even my black outfit that shows off my muscles. I wish I'd bought a razor and had shaved.)

First she talks to Tuesdee.

"You're pretty gown up for never coloring before, but you're doing a good job."

"Ummm. Waaa...."

She turns to me. "I saw you showing him how." Then she says, "I mostly stopped because of the great vests you're wearing. Where are they from? They look as if they belong in a museum. Could I get one?"

I'll risk it...though what's to risk? We're both already in trouble.

First I'll make sure she's the woman, though I like her even if she's somebody else entirely and doesn't need rescuing. But my duty is to the woman I was to kill.

"Did you move here from the Greek Revival house?"

She looks at me in a different way. Appraising. Thinking. Yet again, dark eyes to dark eyes. I can see she recognizes me—from our faces, so close in the light of my thumb light? From my kiss?

She looks down at my hands as if trying to judge their strength. She says, "I know you."

I tell her the truth, all of it. And how now I'd like to save her...bring her with me. I ask her if she knows why she got "marked." She says because of her man, but he was her "mark," too. She says, 'I've done what you've been doing. I failed them, too, but if I kill you tonight, they'll make things right for me again."

She was to wait for me with a collar protecting her neck and her hands ready to grab my neck. If successful, she'd be back in their good graces.

I tell her we're being watched right now, even as we sit here, and she says she knows that already.

"Leave with us now. Don't go back for anything."

"But shoes!"

She's wearing high heels with the bottom of the heels about a quarter of an inch wide. They won't last a minute. But I can see on her face the eagerness to come.

"I know where we can get some boots on the way out of town."

I'm thinking: And long underwear.

"Where are you going?"

"Back where this boy comes from. Mountains. You'll get a vest. Besides, you can have mine right now."

When Tuesdee hears this he shouts, "Waa. No. No go. I'll stay here."

I know I can't make him do anything. He followed me because he wanted to. Even if I'd objected he would have tagged along behind. Funny little old-man boy. For all I know he's fifteen...sixteen, or, on the other hand, seven.

"Please come. At least tell your ma and pa where you'll be and say goodbye. And how are you going to live down here? Even with my money? You don't know anything about it here."

"I can."

"You don't even like the food."

That sets him thinking.

"How will you live?"

"I saw all what *you* do. The park and that. Hamburgers."

It's not until I tell him we can't escape without him, that he looks as if he'll help us. "And we need you to lead us when it's dark. It's our only hope to out-run the people who would kill us if they caught us. Please, at least do that for us. If we can't keep on in the dark without lights, I don't think we can escape them."

If it wasn't that I wanted to take him home I'd not go back the way we came. When we get there I'm going to head off into new territory. Maybe a whole other mountain.

Finally he says he'll help but he won't go all the way. Maybe later I'll be able to convince him to come all the way up to see his ma and da.

As we start off, I finally remember to ask her name. I've wanted to know it all this time, but she won't tell me. She says, "Call me Birdie for now and I'll call you whatever you want. Besides, when have people like us ever used real names? I've been Jane and Betty and Ursula. Even Thomasina."

I not only don't know her name, I don't know her at all, and yet here I am leading her away and not only to save her life, I'm in love...with a figment of my own imagination. I keep thinking about kissing her again and wondering how she'll respond. I keep thinking we'll live happily ever after in the mountains, but that takes a certain kind of person. She would have to love the mountains as much I do.

And yet she's as "marked" as I am. She has to live hidden or not live at all. That is, unless she kills me.

We move fast. She's as strong as we are. Of course she is.

If anybody follows us, we don't see it though we keep looking and listening. Maybe they're glad to be rid of us. Why should they bother with us anymore?

But isn't it important to make us an example of what happens when you disobey?

By nightfall we're far up and beyond the first hills, but we keep on climbing. I bought flashlights as Birdie was getting boots and long underwear, but we don't use them. It will be an advantage to have Tuesdee lead us in the dark. I tell him to stay away from the trails so we stumble on over rough ground. Mostly straight up. At midnight we cross over the first high pass and come down into the trees again. We don't sleep until morning, Tuesdee, as usual, cuddles against my back and Birdie lies behind him.

Though I've made her up, so far I still like who she really is. Actually I like her better than I could have made up. I didn't know she'd have such a good sense of humor.

We wake at noon, nibble on nuts and raisins as we go on. And we sing. I teach her my songs and she teaches me hers. She already knows the Sky Waters song. (She says, "I've know it since I was a child.")

And then, silently, suddenly, and even though we're above the tree line and there's not much underbrush for hiding…magically, here's Pa and Oh Pa.

(I could learn a lot about hiding from these people including Tuesdee.)

First thing Pa grabs Tuesdee by his ear. The Oh Pa twists his arm up behind his back. I think to protect Tuesdee and then think I'd better not. It's Birdie who stops them. Her iron grip on their wrists.

My woman!

Is she mine?

There's a moment of scuffling. Then we sit in a circle on the ground, and nod and smile at each other. It seems, no hard feelings on their side or on Birdie's or even on Tuesdee's. I know he's used to that treatment. I pass out nuts and raisins and the last of our hiking bars.

Tuesdee keeps saying, "No go 'ome." They talk slowly to us, but they talk so fast to him in their odd dialect that I can't keep up with them. They're doing it on purpose to keep us from understanding. There's much shaking of heads and gestures, but they seem to know as well as I do that nobody can make him do anything.

They say, "Maybis Ma?. Maybis Ma?" But Tuesdee keeps saying, "No," and "Maybis later."

They give up.

I trade two of our new flashlights for another vest. That only leaves one light for us, but the batteries on all of them will wear out soon, anyway. I don't know why Tuesdee's people like those so much when they can see in the dark.

Turns out Tuesdee has decided not to go to town, but to come with us. I think he's in love with Birdie, too. I was worried about him trying to live in town, so I'm relieved. Though I'd rather Birdie and I could be off by ourselves. Still he knows how to live in the mountains. He'll be a good help. We can live as his people do, moving every few days, hiding our shelters every morning. Putting out false trails.

After Pa and O Pa leave, we veer off and head for the mountain Tuesdee says his people call The Wrong Way Up.

Much later, when we're sitting above a muddy pond that, even so, reflects the full moon— Birdie leans against my shoulder and Tuesdee sits at our feet— I say, "Let me tell you what's going to happen.

"Because of you, Tuesdee, Birdie and I won't ever be found by the men with choking hands. And even if one does find us, the mountains will have changed him into a whole other kind of man. Tuesdee, I'll teach you to read and later you'll find your way back to your ma and pa and after that you'll go down and dig up my money and go to town and find out all about a different kind of life.

"As so often in the mountains, there'll be lightening and hail but we'll pass through all that safely. We'll walk through fields of flowers and butterlies. There'll be views that make us shout with joy. The sky will be so full of stars we'll feel as if we're falling off the earth, right into the milky way."

But wait, will Birdie put up with living with only us?...mainly me? And for years and years? People need other people. I wonder how long our life in the middle of the mountains can last. I told them our future, but there's a future where we chase each other back to town. I would be the one trying to catch up with Birdie.

Still for now, our only duty is to the road and after that, the path. There's the comfort of the trail. The rhythm of our steps....

Some say each step is a prayer. Some say each step is a song. And we do sing.... By now we don't believe there is a Sky Waters, but we don't care, we'll keep looking for it anyway.

In the Time of War and Other Stories of Conflict/Master of the Road to Nowhere and Other Tales of the Fantastic, 2011

The News That's Fit

The man who brings the news sometimes stays away a long time even when there must be plenty of news to tell. Or so it seems to us. He usually comes about every twelve or fourteen days, but we've been waiting for well over a month now. That's never happened before.

Considering the journey, everybody's nervous for fear something has happened to him on the way. Or we wonder if the news is so bad he doesn't dare bring it. Or it might be so embarrassing...so sexual maybe...that he doesn't want to talk about it.

But surely there's some interesting news to tell after four or five weeks have gone by: A wedding where the bride ran off with another man, or the death of a boy who thought he could fly, a six toed baby, a horse who can count.... If he doesn't come to tell us we won't know anything about any of these.

Our newsman seems nice enough, but we don't trust him. He's from down there. I like him, though, and for the exact reason everybody else is wary of him...because he's *not* from here. Not that I trust him anymore than the rest of us do.

We always keep a watch down the switchbacks to see if he's on his way up. When he comes, he plays a fancy tune on his flute to call us to the center of town. Sometimes he picks flowers along the way and gives them to us women.

Once in a while he brings us things we never see around here, a harmonica, an orange, balloons… once a half dozen flutes just like his. The things can't be heavy, he has a long hard way to go. Now we wonder if he's quit this job and didn't even come to tell us the news of his quitting.

Of course he could be drowned in the rushing rivers, or lying in some gully with a broken leg. They say there's a wobbly hanging bridge. They say there's two mountain passes. Our newsman says it takes him a week to get here. He says there's many dangers along the way and that the hanging bridge is ready to collapse.

I'll go and look for him. After all, I'm dispensable. I have no children and no family left. I'm not good for much else than running off on what may be a useless journey. I'll gather up the news myself. And I have one of those flutes, though I can't play it. I'll bring it and learn to play it on the way. I'll surprise everybody when I get back.

They'll say, "What do you know about helping a wounded person? or about camping out on the trail? And you don't know good news from bad." They'll say, "You're too old" or, "You're too young. And do we need the news? Look how we're getting along without it." But after all those they'll say, "Bring bandages and something to use as a splint."

I not only pack up bandages and a splint, but special herbs in case he's lying along the trail in pain. I start down the switch backs, everybody waving until I round the corner of the cliff. They call out, "Bring us some surprises," and, "Bring us good news." I've never been especially good news before, but maybe I can be now.

No matter what they say, I *do* know something about news. I know the price of eggs down there isn't important to us up here. I know scandals are interesting even when we don't know the people involved. Murders are always good. And news is important. You can't be an educated person without knowing who died.

I bring a big note book. I don't trust myself to remember things as our newsman did. Besides, I like to draw.

As I go, I keep looking around for him. I look over cliffs. Behind boulders. Even when the streams are far below, I study them. It makes for slow going.

The first evening I get out my flute. I don't make much progress. I learn one simple little tune. Sort of. My fingers don't stay on the little holes. Our newsman could do trills and rills and flourishes and he doesn't have a flute any fancier than this one.

Next day I find a land slide has blocked the trail. *Big* landslide! *So*…. No wonder. It takes me half the afternoon to climb around it. A dangerous climb, too, but I keep reminding myself there's a whole new life out there. And maybe other news to hear that we don't know anything about. The big note book I brought is heavy and I think about leaving it. Though maybe not yet. This may be the hardest climb and I've already done it.

To be a news gathering person you have to be spry. Our newsperson was…

is spry. And he's all muscle. For sure he could climb above and around the landslide better than I did. I hope he isn't at the bottom of this pile of fallen rocks. I begin to feel even more worried than I already was.

I've always liked him more than I should, but I'm pretty sure he wouldn't care for any of us from up here even though he brings us sewing needles sometimes and always flirts. (Once he leaned so close…his black eyes….And I knew mine were only a pale greenish tan.) But we're too countrified. All we know is what he tells us.

I keep on, slowly, looking for signs of him. Every now and then I think I see him partly behind a boulder. I climb down to it, but, so far, it's never him. I pass the hanging bridge. It hasn't collapsed. As I cross it, I study the river and rocks below for a body.

Another two days and I begin to see terraces and goats and goat herders. I'm getting closer to where the news begins. Even with all that looking behind every other rock, it hasn't taken me a week.

At the last high hill, I stop and look over at the town below before going in. It's so big it's scary. Where I live everybody knows everybody else, but I don't think that can be true here. I stand there a long time trying to make sense of the place. Streets curve and curve… more and more of them… around a large central square. Even this early in the morning, I can see there's already a lot of action down there. The news that's told in that square must be great and grand. I study the streets so I can find my way to it. I see odd places where houses have all fallen down in a row.

I didn't find any sign of our newsman along the way so I'm worried. Should I look for his mother and tell her something might have happened to her son? His name is Flimm but I don't even know if that's his first name or his last.

It's all downhill now. I trot along. I'm scared but excited about my future life…I know for sure it will never be the same.

It's a nice smooth road except for a couple of spots nearer the town, where there are such big holes they cut it right in two. Why didn't our newsman tell us about this road? Also about how big the town is? My people would love to hear about it.

As I come into town I can see right away how countrified I am. My pants are too wide and loose. We always have big bright sashes but nobody here does, not a one. And I don't see anybody with their hair tied back and up in a knot on the top of their head.

I find my way to the main square. It's early and they're setting up a market just like we have only this one is much bigger. Right in the middle, there's a fountain with a naked lady. Or there used to be. Thank goodness her top half is mostly broken off. I'd be embarrassed if it wasn't. The bottom part of her arm is still there, against her hip, and still holds a vase out of which a trickle of water is dribbling into the small pond below, but the pond is cracked and there's only a little puddle in the bottom of it. A woman is sitting on the edge and holding up a teapot to catch the trickle.

People are putting up stalls and tables. At one stall they're already selling a sort of pancake with fruit in it. Next to that there's someone cooking sausages. Suddenly I'm hungry for food that's not dried. I never thought about needing money. None of us did. I have all these useless bandages and herbs and a splint, but not a single cent. We should have realized it would be much more civilized down here and everybody would need money. I wonder if the news is also more civilized here than our countrified news up there. No wonder our newsman never mentioned smooth roads. They're used to that. It's probably the winding trails that are news to them.

I sit down, my back against a ruined wall, and watch. I'm less conspicuous sitting down than walking along in my odd clothes. I nibble at my dried food and watch people drinking red and yellow drinks and a fizzy drink that's surely beer, and wish I had some money.

A giant horse walks right by me only a few yards away. He's led by an ordinary sized girl. We only have burros. I do know about horses, but I didn't know they could get this big. I'm sure that horse is here in the square, to be put on display because it's the biggest horse in the world. That certainly is news my town would be interested in. Also all these different clothes.

I take out my notebook and begin to draw. I draw people in tight pants or short skirts with their lacy underwear hanging out below. I draw the big black horse towering over them. I even draw the broken statue of the fountain. I wonder why our newsman never thought this broken lady was news. And he never drew things. I think my people will like my news at least as much as his.

There are lots of fruits and vegetables here I never saw before. (Some have warts. Some have long curved necks. Some are purple.) And the vegetable we use the most up there isn't here at all. Not a single one. I draw the odd ones, though without color they won't show very well. I write, "orange", "red," and, "purple" under my drawings.

I draw the lady in the striped skirt across from where I sit. She's selling silvery jewelry and making new things as she sits there. Her crutches are beside her. She only has one leg. Next to her is a person selling fish. He only has one arm. They're sitting on chairs that fold up in a clever way. I draw a diagram of how the chairs work. Over on my side there's a man setting up an easel. He asks if I want my portrait drawn. "For only ten," he say. I do, but I have to say no, because I don't have any money.

Then I realize I should write out the news of our newsman. How he's most likely crushed under that big landslide. I put in how hard it was to climb over and around the slide. I do such a good job about him being crushed and smothered I actually make myself cry.

I look up at the bustle of the square to calm myself. By now it's crowded and noisy. There are more different kinds of clothes here than up home, but even so not a single person is dressed at all like I am.

That big horse is standing there, at the back of a stall, *not* as if on display and nobody is paying any attention to it. It's as if all their horses are this big. Nobody is paying any attention to the fountain with the bottom half of a naked lady either. So this... *all* this, is what it's like to be civilized and citified.

And then, across the square, there he is, Flimm himself. Looking perfectly all right— obviously not thinking about us and the news at all.

I feel all trembly. I always do whenever I see him...because of his black, black eyes...because of his black hair, his...yes, his ugly weathered face.... Only now I'm also all trembly with shock and anger. He's forgotten all about us. And he's with a woman. Much more beautiful than any of us. Her hair is not only as wonderfully dark as his, but long and wavy. We, up there, mostly have lank pale hair and it's hardly ever wavy.

How can he have forgotten us like this? ...not even tried to send somebody else? Though maybe he did and that's the person who got crushed in the landslide. I shouldn't judge. Not yet.

He's not dressed at all like he is up there, where he's always wearing his mountain climbing clothes. What he has on now fits better and is shiny and smooth. He looks wonderful. Still just as ugly but cleaner and freshly shaved and combed.

Here's lots of news my people would like to hear about, but I'd hardly know how to tell it. I need more facts and I know enough about news to know it shouldn't just be my angry opinion right now. News is supposed to be done with both sides in mind and never in a temper. I need to keep my own opinion out of it. He's the one told us that. He never ever told us what he thought about the news he brought. When we asked how he felt about things, he'd look sly and make jokes.

I know all about everybody's life up there but I know nothing of his. In fact, now that I see this place, I know that I know even less about him than I thought. If he's married, we don't know about it, though he certainly flirts with all us women. And we all have hopes but we never talk about it. We all think: What if he took one of us down and up, and up and down, and all the way to town? What an adventure that would be! Except now I've gotten here all on my own.

I think to yell: Hey it's Darta! I'm here! All this way by myself. For you. In case you were hurt along the way.

But I wonder if he'll remember me at all—though he'll recognize the way we dress. Then I think to hide and watch... see where he'll go, what he'll do. I sit still and carefully don't look straight at him. I'm thinking how I've come all this way to find him. I've looked over every cliff in case he's lying there dead or hurt. I've written his death down. I've cried for him, and here he moves along the stalls hanging on to a beautiful woman's elbow.... I have to hold myself back from attacking him. But news people never do that.

When he and the woman start to leave the square, I get up and follow. I stay well back. I try to keep behind people and in the shadows.

Then I see the smallest dog in the world. No doubt headed towards the square to go on display next to the biggest horse. He's carried in a fancy little bag by a lady in the narrowest skirt I ever saw. It has a big slit in the side, but even so she has to take small steps. Also she's wearing the highest heeled shoes I ever saw. I suppose she's going to the square to show off her skirt and shoes. I stop to watch, just for a minute, to admire how she manages to walk as well as she does… and I lose Flimm.

I hurry around the corner (glad for my flat shoes and wide pants) and then around a different corner, past a long row of fallen down houses, but I only get more and more lost. Then I hear a flute in the distance, playing with the trills and flourishes exactly the way Flimm plays. I follow the music around a corner and there, sitting on the ground….

I'm too angry to be a proper newsperson. I look around for a rock to use as a bludgeon, but there isn't one handy, even with those fallen down houses just around the corner. I'll attack anyway. He's sitting down. I'll kick….

But it's not Flimm.

I fall over backwards trying to stop myself.

It's a ragged round faced boy. Hardly in his teens. He's wearing loose dirty clothes. His face is full of odd little wounds. He's nothing at all like Flimm.

I lie there saying, I'm sorry, over and over. And the boy is saying, "But you didn't kick me, you just almost did." And, "Thanks for not doing it."

He helps me to sit up and gives me a drink from his water bottle.

How am I going to find Flimm now? He shouldn't get away with this. We thought he was our friend. If he needed a woman, we had many. Maybe not as beautiful as those down here, but even though unsophisticated, quite nice ones.

And then there was me. And I'm getting more sophisticated every minute.

I sit down next to the boy, take out my note book and cross out everything I wrote about Flimm. Then I draw the smallest dog in the world and the woman with the tight skirt. In spite of Flimm being alive and well, I'm glad I came. This place is interesting. I also write about the boy playing the flute. His name is Jall. Later I'll ask his age and write that down, too, but he's gone back to playing his flute. I've practiced every single night on the trail and I still can't play very well. This boy, as Flimm does, has a flute no better than mine, and he can play all sorts of fancy things. I wonder if he can teach me some of those rills. I don't have any money though, and everything here is so civilized it takes money.

I still feel like kicking somebody. I'll have to tell everybody back home that Flimm dropped us and without a word. I'll tell them these people are not our kind at all. They even pronounce half their words all wrong. They call the square the squire. They eat all sorts of odd things…. No wonder our newsman has such a long nose.

I write all this down and then take out my flute. I play one of my simple tunes. (By now I know five.) The boy and I both laugh at how simple it is and how badly I play it. Then we play together, me, the simple tune, and he, the ornaments and harmonies around it. I had no idea I could ever sound this good. Of course it's what he's playing that makes me sound so great, it's almost as if I can really play.

Somebody drops coins into the dust in front of us. We laugh again and play some more. After a bit we gather up our coins. "We ought to go to the square," he says. "You should stand up there in your funny clothes and I'll sit beside you and play the ornaments."

I'm thinking how I could eat some of those odd fruits. Maybe have my portrait drawn.

So he leads the way to the square. He has a really bad limp. He could never climb up to visit us. Even with me helping, he'd never get across our mountains.

We pick practically the same spot where I sat before, only now it's sunny. The portrait man has moved farther down into the shade. I stand and the boy sits at my feet. We make a good team and my clothes are an asset.

Though the portrait painter has lots of customers, he comes over to draw us and then again and again because people buy his pictures of us for more money than they pay for their own portraits. He says my costume helps, and I think: What costume? But to them I guess it is.

We play all day and make a lot of money. More than I ever had before. And the portrait painter gives us some of what he makes on our pictures, too. He says it's only fair. And then he gives us one of the pictures of us and Jall says it can be mine.

Then we buy some fruit and I get myself a sausage.

This is all really good news. I can't wait to go back and tell about it. I'd bring Jall back, too, if he didn't have such a limp. It is nicer there than here. Here they don't even have one single great view, not a one, though they do have everything else. I wonder if I could bring the smallest dog in the world back with me.

I do keep looking out for Flimm, though everything is so interesting I forget to be angry. I keep wondering if Flimm and I could sound as good together as Joll and I do.

When the market begins to thin out, and people start to undo their stalls and pack up, They hitch that biggest horse in the world to a huge cart. Again, a girl no bigger than I leads him off. I wish I'd had the courage to go up to that horse and stroke him the way she does.

Jall and I divide up the money. I didn't bring anything for a purse so I put my share in with the last of my dried food. I wonder if I have enough to buy that smallest dog in the world. Or that horse. Though I don't think I could get that horse across the hanging bridge and all the way home.

This is a very exciting place, everything here is news, but I still need to find Flimm. How do people find people around here? His safety is all my people really want to know about. They'd like the biggest horse and the smallest dog, but they wouldn't be satisfied until I told them about Flimm. I should have stopped him when I first saw him even though I was scared to. I felt so angry and trembly I wasn't sure what I'd do.

Jall and I decide to spend the night right here where there's a little water for washing and to drink. The sound of the dripping fountain is pleasant and soothing. In the morning he'll help me find Flimm.

We stick to our same corner next to the tumble-down wall. It's out of the way.

But even with the soothing sound of the fountain, I can't sleep. I can't stop thinking about Flimm and that woman and how silly it is to be in love with somebody from here that I hardly know.

Maybe I'm in love with him simply because he brought us the outside world. Or simply because he's different. Or because he jokes all the time. But there must be lots of men like Flimm down here. I should look around. It would have to be somebody who doesn't limp if I want to take him home and show him off up there.

Just after I finally get to sleep, first thing in the morning....

...someone shakes my shoulder.

"Darta. Darta."

Here *he* is...looking down at me. The slicked-up Flimm.... All in black, freshly shaved, hair combed, and I, for sure, the opposite.

I wake as if to a happy dream.

He remembers my name!

He asks a whole row of questions: "What happened? How did you get here? Why? What's wrong? Are you all right?"

As if the news was the other way around, from me to him.

He says it was one of those drawings of us that showed him where we might be. They're all over town. They show the corner of the square and the ruined wall.

I'm still half asleep. Is it really him? I say, "I looked for you all along the trail. We thought you were dead or hurt. I cried for you."

I reach up. He...for heaven's sake, kisses my hand...a *long* kiss...lips so warm and soft. Sits down beside me.

I say again, "I cried for you."

Then I actually do wake up. This is no dream. Here I am, rumpled and dirty, dressed in clothes nobody wears down here, and he, so clean and citified. What chance do I have? And why is he always flirting? Doing odd things like kissing hands?

I'll make the news myself. I'll *be* the news and I don't want to see both sides. Even Flimm has said there aren't always two sides to things.

Besides, how come such an ugly man gets to have such a beautiful woman as that one he was walking with yesterday? And here he is being flirtatious even to me right now, and enjoying himself. How can he be so happy after all our worry?

I attack.

I catch him by surprise. Right away he's down on his back trying to defend himself. He doesn't hit out at me at all but I hit and hit. Scratch and bite and kick.

Jall wakes up. He's a skinny lame boy so he can't be much help,

But instead of coming to help me, he starts to play the flute. A sad wavy tune. That stops us. And almost right away. Or rather stops *me*. Flimm was just protecting himself.

I sit back. News people don't cry. Is it the music or just everything in general?

What with Jall playing that sad tune and the surprise of it, I'm calm but Flimm isn't. He grabs me, one strong hand on my arm. I'll bet I'll have bruises there.

I've never seen him angry. He didn't hit out at me as I was hitting him, but now he looks as if he'd like to. He looks scary. I can see his jaw clenching and unclenching.

I duck down and try to pull away. I know he's going to hit me and I deserve it. Except he doesn't.

"What's all this about? Why?"

"For you. We worried. There was a land slide. We thought the hanging bridge had broken. I looked for you in all the cliffs."

It's then I begin to actually cry.

He tries to put his arm around me to hug me, but I pull away. "You're in love," I say.

"What are you talking about?"

"I saw you yesterday. That woman."

He starts to laugh. I know him well enough to know he laughs about everything, but even this?

"I'm in love, yes, with your mountain village and all of you gentle, sweet women. You're not like the women down here. I prefer how sweet you all are compared to the town women. How innocent…."

"I don't believe it."

"Look around you. Wouldn't you want relief from this?"

And suddenly I see.

"I never told you of the war. I never told you of these bombed out houses. Look at his ruined wall…. Our broken fountain…. The news I brought you was always false."

How could I not have seen it right away, back at the bombed out road? What kind of newsperson am I to be so blind? He said, "How sweet" we are. He's right, we're much too sweet. But is it my fault if I'm innocent, since he never told us anything real?

"And I never worried you with our epidemics. How many of us died…. Look at this boy's pock-marked face."

Jall, too. I never thought. …all this really real news….

"You were our hidden garden…for the Preservation of Innocence. I came back and told news of you to the town. I brought your births and deaths and marriages back here. Now there's no longer the time or money for the trek out there. We'll miss hearing about you. We were all in love with you."

"But you taught us the news was honorable. You said it should be even handed. Fair. And true."

"We needed you to be as you are. Our world was falling apart. We kept thinking: At least there's our mountain village, safe and sound."

"If you won't bring us the news, *I'll* do it. And my news will be real."

"There's mountain storms. There's rockslides. Steep drop offs. A woman can't do it."

"Of course I can. I've just been through it. And, look, my notebook is full of news. I drew the news, too. The biggest horse, the smallest dog… It's all here."

"Stay here with me. Come and meet my mother. She has always wanted to meet one of the sweet women from the High Hidden Garden. Nothing good will come from telling your people the real news. Come."

"No!"

I can't believe I'm refusing him. I always thought, if I ever had the chance, I'd run away with Flimm without a second thought.

I don't want to hurt him. I tell him I'm tempted, "But I'd rather bring real news to my people. They deserve it. They don't want to be somebody else's High Hidden Garden for the Preservation of Innocence."

Asimov's Science Fiction Magazine, June 2011

The Mismeasure Of Me And How I Saved The World

I've always wondered who I was. I took time off to find myself, but I could only afford a year and that wasn't anywhere near long enough. Maybe later, after I accumulate more money, I can try again. But even now I do take little bits of time, every weekend or so, to think: Who am I?

That one year when I had the time and money to use some for finding me, I went up into the mountains. I sat at the tops of cliffs, looking down at the views of the valleys below and tried hard to think about myself. Every time I found a still pond, I'd look in it and study my face and wonder what it signifies, as: What does it mean to have striking blue eyes, a wide forehead, and naturally curly hair?

But as of two days ago, I particularly need to know a lot more about myself. Thing is, I met a man I like a lot and I want to present him with the real me.

When he asked me out, it scared me. I felt right away that I needed more substance. So I said, "No," but I said," Later." I tried to look as if I wanted to go but was just too busy. I looked deep into his eyes, trying to convey that I liked him.

Since he wasn't at all pleased at my postponing our date to a week later, I think he might actually be as interested in me as I am in him. All the more reason to go off, and in a hurry, to see if I can get any more information about myself. If I find out anything... even a little bit...in the long run it'll be worth it.

On the other hand, regardless of who I might turn out to be, should I be mysterious? And then maybe I wouldn't ever have to go to the bother of finding out who I am. Perhaps I can be mysterious even to myself.

(Maybe I shouldn't have given him that long longing look right into his eyes. That can't be mysterious.)

Should I refuse to answer any personal questions? Being born right outside of Detroit isn't very glamorous.

Some day maybe he should come along. We could both look out at the spectacular views and think about me.

That year of finding myself, I had made sure I was cold and so tired I could hardly put one foot before the other. I starved myself. Though I sneaked a bite here and there when I got really hungry. I was hoping to find my totem or my real name. And I actually even saw a vision, but afterwards I was the same old me. Not a single new understanding that I could tell.

What I saw was nothing I could take for my totem. Before me, hovering over the valley as if atop a cloud, lay a city all made out of red rock with domes and towers and fortifications, but I wasn't sure if it was really a city or just an odd formation of cliffs full of holes that looked like doors and windows. I don't see how I can make that my symbol. I was hoping for an animal or a tree. Even the wind or water can be a totem. Though perhaps a cliff can be a totem, too.

So off I go again.

When I come back I suppose my hair will look a fright.

The first day out I find a big rock to sit on. As before, I empty my mind of all but the view and wait.... And wait.... And wonder....

I wonder what kinds of things this man likes in a woman. I already know most men like a quiet woman who agrees with them. They like somebody who picks up the things they drop.

And then I interrupt myself and bring my thoughts back to me. I wonder, how does one become mysterious. Isn't that what a woman should always be? And one way is simple, don't talk too much. What is hidden is always sexier than what is shown. What I don't say will always be more important than what I do say.

I hike on, deeper into the mountains. I sit at the top of cliffs. I admire views. And then I come upon it.... I'm on a drop off across from a red cliff that looks kind of like a city full of doors and windows. It's just like my vision on my other trip. Nobody could possibly live there without being able to fly. And I do see black creatures... perhaps ravens?... flying about it.

This cliff is so interesting it looks as if it might broaden one's horizons just to be there.

The closer I get the larger the crows seem. They're actually flying people. I'm dreaming of course. This is my totem vision at last. No need to be careful. None of this is real. Perhaps I, too, can fly.

I stand on a big boulder and try to take off.

But you can dream a fall, too. You can dream scratches and bruises and tears in your clothes. You can dream you can't get up and you're not even half way over towards the cliff. I shouldn't have been so careless, running off as though I could fly. It evidently isn't that sort of dream.

But there's a sudden wind and a flapping sound. There's dust blowing up. I dream beady black eyes, round as buttons. I dream a man thin as a crow. Nose like a beak, a little V shaped smile.... Sits beside me, all knees and elbows. His clothes, all black.

I dream him speaking a foreign language full of Ks and coos. I understand that he's flown down to help. I know he'll carry me off to his cave house in the cliffs.

Funny, though, he walks me down and over to the cliff houses. I was hoping he'd fly me. Dreams are so often full of flying I wonder that he doesn't.

As we limp along he talks his Ks and coos. I have to guess what he's saying. He's much more interesting than the man back home that I'm out here finding myself for, though they both resemble crows.

Now that I'm close to the cliff, I dream they're pretending not to know how to fly. No doubt because of me being there. They climb around with ropes and flimsy ladders. They don't want me to know about their flying. That probably has some deep meaning that I won't be able to figure out until I wake up.

His arms around me, he helps me climb the steep rope ladder to one of those holes in the cliff. Inside, he helps me to a sort of air mattress on the floor. I shut my eyes and try hard to fall into a deeper sleep because I hope, when I wake up, I'll be back in the real world and won't feel pain anymore.

Try as I might, I don't sleep a deeper sleep. In a way I'm glad because I can experience this place and this man for a bit longer, though I wish I'd stop dreaming pain. Perhaps I'm actually in pain in real life.

I give up and pay attention to where I am. It's as red on the inside as it is on the outside. The man in black sits on a red lump, silhouetted against the red walls. He hums an odd buzzing hum. I wonder that I'm dreaming such a sound. Perhaps I'm already home and the refrigerator is acting funny. Or is a bee flying around me as I sleep somewhere out on the ground in the mountains?

Perhaps this dream is all about that man I'm trying to find myself for in the first place... not about me at all.

I look at the man through half closed eyes so he won't notice. A handsome profile with a nose worthy of consideration. A bird of some importance. A bird to be reckoned with.

He says... I think he says, "Relax," but how does one relax when all banged up? To avoid the pain and get back into the real world, I tell him, "Wake me up."

I've always liked sad skinny men with brooding dangerous looks. Even so I say again, louder, "Wake me up."

But he doesn't understand. Or maybe he knows he'd disappear right out of my life if he did.

I ask him, "Bird or man?" And when he looks puzzled, I ask, "Crow? Caw, caw?"

That makes the sad man laugh.

If it's my dream, why can't I have what I want in it? Well, I do have the right man for once. That's one way I know it's all a dream.

Though I guess I know who I am now.... The one with the swollen and scratched nose, lump on forehead, a limp, though I still have blue eyes and naturally curly hair. But maybe that doesn't matter anymore. I'll have to act a whole different way. Like bring the coffee kind of thing. But I'd do it for this man anyway. Except sometimes the more you do for them, the less they notice you.

But he's getting something for me now. Broth with what looks like worms in it. Tastes of the earth but not bad. I sip all the dream broth and dream that I feel better afterwards.

He looks at me—those glittery black crow eyes—and says what could be, "Are you feeling better?"

If he had leaned any closer I'd have kissed him. After all, it's my dream, I can do as I want. And yet, even in my dream, I was too shy. I looked away. I pretended not to notice though I felt his warm breath on my cheek.

Maybe I should tell him not to wake me up yet.

He has moved away and sits on his red lump. On the wall behind him I can see the shadow of huge black wings. Wings to lift a person have to be enormous. I hadn't thought they'd need to be so huge. If he wanted to, he could fly me to wherever it is I'm sleeping back in the real world.

He says something again in Ks and caws. Goes to the doorway and raises his arms exactly like a cormorant drying his wings. Of course he can fly.

But what if I'm a prisoner now that I've discovered them? If, that is, it's not all a dream. Though why wouldn't it be a dream? People living in holes in red cliffs pretending they can't fly when they can?

I move to the doorway, too. There's a steep drop off. Even though there's a rope, there's no way I'm going to be able to leave here by myself and I already know this isn't a good dream for flying.

Outside, the crow people are all over the place, up and down the cliff, but nobody is flying. They're still pretending not to be able to.

He holds my arm to make sure I don't fall. Then brings me back to his lump of a chair.

They always say not to fall in love at first sight, but if this is my dream, it's all right. I have dreamt his solicitousness. I have dreamt the look in his crow eyes.

And there's that odd buzzing sound again. Does he think that's singing?

Then, "Nay, nay," he says, and those words are clear. The rest I have to guess. He says that nobody must know about them. That they're here to wait until it's the proper time to attack. "Clack," he says, and "Quack."

It all makes sense. And I'll bet you can hypnotize people with that humming and buzzing. Or put them to sleep. (Not me, though, since I'm already asleep.) They'll put the whole world to sleep when they decide it's time to take over, but I'll save us.

Would I really dream that? I must be full of thoughts of revenge. Probably it all started in the way nobody takes me seriously. You can't have blue eyes and curly blond hair, be barely five feet tall and have people listen to what you say.

Or is he telling me I'm beautiful in spite of scratches and bruises? Is he asking me to stay? But can I make him worm soup?

Not even in my dream.

But on the other hand, how to save the world? And can I do it all by myself? Bring down the whole cliff for instance? Find the pillar that holds everything up and find a way to undermine it.

Or could I bring them smallpox or some similar disease they would have no immunity to? Maybe a kiss would be enough to do it. I should have kissed him back when I had the chance. How many people would I have to kiss to start an epidemic?

Assuming, that is, that this isn't a dream.

Whether it is or not, I'll start kissing people. Of course I might make myself sick instead of them. Some sort of bird flu. But I'll risk it for my country.

Now isn't this strange? A. I'm so resentful I dream aliens are taking over the world and, B. I dream that the way to save the world is that I have to kiss them all. I'm having a hard time figuring out what this dream means.

I come close and put my hand on his arm. Nothing but bone and muscle. Just like a flying man would be.

Should I ask?...or just do it?

I look up at him and purse my lips.

(I'd never do such a thing in real life.)

He doesn't get the point or doesn't want to get it.

To start an avalanche would be a lot harder. I'd have to get up on top of the cliff and find boulders I can pry out and launch over the side and it might not work anyway.

But then, and lucky for the world as we know it: A whole bunch of them crowd into the cave to get a look at me. I kiss them all Hello. I say, "This is how we do it with my people." And they say coo and caw and then let me kiss them again, though I never do get the chance to kiss the man I really want to kiss. Lots of dreams are frustrating like that.

I don't wait to see them sicken. I climb down the cliff on those scary ladders and knotted ropes, and hurry towards home.

I know who I am now, though I still don't know who I used to be. I don't know if that matters anymore.

Finally I'm tired enough to fall into a deep dreamless sleep, and then I wake up into the real world.

Odd, though, I still hurt all over.

So, to summarize my waking up and my returning to the civilized world: Bruises, scratches, a limp, tangled hair (when you have naturally curly hair and don't comb it every day it gets into tangles that are impossible to comb out), maybe bird flu (I do have the sniffles). Lets see how that man I was out trying to find myself for likes me now that I've found me.

Except after meeting the man of my dreams how will this one measure up? He'll probably talk too much. I prefer coos.

And we do meet. A nice restaurant. I'm sunburned and freckled, bruised and scratched. I limp. I've cut the knots out of my hair. It does look funny. But he isn't the best looking man in the world. Except when have I ever liked good looking guys.

And here he is, all in black. Again as up in those cliffs, I think I see the shadow of huge wings on the wall behind him, though that can't be.

I sit down across from him. I say, "I could learn to make worm soup."

Lady Churchill's Rosebud Wristlet, #27, August 2011

Danilo

Lewella is pretending she's getting married. Of course to a stranger none of us knows. "Someone from the North," she says. He'll come for her in the spring. She has to have a trousseau. Especially things they don't have up north. But we mustn't go to any trouble. She'll only be able to take one small bag. Besides, she's not sure about what they don't have up north, anyway.

First of all who would marry her? She's too old and she has a limp. Her hair is always flying off in all directions and it's mostly all white. Nobody around here would look at her twice. Nobody has so far.

"What's he look like?"

She has it all figured out. "Oh, not handsome."

(We guessed that already.)

"But I like his looks anyway. He's thin. He has a long nose. Like most men, he doesn't talk much and never about what you want to hear. Especially never about love. But even so he's very nice. Looks back to see if you're following along all right. Helps you up if you fall."

"What's his name?"

She's not ready for that question. You can see her thinking and then answering too quickly and...you can tell...blurting out a name she doesn't even like. "Don, I mean Dan. Uhh, Brown...lee. Brownlee."

She's mad at herself for not thinking up a name beforehand. "So," we say, "Dan Brownlee?"

"The Dan is short for his real first name."

"So what's his real name?"

"I'll ask him when I see him."

"But you said that wouldn't be until the wedding."

"He might come by before that."

She's set the date, ten days into April.

I gave her two old towels I was going to throw out. She didn't get the joke. She thanked me as if she really liked them. Right away she put them in the little bag where she's keeping the things for her trip north. Doesn't take much to make her happy which doesn't bode well for Don... I mean Dan... Brownlee being anybody special.

So far, besides my towels, she has a little silver comb, a bar of honeysuckle soap, and a lacy collar she's going to sew on to her best dress for her wedding. She's also been sewing herself a nice warm coat for up north. She'll bring along a pan and spoons and her daddy's old hunting knife.

The coat she's making is made of a couple of dozen rabbits. I hate to see all those white jacks gone to make a coat she'll never need. Course she can always change it into a blanket. Even here in the south, the nights are cold.

Well, if pretending to get married makes her happy for a while, why not? She has little enough to enjoy. A pretend life is better than nothing, but we wonder how she'll be, come April tenth.

Later when I tried to give her another wedding present...a real one this time... a little bone spoon... she said she had enough things by now. We all wonder, is she ashamed to take more presents when she knows the bridegroom doesn't exist? That was a small spoon and had a little snail carved into the end. I liked it myself and, since I was ashamed about giving the old towels, I wanted to make up for that with something really nice. And it isn't as if it would take up much space on the way north.

Next thing we know, she's hung up a picture in her front room. I can't believe it. We've no idea where she got it. A deeply lined face and just the right amount of grey at the temples for somebody her age. (And my age, too.) Black eyes. In the picture, they seem to look deep into you. As she said, not handsome, but he has his own attractiveness. Very masculine. I can see why she picked this picture. I could go for a man like this myself.

He seems pretty well dressed compared to us. Why would somebody like that want anybody from around here? How did they get to know each other in the first place?

But...I don't know...makes me want a picture on my wall, too, except where would I find one as good as hers? Or even not that good?

She says his name is Danilo. Now where'd she find that out? and when? Made it up, is what she did.

She does spend her free time alone in the woods, but I do, too, and I never run into anybody out there but us.

I watch her out my back room window. Lately I've followed her several times as she went out walking. She sits and hums to herself. Bees and hummingbirds fly around her as if she's a flower and even when she's not wearing red or yellow. There's a jay that comes and hops around her feet and she feeds him crumbs. That's all that happens. Once a streak of sunlight shined down sideways through the trees on to her tangled white hair and made it glow in a magical way. Not for long, though.

Sometimes I get to thinking Danilo is real and I wonder what he'll think of those frayed old towels I gave. How will he judge me? And all of us weavers and cheese makers? Our mushroom drying roofs? Our mulberry wine?

People seldom come here except by mistake. We're off the beaten path. We're quaint. The people who run across us say how unspoiled we are. I think if you're ignorant, then you're spoiled. But, like everybody always is, we're ignorant of our ignorance, you could say. This is the only life we know.

The business is owned by men who live in town. People say they grow fat on us. We hardly ever see them. I ask, "Lewella, Is it one of those men?"

"Oh for Heaven's sake, of course not. How could you think such a thing?"

She's right to be insulted. Nobody would want one of our bosses even as an imaginary husband. Or, rather, *especially* never as an imaginary husband.

She talks to herself even more now than she used to do. I suppose it's him she's imagining beside her. I'm wondering what that's like, so I start mumbling to myself and think of Danilo beside me—ugly but *so* manly. In my daydream he needs a shave. I have him name the birds, the flowers.... He would know them better than I ~~do~~. He would explain why the owl can fly so silently. He'd tell me about the splints of a horse's leg. How the roadrunner has a foot with two toes in front and two in back like a parrot's....

But Lewella doesn't wait till April comes around. I suppose she hasn't even fooled herself and she's ashamed. She gathers up her wedding presents into a big plastic bag and leaves in the middle of the night, as if to avoid all of us, and so as not to have to say goodbye.

I saw her gathering up her greens the night before. She didn't pack up Danilo's portrait. Too bulky I suppose. I had the thought I'd go steal it after she'd gone, but then I thought maybe I'd better pack up, too, and follow. See if she gets any farther than the first village. Besides, she needs looking after. She's as innocent as a six year old. I may not be much better myself, but I might be able to keep her out of trouble.

I wrap up in my big black shawl and follow. Off we go. Is this north? I don't think so.

She carries this little beaded purse on a long handle hung over her elbow. The rest of her stuff is in that plastic garbage bag hung over her shoulder. She carries another smaller plastic bag with her food. Everything I bring, food and all, is in my little backpack.

She doesn't hesitate at the village. Goes right on by, as if she knows where she's going.

I'll keep following and when she's all worn out and has eaten all her greens, (For sure she took a ball of cheese. I will, too.) I'll confront her and bring her safely home.

She stops to eat greens and cheese when the sun is high. I stop, too, and eat some of mine. Then off she goes. This is still west, not north.

Seems as if she thinks she sees him all over the place. A farmer on a tractor looks like him. She runs off into the field to check. The zucchini seller at the roadside stand looks like him. She stares under his big farmer's hat. There's a group of people having a picnic in a farmyard. She must be thinking one of them might be him. She rushes in.... But he's not there. They give her a big slice of watermelon. It's a hot day. Makes me wish I had some, too, but I'm not the kind of person, goes rushing off into other people's parties.

I'm so embarrassed for her.

This is how the day goes.

Her big coat comes in handy that night. I wish I had one like it. I'm tempted to admit I followed and crawl in with her. I'm well back, though hidden in the same copse she chose. Earlier we had passed an orchard and we both stole apples.

The next day is exactly the same. Very embarrassing. I'm glad I'm pretending I'm not with her.

That night we sleep (separately) hidden in a corn field and eat some of the corn even though it's the kind for the cows and is tough.

Good I'm keeping an eye on her. She'll talk to anybody. I'm worried she'll make somebody angry or that somebody will steal her coat. It's the only thing she has that's of any value. That is, unless she has her lace collar with her. She probably does since she wants it for her wedding.

Then there's a whole day with nothing but wheat and alfalfa fields. Things are getting farther apart and emptier. We have to sleep in a wheat field.

She finally does turn north. That's when I decide to catch up to her. I don't want to spend another night freezing.

She doesn't seem surprised to see me. Did she know all the time I was right behind her?

First thing I say is, "There's no such person as Danilo and you know it."

"There's his picture to prove it."

"That's not even a real name."

"Yes it is. I looked it up."

"Come on home."

"But maybe over the next hill. Who knows who'll be there."

"More wheat, is what. And look around you. There aren't any hills anymore."

I tell her she's crazy, but she doesn't even care if she is or not. I say it's dangerous out here.

I grab her wrist and try to pull her back. We struggle. I lose. She helps me up and out of the ditch. She says, "*You're* the dangerous one."

Well at least I get to spend the night under her big coat with her, warm for the first time since we started. I'm so tired even her humming herself to sleep doesn't bother me.

Next day I still lag way behind on purpose I can't stop her from peering at men— close up under their hats. (She likes big black cowboy hats the best. I guess she thinks that's what Danilo would wear.) I'm worried she'll peer under one too many and I'll have to rescue her.

She's limping even more than ever. Seems as if both her legs are hurting now. (Did I do that to her when we fought? But I'm the one with bruises and pinch marks.) I keep saying we should go back before she gets so she can't walk at all, but she won't stop.

Between us we have enough money to take the bus home—over sixty dollars, most of it mine. Though if we get too far away it won't be enough. The bus goes right to our village. We'd have to walk the rest of the way… to our "quaint" nowhere. She says we have to save the money for emergencies. I tell her, the way she's hobbling along, it's an emergency right now, but she finds two stout sticks for canes and keeps going.

The next morning she decides to wear her lacy collar. She pins it on her pink t-shirt. She does look quite fancy, long as you don't notice the safety pins and those two dead sticks she's using for canes. The collar is really quite nice. It's tan/gold with a design of vines and leaves and gnarled trees, all almost the same color, just a little more goldish, but I doubt if wearing it is going to help us find Danilo.

Then she sees somebody who looks—to her anyway—like Danilo. "It's him!" she says. Yells, that is.

"How can you think that? He's too short and doesn't even have black hair. I wish you'd brought the picture. With that, I could prove it's not him in half a second."

"What are you saying? It's just like the picture. Cute and chubby."

How can she think that? I ask this man what his name is, but Lewella is already calling him Danilo, so of course he says, Danilo.

I say, "You know there's no such name."

How can she think it's him? He badly needs a shower, (but of course we do, too.) Is tit just hat he has a big black hat?

He asks her how come she's wearing that beautiful lace collar? "What's the occasion?"

"You," she say. "I knew you were coming."

Oh for Heaven's sake.

This Danilo is no taller than she is and has a kind of pale, pasty look that's nothing like the picture. He's chubby. I'm wondering, is she going blind?

We keep walking. He follows. He says, "How about that sunset, huh?"

That doesn't sound anything like the man who would have told me why the owls can fly so silently.

Though he pretends not to, he follows us as we look for a sleeping place. I see him watching from behind trees as we settle in. This is a nice little park with a stream and picnic tables. We go to the far end where it's woodsy and hide in the bushes. Lewella takes off the collar and spreads it out on her bags so it won't get wrinkled.

After we're settled in, I sneak back and see that man crawl under one of the tables way at the front of the park. I don't trust him so I try to stay awake to guard us but I fall asleep sitting up leaning into the bushes. I guess I sleep even harder than usual because of trying to stay awake. Of course everything we had of any value is gone except her coat... that lace collar gone, and our sixty-six dollars.

"I told you and told you it was dangerous out here. He could have murdered us for your coat.

I want to blame her for thinking he was Danilo and for wearing that lacy collar, but she's about to cry.

"I'll bet he's already got it all wrinkled. Now what'll I wear to be married in?"

"We'll find another one."

"Not as nice."

"Probably not, but *you'll* be just as nice as ever."

That makes her feel a little better.

"Next time let *me* say if it's Danilo or not."

Now that we've lost the bus fare, I wish we'd turn around while she can still walk at all. I try to fool her with the wrong direction, but she seems to know exactly which way she wants to turn.

I'm still lagging way behind. When we get together that evening in order to find a place to sleep, she suddenly appears with a ... what looks like... a diamond ring and I know she hasn't been near to any K Mart or Wal-Mart that I could see. Besides, we don't have a cent. I don't ask. I refuse to pay attention to it even though she keeps waving her hand in front of me. Has she taken to stealing? Well the next minute we do steal... corn on the cob out of a back yard garden. This time it's tender and good even though raw.

We're getting thin and we're always hungry. Well, I am. Lewella looks just about as usual, though she's limping more than ever. "Why don't we just go back and wait for April tenth to come along? Please."

That evening we come to a little town and find a nice big park. Unfortunately it's across from a bar and there's a drunk sitting on a bench near the baseball diamond. He's wearing exactly the kind of hat Lewella keeps looking under all the time. The way he's sitting his face is easy to see. His hat is tipped way back. he's unshaven. But....

I hurry us past so she won't notice, though she might not recognize him anyway, since before, she picked that funny pasty, short man. Besides, she keeps looking at her ring.

This man is thin and tall. Sitting, legs wide apart, leaning back, asleep or just too drunk. You'd think he'd be hurting his neck that way though maybe the hat helps soften the bench edge. I can smell the alcohol from the path. He's snoring, his mouth is open, his teeth are crooked, he has a lump at the bridge of his nose.... But... I can't help it...I find him as attractive as I did his picture.

It's a big park. I take us way to the back, where there aren't any benches or paths. I settle us behind a row of bushes just out of reach of the sprinkler system. I know that'll be turned on at night. It'll be easy to get a drink.

Lewella can't help talking about the ring. "Isn't it nice. Look."

I don't.

"He knew how bad I feel about losing that collar so he wanted me to feel better. At first we'd decided we weren't going to have an engagement ring, you know."

I tell her I'm not going to say a single word. I turn my back and get ready to sleep…or seem to sleep.

Here he sits only a block away… snoring … snorting….

But he exists! I'm all atremble.

After Lewella is asleep I get up and go back to that bench. He's still in exactly the same position though it's been quite some time. I say, "Dan?" and, "Danilo?" a couple of times, but he doesn't wake up. I sit on the edge of the bench and examine him. A lined face just like the picture. And tired…eyes with dark circles under them. The mustache a little longer than in the picture and there's more gray at his temples. The silky black shirt looks expensive. The vest is gold and tan with all kinds of curlicues. It reminds me of that fancy collar Lewella had. Same curling vine-like designs and gnarled trees. Since it's getting cold, I think to reach over and button it for him, but he's too smelly from drink and what if he woke up with a jump when I touched him? And the more I look, the more I'm glad he didn't wake up when I said, Danilo. I've had this chance to study him.

I like his looks so much I hate to go back to Lewella but I need to crawl under that coat of hers and warm up.

We wake to the smell of coffee. Instead of being stolen from, here's a meal, two hamburgers and two cups of coffee all still nice and hot. We haven't had coffee for a long time. How did somebody do that, and so we woke up just at the right moment?

I don't take a sip or say a word. I rush out to that bench, but he's gone. Of course he is. Why didn't I stay there and wait for him to wake up?

I go back to where Lewella is enjoying her coffee. "See," she says, "He's real enough to bring us breakfast."

I don't answer. I feel glum. Did he give her that ring? Why did he have to get so drunk?

She hobbles off much faster than usual. I suppose the coffee did it. This time it really is north. She walks on humming to herself even louder than she usually does. (It never has a real tune to it.) I lag farther behind than usual. I'm glad she never saw him. But she was so wrong before, she might not have recognized him anyway.

But I have no business falling in love with her man. Not to mention falling in love with a drunk.

Except a drunk who brought us coffee? Was it him?

Maybe that diamond ring is really real.

I'd have another fight with her about leaving this park and Danilo if I wasn't sure she'd win. How can she when she's so much smaller than I ~~am~~? She knows exactly where to pinch and squeeze and how to trip up a person. Where did she learn all those tricks?

We've hardly gone but an hour when— I can't believe it— here's another little chubby man with a big black hat and Lewella is heading right to him with that eager look of hers.

For Heaven's sake, not again.

I shout. "Let him tell you his name first," but she's already yelling, "Danilo."

"Remember what happened last time? Your lacy collar?"

Except for the hat, he's all in tan-on-tan camouflage. As she nears him I can see he not any taller than she is.

He's so busy looking at the sky, where, way, way off, there's a flock of geese flying south... that she has to tap him on the shoulder before he notices her yelling at him. Then he points and says, "Look! Look! Look!"

And we all do.

This man, unlike the other one that turned out to be a robber, has a very nice little V shaped smile. At least that.

I back away even farther. Best not to let him see I'm with her. Though I suppose he knows it already.

I can't understand how she can think this little man is Danilo.

He has one of those scooters. Also painted in camouflage tans. I don't see how two people can get on that and with all her packages, but they do. Good they're both small.

I yell, "Wait!" I rush forward, but I'm too far away.

And there she goes—putt, putt, putt, and lots of smoke—without a second thought about me. But I'd do the same, and anyway, I was pretending not to be with her, why would she say goodbye?

I wave, but she doesn't notice.

Something about that tan scooter and his tan camouflage and all that smelly smoke... I don't know what...but they disappear before they get to the corner.

She left her two stick-canes as if she will be magically cured of her leg problems. I wonder if she will.

She probably would have done a lot better without me following her around. Her innocence would have saved her...those blue eyes...that luminous quality....

And she went off with her white coat of jack rabbit fur. Who ever heard of that until she made one? It was getting dirty, though. And she took those worn out towels that I'm sorry I ever gave to her. I hope they come in handy sometime, at least as rags.

I hope he's not a drunkard like the other Danilo.

So here I am, no money, no diamond ring, no lacy collar and even no rabbit fur coat to keep me warm at night. And I'll bet whoever gave us coffee and sandwiches isn't going to do that just for me. She's the one with hair like a little white cloud and a magic innocence that calls down humming birds. I'm just as innocent and ignorant as she is, but I don't expect to get any diamond rings.

I look up at the sky where the geese were flying south. Only now there's nothing there except one little puffy cloud that reminds me of her.

I watch the cloud for a while and then I head back to that town where *my* Danilo is. I check that bench, but it's too soon for anybody to be drunk and collapsed there, so I head to the far end of the park, back where we spent the night. I miss Lewella, not only for her coat. I even miss that cheerful tuneless humming.

I'm not only cold but hungry and I hardly slept at all last night. I curl up in my shawl and try to sleep before it gets really cold. I push leaves up around me though I don't suppose that helps much. Later I'll see if… *he*… might be out on that bench.

The moon is high and almost full. This time he's turned sideways, curled up, long legs almost at his chin, and with his cheek against the hard edge of the bench. Again, his rumpled big black hat is saving his cheek a bit. It's cool so he's all buttoned up. He smells of alcohol again. I sit down at his feet and right under the bench, there's a crumpled up twenty dollar bill. It could have just fallen out of his pocket or it could be for me.

I don't take it.

I look at what long fingers he has. I look at the bump on the bridge of his nose.

I wait. After a while he turns from his left cheek on the back of the bench to his right cheek on the back of the bench. As he turns he gives a big snort.

I wait.

And even though it's cold, I fall asleep.

When I wake it's already morning and he's gone. But the twenty dollar bill is still there.

Just as I reach for it, a boy runs by and scoops it up.

I sit on the bench and think.

So what about him sleeping on a bench? Doesn't he have a home? Will he whisk me off to a life of sleeping on benches? Not that he wants to whisk me off anywhere. Would I agree to that? Yes I might and there I was criticizing Lewella for her odd little man.

Would I get to go off in a cloud of smelly smoke to some magical tan on tan place like she did?

Then I think about coffee and eggs. I search in my pockets to see if there might be any coins I hadn't noticed but there aren't any. Maybe if I go where the food is.

I check up and down the street but there doesn't seem to be any place nearby except that bar. It's closed now.

I go on farther down the road and find a gas station with food. I go on farther to farm houses with gardens and fruit trees. I sneak around and steal. Zucchini doesn't taste that good raw but they have a lot. I don't think they'll miss one. And they have grape vines along their roadside fence.

But nothing is the same without Lewella to look after and to share with. Though it's a lot easier to steal without her hobbling beside me… not paying attention and singing. I think people noticed every time and just let her steal. I'll bet they won't let me if they see me.

I spend the day more or less in a ditch…. Well… in a ditch. I feel better after I eat and I'm warm in the sun so I have a really good sleep all afternoon. Wouldn't it be nice if another coffee appeared just as I wake up? But naturally, none does. I steal another zucchini and walk back to town. It's getting dark. I'll go to the bar myself.

As I near I hear music...an out of tune piano. It sounds cheerful. No wonder people go to bars.

I'm getting awfully grungy. Like that white rabbit fur coat, I'm grimy all over. Leaves and sticks in my hair. I haven't washed it or myself since we left. It's getting to be fall. Pretty soon it'll be too cold to wash even if I find a nice secluded pond.

I try to make sure all the dirt and sticks are out of my hair. I've been using Lewella's silver comb and it's gone off with her. I have to use my fingers.

I've never been in a bar before. I hope I'm not too dirty. Aren't bars usually kind of dark inside?

Somebody is playing rills and trills and arpeggios all around the melody and people are singing, Pack up all your cares and woes, bye, bye blackbird.

I go in. It's a small narrow bar, but seems to go way, way back. I can't see how far. In front there's hardly room for the piano and five or so tables.

It's decorated as if we're in a forest. In the back it seems to open out. Even looks like the moon is just coming up, way back there behind the trees. As if it really is a forest and as if there's no end to it. It's full of magic lights as if people with flashlights are way back there in the trees. I wouldn't dare go there.

There's a crowd standing around the piano but I can see there's even a long green vine winding up and around the side of it. There's a big black hat on top and beside the hat a glass of light liquid. They're all singing Whispering grass... don't tell the trees. That seems appropriate. Everybody seems to know all the words.

At first I can't see who's playing, but I see a black silky shirt sleeves and a golden/tan vest, glistening even in the dim light. I move to the back of those standing close. He looks serious...businesslike, but so many extra notes and flourishes it's as if it's all a joke. Every now and then he sings, too, but it sounds more like growling.

I don't know what to do. I move away and sit near the door and listen and look around. Now he's playing Has Anybody Seen my Gal? Five foot two. Eyes of blue.... That sounds just like Lewella.

Now that my eyes are more adjusted to the dim light, I think I see her... I'm not sure.... but Is that her and her Danilo, way back there under a tree at a little table with a flickering light? Both wearing tan on tan camouflage? I'm pretty sure it's her because of that mess of white hair. I'm even more sure when I see that diamond ring catch the light and flash a beam out towards the front of the bar. It's a real diamond all right. A phony one couldn't do that.

And then this Danilo stops playing and swings around on the stool so he's facing all of us... takes a big drink from that glass. He's sweating all over his black silk shirt.

Do I dare?

I dare. I join those standing close around the piano.

Right away he looks straight at me and smiles. (And his eyes are just like in the picture, they seem to look right through you. And even so are welcoming.)

He says, Hello, just to me. He reaches and plucks something from my hair. "You have Bindweed in your hair."

This is my Danilo, the one who knows all about nature.

"I'm a mess."

He reaches again and picks more of it out. "Did you know the other name for Bindweed is Morning Glory? Is that what you are?"

"I'm too tired to be Morning Glory. And I haven't washed in days."

"You smell of fresh hay. And of the earth. Jenny? You're Jenny aren't you?"

"My name is Mary Ellen. But you're Danilo."

"My name is Jack.

***Asimov's Science Fiction Magazine*,** September 2011

The New And Perfect Man

To make sure our child would turn out better than any other child, my wife and I bought the most expensive Graham/Gallagher box. This is a new version of the old Skinner box. It can be expanded to fit several ages. There are age appropriate science projects you can add every six months. The child can stand up in it. There are railings so he can learn to walk. There's a red button he can push for water, a blue button for milk, and a green one for juice. Toys he can reach hang from the ceiling. There's a soft floor to fall on or sleep on. As he gets older, the walls unfold until it becomes a large room with desk and book shelves.

While he was in the womb, we listened to a lot of the best classical music. Not just Bach and Mozart as was recommended, but contemporary classical, too. We wanted a contemporary man. We hoped he'd go way beyond us. We didn't expect him to agree with our old fashioned way of life. We didn't want him to.

I listened, too. I wanted to take part. I know how much a father matters.

(When we decided on the name Amos, we were under the impression that Amos means beloved, After all it seems to have amo, amas, amat in it. Then we found out it means a burden.)

He wasn't going to hear any bad words. He wasn't going to see any violence or any sex. We would home-school him though the box would do most of the work. It was also programed to stay up to date on science.

We had chosen each other carefully, too. We both knew we wanted a special child. Why have a child if it turns out to be just anybody?

We researched nutrition for Madeleine while she was pregnant and, of course, for the baby for later on. We wouldn't allow chocolate or candy or white flour or coffee or coca cola in our house. Green tea would be our drink and milk and juices for the child.

And then we found out by ultra sound that...(but they weren't exactly sure...it was hard to see...the baby was in a bad position...they could be wrong...but they were pretty sure)... the baby was a girl.

We said, Oh well, and, That's fine with us. As long as it's a healthy baby, that's all one could wish for. Maybe it really was with Madeleine. We didn't talk much about it after that. But no reason, we said, to stop our plans. We would make the new woman, though that didn't seem as important as having the new man.

We didn't think of a girl's name. We still hoped it would be our Amos.

But the baby was, indeed, a girl.

We're both handsome people but the baby was funny looking. That didn't bother us. Most babies are. We were sure she'd grow out of it. Unfortunately, as she grew, she didn't seem to be getting any handsomer. She went from bald to lank straight brownish hair. She went from a narrow face to an even narrower one. She did have rather nice eyes that sometimes looked green and sometimes looked tan. Her mouth was too big, but she smiled a lot. Sometimes it seemed she thought she had to. Madeleine and I discussed that, but couldn't figure out how that could be.

One good thing, she was very smart. And she walked at nine months.

To hasten her reading, for a while we put labels on everything. Madeleine wore MOTHER. I wore DAD. Madeleine thought FATHER would be better but I wanted to be DAD like my father was to me. We marked the bed, BED, bathroom, BATHROOM, chair, CHAIR, and so on. We put ME on the child herself.

There was a cat and a dog that visited now and then. We didn't want to own any animals but we didn't want our child not to know what they were like. (They wore their labels, CAT and DOG, and later CALICO and JACK RUSSELL.) We had parties. We invited other children. All the visiting children loved the Graham/Gallagar box. They pushed the buttons till the box ran out of milk and juice.

Even though there were loving arms in the box that would hug her any time she cuddled into them, we knew she needed our arms some of the time. Every day we scheduled a family time, all of us together, talking and hugging.

We kept smiling. We hummed and whistled. When the Graham/Gallagar box added a clock, it was a bird song clock. Every hour it chirped a different bird song with a picture of the appropriate bird. Now there's a piano keyboard and a guitar. We opted for no computer until later. We may be wrong about that but we'd heard that it sometimes gets to be the only thing the child pays attention to. There is a TV there but it only allows educational programs.

We planned to take her on a world tour as soon as she was sixteen: the pyramids, the Eiffel Tower, Venice.... Even though nothing has quite the same meaning as it would have had if she were a boy.

But this may never come about.

She's gone.

She's twelve.

Unfortunately we let a whole afternoon go by before we checked on her. It was dinner time before we discovered she wasn't in her box.

Did somebody steal her? Do they know how valuable she is? Will they treat her as if she's just an ordinary girl? Will they ask for a ransom? And if so, when?

It's a big world. Bigger than I thought. But I don't need to be scared, I just need to be clever. And get away from our house fast.

First thing I want to do is climb a tree. Way, way up. I know it's not the smartest thing but I want to do it anyway. I run and run until I find a really tall one. I find out I'm good at it, too. And I find out I love heights. It's so different from being in a box…and yet I love my box, too. It looked after me.

I've been planning this for a long time. I've been stealing money for months. I picked a good time to leave. Mother has trouble sleeping so it couldn't be in the middle of the night, but when she takes her nap she's really out so I leave in the afternoon. Just before I go I cut my hair. I'm not very good at it and I can't see the back, but I'm pretty sure I look like a boy.

I have an apple and nuts and I ate a lot before I left. In fact I ate so much I'm uncomfortable. I'm so stuffed I can hardly move. I wear one of my dad's white shirts. He's got so many he won't miss it. And a pair of his old pants. It's good I'm almost as tall as he is.

I don't think either of them liked me growing so tall and skinny so fast. I passed Mother last year and now I'm almost up to Dad. And they're both tall people.

I picked a rainy day. All the easier to get lost. I put on a plastic garbage bag for a raincoat. They'll probably call the police before twenty minutes have gone by. Though maybe not. These days they don't check up on me as often as they used to. Now my Grahm/Gallagar box is as large as a large room and I've told them over and over that I need them to leave me alone so I can get my homework done. They're happy to do that. I've notice ever since I was little how much of a bother I am. The box is my real parent. It sang to me and read to me whenever I wanted it to.

It wasn't good climbing tree weather, kind of slippery, but I managed. I watched everybody from up there. Everybody had an umbrella and nobody looked up.

First night I find a big cardboard box just my size. By then it has stopped raining and the box is almost dry. Besides, I have my plastic bag. I feel comforted in there. Boxes are my friends. It reminded me of my box when I was little and it was much smaller.

Next morning I check myself out in store windows. I see I make a pretty good boy. Tall and lanky. With this haircut, I don't think anybody would take me for me.

I've never had coffee before, nor a doughnut either. I've never been to a diner. And I've never been anywhere at all by myself. I stop at the first little coffee shop I see. I get out some of my money. I have a lot. It's good Dad's pockets are big.

I sit there a long time. I do get some funny stares but maybe people always do that. What do I know? But it could be, since I cut my hair myself and couldn't see the back, I might look funny back there. Anyway, I'm looking around at everybody, too.

I'm feeling really good. When I leave I stride off taking big steps like a young man would do. Though, just like Mother said it would, the coffee makes me shaky. I didn't like the taste much either. I'll go back to milk.

I find a park and sit down on a bench. I watch the pigeons. I should probably be trying to get farther away, but I need to watch and learn things and I want to feel how it is to be out here by myself.

I watch the little kids. Some have toys that have no other use than to be toys. Soft fuzzy things that wouldn't teach anybody anything unless you count how to hug. I never had one of those. I wonder if I'm too old to have one now.

Then I see, under the swings, something purple. I go over and pick it up. It's only a little bigger than my hand. Too small to hug, but I like it. A little purple dog or maybe catish thing. And it fits in Dad's pocket so nobody has to know.

It's dirty and chewed on. For sure Mother wouldn't want me to have it, but right now I'm not so clean myself.

I sit and eat my apple. I wish I knew how to drive a car. Think of all the places I could go. I've only seen the countryside from my parent's car and I haven't seen that very often.

For lunch I go to McDonalds for a hamburger. I do know a few things. Those children that came over now and then so I'd get socialized always said McDonalds was really good. And they were right.

Now I'm going to go on until I get out of town. I've never really been out in the country so as to walk around in it.

Then I meet this dog. He follows me. He's much too thin. I know dogs don't eat nuts so I use some of my money to get some dog food. Then I need to get him a dish so I can give him a drink of water. We can both use that.

I name him Skippy. I never named anything before.

I don't need that cuddly toy now that I have a real thing to hug. I don't throw it away though, I leave it on some steps where some little kid can find it.

Then I realize I ought to choose a name for me. I'm thinking Bill or Tom or maybe Sam. Short names seem more like boys even though Dad's name is Avery.

Skippy and I walk all day and we haven't even gotten outside of town. In the evening we go to another McDonald's. We both have hamburgers. Then I look around for another box for the night but I don't find one. Skippy and I just find a dark corner behind bushes. We don't sleep very well.

It isn't until the next afternoon that we get away from town. I've been to places like this by car and flown over them twice when we went to Grandma's, but being right in it is different.

They didn't want me to have anything to do with Grandma. She didn't approve of the box and didn't keep her mouth shut. She lived a long way off in Chicago so she couldn't have been much trouble for them.

If she was alive I'd go to stay with her. I was nine when I saw her for the last time. Mother said she was bad for me. That's because she spoke out in front of me and she knew I understood her. In fact mother said Grandma had talked in front of me on purpose, so she didn't deserve to ever see me again. At the time I agreed with Mother, but I don't think I do anymore. Why should Grandma never see me again just because she disagreed? I know she really liked me and she hugged just as if she was the arms in the box.

Thinking about her being gone, I cry a little bit even though I hardly knew her. Skippy cries a little, too. And then we find a place to spend the night. Just bushes, like the night before.

As soon as we get out into the real countryside, Skippy and I leave the road and go off into the fields and woods. There's bugs. We find a teeny little road that leads to a lake. We decide to stay there and enjoy ourselves. We run up and down the beach. We look under logs. We chase frogs and turtles. From all those science programs I saw, I had no idea they were so hard to catch.

We forget about food. We don't think about it until we're already hungry. I guess that's a sign I've been looked after too much all my life. I never even had to wait for a meal. So now we have to find our way back to the big road where there are places to eat, but it's getting dark. We may have to go to sleep without any supper. I think Skippy is used to that, but I'm not. I wish I'd bought a couple of extra hamburgers to bring with us.

It gets so dark. I've never seen it this dark before. And the stars! I never saw those either. Not like this. At first we thought we'd go to sleep under some bushes, but the sky is so wonderful we lie out in a clearing. We see some falling stars. We don't sleep much but we don't want to. I wonder when I'd have had a chance to see this if I'd stayed home. And I probably wouldn't have seen real minnows swimming around either. That's another thing, I didn't know they were so small.

We're so hungry we can hardly stand it. Even so Skippy is still skipping. We get back to main road and start walking. We don't find a McDonalds. We have to make do with a diner. We woke up so early it's only eight o'clock when we get there. We share a bacon and eggs but they make us eat outside because dogs aren't allowed.

I haven't been thinking about where I'm going. It's just away. I should make plans. I think I'll try to get a job pretty soon but I'd like to be in a really nice place when I do it. Maybe near a lake.

And one of these days, or rather, dark nights, I'm going to go around looking in windows to see how people live. I've learned a lot from books and science programs, but it could be like seeing those stars. Reality is different.

I see somebody not far from the diner hitch hiking. I do that, too.

Turns out people don't want a jumpy dog in their car, but I finally get a ride with people who already have a dog. A nice friendly one. He's happy to have Skippy along.

When I say I'm willing to go anywhere, the people are suspicious but they give me a ride anyway.

That's the first time somebody calls me, Young man.

I've never been in such an old rusty car. I'm having a lot of wonderful experiences.

There's been no ransom note. We're beginning to wonder if she ran away on her own but why in the world would she do such a thing when she has the best of everything right here? When the police found her cut-off hair, they said she must have done that to herself and they refuse to look for kidnappers.

We told the police how special she is. We showed them the Graham/Gallagher box. We tried to make them understand that this wasn't just any sort of room. We told them how much it cost but we don't think they were impressed. I suppose they were jealous for their own children. After all, it's not every child can have such a wonderful education.

"She's the new woman," we said, but we couldn't make that clear.

Thank goodness she's a tall girl and will stand out. We believe she grew so tall so fast because of all the good nutrition we insisted on.

There's a man and woman in the car. Both wear blue jeans. I always wished I had a pair but Mother didn't want me to have them.

They ask me where I'm from. I say around the corner from that diner. I ask them if they know of a job. I say I'm eighteen. I thought that would be OK since I'm so tall. Nobody ever believes I'm only twelve.

They say they're going to a place where they can pick apples and do I want to come along?

Their names are Jan and Tom. So I'm thinking I won't say I'm Tom. I say Sam. Their dog is named Pet. Tom has a scraggly beard. I've never seen a bearded man in the real. I know about that, though.

It gets to be so pretty and farmish and I'm thinking maybe this will be a good place for me to stay. I do love farms.

For lunch we stop at another McDonald's.

At the apple place anybody can work. Later some high school kids come after school. Everybody picks till it's too dark to see.

Such wonderful hard work. I do a good job, too. Everybody says so. The ladder is rickety but I don't care. I love to be up high in the trees. Except now that I've seen these high school kids, I'm thinking maybe I'd better not say I'm eighteen anymore. I'll bet Jan and Tom didn't believe me anyway.

But I've never been so tired. I practically fall off the ladder at the end of the day and I'm too tired to eat supper.

We're staying at a funny little motel. The bed is lumpy but there's really nice pictures on the walls, one of kids with fishing poles and one with children on a swing.

I sure learned a lot, and a lot of new words I never heard before.

All night long I dream I'm picking apples. I wake up really sore. I can hardly move. I decide I won't even stay for my pay. We have a lot of money. Right after breakfast Skippy and I just walk away. I'm a little teensy weensy bit sorry, because I've never had a chance to be so close to a man with a beard.

Down the road there's a group of houses and a little store. Right outside on the store's porch there's a batch of newspapers and one of them has a picture of me on the front. Two versions, one with me before I cut my hair and one where they did a version with me with my hair cut. And here I am standing right beside them. There's one big difference, though, right under the picture it says, " a twelve year old girl," and they don't know I have Skippy.

I don't dare buy a paper. We move away fast. We don't know what to do. I'm learning so much and having so many adventures. What will I do if they find me? I won't go back. Can they make me? I guess they can, considering I'm not eighteen.

A big hat would help, but I'll have to buy it in a place without newspapers.

A big bruise on my face would be nice, too. Or some cuts so I could have a bandage. Or I can have a bandage anyway.

So we get out of there fast. Walking. I was thinking of hitchhiking again but I don't think I should.

Finally we get to a pretty big town. Nobody pays any attention to me. I buy a red baseball cap, a pair of blue jeans, and a boy's sweater. It's not wool or silk or anything like that. It's red, too, and has a little dog on the front. Mother would say it isn't in good taste but I like it a lot. I'm not sure what good taste is and I'm not sure why bad taste is so wrong, but maybe if I'm dressed in bad taste, Mother might not recognize me. I get a red knapsack, too. These are the first things I've ever bought for myself and picked out by myself. (So far I guess everything I have has been in good taste.)

I also get some large band aids and put one on my chin. I remember to move most of my money to my jeans but I leave some in my dad's pants pockets in the knapsack.

Then I buy a newspaper and we go to McDonald's. They don't let Skippy eat in so we have to sit outside. Skippy always waits for me even though we don't have a leash. We're a team.

The article doesn't say anything about me being a boy. And they say I ran away on my own and nobody knows what direction I went. They write that I'm ignorant of the world (but I'm learning fast) and my parents fear for my safety. They write: "Her parents have great hopes that their experiment in learning will make a new kind of human being." There's two pictures of the Graham/ Gallagher box, one from years ago when it was much smaller and one from right now. You'd think I'd feel homesick for it when I see those pictures, but I don't.

I don't know if I dare go to a motel by myself. And from the way those high school boys looked I don't think I dare say I'm much older than fourteen. I've never heard so many bad jokes as I heard with those boys. I don't know enough to be like them yet. Those children that visited now and then were Mother's choices as suitable for me. I guess she didn't want me to hear any jokes like those.

I see lots of boys with caps and jeans just like mine.

This is just the right kind of town for me to spend some of the night looking in windows to learn more about what life is like for people who don't have to grow up in a box. This town has all kinds of houses with yards. Big ones and little ones. Lots of bushes and trees. I could climb trees and look in upstairs windows.

I pull my cap down over my eyes and we walk around town until it's time for more hamburgers.

We find a nice neighborhood for my study. First we sit in a little park with slides and swings. That's another thing I never had a chance to do, so we swing and slide for a while. There's nobody else around or I wouldn't dare. When it's dark enough we go off to look in windows.

Skippy seems to know we should be quiet. He doesn't bark much. He was good in the motel, too. Nobody knew he was there except me and Jan and Tom. Pet was good, too.

In the windows we see people eating things mother wouldn't allow, but mostly we see people watching TV.

When we hear sirens we hide. A police car stops right at the house we were just at. I see three policemen wandering around the yard and then they start snooping around the neighboring houses. Looking under bushes and in tool sheds. Earlier this evening I saw people walking their dogs so I come out and pretend to be walking Skippy. A policeman comes right up to me. He asks me if I saw anybody snooping around looking in windows. A peeping Tom, he said. Mother and Dad said not to lie. I say, no, I didn't see anybody. That's the truth. He lets us go.

I guess people are scared of somebody walking around in their yards and looking in their windows. I should have realized that. I would be, too.

We go back to the little park and Skippy and I stretch out on a bench.

That's where the police pick me up.

I don't lie. I say, yes, I'm the one that's the peeping Tom.

(I never heard those words peeping Tom before. I wouldn't have done it if I'd known it's some kind of crime.)

But I might not have told the truth if I'd known they'd not let Skippy come with me to the police station

I say I'm Sam Tomson. I say I'm fourteen. I say I'm really sorry.

They call me a pervert. "You scared an old lady half to death."

They feed me stuff Mother wouldn't approve of at all, some real sugary phony juice, and even pie. I can't eat anyway. I keep worrying about Skippy. Even though I'm supposed to be a boy, I cry a little, but not in front of anybody. If I ever get out of here I'm going back to that park and try to find Skippy. Is this the way real life always is? Is this what Mother and Dad wanted to keep me from?

She's all right. Our wonderful new woman. We hope nothing bad has happened to her. We're afraid she might not tell us if it had.

We bring the doctor over right away, and find out she actually has mange. After all the things we tried to save her from....

We may also get her to a psychiatrist, though I understand they don't always side with the parents.

She says she had a dog and we told her we'd buy her another one but she only wants that one. She won't talk to us except to ask for her dog. We keep telling her that's the one that gave her mange and goodness knows what else, but she doesn't seem to care.

All our special diet and education, the early reading program, the music, the art, the science.... Has it all gone for nothing? Is she just an ordinary person? She even said it. "I don't want to be special, I just want my dog."

We put her right in her box and let her rest there. It wasn't as easy to do as it usually is. I actually had to use physical force. We lock her in. Then we add a whole new program: Elementary French. We tell her we're going to Paris. Even if she doesn't want to go, she'll appreciate it later on.

We're thinking of having one of those ankle devices put on.

Madelaine can't believe the tasteless clothes she bought for herself, and that any daughter of ours could actually like that cheap gaudy sweater with a puppy on the chest.

We did consent to advertise for the dog and to give a reward for his return. She drew the picture for the ad. She never was good at drawing though she does excel at many other things. So far no response. We're just as happy. A stray must harbor all sorts of diseases and bugs. It's a wonder she doesn't have fleas.

Postscripts #24/25), 2011

All I Know of Freedom

I'm making do with less. And then less and less and less. I'm even eating less. But I don't know if it's better to eat a lot so as to live off my fat later on, or eat less so as to be in practice for not having enough food. I've heard, though, that if you're fat, you stretch your stomach so you need more food to feel satisfied, so I've decided it's better to shrink mine.

I'm practicing for getting out of here.

I won't be able to take anything but the clothes I'll be wearing and what I can stuff in my pockets.

Also I'm hardening myself up for the cold. Sometimes I sleep with the window open no matter what the temperature. I live in the attic. Nobody notices what I do up here. I even have a book though I don't know how to read it.

If I keep quiet and do my jobs I'm practically invisible. Just like Mother said: "It's always good to behave yourself so as not to get noticed." She also said, "Stand up straight, say thank you and please." I don't. I keep quiet and hunch over so as not to be seen.

I was sold for quite a respectable sum. Or so Mother told me, and proudly. I don't blame her. I presume she had to do it. And these are not the worst people to be sold to. I've heard some get beaten. These people don't do that.

Trouble is, now that I'm getting breasts, I can tell that they're beginning to see me no matter how quiet I keep.

I tried to leave before but I didn't get far. I was too young. I didn't realize how hard it would be and how I'd *have* to be tired and hungry—how I'd have to maybe be freezing or wet. That's part of running away. This time I'll be ready. That time I came back by myself. They didn't even know I had gone.

When they took me, they promised they'd let me go to school so I was glad to go with them, but they never did let me. They kept saying, "Next year," and when it was next year they still said it. Pretty soon even they stopped saying it because it was clear there wasn't going to be a "Next year" for me.

There are lots of books around. More than anybody would ever need. I thought maybe I could teach myself to read. I looked at captions under pictures, but there aren't very many pictures and that hasn't helped much. If I waited till the baby was a bit older, surely there would be some simpler books, but I'm not going to wait.

When they first took me, it was just great. I couldn't believe my luck. Plane rides and hotels. Wonderful food—though some of it so odd I didn't dare eat it, and I was homesick every now and then for lentils. They got me the first frilly blouse I ever had...and that was the last, too. It was tan and silky. I did all sorts of things I'd never have had a chance to do except for them—as they kept telling me. That's when I thought I really would get to go to school.

They kept telling me I should be grateful—and I was. Actually I'm still grateful, but I think I've paid them back enough by now. I don't know how long I've been here. I wish I'd had the sense to mark off the years.

The one good thing is, they never whip me. That's what they used to do back home and it's one of the reasons I wanted to get out of there. They always talk sweetly. My so-called father calls me a hundred different things. They all sound good. "Madam, If you'd be so kind... Miss, by your leave." Talking that way is his joke. Like, "My dear, clean the toilet and be quick about it. Sweetheart, change the bed and wash the sheets." (He doesn't even say sweetheart or my dear to his wife.) Now and then he says, "Miss whatever your name is...." He really does forget my name and that's why he says, Madam and My Dear. That's odd, too, because they're the ones named me what they wanted me to be. My real name was much too long and complicated for them to remember. They never even tried.

Now that I'm getting breasts my so called father is looking at me in a different way. All that fancy language he talks, all those Madams and Sweethearts, Dear Ladys, and By your leaves might turn into something entirely different. He pinched my breasts as though to see how much they'd grown.

My so-called mother, ("Call me Mother in front of people." Though people hardly ever come here.) ...she was the one decided what to name me when they took me. She wanted something simple and easy to say. She calls me B. I do know that letter. She spells it Bee. I know A and C, and E, and some others, too. I like O.

Here, I have to do what I don't want to all the time. I mean *all* the time. Easier to list what I *don't* do than what I do. And I can't think of a thing I don't do.

They'll miss me when I'm gone. I'm going to have to be careful, though I don't think they can risk setting the cops on me since I'm here illegally. I didn't realize that until recently. I'm a secret. They bought me when I was ten. To get me in the country they pretended I was their daughter and got some sort of phony passport.

I don't want to do anything to put the baby in danger. I'll leave at night when they're home. I'm sorry for the house plants. I don't think my so called parents will remember that they'll need to water them. Maybe they'll forget about the baby, too. At least it'll make a fuss.

There's a big wall around their place and an iron gate that's always locked. There's broken glass along the top of the wall and sharp points on top of the gate. They say to keep robbers out, but I think it's for keeping me in.

But I have the gate key now. They've turned the house upside down. They've frisked me and more than once. He did it. Looked everywhere on and *in* my body. Then, for the first time, they whipped me. I almost told them where the key was, but I managed not to. Finally they got tired and stopped. Then my so called father scared me in another way than pinching breasts. He said I was a pretty girl but he could make it so I wasn't if I didn't behave myself.

But they're not all bad. They were kind enough to give me a day to rest up after that. I guess they knew I'd need it. "Mother" even served me supper in bed. She said, "You'll get breakfast in bed, too, if you show us where that key is." They were extra nice all day (I got dessert. I got a heating pad on my sore spots) but I said I didn't know so I didn't get breakfast in bed.

Next day I pretend I'm worse off than I am. I hobble around and sit down (sideways) whenever I get to sit. They'll never think I could go off tomorrow. Weather report says rain. Perfect.

Middle of the night and I'm off—my pockets full of peanut butter sandwiches. Now all I have to do is find a school. I'm not sure what a school looks like even though I've seen pictures. I know sometimes it's a little school and sometimes it's a great big building school. At least it should say school on it. I can read that. It's got two Os.

After I let myself out, I hide the key under a big tree next to a parking lot a few blocks away. I dig it in nice and deep. That's what I did last time I ran away and how I got back in before they found out. That time they didn't even know the key was gone. They'd left it on the hall table.

It's drizzling but I have a big black garbage bag over me. I walk on down the road, turn a corner and then another corner. Walking anywhere I want. I keep turning corners just because I can.

This right now is what it's like to be free. Sometimes I run even though I have a lot of heavy stuff in my pockets. Sometimes I hop and jump. All I know about freedom is what I know right now.

I turned so many corners at first I don't suppose I get far, but now I'm getting somewhere. I've taken smaller and smaller roads and this one is the smallest of all.

Then I hear something crying. I hold still and listen. There's a big bush by the side of the road that would make a good place to hide. That's got to be where the creature is. I move closer. The crying stops.

Since I don't know what it is, I'm a little worried about reaching around in there. But I'm thinking how I know what it feels like to be wet and homeless even though I haven't been that way very long.

I crawl under the bushes and feel around until I touch wet fur. The creature cries again. It doesn't bite me. I pull it out and under the streetlight.

It's nothing but skin and bones and so dirty and matted, I hardly know what it is. But then.... It's just what I've always wanted and knew I'd never get to have. I even have a name all picked out. I don't know yet if it's a boy or girl, but I'll call it Mr. O'Brien. There was once a man came to visit my so called parents and that was his name. I was in the kitchen cleaning up and he looked in at me with curiosity and kindness. I would have said something but he took me by surprise. They usually kept me hidden when people visited. If he had come again I would have been ready to say something, or I'd have made some sort of sign, but he never came back. Usually when there were guests "Mother" locked me in the attic. I only saw that man for a few seconds, but I'll remember him forever.

This Mr. O'Brien here is some kind of puppy, I don't know what kind. It's mostly brownish unless this is dirt. I hope we get to be friends and that it grows up to be big and dangerous. I'd like to see my so called father try to come after me then.

I put Mr. O. in with me, under my big black garbage bag.

We walk until there aren't any more street lights. I'm looking for the real Mr. O'Brien, or a school, whichever comes first, though right now any dry warm place would do.

But no good place comes along. Then we see a big dog house at the end of a dog run but no dog there and it's quite a ways from the house. At least it's out of the rain. We crawl in. I get stiff all curled up there and have to stretch my legs out into the rain. We don't sleep much. We leave as soon as it's even a little bit light. I share one of my peanut butter sandwiches with Mr. O'Brien.

That morning just about at dawn (we've already walked for a while) I see a school way out here in the middle of nowhere. At least it says SCHOOL on it. It's no bigger than a little house and has a big back yard with an old sand pile and a slide and two swings. I know about those from a long time ago.

I push on the doors and look in the windows. It looks abandoned. But what a nice place to hide. Two rooms. A few little chairs and tables. It would be nice if some books were still there, too, but I don't see any.

Except I can't get in. I try all the windows but I don't want to break any.

We give up and go on.

I share another peanut butter sandwich with Mr. O.

At evening we come to another school. This one is entirely different. It's big and it looks scary. It says SCHOOL on it but almost all the people there are grown ups. And some look very old. They're kind of raggedy, too. The men have beards and the women wear long skirts. There's a big banner right under where it says SCHOOL but of course I can't read it.

They're all very busy, but not doing school-like things. They've rigged up all sorts of unschoolish tents, and there are canvas shades over what looks like a cooking place with lots of pots. In the big back field, they're building a huge shiny long thing with no windows at all. Hard to tell what it is because of the scaffolding around it. It takes up the whole field. People in neat while coveralls are working on it.

I'm going to ask somebody what's going on, but I'd like to ask a kid, except there aren't very many around. Odd, but all the kids I see are girls and they're all wearing skirts.

I wait and watch a long time. Good that Mr. O'Brien seems to like being with me and that he's a nice quiet dog. We're both the shy type.. We share another peanut butter sandwich. We're going to run out pretty soon.

We're sitting behind some big bushes to eat and we're not paying attention. All of a sudden here's just what I wanted, a girl about my age practically right beside us. She's wearing a long torn dirty skirt.

First thing she says is—that is, after we stare at each other for a couple of minutes—"I wish I could wear blue jeans like yours, but they won't let me. Skirts are always in the way. Are you trying to hide? What's your dog's name?"

"Mr. O'Brien."

She sits down right next to us and looks as if she'd like to share our sandwich with us, but I can smell what's cooking in those pots under the canvas shades so I know she'll get food.

"Why are you hiding?"

"We're not. We're just having lunch. What does that say there, under where it says SCHOOL?"

"Can't you read?"

I really am embarrassed. I almost say I can except I need glasses. But I decide not to lie.

"It says, PREPARE, THE END IS NIGH."

"The end of what?"

"The world of course, silly. "She looks at me as if I really am dumb. "It's in the middle of ending right now, can't you tell? Everybody knows that. All you have to do is look around. And look how hot it is already and it isn't even lunch time."

Have they kept me so isolated back home I don't even know it's the end of the world? I wouldn't be surprised, though. When I was cleaning up in the kitchen, I heard the news when they listened to it and things did sound bad. Lots of wars and earthquakes and horrible toxic spills and even right near us there was a gas truck crashed into a house and exploded and killed everybody and burned up four houses.

"You have to get ready," she says.

"How? What should I do?"

"You can join us. We're going to a better world. We need more young girls. It's going to take a long time to get somewhere and it's the young women who'll have to have a lot of babies on the way so we can start up the new population. We won't need a lot of men. I'm going to have all the babies I can. I'm precious. You would be, too, if you joined us."

I'm thinking how lucky it is that I ran into these people.

"If I join can you teach me to read?"

"Sure, and I'm good at reading."

I can't believe my luck.

"You can't bring a dog, though. You'll have to get rid of him."

"Right now?"

Maybe I'm not as lucky as I thought.

"Well, pretty soon, anyway. You can find it a good home, though I don't suppose this world will last much longer what with all that's been happening, but dogs don't live a long time anyway. He might die before the world ends so that's all right. "

Not so all right with me.

"Come on, they'll be glad to have you join up. I'll ask them if you can keep the dog till we leave. They'll probably say yes because, like I said, they really do want more girls like us." She says again, "We're the most important ones of all."

Turns out they do want me. I make them all happy, especially when I say I'm running away and my people wouldn't dare tell the police since I was illegal in the first place. They think I've come to the exact right spot. "Sent by God," they say. But they sure don't like Mr. O'Brien. ("That's a growing dog. He'll eat a lot.") I promise I won't ever take more than my share and I'll split my food with him. I tell them I'm used to making do with less.

Turns out Eppie... the girl.... (It's short for Hephzibah. Her mother has a funny name, too, Ziporah)...is a bit younger than I am, she's only eleven. Turns out she and I will share a little tent behind her family's big one. Mr. O. will sleep in there with us. (Her parents sure don't want him around. He's getting not so shy and is very bouncy. I have to keep an eye on him all the time. He likes to chew shoes.)

They take me inside their space ship and show me where I'll be living after we leave. The rooms for mothers are all along the side and the nursery is across from them. What looks like the walls will be the floors after we get going. There's a play room for when the babies get older. It's full of all kinds of great toys, most I never saw before in my whole life. Well, I do know my so called parents kept me ignorant but I didn't know how much I didn't know. But now that Eppie is teaching me to read I'll be able to read all that. Books can tell you everything you need to know. I've got a really good start. Eppie says I'm going faster than she thought anybody could. I think I actually did learn something just looking at those books and thinking about the letters.

I do a lot of work here but, since I'm free, it's entirely different. They tell me I'm one of their best helpers because I know how to do a lot of things and I'm a pretty good cook, too, and getting better.

Those people in white have better tents than the rest of us do, and the head preacher even has the whole upstairs of the school just for his offices and living space. We listen to "our" radio station all day long. They... we keep asking for more money all the time though they seem to have a lot already. They keep saying, God will reward you for your generosity.

Meanwhile my breasts are getting bigger all the time. I'll have to get a bra some way. Eppie hasn't reached that stage yet so I don't think I can ask her anything. I don't feel close to Eppie's mother, but she's the one, comes to me and, about another thing, too. I didn't know anything about that either, which shows how I wasn't told anything back at my so called home. Eppie's mother keeps saying, "Isn't that nice. That means now you can have babies. We're going to need lots." She says, "I'll be taking care of you. I'm the midwife."

Things are moving right along—not only with my breasts. The scaffolding is off the space ship and they're about to stand it up. There's a new kind of scaffolding for that. Also there's been a lot more end of the world disasters, floods and earthquakes, and right here a tornado that ruined a lot of houses in town and killed eight people including a baby, but it went right around us so everybody here knows that God is in favor of what we're doing.

There are only four young men that are supposed to be our... "husbands." I guess you'd call them. They're supposed to be the fathers of all the new babies. They're only bringing a few males compared to females. They said they're the best and the healthiest. Only one looks like the sort they're talking about...sort of a hero type...curly yellow hair.... He doesn't appeal to me at all. Too good looking. I think I'm sort of in love with the real Mr. O'Brien. He's not handsome, but I could see on his face how kind he was. The other three "husbands" are young. One, like Eppie, is only eleven.

Then that oldest handsome boy, Jed (for Jedediah) ...grabs me and kisses me before I hardly know what's happening. I had been out throwing the garbage in the garbage bins and he followed me and pushed me down behind the bins. That boy.... He goes around grinning and looking us girls over. He knows he's one of the few fathers and he's already lording it over everybody, like he thinks he's the most important person on the trip. I suppose most everybody picked to be one of the fathers would act that way, but I sure don't like it. Eppie and I feel special, too, but we don't go around as if we were queens.

Thank goodness Mr. O'Brien is with me...as he always is. I try to fight the boy off and then Mr. O'Brien actually bites him. Grabs his wrist and pulls him away. Draws blood. The boy kicks Mr. O. hard, but Mr. O. doesn't stop. Grabs him by his pants leg and rips it.

The boy says, "Look where he bit me."

"It's just scratches."

"You have to sew these pants up," and I say, "OK," and he says, "Not only that, but you're going to have to do this one of these days, why not now? We can get things started."

He's been boasting about exercising everyday up in the ship's gym. I could feel how strong he is. He probably was chosen for his good looks, too. I don't want to ever have a stuck-up little baby that looks like him.

"You're not the only boy that's coming."

"One of these years you'll have to pick me. That's the rule. We have to mix up our genes."

"Maybe you'll be dead before it happens. Or I will be. I hope so, anyway."

He squeezed my breasts even harder than my so called father did back there at home. This is the first I start thinking about what really is going on here.

Just as I wished him to, Mr.O protected me. Even bit hard enough to draw blood. I feel safe with him around.

Eppie and her family are going to be away for a couple of days while they go say goodbye to Eppie's grandparents. They have to leave Eppie's little brother with them. He can't come because of a heart murmur. Lots of others are off to say goodbye, too. People over forty aren't allowed to come. I can see why. They wouldn't last long enough.

I'm going out to find Mr. O'Brien a good home. ("The dog has got to go. We can't be a Noah's Ark. The lord will supply the needed animals when we get there." Actually they're bringing some cows and chickens but just so as to have eggs and milk for the trip.) They're telling us younger ones to get ready to name all the new kinds of animals we'll find when we get there. There won't be any need for meat so God will leave those animal's out.

I don't ever need a leash. Mr. O. sticks right by me all the time. I think he remembers that I rescued him and warmed him with my own body. I'll bet he remembers sleeping in that dog house.

He's gotten pretty big now, just as I wanted, and he'd willingly die defending me if he had to. He's exactly everything I wished for.

It's so hot everybody in town is just sort of waiting for it be fall and be cooler. The town is all shut up during the heat of the day. Even lots of stores are closed from noon to three. People are at the movies or sitting next to their air-conditions. Some people spend a lot of time walking up and down in the big cool grocery store and the K Mart. Eppie says, "Where we're going it'll be a wonderful new world like this one used to be. God will make it so.

All around town I tell people what a great dog he is and why I need to let him go. After a while I only try where they already have a dog. Nobody wants him and lots of times I wouldn't want him at some of those places either.

When people find out I'm from the end-of-the-world people, they laugh at me. Turns out they call us crazies. One lady said I looked nice and neat compared to some of them, though, she said, Mr. O'Brien looks like he belongs with them. Then she said why didn't I clip him some so he'd be more comfortable in this heat. I hadn't thought of that. She has three dogs of her own and a big fenced-in yard, and she's really nice. She said she boarded dogs and also clipped dogs for people and she knew I couldn't afford it but she'd clip Mr. O. for me anyway.

We went up on her closed in porch where it was cool and she got water for Mr. O'Brien and ice tea for me. There was a parrot there and she told me to hold out my hand and he flew right to me. Then she got out her clippers and showed me how he should be clipped, and even let me do some of it. Mr. O. looked a lot better after we got through with him. I asked again if she wouldn't take him. She said she couldn't afford the food for such a big dog and she said she already had two cats and the parrot and her three terriers and she needed the rest of her space for boarding. Then she says, "Why don't you take him out in the country to some farm? If I was Mr. O'Brien, I'd like to live on a farm with lots of room and work to do."

That's such a good idea. I say I'll go look right away.

"But," she says, "if I were you, I'd not go with those crazies. They really are crazies you know. Why don't you come over here and work for me? You've got a knack with animals and I could use a helper."

I don't know what to say, so I say, "But they taught me to read."

She looks at me funny, then realizes she's staring, and looks down at Mr. O. instead, as if she doesn't know what to say either. Finally she says, "Great dog. If he were mine, I wouldn't get rid of him for anything."

I do find a good home for Mr. O. way out on a farm. They're going to change his name to Buster. I'm thinking they'd like his name if they had ever met the real Mr. O'Brien. They're going to keep him tied up until he gets used to them and to me not being there, otherwise he'd follow me back. As I leave, I hear him barking and barking, and then it changes to crying. But they said he'd get used it. They said it always takes a while. And it was cooler out there and there were other dogs and lots of other animals. I would have liked it there myself. But now I'm thinking I gave away the only thing I ever loved, and the only thing that ever loved me.

And then I worry. It was a long hot walk out of town, are they going to give him water? He needs it right away. They seemed like nice enough people but sometimes people forget or don't notice.

As I get back to the group, here's Eppie. She can see that I've been crying. Also that Mr. O. isn't with me.

She says," Good. You did it. That dog was just too big. I'm glad he's out of our pup tent. Can you picture him bouncing around in a space ship!"

I have to admit he took up more than his share of the tent. I say, "I'm worried he's thirsty and they won't give him water. Maybe I should go back and check."

"Are you going to be worrying about that dog all though the whole trip?"

She's right, I *am* going to worry. I say, "Maybe I shouldn't go with you."

But then she gets all upset. "Oh no." She practically yells it, and hugs me. "You're my best friend."

I think I'm her best friend because I'm so ignorant about the world that she can keep telling me things. I do learn a lot from her but I know some of it's wrong. Though I'm certainly grateful for those reading lessons. She wants to be a teacher and she's good at it, but I'm not really her best friend, I'm just her best and most willing pupil.

We've already packed up most of our belongings and arranged them in our state rooms. My room is next to Eppie's, just as we wanted. The rooms are small, but they have big metal mirrors so they seem larger. We had our choice of colors. I wanted mine to be all woody colors: tans and browns. I knew it would be a long time before I saw any real wood. Eppie's is yellow and blue and white. She put her favorite pictures on the walls. They had to be glued down tight. She couldn't put up pictures in the pup tent but she had these all ready to go. Funny to think of those pictures of handsome men...I guess they're movie stars... going all the way off to Paradise where they'll be old men or dead before we even get there. I wonder why she even has them.

I guess I'd most want a picture of Mr. O., but then I'd never stop thinking about him. Except I don't want to ever stop. Besides, I don't know how to get a picture, anyway.

There's a big rally our last night on earth. They talk about the beautiful world God will lead them to out in Proxima Centauri. They keep calling it Paradise, but the moon is out and almost full, and I don't see how any place can be more beautiful than right here. Besides, this world has Mr. O. in it. I do know my so called father and mother would never find me on that new world, but even so, I'm not sure I want to go. Besides, Mr. O. would keep me safe. He did it before.

The preacher (dressed all raggedy like we're all supposed to be because of renouncing worldly things.) He says… shouts, "And so this evil world will soon burn as if it's hell itself. Parts that don't burn will be covered with water. Already dozens of islands have been lost to the sea. Soon every river will be poisoned. You know it. You know it. You see it already happening Look at Godless New Orleans. Look at Voodoo filled Haiti. How God punished them.

I will not be among you, I'm old and I'm not the best of the best, but you are. You're the chosen."

The moon is so bright I wouldn't even need a flashlight. There's a little breeze and it's cool for a change.

"…and there will be the winds of a hundred hurricanes and they will last a hundred years, and the earth will shake…. You know it. You know it. You've seen it already."

I pretend to head to the bathrooms. Eppie says, "Wait a minute. This is the best part. He's telling about earthquakes that never stop." But I keep going.

"… earthquakes that never stop…I say again *never*. Never! Imagine it. Imagine."

I reach the farm in the middle of the night. The other dogs there bark like crazy. Luckily they still have Mr. O. tied up in the front of the house. He's almost chewed through his rope. He'd have been free in another day or so. We hug and he cries with joy and so do I. The lights go on in the house and I untie him fast and we run, but not towards the end-of-the-world people. Maybe we can spend the night back in that dog house.

In the dog house we find a half dead kitten. We can't do anything about it until morning so we all just cuddle up together. From now on I'm going to do the opposite of the end-of-the-world people. I'm going to take in animals, and Mr. O'Brien and this kitten are the first ones.

Except the kitten dies in the night. It was just too bitten up and I didn't have any way to help save it. I had thought about that woman who did grooming. She'd know how to help, but it died before I could get it to her. At least it didn't have to die alone. I told it I loved it and that it was a good kitty. I hope it understood.

The end of the world people leave in the morning. We hear the great roar and see the flash of their going. It lights up the whole sky. It's exciting, and for a minute I wish I was with them. I shout and Mr. O. gives a howl. Then we run, as if to follow it.

We run. And run and run and don't care where. All of a sudden here's that little two room school that looks like a house. This time I don't think twice. I break a window and we fall inside, all worn out.

We lie there the rest of the day feeling sad...about Eppie being gone, but glad we're here together. We don't even worry about not having anything to eat. When it gets dark, we sleep.

But in the morning, we're hungry and thirsty. There's no water here that works. Everything is turned off. No electricity. I find how to turn the water on under the house. I know about that from home, but I don't know how to turn on the electricity. At least we have something to drink.

I don't know what to do or where to go or how to get food, and then I think about that lady who said I'd be a good helper.

Mrs. Sindee feeds us and I get hired and I'm going to get paid.

Things do get worse. Everybody wonders where fall got to and if it'll ever cool off. And there's earthquakes where they never had them before, even one right here, and then Mrs. Sindee gets flooded out. I help her clean up after the water goes back down. Good thing is, people go on wanting their animals clipped and boarded sometimes and it finally does cool down. In fact it gets too cold. Mr. O'Brien and I and even Mrs. Sindee...we don't even care. We wear our long underwear and Mr. O'Brien grows a heavy coat of new fur.

Mr. O'Brien and I live in that old school and so far nobody has found out. And whenever we find a wounded bird or cat or whatever, we rescue it. And everything we rescue turns out to be the best there is just like Mr. O'Brien. We're all making do with less, but we already have seven books.

I wonder if they'll ever reach Proxima Centauri.

***After: Nineteen Stories of Apocalypse and Dystopia*, 2012**

Riding Red Ted

Advice to the riders of the humpbacked heighthwricks

General Gaba Niri

Part One

Sit well forward, your inner thigh in the hollow between their front leg and their stomach. This is the steadiest seat from which to wield your weapons should that be your purpose.

They can use their dewclaws as a real thumb. We recommend they be removed.

Never wear clothes that rustle or shine. The heighthwricks will shy.

They're utterly silent because of their padded feet and lack of a voice box. A whole herd can sneak up on an army.

Place the bit well behind the teeth and facing the lower jaw. It's the lower jaw that's the most sensitive, so this will obtain the most obedience.

One of their wings is always pinioned. There's no use having a flying heighthwrick. Even with you on their back, they'd escape to their home peaks.

Don't try to see if they can fly by pushing them off a cliff. They'll die from the fall.

Impossible to tell if male or female. If female, an infertile egg will be laid now and then even if no male is present.

You may think I repeat myself needlessly as I say again, keep your head turned to the side and never wear anything that sparkles or squeaks, but it cannot be repeated too often.

As with all beasts, mount from the left side. Though we seldom wear swords any longer, that is still the side from which they're trained to be mounted.

My beast has the dewclaws recently removed. The scars still look raw and painful.

The book said: *If simple enough, they can learn their own names.* I named him Ted.

I poke a stick into his cage to see how he'll react. (I'll call him "he" until I find out otherwise.) I wish the beast could roar instead of sigh that breathy sigh.

He rears. He leaps. What a magnificent creature! That iridescence makes him hard to see. As he reared I couldn't tell his head from his wing.

I poke him again.

Again he leaps and glitters. Again he breathes that long breath out. He may not have a voice box, but he sounds dangerous even so.

I throw in the haunch of a ruminant. In spite of those rows of teeth, he swallows it whole, in one gulp. I can see the lump of it passing down his neck.

If you keep the head tight in it's harness and the mouth clamped closed, you can spend the night under one of the wings. There you'll be safe from all other dangerous beasts.

Heighthwricks can go for miles at a trot, but at their fastest only in short bursts. At an out and out run, they'll pump their useless wings out of habit, or perhaps out of hope. That doesn't help their speed. In fact it slows them down. The rider will not be able to tolerate that kind of bouncing for long.

We'll see. I'm in better shape even than most other military men.

Also we'll see just how far and fast he can gallop.

They said I should practice with my beast before setting out but I'm an athlete in peak form...as all soldiers should always be. Also I have to be in Tanarara by tomorrow.

This whole place is new to me—a volcanic land of rocky towers and deep canyons with rivers at their bottoms, interspersed with sections of desert. It's red and tan and black. Also I've never before seen creatures like these heighthwricks.

They hired me from across the three seas. I'm from a green land full of scurrying creatures and bugs (I don't miss the bugs), of little streams instead of rushing rivers, of rolling hills. We have no heighthwricks, nor would heighthwricks thrive in our damp land. General Goba Niri writes: *Heighthwricks need the dry climate of the high desert. They get dragon fleas and wing rot in damper lands.*

When I arrive, I'll wear my medals although my rank alone should serve to astonish.

Next morning Ted sighs as I wake him with a poke. That's a deep-in-his-throat sigh lasting several seconds. I'll take that as a roar. General Niri: *As to the wake up poke, in the withers is best, and it needs to be hard or the beast won't notice it.*

I say, "Rise and shine," and shine he does. The sun's not yet up, but I have to put on my sun shades.

He's already been saddled and strapped, and the cage, folded now, is attached behind the saddle. Well back so as not to interfere with me.

I climb the several steps of the mounting block, launch myself across to the saddle, sit, heels down, legs in the dip between the forelimbs and the stomach. I don't worry about sitting straight-backed, I always sit that way.

We hurry to cross the plain before the sun is high and the desert heat begins. I'm glad to see Ted has a fast trot and even a good brisk walk. General Niri wrote that that walk would be unusual. Perhaps Ted is as anxious as I am to leave the capital. I've never been a lover of cities. We're two of a kind.

Soon after sunrise, I stop and remove my uniform. I cover my shoulders with a loose white shirt. The military cap of my rank is a fairly good sunshade.

When the sun is hot and high, we finally come to the edge of the first canyon. From the cliff edge, the river below shines like a mirror. It'll be nice and cool in the canyon and the water will be cold. I'm already thirsty.

. Had they not pinioned Ted's wing, he'd have leaped across the canyon in a few seconds. Instead, we start down the zigzag path into the shade. It's instantly cold. Ted keeps at a nice jog. He's not sure footed. When he stumbles he balances himself with his wings which causes him to stagger. By the time we finally reach the river I'm, I must confess, a bit…more than a bit… sea sick. I slide down his flanks, glad to dismount. We lean and drink, side by side. I feel a fellowship. I can't help smiling at him, but I remember the book of instructions: *They can seem tame, even friendly, and then suddenly strike.*

We rest until I feel less nauseous, and then I move Ted to where the bank is steepest, place him under it, climb it and then drop down into the saddle. (There is a light weight rope ladder attached to the saddle in case I need to use that but I want to learn to do this without it. With all the other beasts I've ridden, there's a mane or fur to hang on to, but scales are slippery.)

Ted leaps across the river, wings spread as if they were of some use, and we trot up the other side. There's one more desert and one more canyon to go before we get to Tanarara.

Tanarara is a canyon city. It straddles the river. They say water runs directly through it's lower streets, washes away the dirt. They say there is no cleaner, cooler place. The city is walled by blocking off the canyon above it and below it. They say there's an iron gate.

By the time we near the Tanarara canyon, I've had to stop three times and dismount to throw up. I wish I'd brought something for sea sickness. Ted wanted to eat the vomit, but I managed to keep him from it. *If you use the bridle to twist the neck sideways as far as it will go, and hook the bridle to the saddle horn for a few seconds the animal will become amenable.*

I didn't have to do that. I started to but he wised up right away. Evidently they had already done that to him. I suppose it's easier to do when they're young and ever after they're frightened by it. They don't realize they've grown strong enough to resist.

I want to take time to recover a bit before entering the village. I'm afraid I'll look as pale and sick as I feel.

I slow Ted to his nice clipped walk. I don't get seasick at that pace. When we reach the Tanarara canyon I don't dip down in to it near the town. We trot west several miles and find a place just under the rim where we'll spend the night. We drink from our pack of stale and warm water and look down at the cool river below. Though there's not much expression in Ted's big heavy face, I *think* I can see in his look the same longing for that cold water that he must see in mine.

It's scary leaning so close to that mouth full of teeth. I'd be hardly two bites for him. He was fed before we left and won't be hungry for another month but the general wrote: *Let me reiterate, it's dangerous to think you're making friends.* Yet one forms a bond in spite of one's self, spending all day together, hot and tired. I suppose the bond is one sided.

I'd be happy to live in this barren land forever if I could have one of these beasts for the rest of my life. This one comes with the job. When I stop the job, Ted will have to go. I could never afford such a creature.

This job suits me. I like the hardships and the dangers. I like that I need to keep in military shape. I like this beast. I think I can be fierce enough to keep the job for a long time.

Even now, tired as I am, I'll do my exercises. After riding all day they're all the more necessary.

I've pulled Ted's neck in and down for the night and closed his mouth by tipping the bit up. Now he watches my odd movements. There's no expression on his face that I can read. His ears are so small no way to interpret them. The tail is quiet. I try to see into his eyes. They are empty. Impossible to know if he's accepting of his ropes and the bit.

It is said that, in the old language of this area, heighthwrick means from high in the rocks or, on the other hand, cave dwellers, but I have always thought it means untamable. Why would such a creature ever consent to be tamed? General Goba Niri

In the morning I trim my beard, dress in my uniform, pin on my medals. I check that the cage is still securely fastened. This time I use the ladder to mount. (We lose a few scales. I'm tempted to dismount and save them, but we'd probably lose even more if I did.) Then we climb back up into the desert for the ride to the town. Of course my uniform is wrinkled and sweaty before we hardly go a yard. By the time we dip into Tanarara Canyon again I might as well not have bothered dressing and washing and trimming. At least my medals shine. At least Ted shines.

The road to the town, though it has to go back and forth as much as any in the canyons, is smooth and wide. Ted can trot at a nice downhill clip.

Then the gates are before us, wide and tall. Even so we loom over them. The river rushes under them. We stop and I dismount. We lean and drink again. We can't help it. The water splashes up around us. Now my uniform is damp, not only with stale sweat but with cold water. Now the knees of the white pants are dirty.

Do I mount and then call at the gate? Or do I walk over and pull the chain that rings the chimes?

Before I can decide, the gates swing back by themselves. I see right away that Ted won't fit through them. I'm going to have to go in alone and looking a mess. Nothing to be done about it.

I tie Ted the usual way, (head pulled down, mouth braced shut). I unfold the cage and again make sure it's firmly fastened.

Do I finally see a kind of smile on lips that can't smile? Or am I judging him, yet again, by my own feelings? But I would be proud if I thought like a dragon...like a raptor. All the better for what I'm sent to do.

I straighten my hat. (It's the only thing I have that's worth straightening.) I limp through the gates. (I'm still stiff from all that riding.)

There's no one there. Is this a clever ploy to keep me from my obligation?

But somebody opened the gates.

The street beyond rises steeply, as it must, to follow the shape of the canyon. The road is wide, but not wide enough for Ted. You can hear the river roaring underneath. I suppose you can hear that rushing sound all through the town.

I walk up the street a bit. Like they said, the town is the cleanest I've ever seen. I'm the biggest mess in it. Even with my medals and my military cap, I'm afraid I may be taken for one of the unimportant people.

There are carved stone benches on both sides of the road. I think it best to sit and wait. They opened the gate, probably they'll come to me.

I get out the official document with the gold seal of the capital, demanding the tithe. It's reassuring to think that no irrelevant person would have such a document.

I move down into the sun so that the gold seal glitters. I polish my medals on my sleeve in hopes they'll glitter, too. I'm sure I'm being watched and I presume there's some sort of weapon trained on me. Perhaps many weapons. A lesser man than I might be frightened.

Actually, I feel calm. It's a relief to be sitting quietly for a change.

A long haired boy appears on the street above me. He walks slowly down. He's dressed in a tunic and loose trousers. He's all in white, as am I.

No, it's a woman.

This has got to be a trick. I make sure my dagger is in place, ready to drop down from my sleeve.

As she nears I see something shine at her neck. She's wearing a chain with a dragon scale as the pendant. I hadn't realized they could be used as jewelry. I wonder what the value is of those I left behind this morning.

She actually sits down on the bench right next to me. I think: How dare she? My hat shows my rank. Can't she see my medals? To have a dragon at all ought to be enough to show who I am. I think to say, Back up.

But I'm dazzled by the dragon's scale. Odd how just one is almost as impressive as the whole animal. When it's just one you can concentrate on the reds and pinks that change to green and blue as the woman moves. I find it hard to look at her face.

She says, "I'm in charge here."

I do look up. She can't be much over thirty. She does have a strong look about her. She means what she says. Even so, I say, "I don't believe it."

"No need for you to believe it."

That sparkling dragon's scale is distracting. I suppose that's on purpose. I try to ignore it and look into her tan/green eyes. She's sitting much too close. I'm used to having more space around me.

I have always believed that you make your own luck. That the poor are poor because of lack of substance. That the rich and successful are so from talent and ingenuity, that we all deserve what we have. I can see that she deserves this job just as much as I deserve mine. There's determination on her face, but I will do my job no matter what.

In her own way she's quite good looking. Her hair (in it's own way), is almost as lustrous as Ted's scales. It's blond with reddish tints. But I'm never swayed by looks. Besides, I like a more aristocratic face. Hers, unfortunately, shows her geneology. And anyway, right now, all my admiration is for Ted.

She may have one scale, but I have thousands. I should ask her how much she paid for that. I may be riding on a fortune. I wonder if Ted would mind if I pulled out several. I wonder if only loose ones fall out by themselves. I wonder how hard I'll have to pull to extract them?

I spent several days at the capital before getting Ted and leaving for Tanarara and yet had not seen dragon scales used as jewels.

I says, "Here's the...."

She says, "We know what you're after."

"I've been hired to bring back the tithe."

"You call it a tithe."

"How much did you pay for that dragon scale?"

"Nothing,"

Of course she's lying. Or perhaps she earned it in a sinful way. She's handsome enough for that. Or was a few years ago. She has good teeth. Country people usually don't. Or perhaps she comes from a long line of sinful women with plenty of money for good food and jewels.

And then all of a sudden... I don't know how I know but I know. I say, "Not possible. You!"

"I'm the tithe."

"You won't do and you know it."

"We have no other."

"I don't believe it. Let me see the others. I was sent here to choose. And from those with blue eyes."

"You'll find no others."

I don't trust her. I don't want her riding behind me even if it's in a cage.

I suppose she'll be wearing that scale if she comes with me. What will Ted do? *Do not wear anything that glitters or shines.*

"I need for someone to sign the document. It can't be you."

"It has to be me."

"I must see your pedigree."

It's just as well I know nothing of this job and nothing of this place. Was that the reason they hired me from across three seas? Have others tried and failed? Have they been dazzled by dragon scales? Have they fallen in love and never come back? But I'm a man of my word. I'm not like other men.

"I have it here."

She unrolls a document that not only has a gold seal, but a long blue ribbon. At the bottom there's a name: Mattia. It gives her age as twenty-five. The legal limit for the tithe. The tithe must be able to bear children for at least four years. I don't think she's that young.

"Where did you steal this?"

Perhaps she deserves to be the tithe from cleverness and know-how. I respect that.

"And what will you do with the memorable men of the capital?"

Does she want a son who'll take over the government? Or can she be so mistaken as to think she, herself, might take over?

On the other hand, why should I care? I can say I was suspicious but had no way of finding any other tithe. I can say the document looked real. I had no reason to doubt, though she did look too old. I can say I'm not a good judge of women. That I thought perhaps the weather in the canyon was hard on the skin.

"Where is everybody?"

"You have no need to see any of the others."

The way she says it, I have another suspicion.

I'll not put up with this ruse any longer. Close behind me there's the door of one of the houses. It's ajar and I see movement behind it. I stand up slowly and stretch. Then I leap over the back of the bench and enter that door.

After sitting in the sun, I can't see anything but shadows. The woman is right behind me. She must have jumped the bench as nimbly as I. She grabs my arm, but doesn't pull me back.

No one in there is dressed in white. Three woman, all young and all strikingly beautiful.

For sure I was supposed to pick one of these.

Mattia (If that's her real name, which I doubt) still holds my arm.

The more my eyes adjust to the dim light, the more beautiful the women become. There's even one with quite an aristocratic look about her.

"And in the other houses?"

"More of the same. But only I am the tithe."

I let my dagger slip down from my sleeve, and at the same time lash back with one leg and trip her. She's good, but I'm better. Except I hold back. I tear her white tunic half way down the front.

Of course the other women turn on me. Before I know it I'm on the floor on my back. I didn't hit out as I would have if they were men. In fact I rather enjoyed the scuffle… and made the most of it. (I managed to pull that aristocratic looking one into a hug. I held her pressed against me for several seconds.) I let them take my dagger. I don't feel vulnerable without it, there's another in my boot.

They sit on me to hold me down. I don't mind that at all.

The aristocratic one won't look at me. She gets the ropes and ties me up, as the others hold me. She blushes the whole time.

She isn't very good at tying. She's too nervous. I can wriggle out of her knots whenever I need to.

They bring me outside back to the stone bench. Other beautiful women come out of the other doors. Is the town nothing but women? And it's odd, most of them have blue eyes. A tithe of the most beautiful would be more than would fit in the tithe cage.

Only Mattia wears a dragon scale. She says, "So this time they sent one military man with a dragon instead of three jailors with donk carts."

That's evidently a joke. They all laugh, and then they're silent. It's so quiet for so long I think of Ted, and I remember: *Heighthwricks should not be left too long tied and inactive during daylight hours. They are intelligent creatures and need stimulation. When they become restless, they will find ways to amuse themselves. They can do damage to their surroundings.*

(I think again how I deserve this beast. How we're two of a kind.)

I'm enjoying myself looking out at all these women, picking out the most aristocratic, but I'm thinking if I have to use that other dagger, this time I'll not spare them. They're quick and clever, and stronger than most women. Somehow they've taken over the village. What have they done with the men? I must fight with everything I have.

I see now why I've been chosen specifically for this job and given a dragon. It's because of who I am. But is it also that I'm not a handsome man? That I'm rather short? That none of the women could fall in love with me? But they knew of my soldierly reputation back in my own land. Should I be proud or ashamed?

I keep my dignity. I sit, at attention as best I can. My hat is lost somewhere but my medals still shine. I turn so that the sun is on them.

Mattia says, "Strip him and take away all the other weapons hidden on his body."

I pull out of my bindings, but they jump me as I'm leaning to get my other dagger. I don't hold back, but there are too many of them and they've been trained to fight. I end up naked. Even barefoot.

They lock me in a tiny room with a little barred window in the door. I can see a bit of another room where a woman stands guard, but not in a military fashion. She sits, leaning back against the wall, and plays a small squeeze instrument. It makes a humming sort of music that reminds me of the breathy hissing that Ted makes.

Most men would be discouraged, but I'm confident I can find a way out of this mess. After all, trained or not, they're only women while I'm in top military form.

I don't suppose I can count on Ted for any help, except, tied down tightly as he is, he may become restless. I think again of what General Niri wrote: *We have no chains or ropes that can hold them. They can break through any bonds when they really want to, though most never realize their own strength. You must see to it that they never find out.*

Just as you'd expect from a bunch of women, the mattress is soft and the blankets warm. There's even a pillow. When they push a supper in through the door flap under the little window, the food is the best I've had.

When I wake the next morning... after a good sleep... I lie quietly and listen. There's just the sound of the river rushing below the village.

Breakfast appears. Again, food as appetizing as the women. Still, this is unsettling. Here, even the lesser women are beautiful, even the one who pushes in the breakfast. Actually she looks quite aristocratic. Or perhaps nobody is less or better than anybody else here. I don't like it. How do they keep track of the worthy?

After breakfast I do my exercises. (You don't need weights to do weight lifting.)

Then two women come and escort me to a basement room nearer the river that rushes under the village. Some of the water flows up to a heater and then down to a small pool. And hanging there next to the pool is my uniform. It's been washed and pressed and the medals polished. And here's even my hat. I could escape from this bathing room but why would I?

As I'm dressing there's some great crashes. They even shake the building. Almost all the water sloshes out of the pool. I can't tell what's happening, but things are being broken. Big things. This land is prone to earthquakes, but it could be Ted. I hope it is.

Things quiet down but I hear the women running around and shouting. I bathe and dress, check myself in the mirror by the door. I look as good as when I first started out, though I suspect I won't stay that way for long.

I find my way to the central square. There's a lot of damage to the gate. Ted for sure. Even the stone pillars at the sides are smashed.

But where is he? Then I catch a glimpse of his sparkle just beyond the ruined gates.

The women are trying to get the debris cleared away so they can use the road. I stride down with military bearing. That is I try to. The road is uneven. I don't achieve the look I'm aiming for.

As I reach the gates I see that the glimmer beyond is the shine of the rushing water, not Ted.

I stumble through the debris. The women stop their cleaning up and watch me. They don't seem to care that I'm leaving. They smile and wave. I feel I'm their joke. Even so, at the far side, I stand and salute them. They salute me back, laughing. All right, so I'm your joke. If they think that hurts somebody like me they're mistaken.

I hold myself back from running away, finally free, and march up the road at a dignified and military pace.

I climb back and forth for several switchbacks, round yet another corner when, there he is in all his dazzle.

Now this is strange. His mouth is still bound partly shut, but even so he grabs me by the back of my uniform, carries me, sets me down a half hour later at the top of the canyon. I'm covered with saliva, my uniform is in shreds, but I feel a great elation… rescued by a heigthwrick! Has that ever happened to anyone but me?

At the top, I take off my gummy torn uniform. It's useless and disgusting. My hat fell off long ago. It's dangerous in the desert without a good hat and something to protect your shoulders. I'll make something for my head out of the uniform.

I turn to mount. As I reach my seat, I see, in the dazzle of his scales, that the tithe cage isn't empty. The door hangs, unlocked, Mattia is there.

"How?"

"Sit down. We're heading east."

I'm not going to stoop to ask why.

But I'm disappointed. I had thought Ted rescued me all by himself. Now I suppose Mattia did it. Though why would she? Why does she need me?

Mattia shows me how to arrange the sleeves to hold my uniform over my head and shoulders. I can't look very dignified with this on my head but Mattia doesn't matter.

She has filled the water jars and brought food. I turn us east. Maybe I'll get rid of her on the way, sneak back to the village for a more aristocratic beauty.

Should I lock the cage? I guess not yet.

When it's about to be the hottest part of the day, we dip into the shade of the next canyon. We go to the river at the bottom. Not like the one in Mattia's village, more a trickle, but enough for us to drink. We sit on the bank and eat Mattia's picnic. Again, the food is the best I ever had.

Odd, how comfortable we—all three of us—are, resting here together. Ted looming over us, that lizard smile of his.... It's hard for me to believe he isn't friendly. I take off the mess on my head. I lie back and look up at sky above the canyon. We've been silent all this time. A comfortable silence. I'm thinking how Mattia isn't bad looking.

I say, "So you plan to take over the capital in the same way you took over your village?"

"If you were a tithe...."

"*You've* never been one."

"Of course not, but.... Last year we sent the men back without their carts and cages, tied to their donks. Your heighthwrick wouldn't go home, but the donks would head for the barn. We weren't expecting someone like you with a heigthwrick. It makes us proud and confident. If they feel the need to send a soldier with a dragon, they must be worried."

"And you control heigthwricks."

"Wearing a scale helps. But your dragon is.... different. She carried you up herself. It wasn't me. I didn't know she could, especially with her mouth half closed."

"She? How do you know it's a she?"

"I suspected, and then she laid an egg. Didn't you hear her crowing?"

"Crowing!"

"Too bad you missed it. We put the egg next to a stove."

It can't be fertile.

"It would be worth a lot to us to have another one exactly like her, especially if we had a military man to ride her."

Can I guess from this, something about a town full of mostly blue eyed women?

I suppose she has my daggers and I can't even guess what else. I should have locked the cage a long time ago. I'm not worried. I'm looking forward to whatever adventure she's about to reveal.

Ted, a female! Theodora? Teddy?

"And you brought me out to this canyon to kill me and keep my beast if I don't say yes?"

"You could stay."

"All we want to do is stop the so called tithe."

With me and my heigthwrick no one would bother them.

"Heigthwricks always want to go home."

"We all do"

"Except for you."

"I like it here. It's rugged and difficult. I prefer the desert brown to the mildness of green."

"So stay."

"Unlike most dragons, yours is definitely imprinted on you. They usually don't imprint on anybody."

Some are more malleable than others. General Goba Niri

Could I stay and defend the village? I and… Theodora? And what loyalty do I have to the capital and its ways? Isn't this a more moral duty then collecting the tithe?

It's clear she's never known someone like me before. She'll have to think fast to best me.

I deserve this animal.. We're two of a kind.

She's really quite attractive.

I tell her I'm not from here, I'm from the land of forests. We have no heigthwricks. She says she could see that from the beginning, my darker hair, my lighter skin. "You must take care not to be in the sun too much."

They can be obstreperous and willful. They try to go their own way.

At the beginning I was careful to keep my head turned to the side as General Gaba Niri advised, but now I ride however I can manage. I'm not paying attention. Too hot. This bunch of white rags over my head and shoulders.

They should never be left unattended for long periods.

They don't eat frequently but when hungry become hard to control.

She says, "Should we keep him or should we do as planned?"

Those who dare to wear a dragon's scale.

As he gets away the dragon rears and knocks him out. Left with an egg.

The aristocratic one is hiding in the back. I stare in her direction. Try to make my eyes speak. If they do or can, I wonder what they're saying.

There are things that could be weapons along the tops of the houses. One can't ever be too careful.

Why do you think there was nobody but me to meet you in the village?

If a hat blows off they'll shy whether the hat is white or not.

I see movement up the street. It turns out to be a cat.

Where are the common people?

A lesser man than I might be worried. A lesser man than I would need to practice. A lesser man than I would wonder.

If the creature should take off on it's own lean forward. Place you head down against the neck. Stay calm. The heighthrick will sense your agitation and become all the more wild.

As with all creatures, their personalities will vary. Some will be more active than others. Some will be lazy. Some will seem to be tractable. None can be trusted. We haven't yet been about to tell just how intelligent they are. Certainly too smart to be of much use in battle. Every now and then one will do something tricky and clever that's not anticipated. Keep a watchful eye. Never let your guard down.

I know better than to fall in love. Lovers lose.

I have gotten too close to Ted.

I'll let the people stay in fear for a while. The tithe.

One beautiful woman? I didn't like the looks of her at all.

The lesser people of this area.

Fish jumping in the river. Jumping their way up river. What comes down to drink. Ted watches.

Ted lays an egg.

Try as I might, I couldn't get the beast to leave the scene.

The mother dragon.

The walled city. No doubt to keep those like me out.

The people back where I come from are all too frightened not to follow the laws of the land. I'm the one who frightens them. That's why I've been sent to this hot landscape of desert and canyons to terrorize this town.

I have been sent with a message to surrender.

They haven't paid their taxes for a long time.

And never got there. Landed in the dragon's world.

There's an arena that they insist I ride in at the start, but I'm anxious to go out and test him on the cliffs. They say they leap as if goats.

I've bought myself the boots and gloves. I have a large hat with a chin strap.

Too smart to go into battle.

Asimov's Science Fiction Magazine, April-May 2012

OTHER BOOKS FROM NONSTOP PRESS

The Collected Stories of Carol Emshwiller, Vol. 1
$29.95 Hardcover (ISBN: 978-1-933065-22-9; ebook available)
"... offers not only hours of pleasure through its dozens of wonderful, magical stories, but also the rare joy of seeing a master's work develop over decades." — Strange Horizons
A MASSIVE COLLECTION of 88 stories. Carol Emshwiller's fiction cuts a straight path through the landscape of American literary genres: mystery, speculative fiction, magic realism, western, slipstream, fantasy and of course science fiction. The first of two volumes,.

Lord of Darkness by Robert Silverberg
Trade paper $17.95 (ISBN: 978-1-933065-43-4; *ebook available*)
"... gripping and compulsively readable." — George R.R. Martin
SET in the 17th century and based on a true-life historical figure, this novel is a tale of exotic lands, romance, and hair-raising adventures. Andrew Battell is a buccaneer on a British ship when he is taken prisoner by Portuguese pirates. Injured and ailing, Andrew is brought to the west coast of Africa where his only solace is Dona Teresa, a young woman who nurses him back to health. Andrew's sole hope to return home is to first serve his Portuguese masters, but it is a hope that dwindles as he is pulled further and further into the interior of the continent, into the land of the Jaqqa overseen by the powerful Lord of Darkness. .

Meeting the Dog Girls, stories by Gay Partington Terry
Trade paper $14.95 (ISBN 978-1933065-20-5; *ebook available*)
"... nonpareil fantastika that will stay with you for a long time."
— *Asimov's Science Fiction Magazine*
A THIEF, languishing in prison for stealing moments, escapes and becomes a chronometric fugitive. Women wait in a long, endless line, night and day, without knowing what is at the end of the line. An otherworldly marble called the Ustek Cloudy passes through the hands of Ambrose Bierce, Amelia Earhart, and D. B. Cooper just before they each disappear off the face of the earth. Whether they are called fantasy, magical realism, science fiction, or brilliant parodies, the stories in this collection—the first from Gay Terry—blend the real and the fantastic in an imaginative and mischievous way. Written in the tradition of Ray Bradbury, Carol Emshwiller, and Neil Gaiman, these contemporary fables present remarkable characters trapped in unusual situations.

Musings and Meditations: Essays and Thoughts by Robert Silverberg
Trade paper $18.95 (ISBN: 978-1-933065-20-5; *ebook available*)
"This delightful collection reflects Silverberg's wide-ranging interests, wit, and mastery of the craft." — *Publishers Weekly* (Starred Review)
A NEW COLLECTION. No cultural icon escapes Silverberg scrutiny, including fellow writers such as Robert Heinlein, Arthur C. Clarke, H. P. Lovecraft, and Isaac Asimov.

Reflections & Refractions: Revised & Expanded Edition
by Robert Silverberg
Trade Paper (ISBN-13: 978-1-933065-51-9; *ebook available*)
NEW EDITION. Chronicling the events and key ideas from the second half of the 20th century in both the world of science fiction and the world at large, this collection of insights and musings from a Grand Master of the genre offers a unique perspective with the edge of honed artist.

Science Fiction: The 101 Best Novels —1985-2010
by Damien Broderick and Paul Di Filippo.; Foreword by David Pringle
Trade paper $14.99 (ISBN: 978-1-933065-39-7; *ebook available*)
"If you want to know the essential science-fiction books to read that were published in the last 25 years, this is your go-to guide." — *Kirkus*
INSPIRED by David Pringle's landmark volume, SCIENCE FICTION: THE 100 BEST NOVELS, which appeared in 1985, this volume will supplement the earlier selection with the authors' choice of the best SF novels issued in English during the past quarter-century.

The Very Best of Barry N. Malzberg Introduction by Joe Wrzos
Trade paper $14.95 (ISBN: 978-1-933065-41-0; *ebook available*)
FOR NEARLY half a century Malzberg has been stretching the boundaries of science fiction and fantasy. Each of the 37 stories in this hand-picked compilation offers Malzberg's trademark vision that is equal parts cautionary tale and social commentary, with a dash of the dark humor so characteristic of his work.

. . . .

Nonstop Library of American Artists

Vol. 1: Arts Unknown: The Life & Art of Lee Brown Coye by Luis Ortiz; $39.95 Hardcover (ISBN: 978-1-933065-04-4) *Fully illustrated, color.*
"A must for lovers of the weird and fantastic." — *Publishers Weekly*
"A smashingly beautiful book … reading this fine biography is like riding a train through the history of three-quarters of the 20th century, and seeing Coye's monsters through every window." — *Asimov's SF Magazine*

Vol. 2: Emshwiller: Infinity x Two
The Art & Life of Ed & Carol Emshwiller by Luis Ortiz;
Hardcover, $39.95 (ISBN: 978-1-933065-08-3)
Fully illustrated, color; A Hugo Award nominee and Locus Award finalist.
"... fascinating .... a must have for anyone interested in SF art, writing, and history." — *LOCUS*

Vol. 3: Outermost: The Art + Life of Jack Gaughan by Luis Ortiz;
$39.95 hardcover (ISBN: 978-1-933065-16-8) *Fully illustrated, color*
FANTASTIC IMAGERY, explosive color, and occasionally creepy creations merge together in this elaborate collection of the work of genius artist, Jack Gaughan. Extremely prolific and popular from the 1960s – 1980s, Gaughan is showcased in this chronicle of a master of the science fiction and fantasy genre. Overflowing with samples of work from the artist's personal archives and exploring examples of his working method.

. . . .

Cult Magazines: From A to Z, A Compendium of Culturally Obsessive & Curiously Expressive Publications
Edited by Earl Kemp & Luis Ortiz
"Contains a wealth of arcane information about many of the oddball magazines that once graced newsstands." — *New York Times Book Review*
Oversized trade paper, $34.95 (ISBN: 978-1-933065-14-4)
Featuring full-color reproductions of hundreds of distinctive cult magazine cover images, backgrounds, histories, and essays that offer a complete picture of a bygone era. ***Fully illustrated in color.***

The Monkey's Other Paw Edited by Luis Ortiz
Trade paper (ISBN 978-1-933065-33-5)
"... a worthy celebration of fright fiction's ancestry...." — *Publishers Weekly*
Subtitled "Revived Classic Stories of Dread and the Dead". This anthology presents new sequels, prequels, retellings, homages, and alternate POV takes on classic terror tales re-imagined by some of the best writers of horror, fantasy, and sci-fi working today including: Steve Rasnic Tem, Don Webb, Paul Di Filippo, Barry Malzberg, Damien Broderick, Alegrîa Luna Luz., and Gay Terry.

The Steampunk Coloring Book
ISBN-13: 978-1-933065-61-8
With a unique and highly popular theme, this activity book takes steampunk enthusiasts on an exciting ramble through a Victorian-Edwardian wonderland that imaginatively blends past and future.

www.nonstoppress.com

www.ingramcontent.com/pod-product-compliance
Lightning Source LLC
Chambersburg PA
CBHW020616310726
48979CB00008B/1503/J

* 9 7 8 1 9 3 3 0 6 5 3 4 2 *